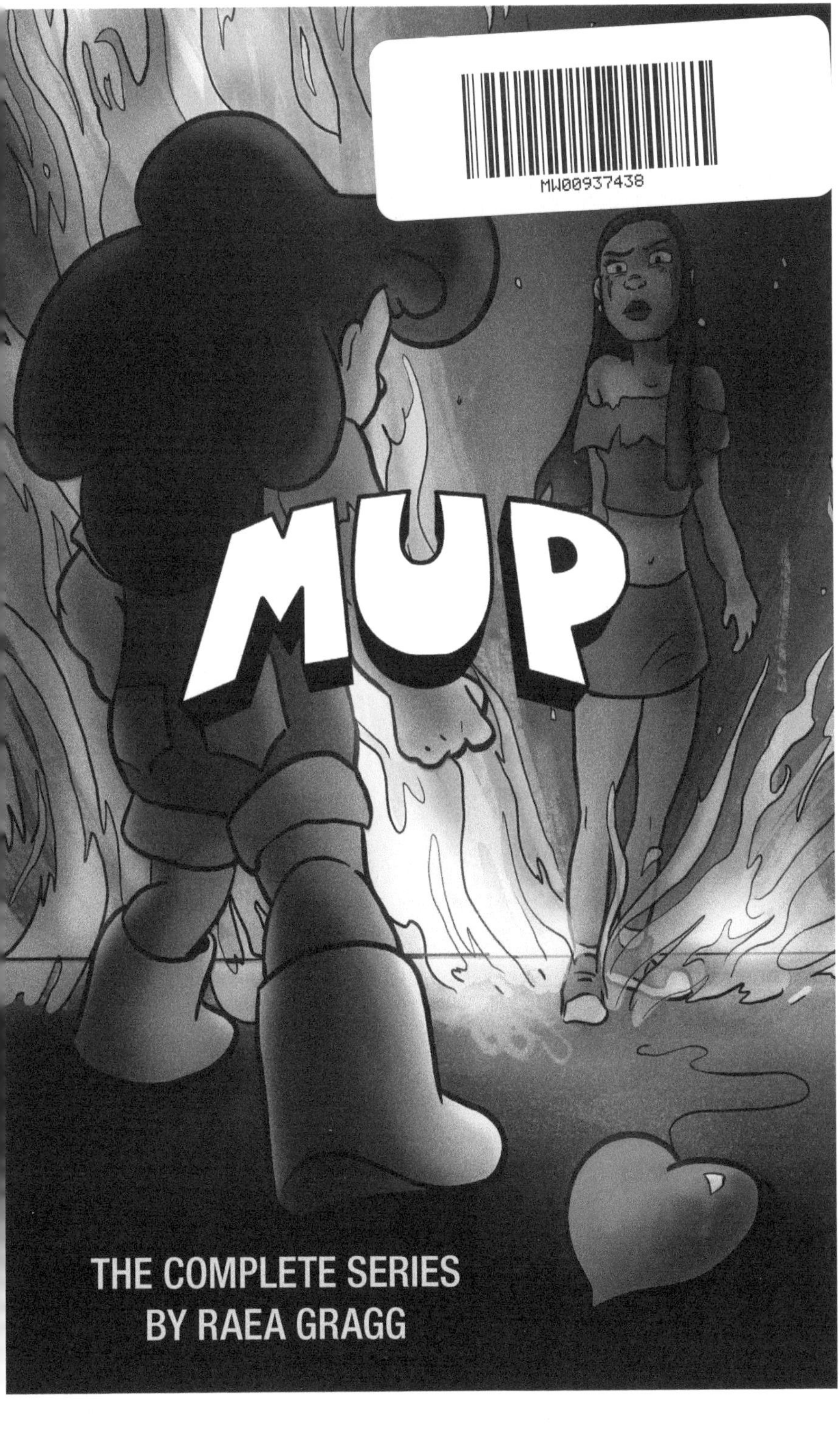
MUP
THE COMPLETE SERIES
BY RAEA GRAGG

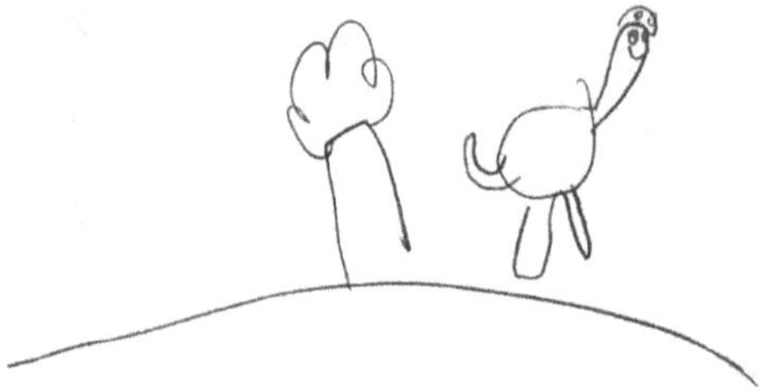

For my sister, Mup

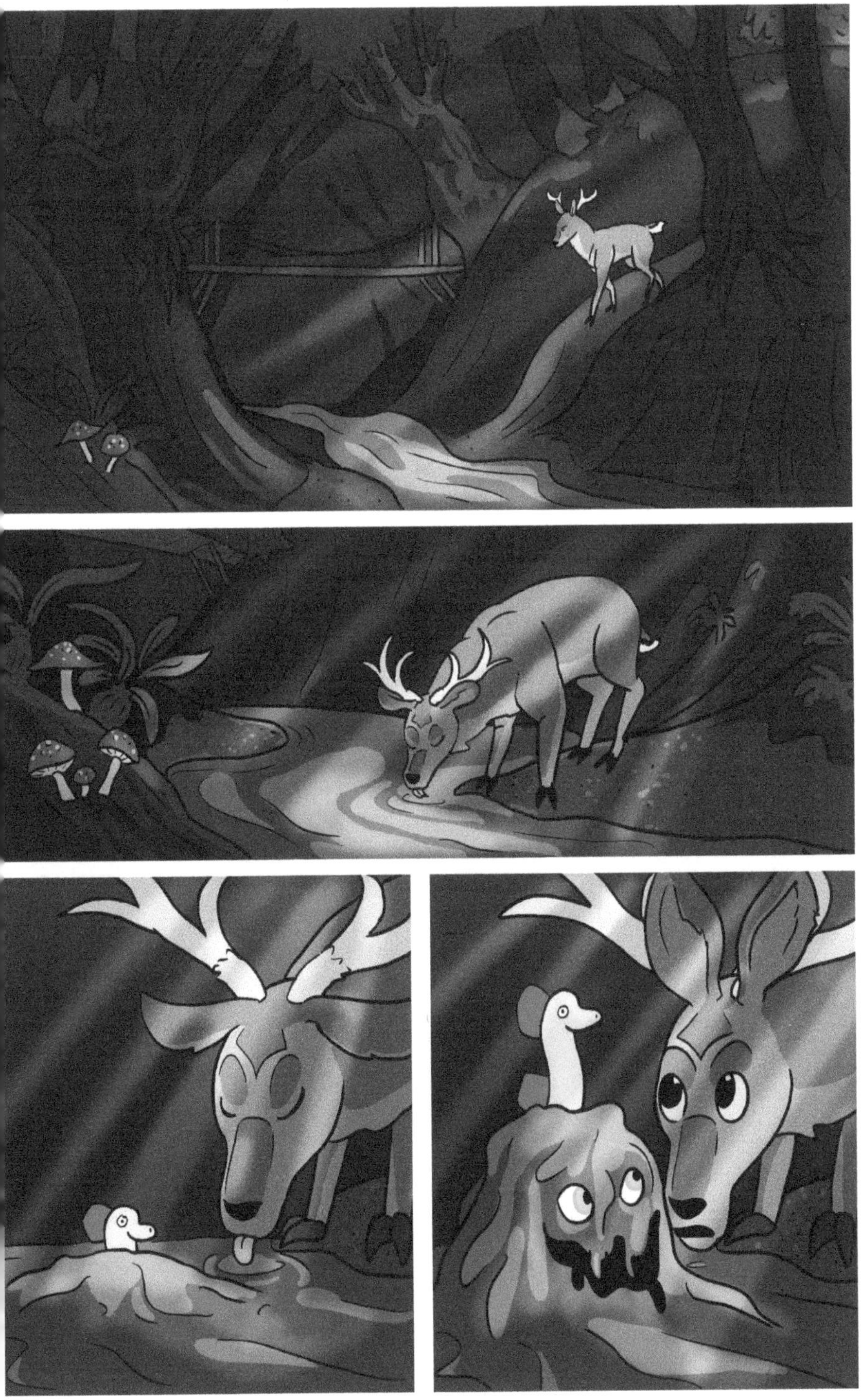

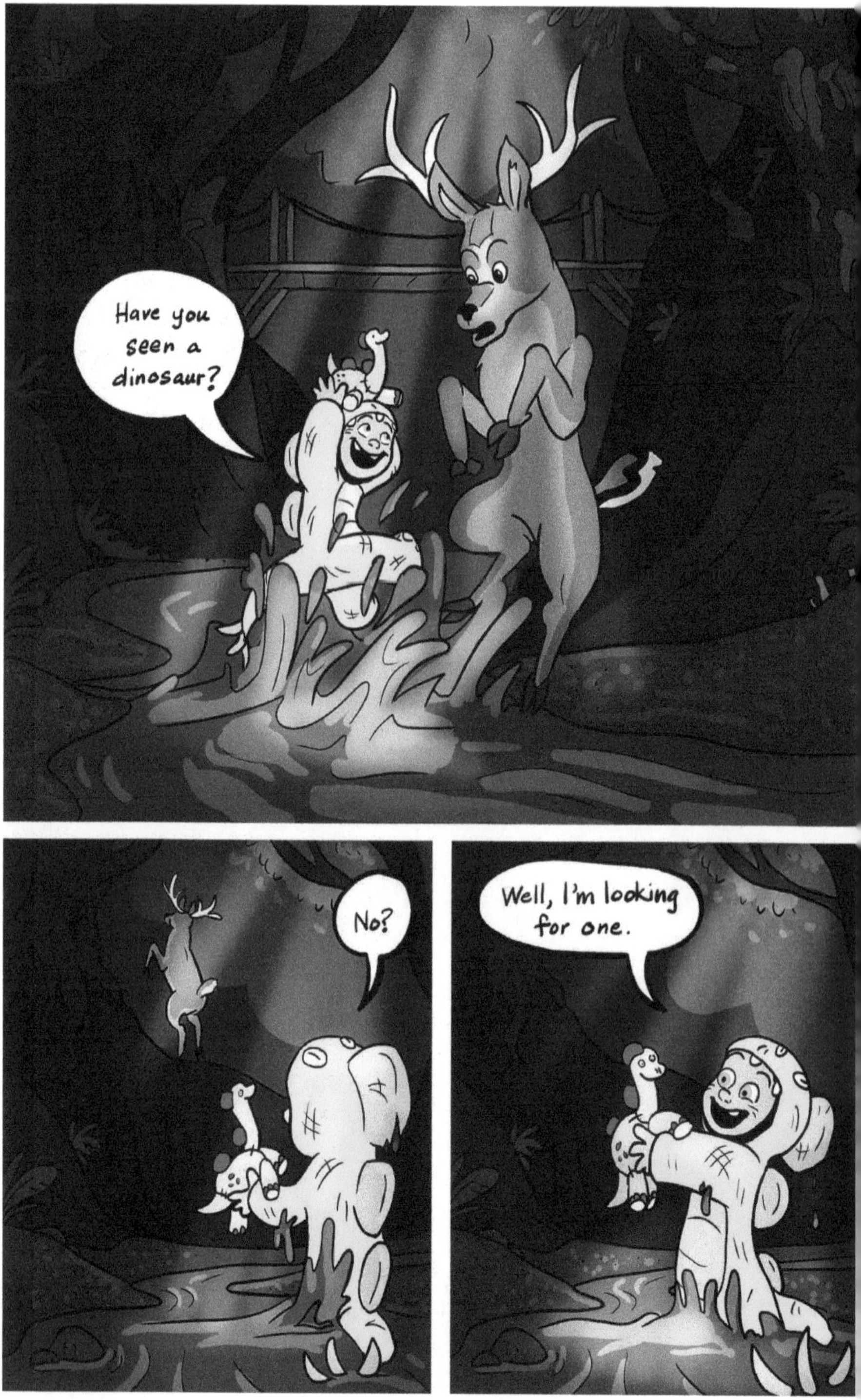
Have you seen a dinosaur?
No?
Well, I'm looking for one.

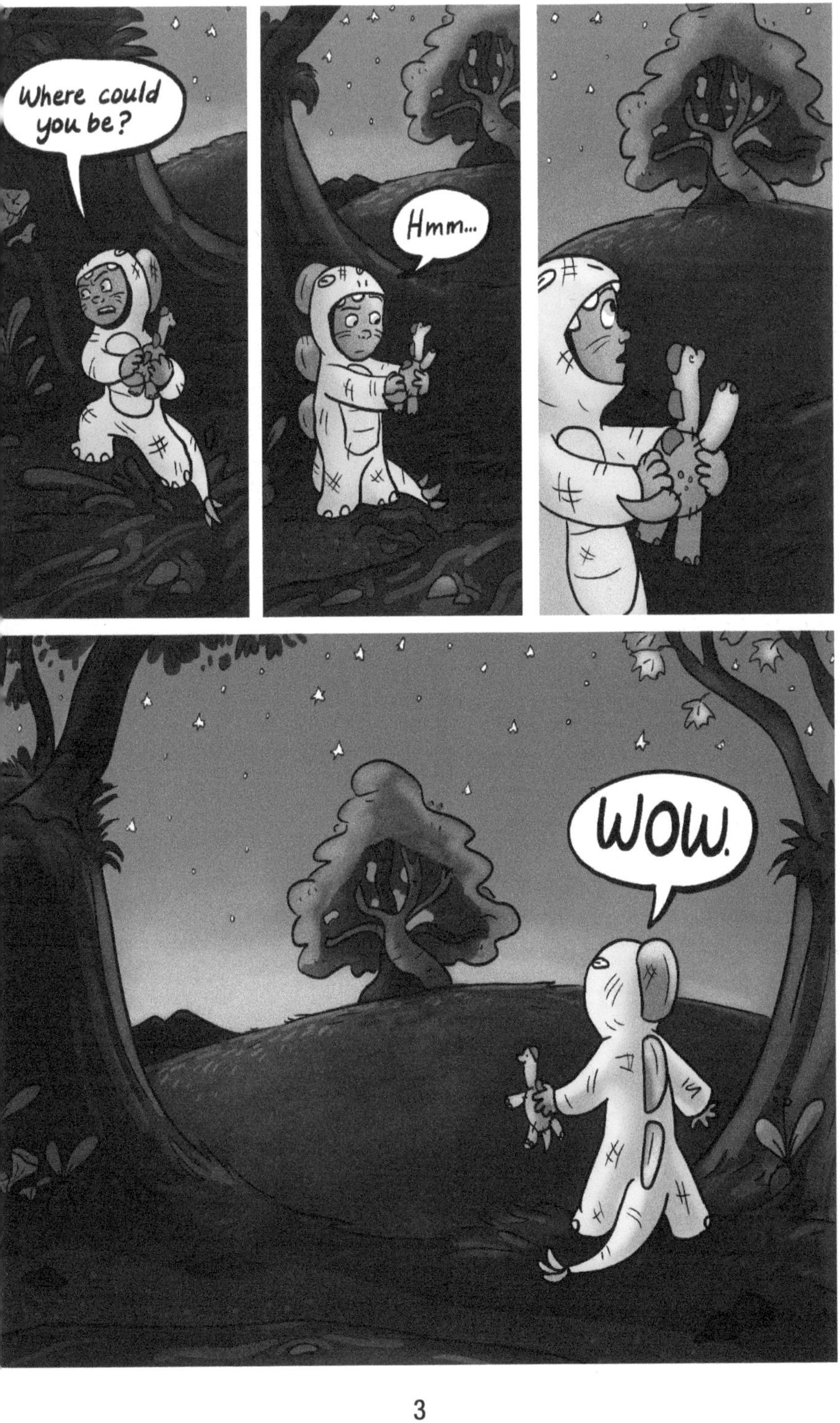
Where could you be?
Hmm...
WOW.

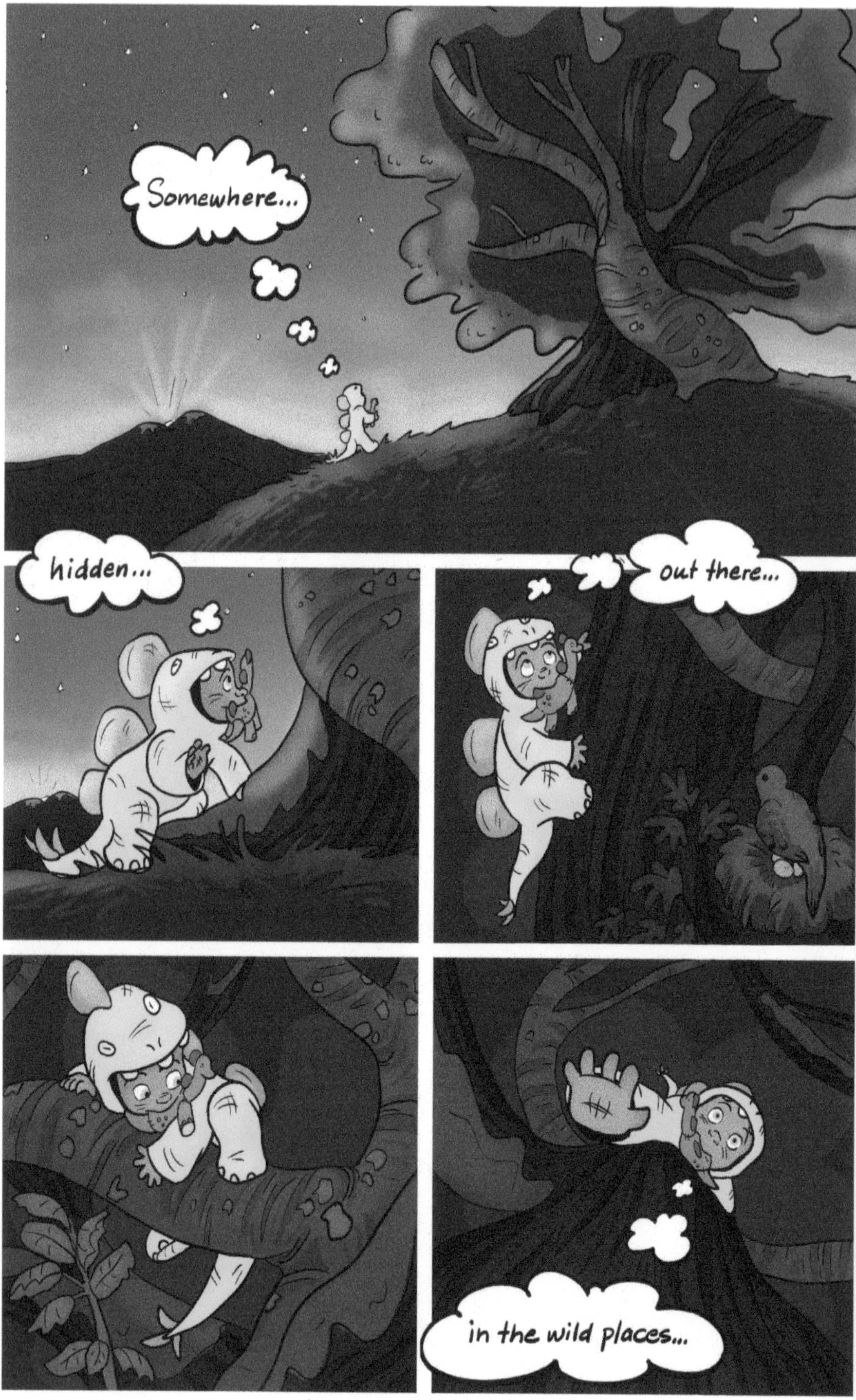
Somewhere...
hidden...
out there...
in the wild places...

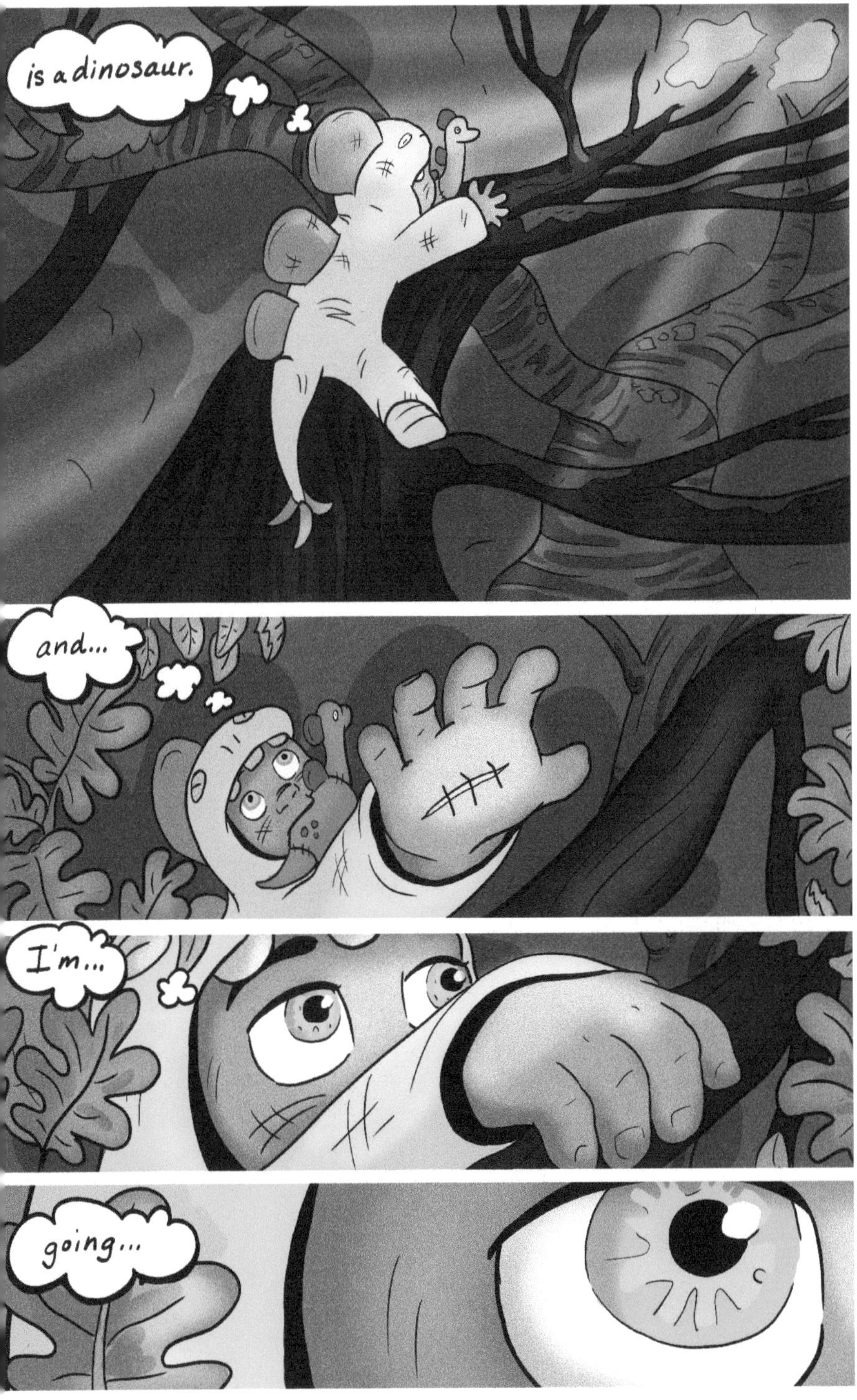
is a dinosaur.
and...
I'm...
going...

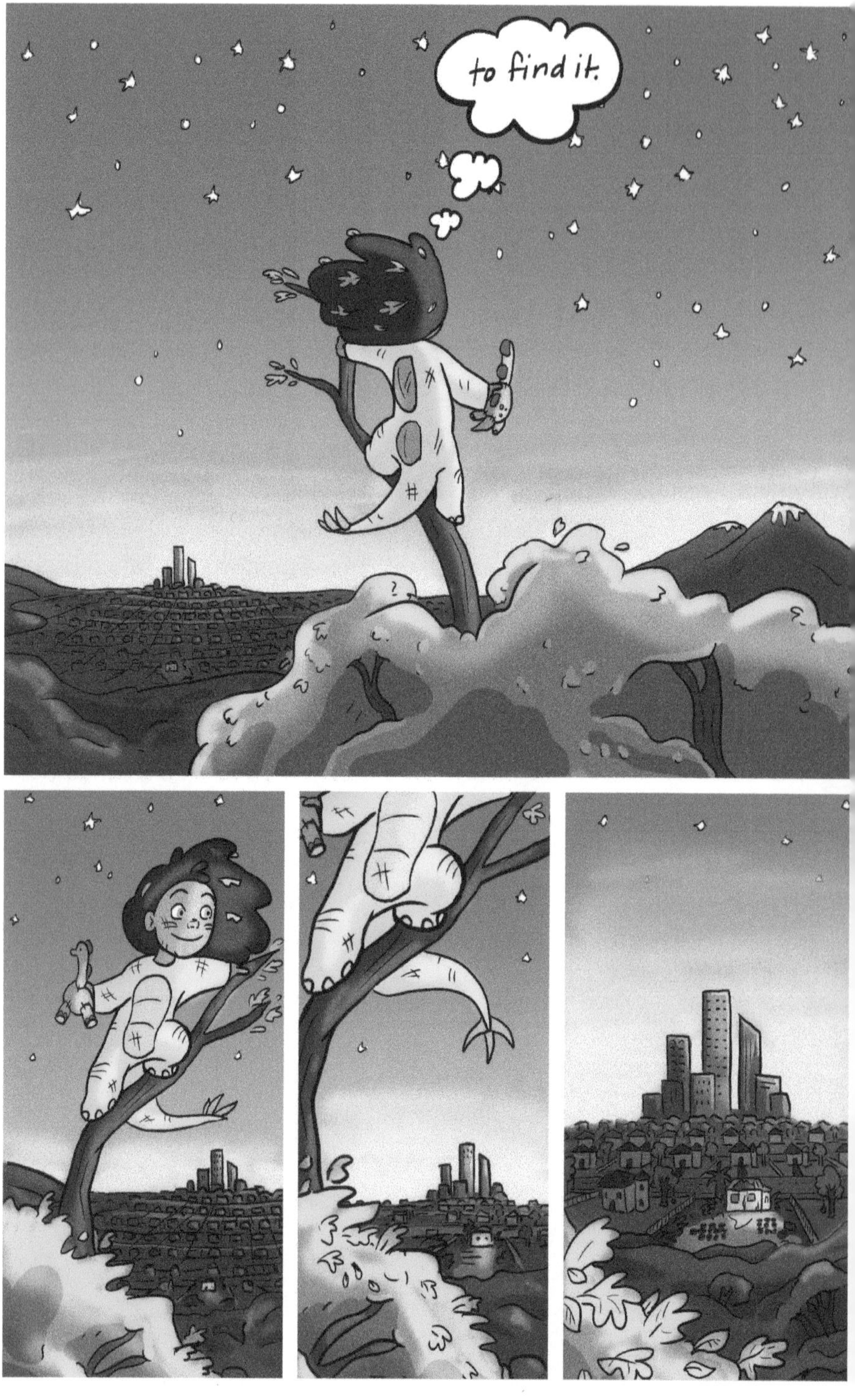
to find it.

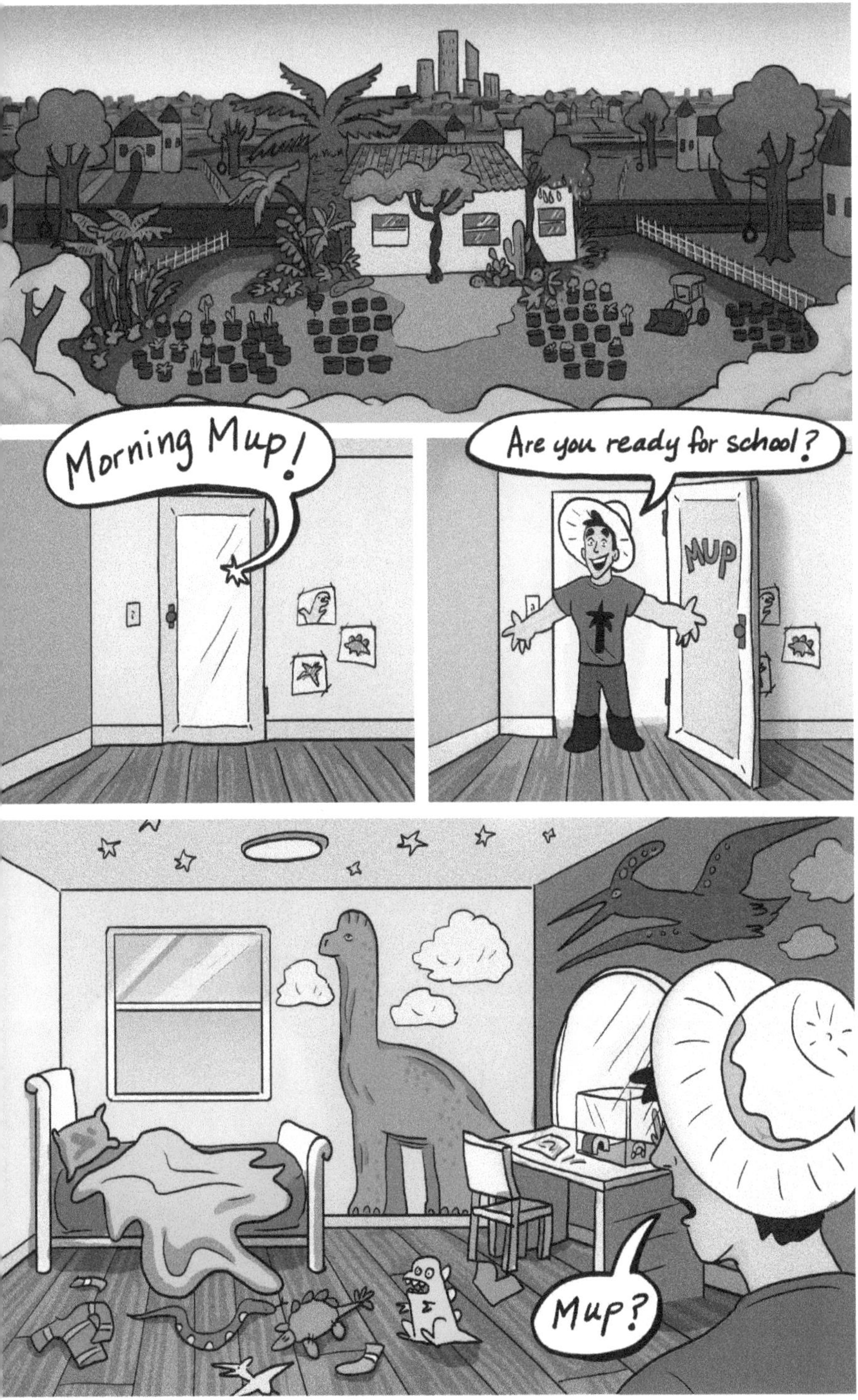
Morning Mup!
Are you ready for school?
MUP
Mup?

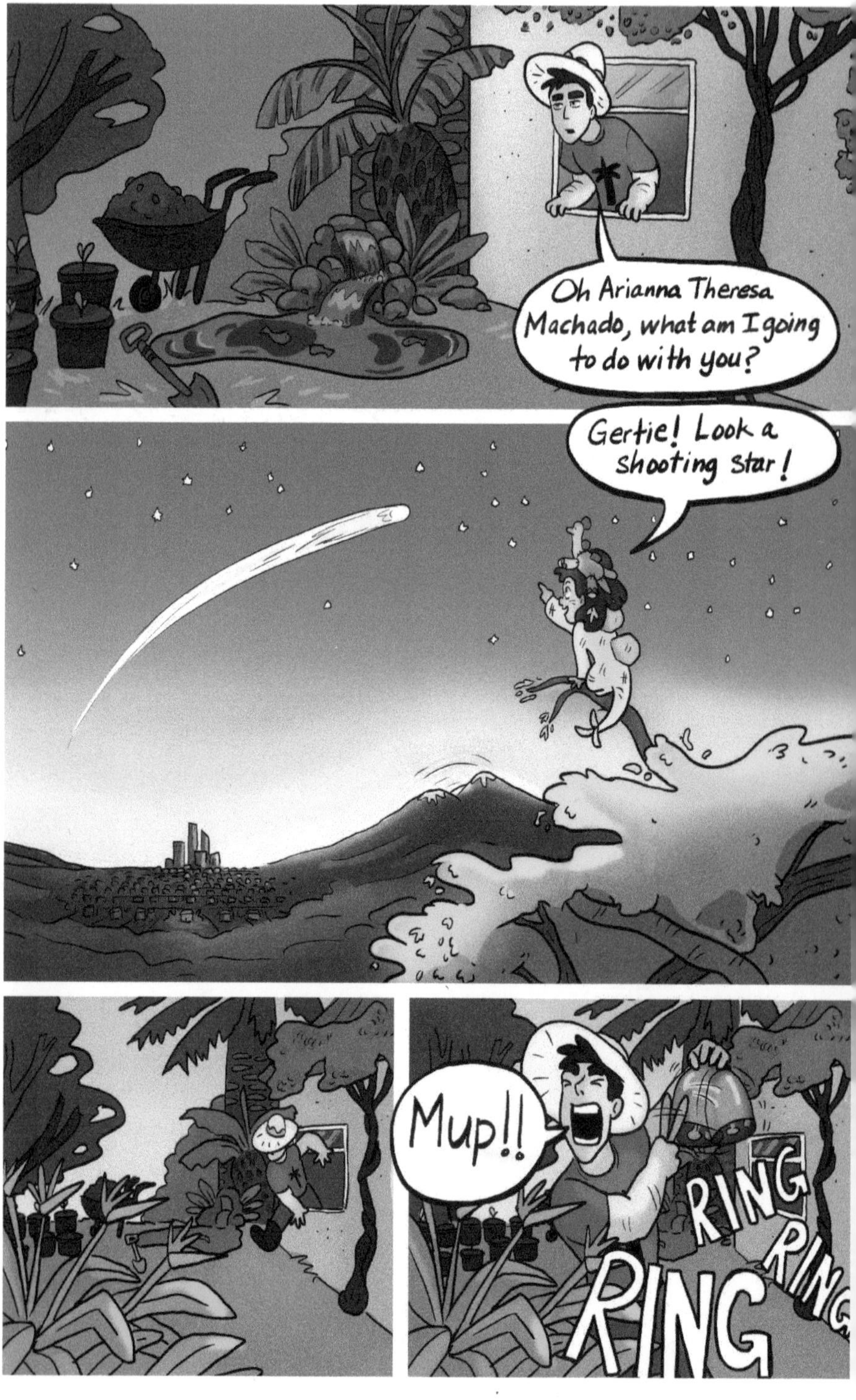
Oh Arianna Theresa Machado, what am I going to do with you?
Gertie! Look a shooting star!
Mup!!
RING
RING
RING

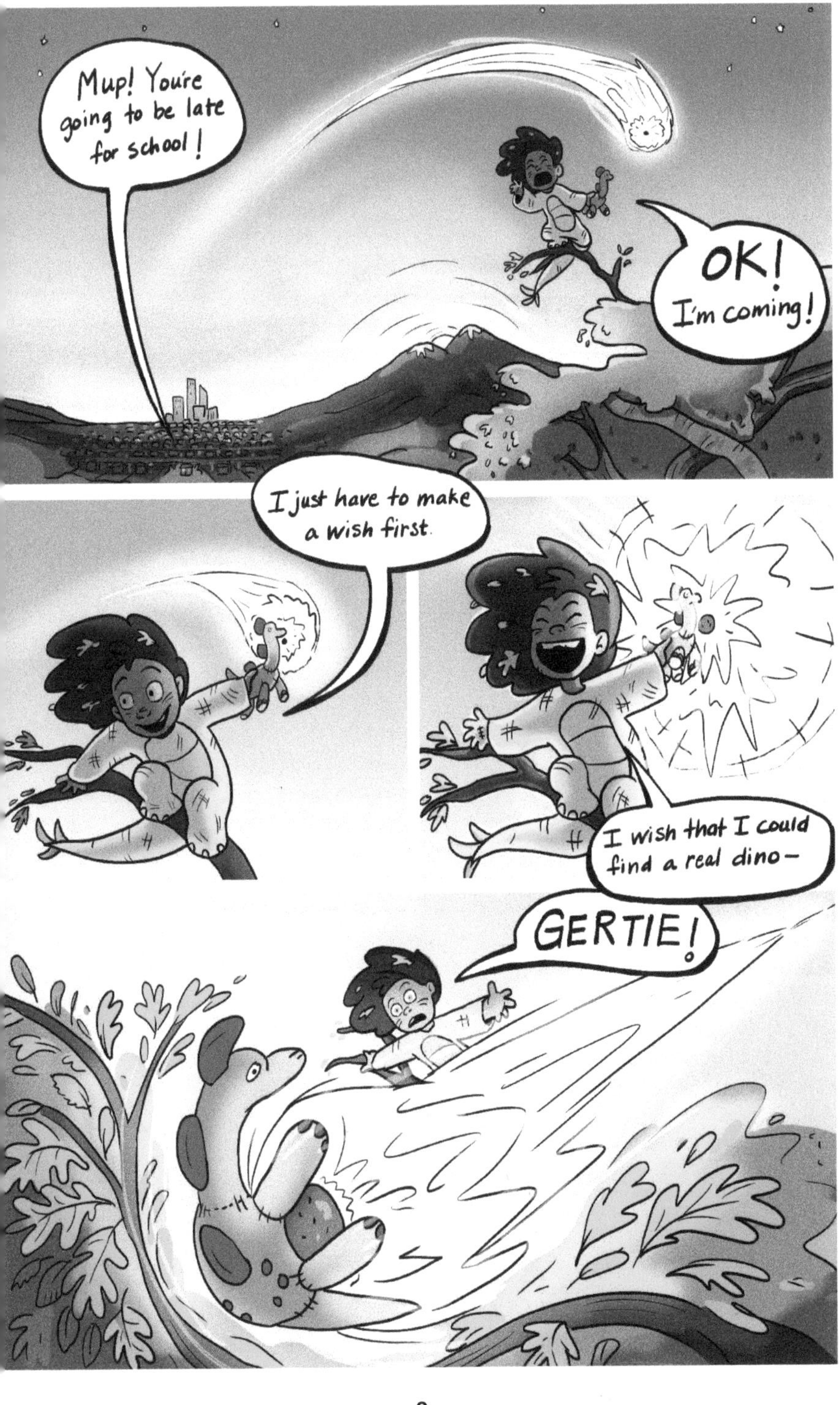
Mup! You're going to be late for school!
OK! I'm coming!
I just have to make a wish first.
I wish that I could find a real dino–
GERTIE!

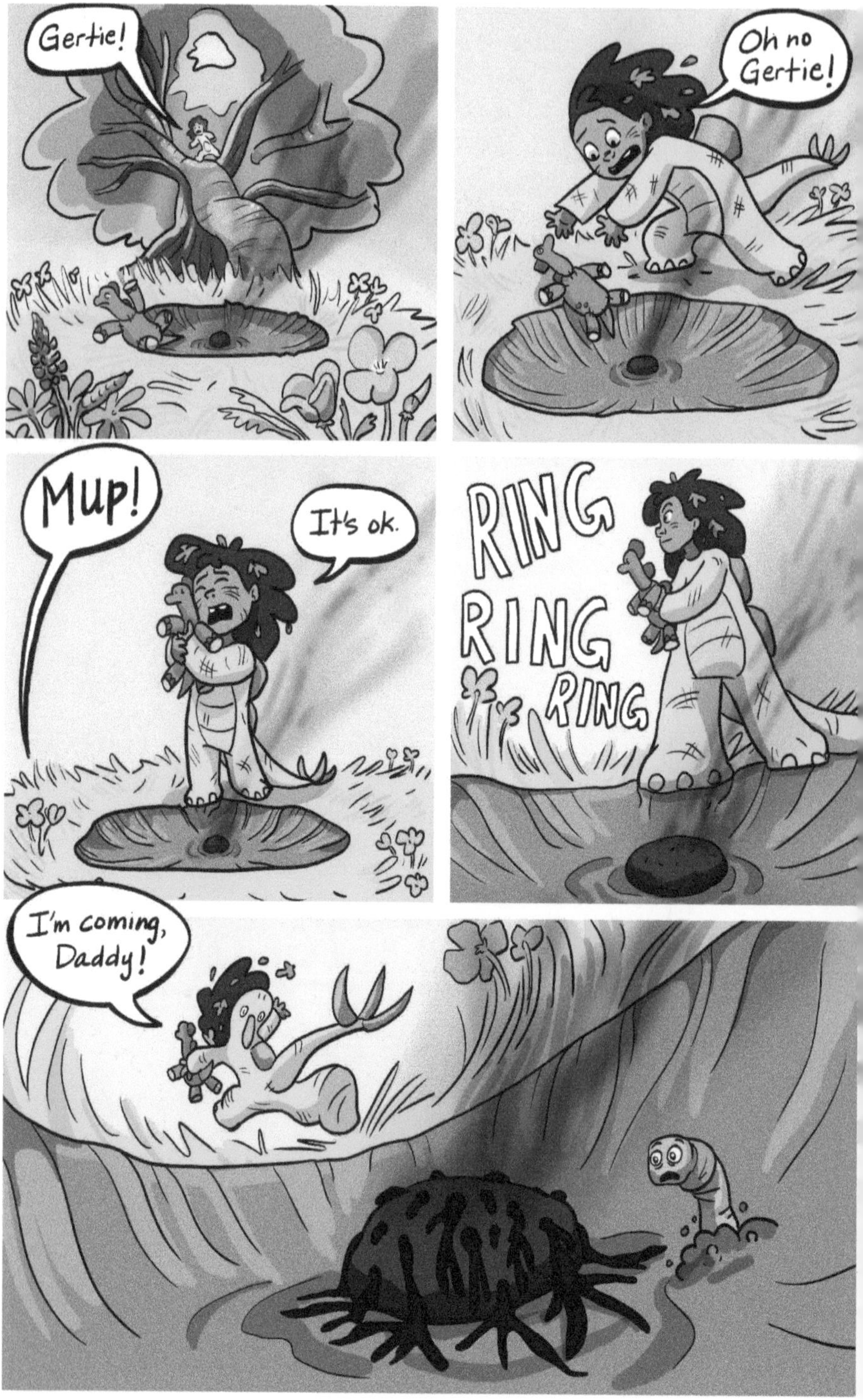
Gertie!
Oh no Gertie!
Mup!
It's ok.
RING
RING
RING
I'm coming, Daddy!

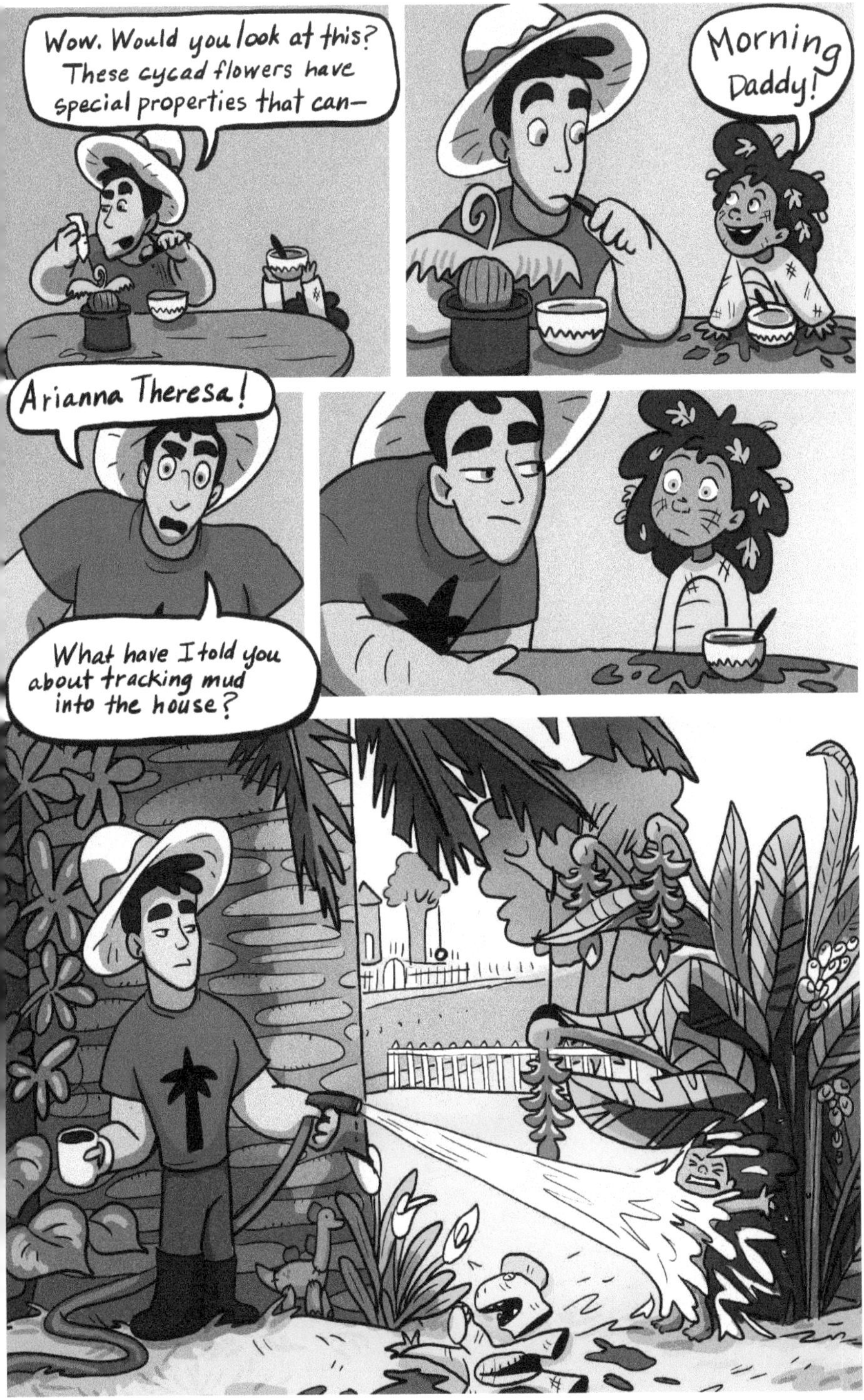
Wow. Would you look at this? These cycad flowers have special properties that can–
Morning Daddy!
Arianna Theresa!
What have I told you about tracking mud into the house?

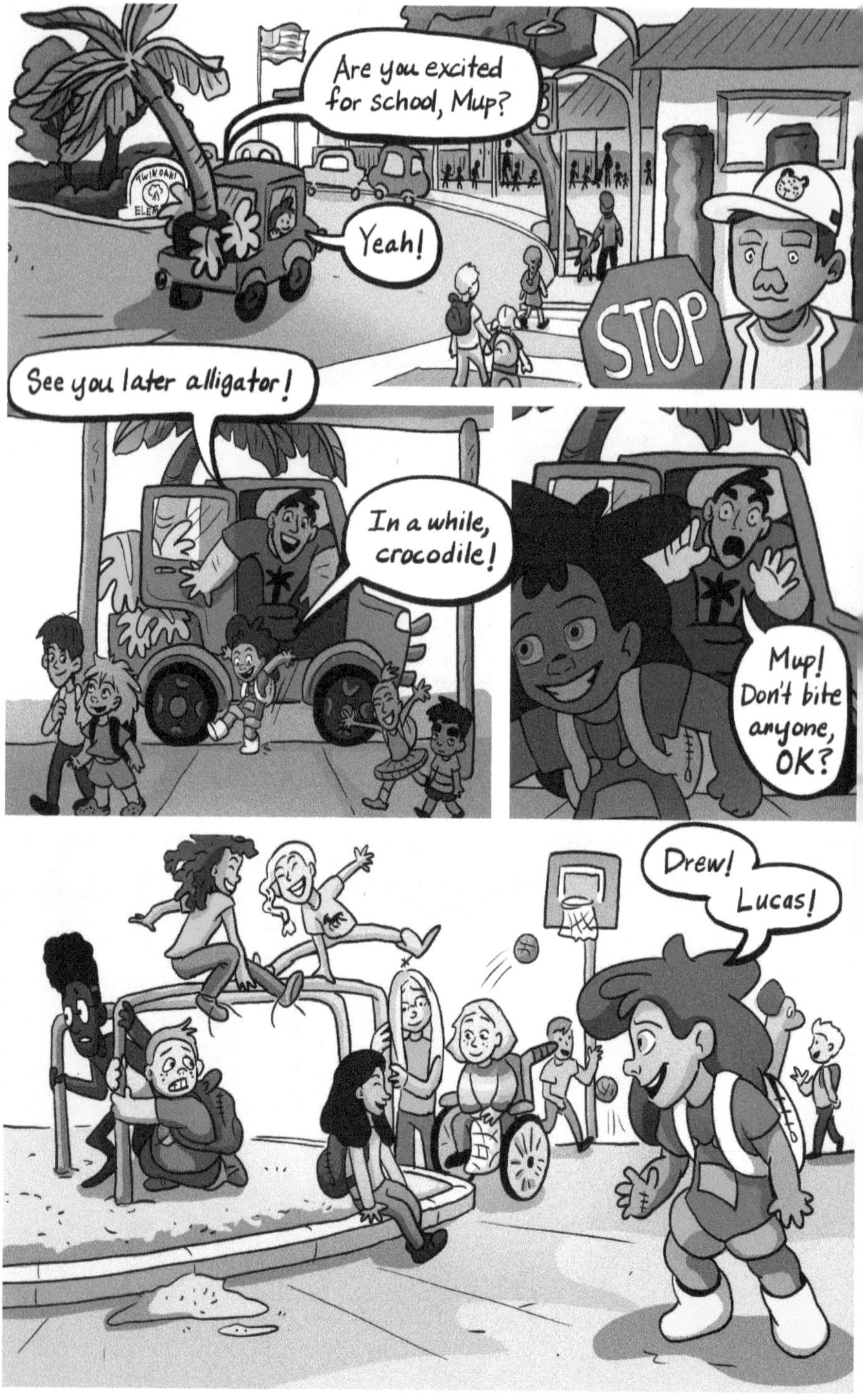

Are you excited for school, Mup?
Yeah!
TWIN OAKS ELEM
STOP
See you later alligator!
In a while, crocodile!
Mup! Don't bite anyone, OK?
Drew! Lucas!

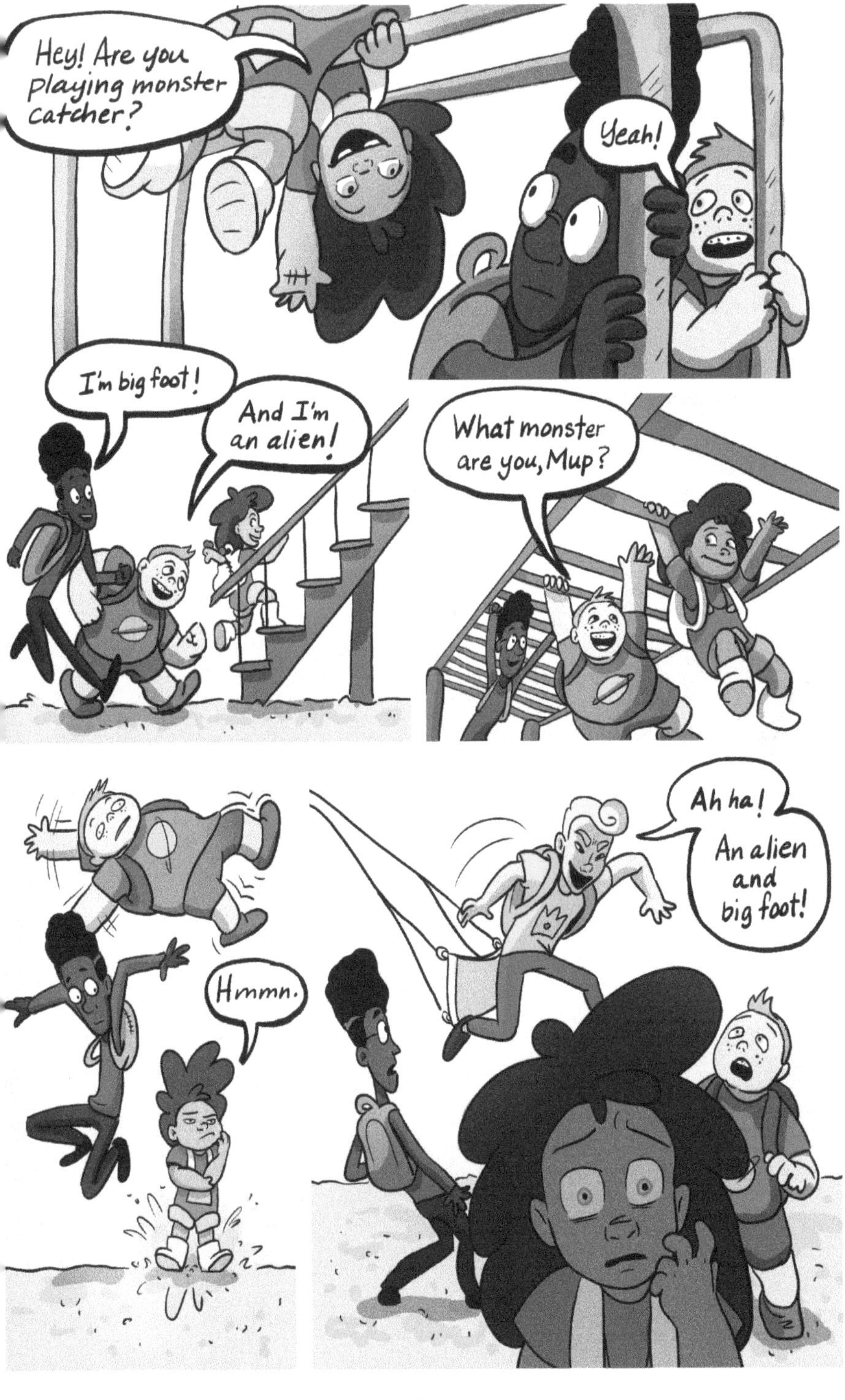
Hey! Are you playing monster catcher?
Yeah!
I'm big foot!
And I'm an alien!
What monster are you, Mup?
Hmmn.
Ah ha!
An alien and big foot!

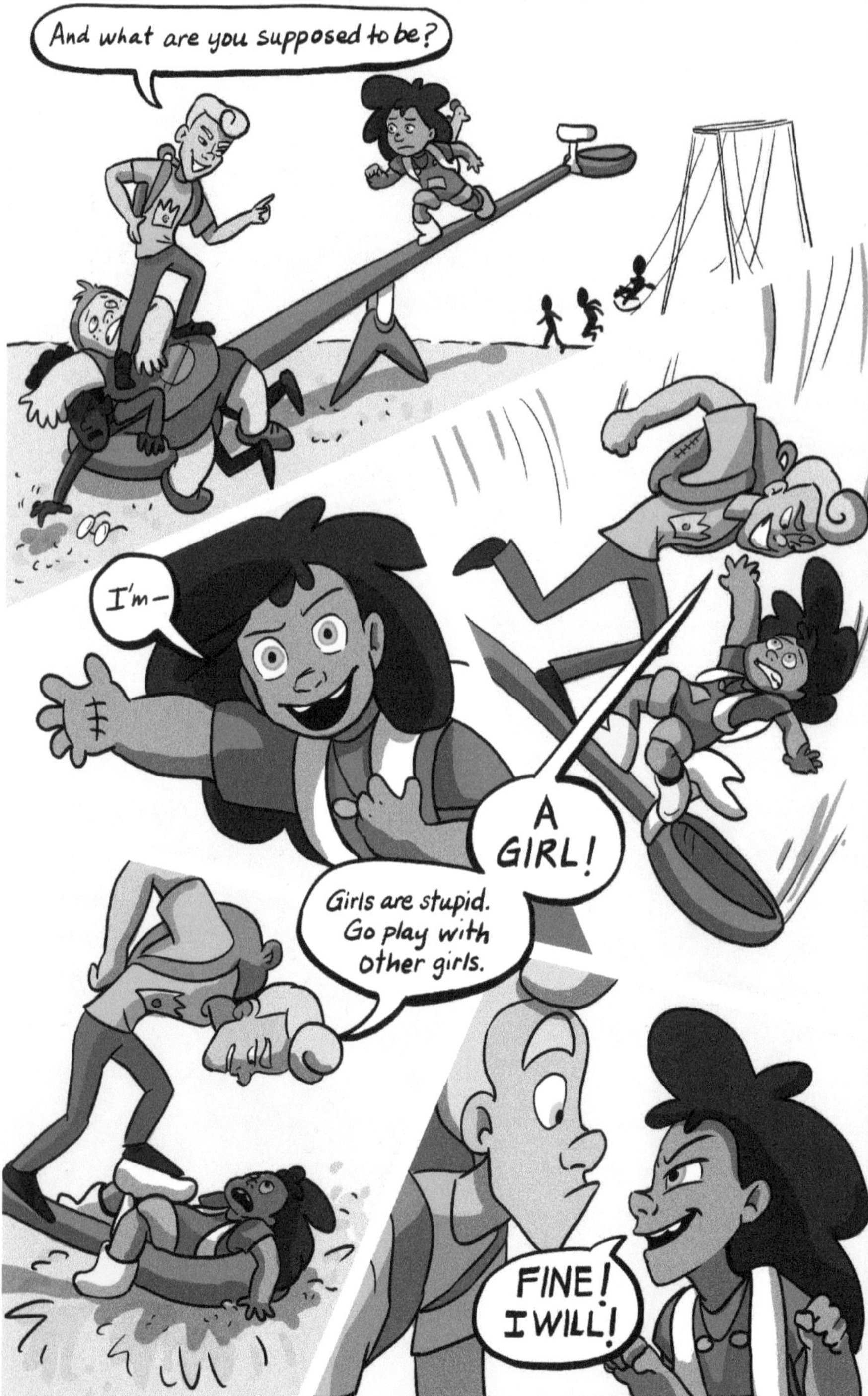
And what are you supposed to be?
I'm—
A GIRL!
Girls are stupid. Go play with other girls.
FINE! I WILL!

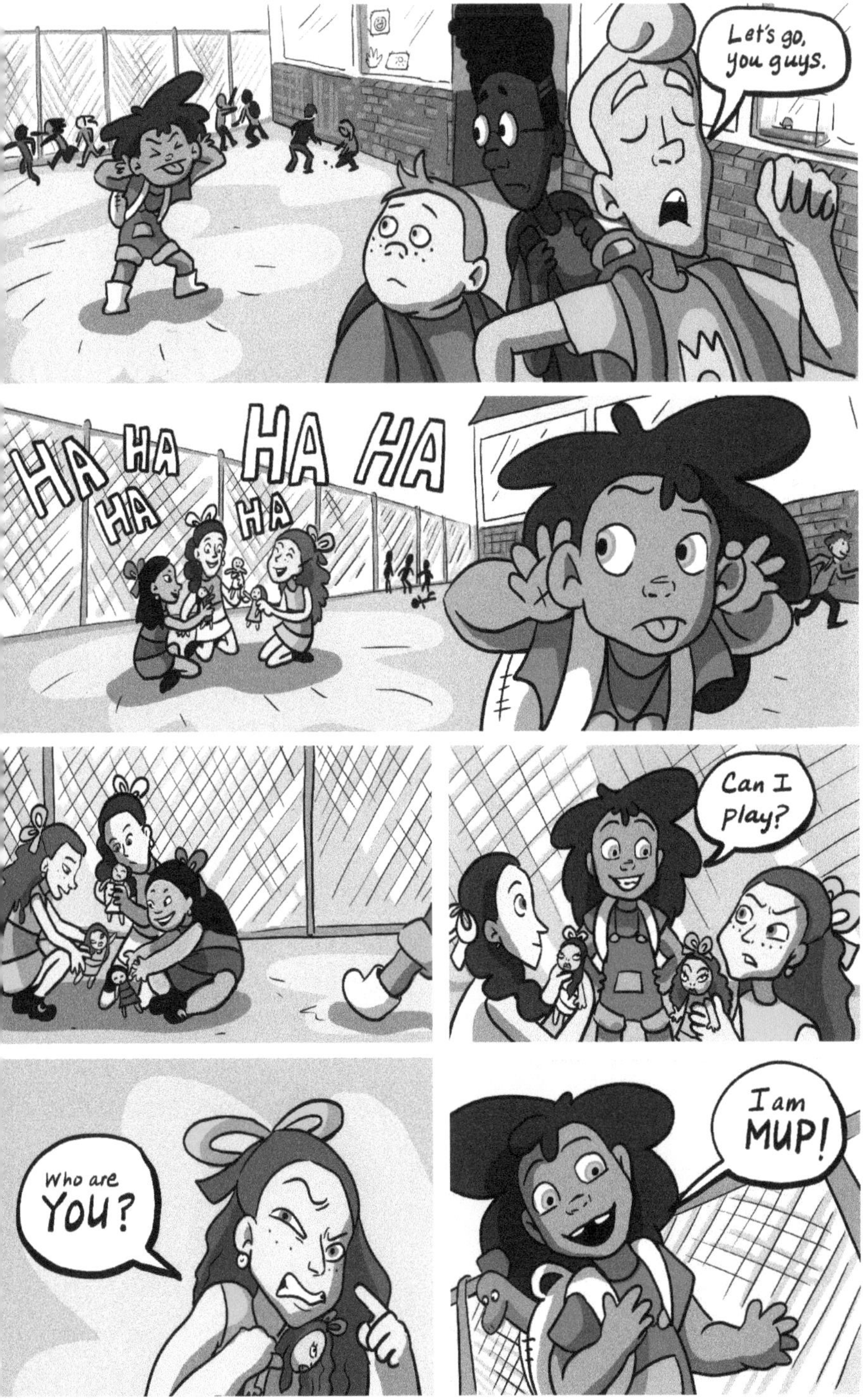
Let's go, you guys.
HA HA HA HA HA HA
Can I play?
Who are YOU?
I am MUP!

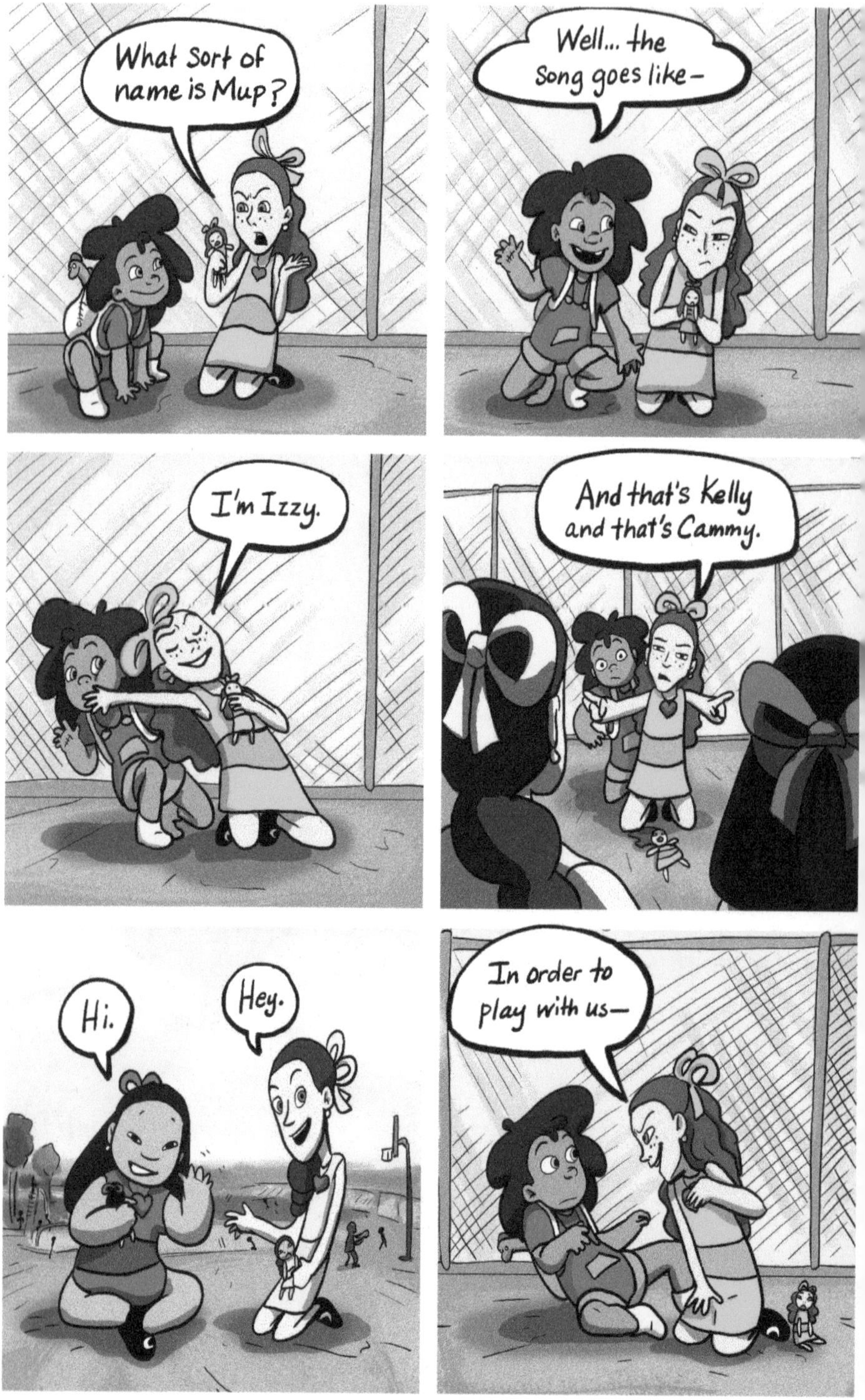
What sort of name is Mup?
Well... the song goes like-
I'm Izzy.
And that's Kelly and that's Cammy.
Hi.
Hey.
In order to play with us-

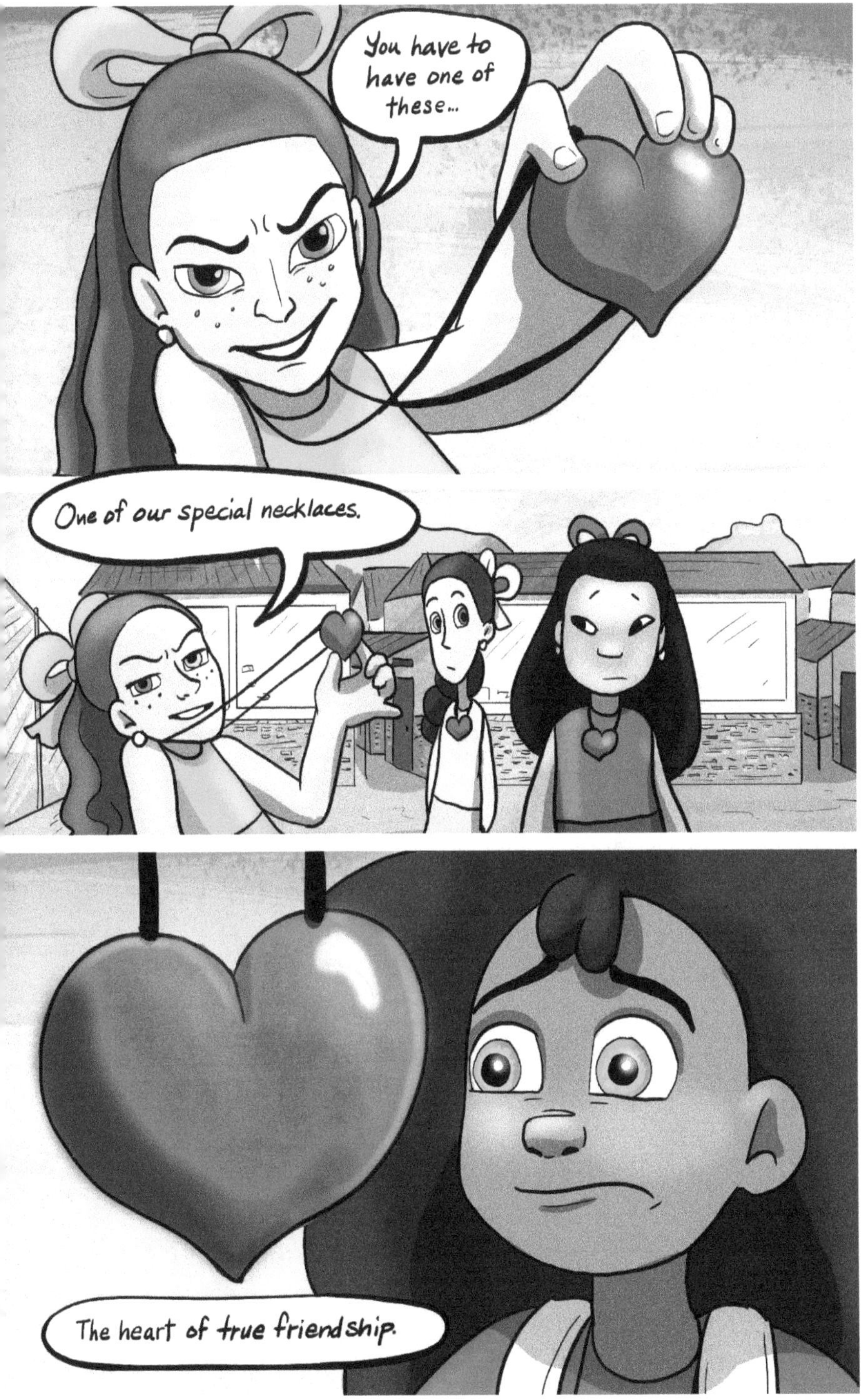
You have to have one of these...
One of our special necklaces.
The heart of true friendship.

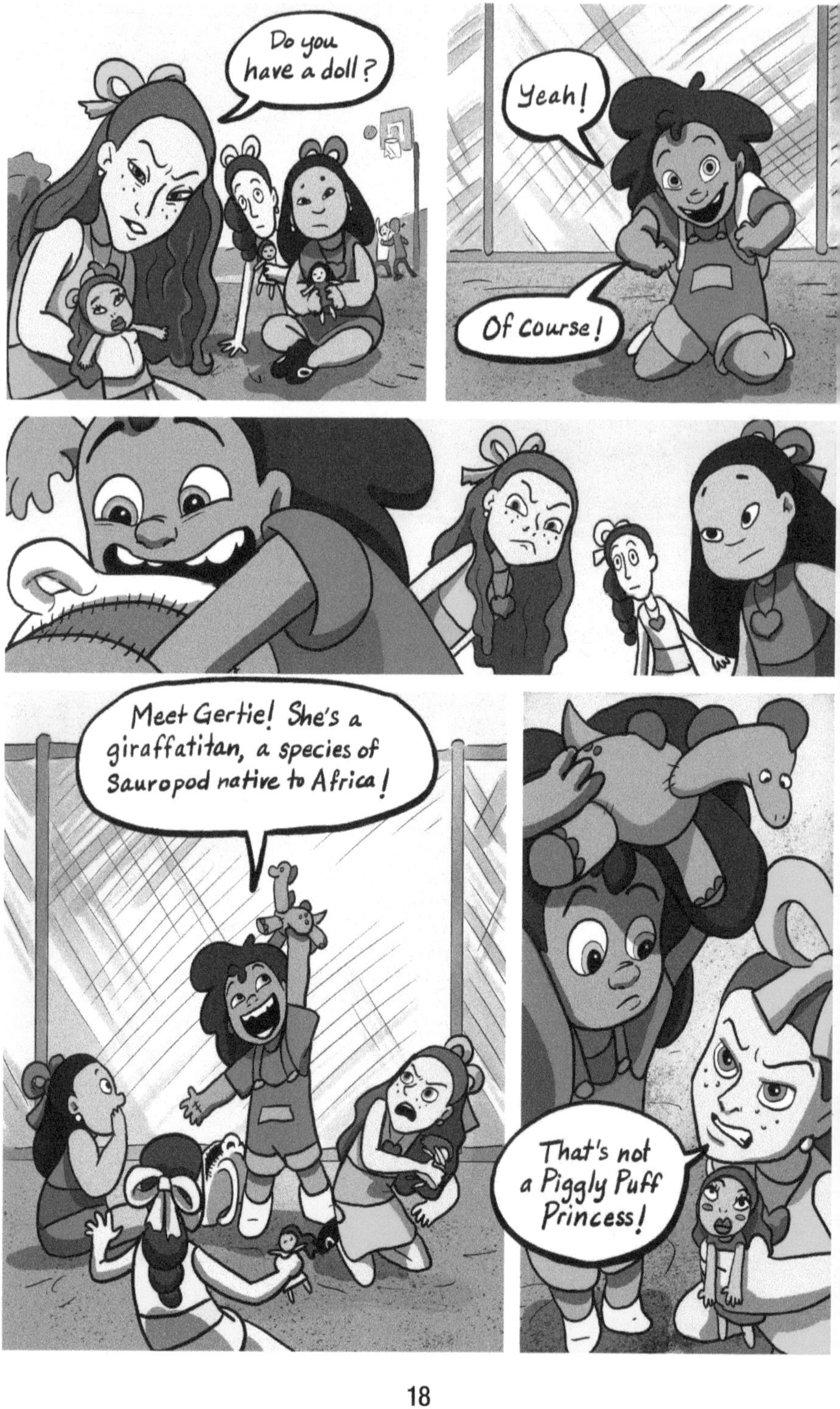
Do you have a doll?
Yeah!
Of course!
Meet Gertie! She's a giraffatitan, a species of Sauropod native to Africa!
That's not a Piggly Puff Princess!

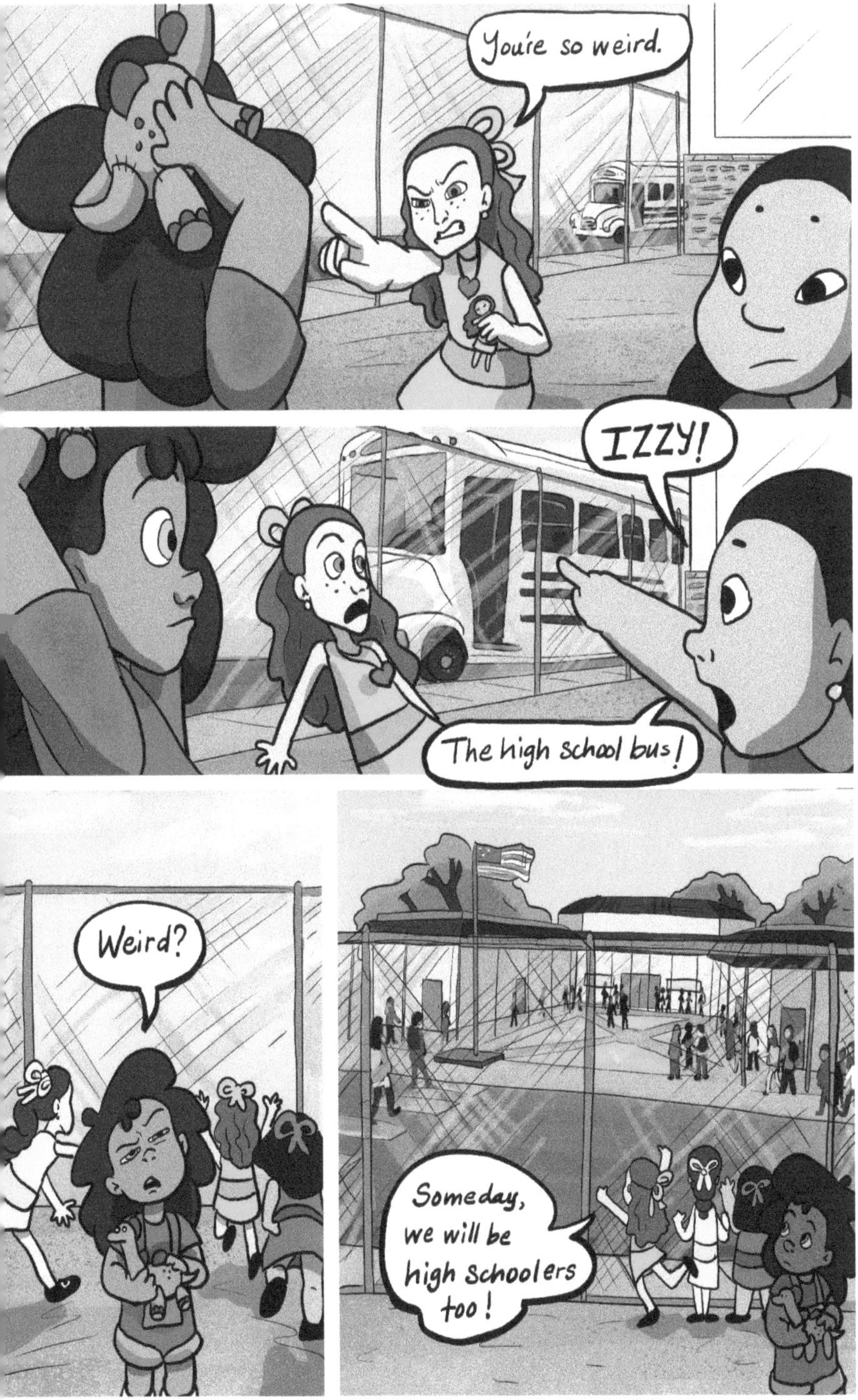
You're so weird.
IZZY!
The high school bus!
Weird?
Someday, we will be high schoolers too!

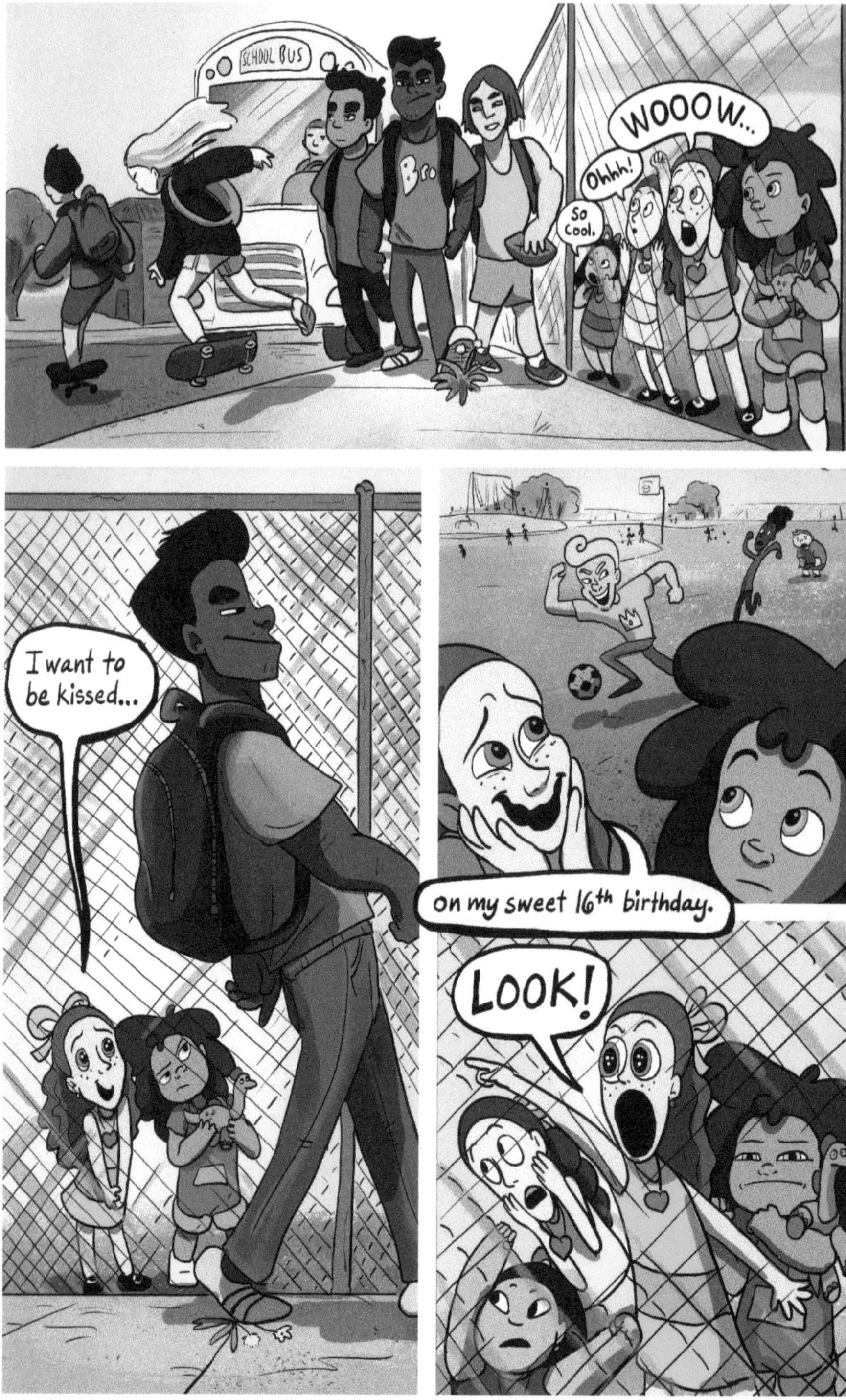
SCHOOL BUS
Bro
WOOOW...
Ohhh!
So cool.
I want to be kissed...
on my sweet 16th birthday.
LOOK!

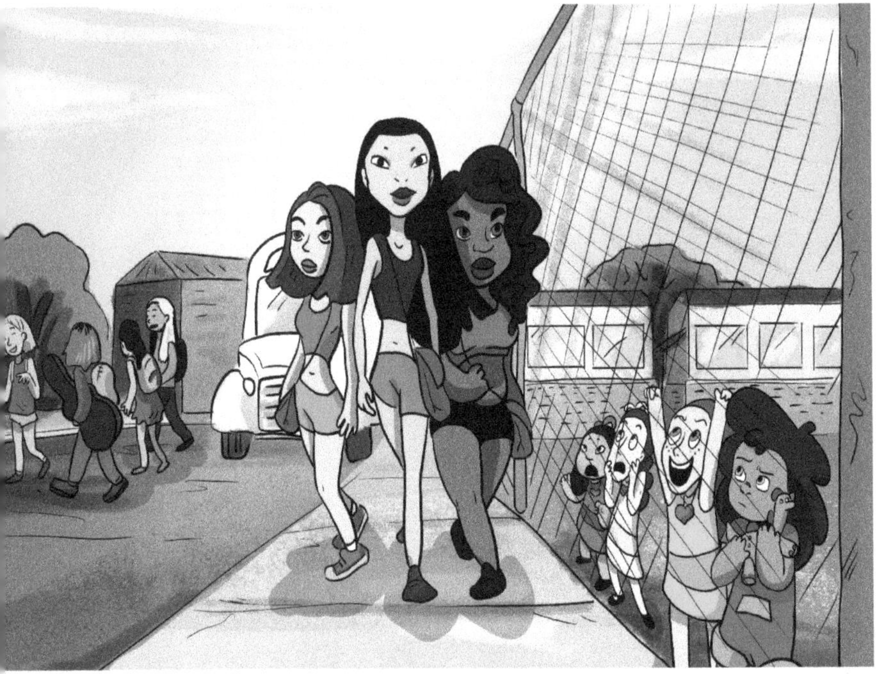

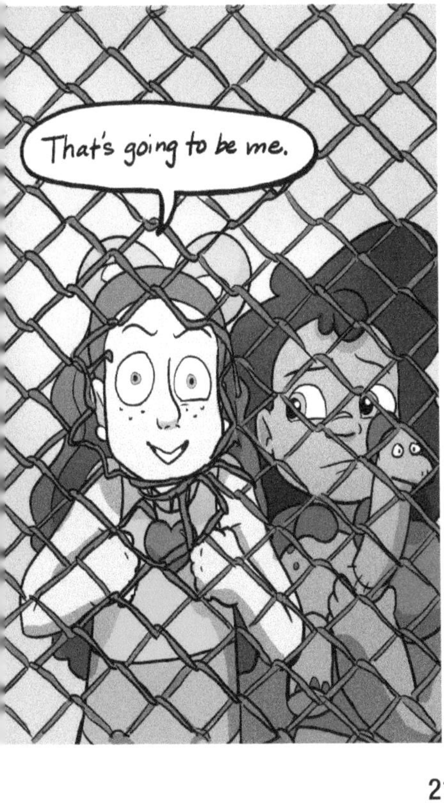
That's going to be me.

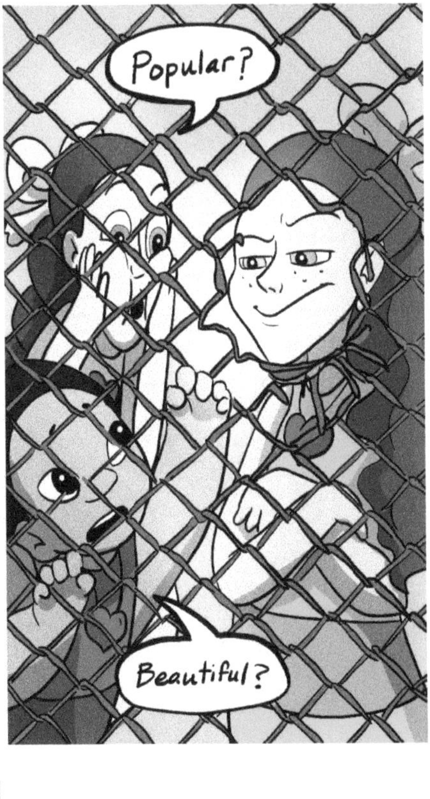
Popular?
Beautiful?

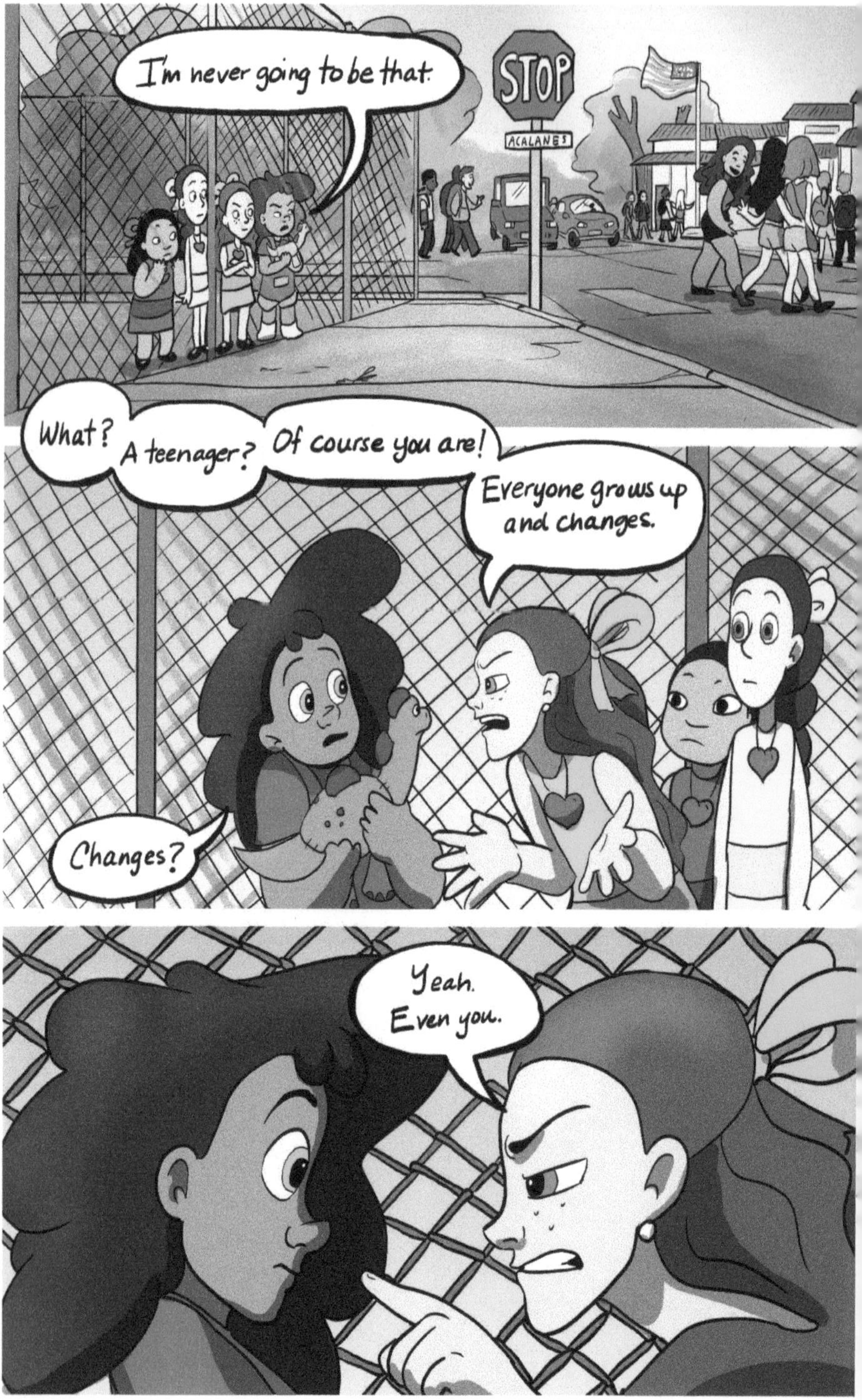
I'm never going to be that.
STOP
ACALANES
What?
A teenager?
Of course you are!
Everyone grows up and changes.
Changes?
Yeah. Even you.

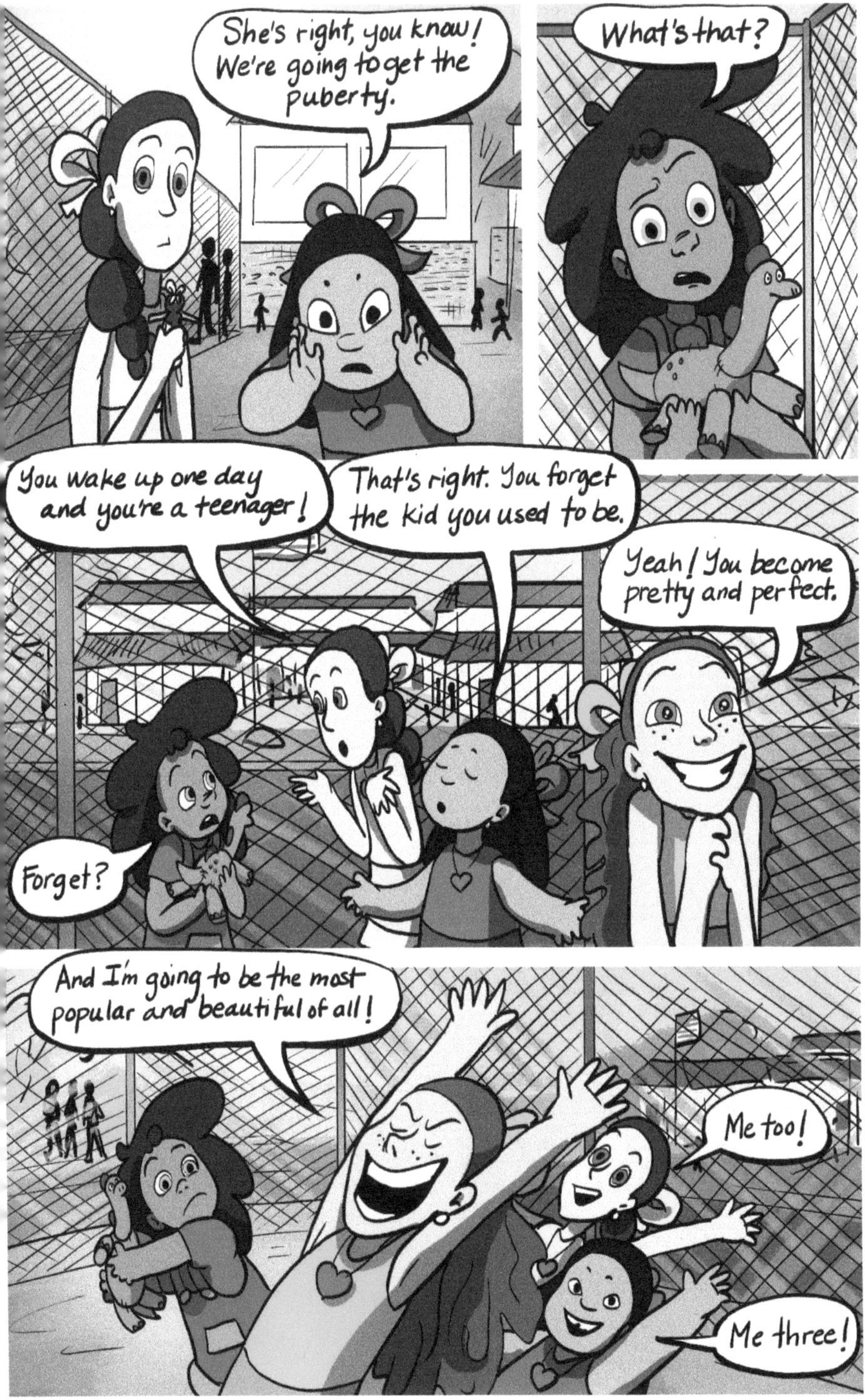
She's right, you know! We're going to get the puberty.
What's that?
You wake up one day and you're a teenager!
That's right. You forget the kid you used to be.
Yeah! You become pretty and perfect.
Forget?
And I'm going to be the most popular and beautiful of all!
Me too!
Me three!

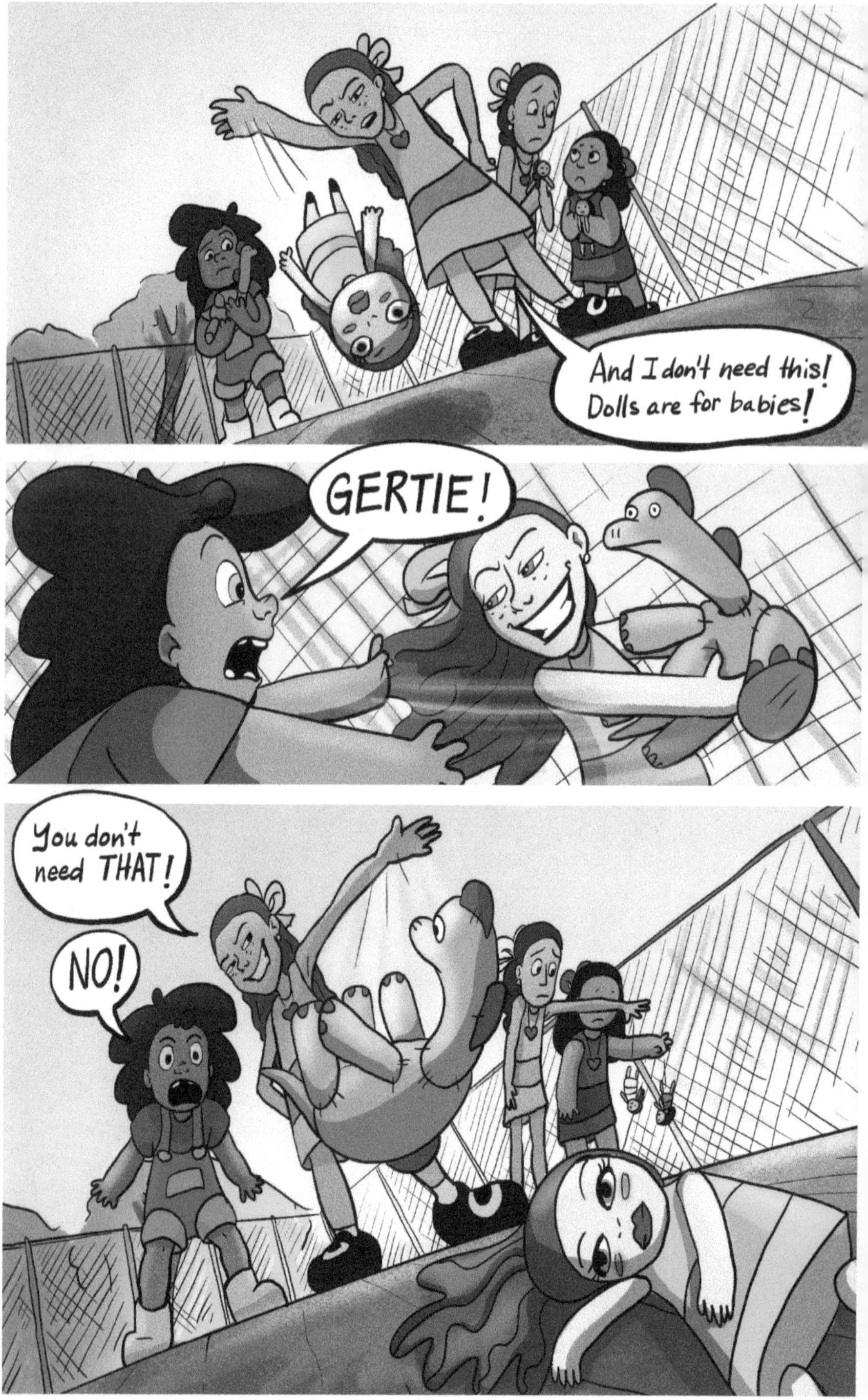
And I don't need this! Dolls are for babies!
GERTIE!
You don't need THAT!
NO!

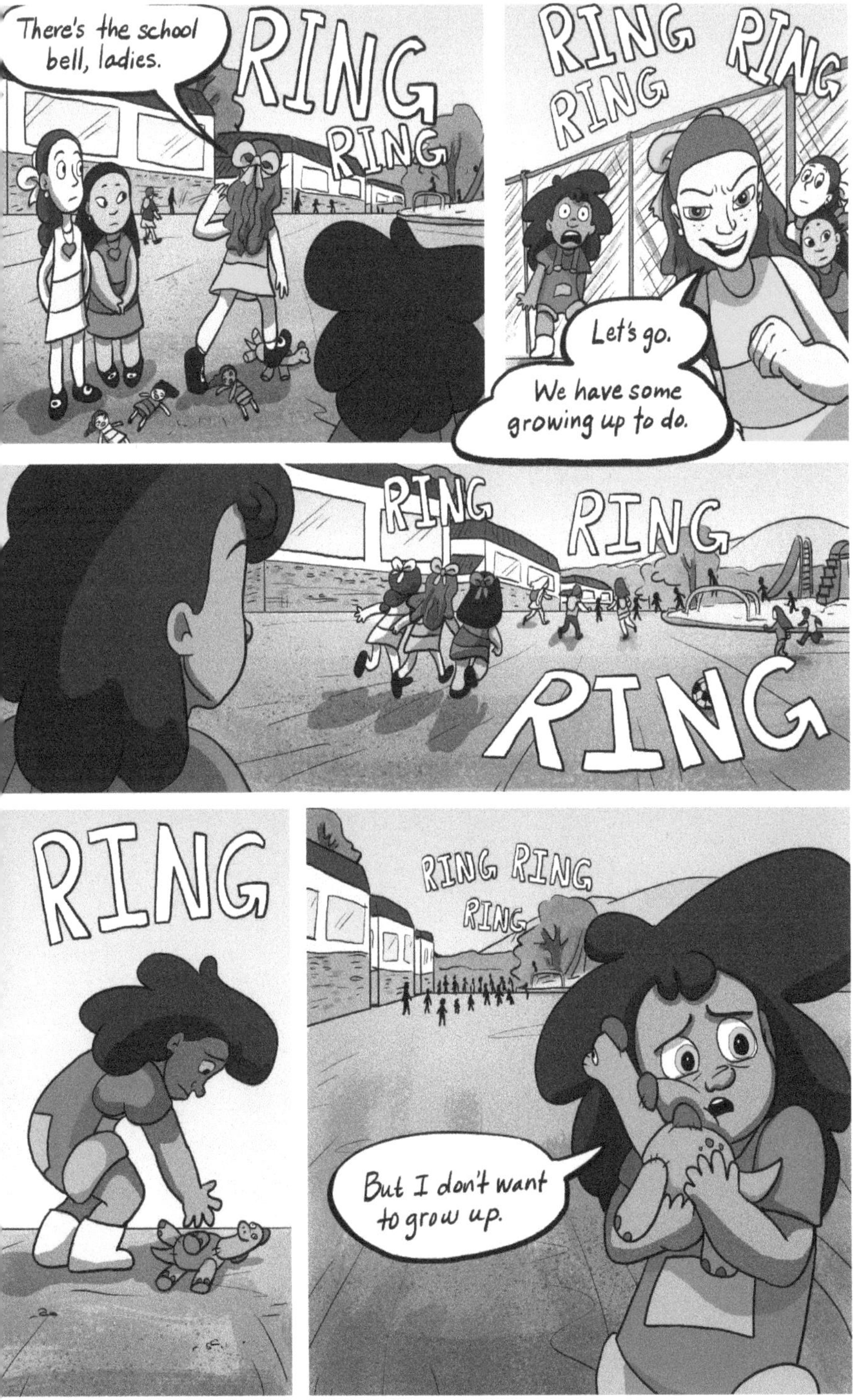
There's the school bell, ladies.
RING
RING
RING
RING
RING
Let's go.
We have some growing up to do.
RING
RING
RING
RING
RING RING
RING
But I don't want to grow up.

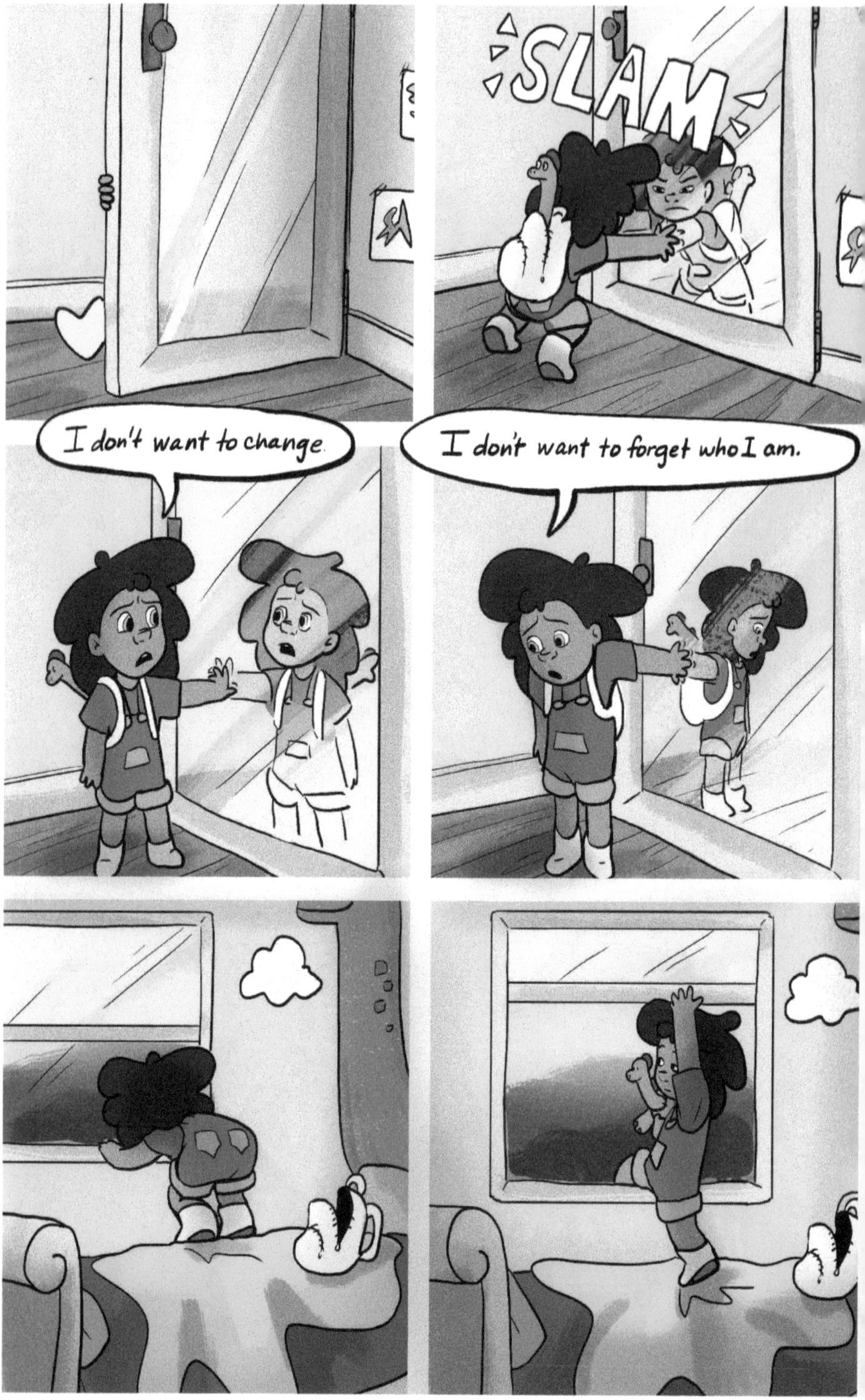
SLAM
I don't want to change.
I don't want to forget who I am.

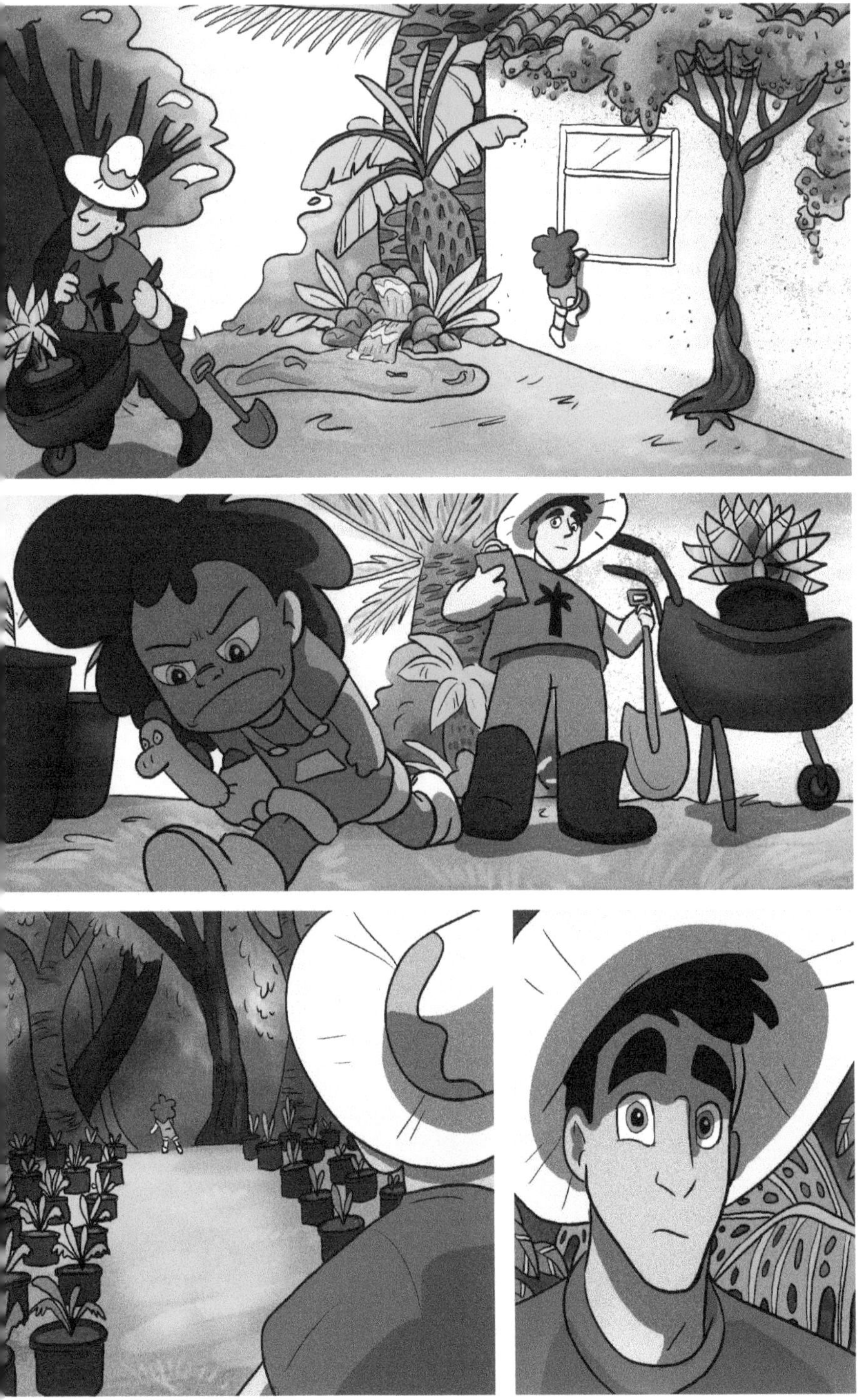

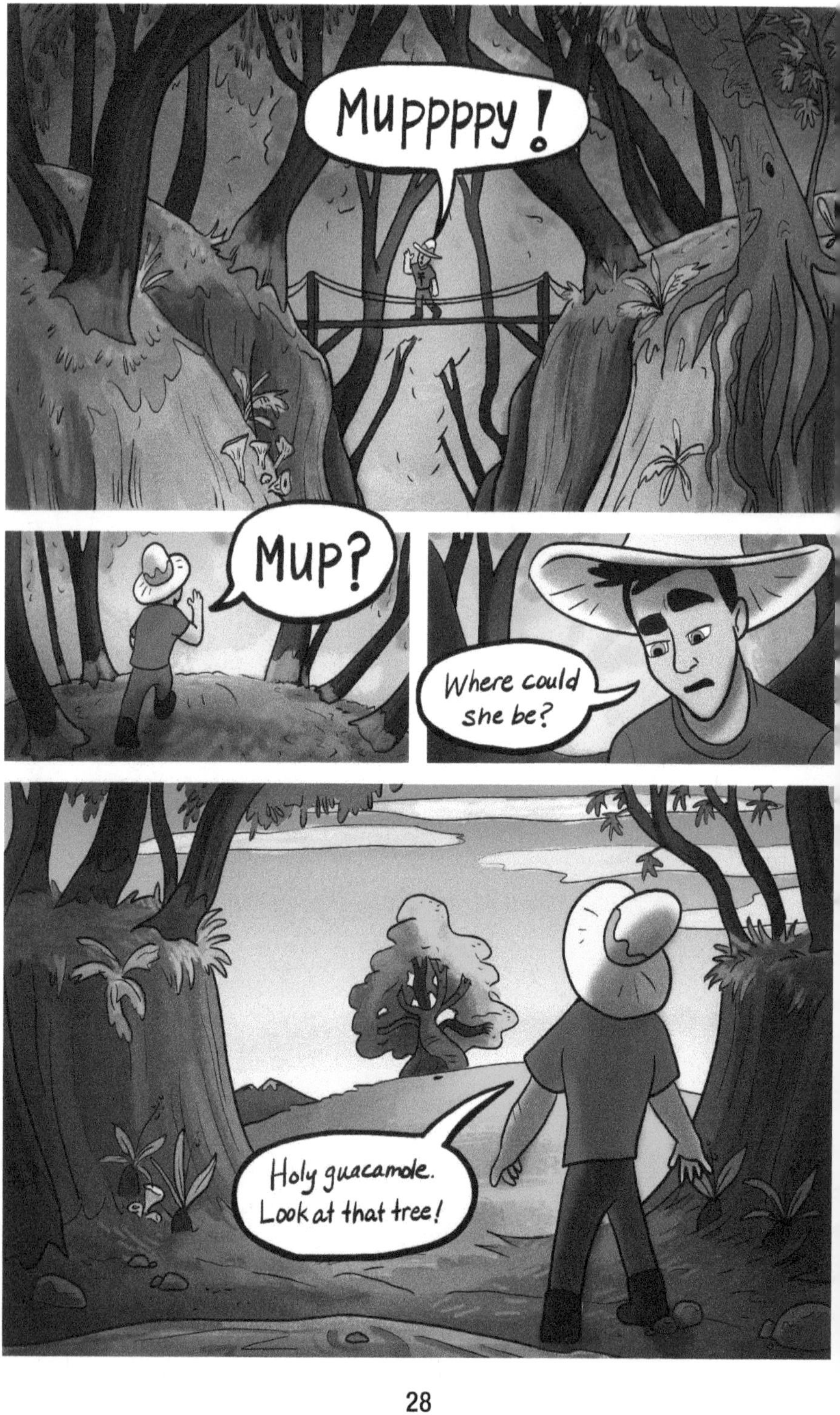
Muppppy!
Mup?
Where could she be?
Holy guacamole. Look at that tree!

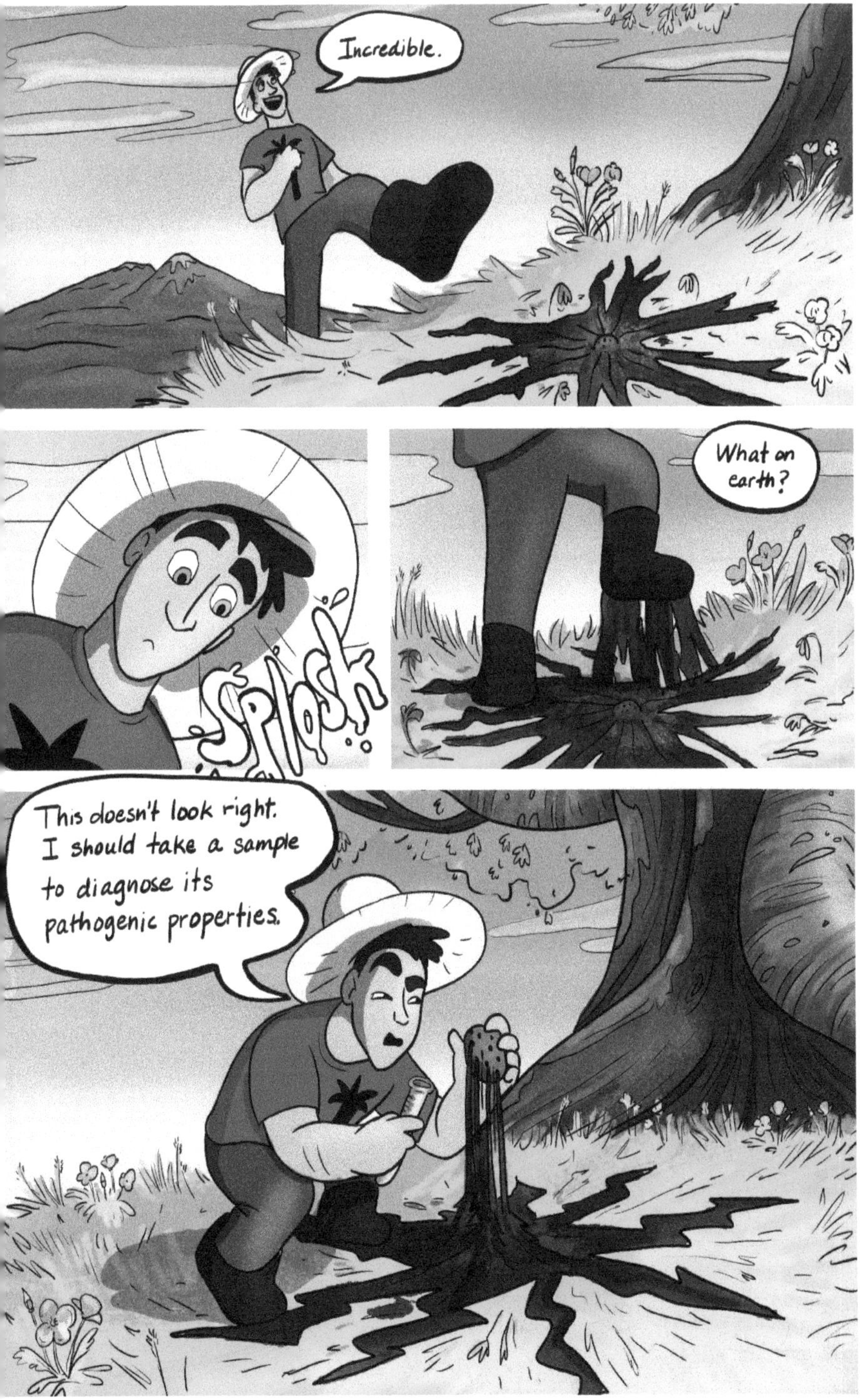
Incredible.
SPLOSH
What on earth?
This doesn't look right. I should take a sample to diagnose its pathogenic properties.

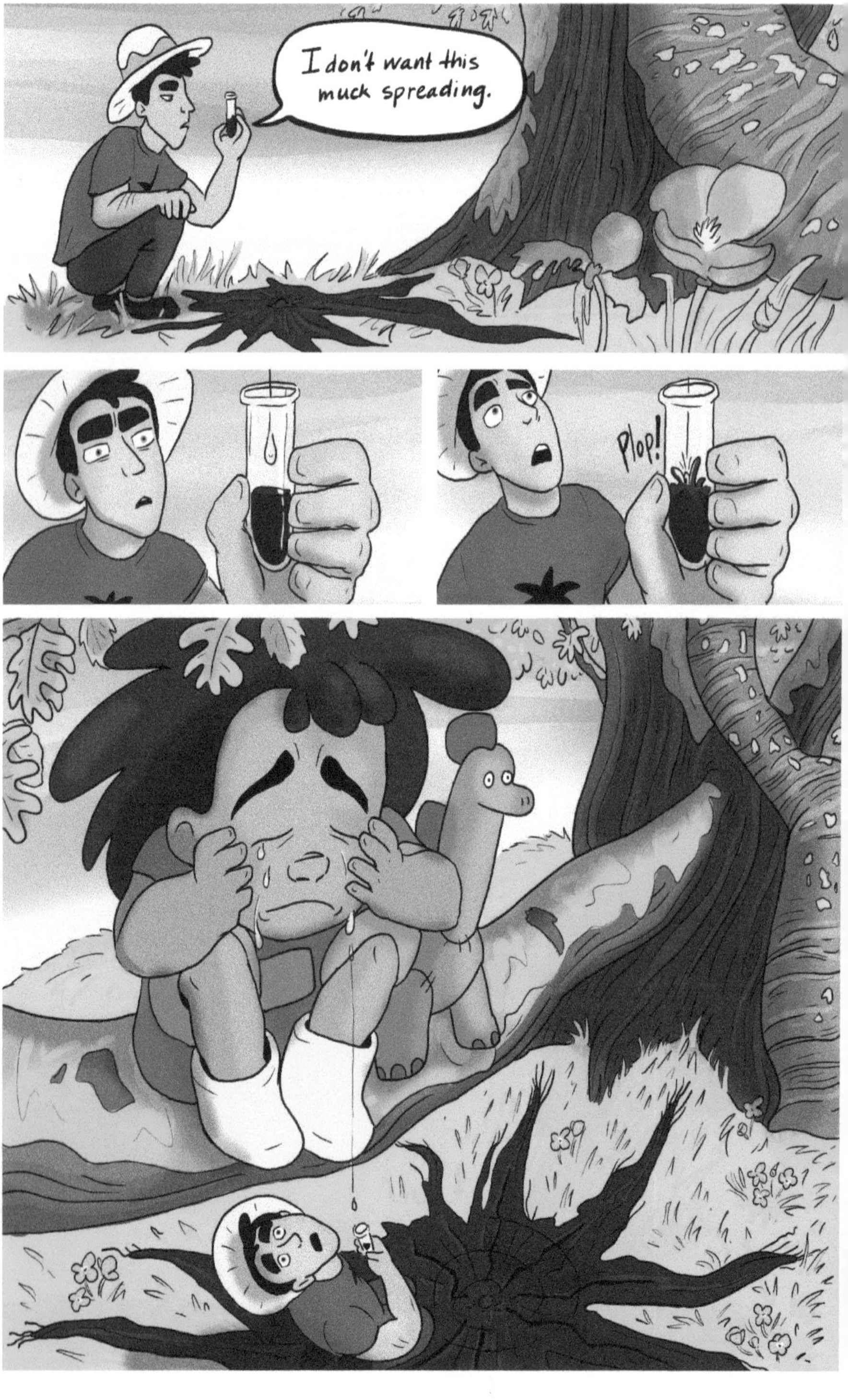
I don't want this muck spreading.
Plop!

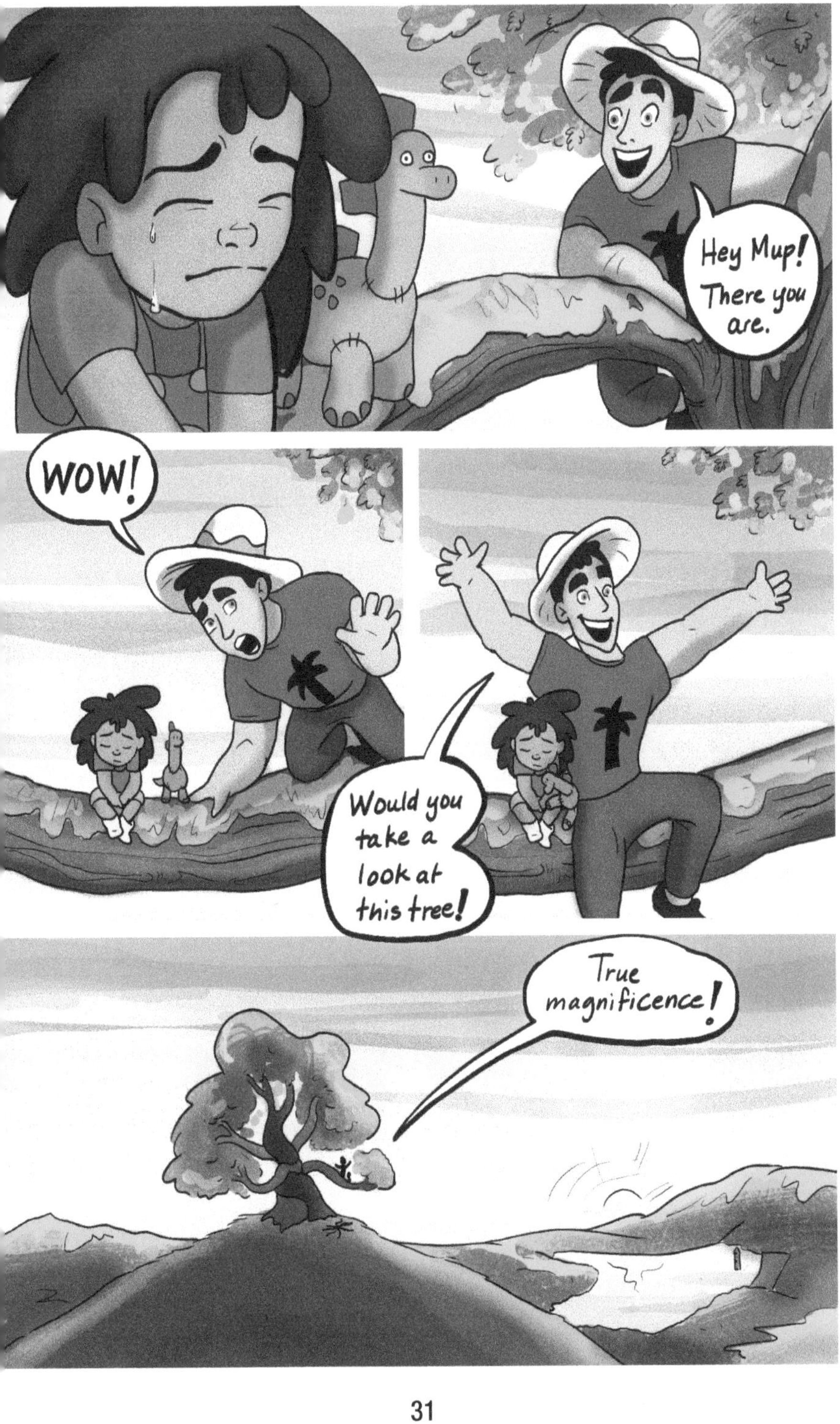
Hey Mup! There you are.
WOW!
Would you take a look at this tree!
True magnificence!

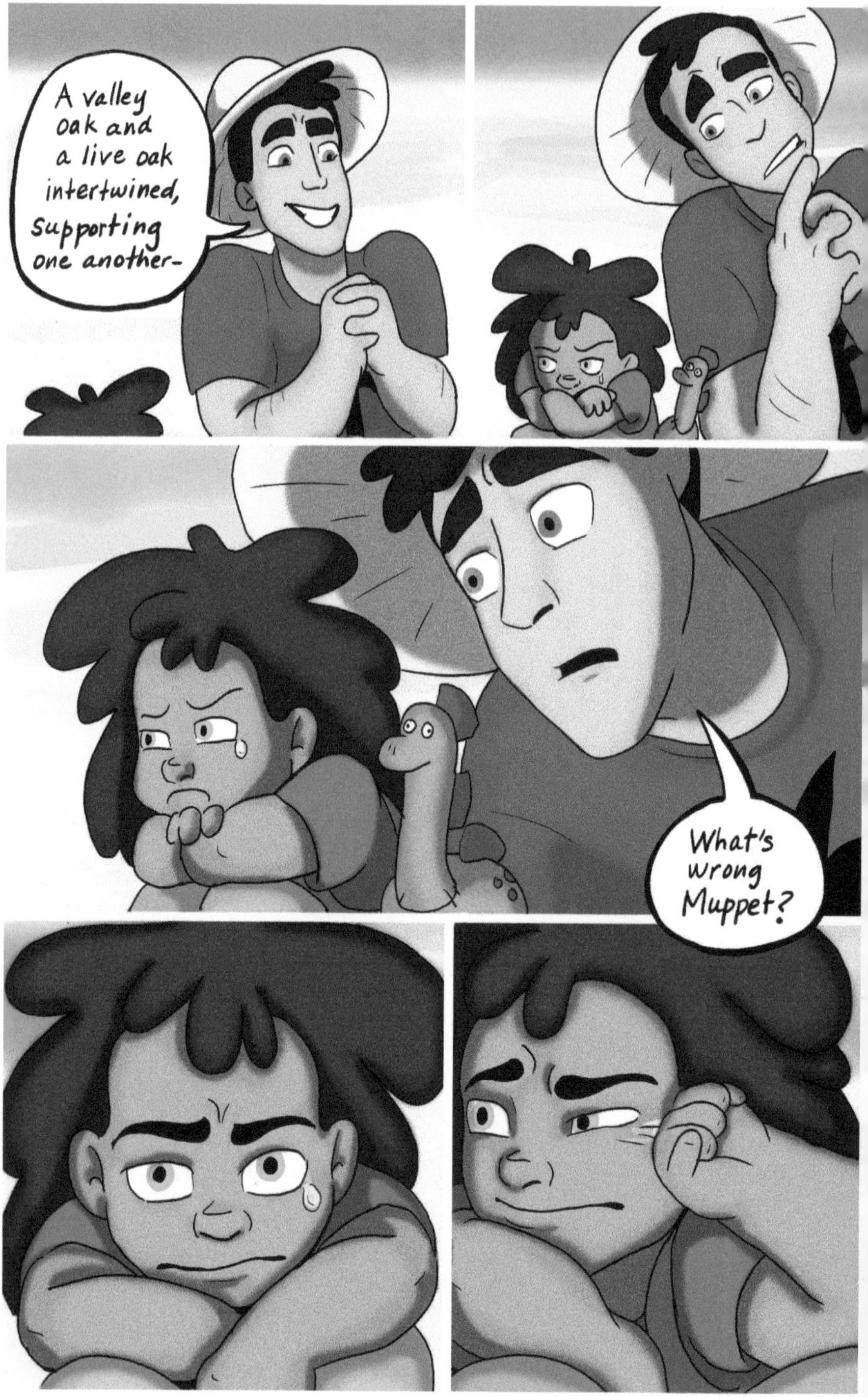
A valley oak and a live oak intertwined, supporting one another-
What's wrong Muppet?

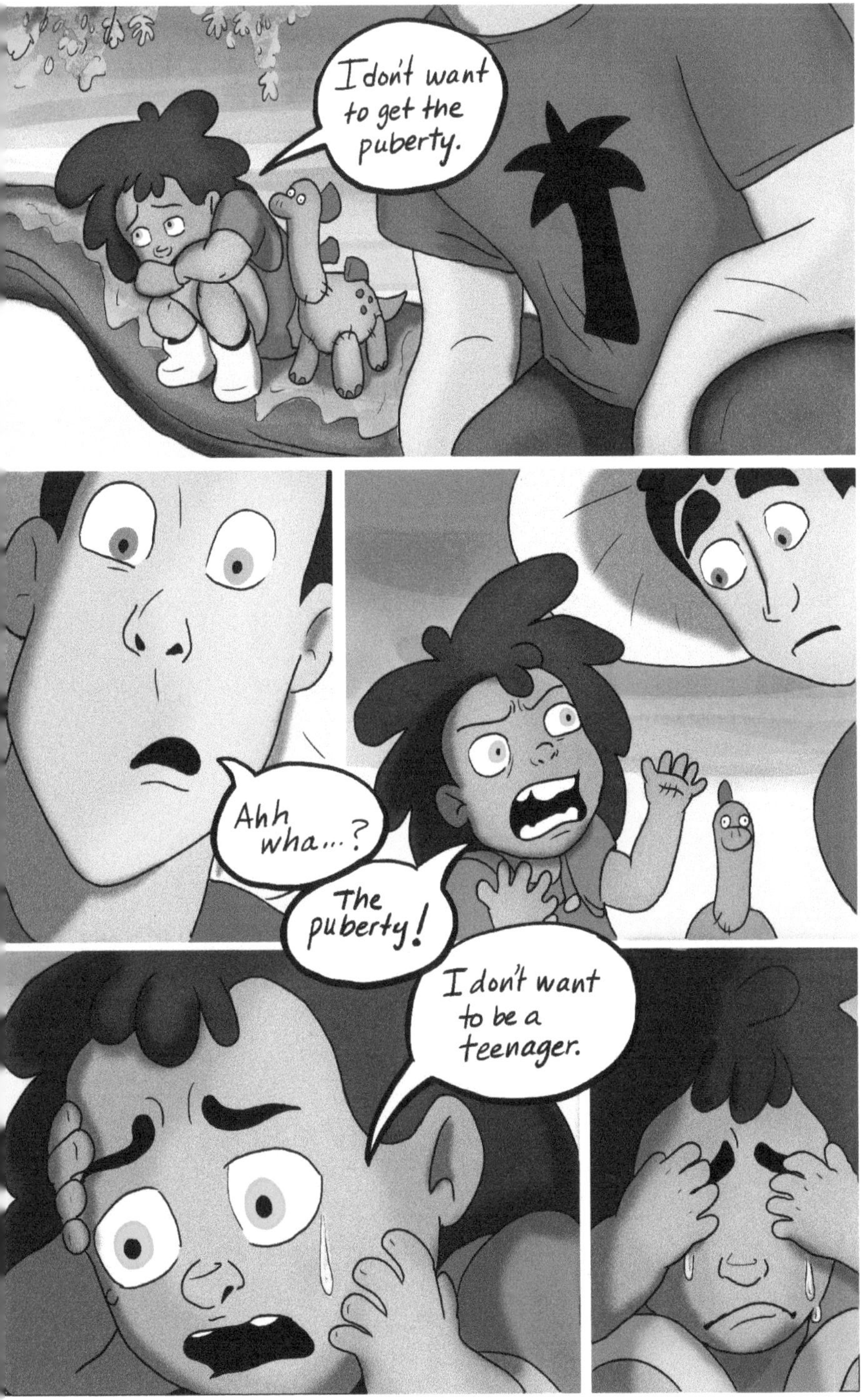
I don't want to get the puberty.
Ahh wha...?
The puberty!
I don't want to be a teenager.

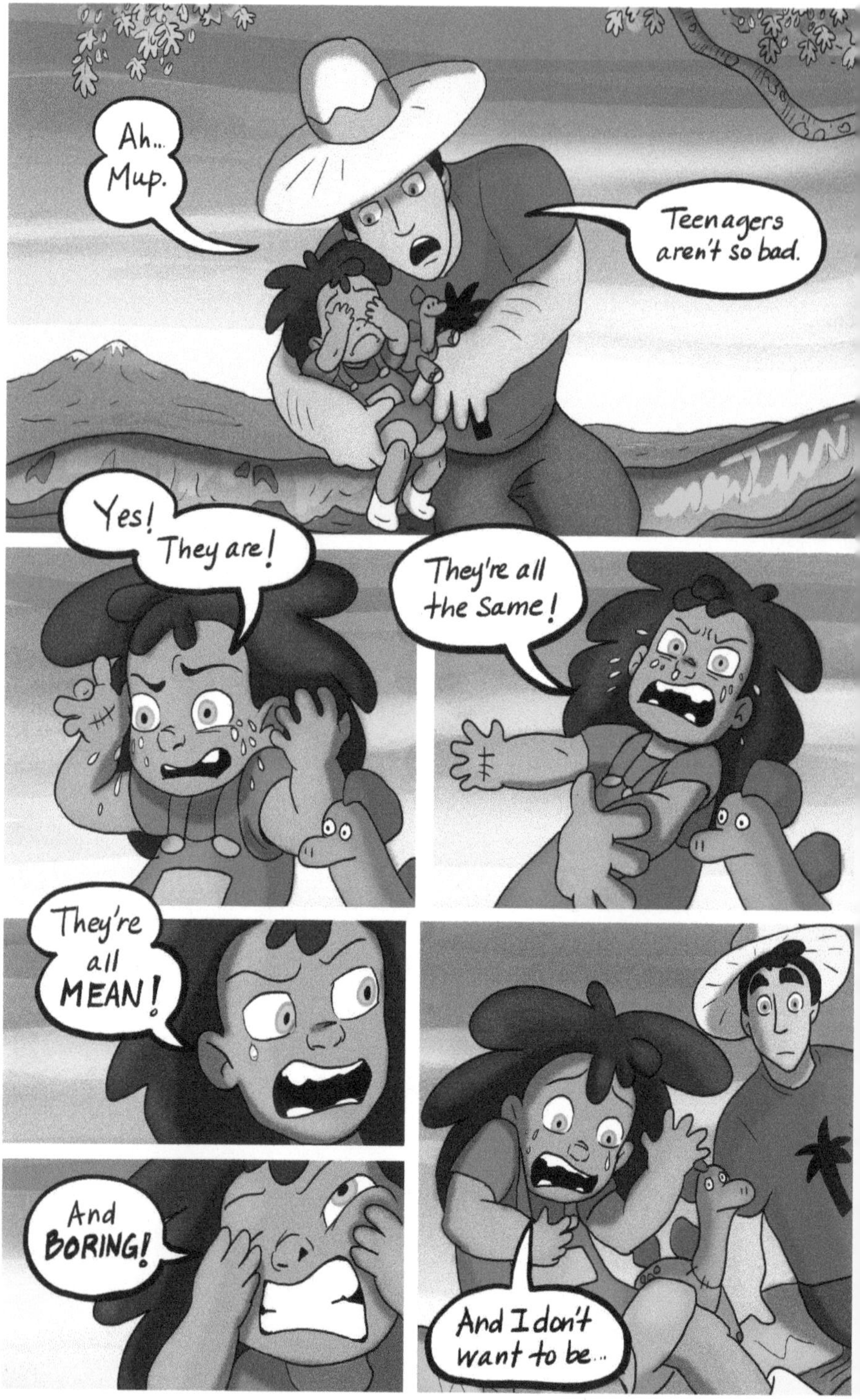
Ah... Mup.
Teenagers aren't so bad.
Yes! They are!
They're all the same!
They're all MEAN!
And BORING!
And I don't want to be...

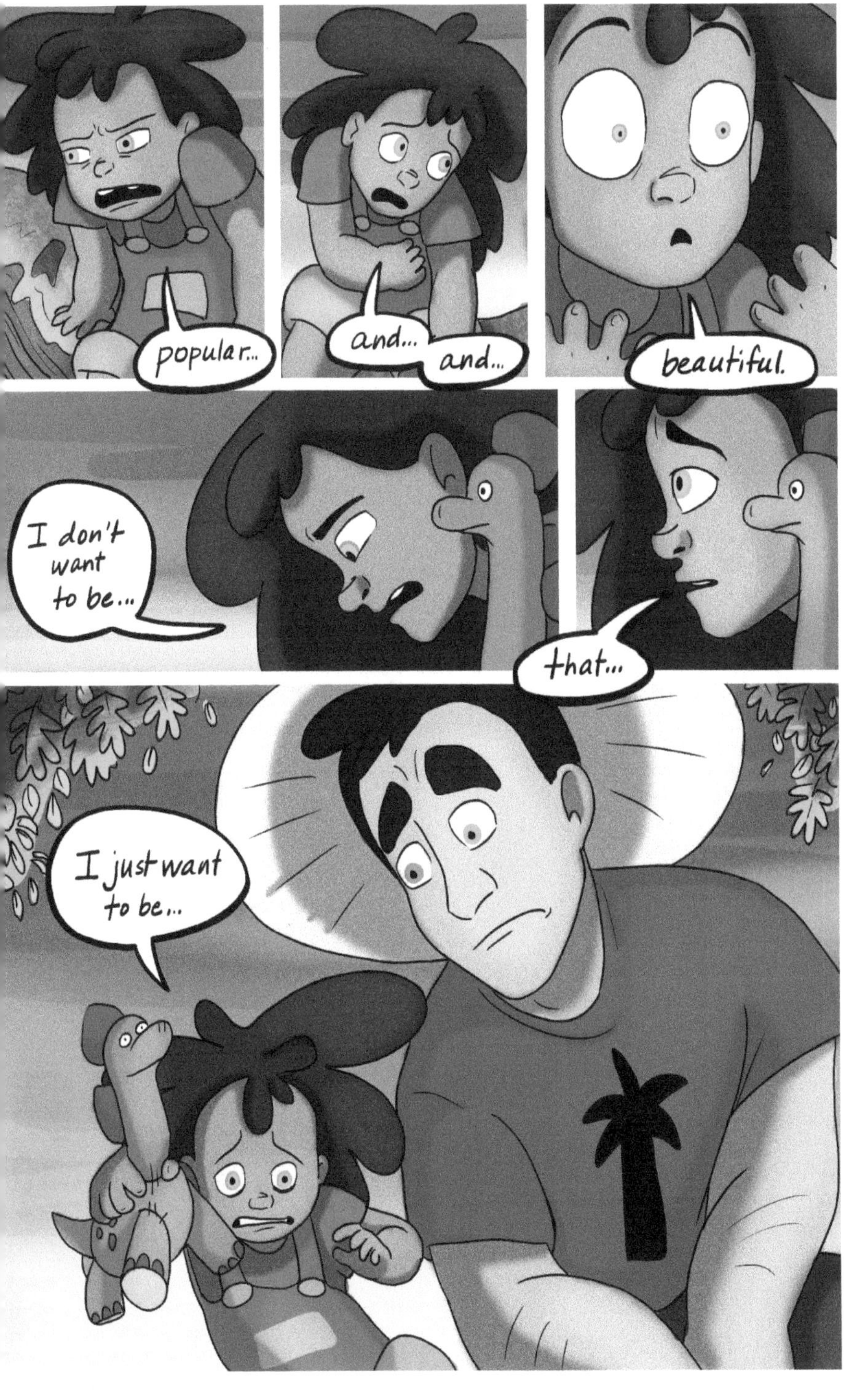
popular...
and...
and...
beautiful.
I don't want to be...
that...
I just want to be...

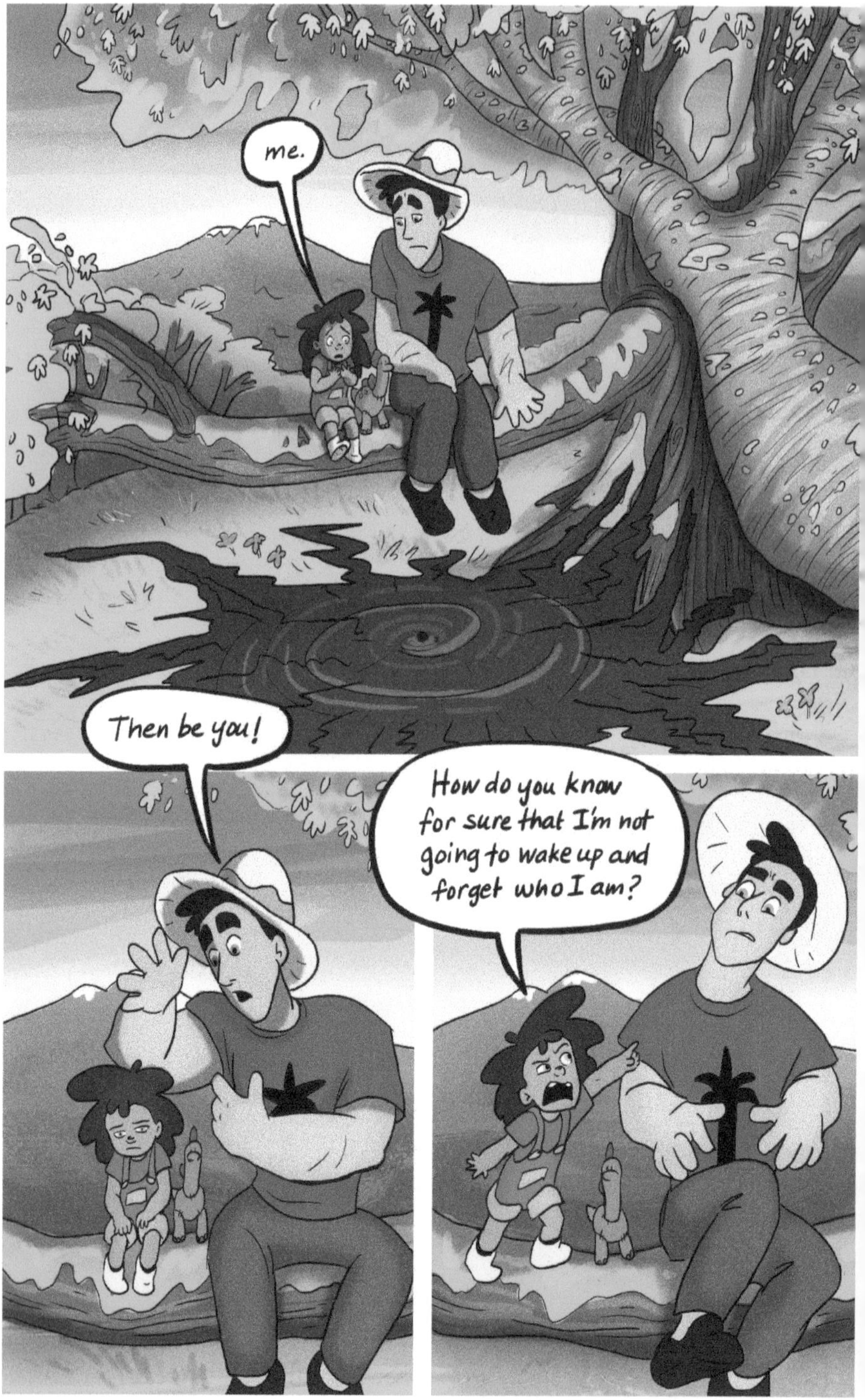
me.
Then be you!
How do you know for sure that I'm not going to wake up and forget who I am?

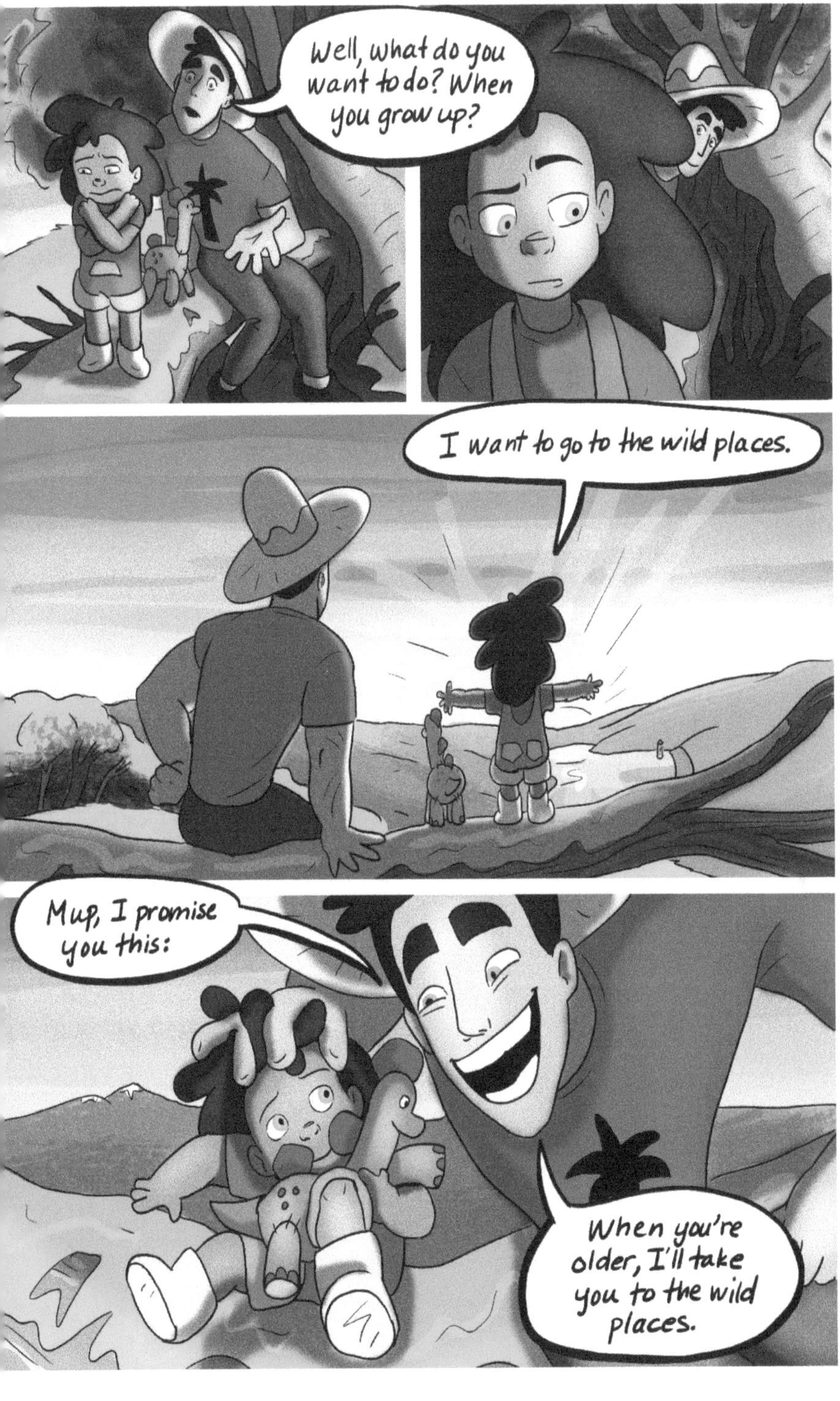
Well, what do you want to do? When you grow up?
I want to go to the wild places.
Mup, I promise you this:
When you're older, I'll take you to the wild places.

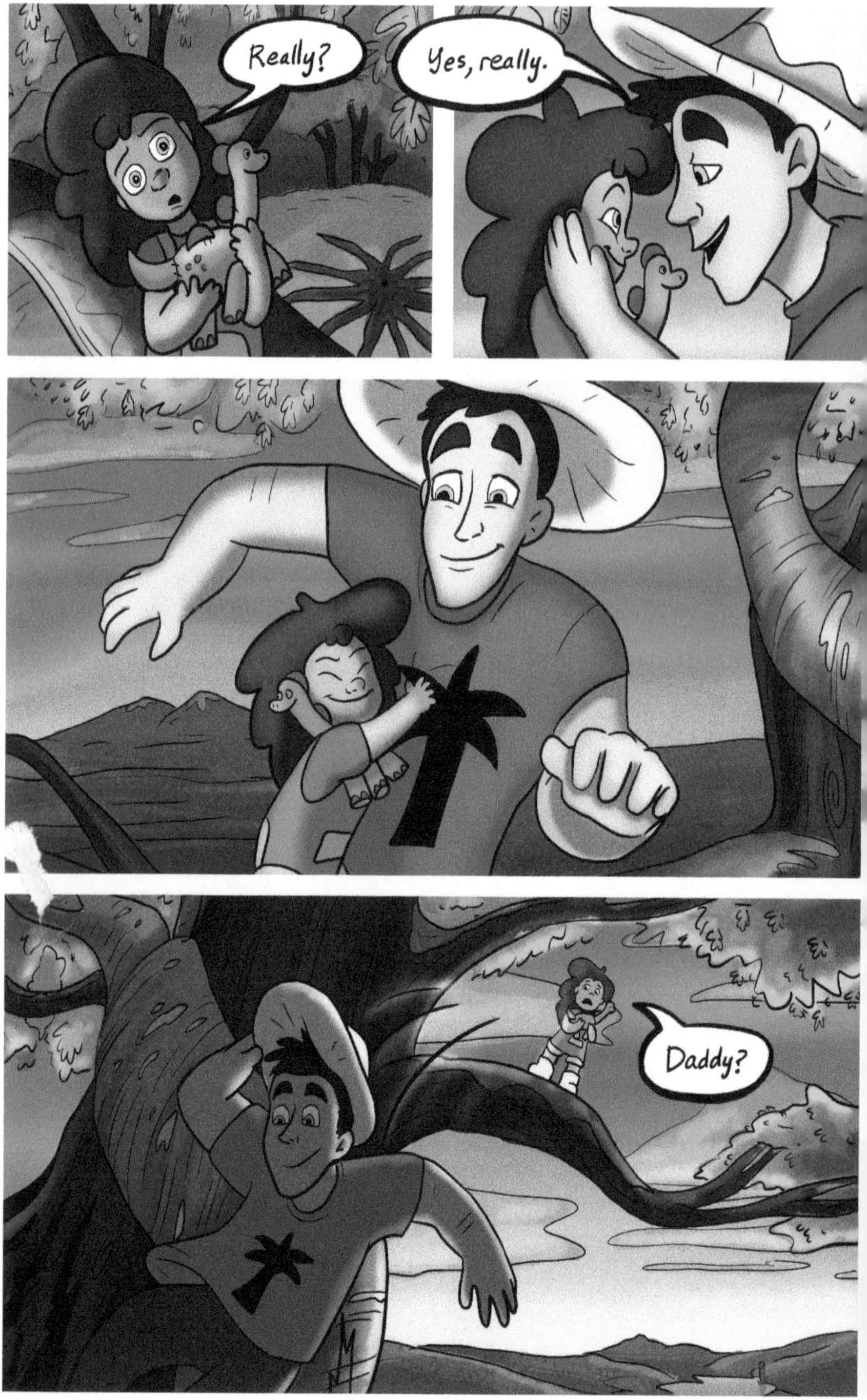
Really?
Yes, really.
Daddy?

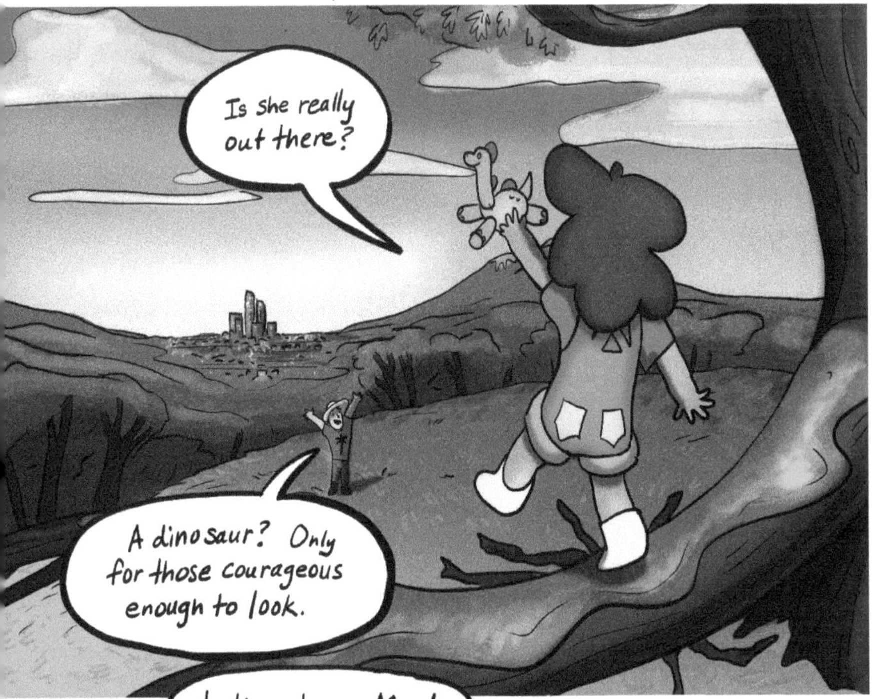
Is she really out there?
A dinosaur? Only for those courageous enough to look.

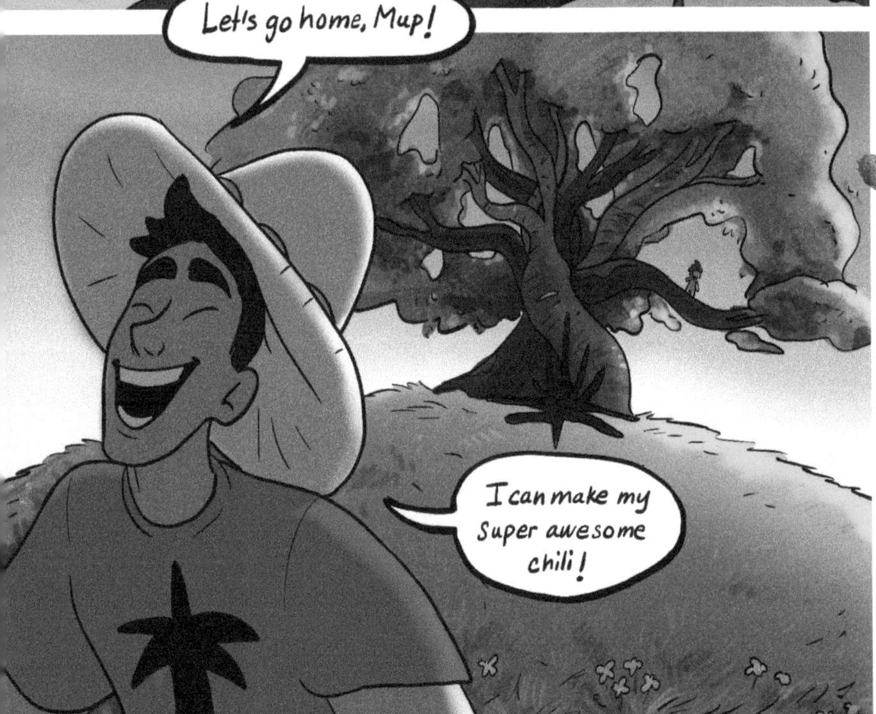
Let's go home, Mup!
I can make my super awesome chili!

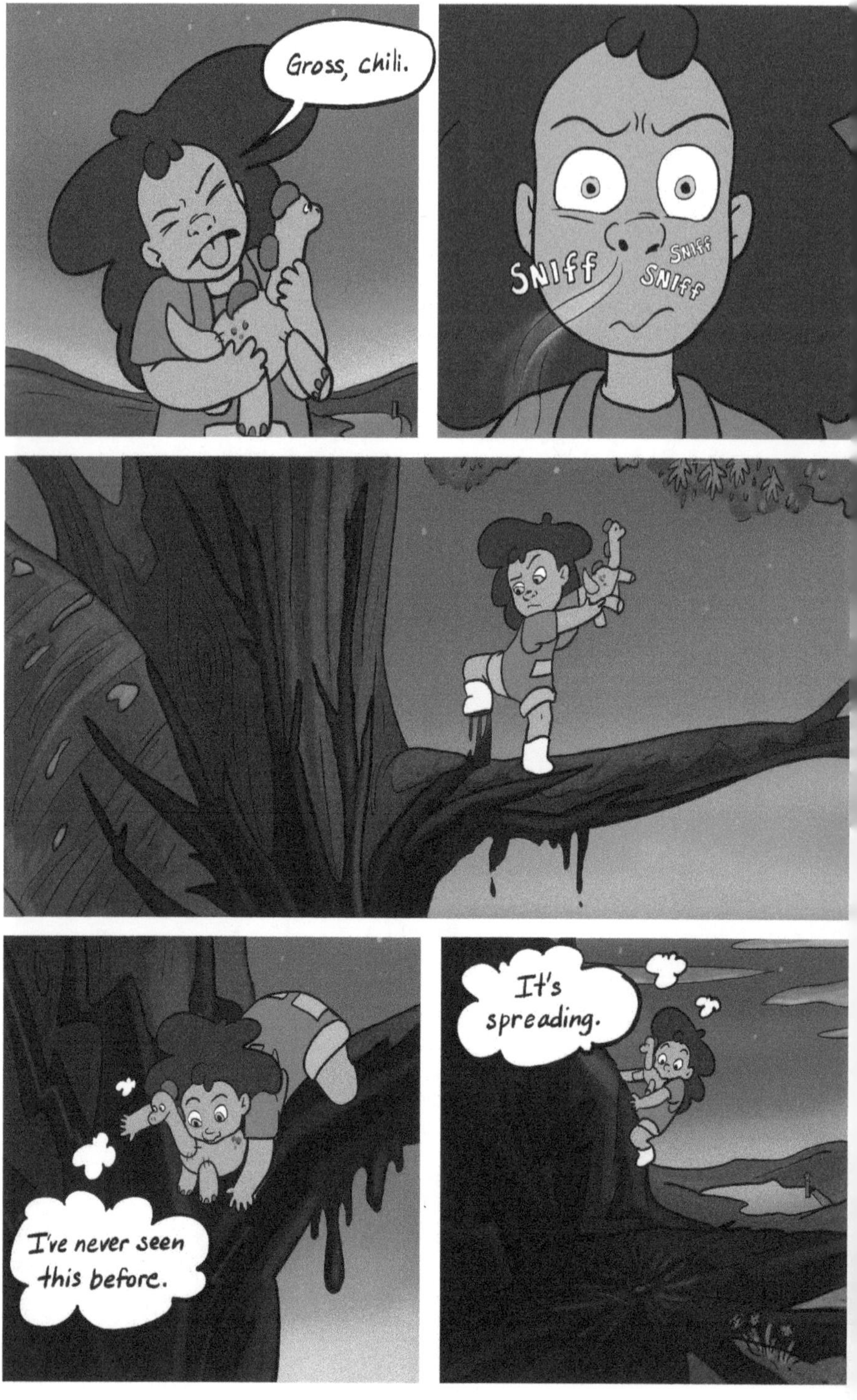
Gross, chili.
SNIFF
SNIFF
SNIFF
I've never seen this before.
It's spreading.

AHHHHHH

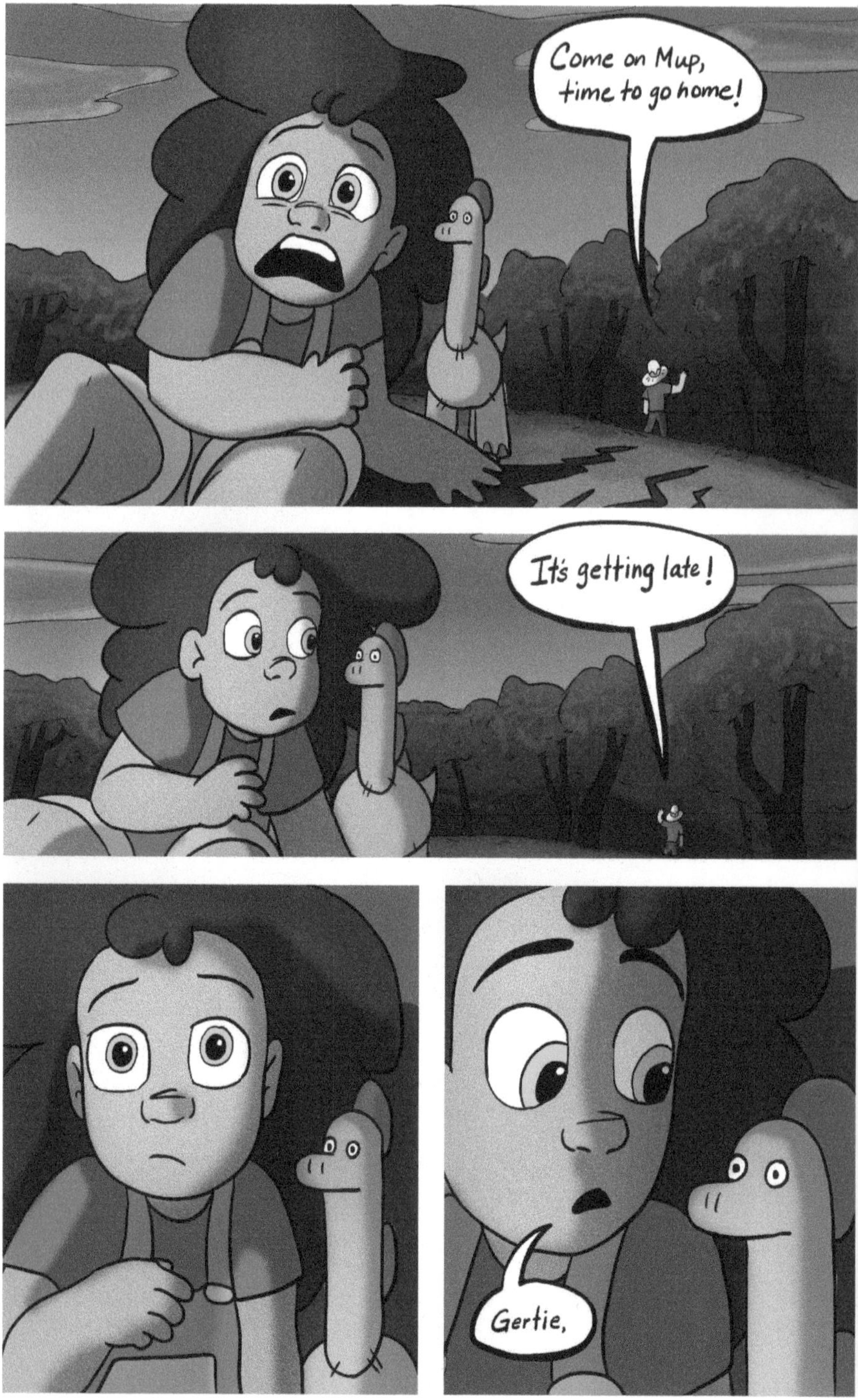
Come on Mup, time to go home!
It's getting late!
Gertie,

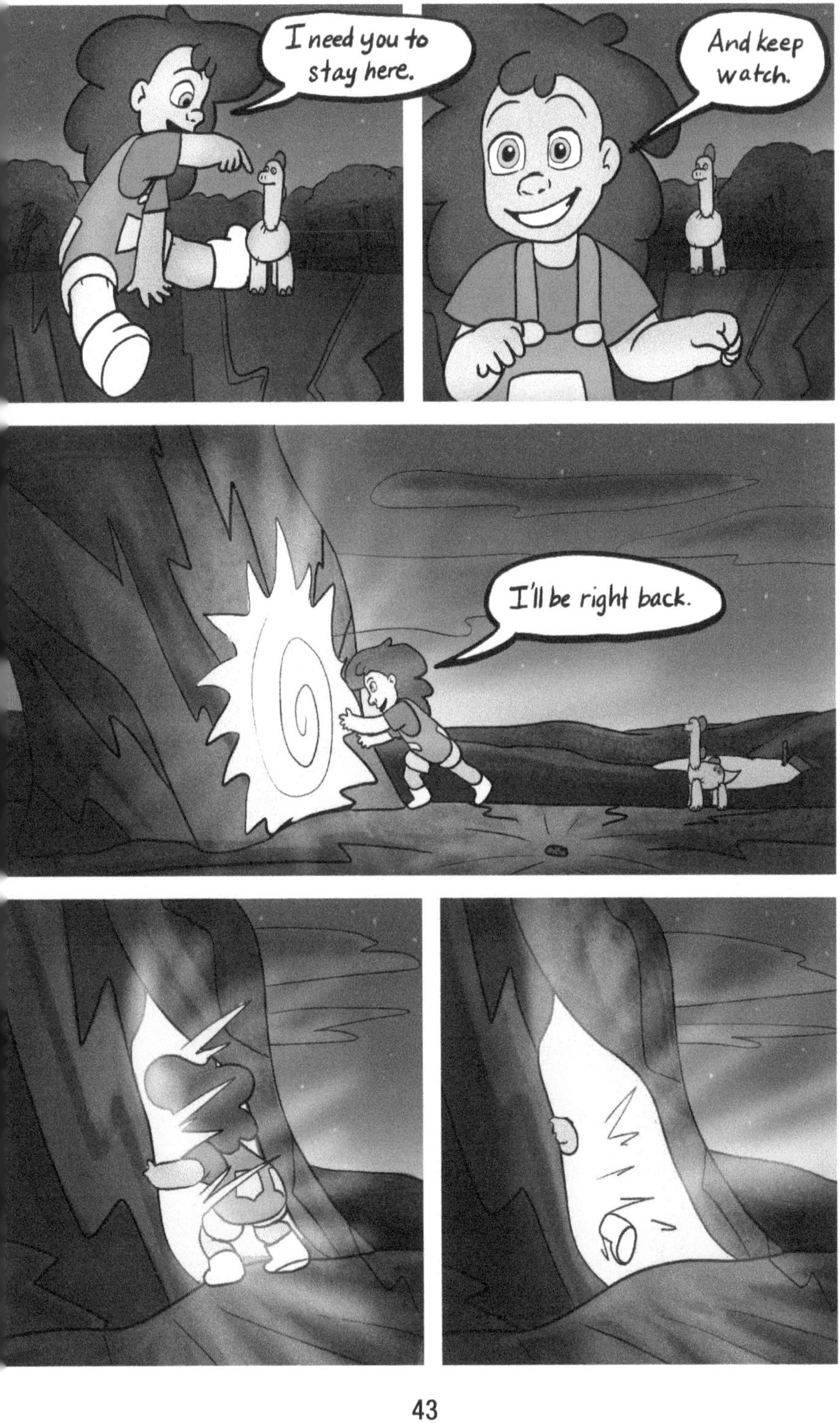
I need you to stay here.
And keep watch.
I'll be right back.

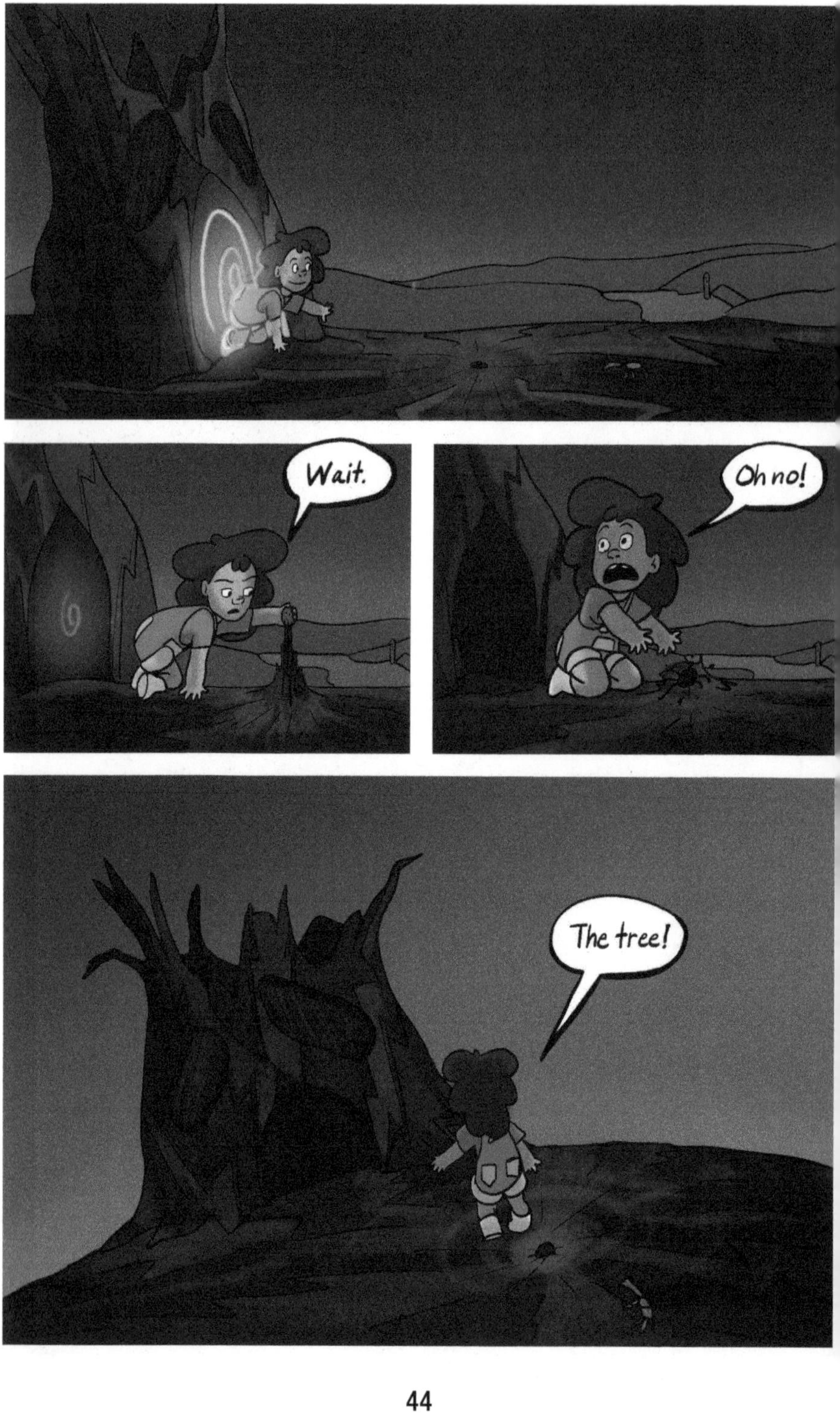
Wait.
Oh no!
The tree!

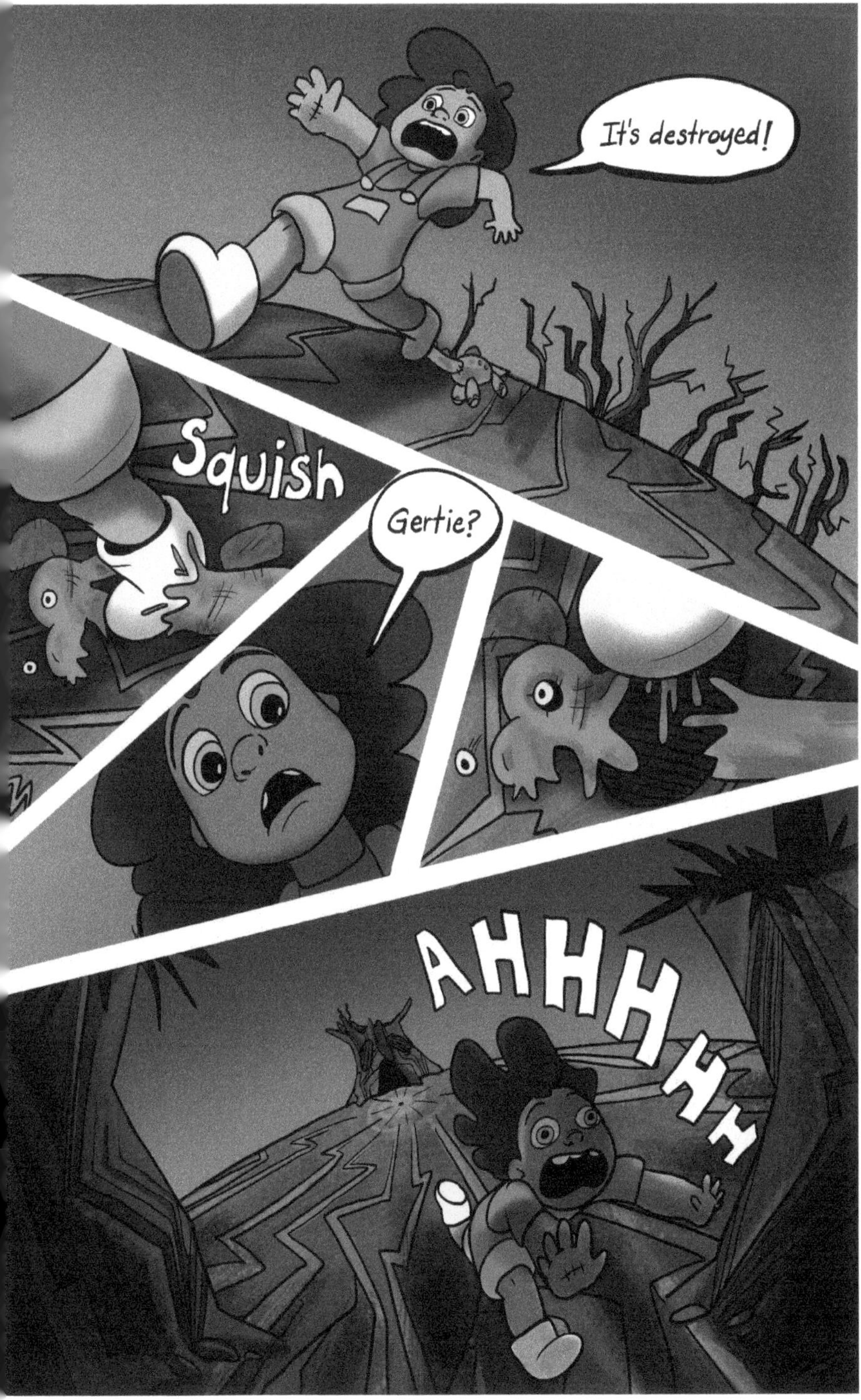
It's destroyed!
Squish
Gertie?
AHHHHH

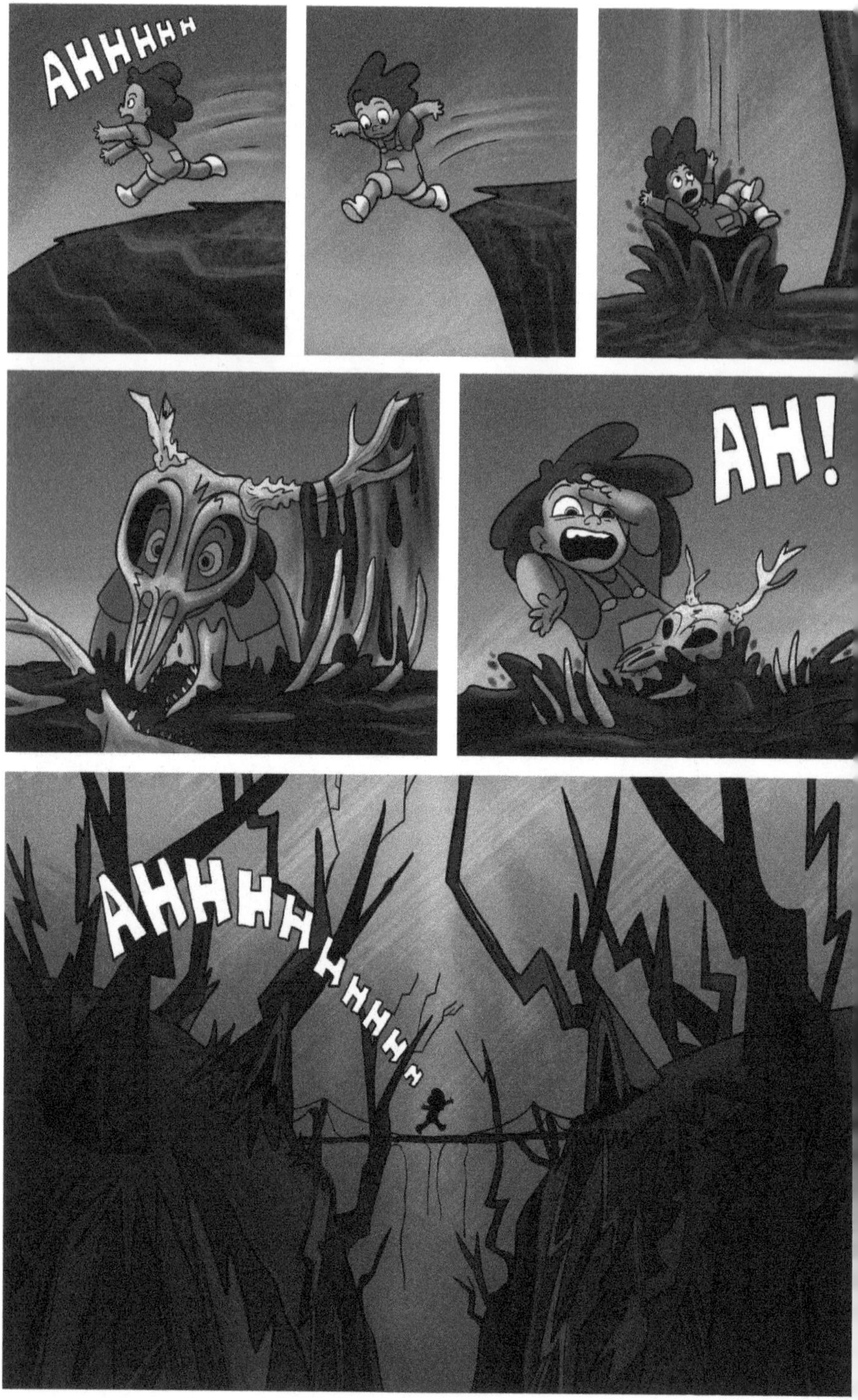
AHHHHH
AH!
AHHHHHHHHHH

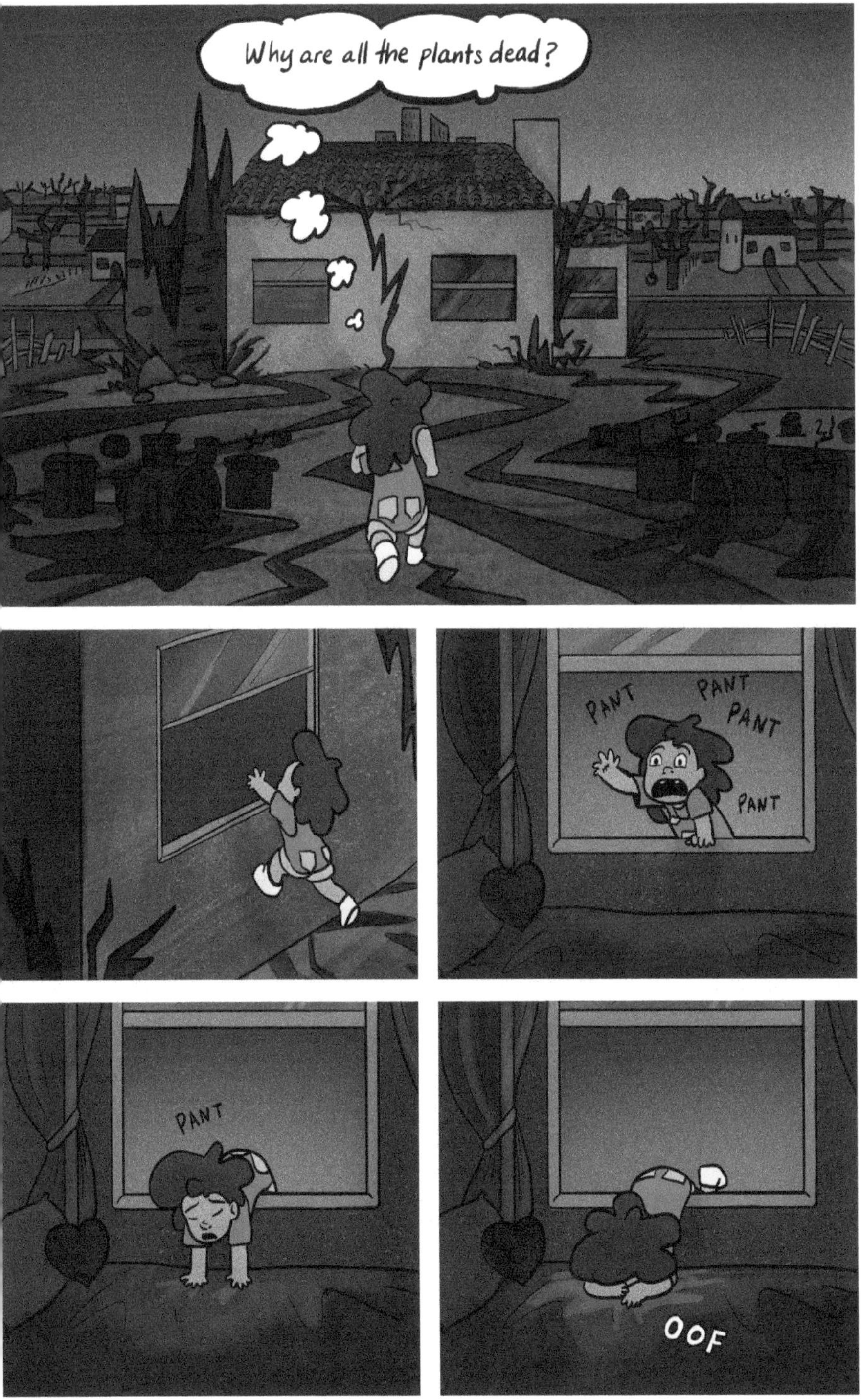
Why are all the plants dead?
PANT
PANT
PANT
PANT
PANT
OOF

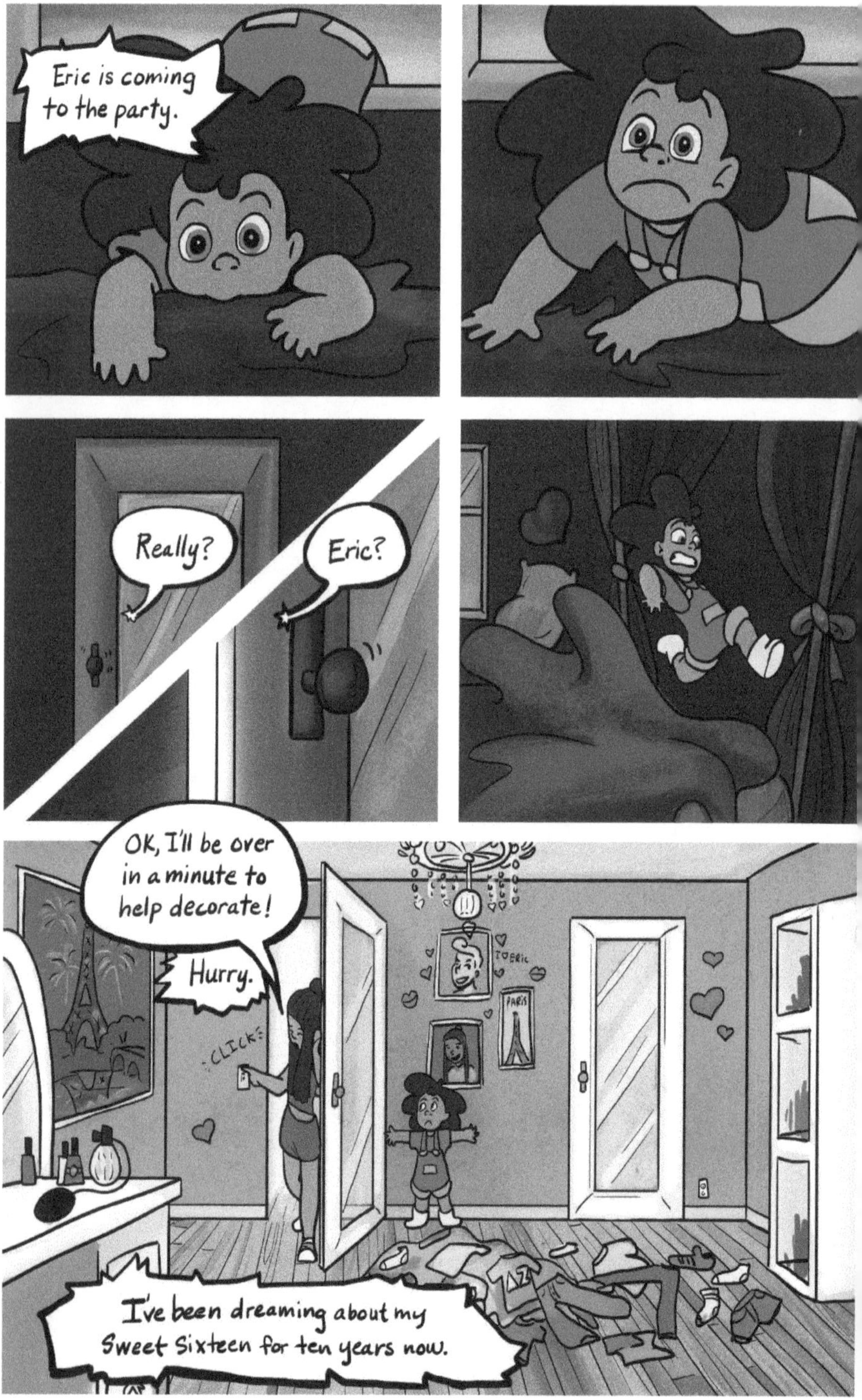
Eric is coming to the party.
Really?
Eric?
OK, I'll be over in a minute to help decorate!
Hurry.
CLICK
I've been dreaming about my Sweet Sixteen for ten years now.

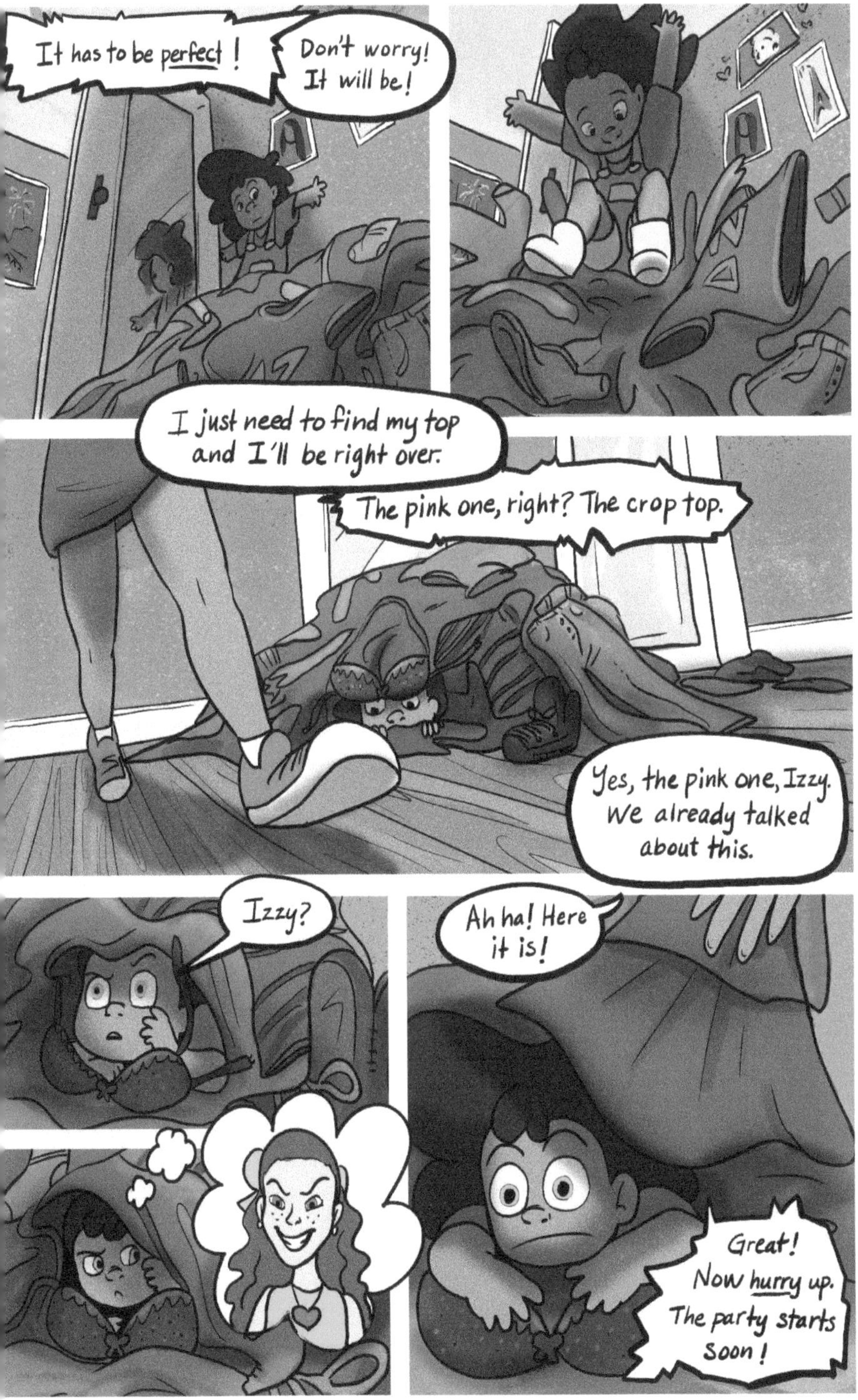

It has to be perfect!
Don't worry! It will be!
I just need to find my top and I'll be right over.
The pink one, right? The crop top.
Yes, the pink one, Izzy. We already talked about this.
Izzy?
Ah ha! Here it is!
Great! Now hurry up. The party starts soon!

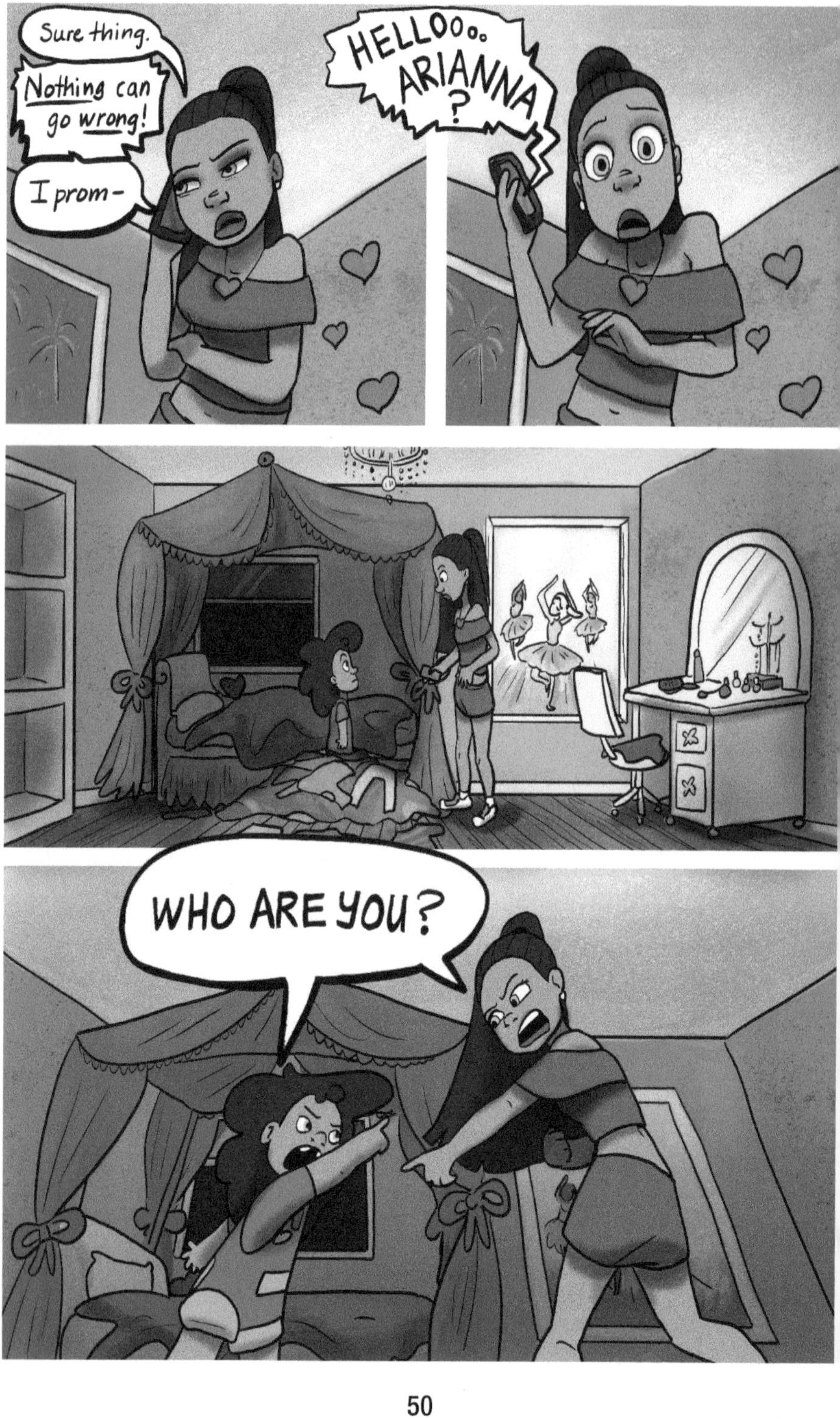
Sure thing.
Nothing can go wrong!
I prom-
HELLOoo ARIANNA?
WHO ARE YOU?

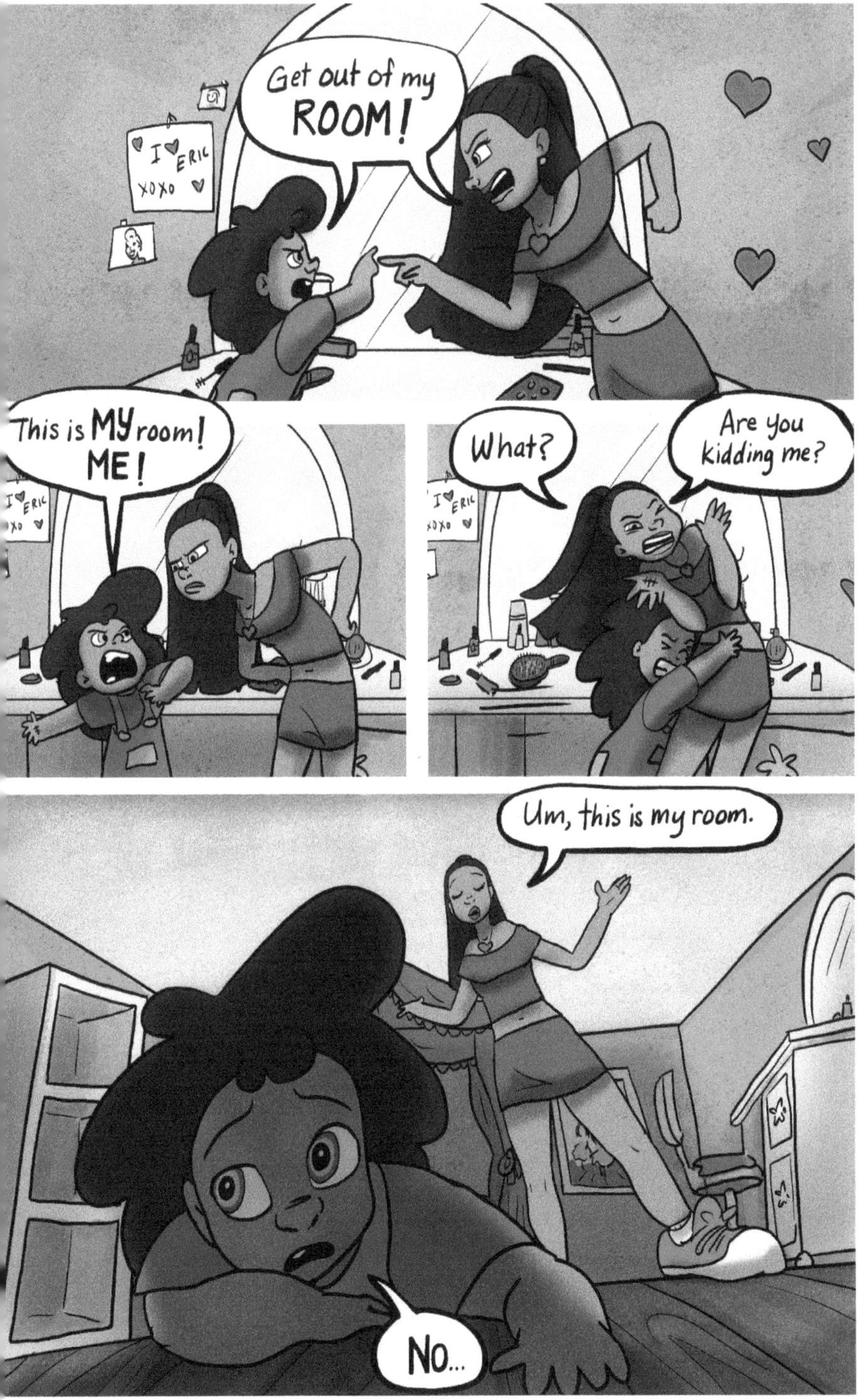
I ♥ ERIC XOXO ♥
Get out of my ROOM!
This is MY room! ME!
What?
Are you kidding me?
Um, this is my room.
No...

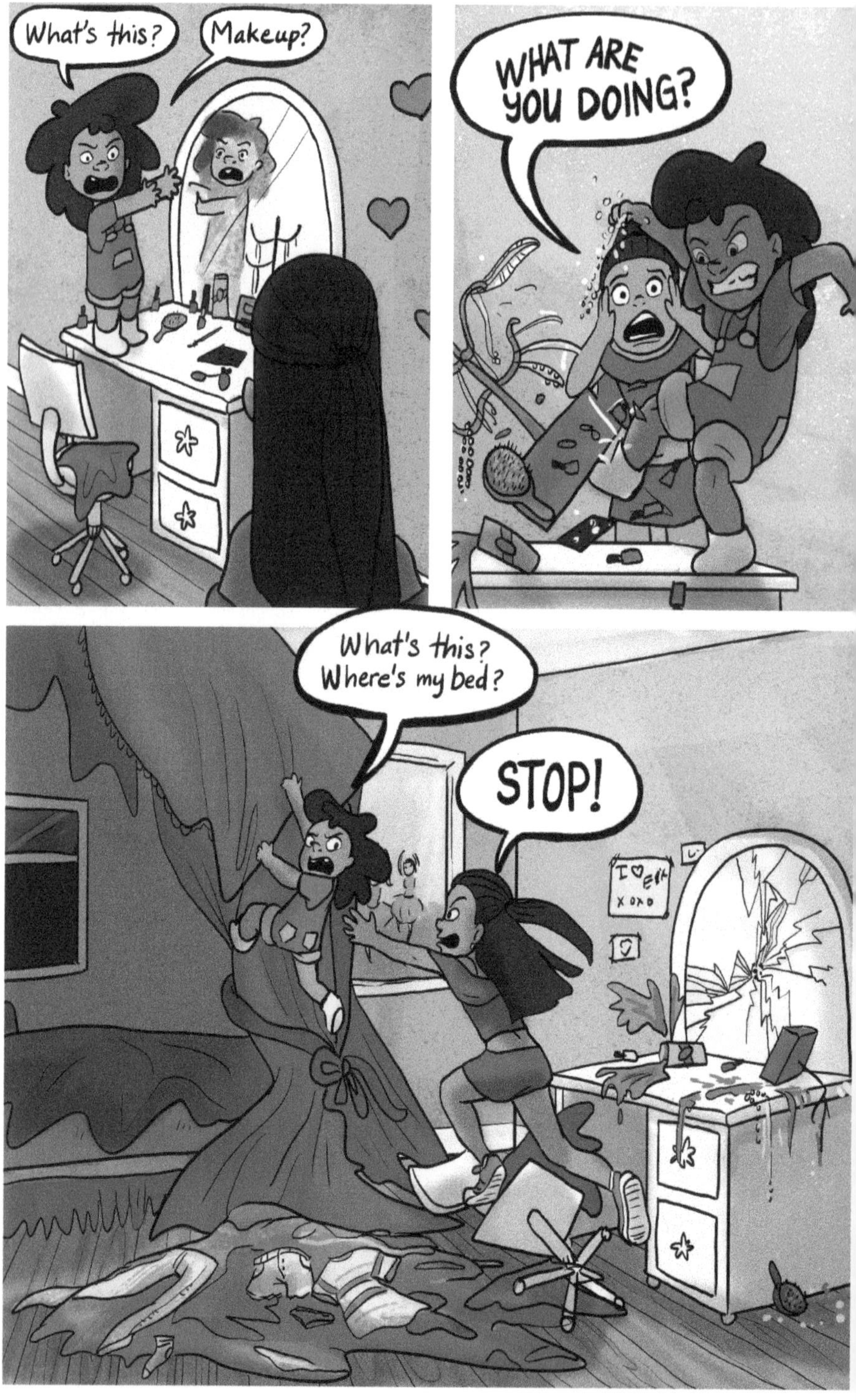
What's this?
Makeup?
WHAT ARE YOU DOING?
What's this? Where's my bed?
STOP!

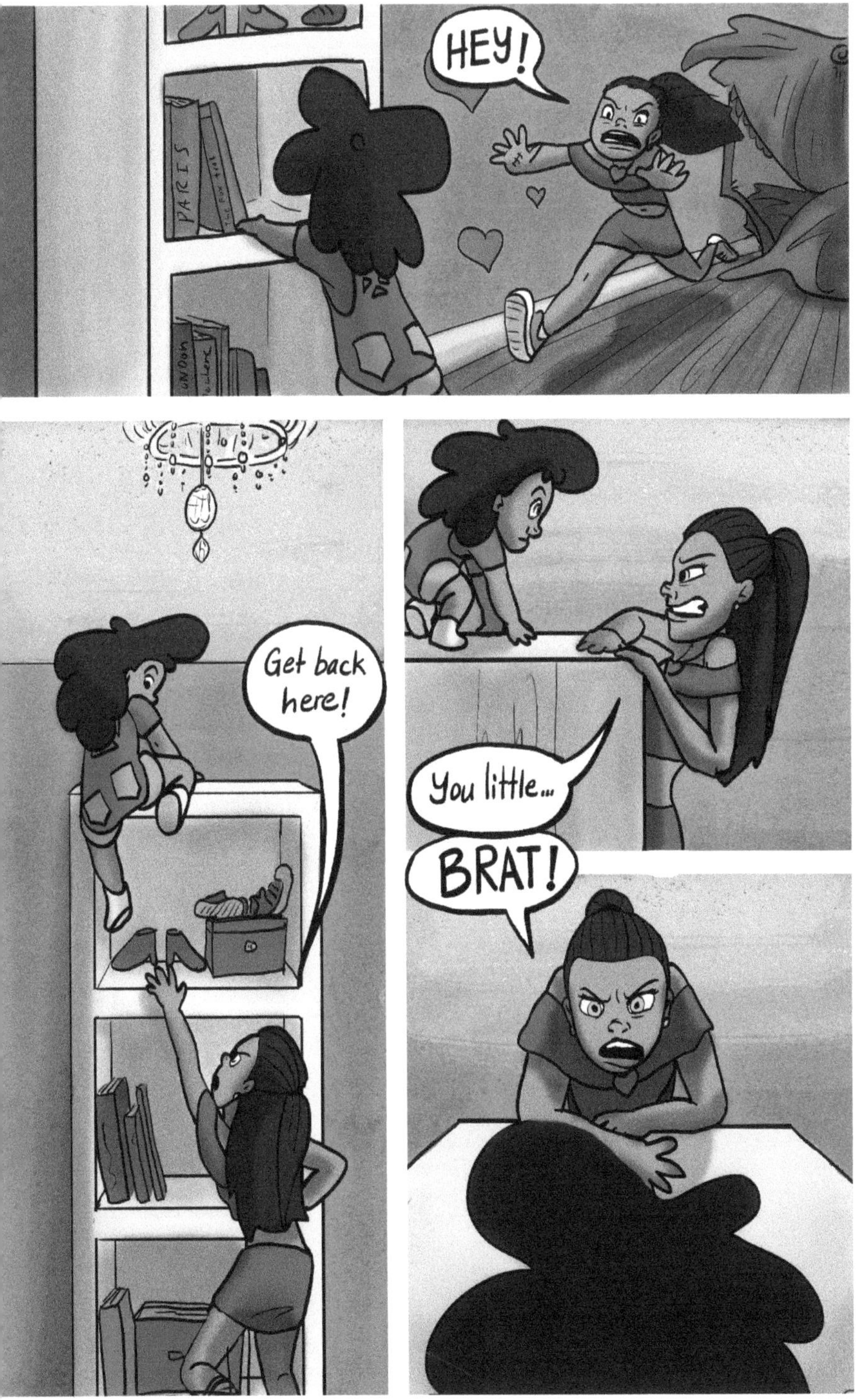
PARIS
HEY!
Get back here!
You little...
BRAT!

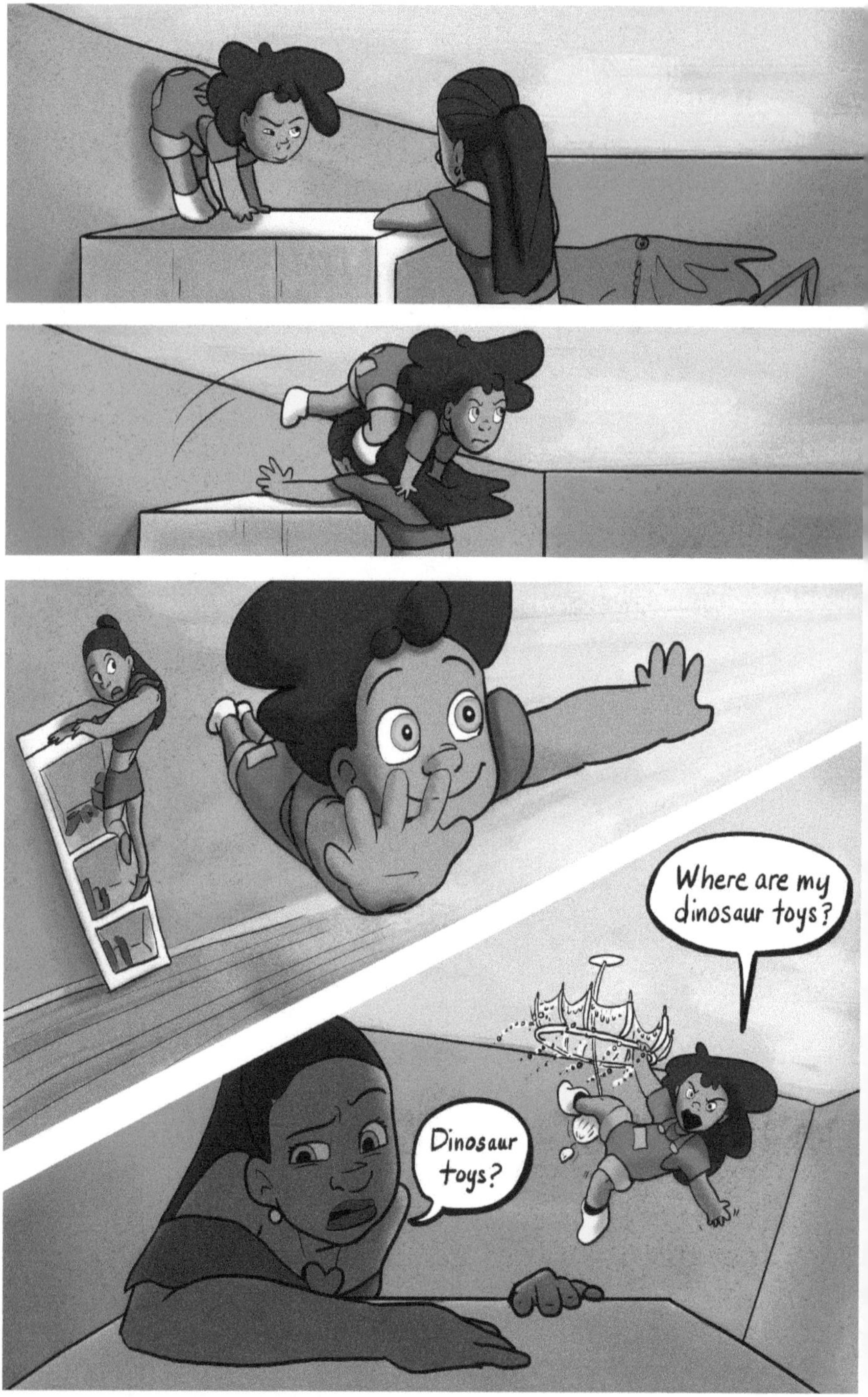
Where are my dinosaur toys?
Dinosaur toys?

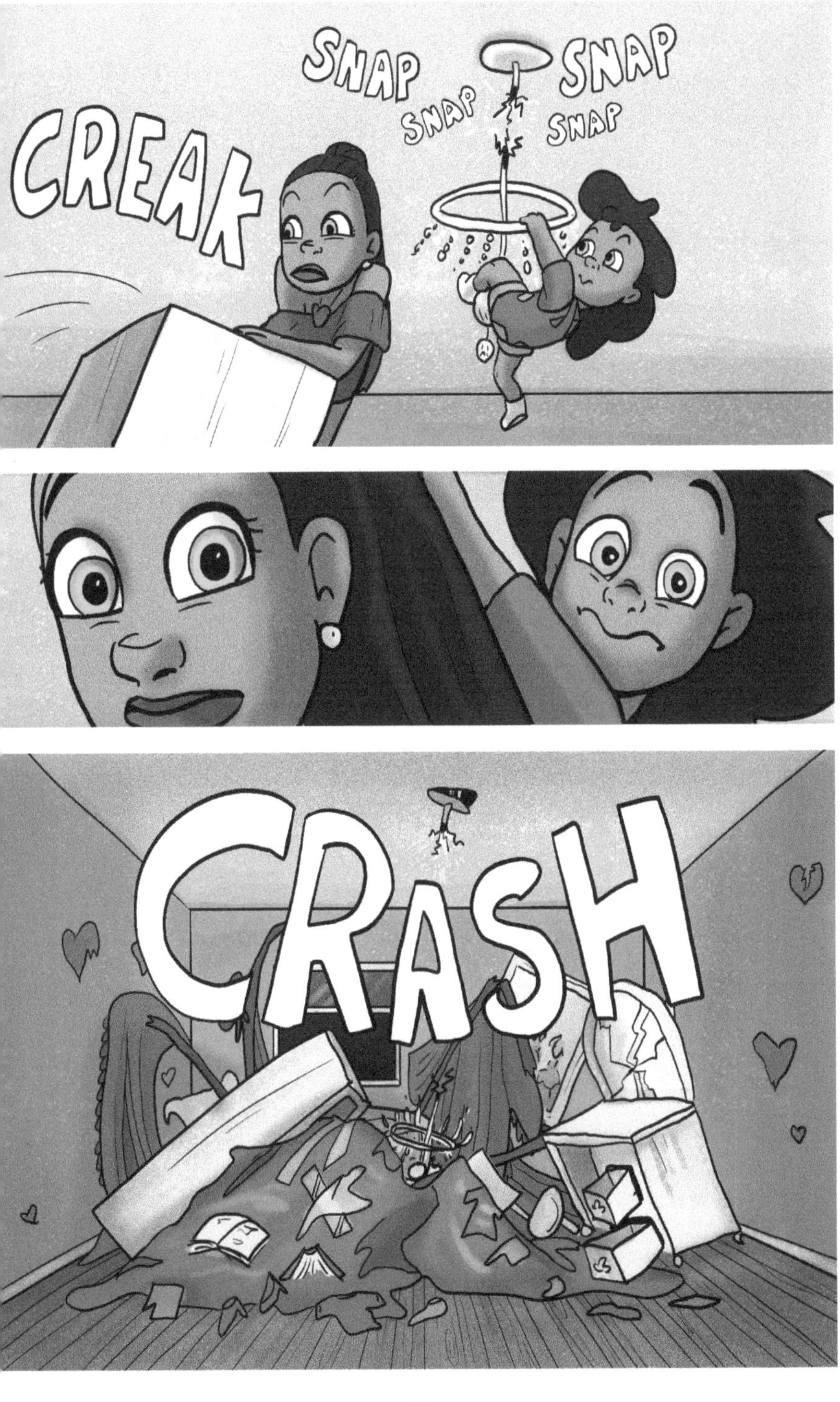
SNAP
SNAP
SNAP
SNAP
CREAK
CRASH

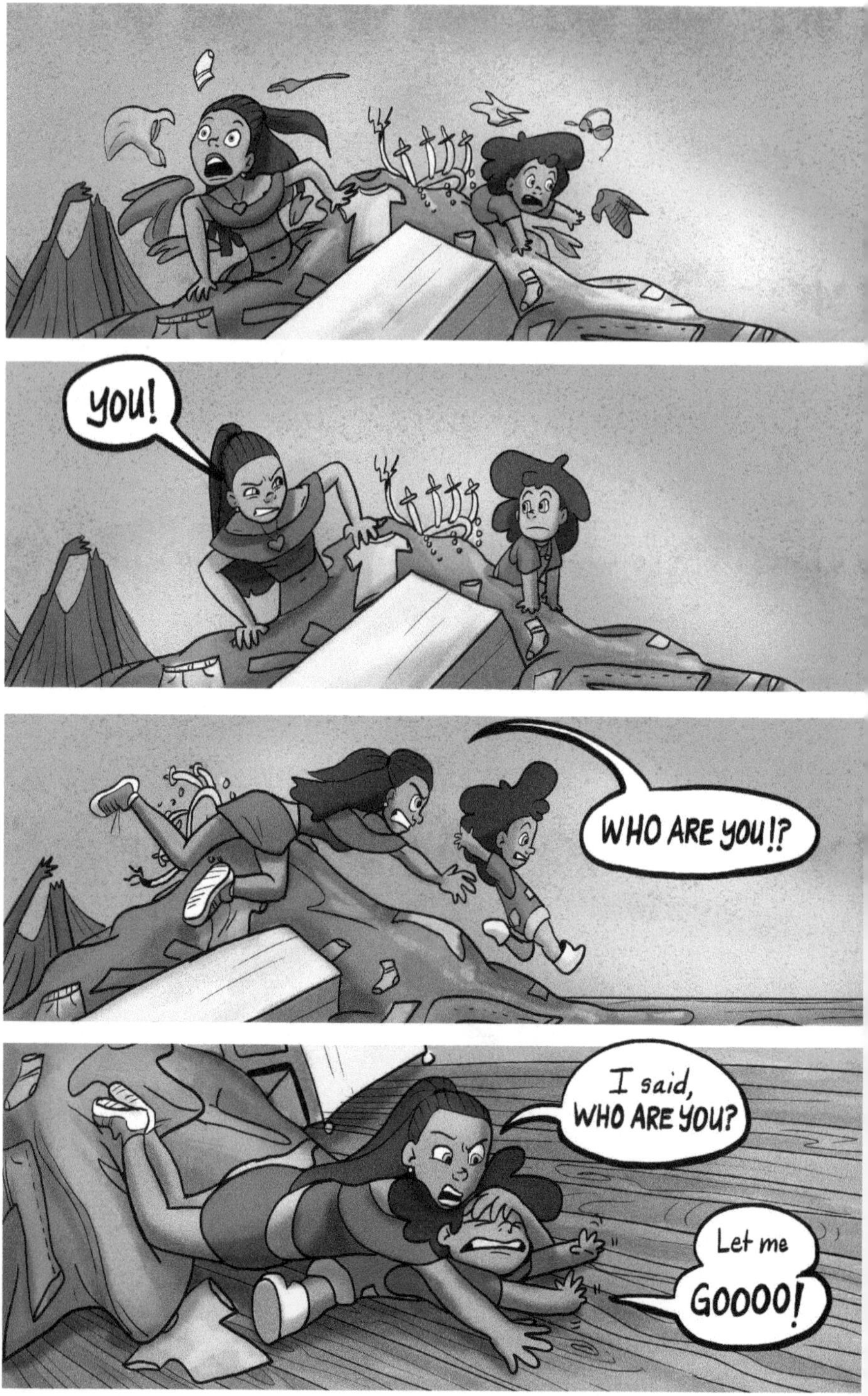
YOU!
WHO ARE YOU!?
I said, WHO ARE YOU?
Let me GOOOO!

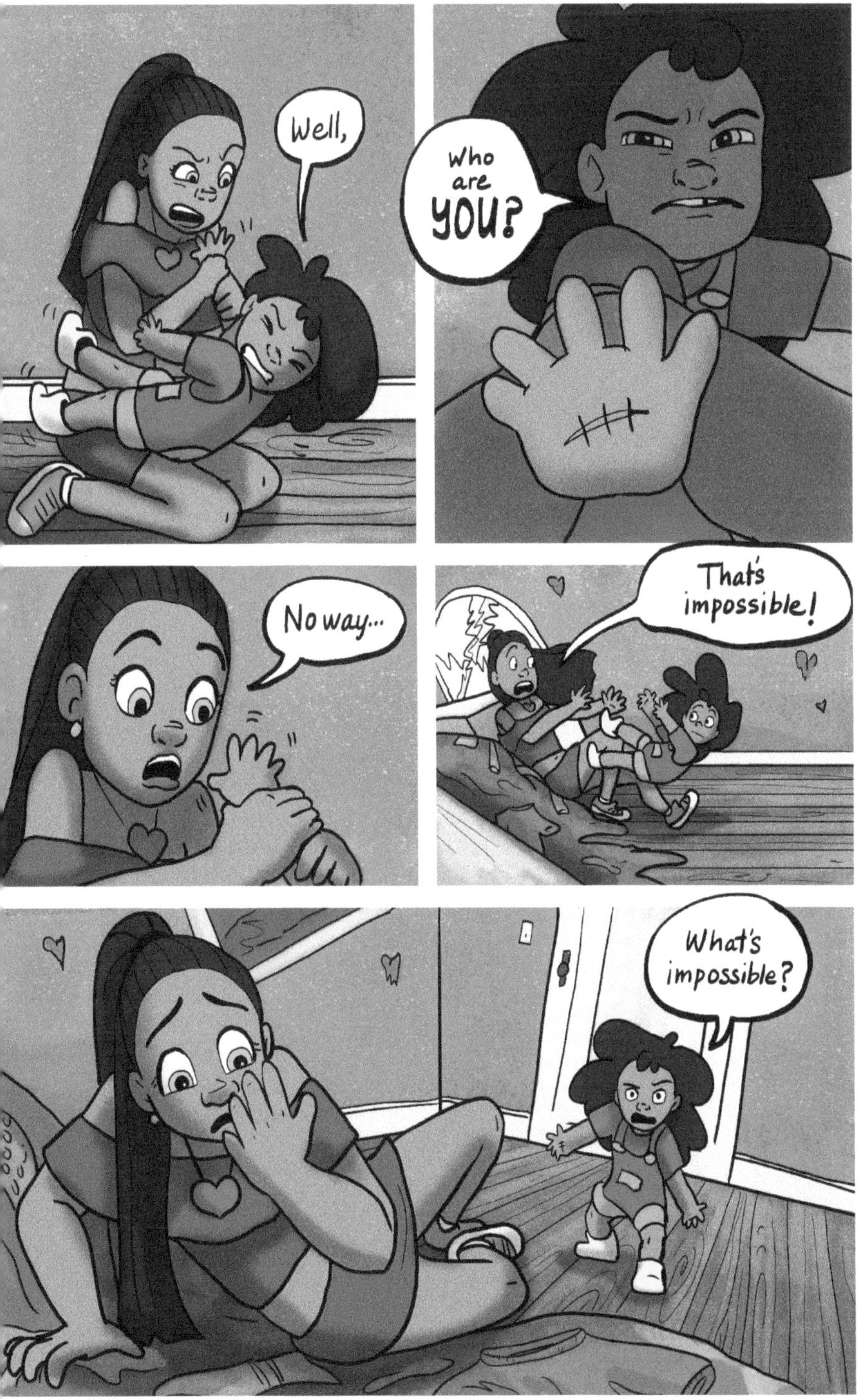
Well,
Who are YOU?
No way...
That's impossible!
What's impossible?

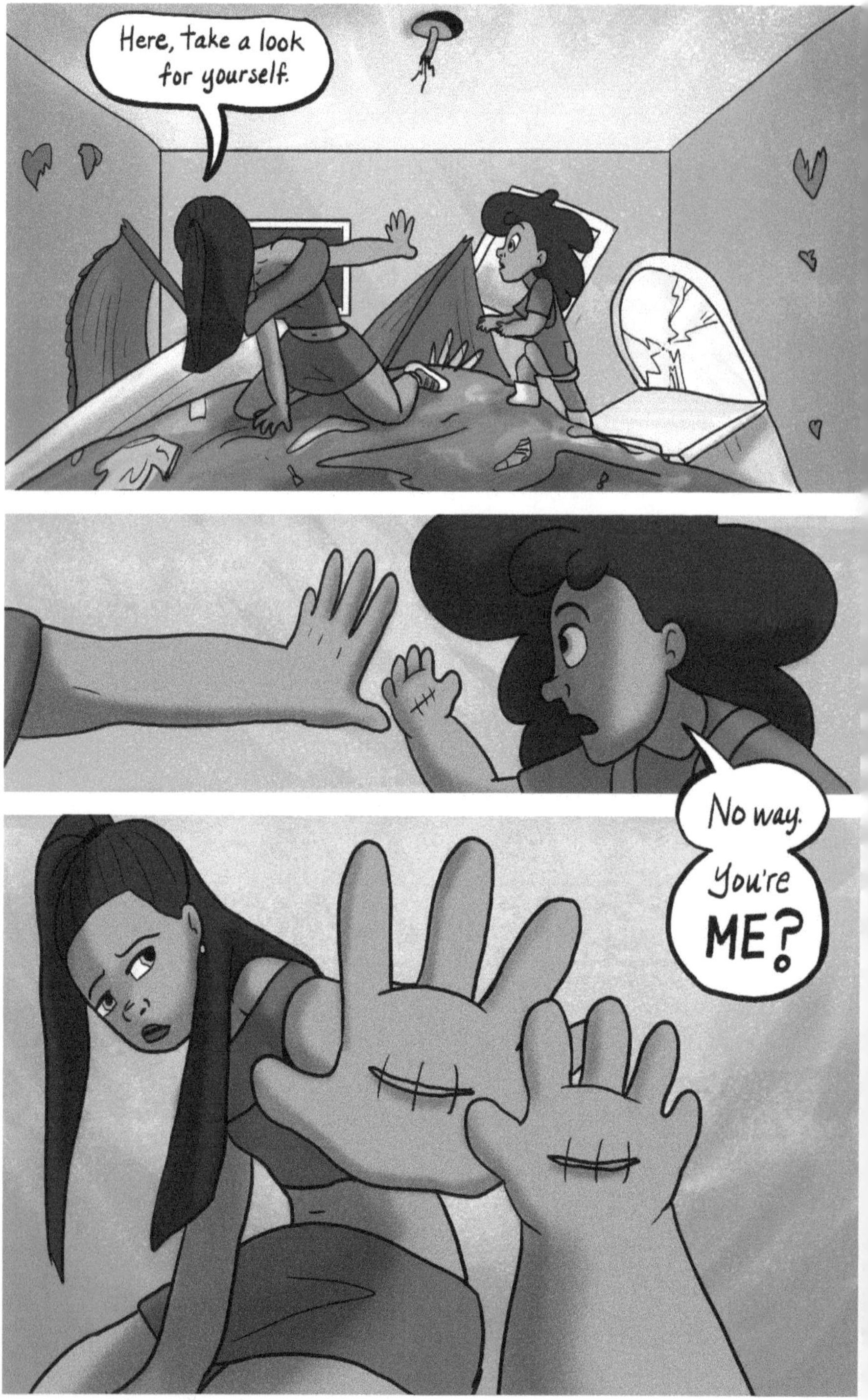
Here, take a look for yourself.
No way. You're ME?

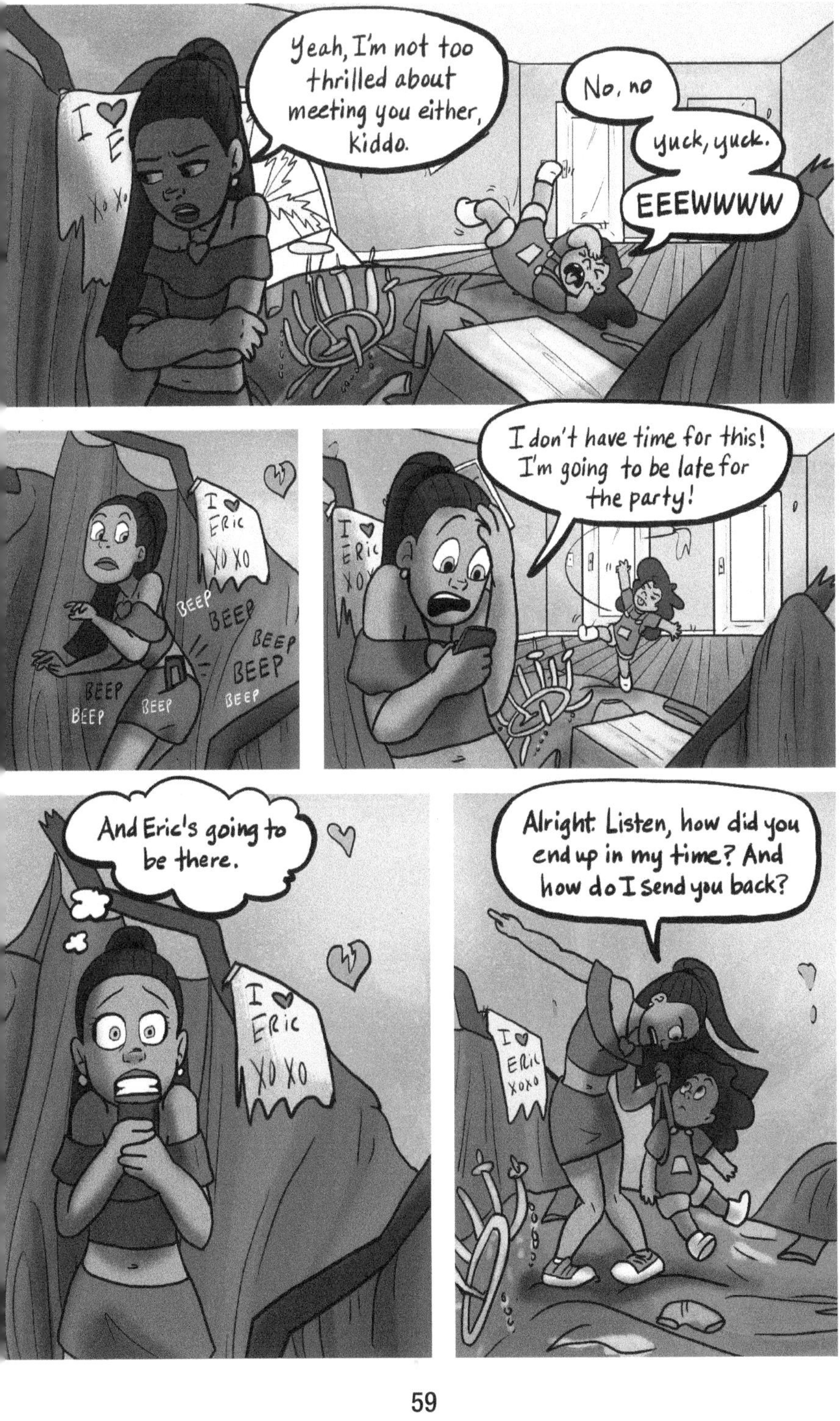
Yeah, I'm not too thrilled about meeting you either, kiddo.
No, no
yuck, yuck.
EEEWWWW
I ♥ E
XoXo
I ♥ Eric
XO XO
BEEP
BEEP
BEEP
BEEP
BEEP
BEEP
BEEP
BEEP
I don't have time for this! I'm going to be late for the party!
I ♥ Eric
XO
And Eric's going to be there.
I ♥ Eric
XO XO
Alright. Listen, how did you end up in my time? And how do I send you back?
I ♥ Eric
XoXo

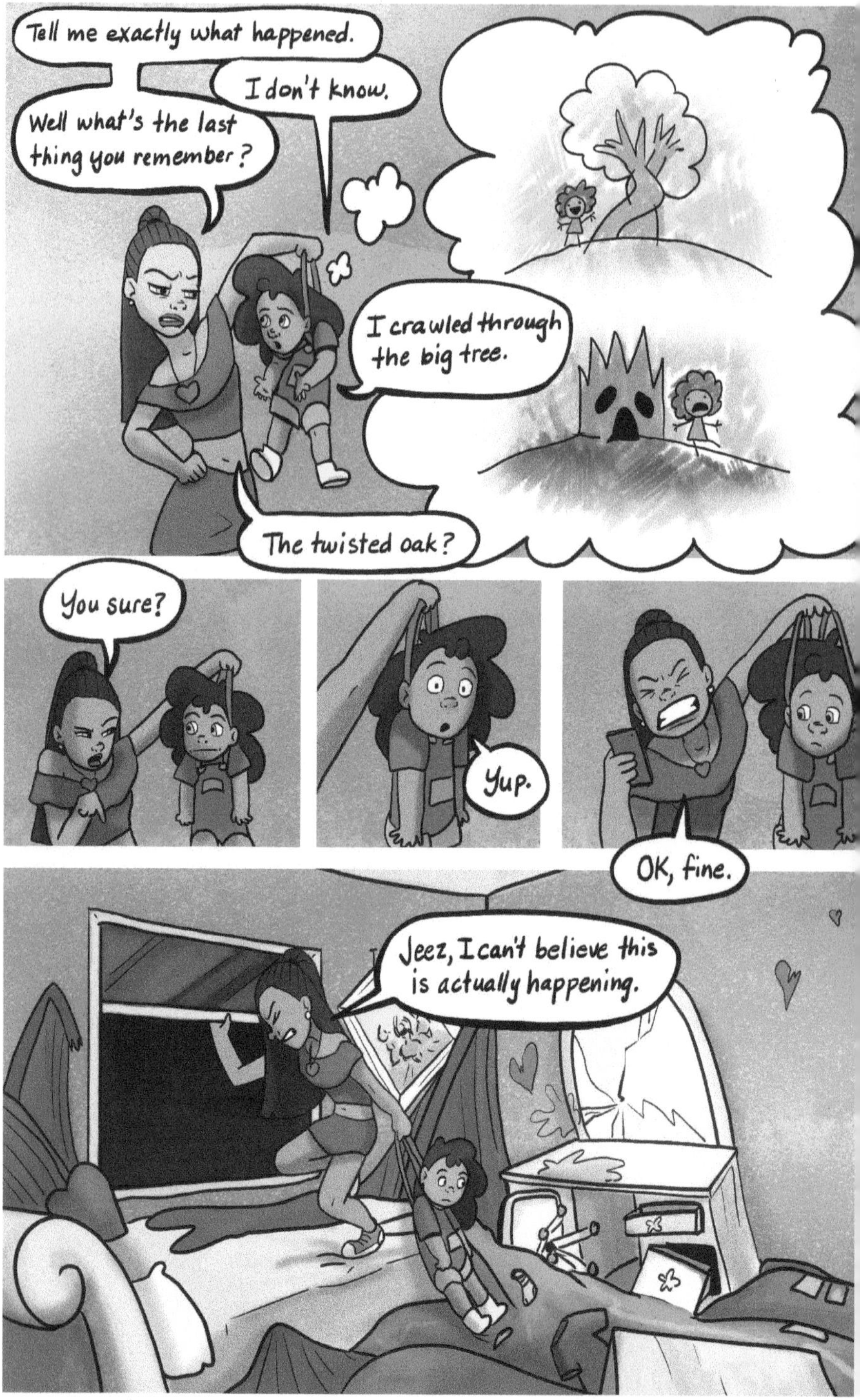
Tell me exactly what happened.
I don't know.
Well what's the last thing you remember?
I crawled through the big tree.
The twisted oak?
You sure?
Yup.
OK, fine.
Jeez, I can't believe this is actually happening.

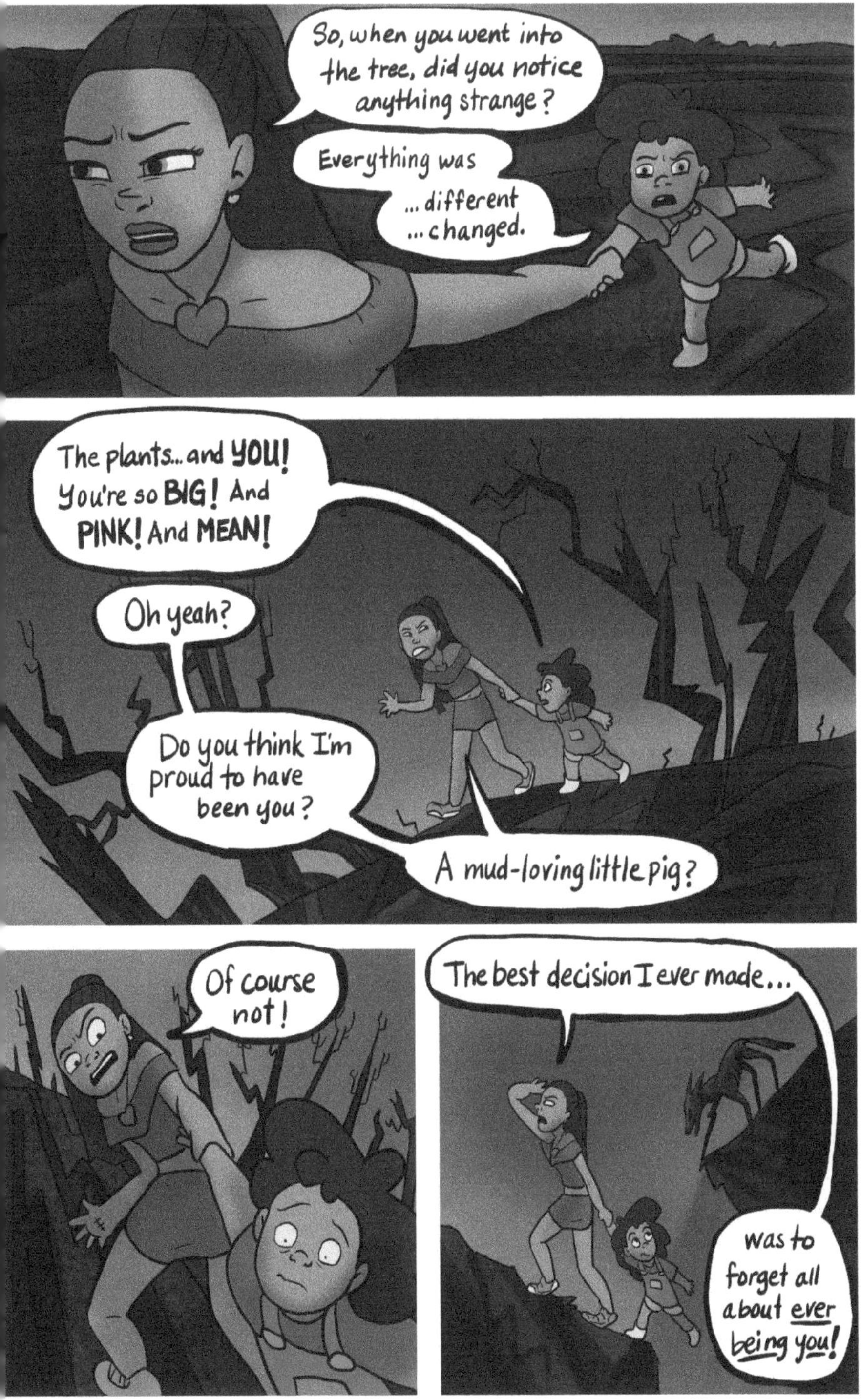
So, when you went into the tree, did you notice anything strange?
Everything was ...different ...changed.
The plants... and YOU! You're so BIG! And PINK! And MEAN!
Oh yeah?
Do you think I'm proud to have been you?
A mud-loving little pig?
Of course not!
The best decision I ever made...
was to forget all about ever being you!

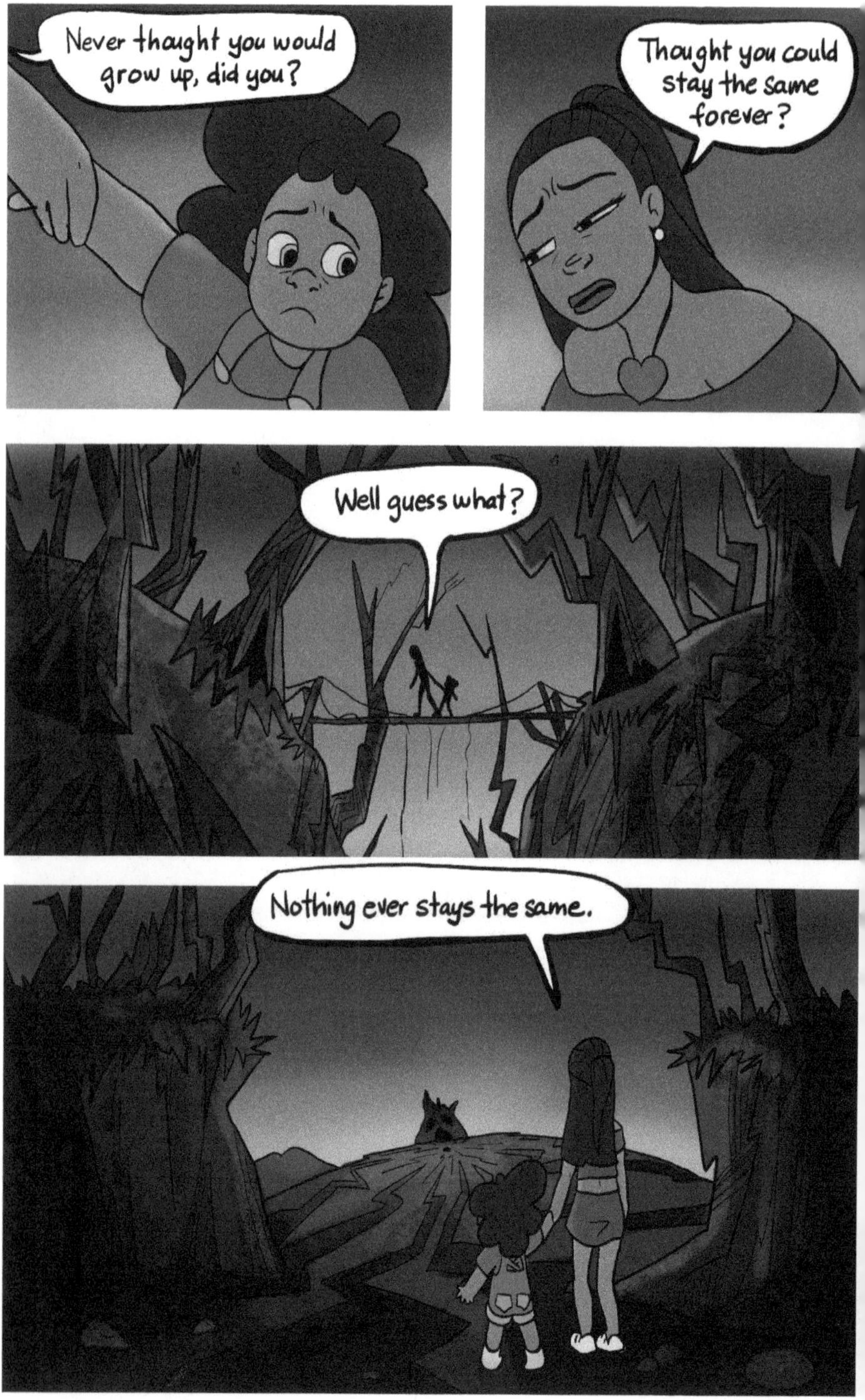

Never thought you would grow up, did you?
Thought you could stay the same forever?
Well guess what?
Nothing ever stays the same.

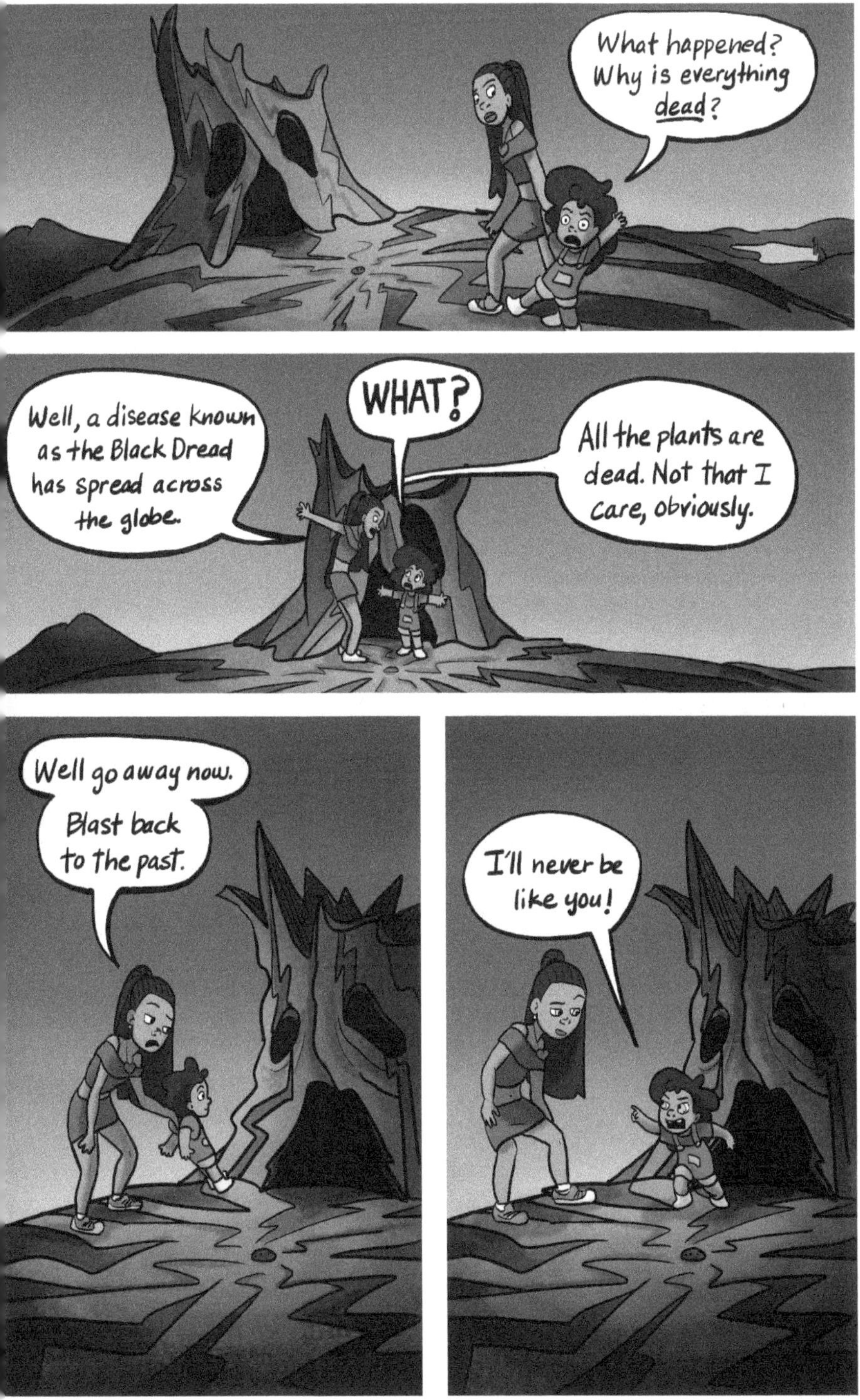
What happened? Why is everything dead?
Well, a disease known as the Black Dread has spread across the globe.
WHAT?
All the plants are dead. Not that I care, obviously.
Well go away now.
Blast back to the past.
I'll never be like you!

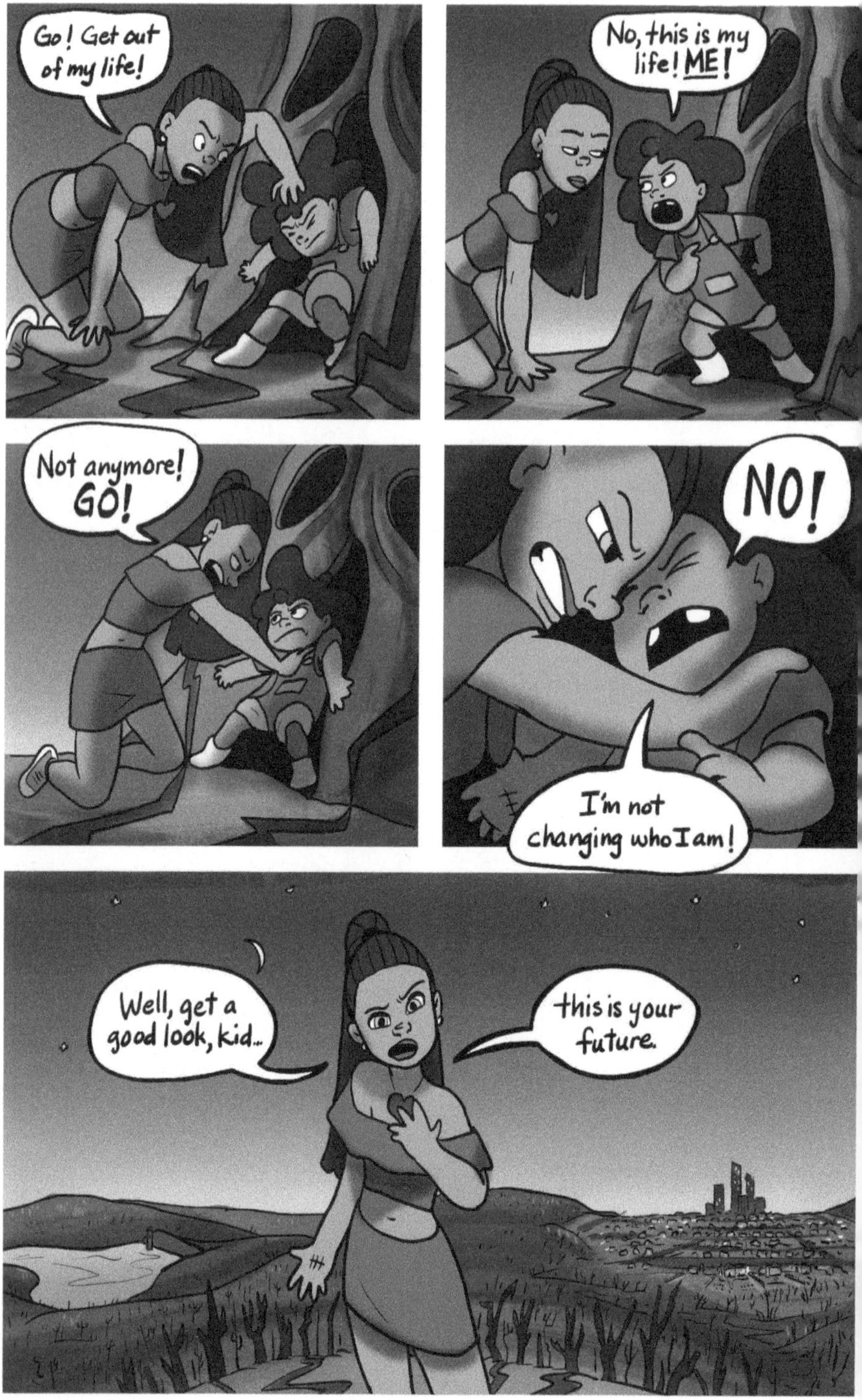
Go! Get out of my life!
No, this is my life! ME!
Not anymore! GO!
NO!
I'm not changing who I am!
Well, get a good look, kid...
this is your future.

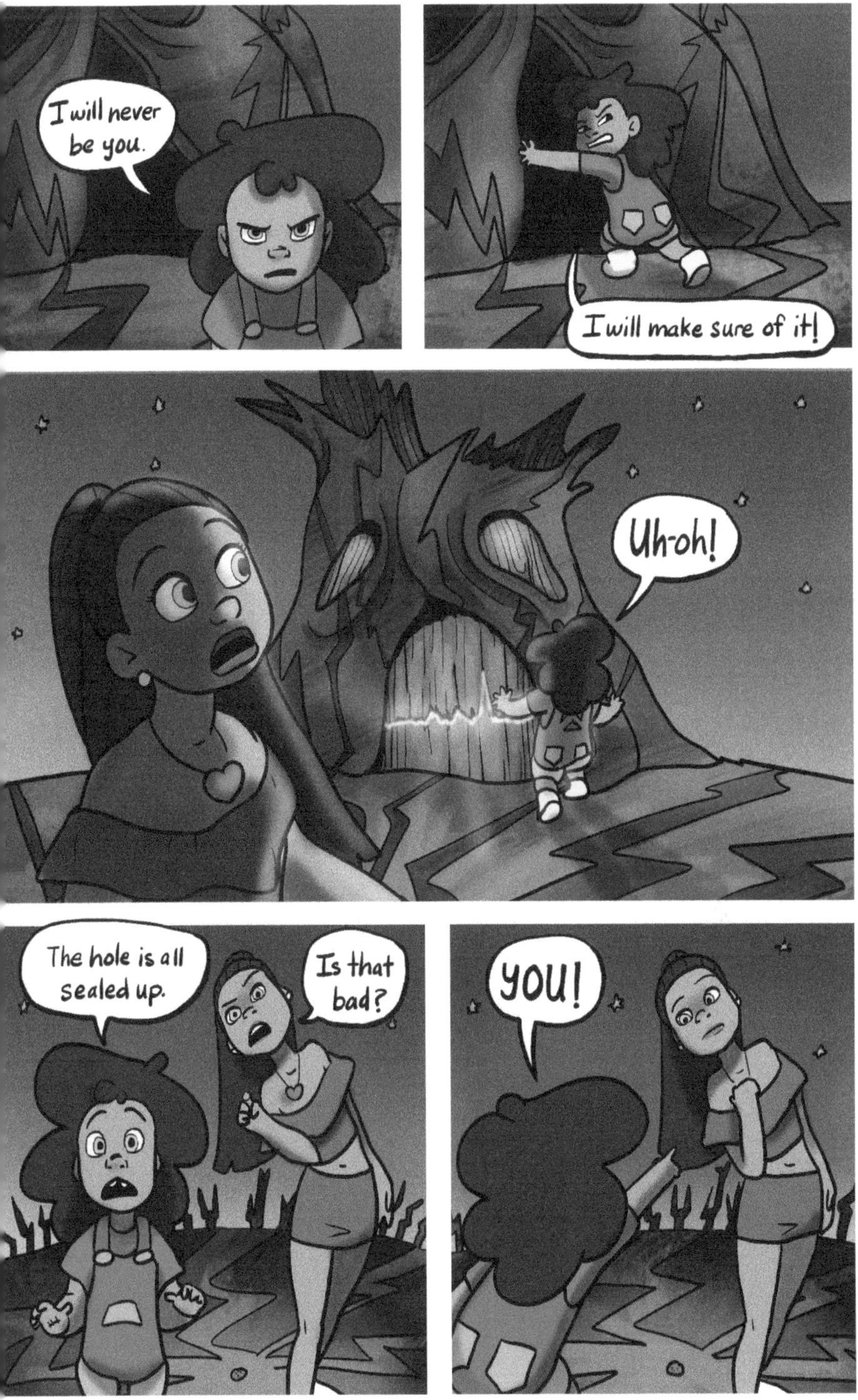
I will never be you.
I will make sure of it!
Uh-oh!
The hole is all sealed up.
Is that bad?
YOU!

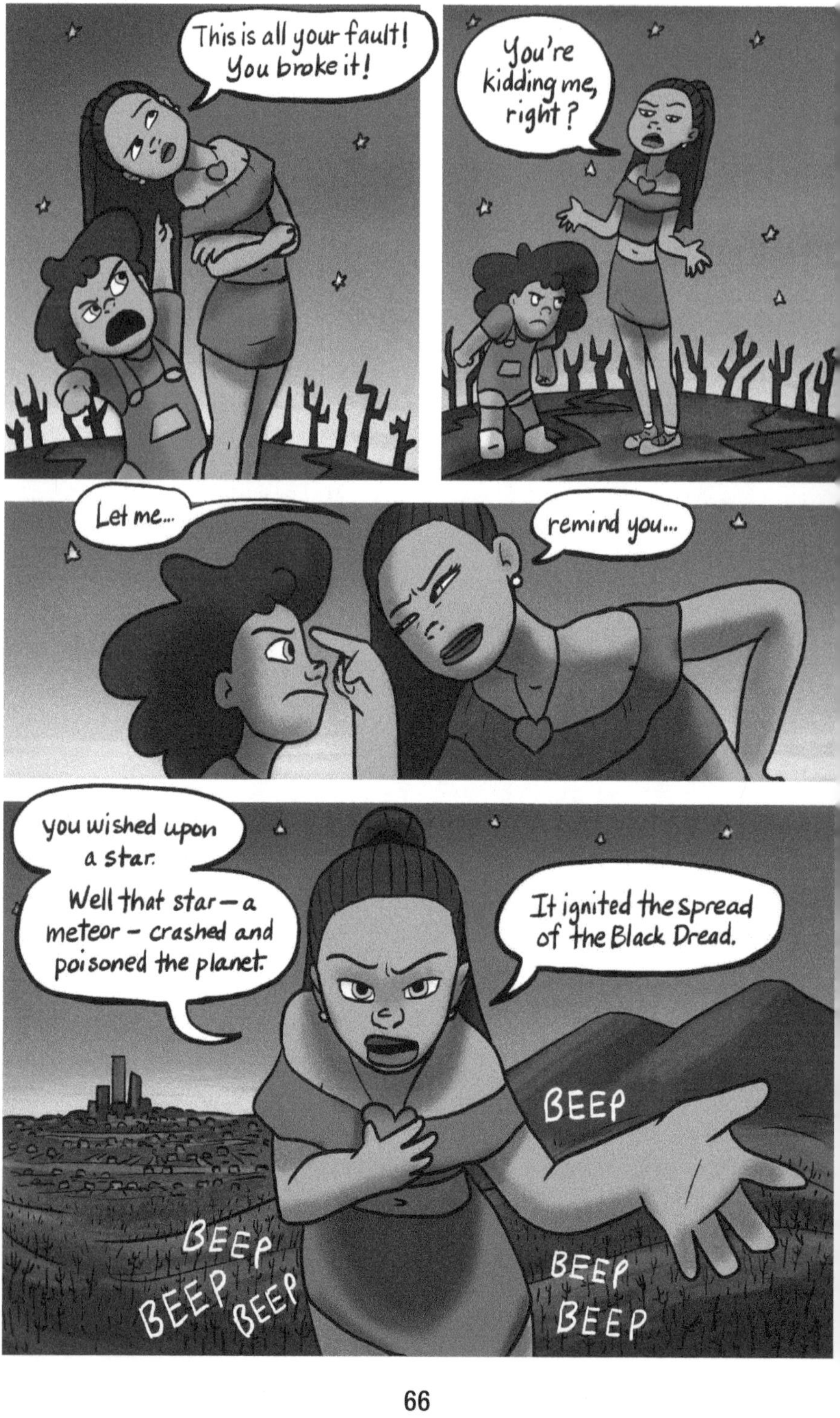
This is all your fault! You broke it!
You're kidding me, right?
Let me...
remind you...
you wished upon a star.
Well that star—a meteor—crashed and poisoned the planet.
It ignited the spread of the Black Dread.
BEEP
BEEP
BEEP
BEEP
BEEP
BEEP

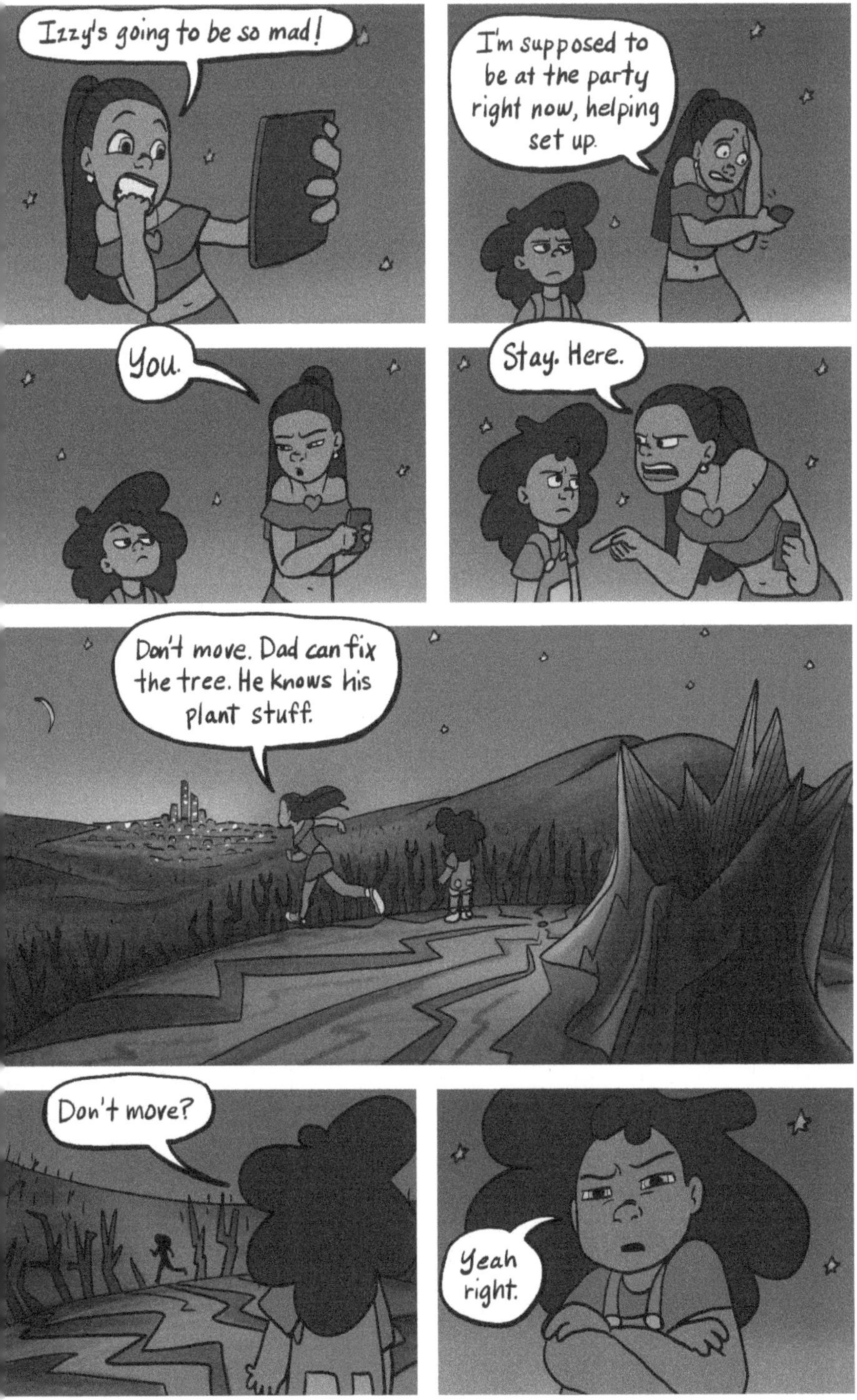
Izzy's going to be so mad!
I'm supposed to be at the party right now, helping set up.
You.
Stay. Here.
Don't move. Dad can fix the tree. He knows his plant stuff.
Don't move?
Yeah right.

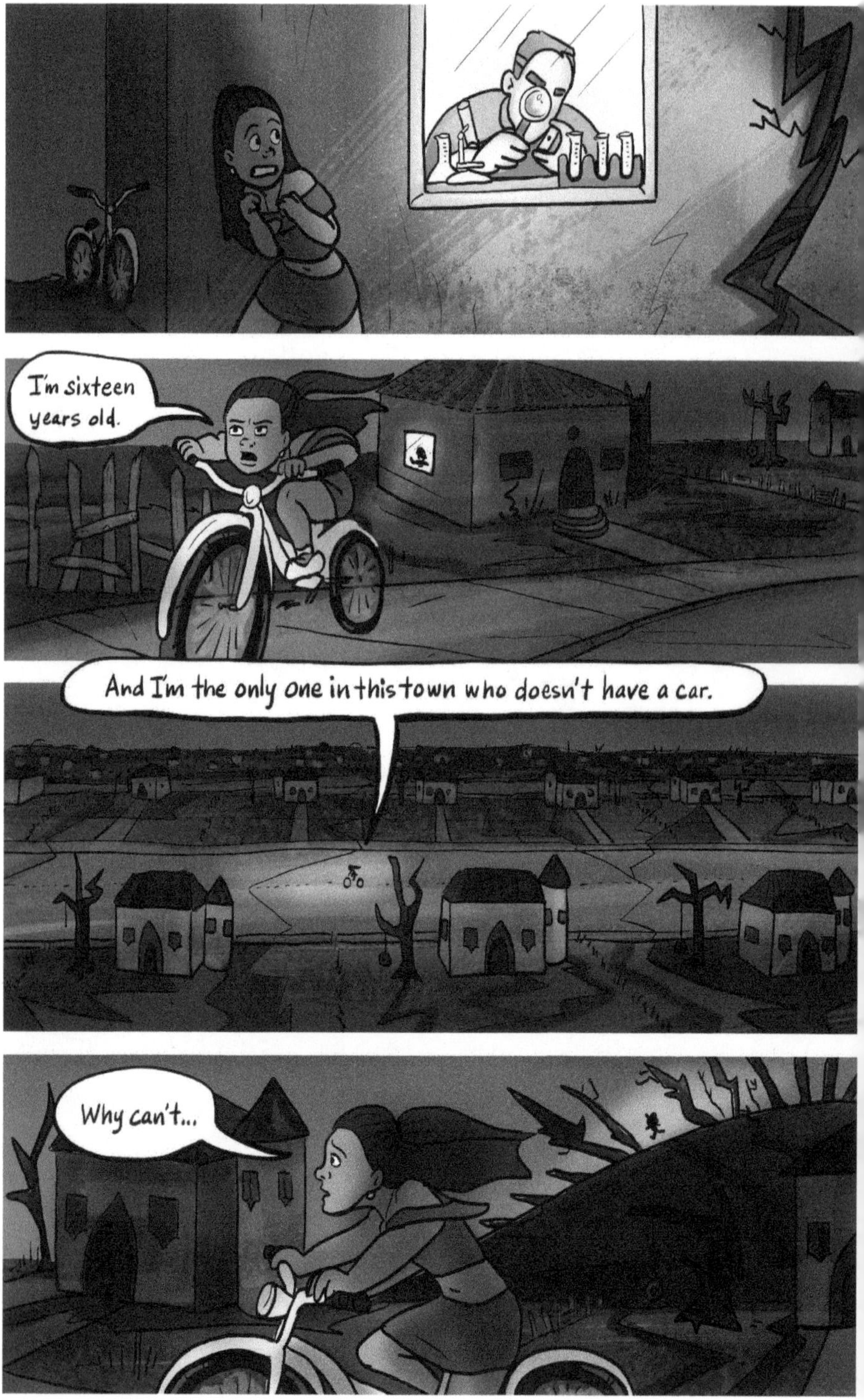
I'm sixteen years old.
And I'm the only one in this town who doesn't have a car.
Why can't...

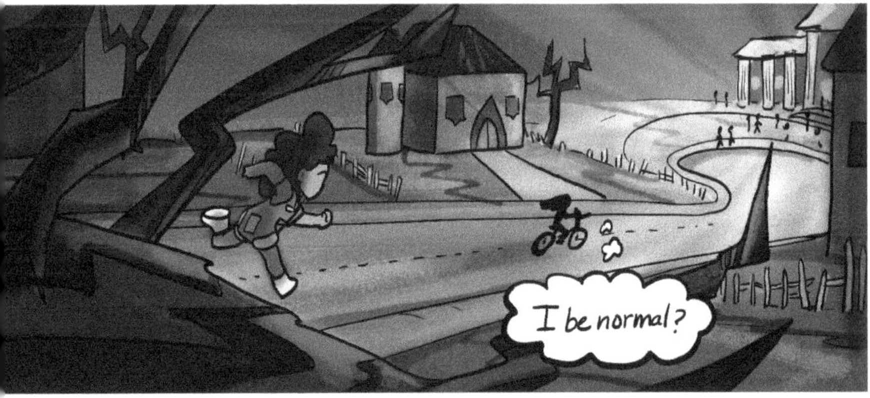
I be normal?

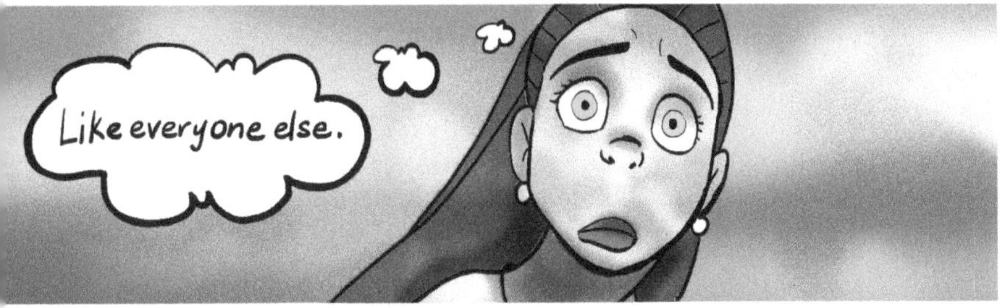
Like everyone else.

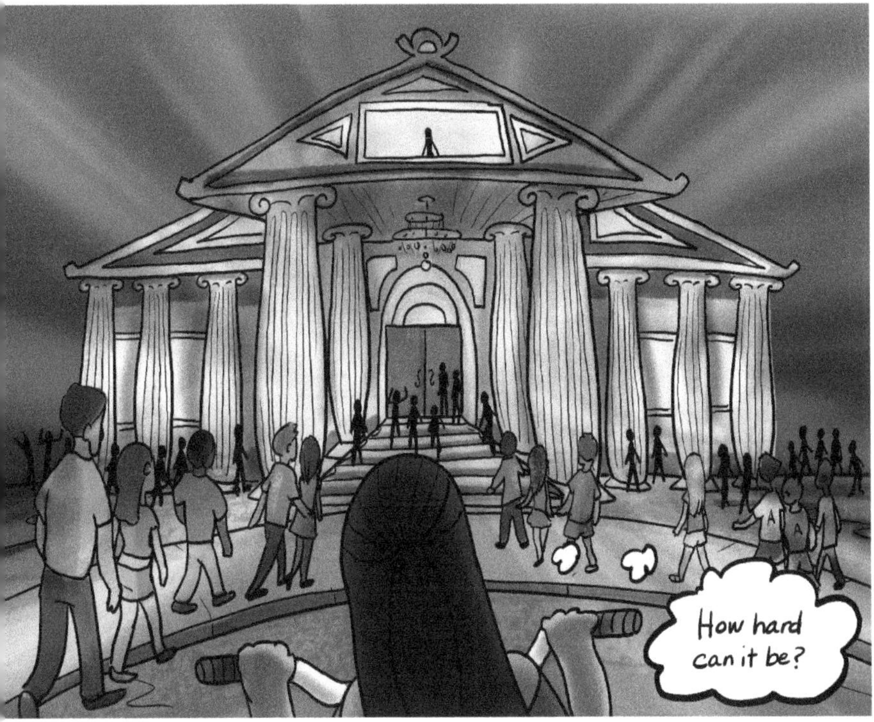
How hard
can it be?

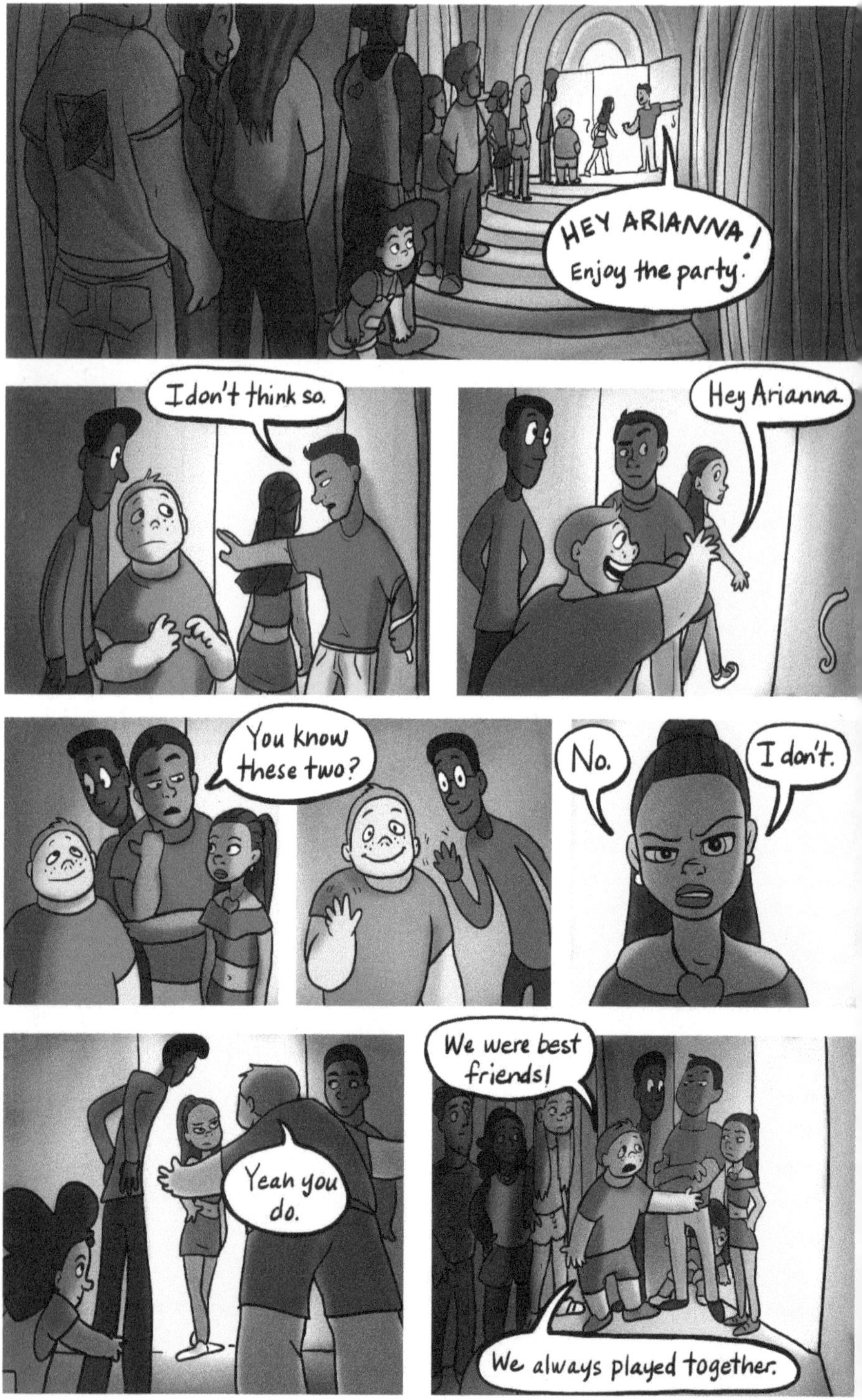
HEY ARIANNA!
Enjoy the party.
I don't think so.
Hey Arianna.
You know these two?
No.
I don't.
Yeah you do.
We were best friends!
We always played together.

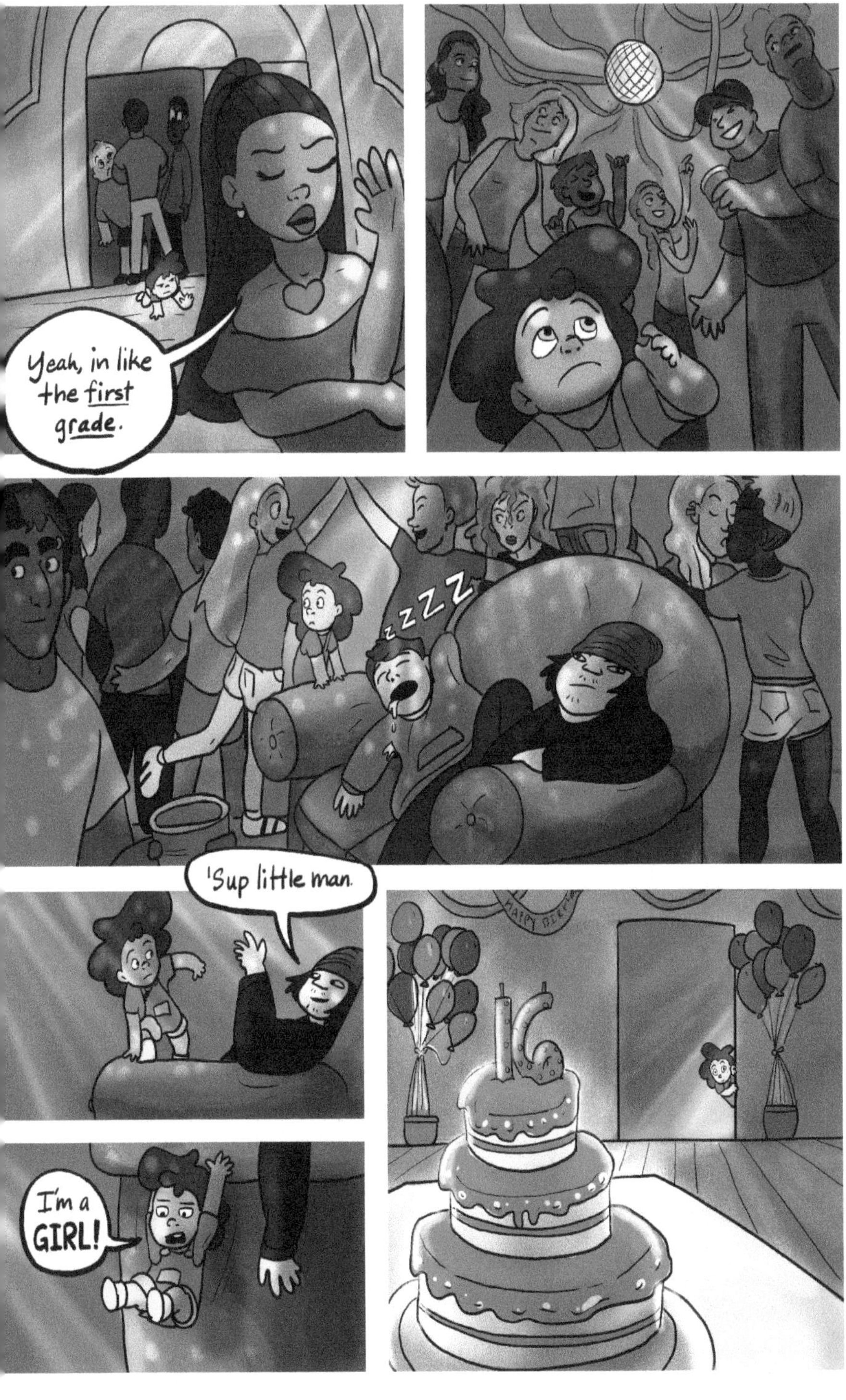

Yeah, in like the first grade.
zzZZZ
'Sup little man.
HAPPY BIRTH
I'm a GIRL!

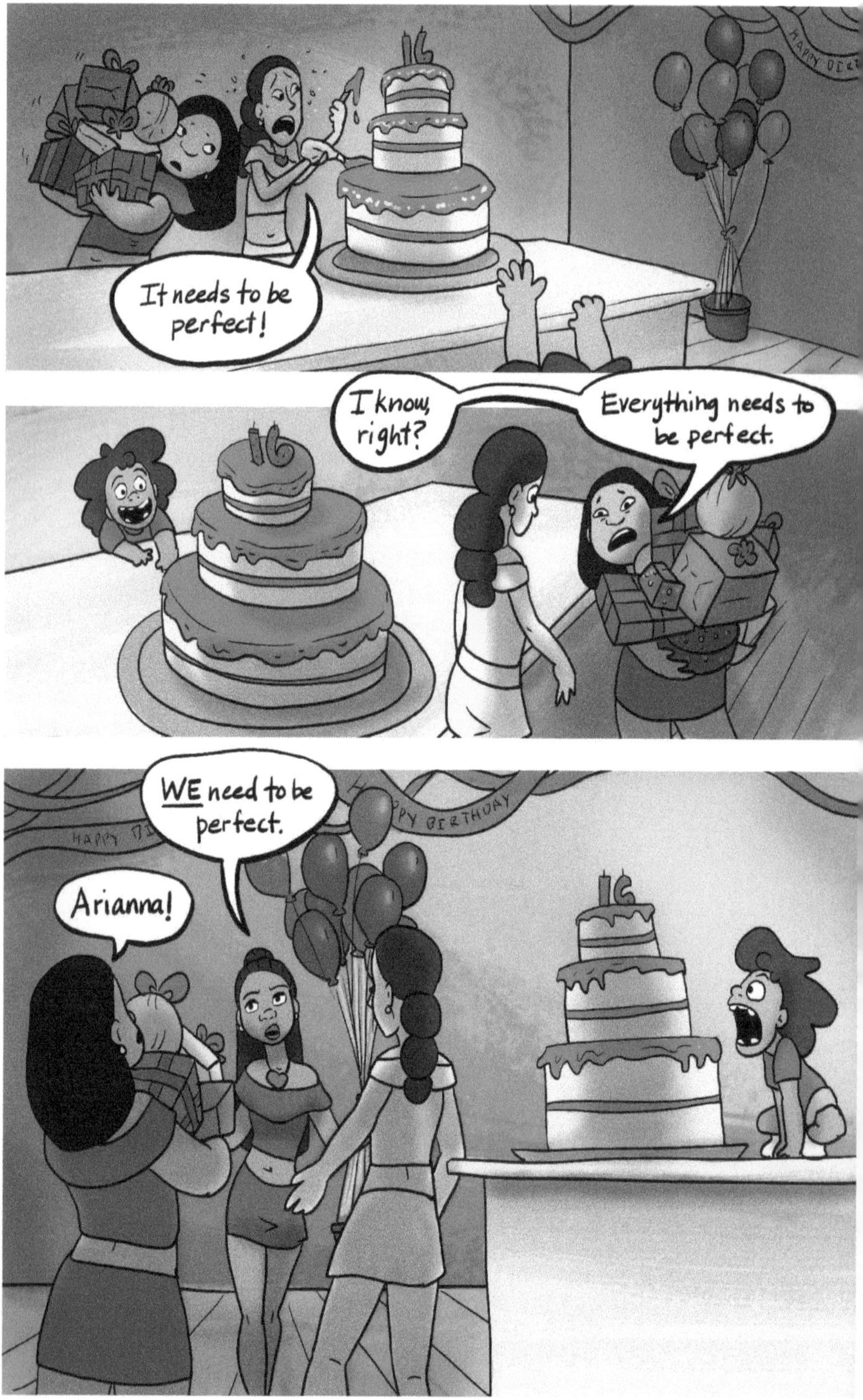
It needs to be perfect!
I know, right?
Everything needs to be perfect.
WE need to be perfect.
Arianna!

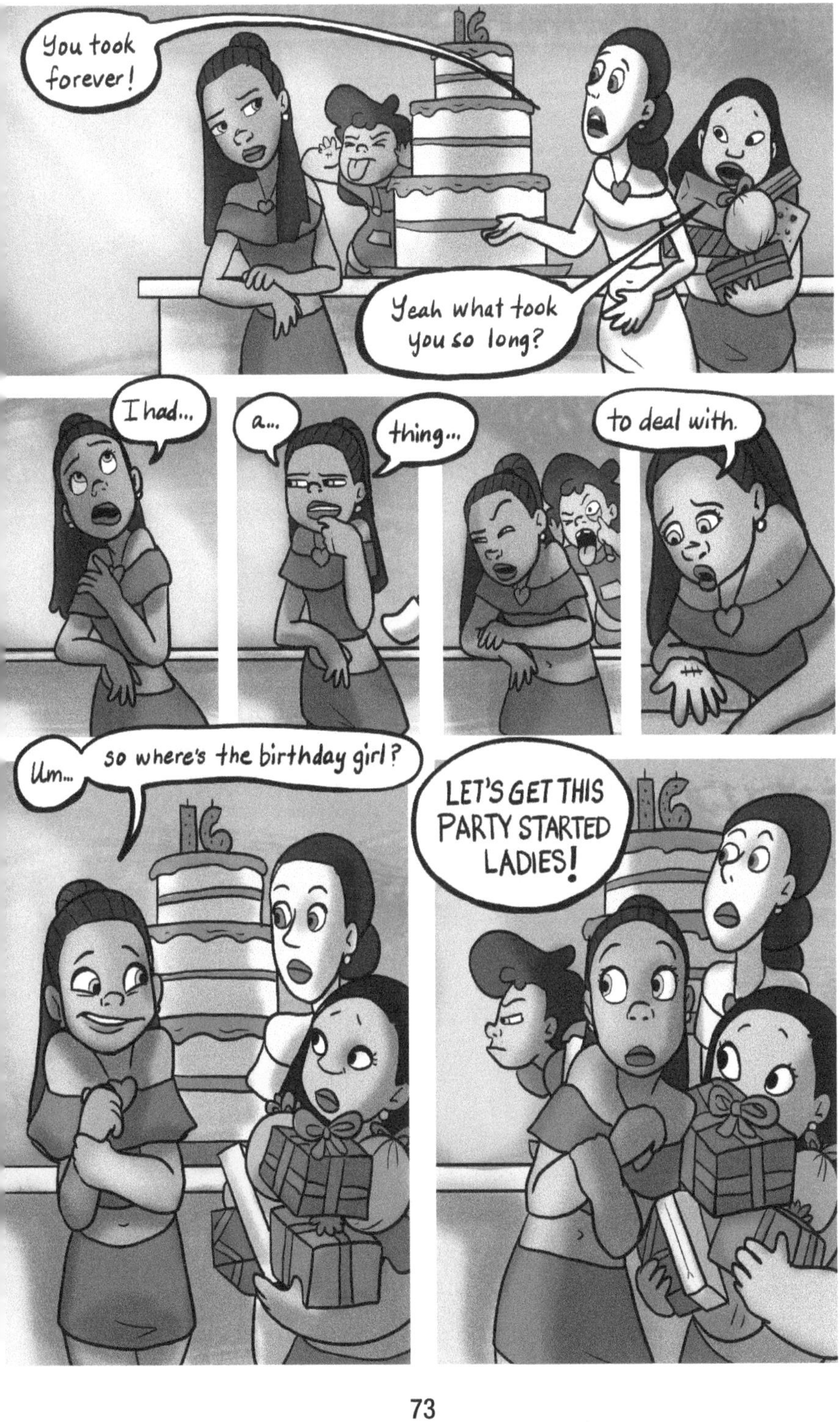
You took forever!
Yeah what took you so long?
I had...
a...
thing...
to deal with.
Um...
so where's the birthday girl?
LET'S GET THIS PARTY STARTED LADIES!

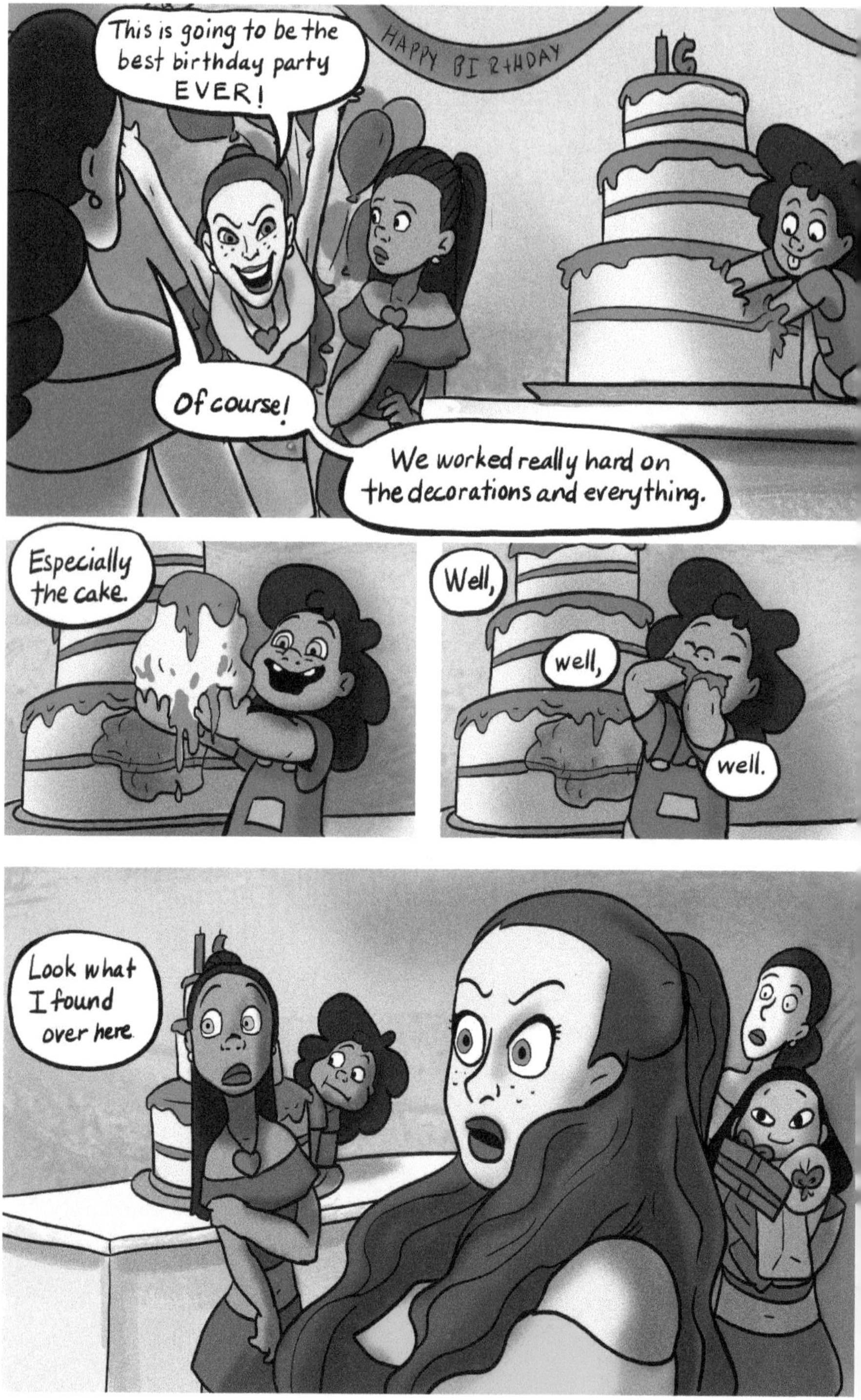
This is going to be the best birthday party EVER!
HAPPY BIRTHDAY
16
Of course!
We worked really hard on the decorations and everything.
Especially the cake.
Well,
well,
well.
Look what I found over here.

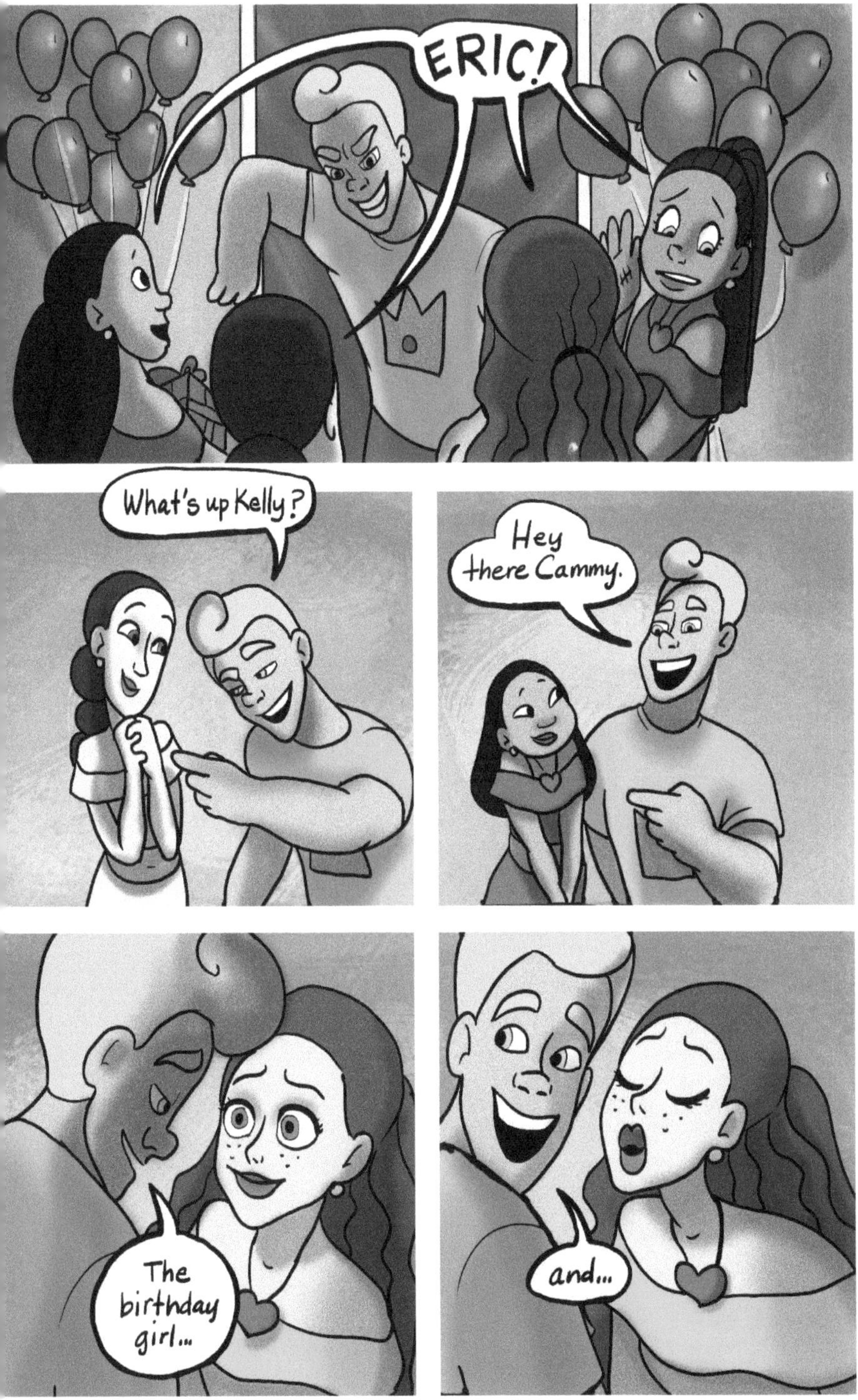
ERIC!
What's up Kelly?
Hey there Cammy.
The birthday girl...
and...

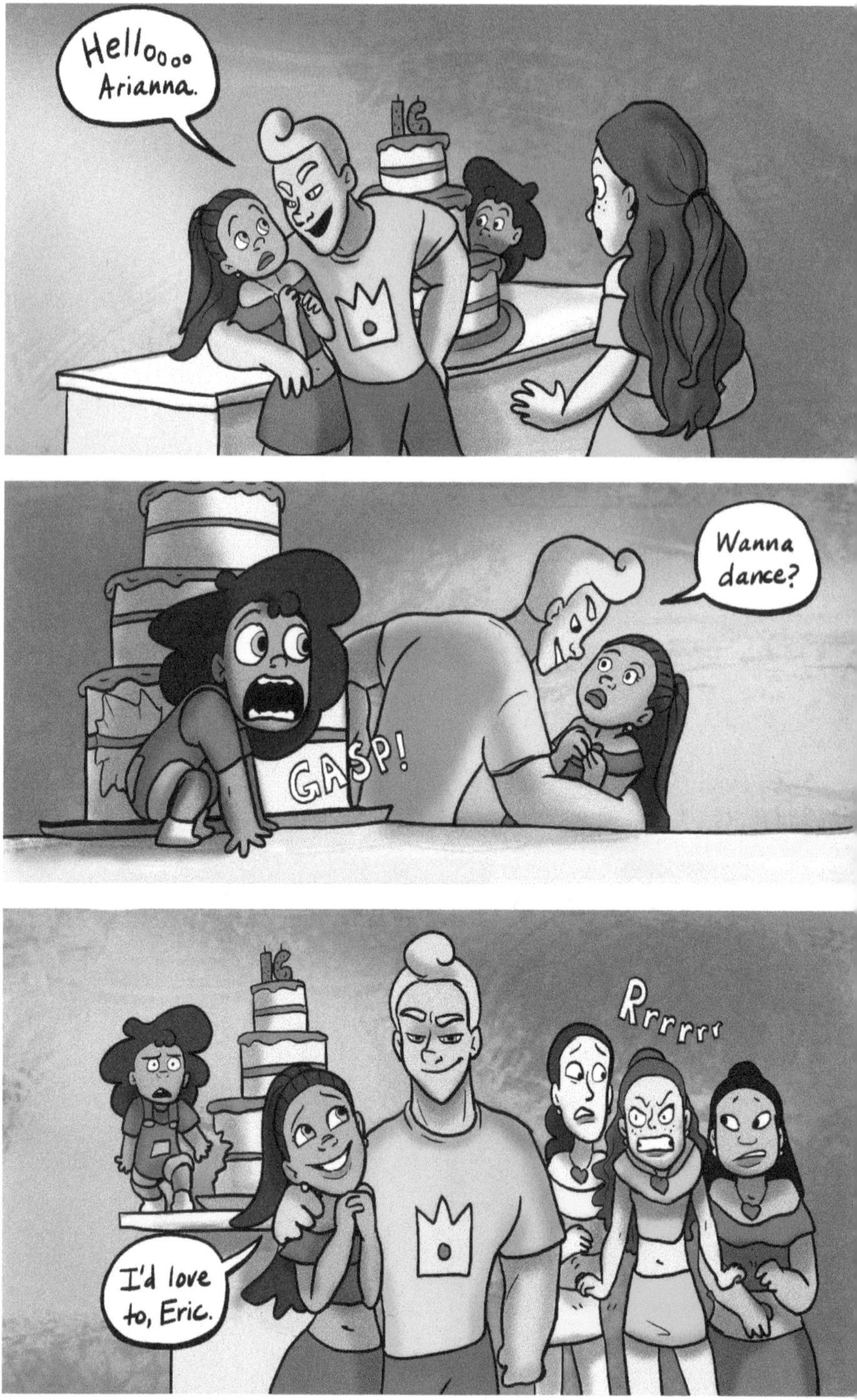
Helloooo Arianna.
Wanna dance?
GASP!
Rrrrrr
I'd love to, Eric.

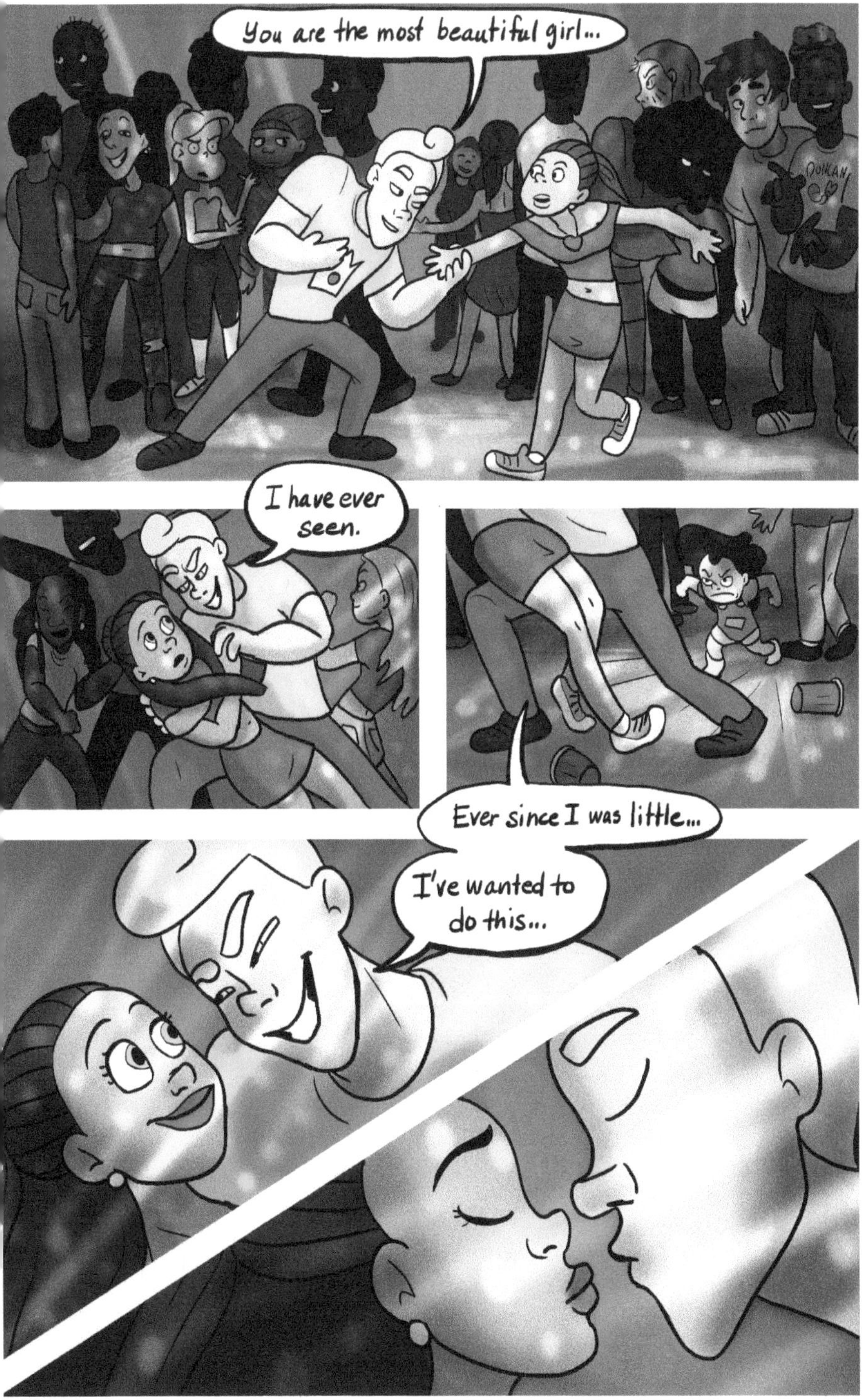
You are the most beautiful girl...
DUNCAN
I have ever seen.
Ever since I was little...
I've wanted to do this...

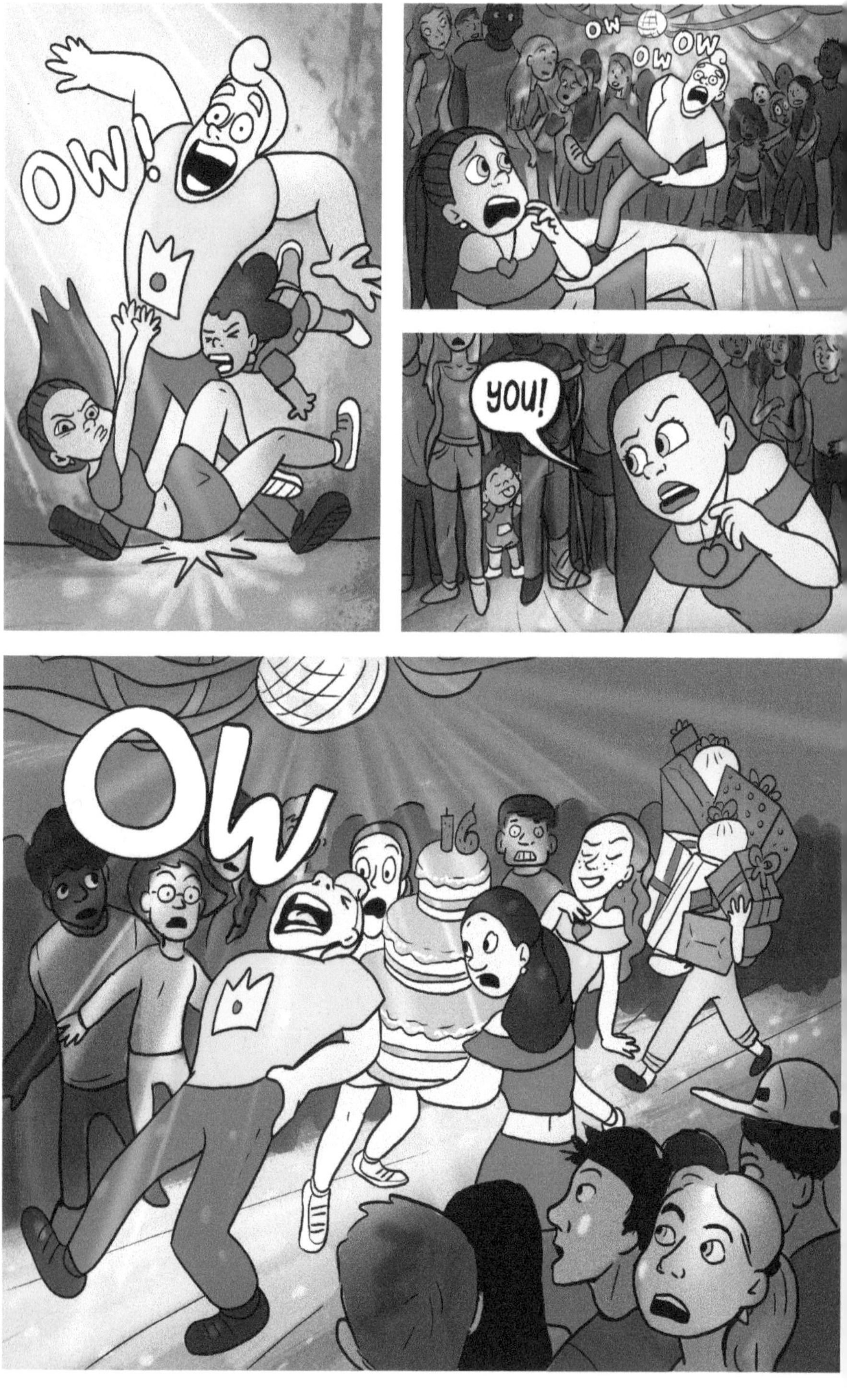
OW!
OW
OW
OW
YOU!
OW

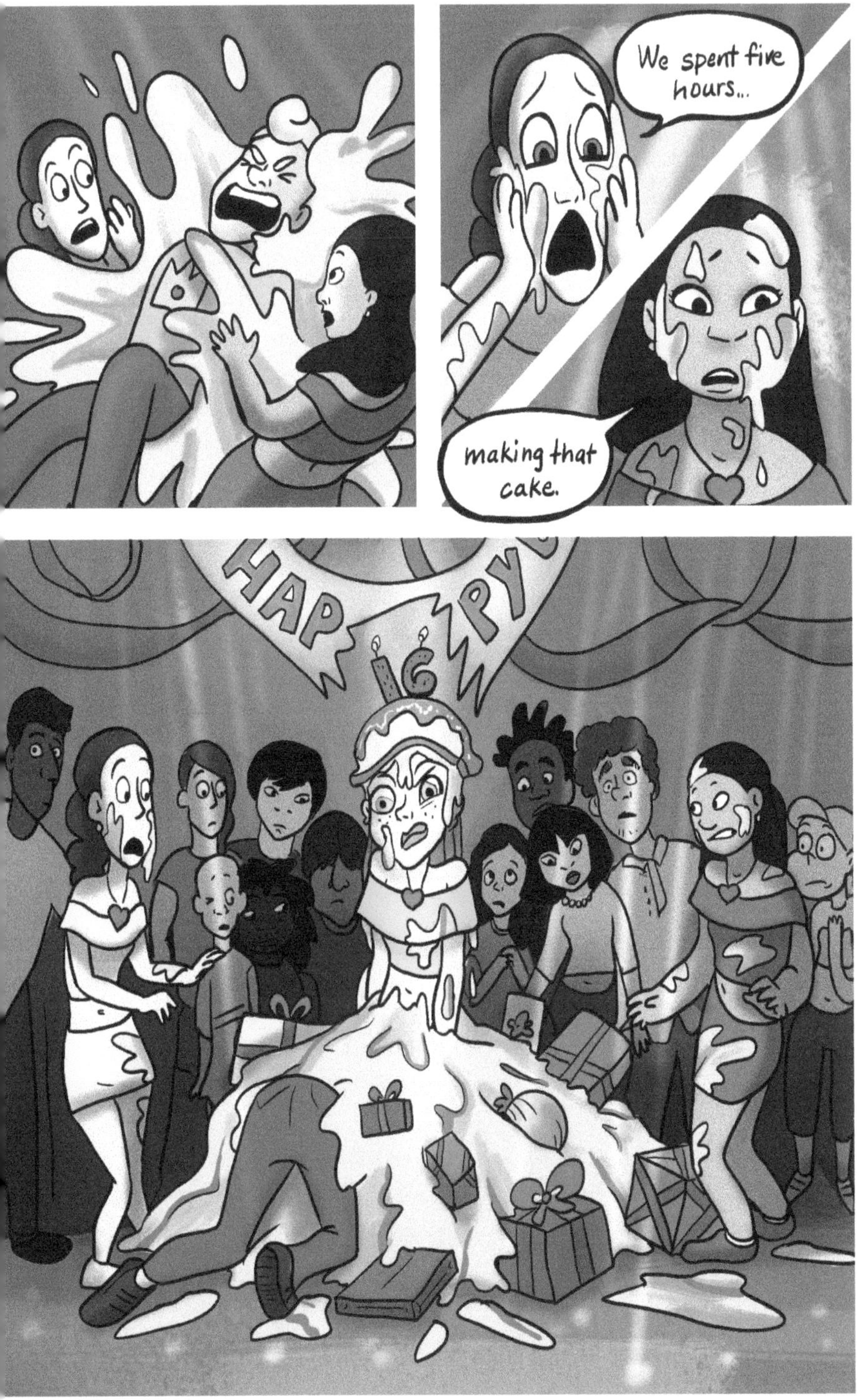
We spent five hours...
making that cake.
HAP
PY
16

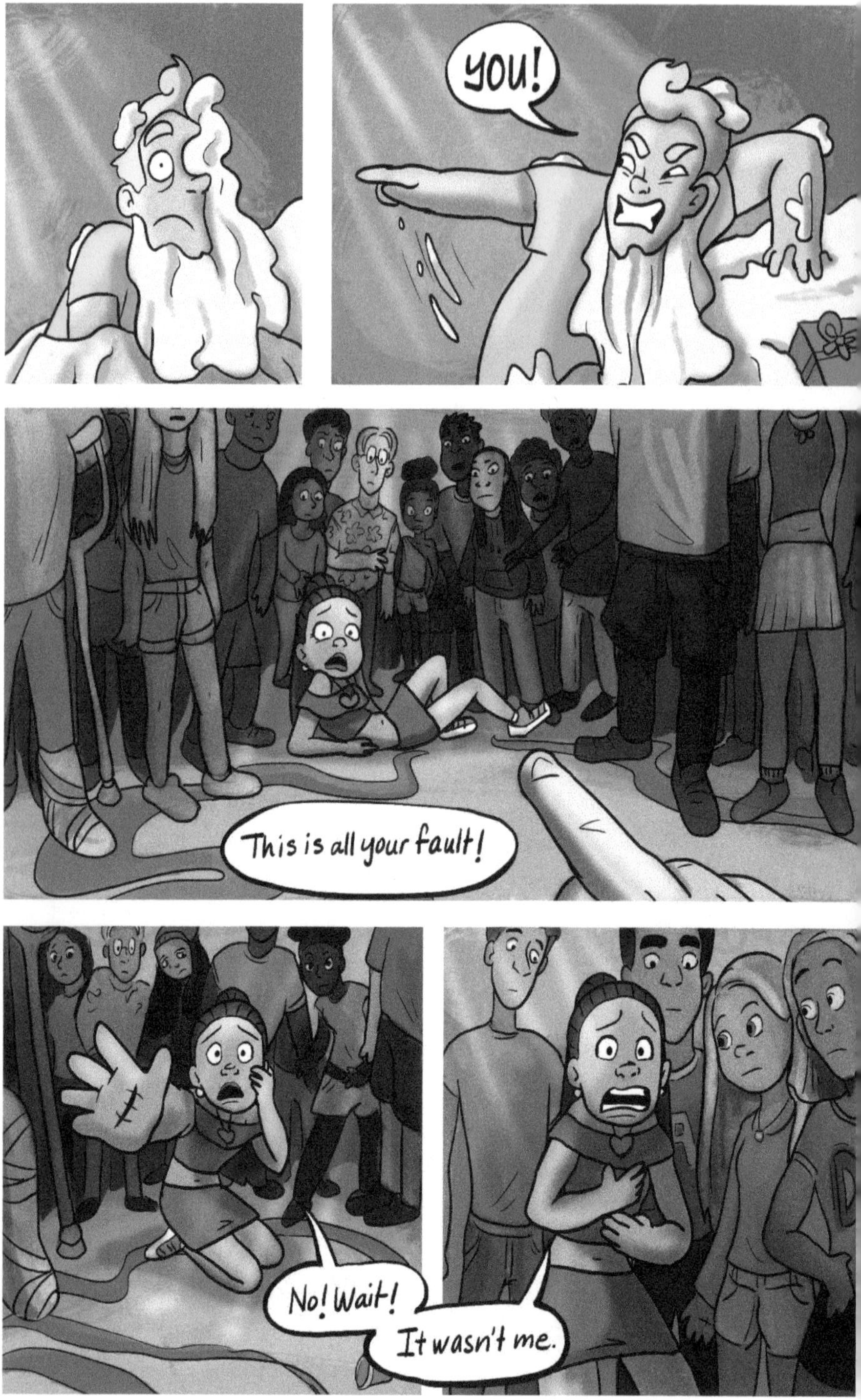
YOU!
This is all your fault!
No! Wait!
It wasn't me.

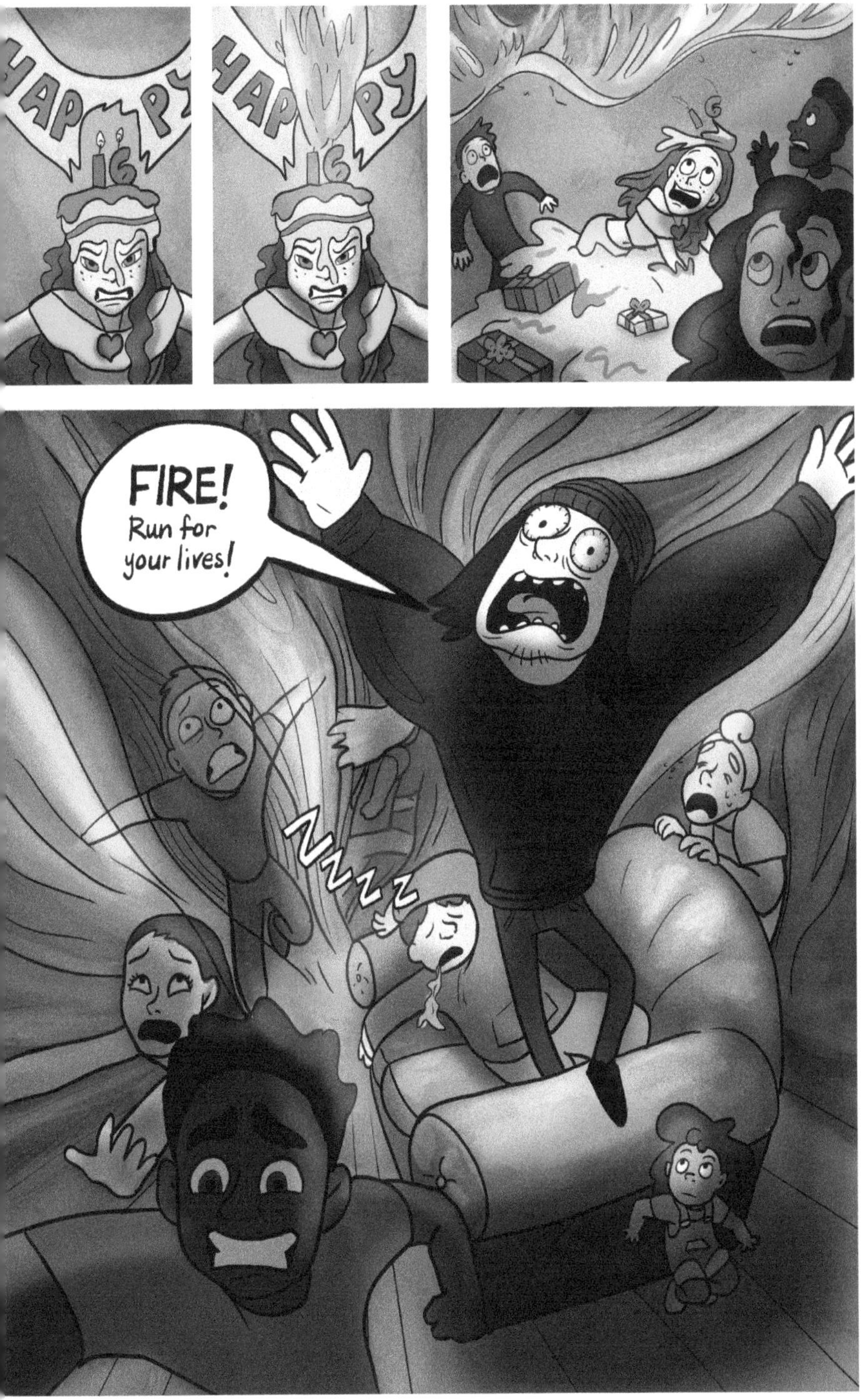
HAPPY
16
HAPPY
16
16
FIRE!
Run for your lives!
ZZZZ

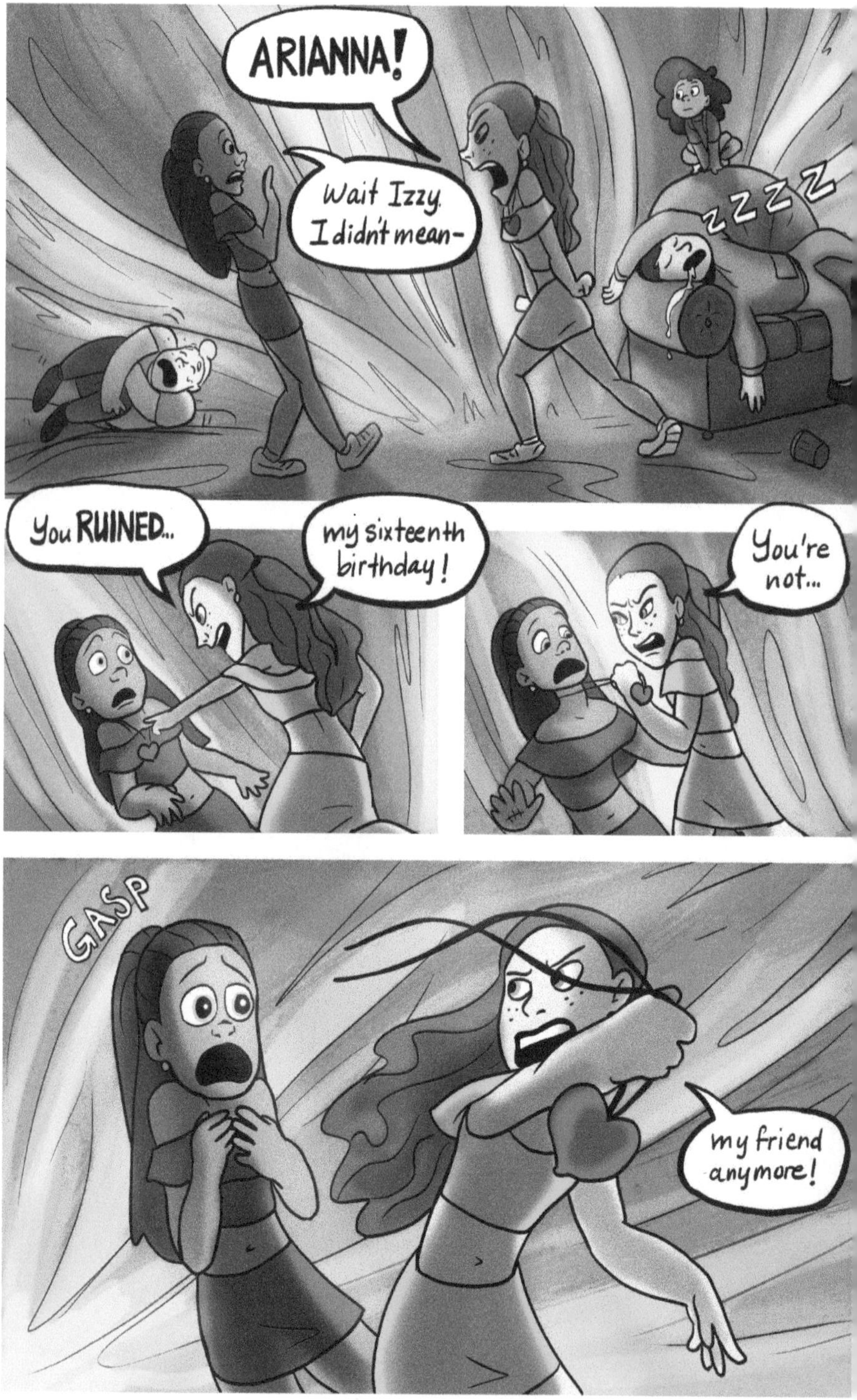
ARIANNA!
Wait Izzy. I didn't mean-
ZZZZ
You RUINED...
my sixteenth birthday!
You're not...
GASP
my friend anymore!

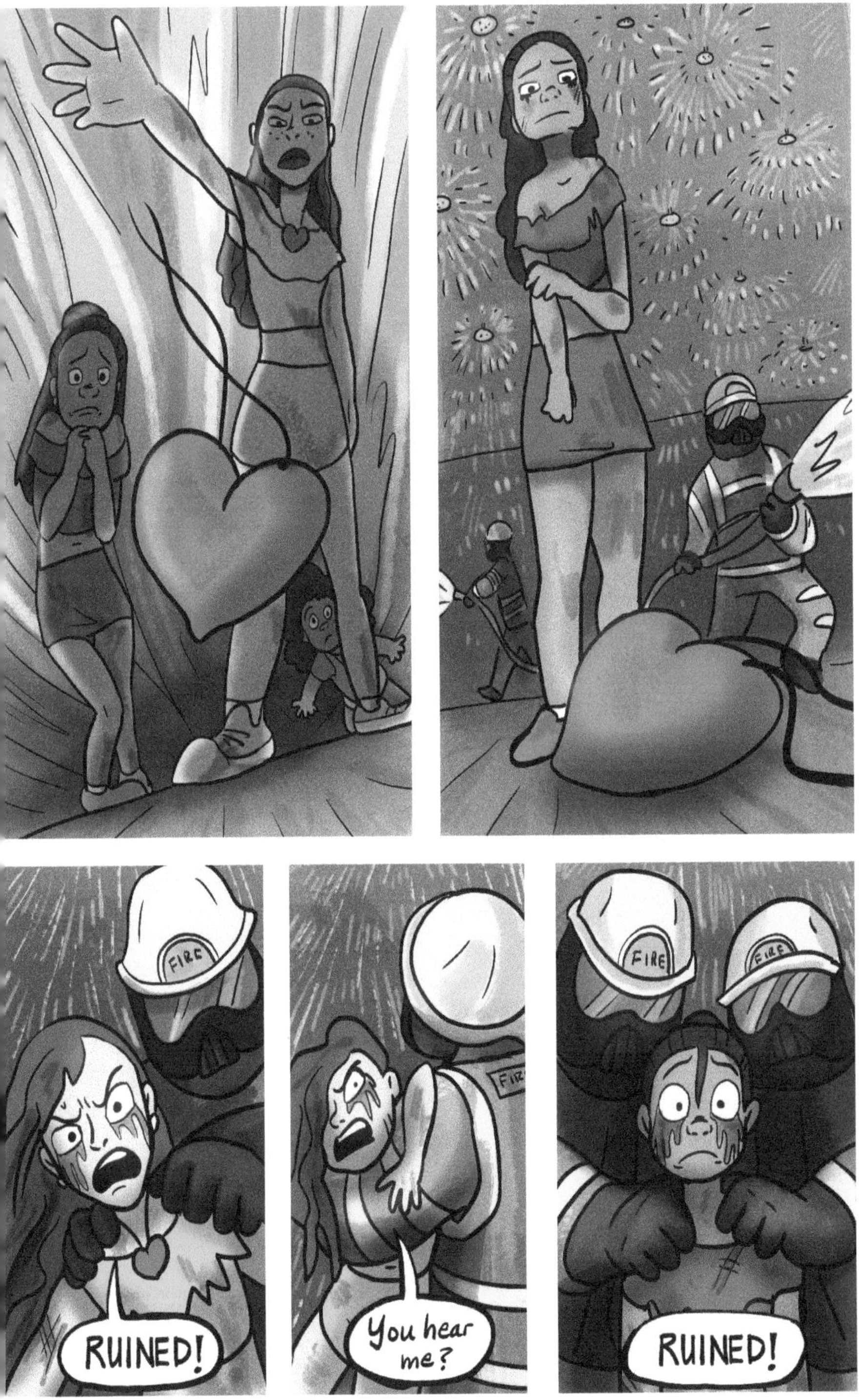
FIRE
RUINED!
You hear me?
FIRE
FIRE
RUINED!

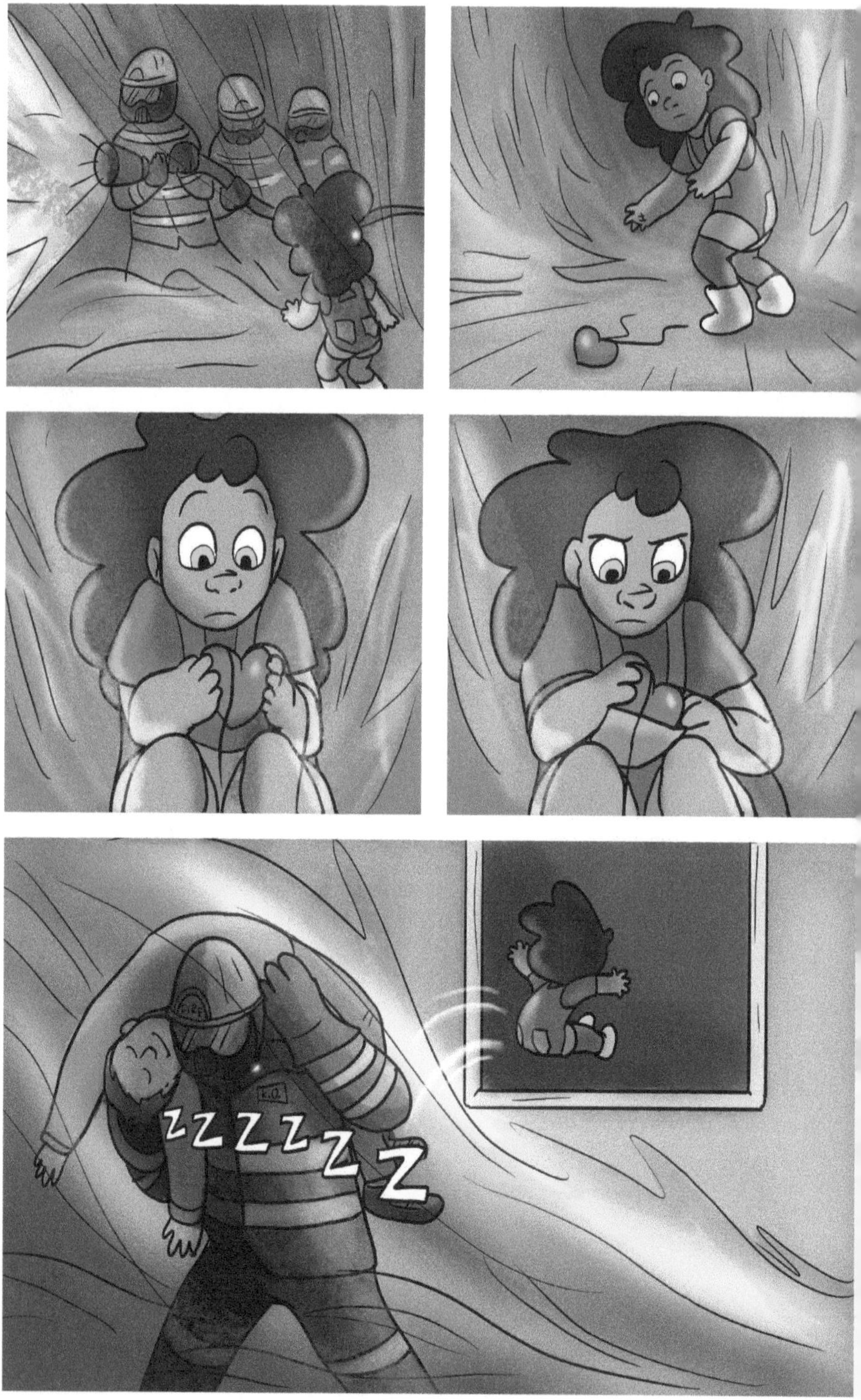
ZZZZZZ

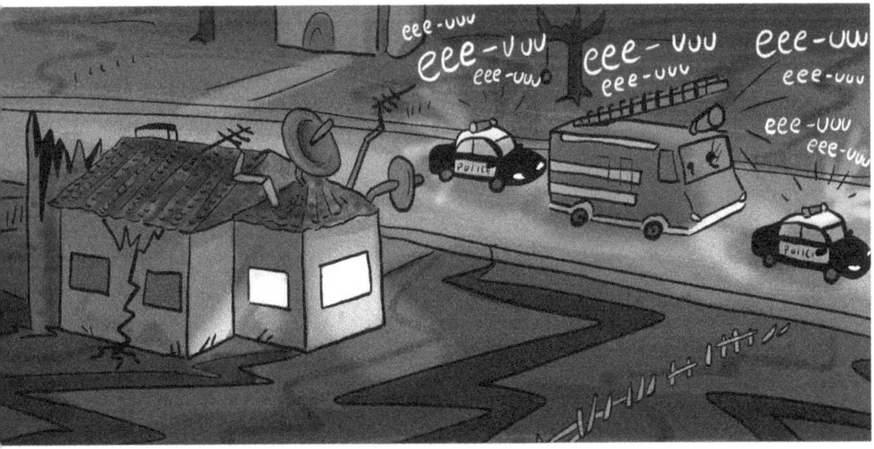
eee-uuu
eee-uuu
eee-uuu
eee-uuu
eee-uuu
eee-uuu
eee-uuu
eee-uuu
eee-uuu
eee-uuu
POLICE
POLICE

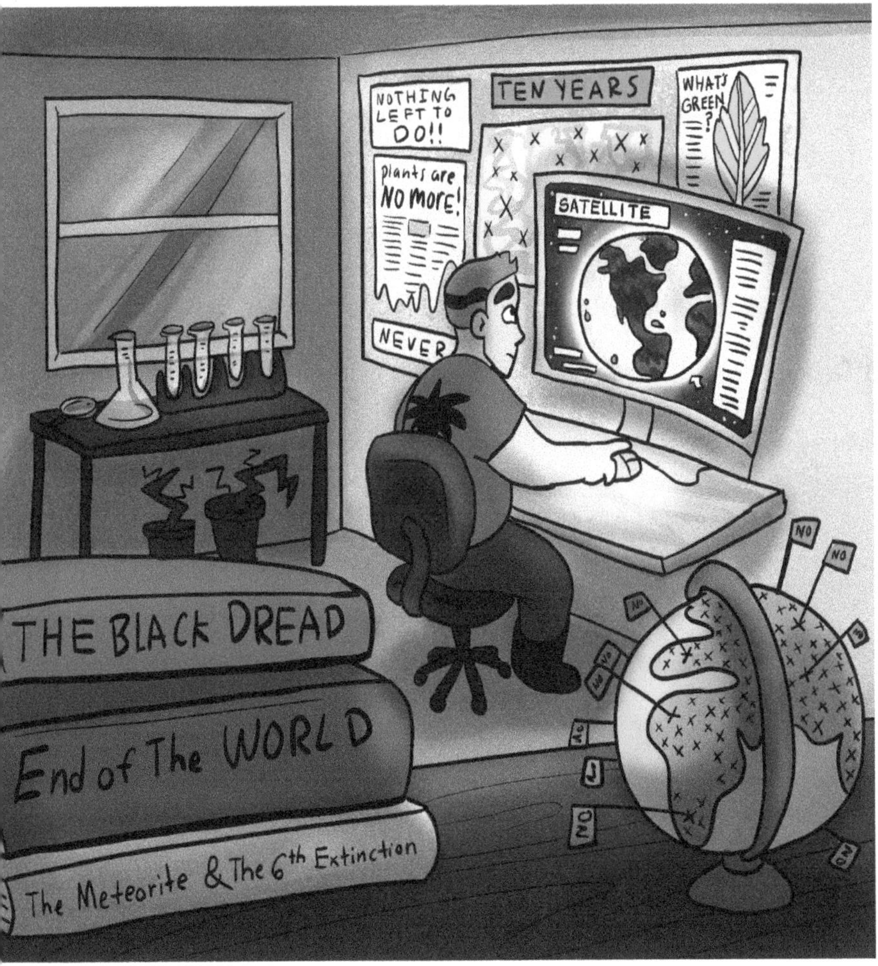
NOTHING LEFT TO DO!!
TEN YEARS
WHAT'S GREEN?
plants are NO more!
NEVER
SATELLITE
NO
NO
NO
NO
NO
THE BLACK DREAD
End of The WORLD
The Meteorite & The 6th Extinction

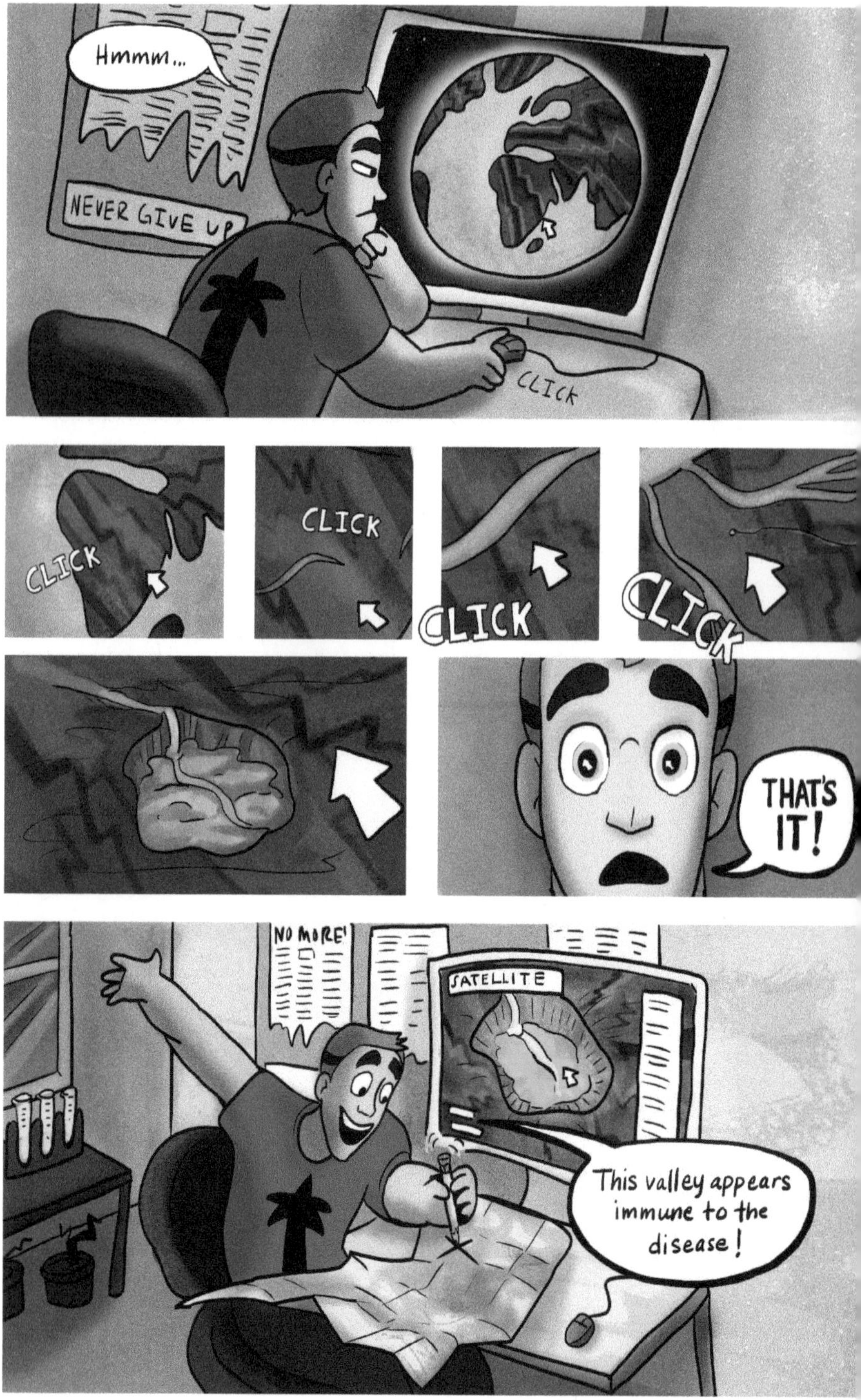
Hmmm...
NEVER GIVE UP
CLICK
CLICK
CLICK
CLICK
CLICK
THAT'S IT!
NO MORE!
SATELLITE
This valley appears immune to the disease!

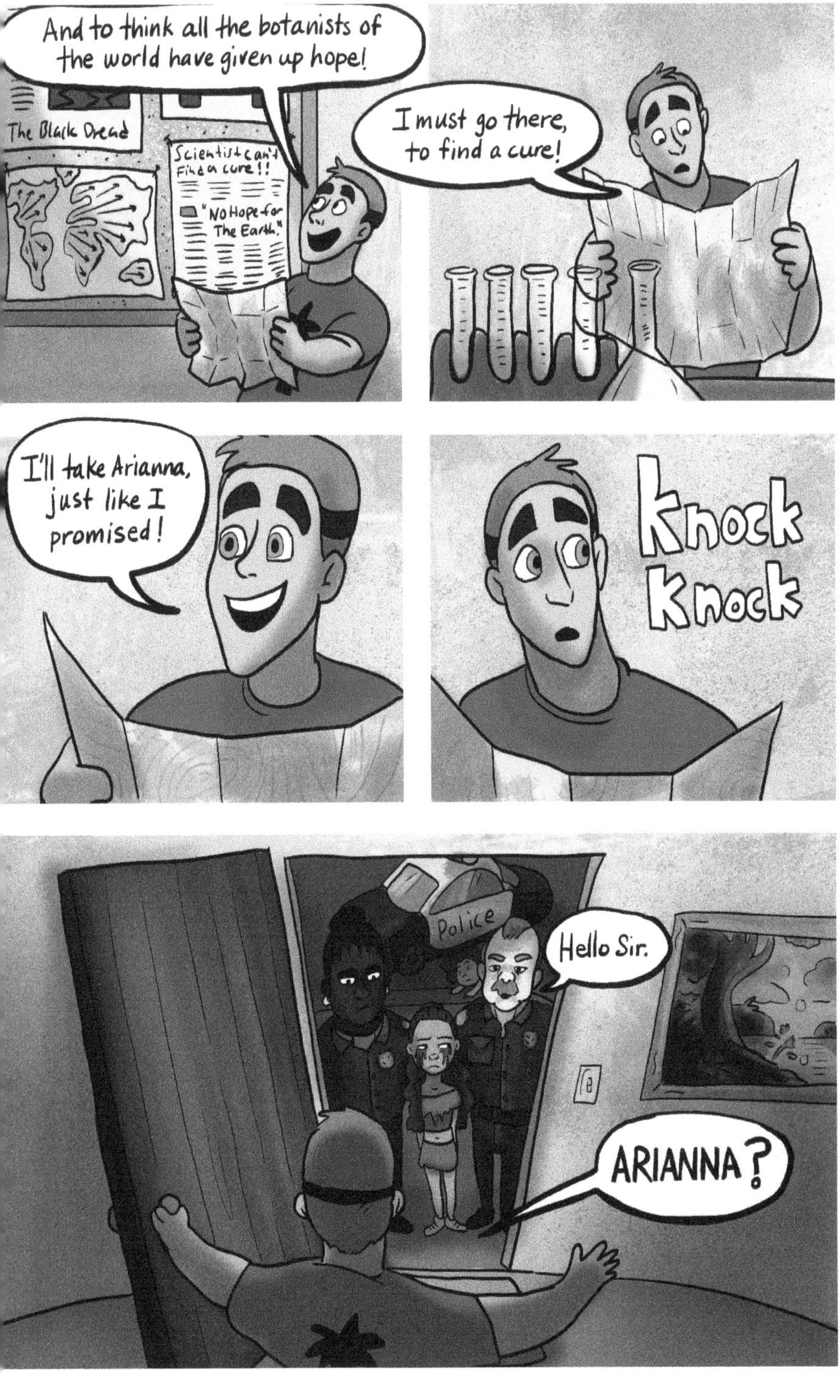
And to think all the botanists of the world have given up hope!
The Black Dread
Scientist can't Find a cure!!
"No Hope for The Earth."
I must go there, to find a cure!
I'll take Arianna, just like I promised!
Knock Knock
Police
Hello Sir.
ARIANNA?

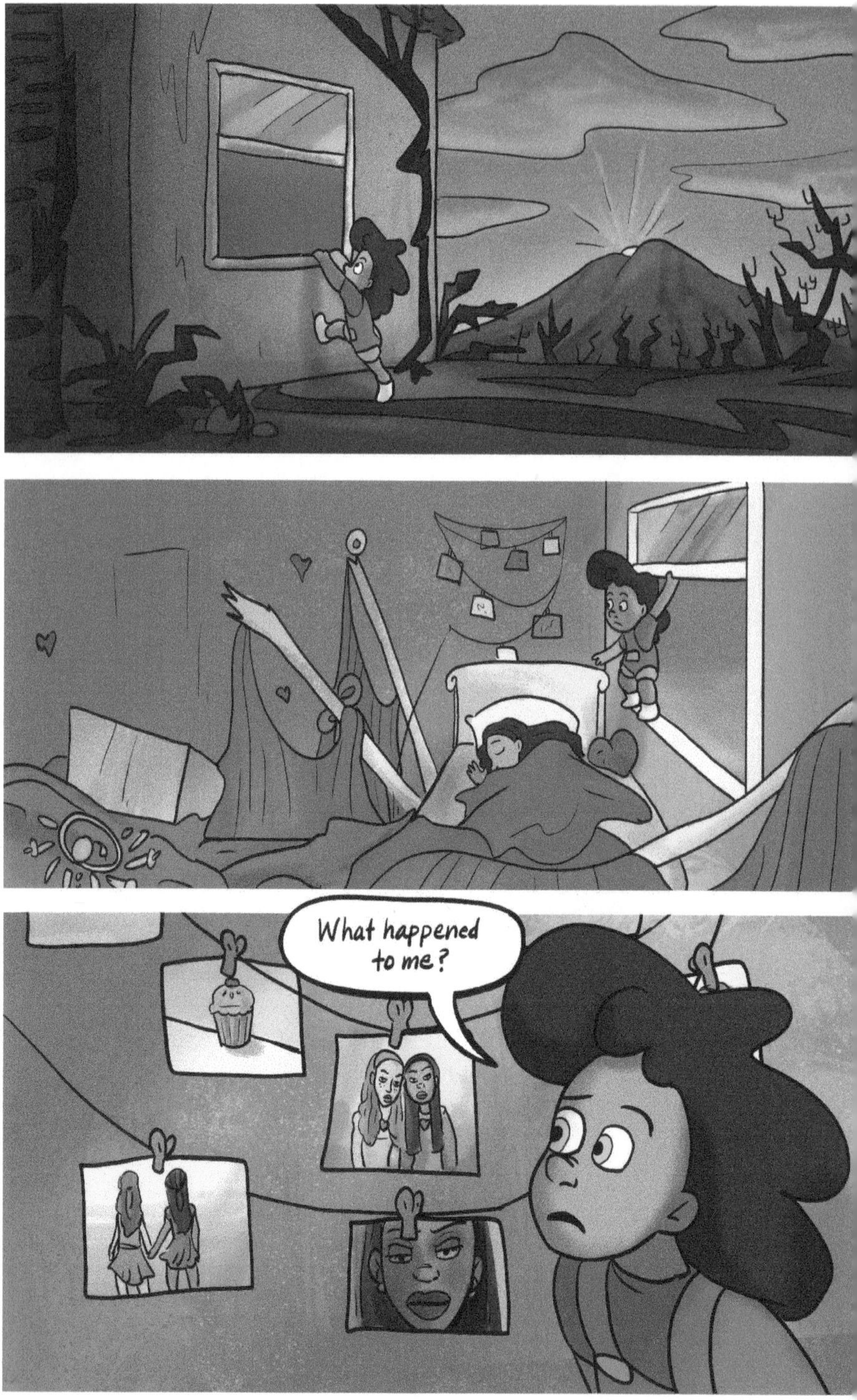
What happened to me?

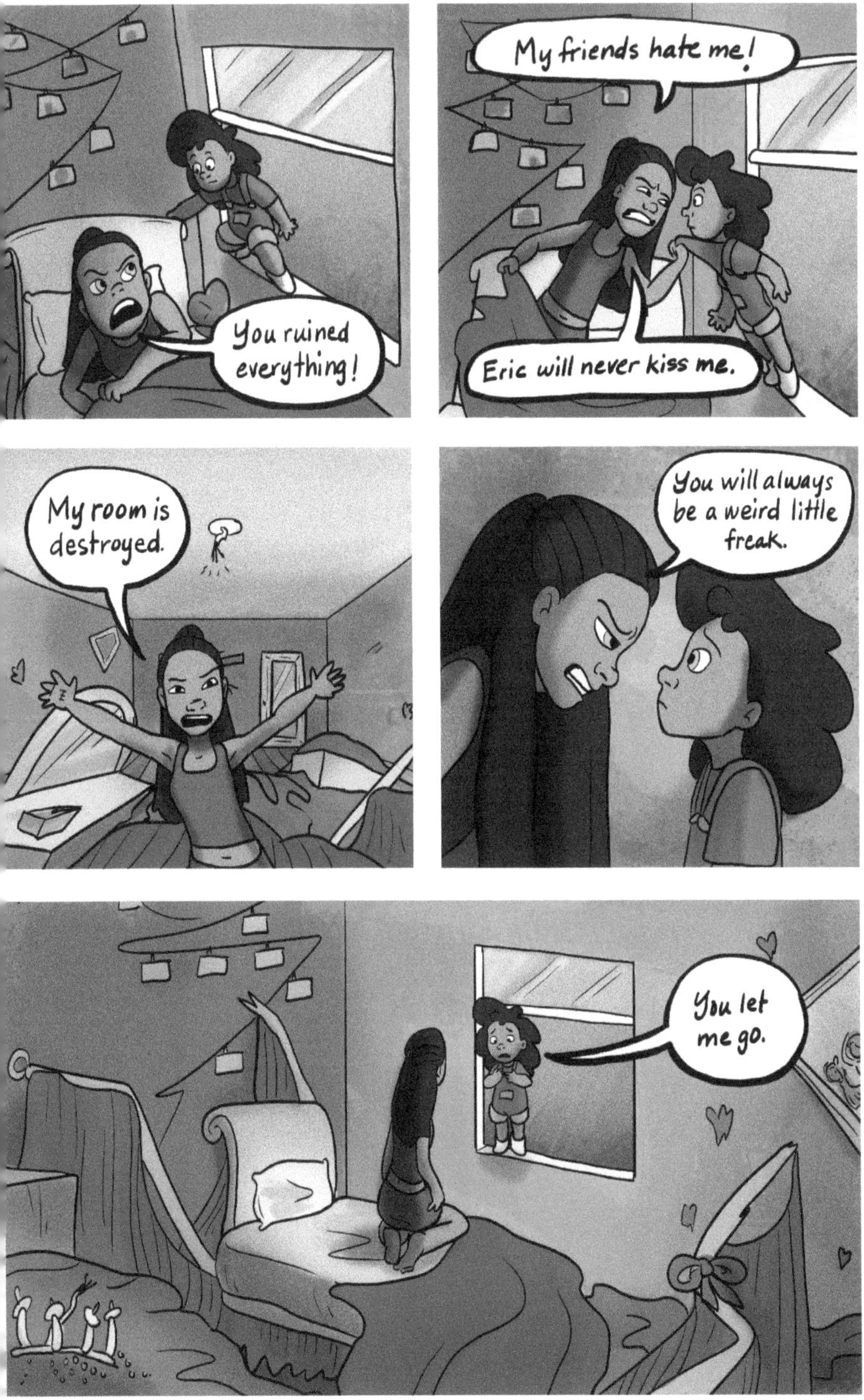
You ruined everything!
My friends hate me!
Eric will never kiss me.
My room is destroyed.
You will always be a weird little freak.
You let me go.

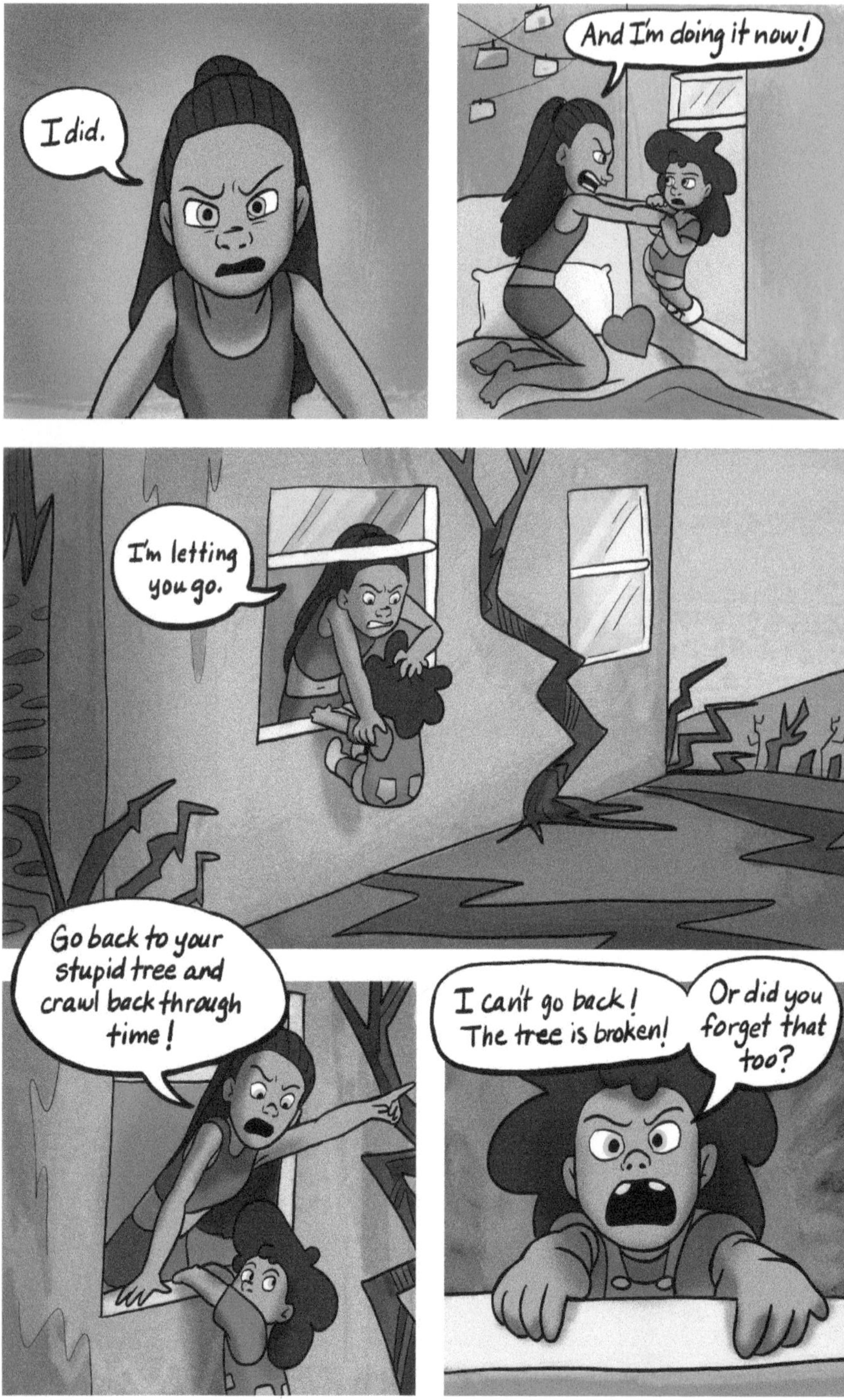
I did.
And I'm doing it now!
I'm letting you go.
Go back to your stupid tree and crawl back through time!
I can't go back! The tree is broken!
Or did you forget that too?

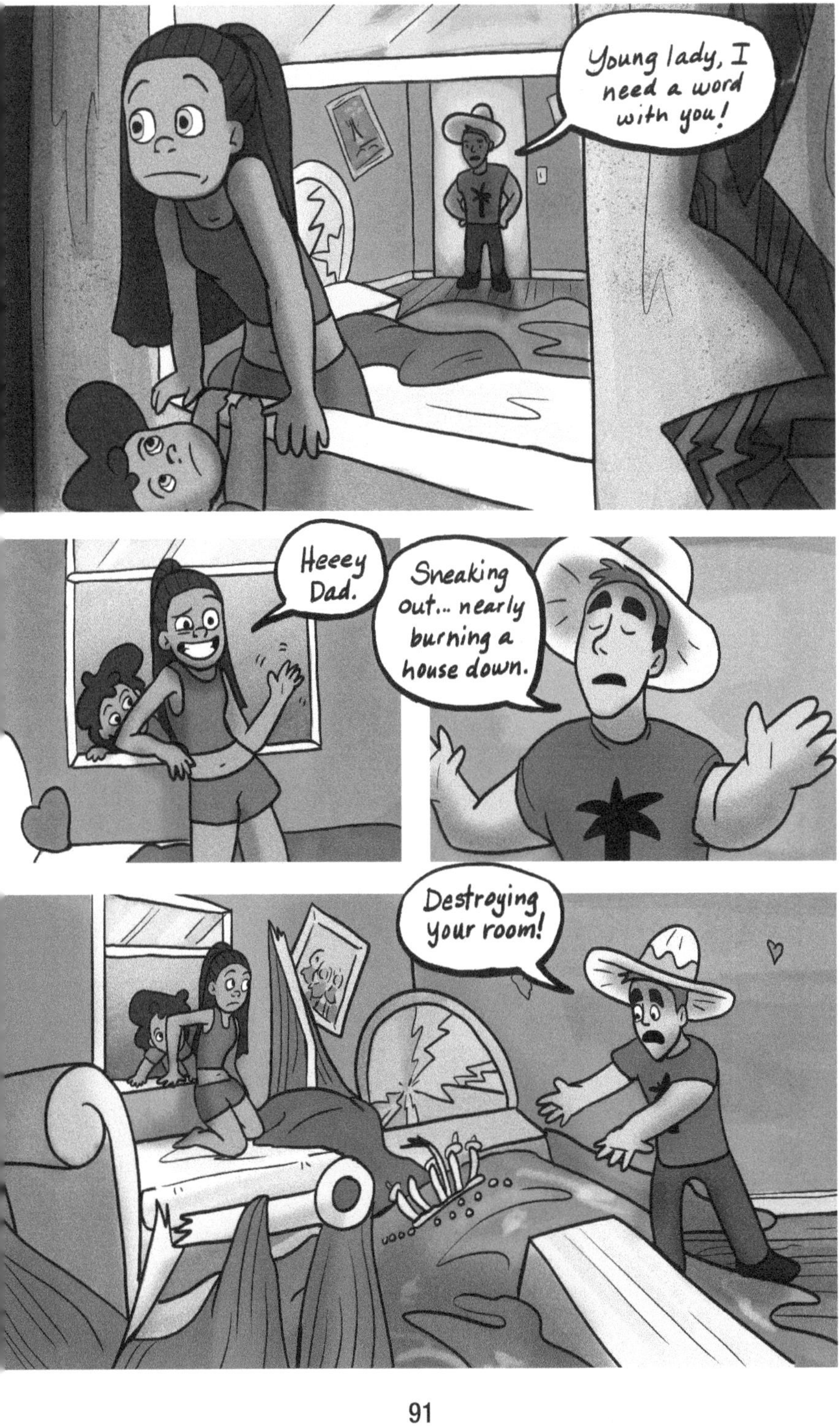
Young lady, I need a word with you!
Heeey Dad.
Sneaking out... nearly burning a house down.
Destroying your room!

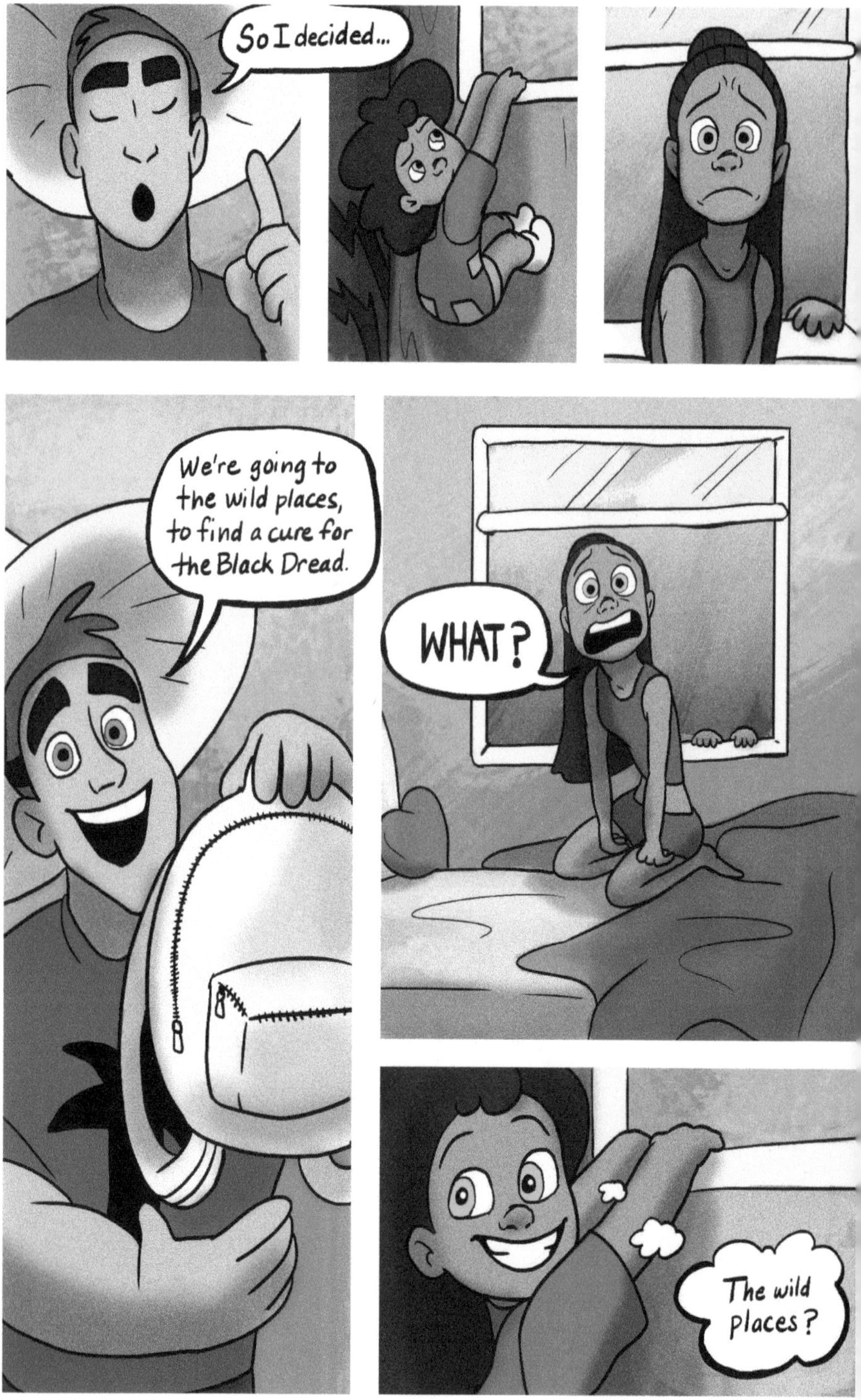
So I decided...
We're going to the wild places, to find a cure for the Black Dread.
WHAT?
The wild places?

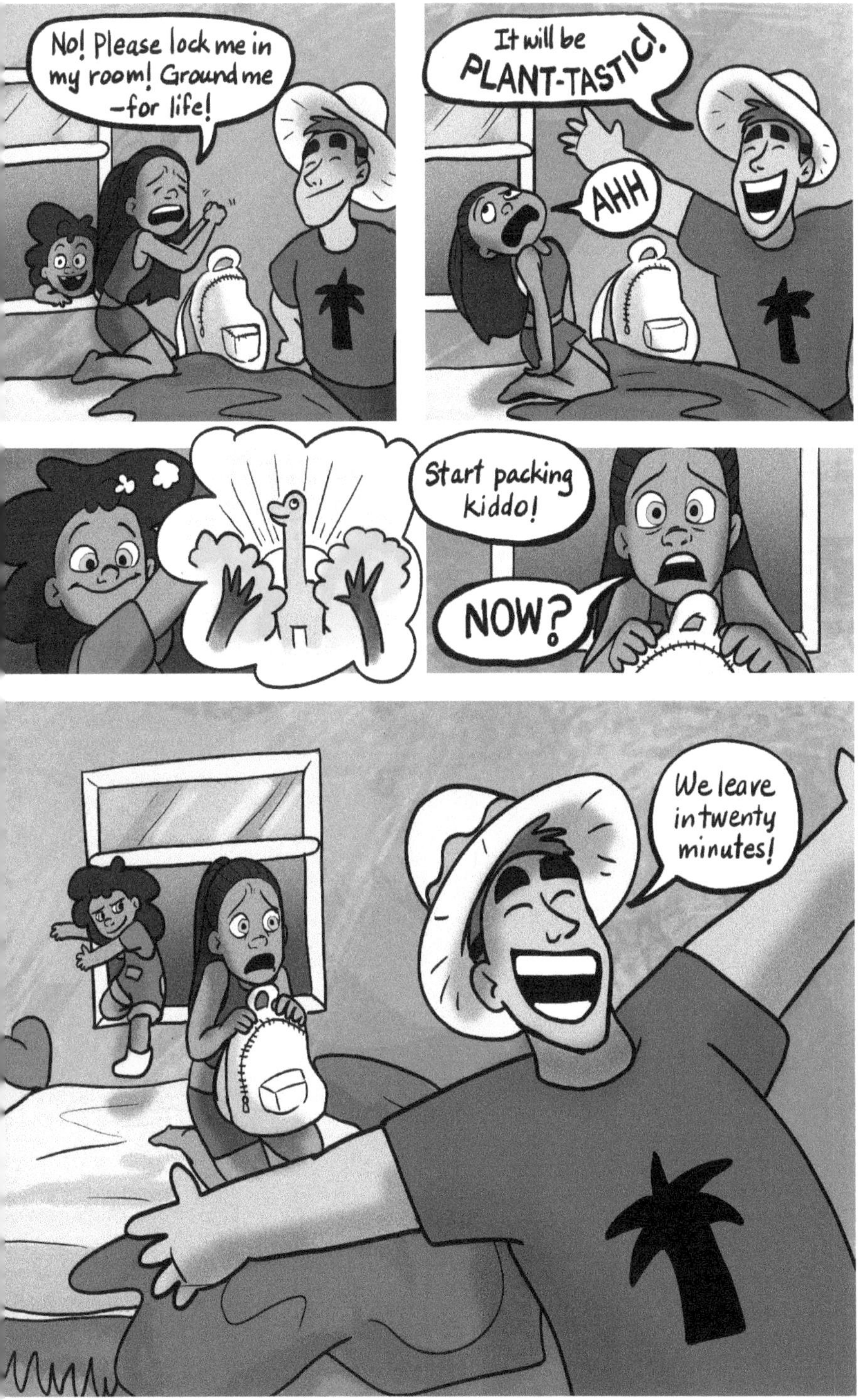
No! Please lock me in my room! Ground me —for life!
It will be PLANT-TASTIC!
AHH
Start packing kiddo!
NOW?
We leave in twenty minutes!

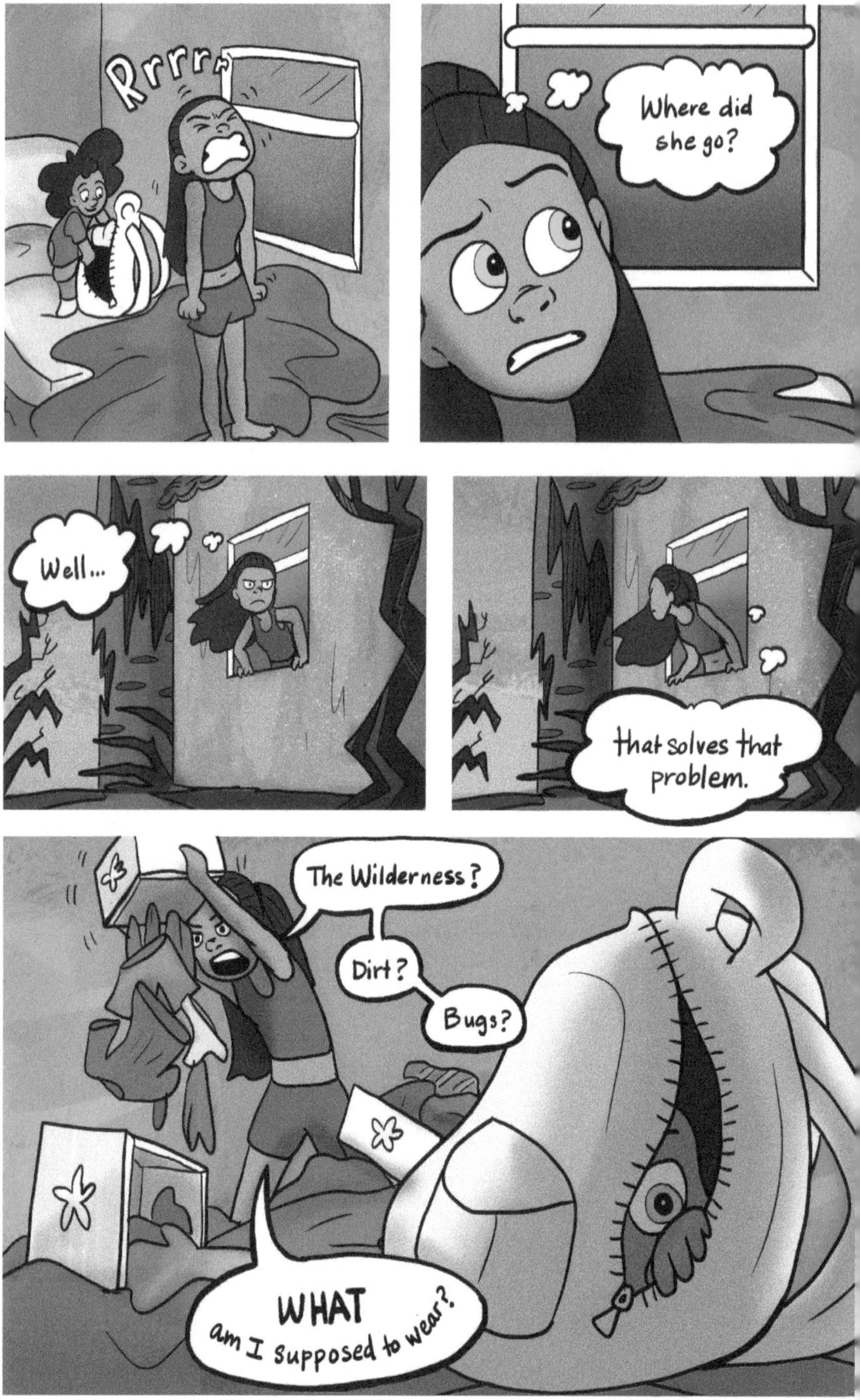
Rrrrr
Where did she go?
Well...
that solves that problem.
The Wilderness?
Dirt?
Bugs?
WHAT am I supposed to wear?

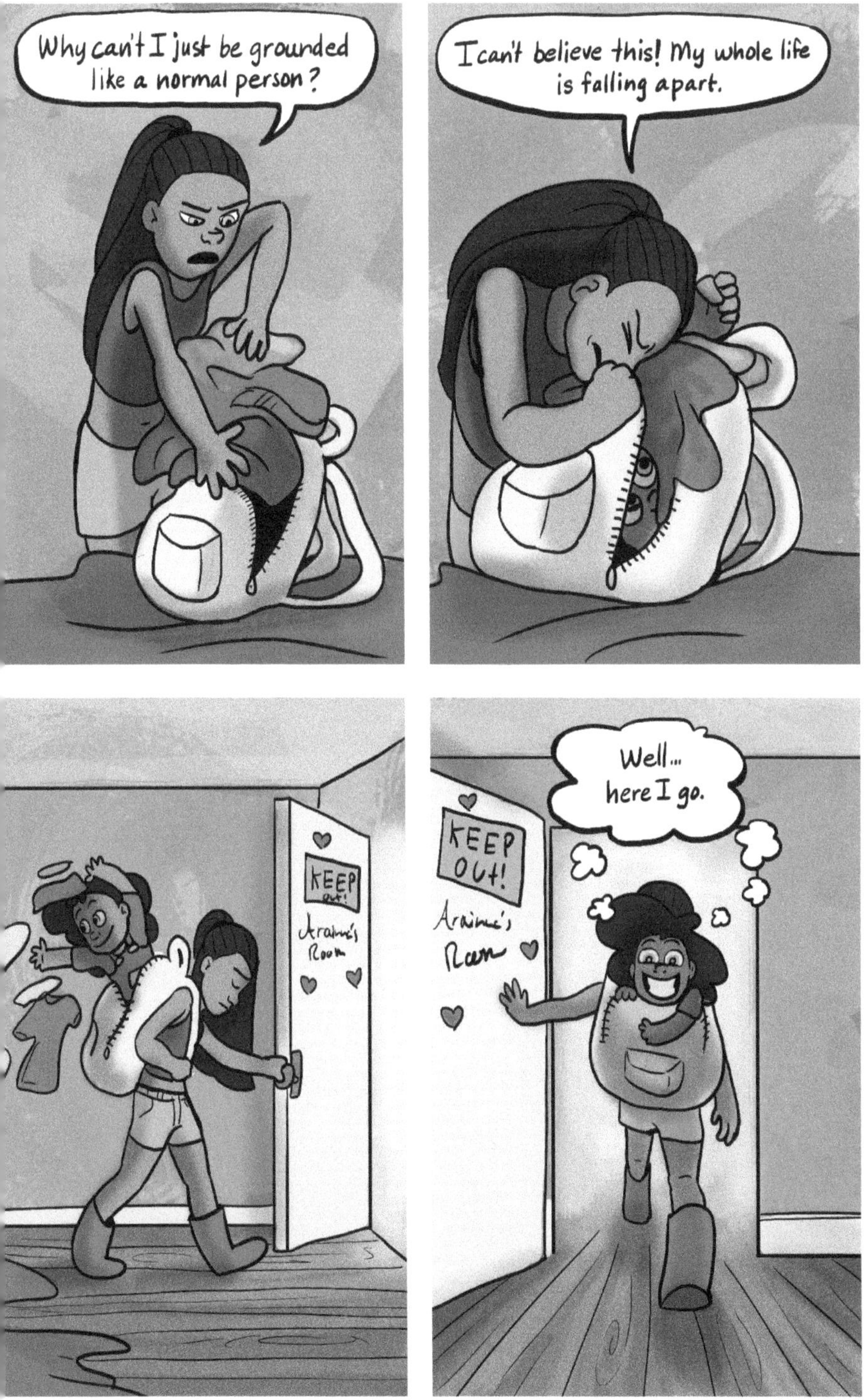
Why can't I just be grounded like a normal person?
I can't believe this! My whole life is falling apart.
KEEP OUT!
KEEP OUT!
Well... here I go.

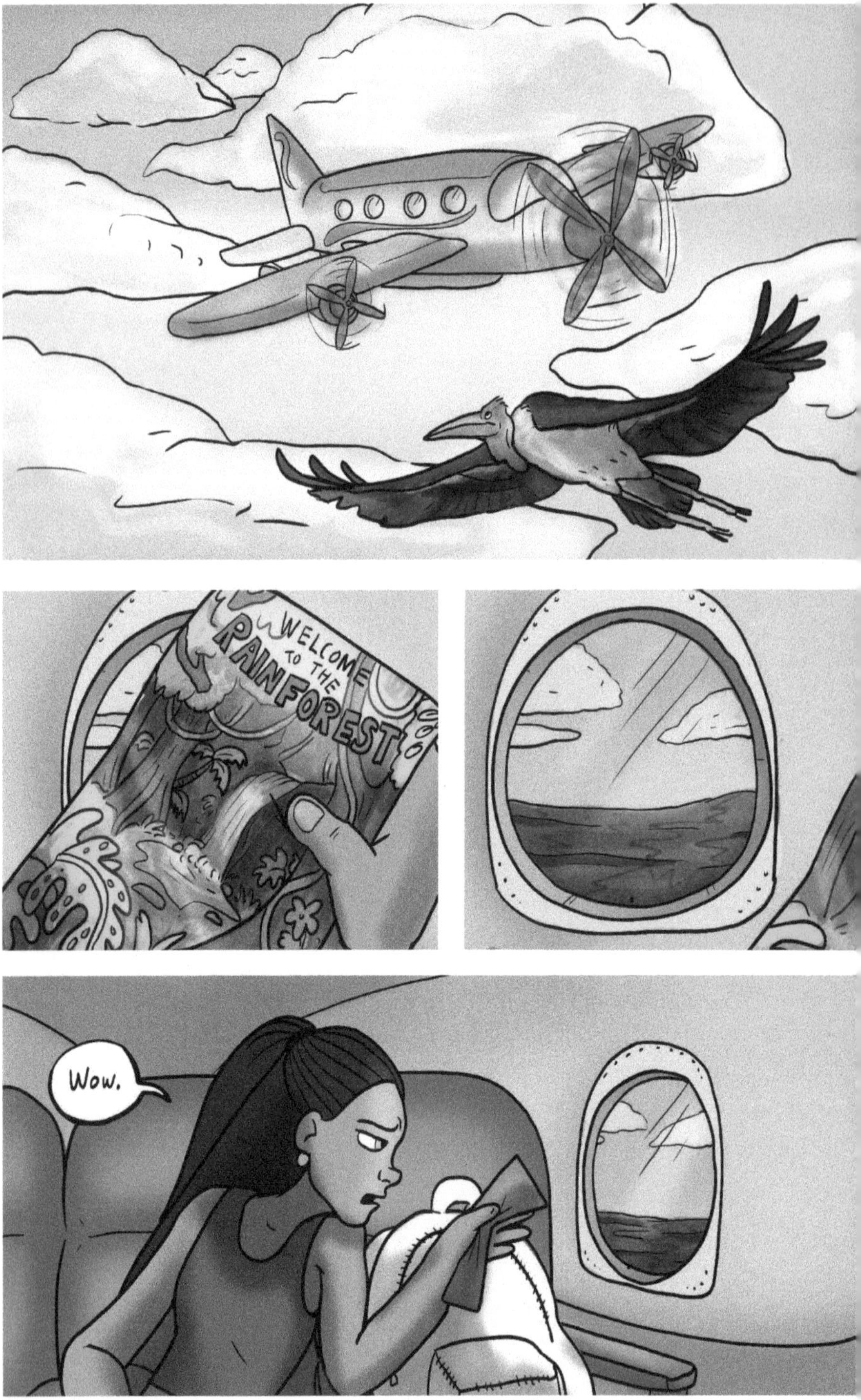
WELCOME TO THE RAINFOREST!
Wow.

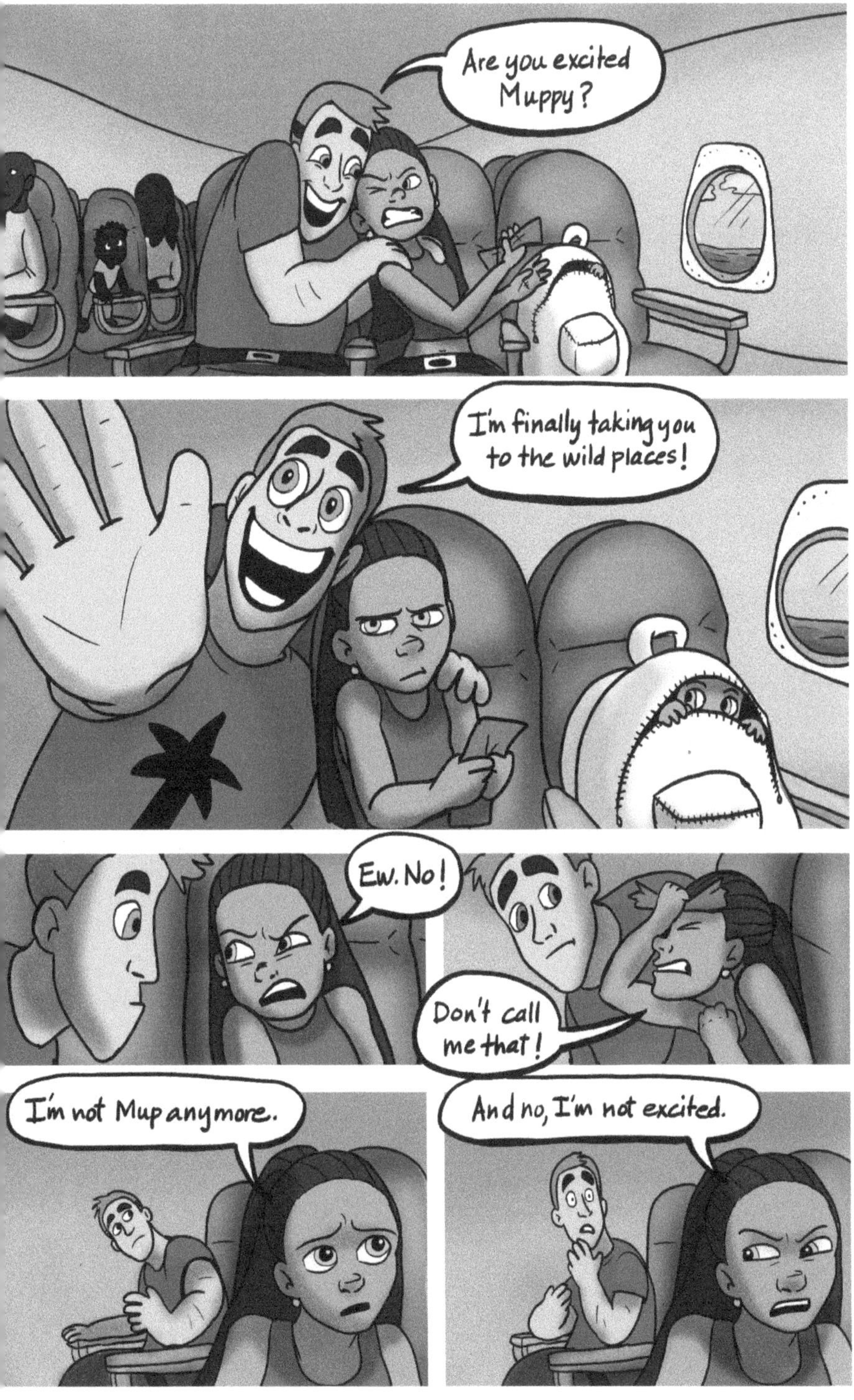
Are you excited Muppy?
I'm finally taking you to the wild places!
Ew. No!
Don't call me that!
I'm not Mup anymore.
And no, I'm not excited.

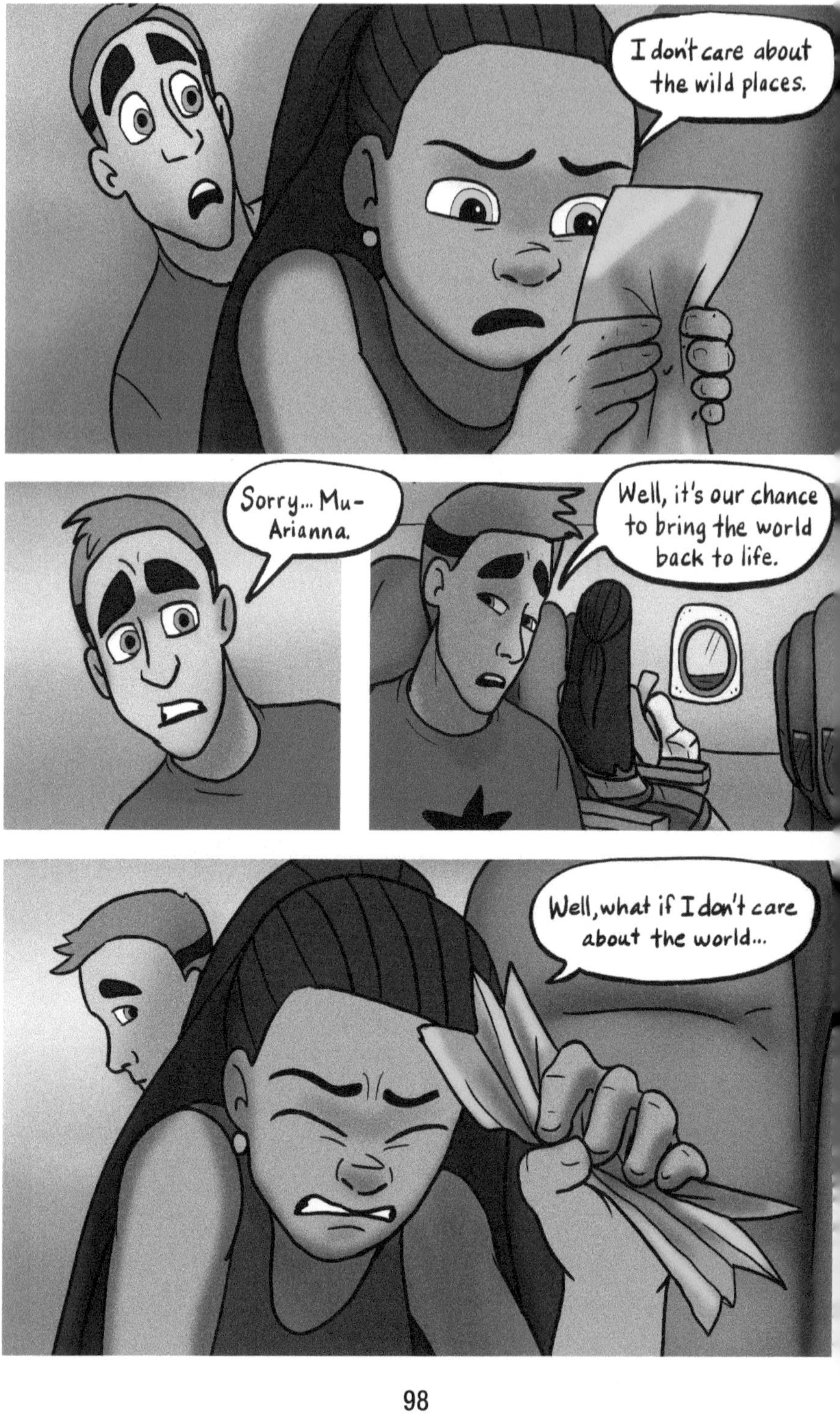
I don't care about the wild places.
Sorry... Mu-Arianna.
Well, it's our chance to bring the world back to life.
Well, what if I don't care about the world...

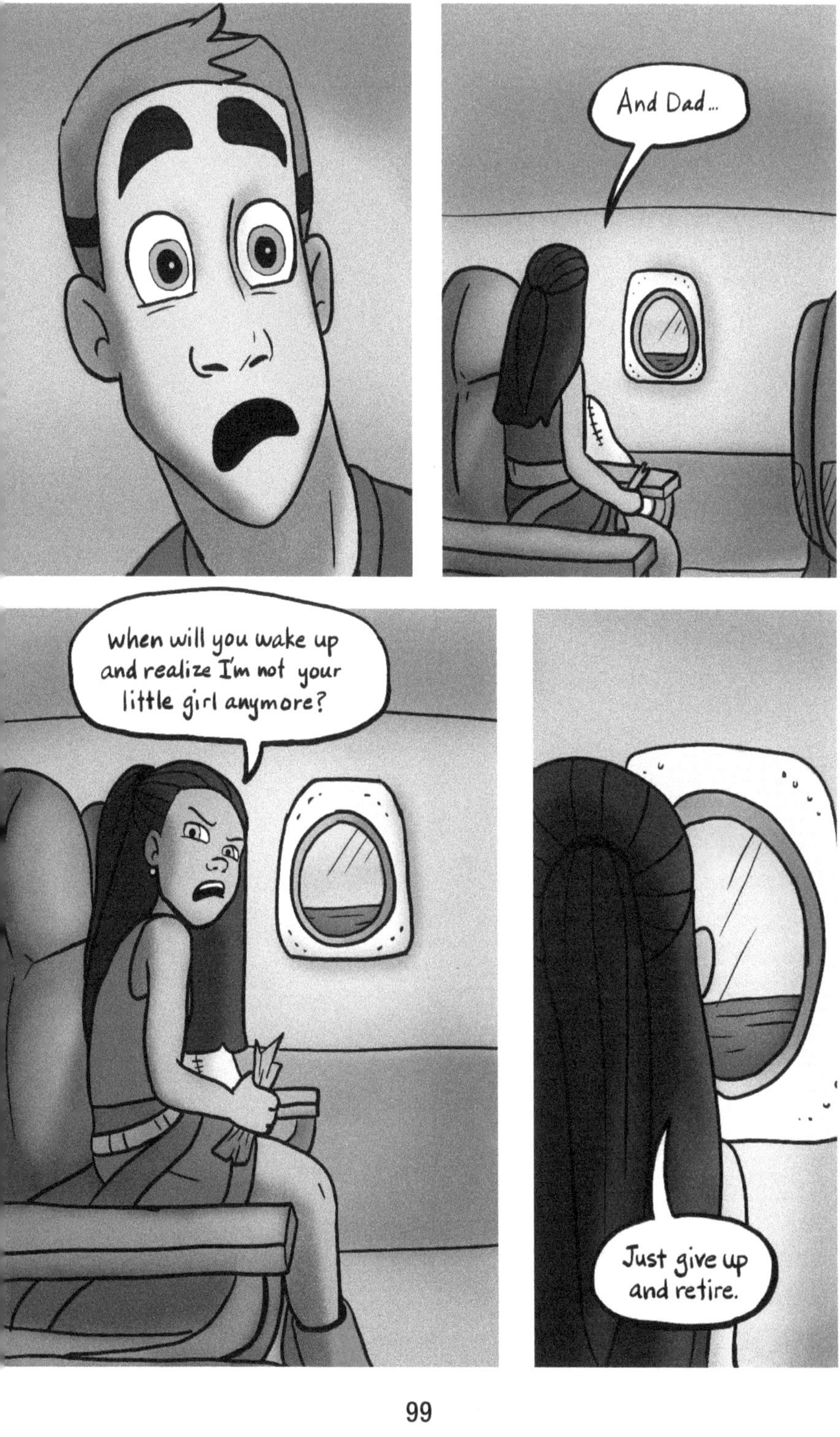
And Dad...
when will you wake up and realize I'm not your little girl anymore?
Just give up and retire.

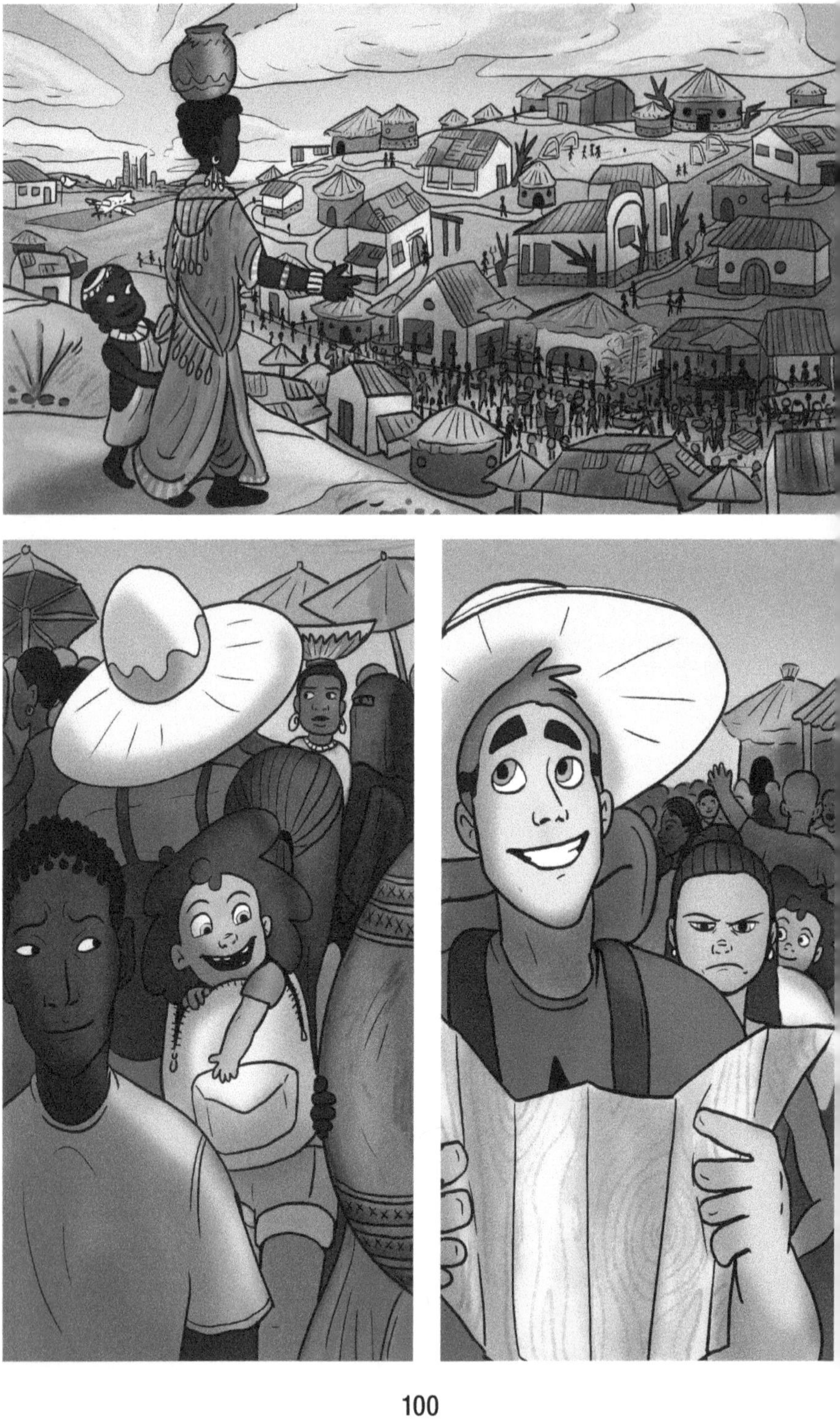

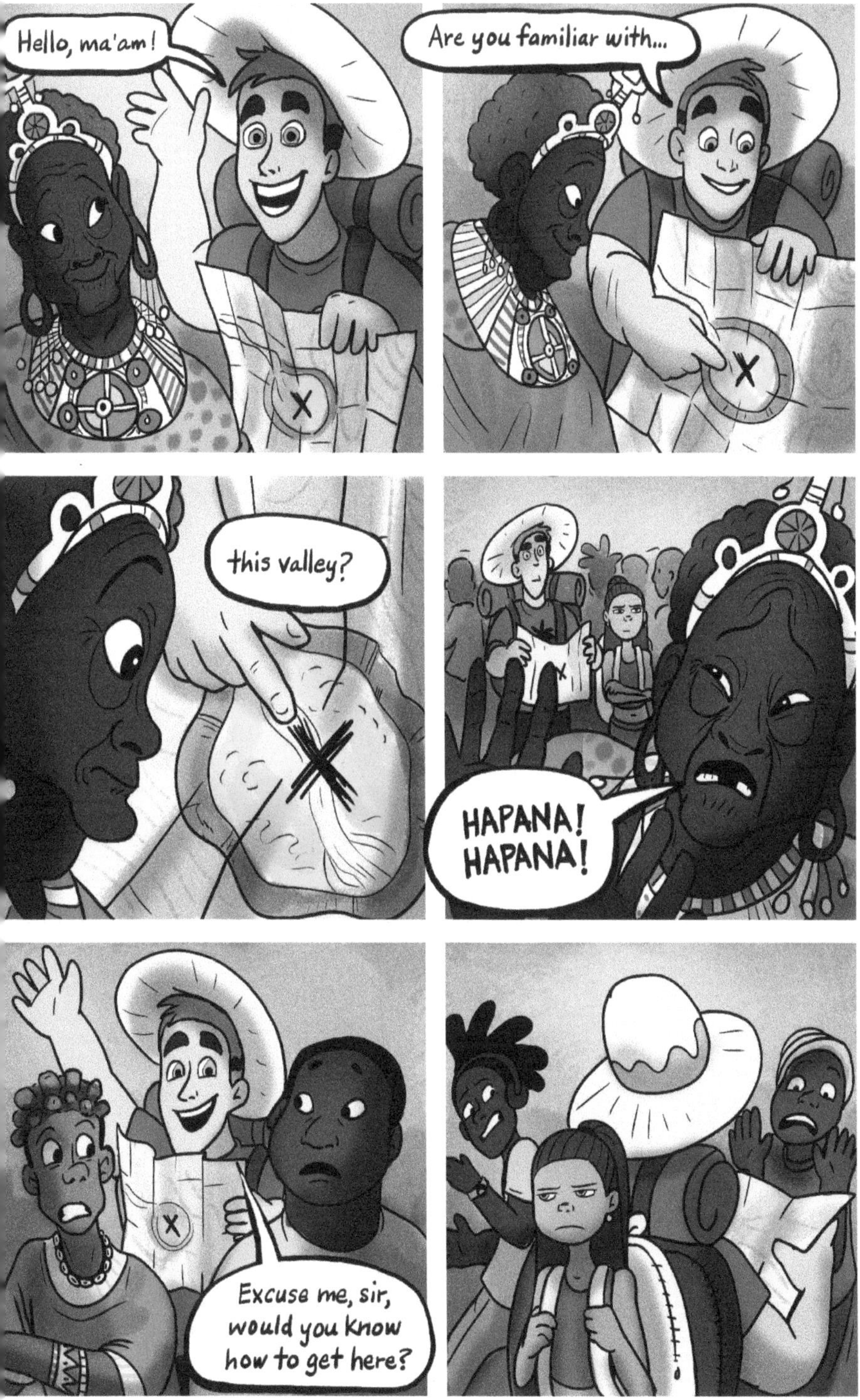
Hello, ma'am!
Are you familiar with...
this valley?
HAPANA! HAPANA!
Excuse me, sir, would you know how to get here?

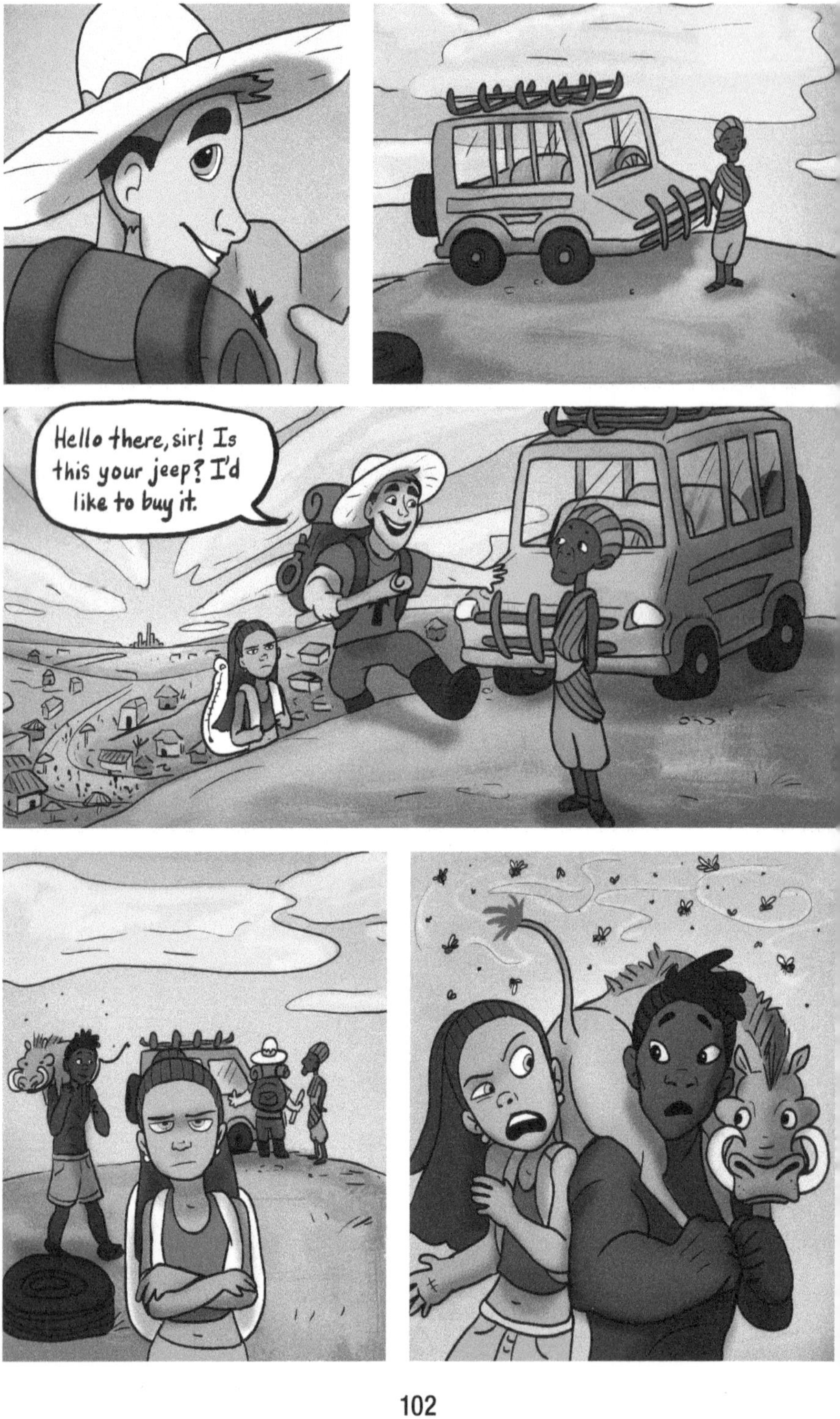
Hello there, sir! Is this your jeep? I'd like to buy it.

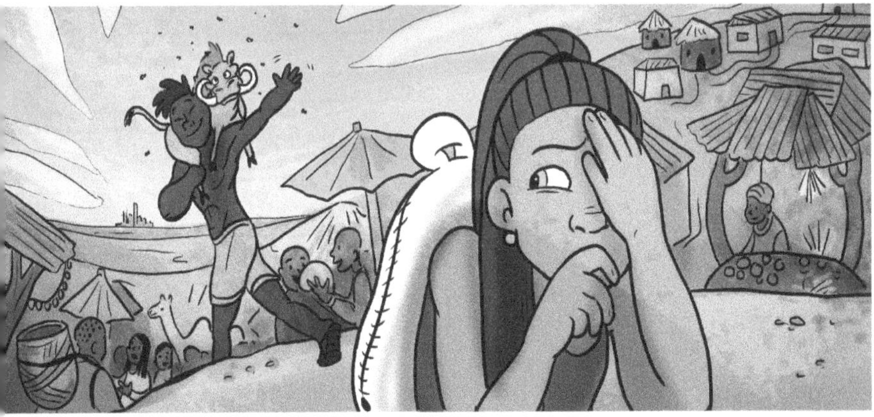

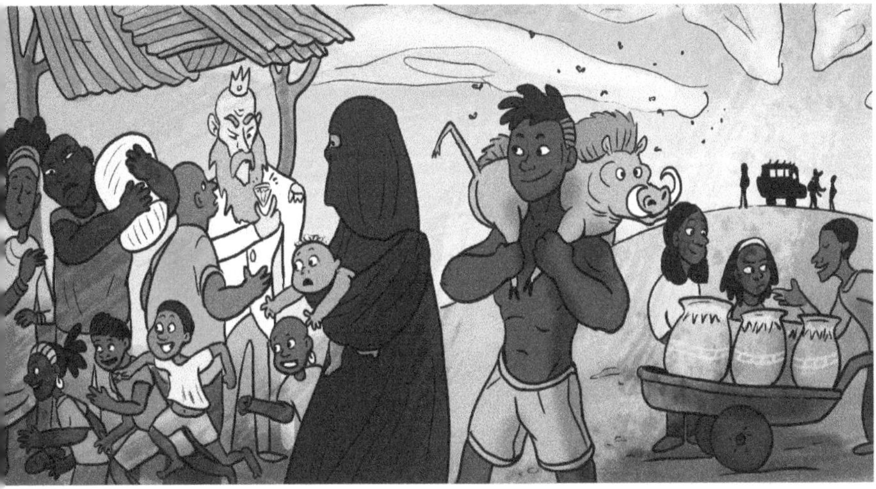

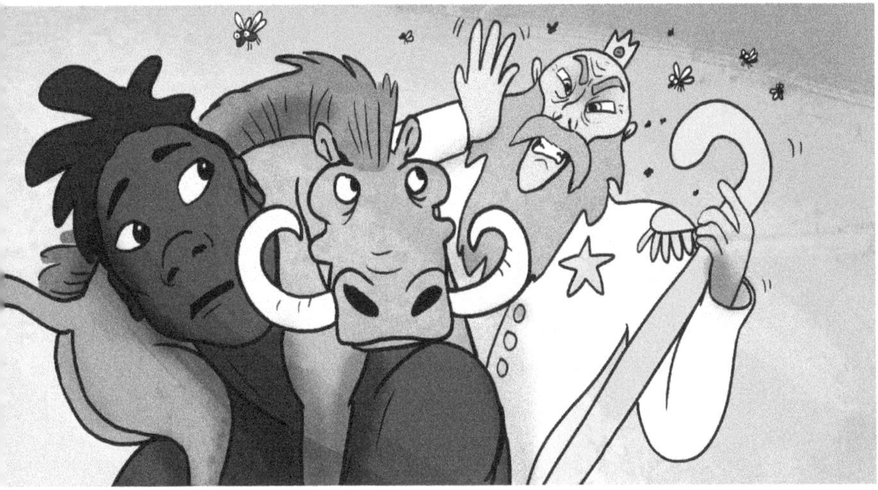

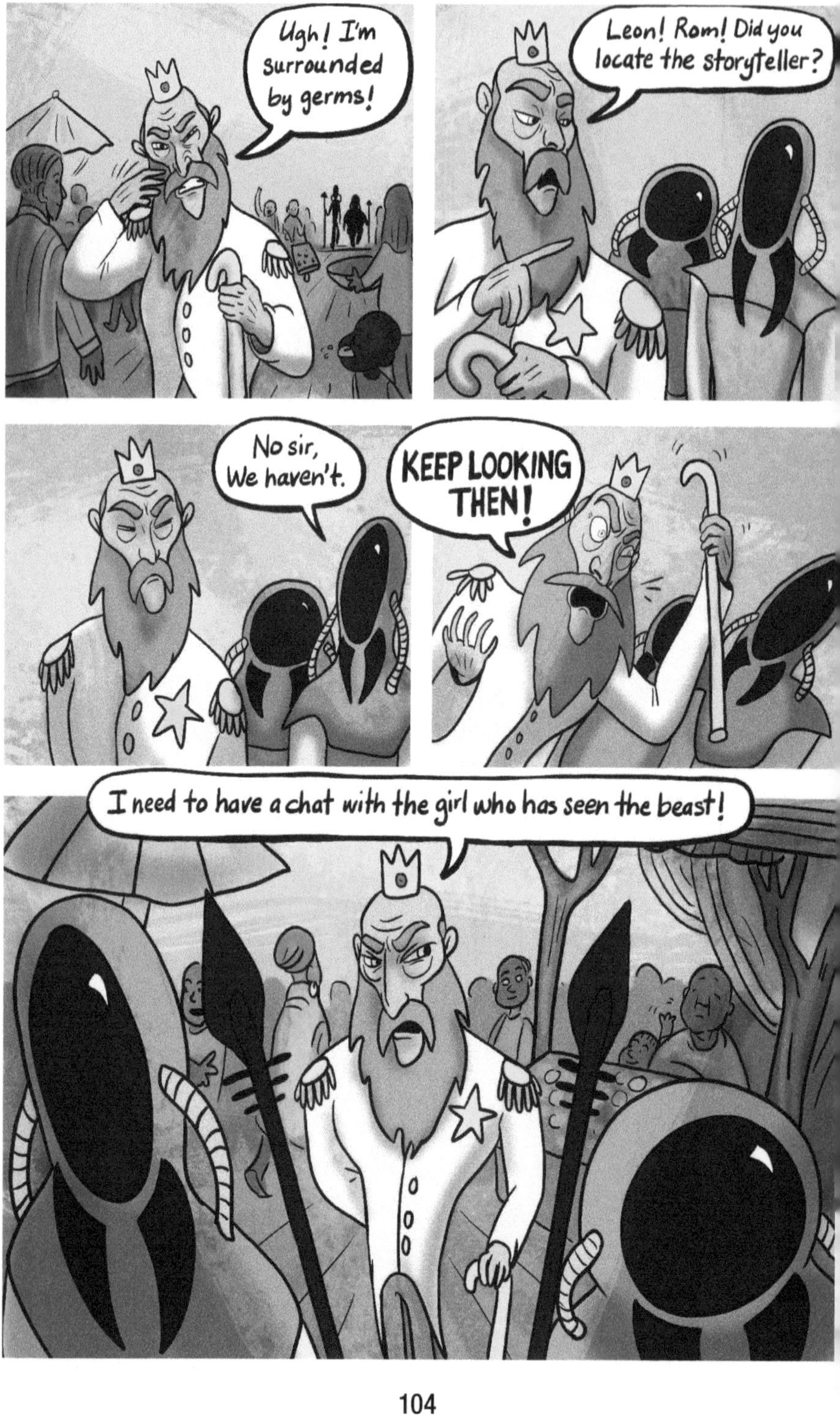
Ugh! I'm surrounded by germs!
Leon! Rom! Did you locate the storyteller?
No sir, We haven't.
KEEP LOOKING THEN!
I need to have a chat with the girl who has seen the beast!

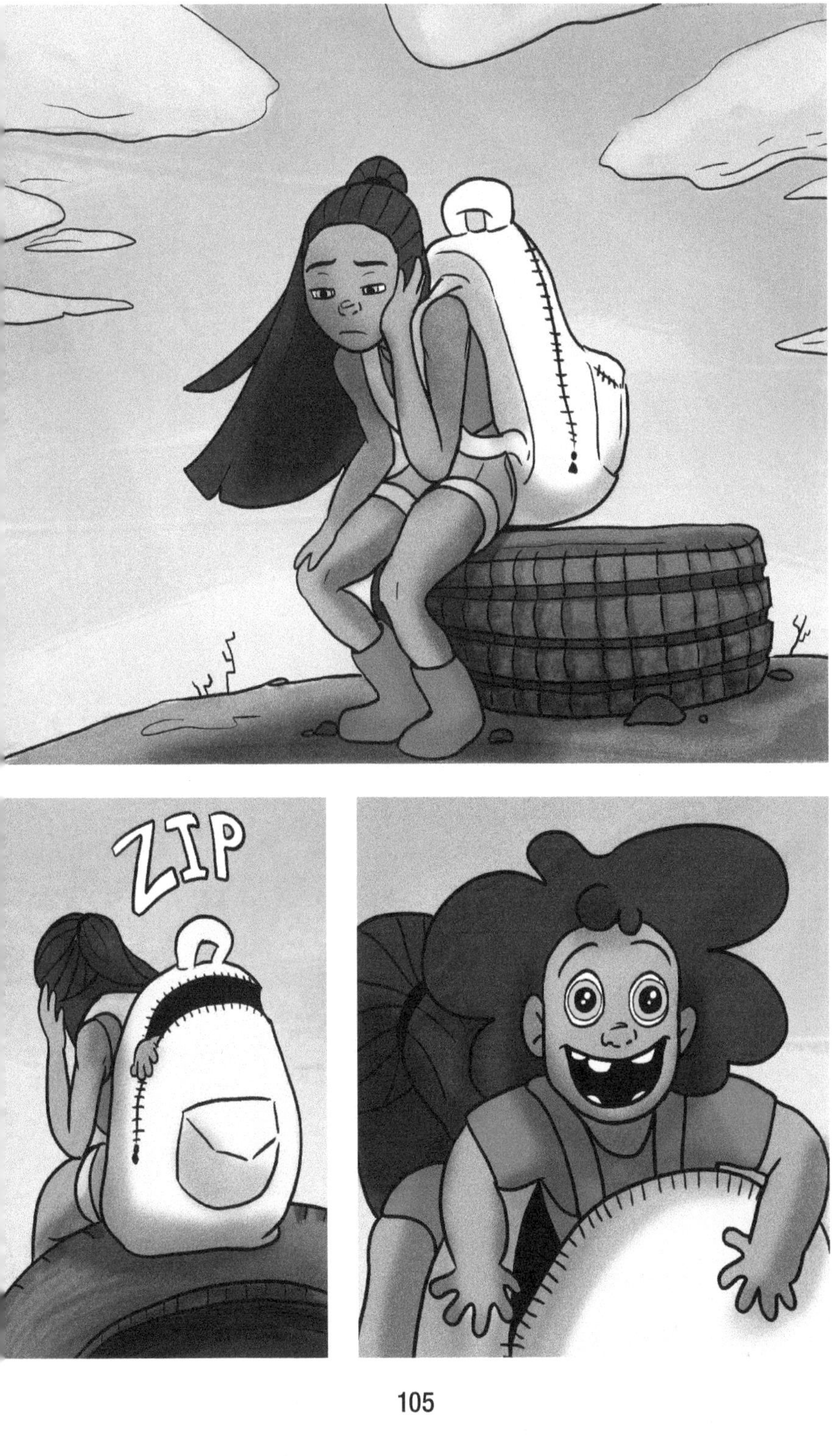
ZIP

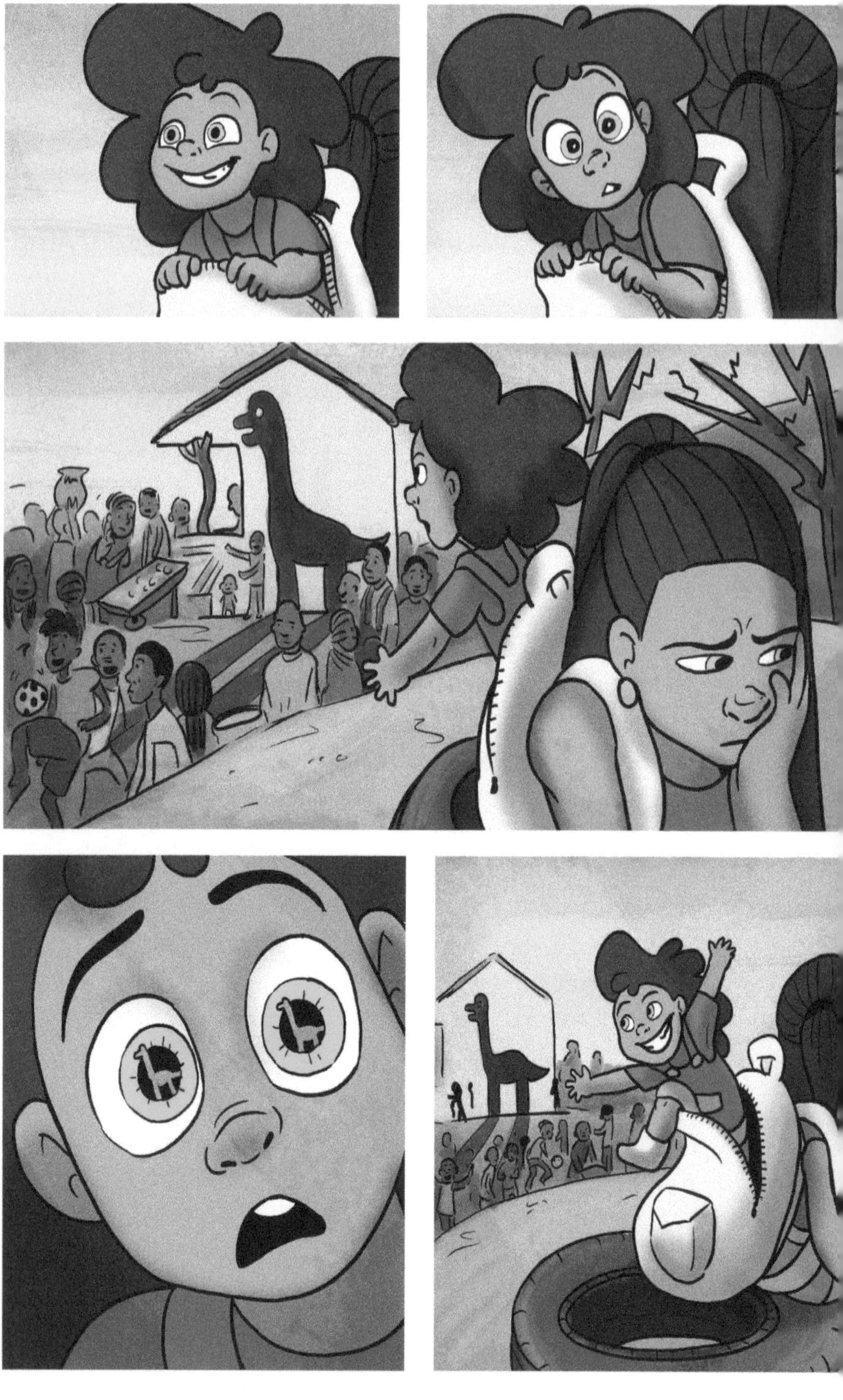

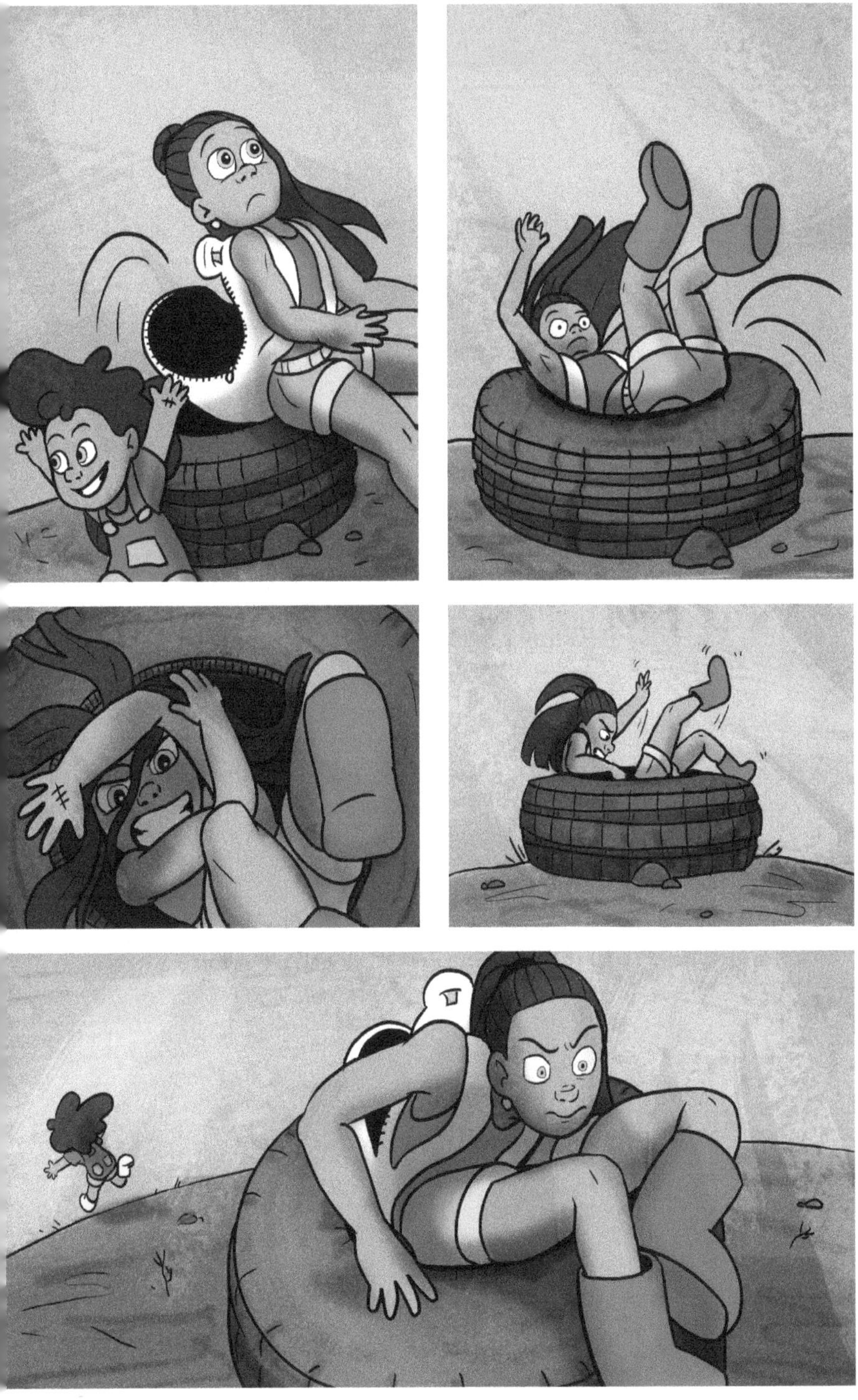

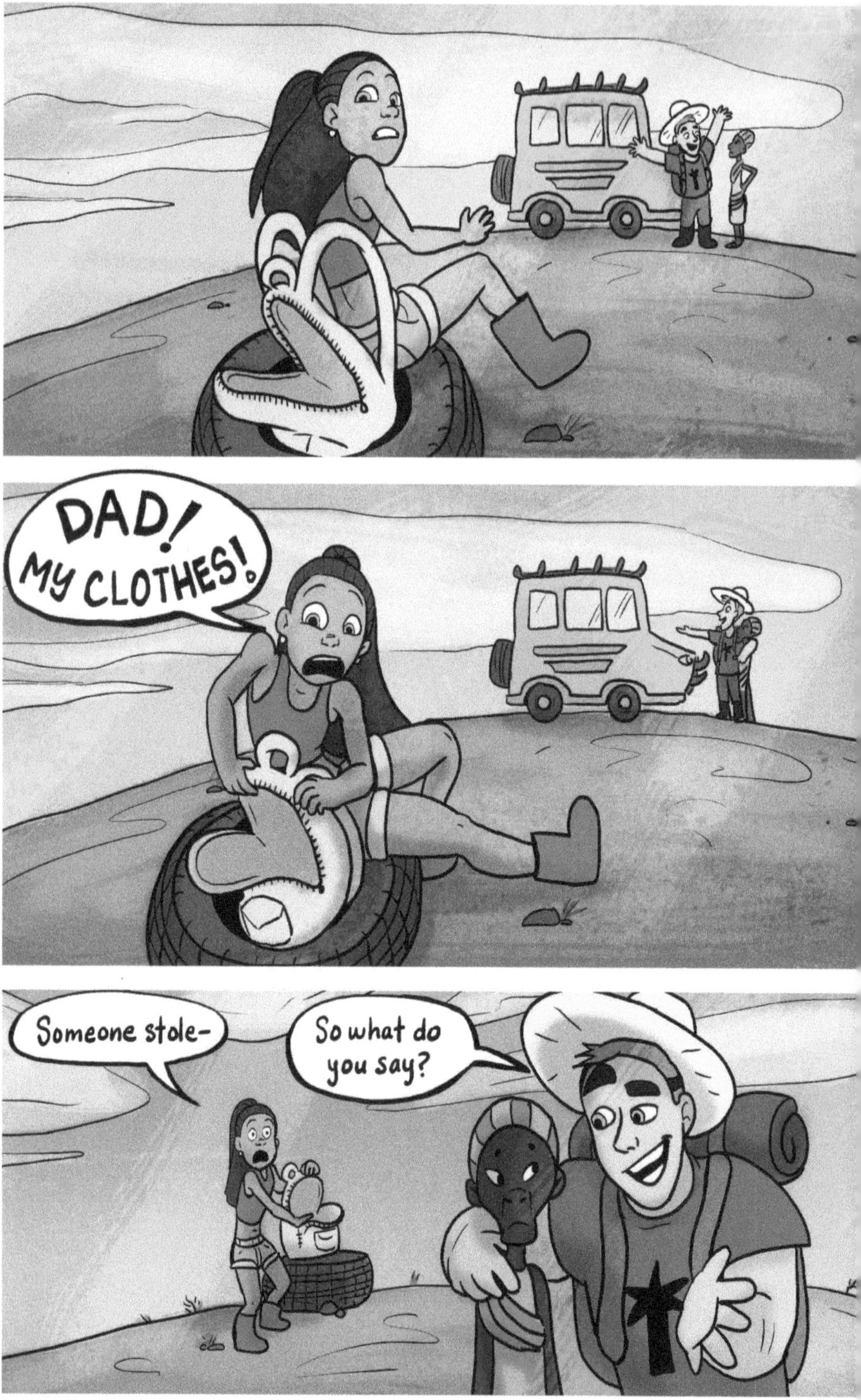
DAD! MY CLOTHES!
Someone stole-
So what do you say?

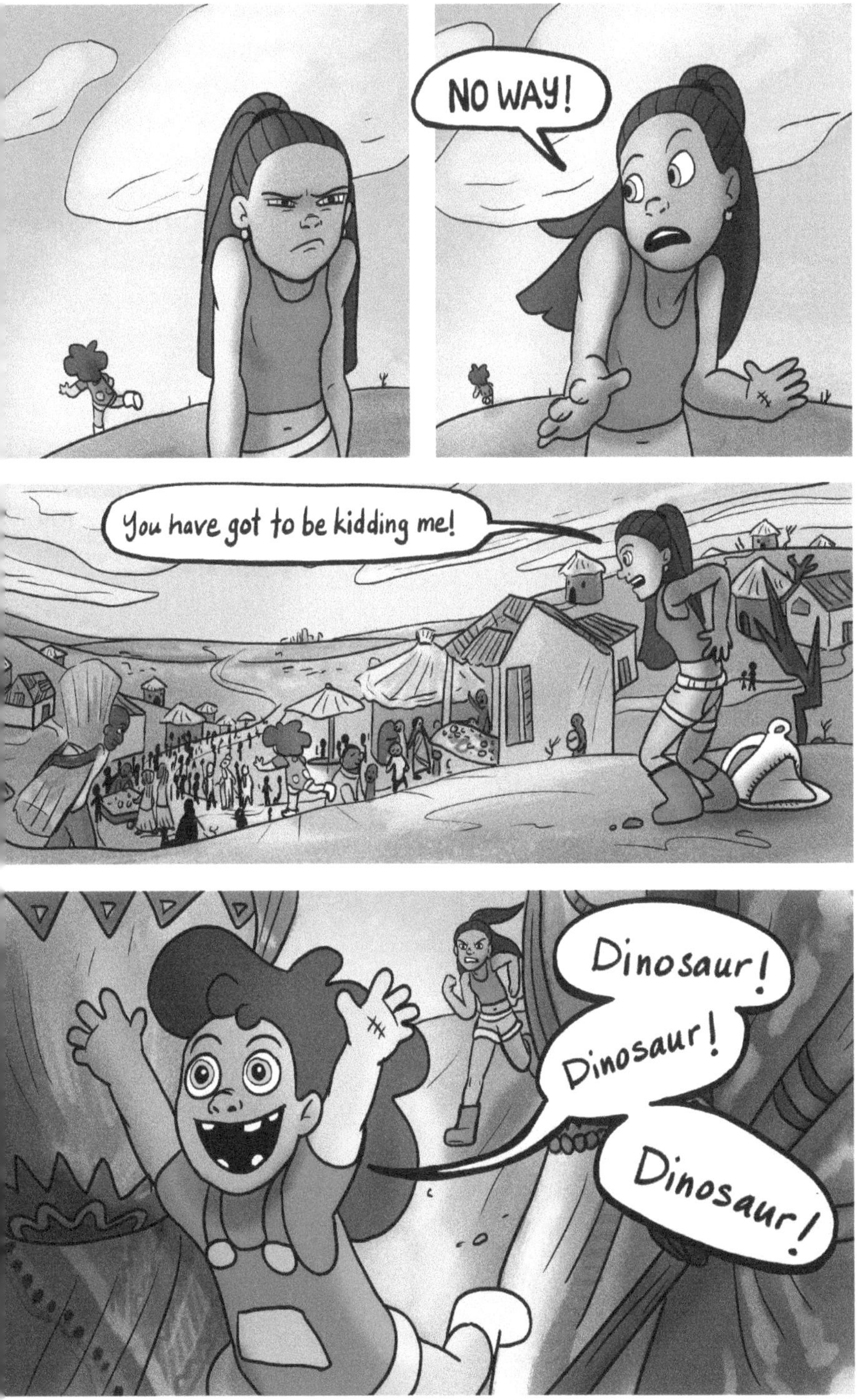

NO WAY!
You have got to be kidding me!
Dinosaur!
Dinosaur!
Dinosaur!

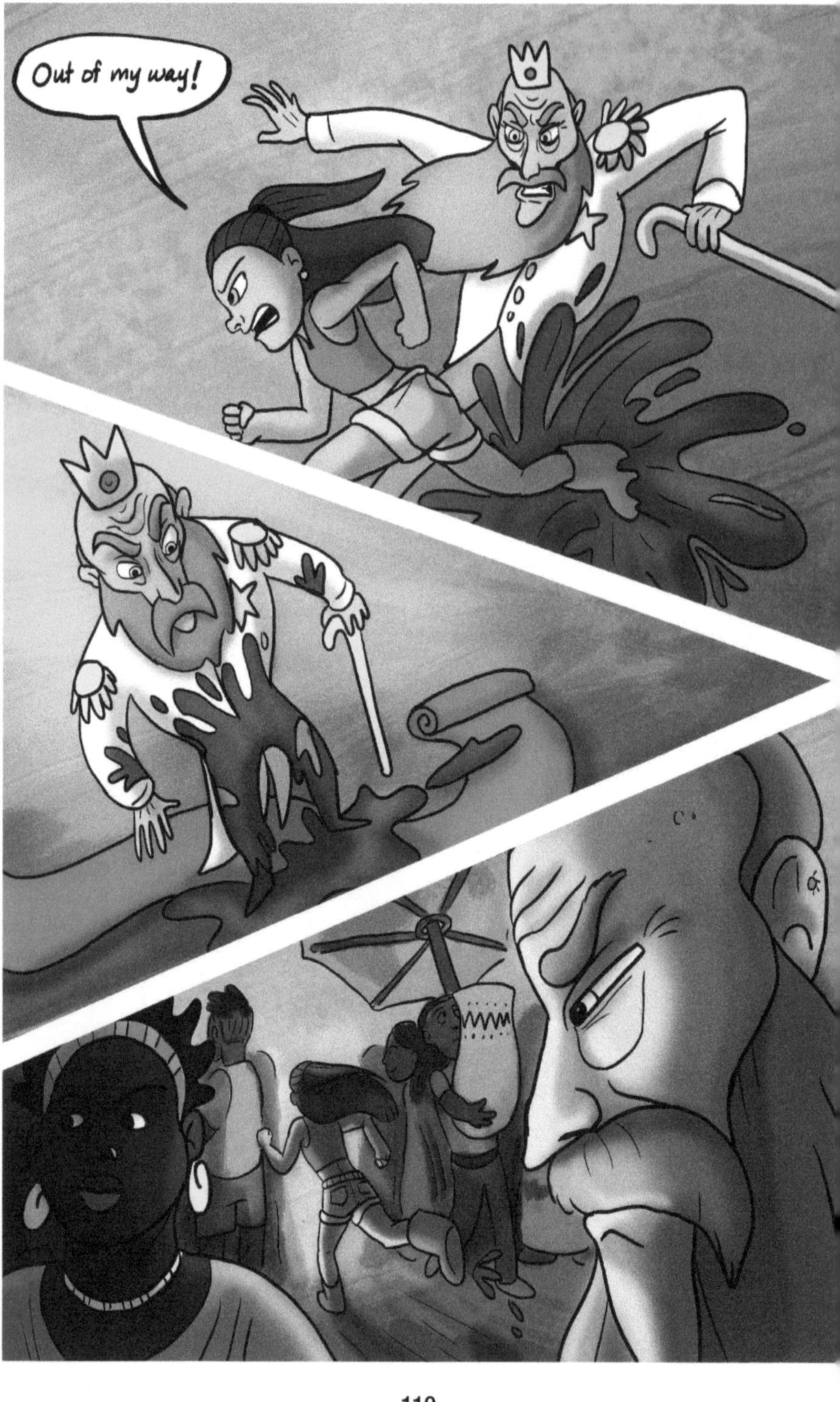
Out of my way!

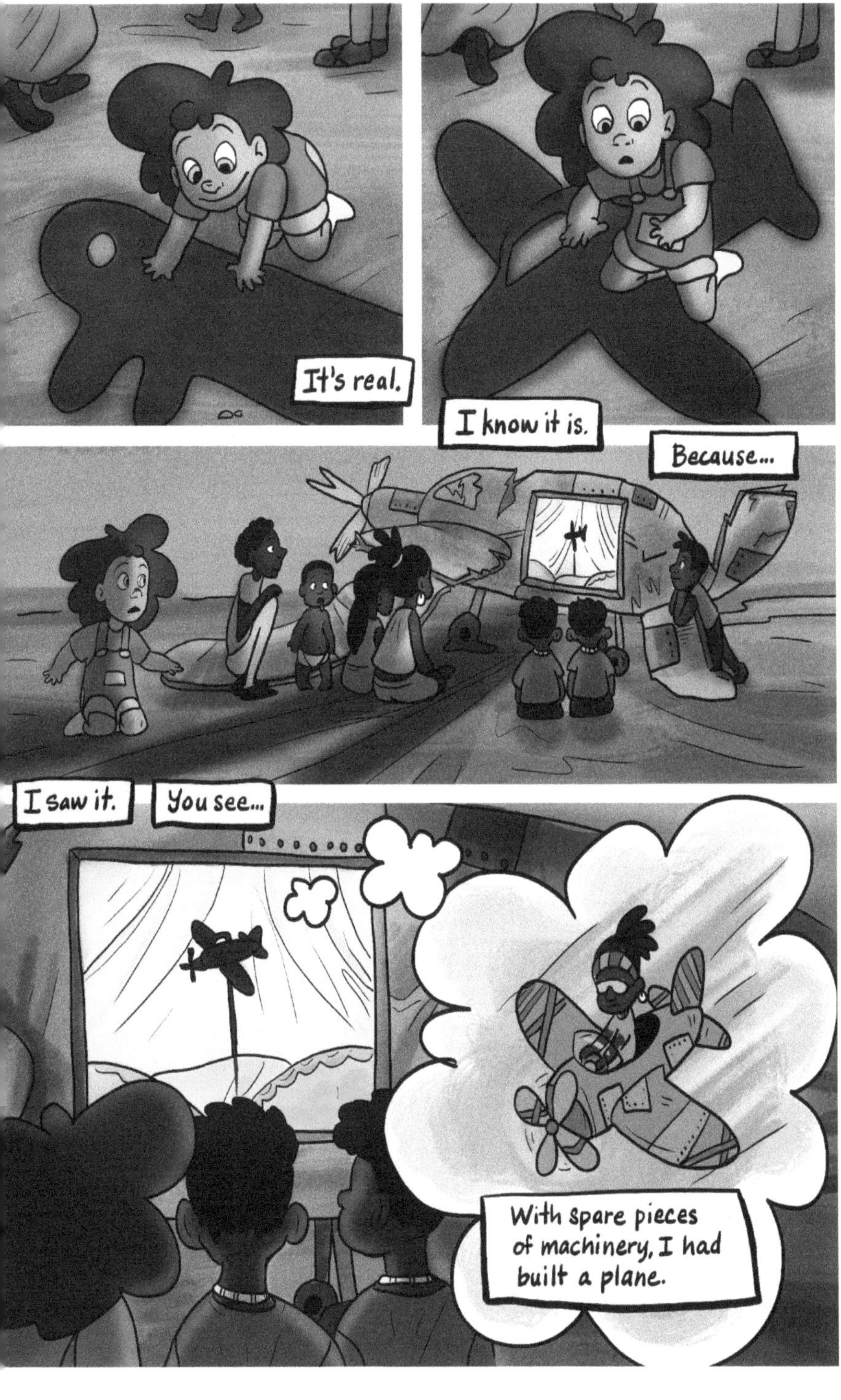
It's real.
I know it is.
Because...
I saw it.
You see...
With spare pieces of machinery, I had built a plane.

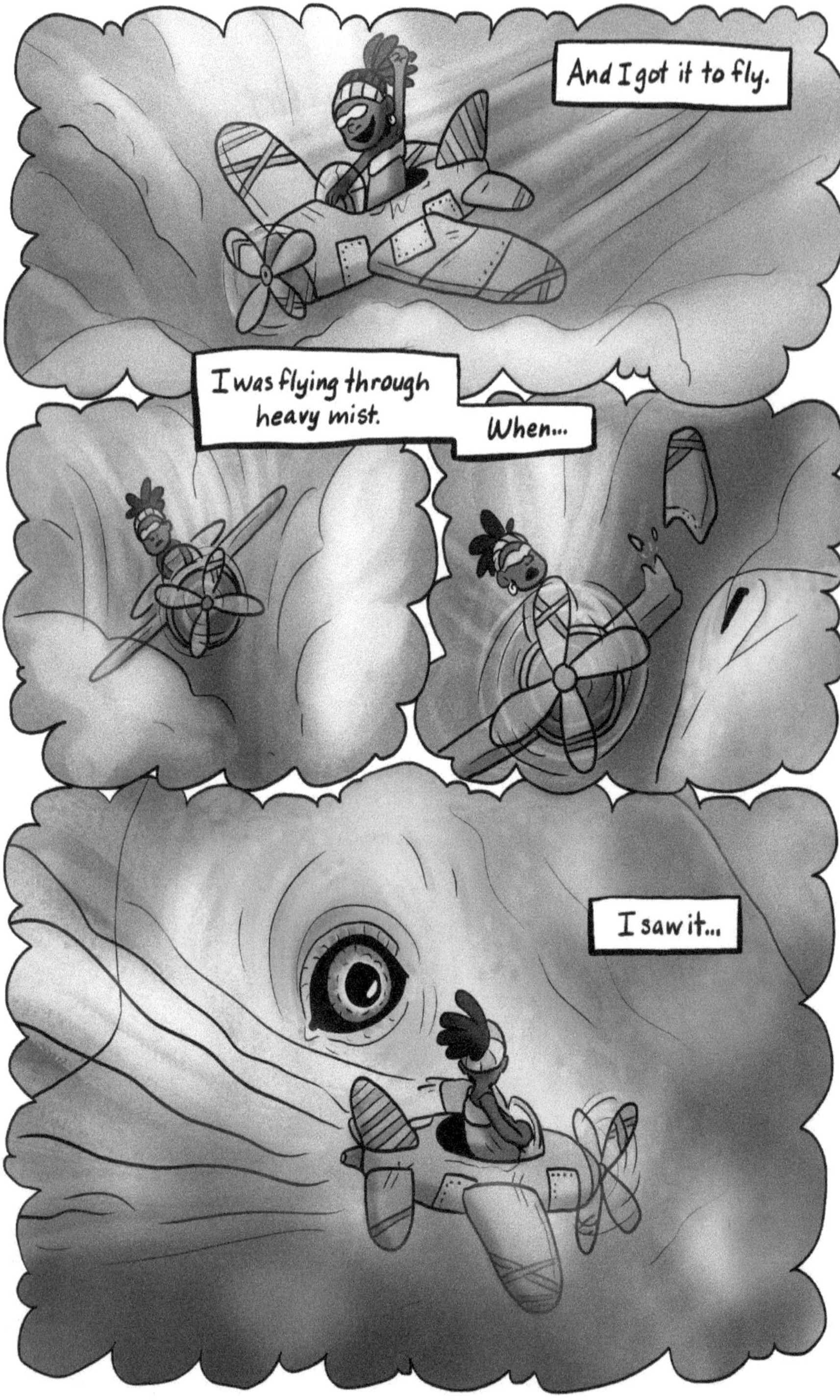
And I got it to fly.
I was flying through heavy mist.
When...
I saw it...

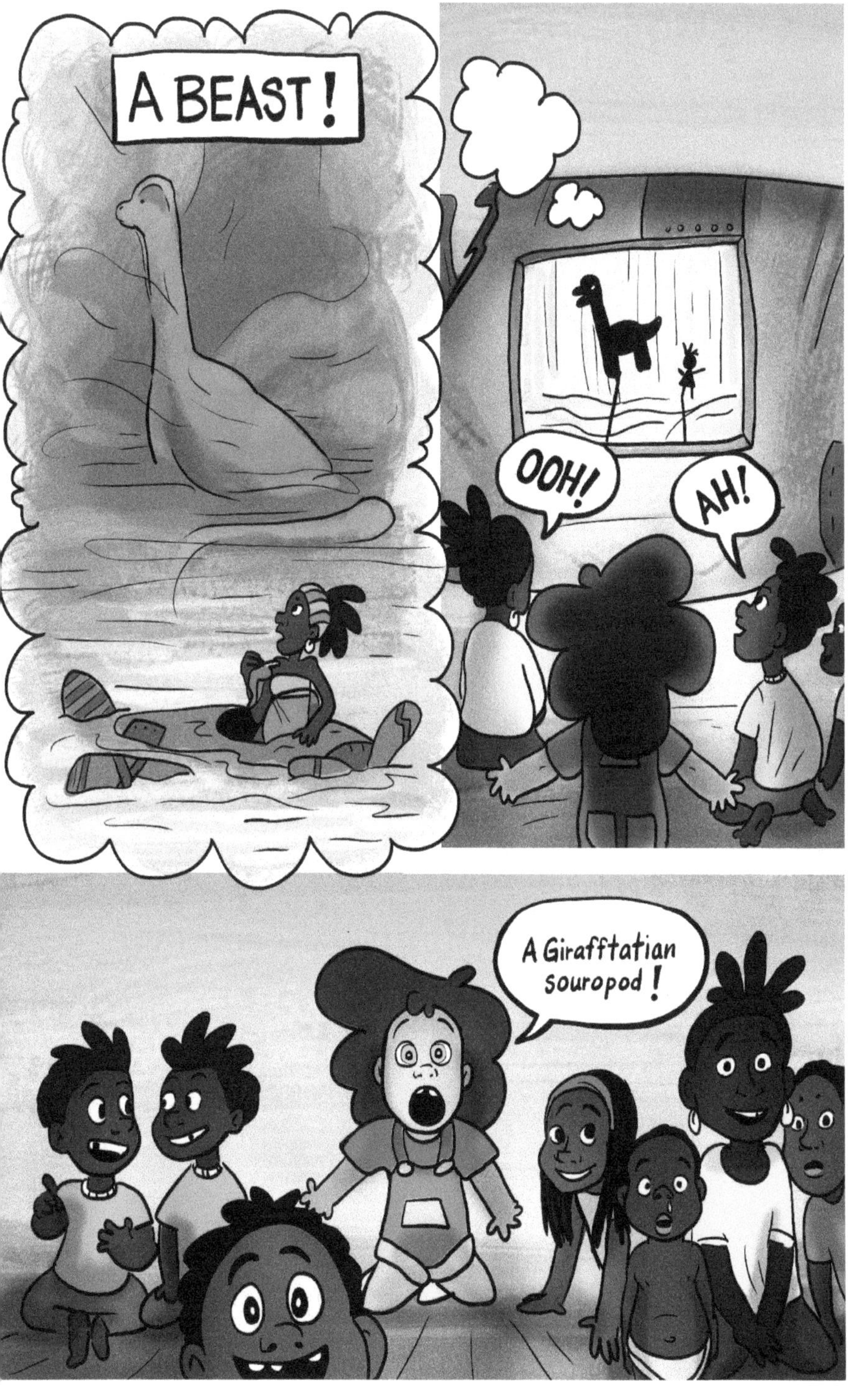
A BEAST!
OOH!
AH!
A Girafftatian souropod!

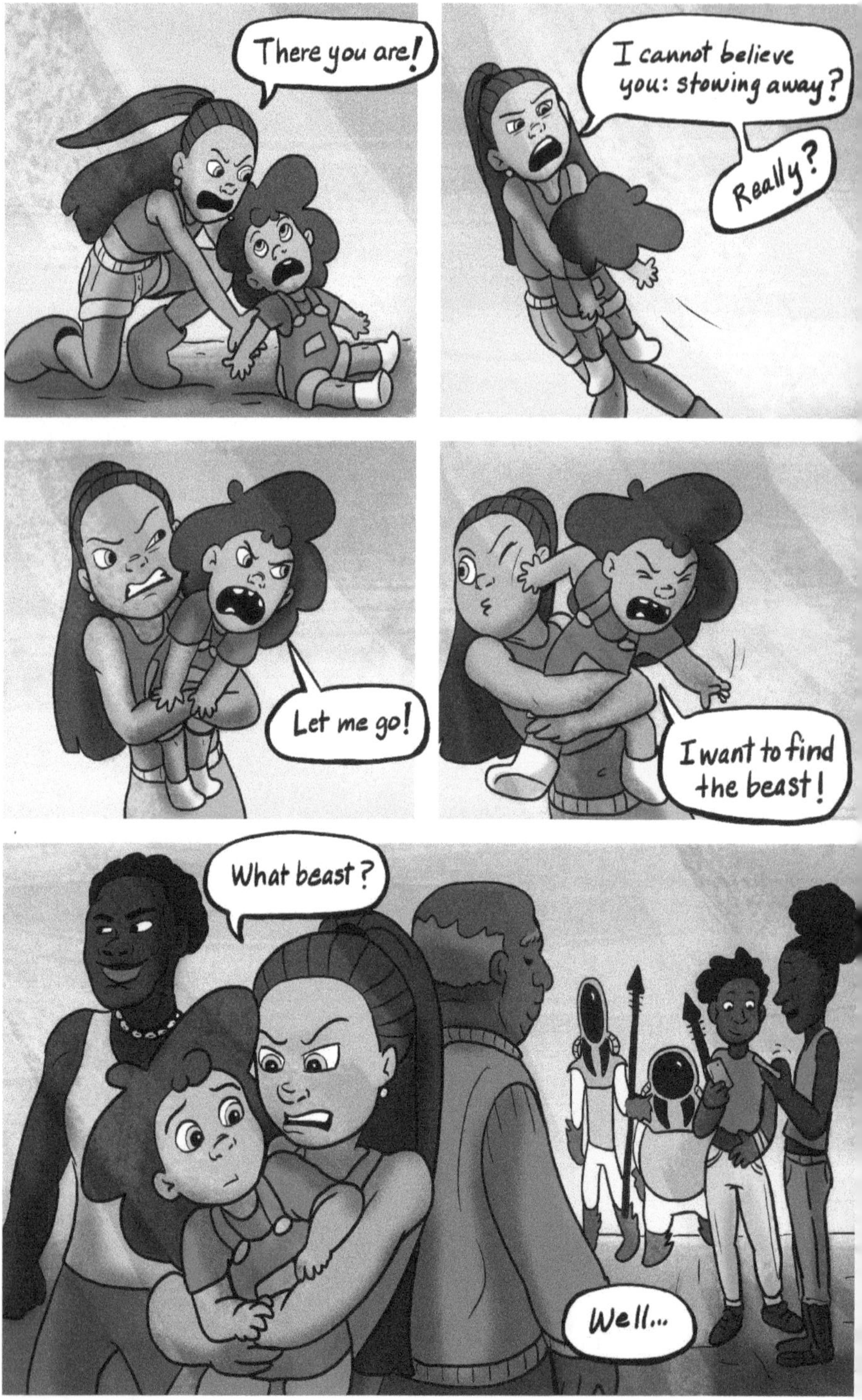
There you are!
I cannot believe you: stowing away?
Really?
Let me go!
I want to find the beast!
What beast?
Well...

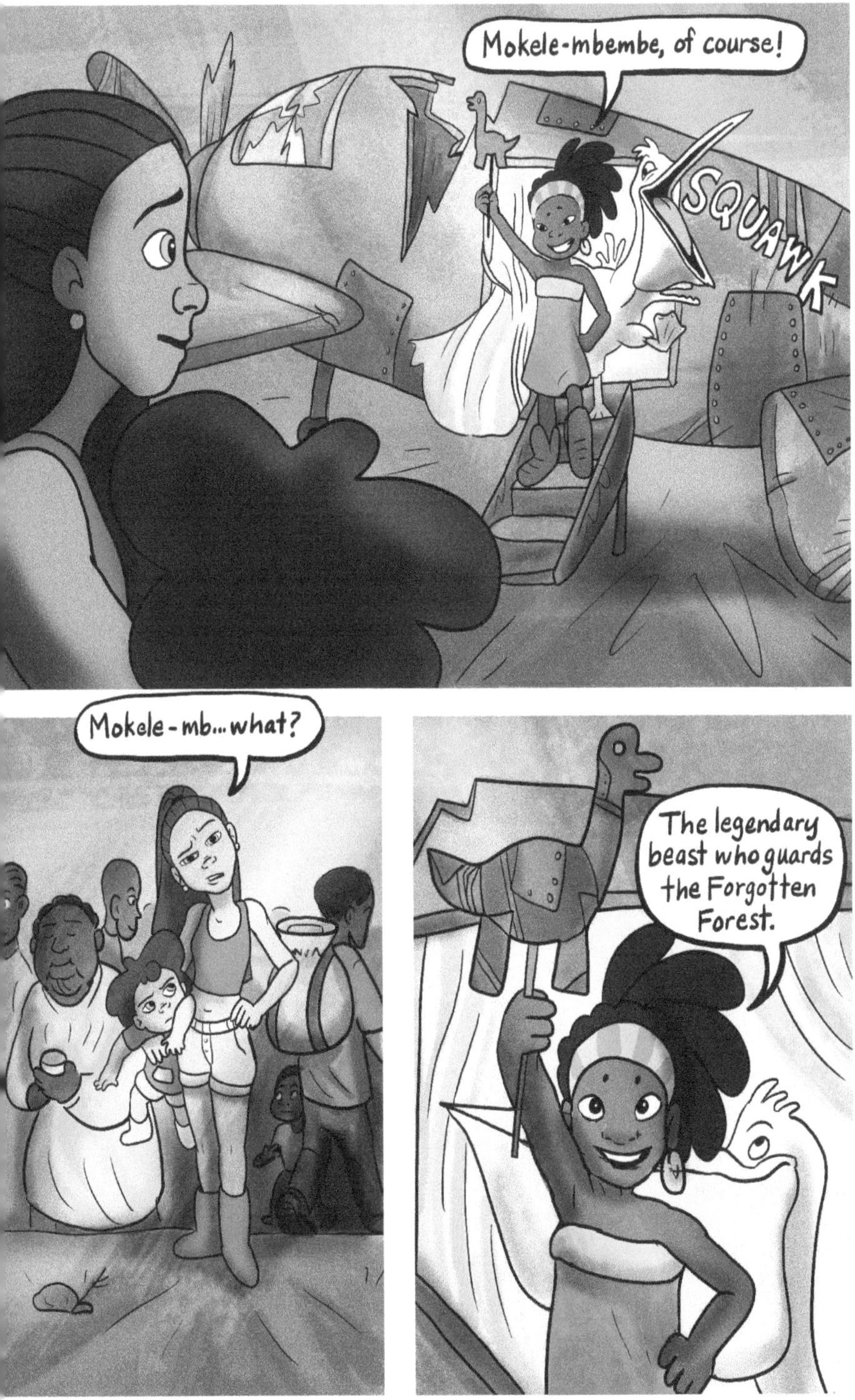
Mokele-mbembe, of course!
SQUAWK
Mokele-mb...what?
The legendary beast who guards the Forgotten Forest.

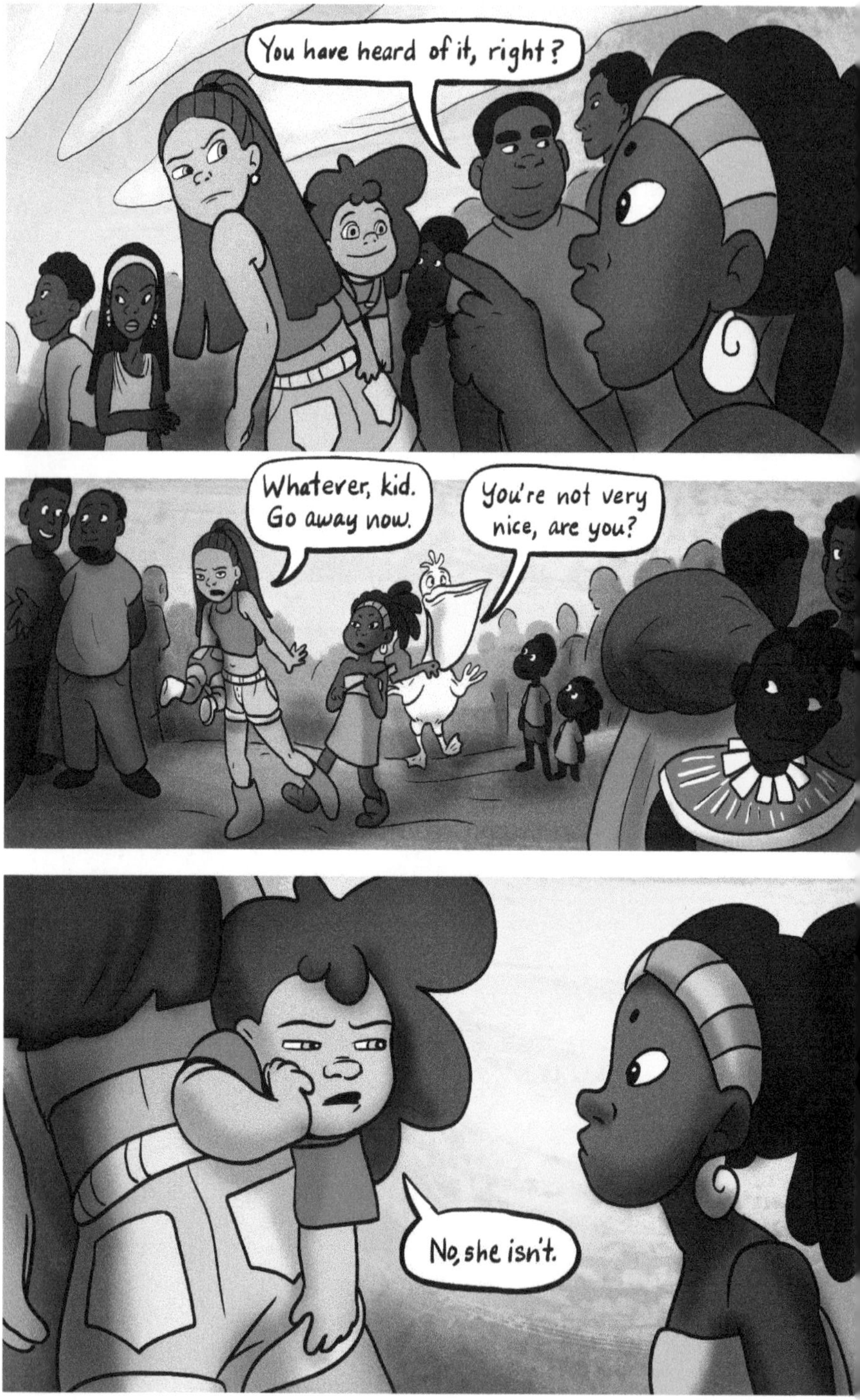
You have heard of it, right?
Whatever, kid. Go away now.
You're not very nice, are you?
No, she isn't.

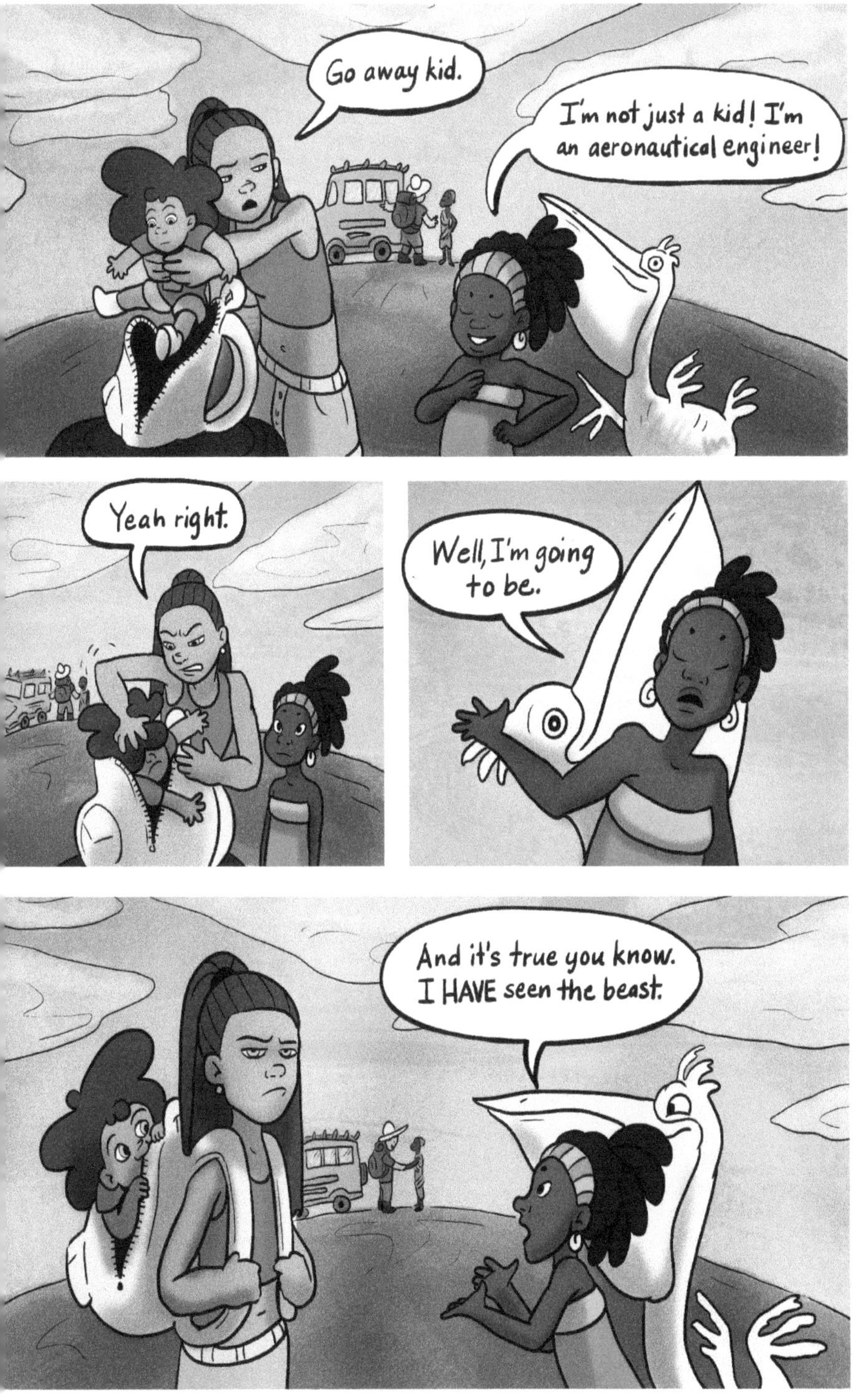
Go away kid.
I'm not just a kid! I'm an aeronautical engineer!
Yeah right.
Well, I'm going to be.
And it's true you know. I HAVE seen the beast.

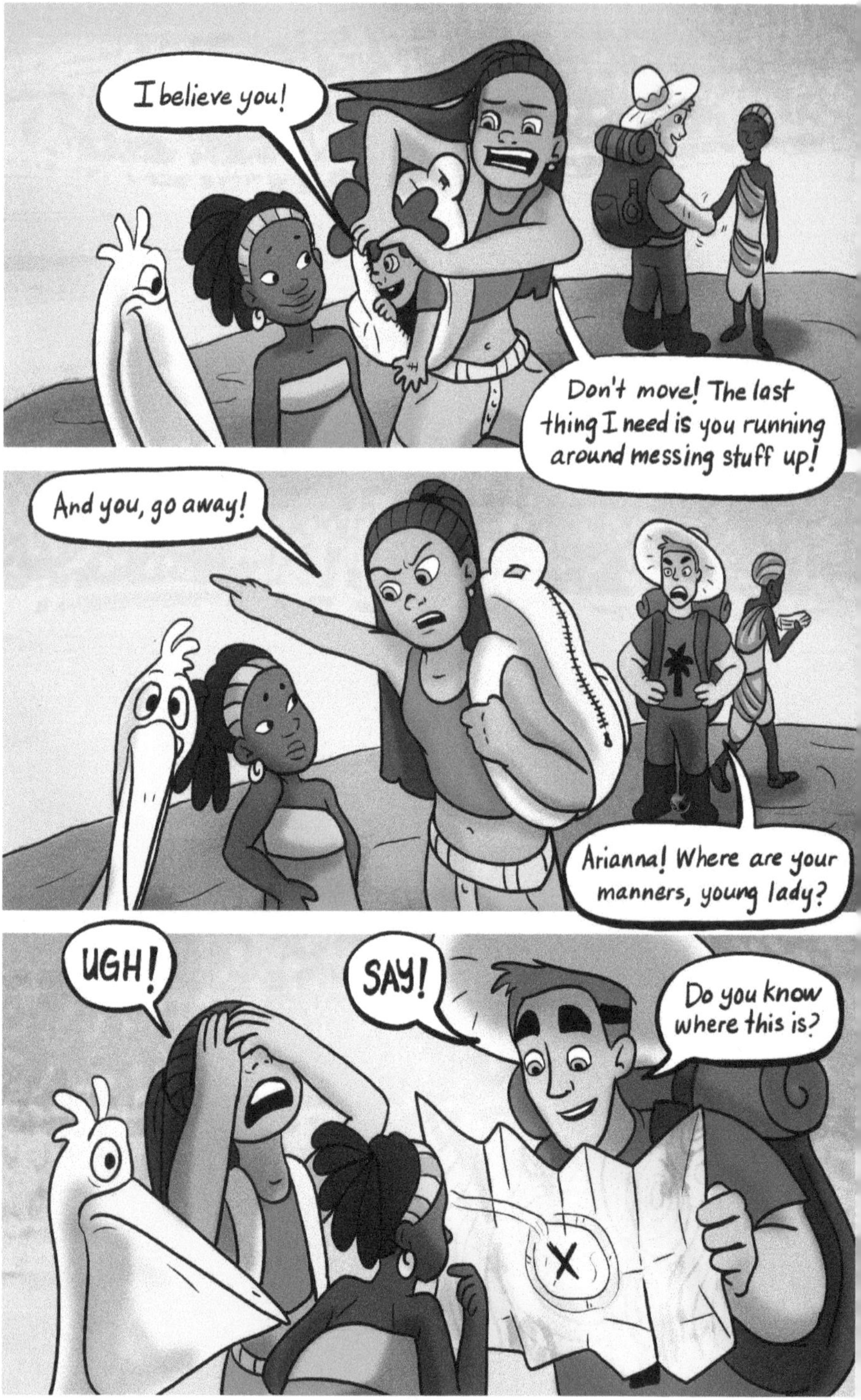
I believe you!
Don't move! The last thing I need is you running around messing stuff up!
And you, go away!
Arianna! Where are your manners, young lady?
UGH!
SAY!
Do you know where this is?

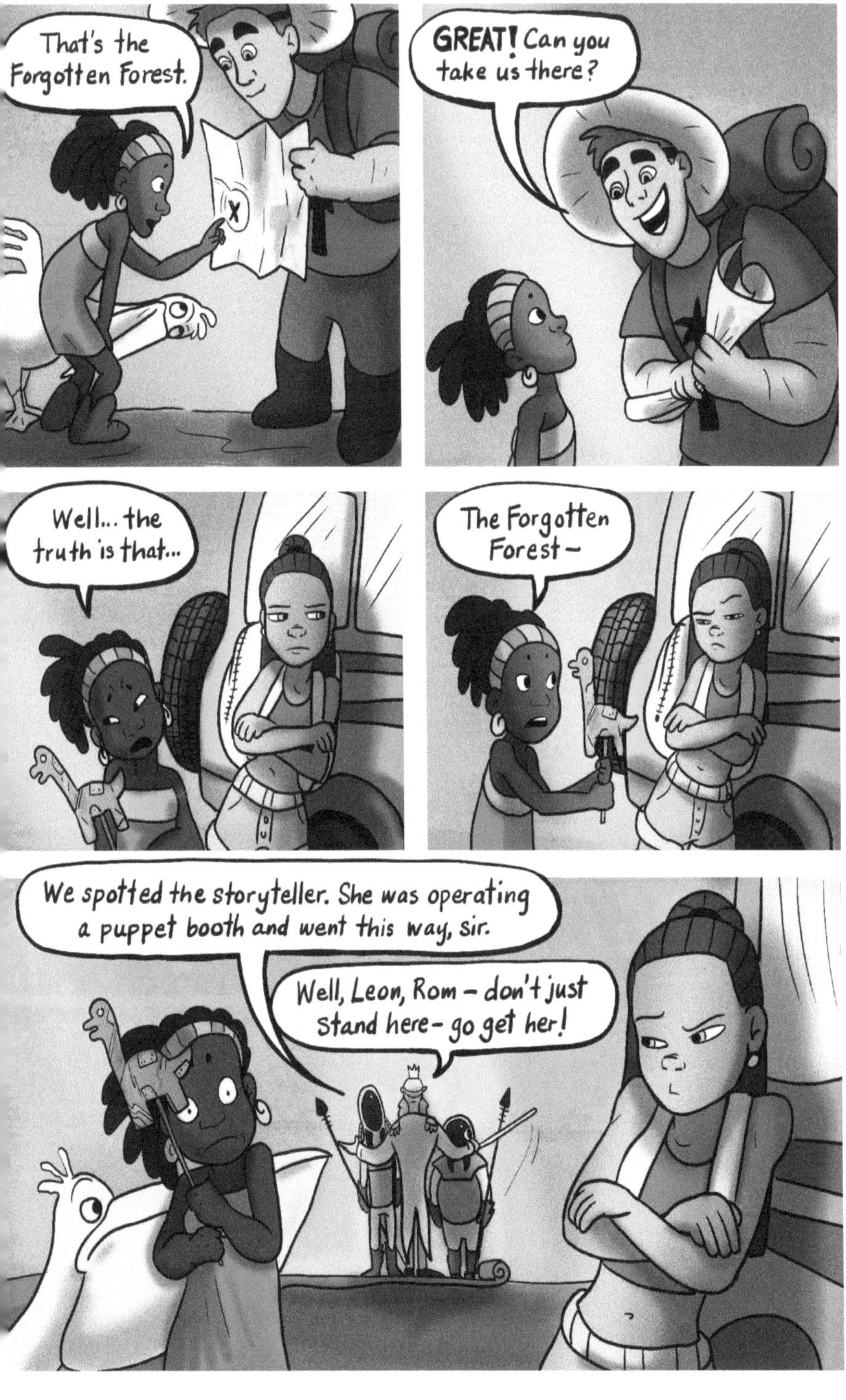
That's the Forgotten Forest.
GREAT! Can you take us there?
Well... the truth is that...
The Forgotten Forest–
We spotted the storyteller. She was operating a puppet booth and went this way, sir.
Well, Leon, Rom – don't just stand here– go get her!

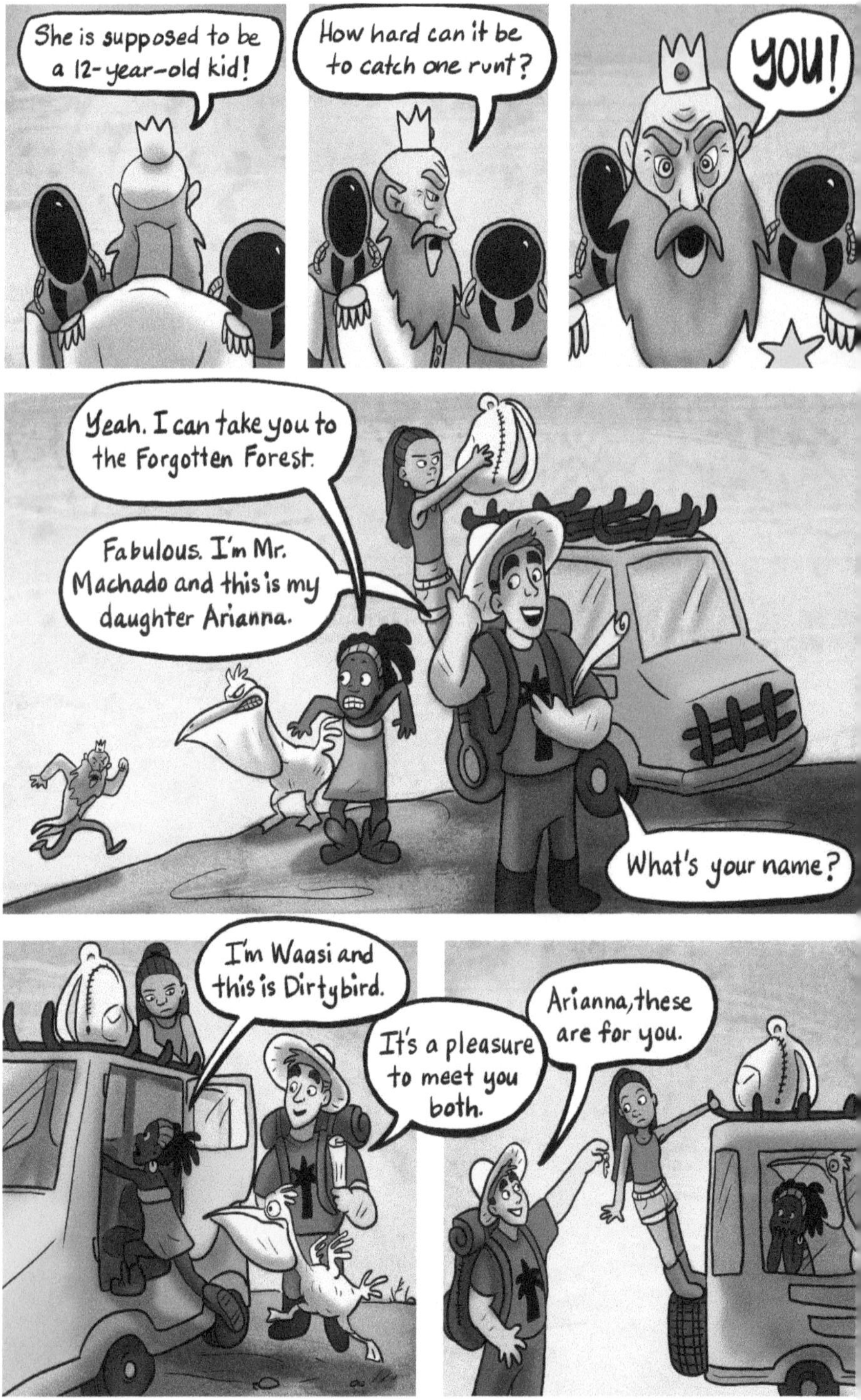
She is supposed to be a 12-year-old kid!
How hard can it be to catch one runt?
YOU!
Yeah. I can take you to the Forgotten Forest.
Fabulous. I'm Mr. Machado and this is my daughter Arianna.
What's your name?
I'm Waasi and this is Dirtybird.
It's a pleasure to meet you both.
Arianna, these are for you.

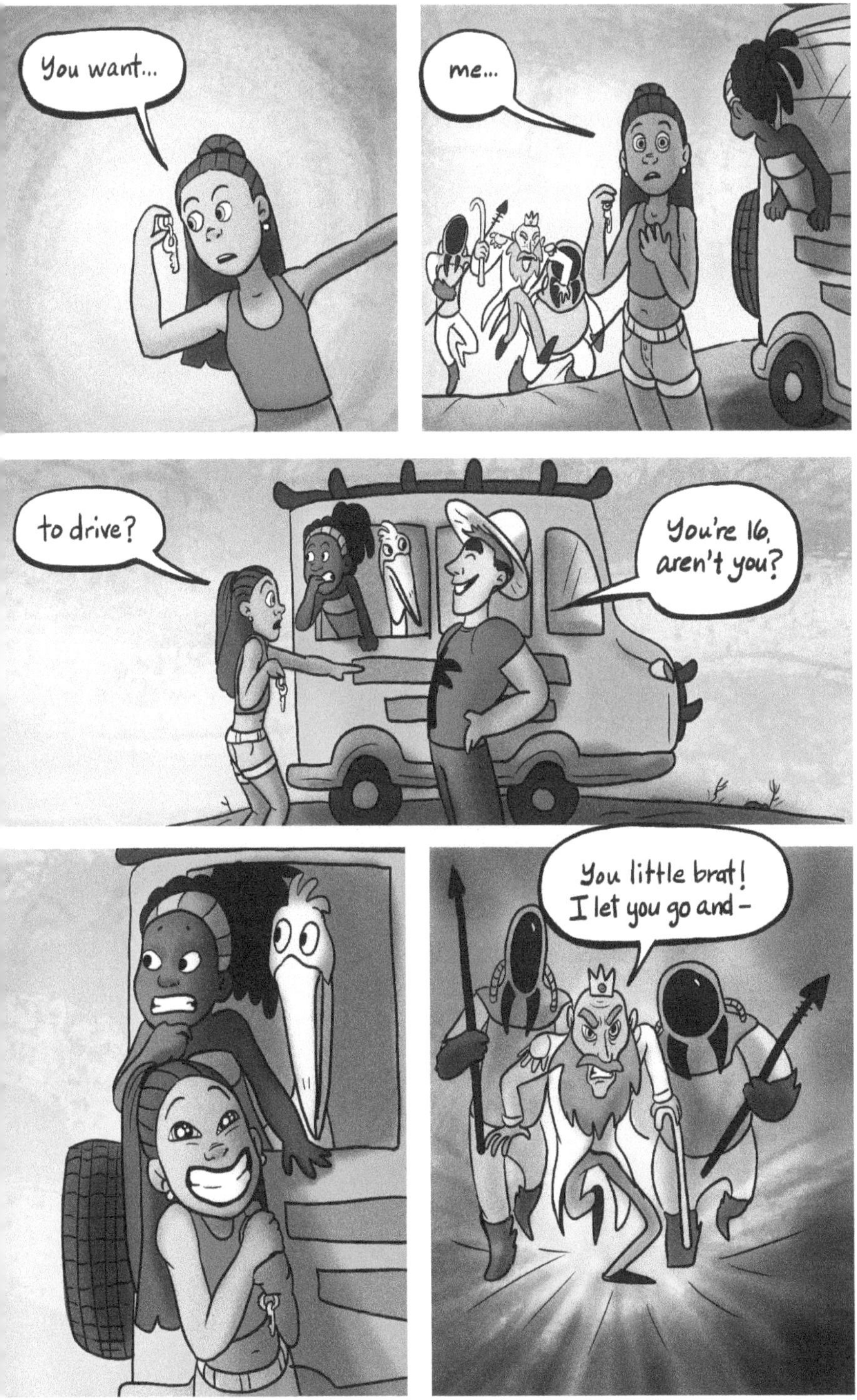
You want...
me...
to drive?
You're 16, aren't you?
You little brat! I let you go and -

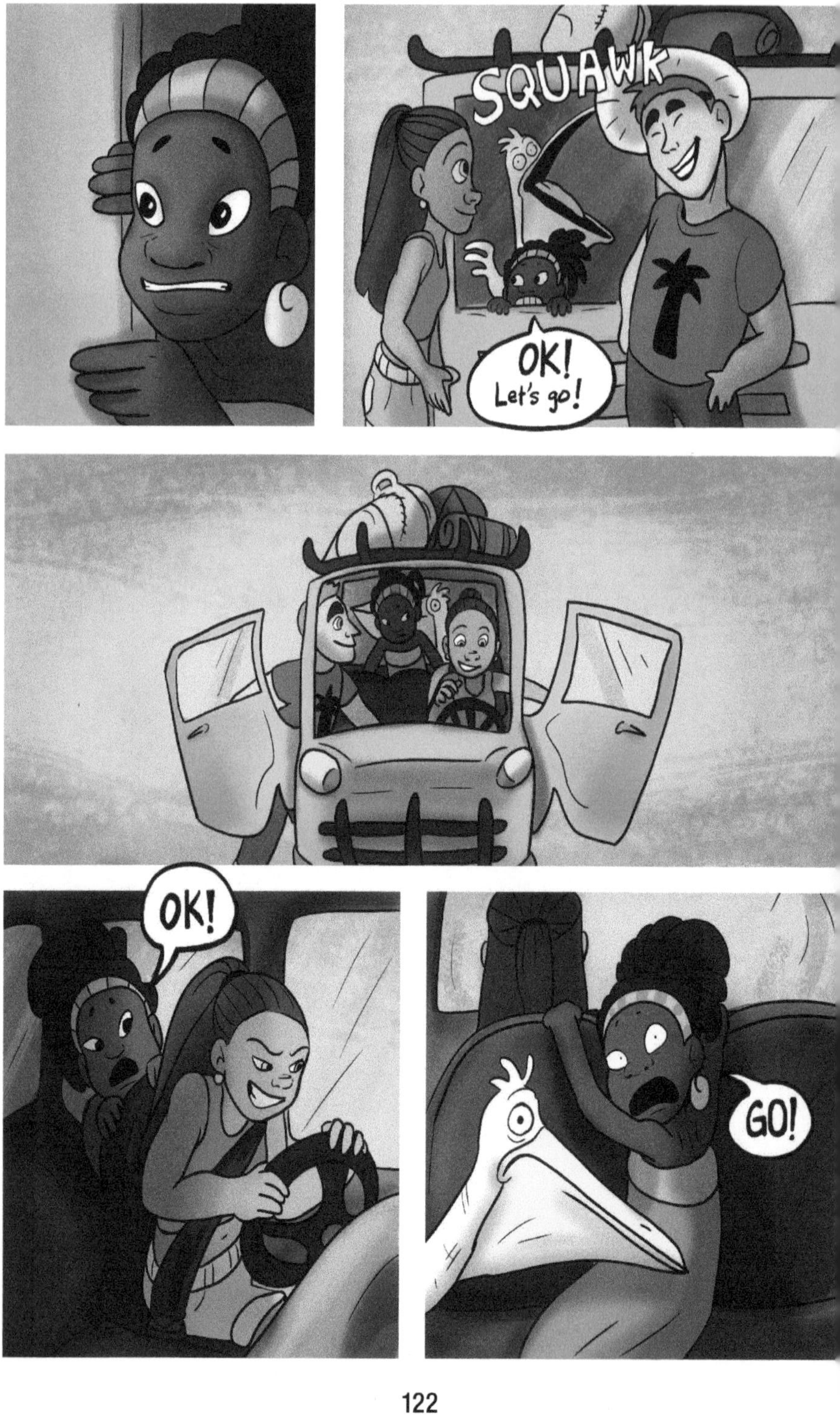
SQUAWK
OK!
Let's go!
OK!
GO!

I let you go once. But not this time, little girl!
VROOM

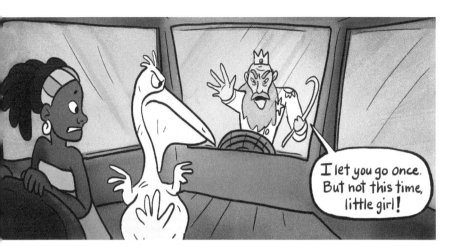

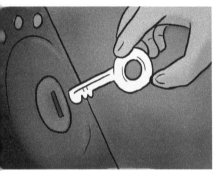

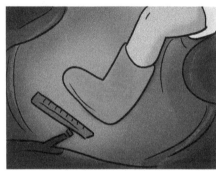

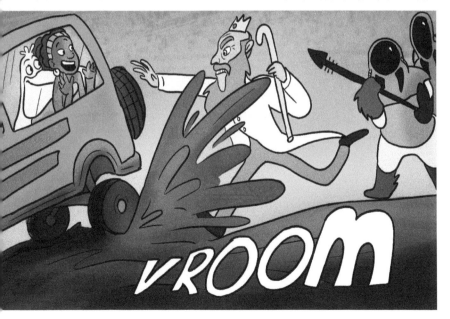

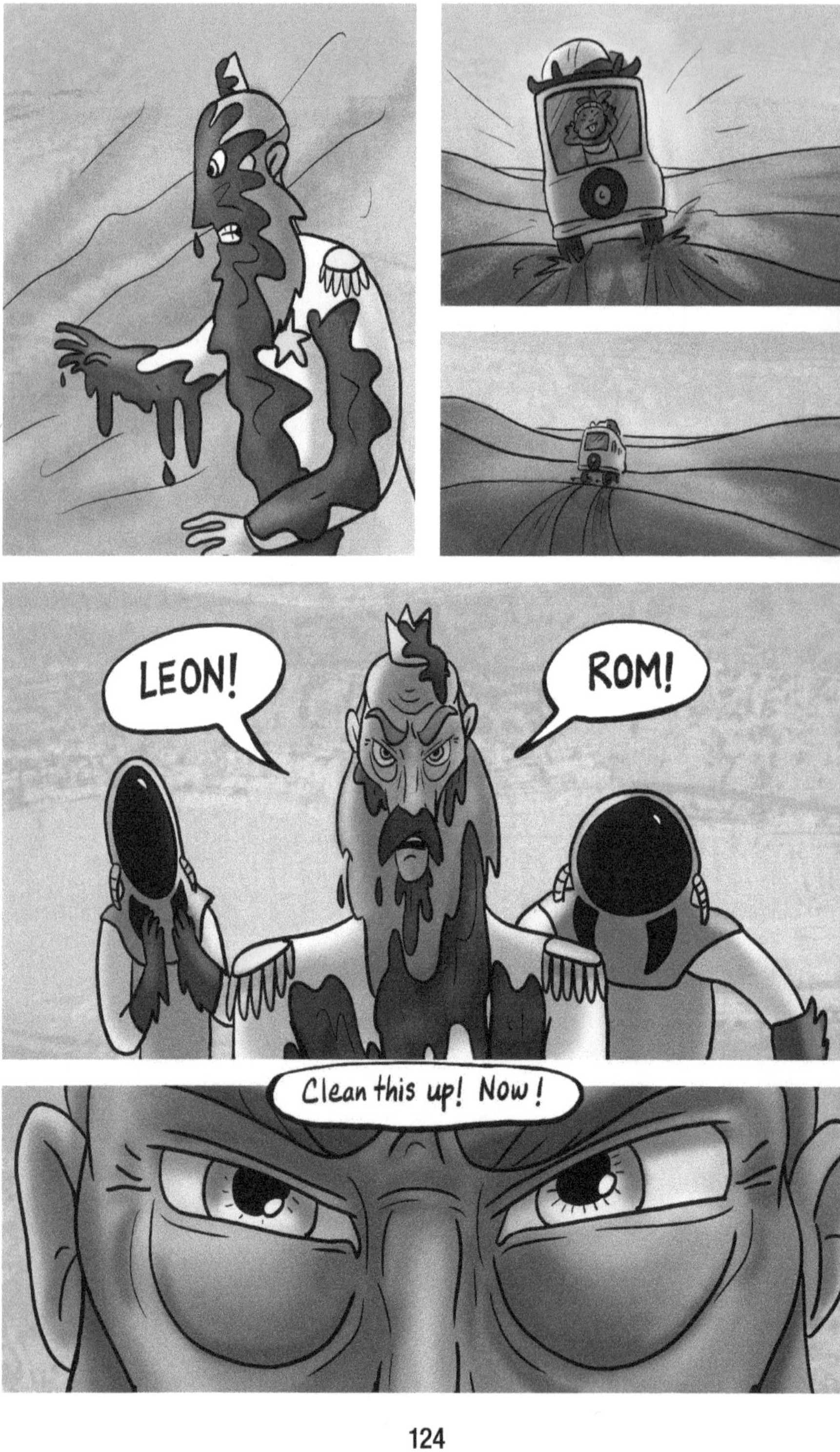
LEON!
ROM!
Clean this up! Now!

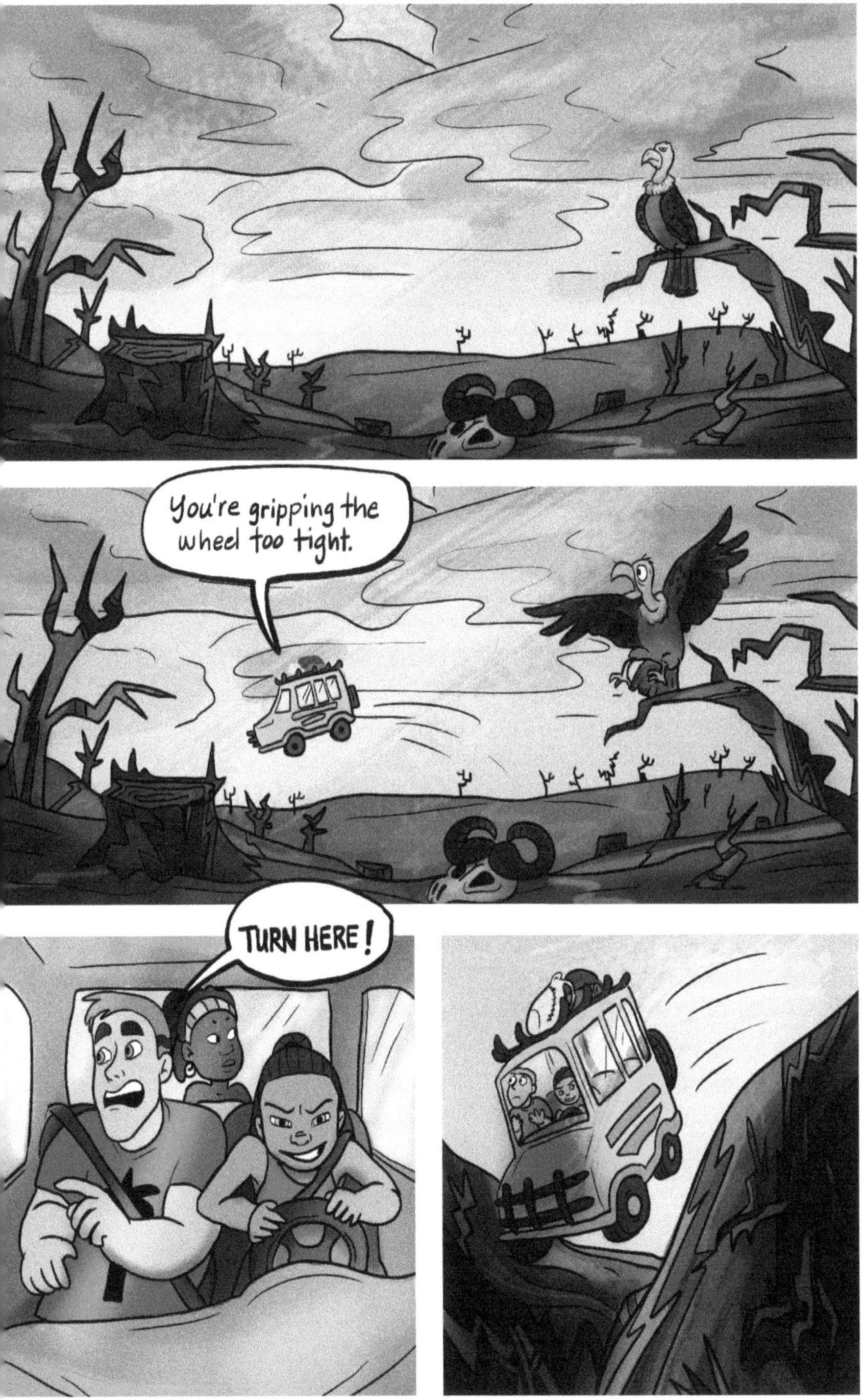
You're gripping the wheel too tight.
TURN HERE!

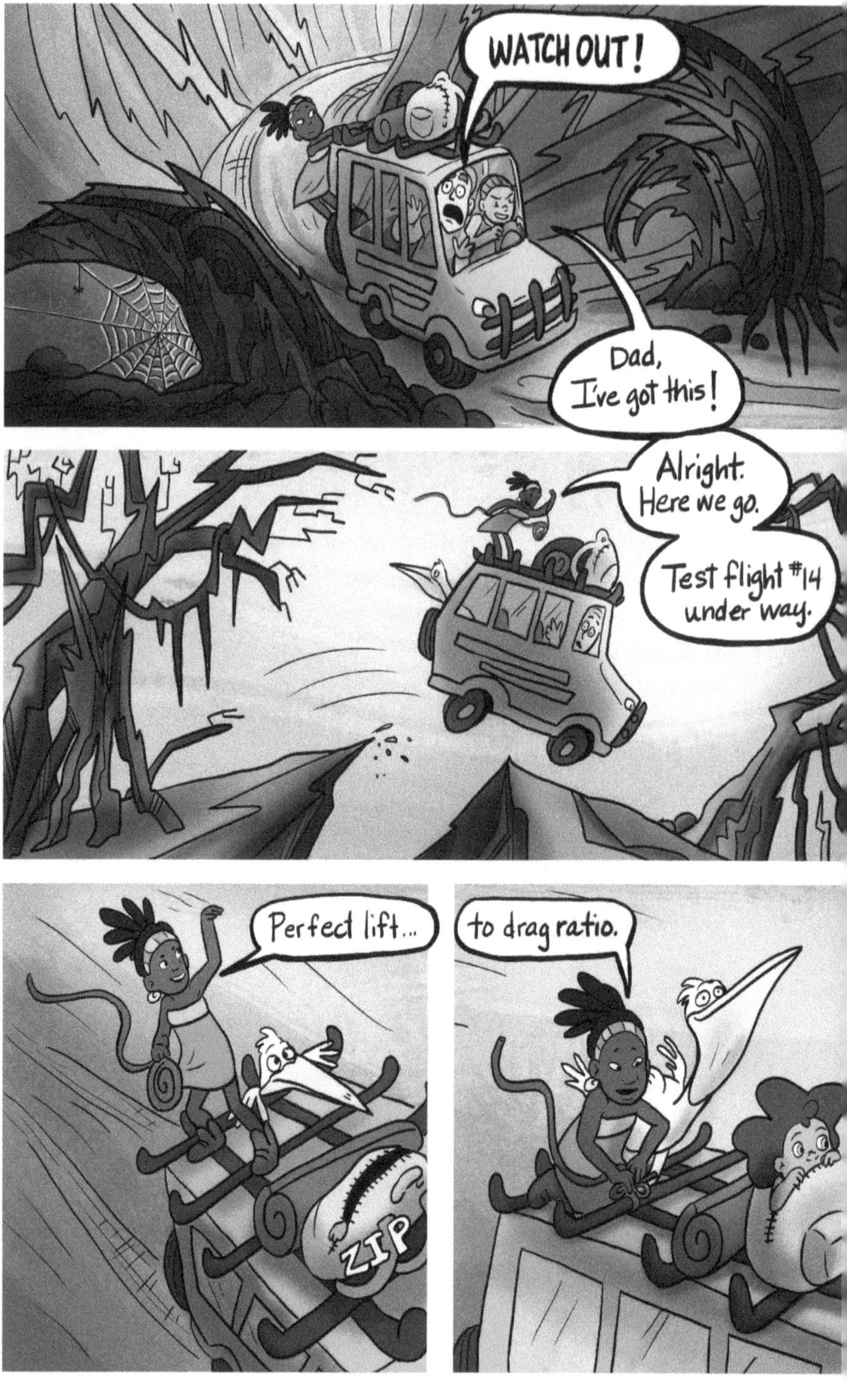
WATCH OUT!
Dad, I've got this!
Alright. Here we go.
Test flight #14 under way.
Perfect lift...
ZIP
to drag ratio.

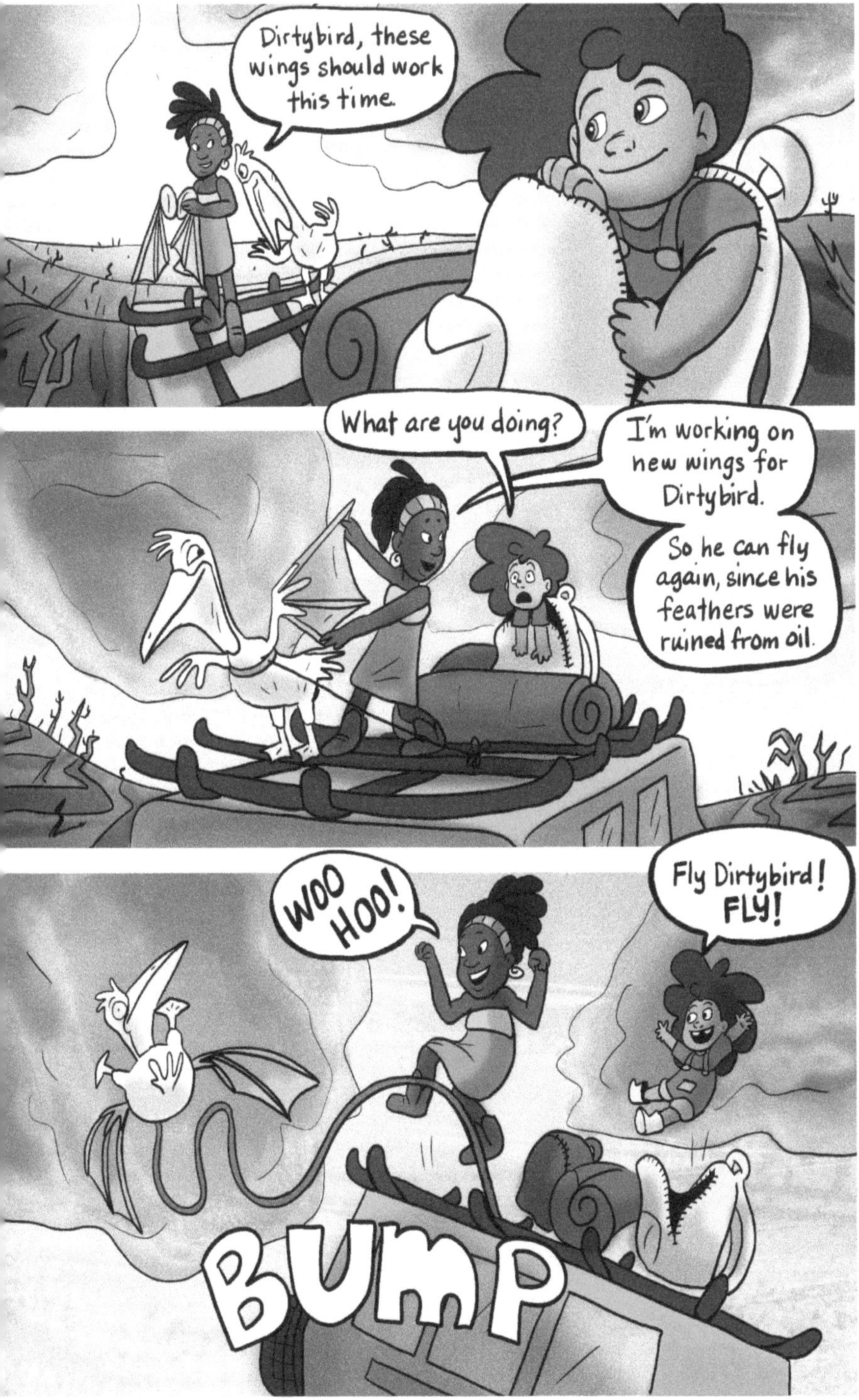
Dirtybird, these wings should work this time.
What are you doing?
I'm working on new wings for Dirtybird.
So he can fly again, since his feathers were ruined from oil.
WOO HOO!
Fly Dirtybird! FLY!
BUMP

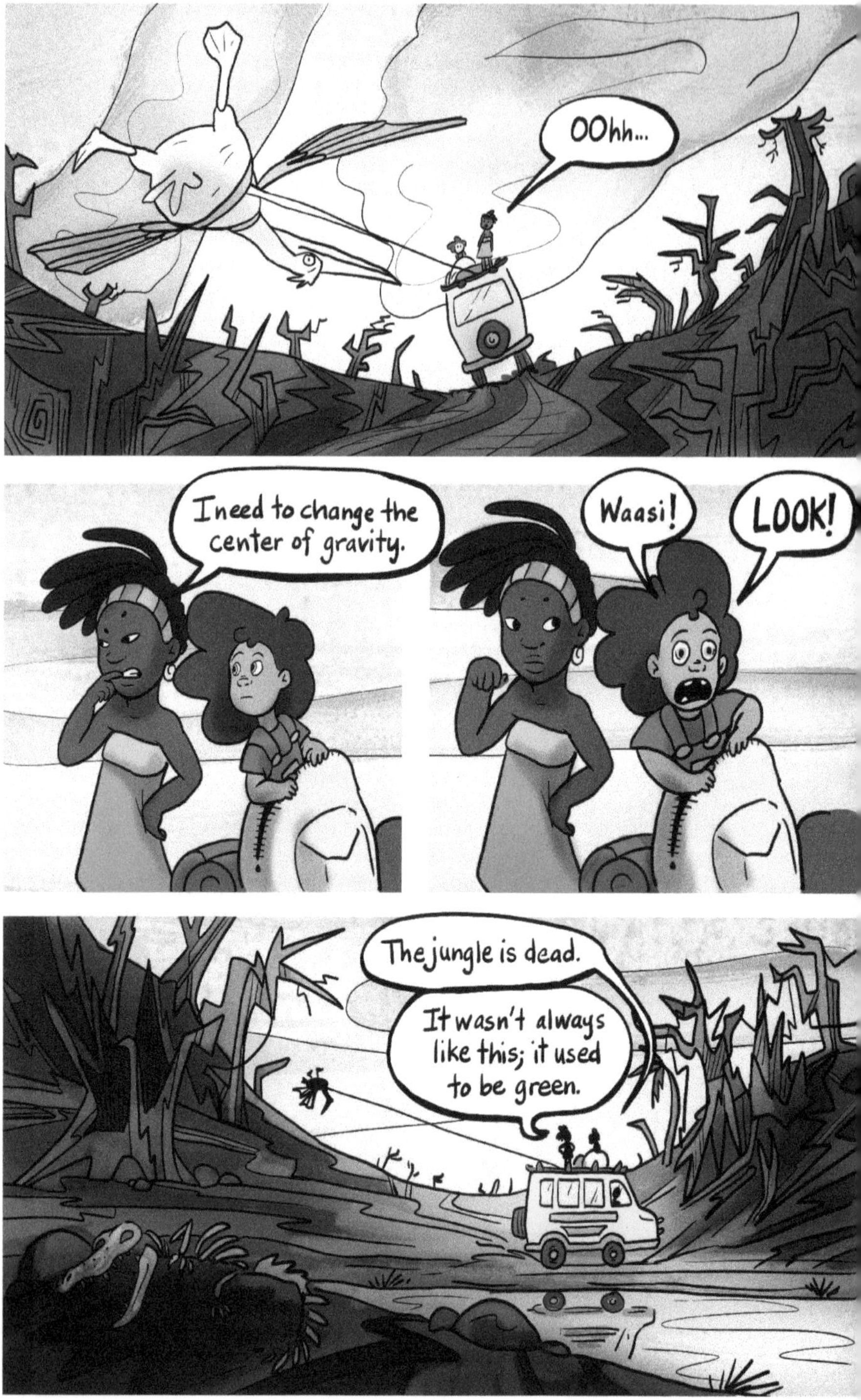
OOhh...
I need to change the center of gravity.
Waasi!
LOOK!
The jungle is dead.
It wasn't always like this; it used to be green.

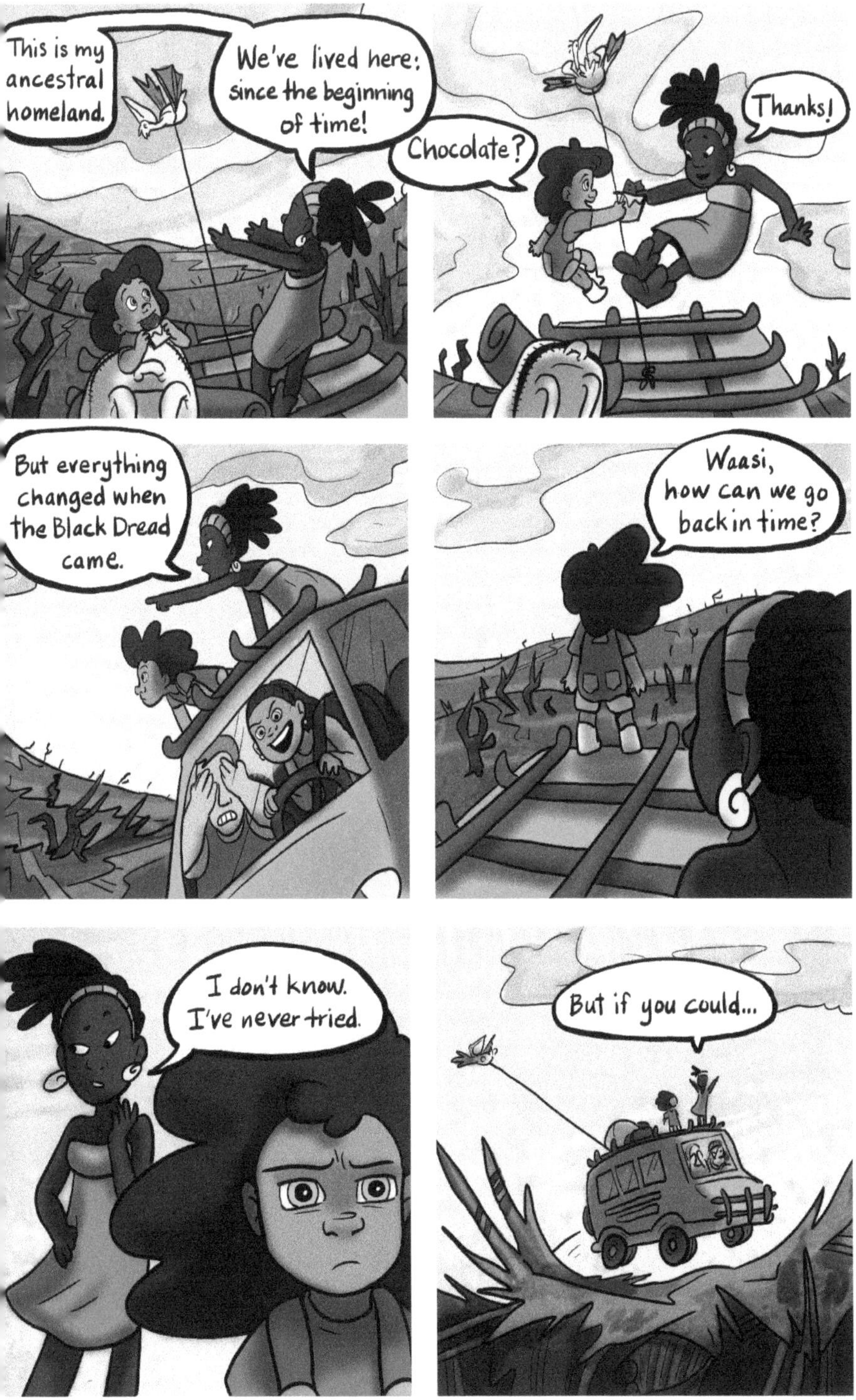

This is my ancestral homeland.
We've lived here: since the beginning of time!
Chocolate?
Thanks!
But everything changed when the Black Dread came.
Waasi, how can we go back in time?
I don't know. I've never tried.
But if you could...

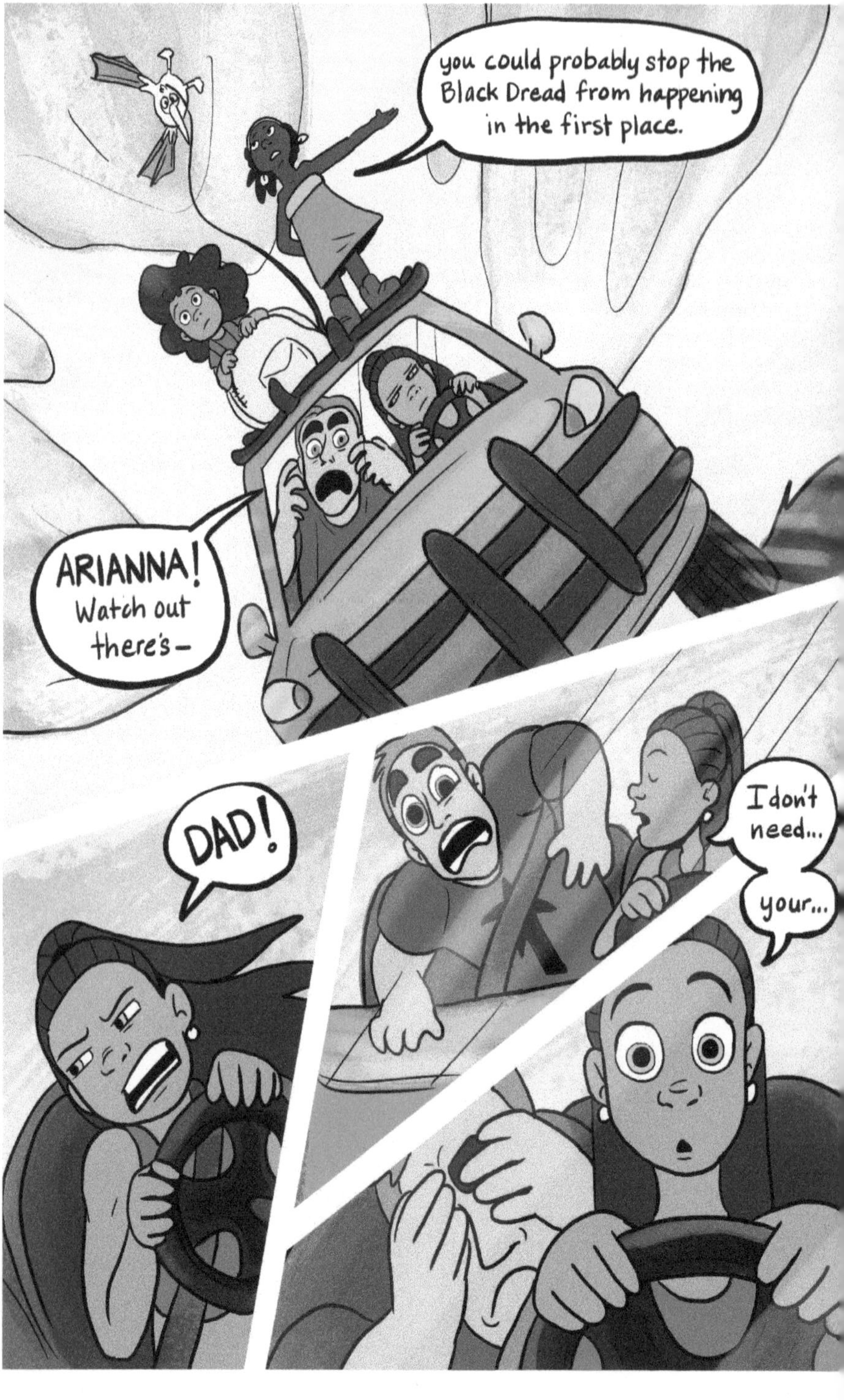

you could probably stop the Black Dread from happening in the first place.
ARIANNA! Watch out there's–
DAD!
I don't need...
your...

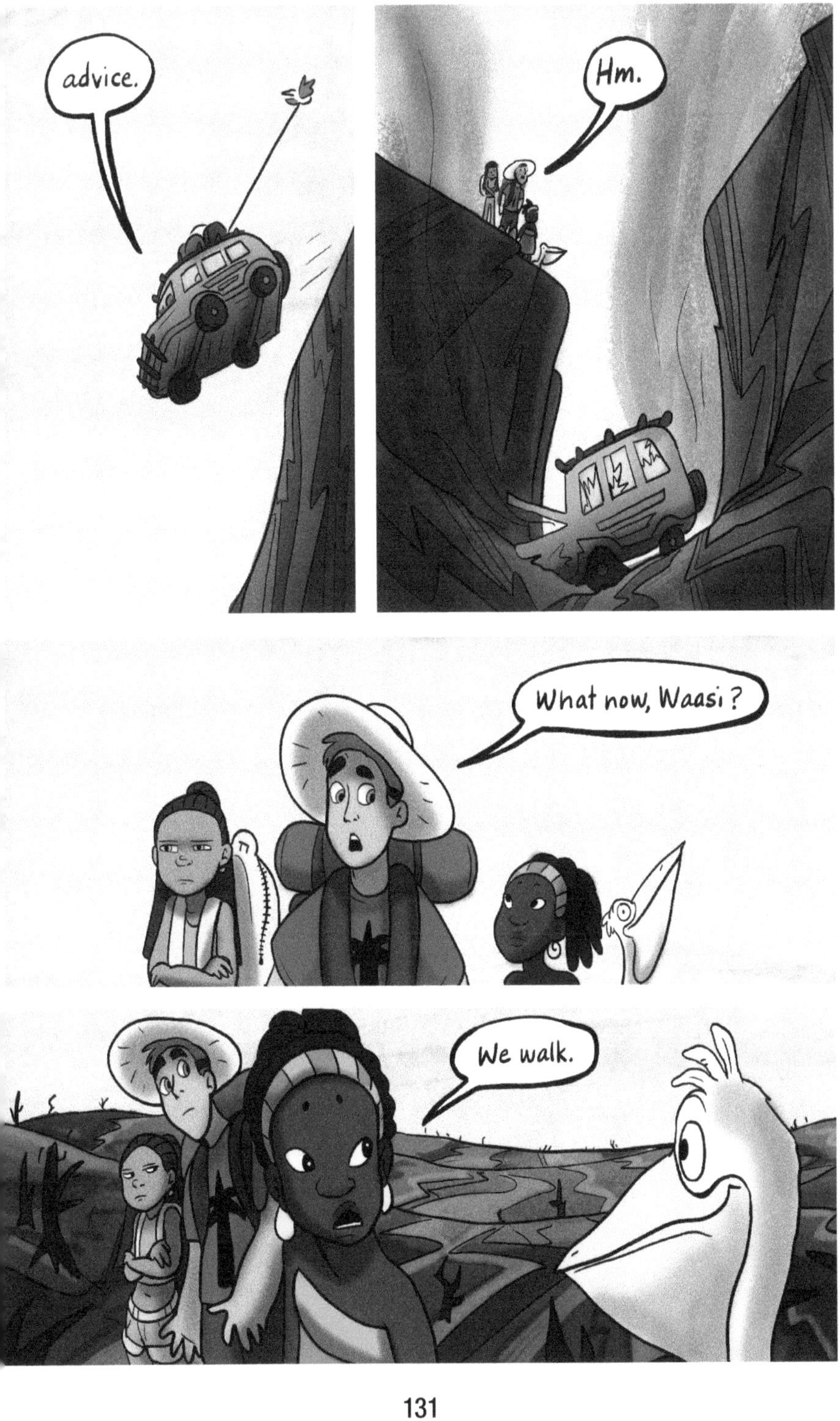
advice.
Hm.
What now, Waasi?
We walk.

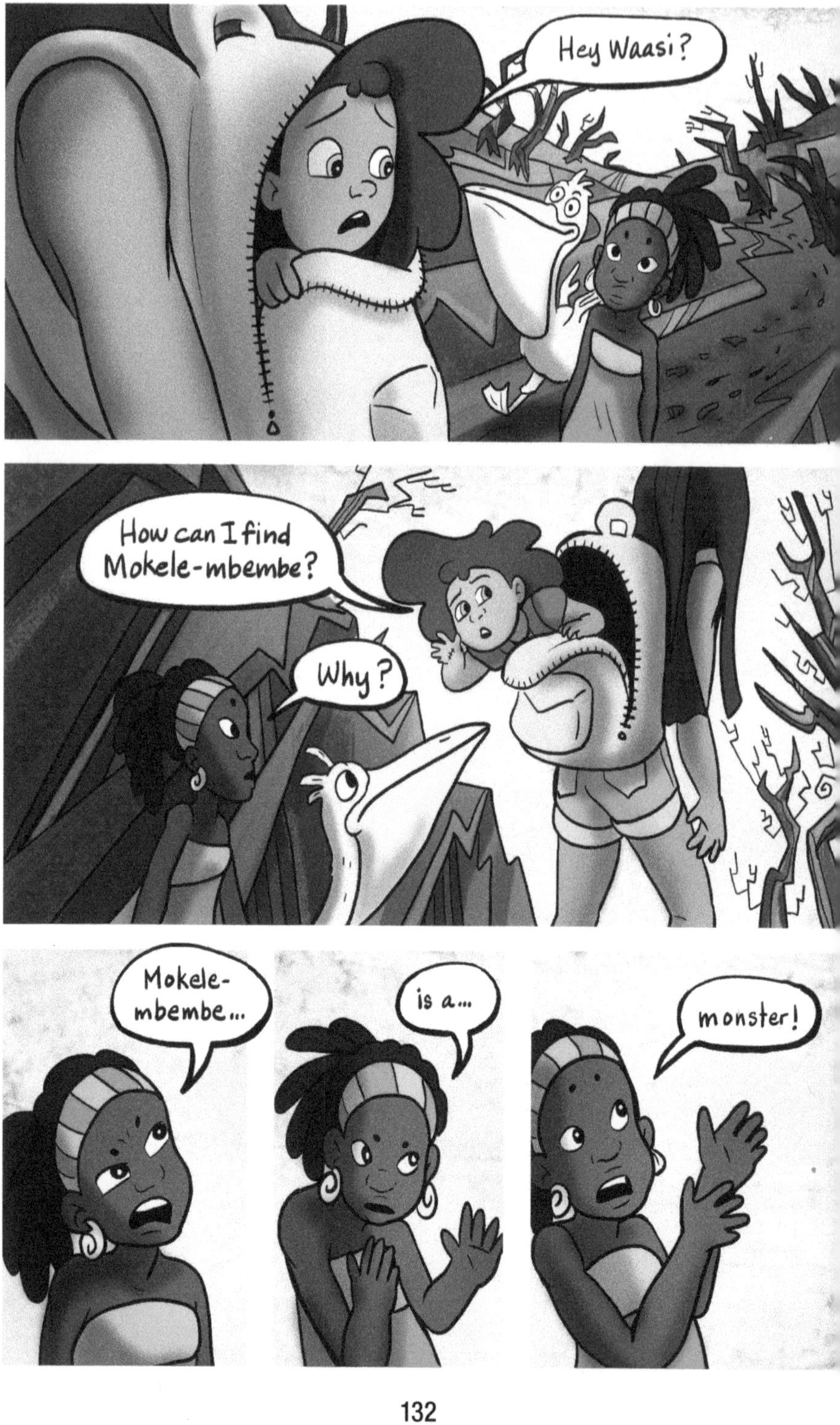
Hey Waasi?
How can I find Mokele-mbembe?
Why?
Mokele-mbembe...
is a...
monster!

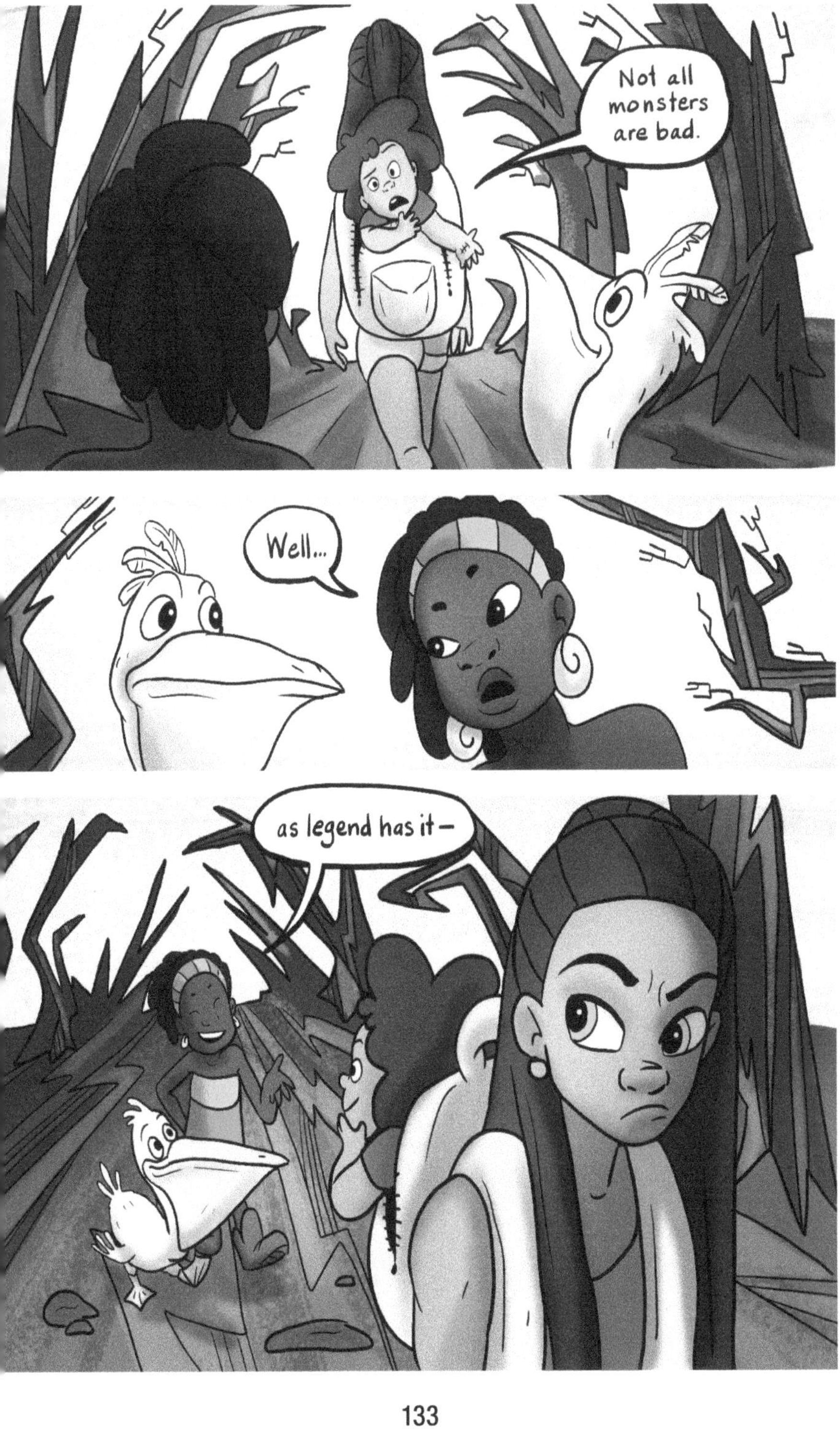
Not all monsters are bad.
Well...
as legend has it—

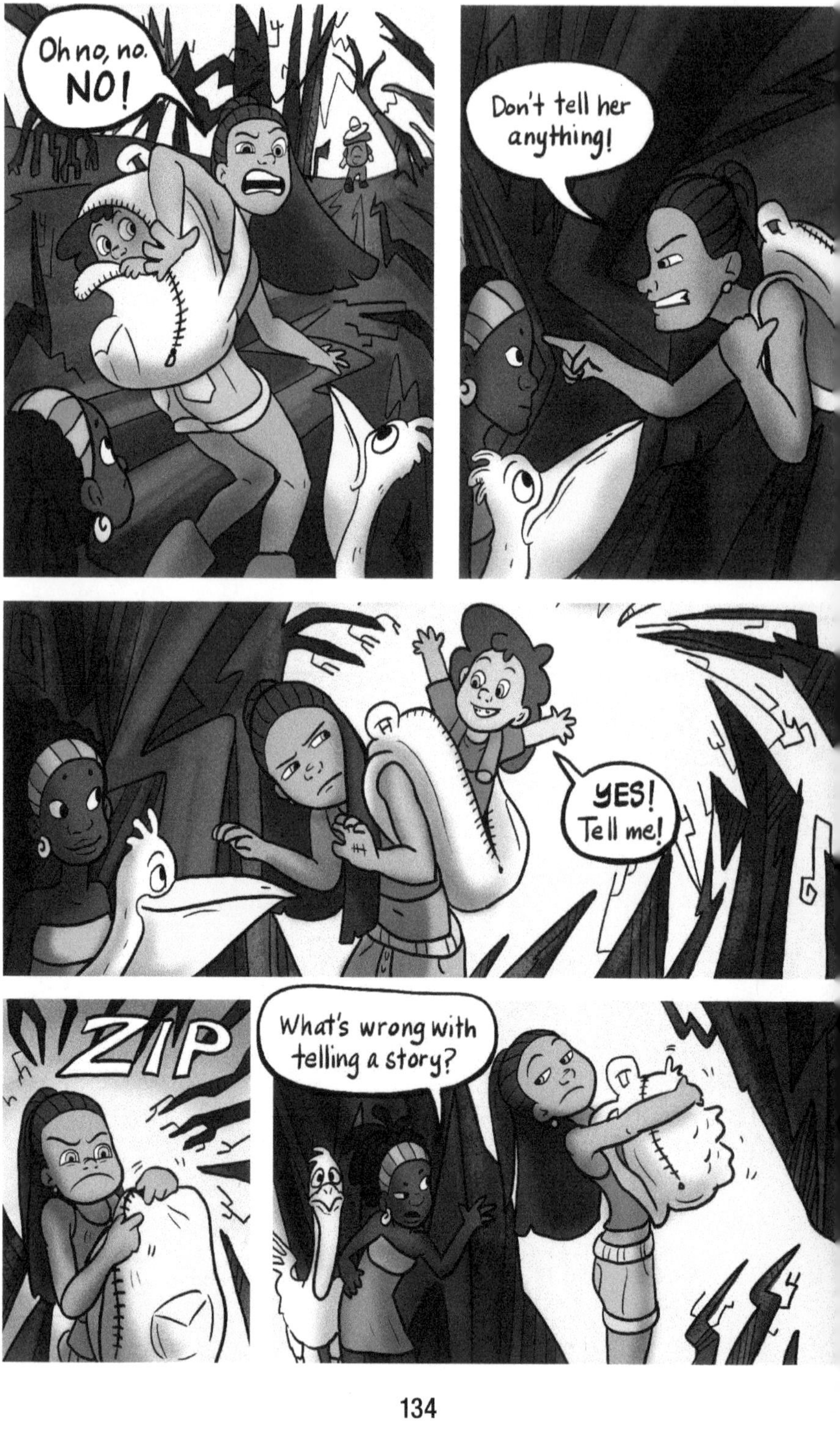
Oh no, no.
NO!
Don't tell her anything!
YES! Tell me!
ZIP
What's wrong with telling a story?

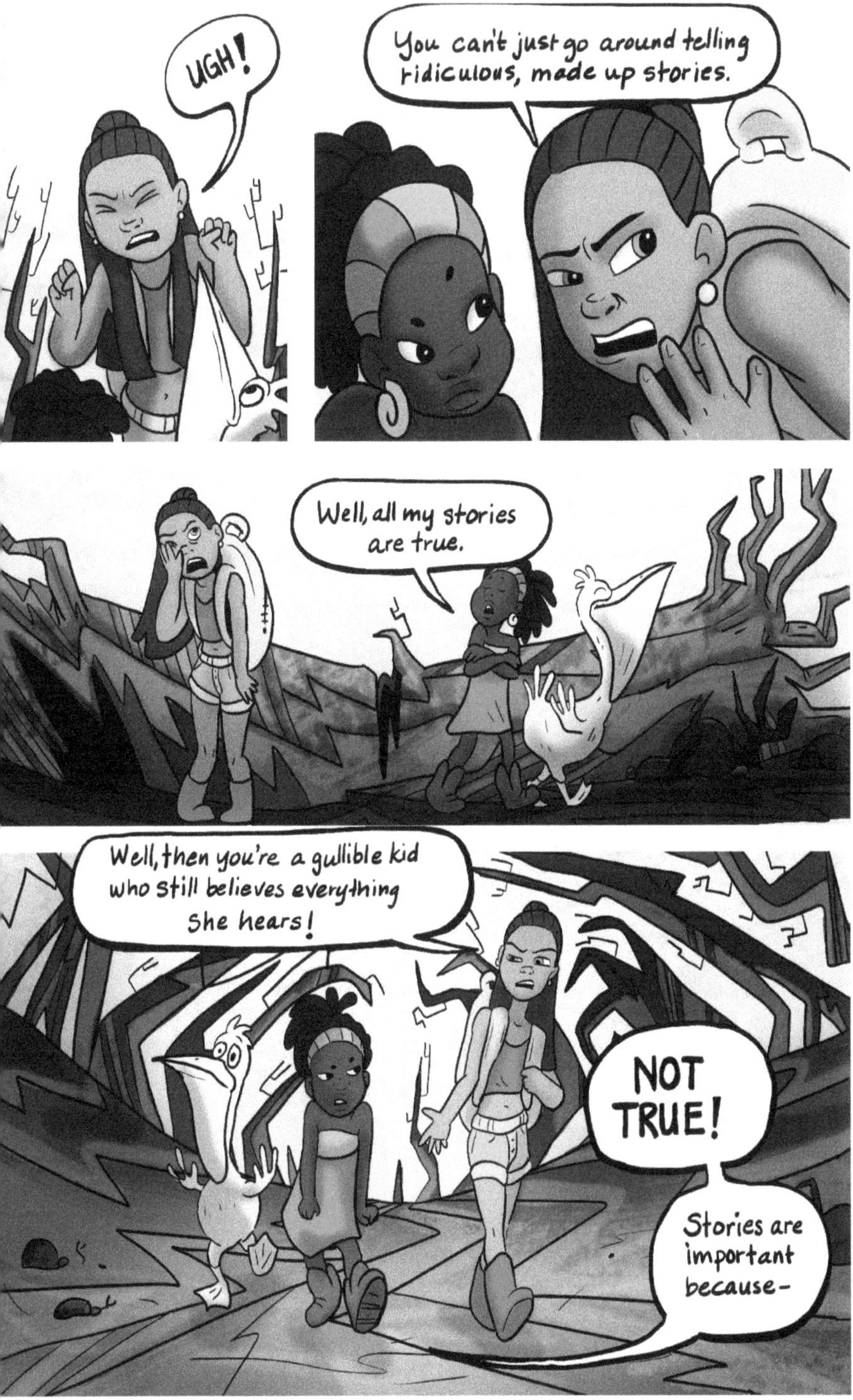
UGH!
You can't just go around telling ridiculous, made up stories.
Well, all my stories are true.
Well, then you're a gullible kid who still believes everything she hears!
NOT TRUE!
Stories are important because-

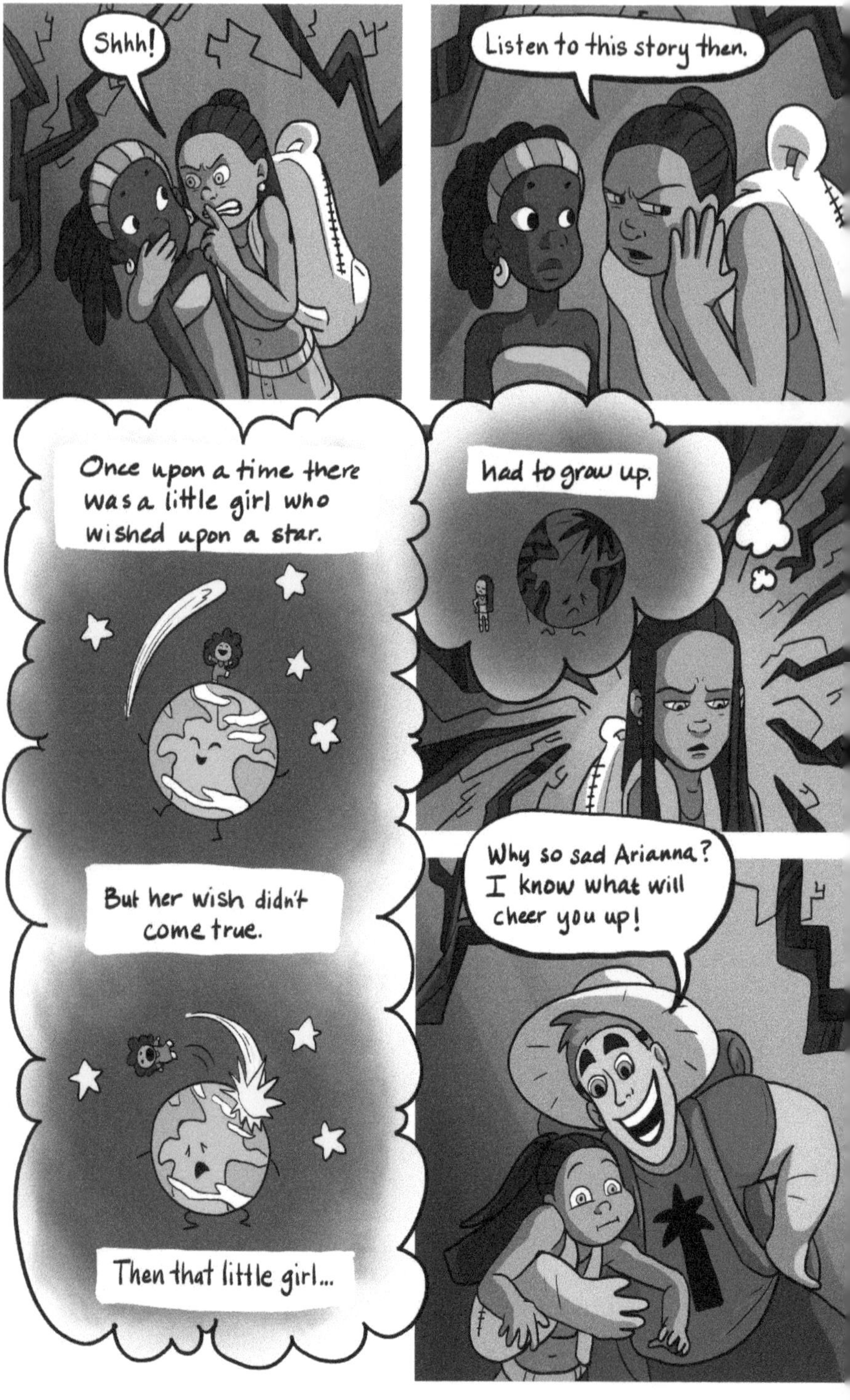
Shhh!
Listen to this story then.
Once upon a time there was a little girl who wished upon a star.
But her wish didn't come true.
Then that little girl...
had to grow up.
Why so sad Arianna? I know what will cheer you up!

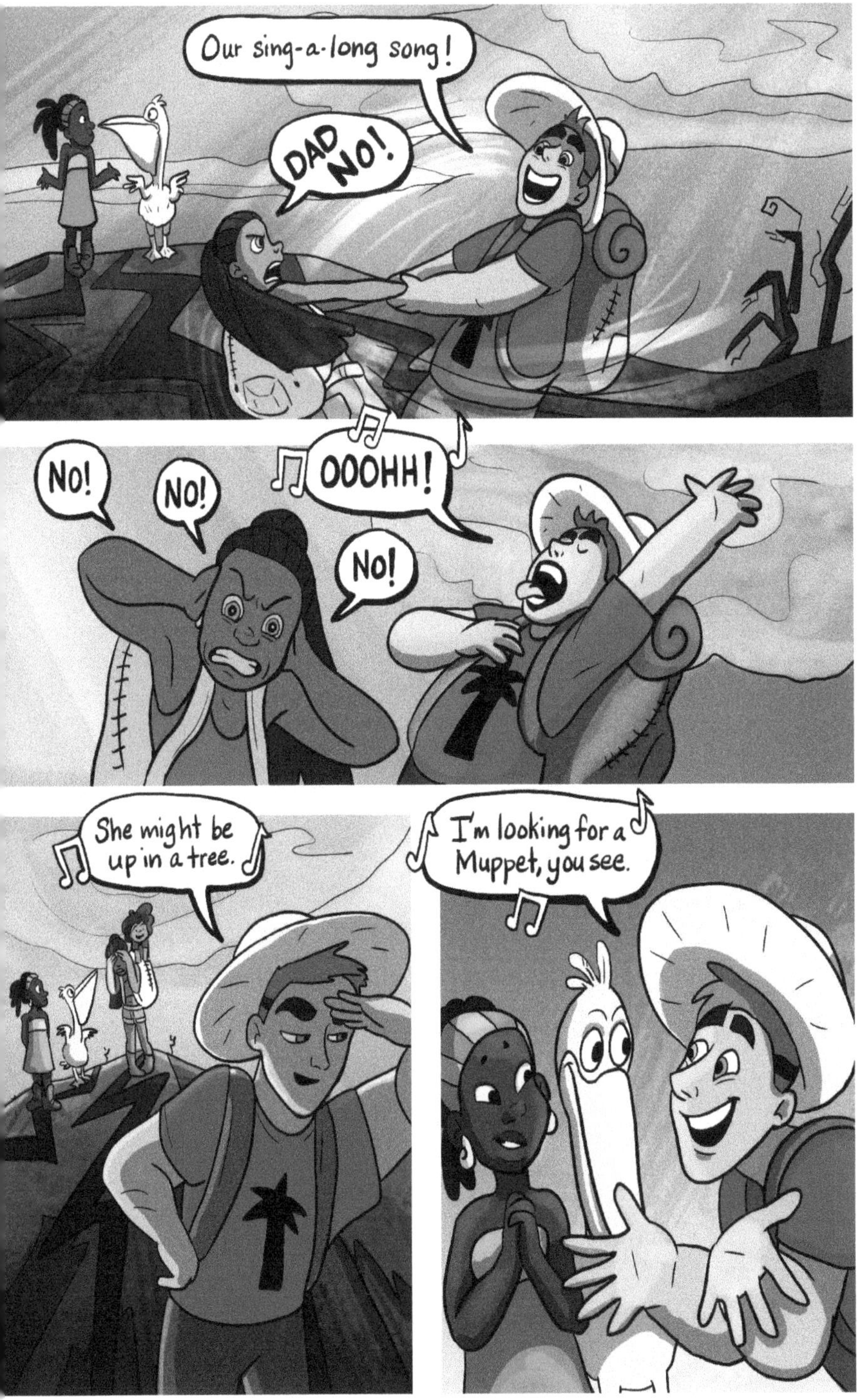

Our sing-a-long song!
DAD NO!
No!
NO!
OOOHH!
No!
She might be up in a tree.
I'm looking for a Muppet, you see.

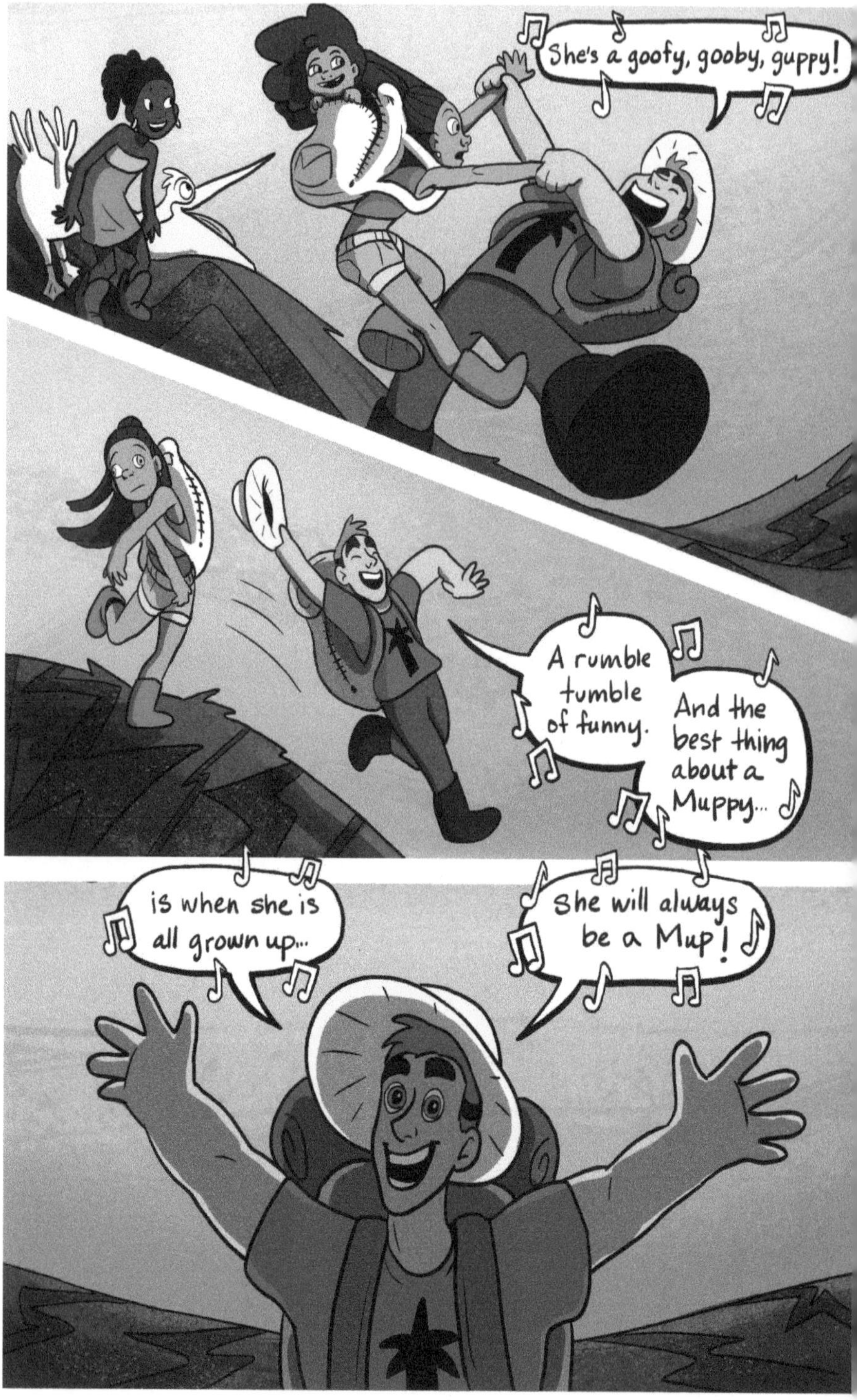
She's a goofy, gooby, guppy!
A rumble tumble of funny.
And the best thing about a Muppy...
is when she is all grown up...
She will always be a Mup!

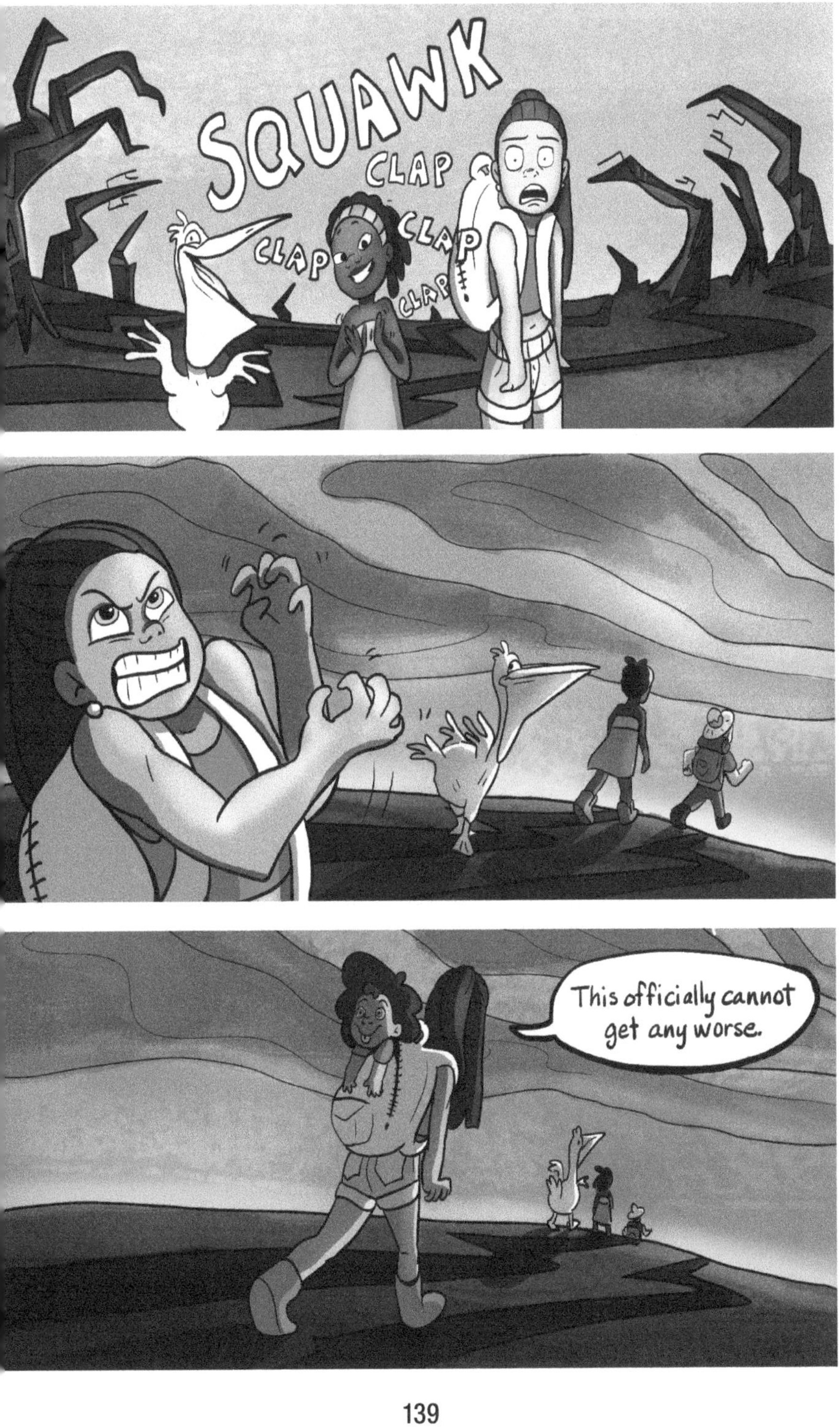
SQUAWK
CLAP
CLAP
CLAP
CLAP
This officially cannot get any worse.

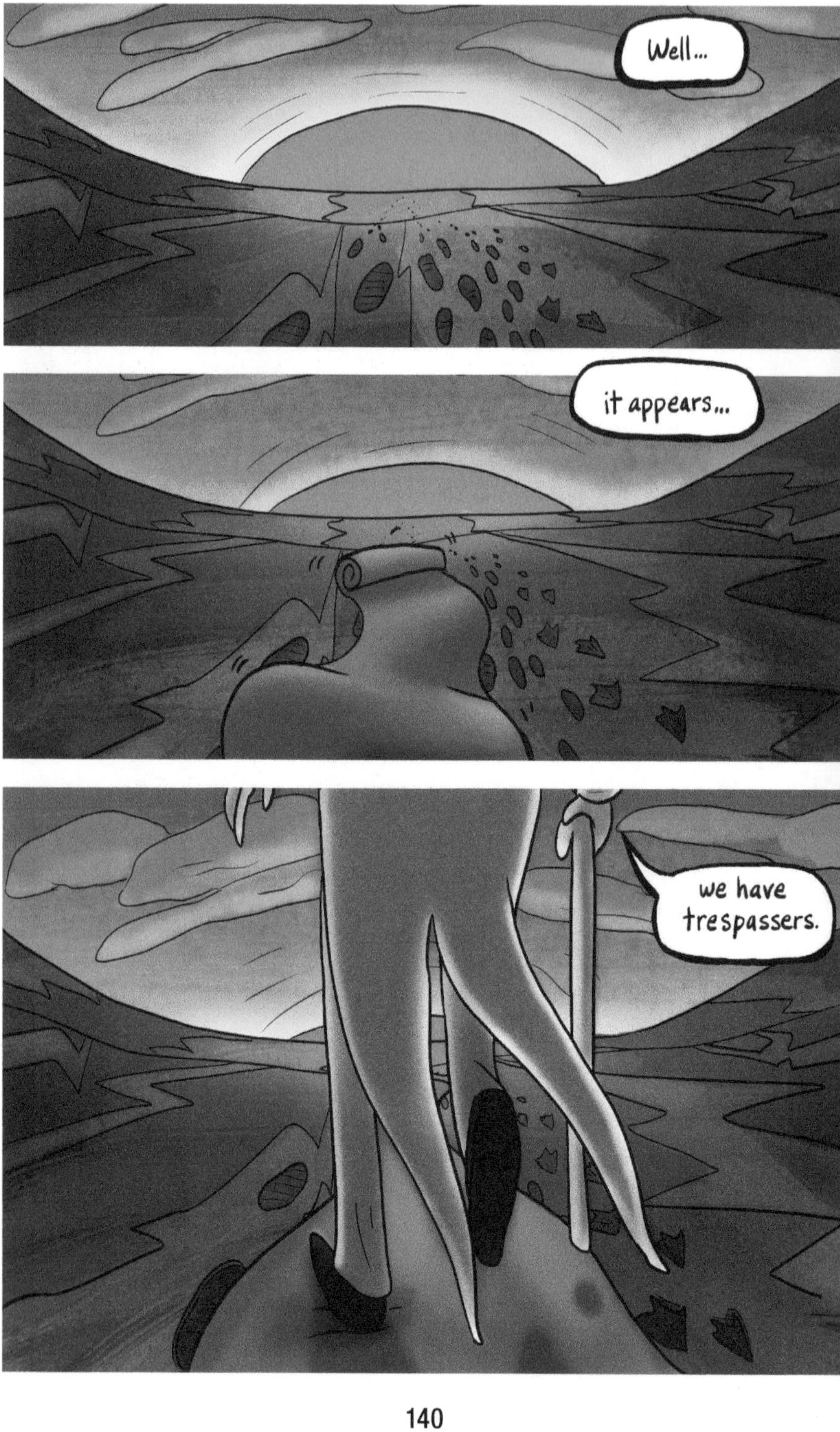
Well...
it appears...
we have
trespassers.

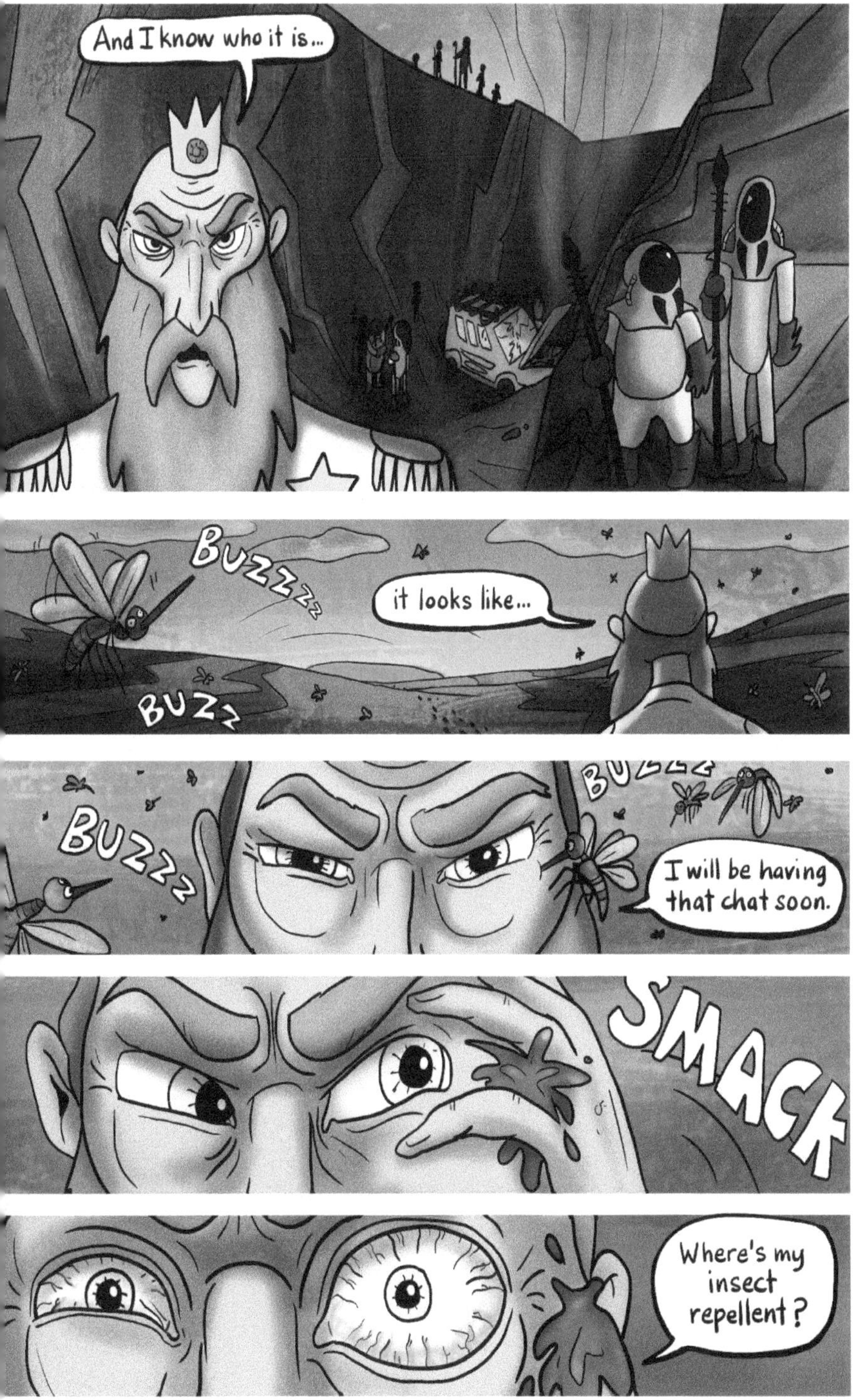
And I know who it is...
BUZZZzz
it looks like...
BUZZ
BUZZZZ
I will be having that chat soon.
SMACK
Where's my insect repellent?

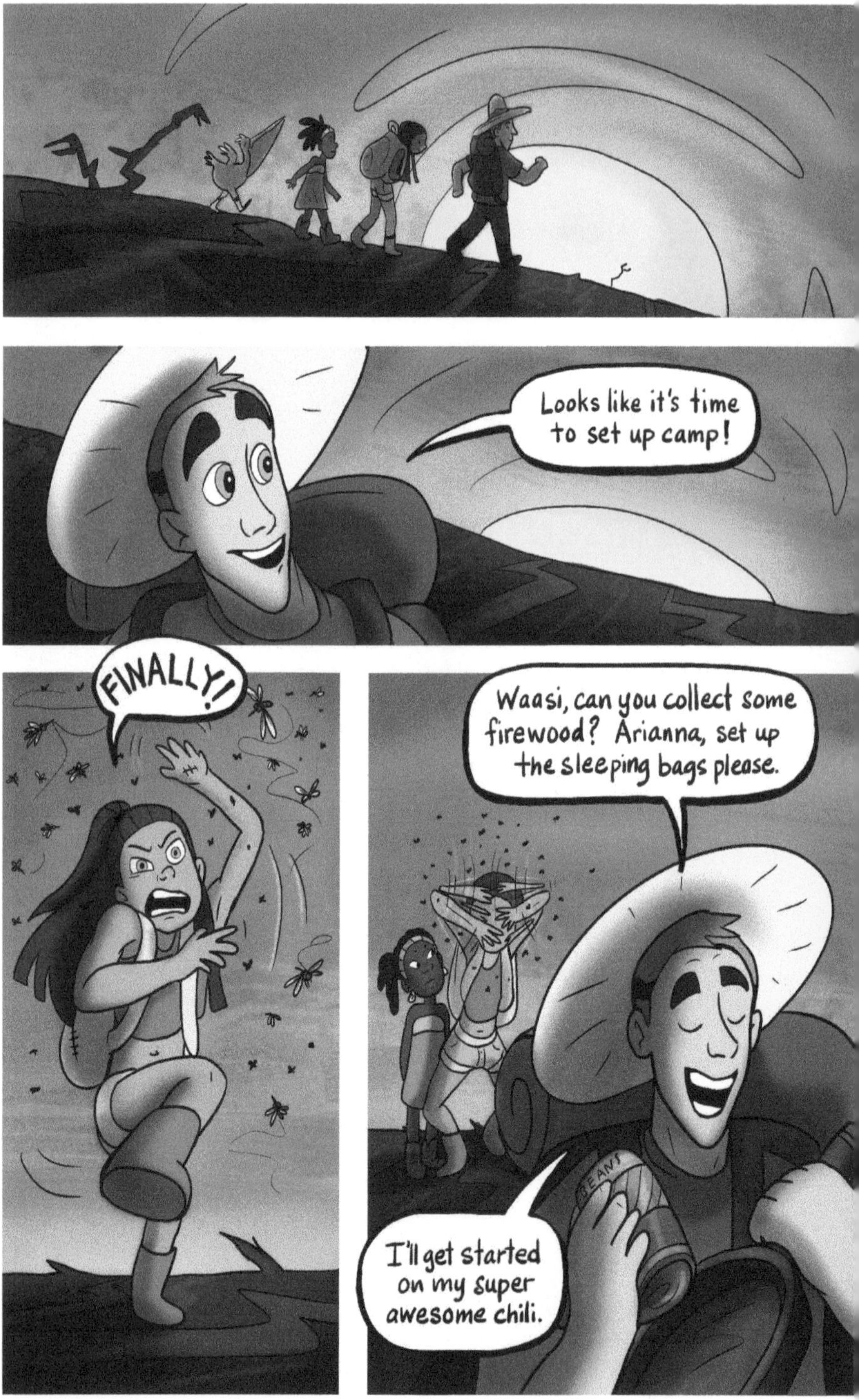
Looks like it's time to set up camp!
FINALLY!
Waasi, can you collect some firewood? Arianna, set up the sleeping bags please.
I'll get started on my super awesome chili.
BEANS

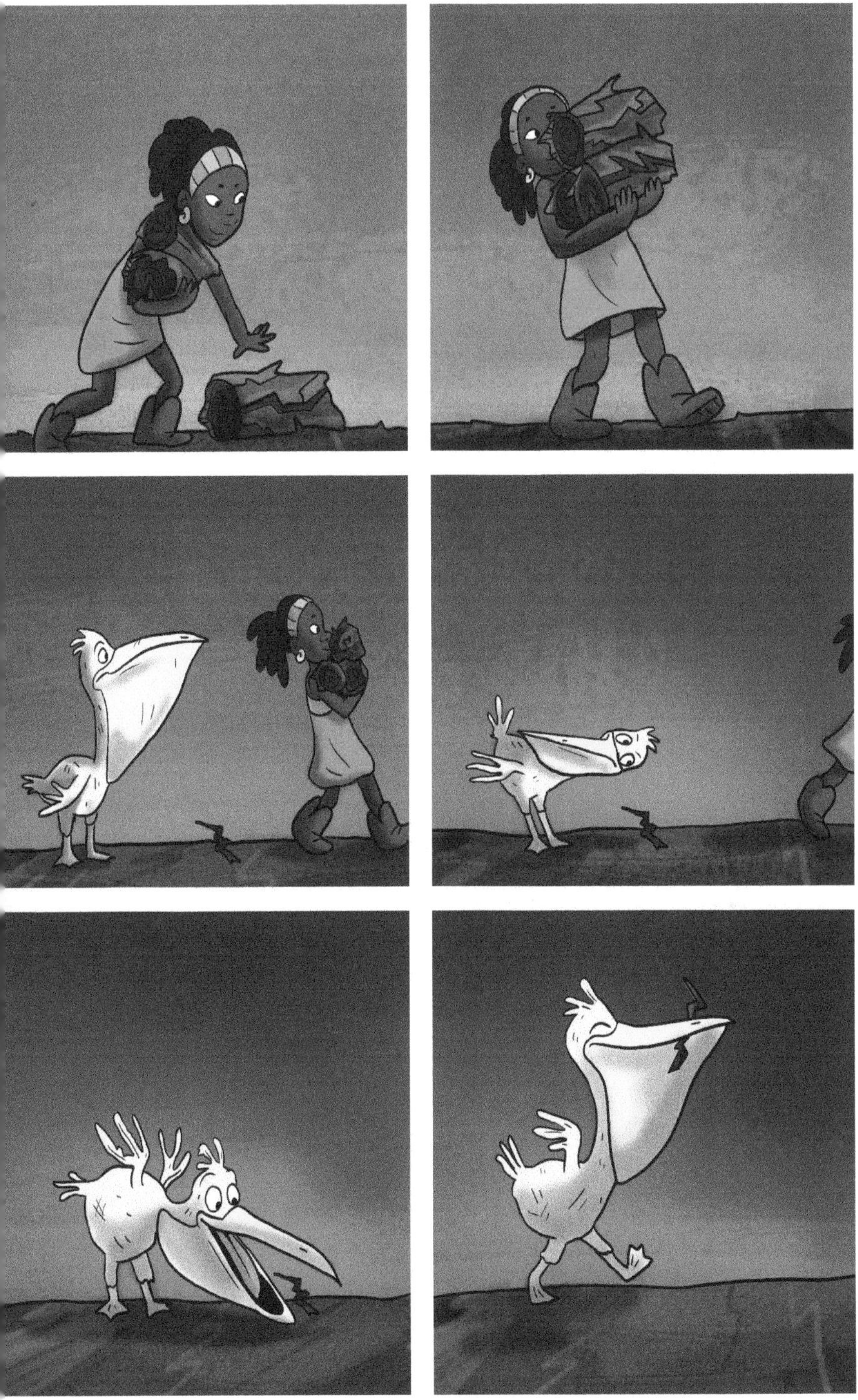

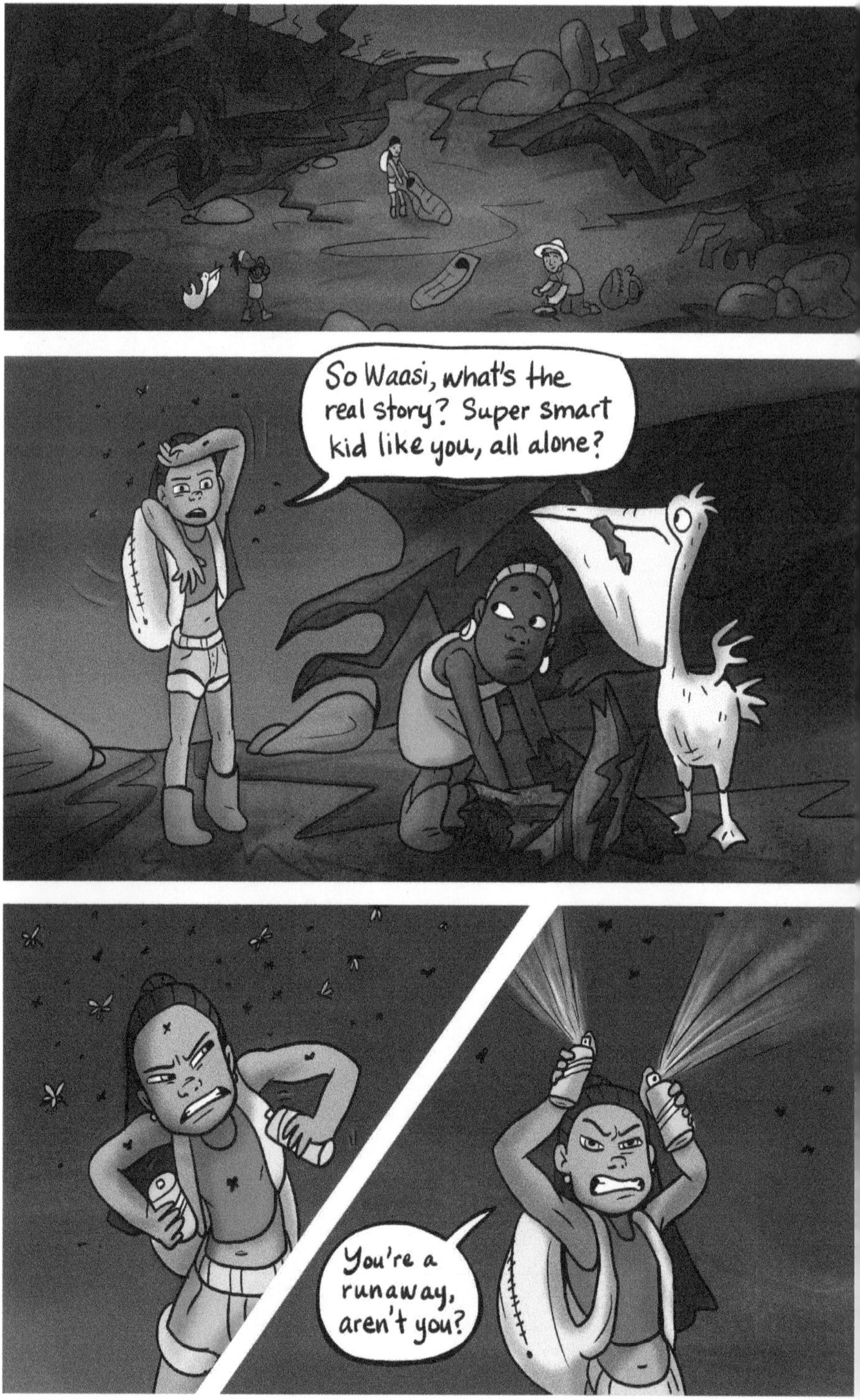
So Waasi, what's the real story? Super smart kid like you, all alone?
You're a runaway, aren't you?

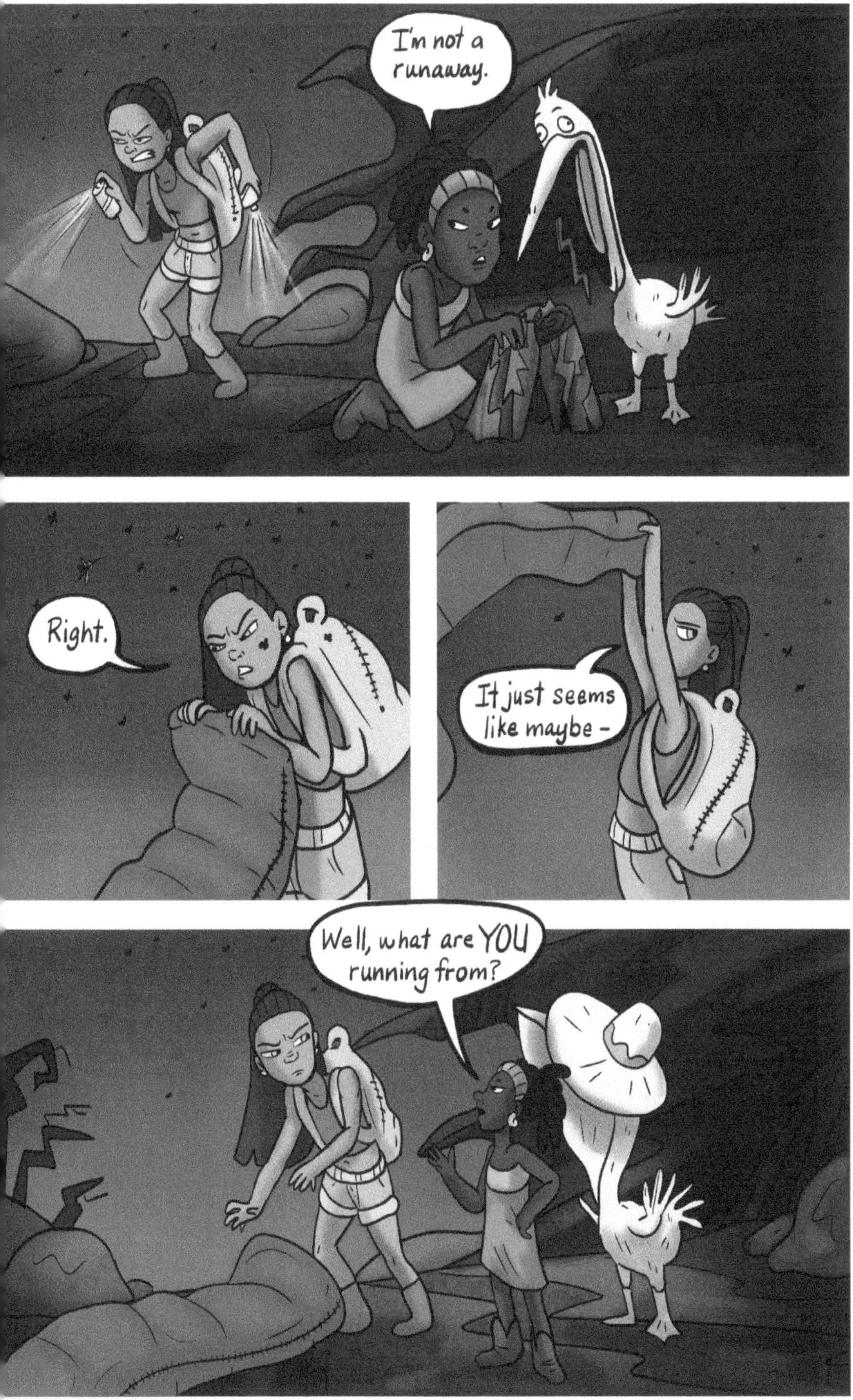
I'm not a runaway.
Right.
It just seems like maybe -
Well, what are YOU running from?

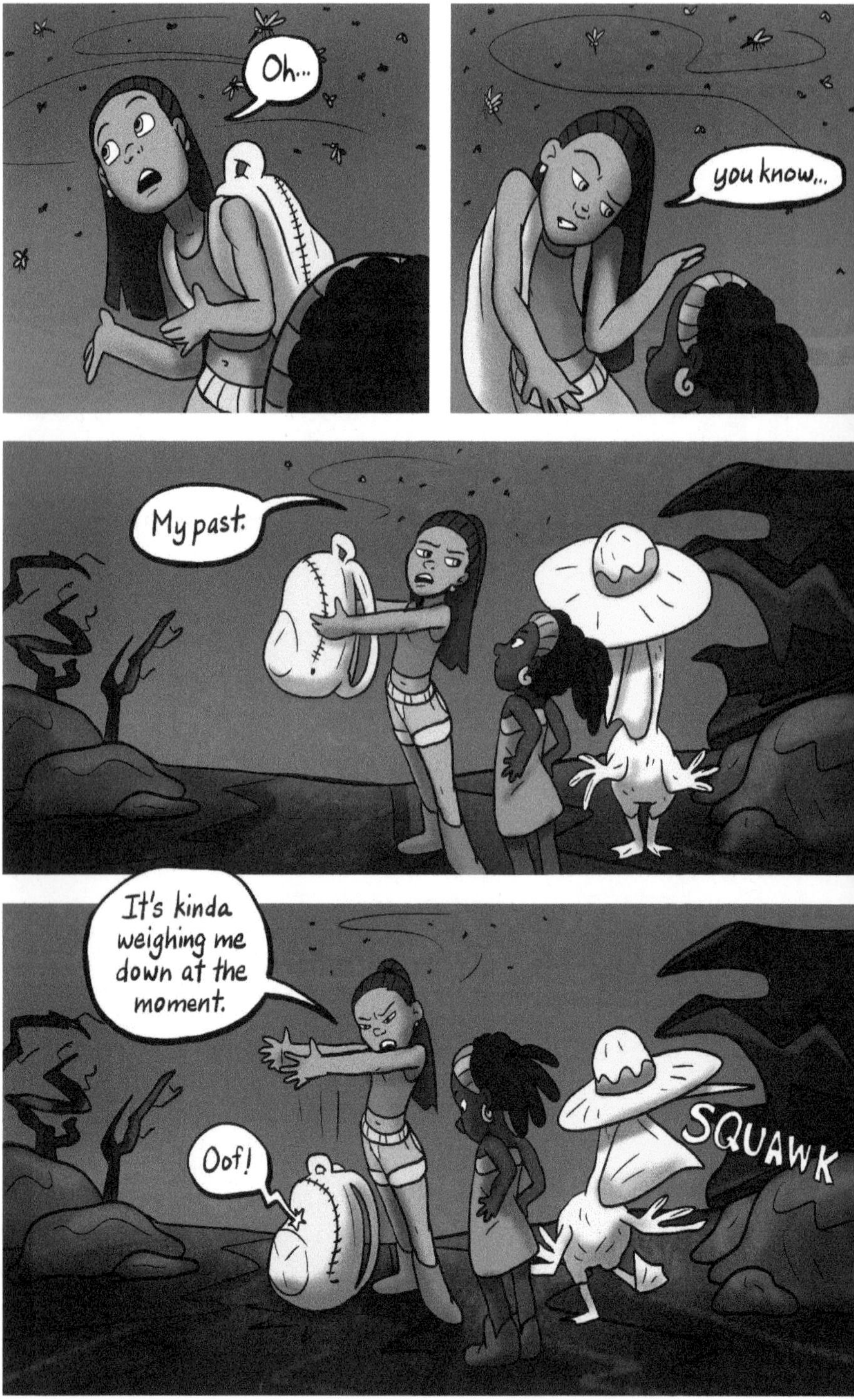
Oh...
you know...
My past.
It's kinda weighing me down at the moment.
Oof!
SQUAWK

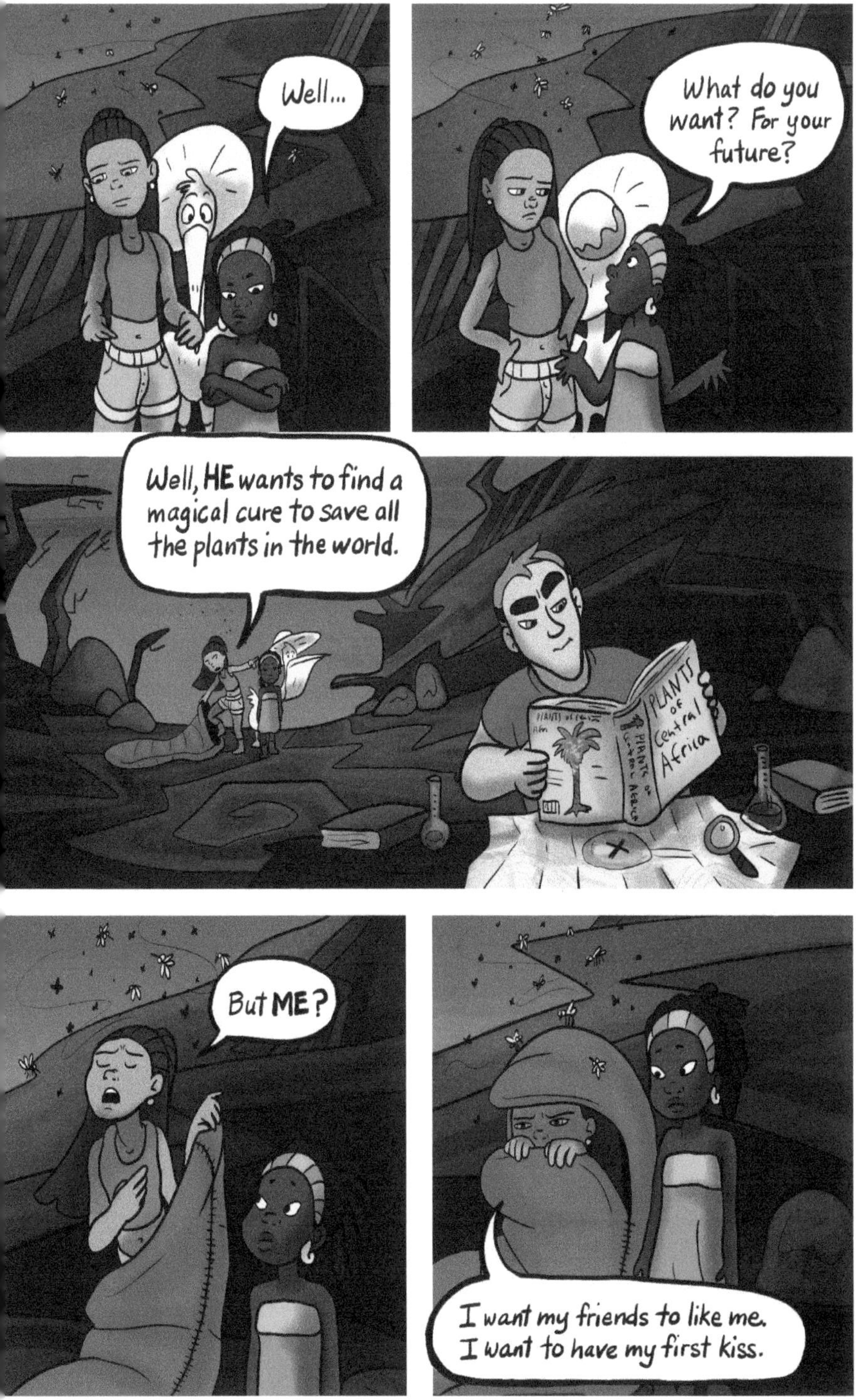
Well...
What do you want? For your future?
Well, HE wants to find a magical cure to save all the plants in the world.
PLANTS of Central Africa
But ME?
I want my friends to like me. I want to have my first kiss.

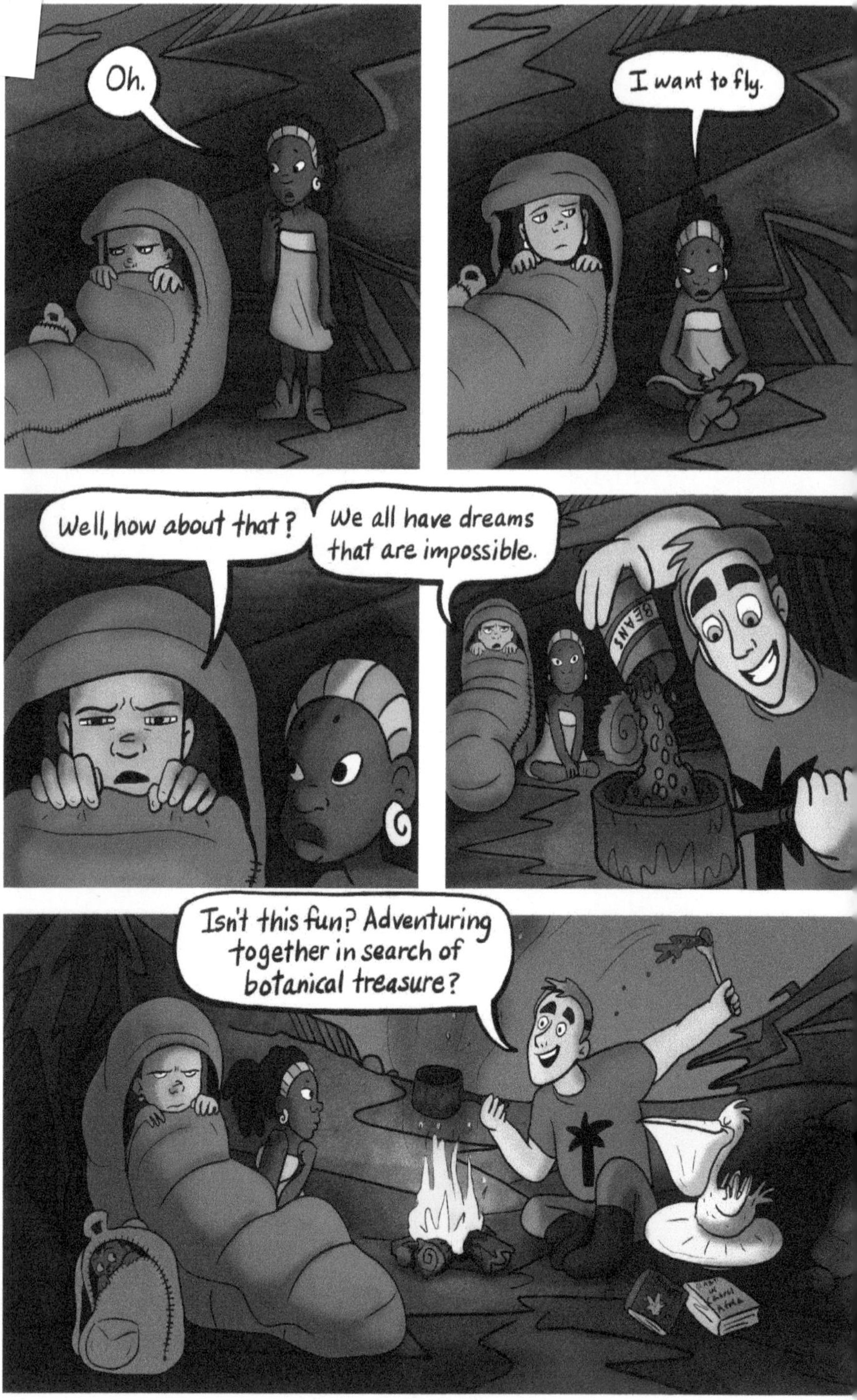
Oh.
I want to fly.
Well, how about that?
We all have dreams that are impossible.
BEANS
Isn't this fun? Adventuring together in search of botanical treasure?

I wonder if we'll see cycads.

Those are prehistoric plants, you know...

dating back millions of years.

Older than dinosaurs even!

Some regions of central Africa are said to have dozens of endemic cycad species.

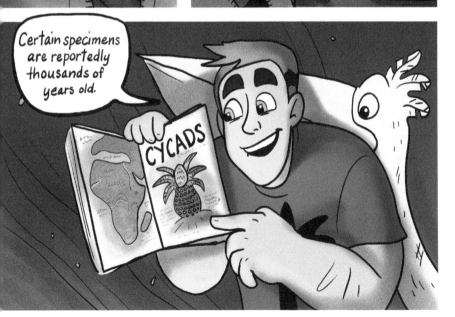

Certain specimens are reportedly thousands of years old.

CYCADS

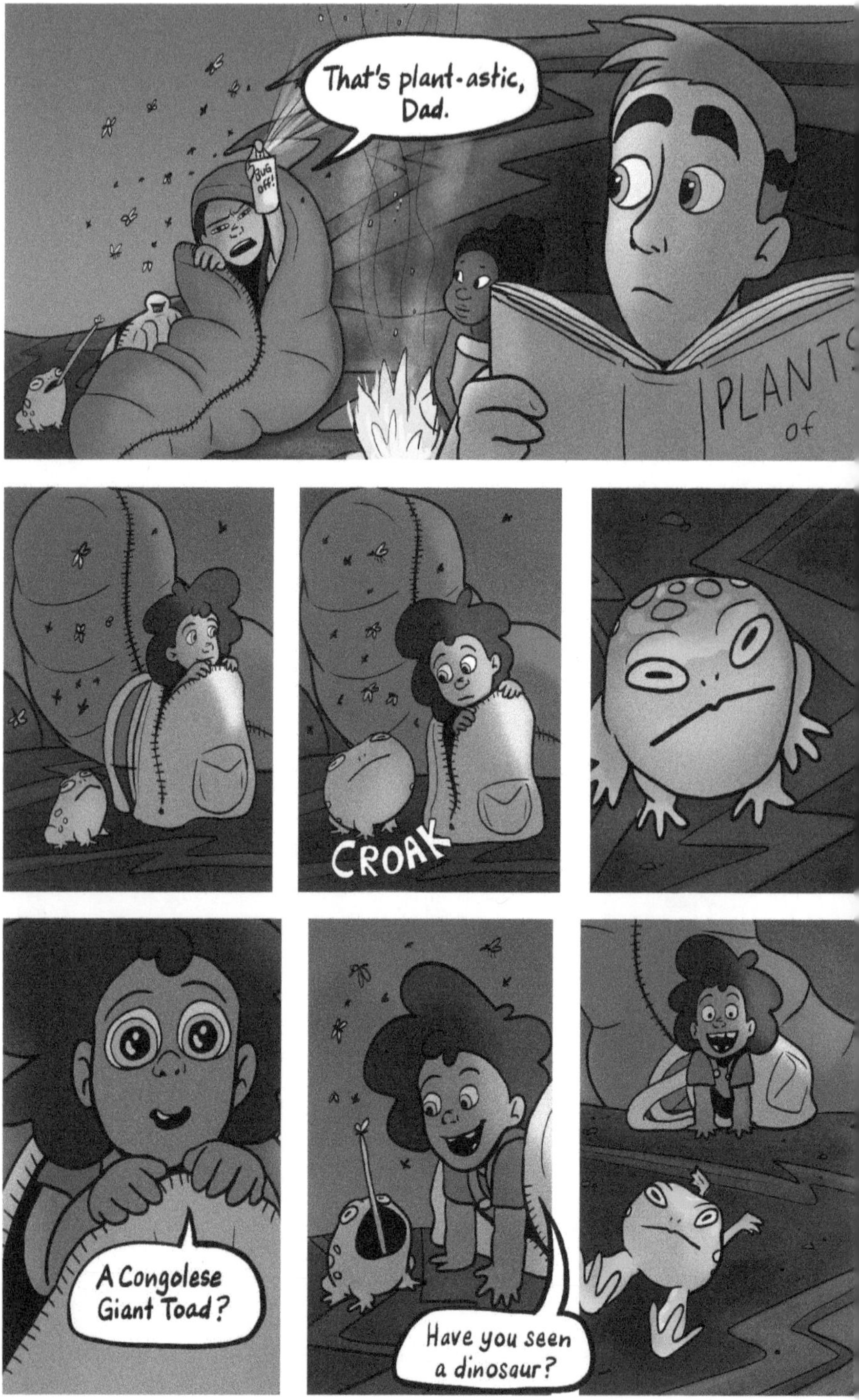
That's plant-astic, Dad.
BUG OFF!
PLANTS of
CROAK
A Congolese Giant Toad?
Have you seen a dinosaur?

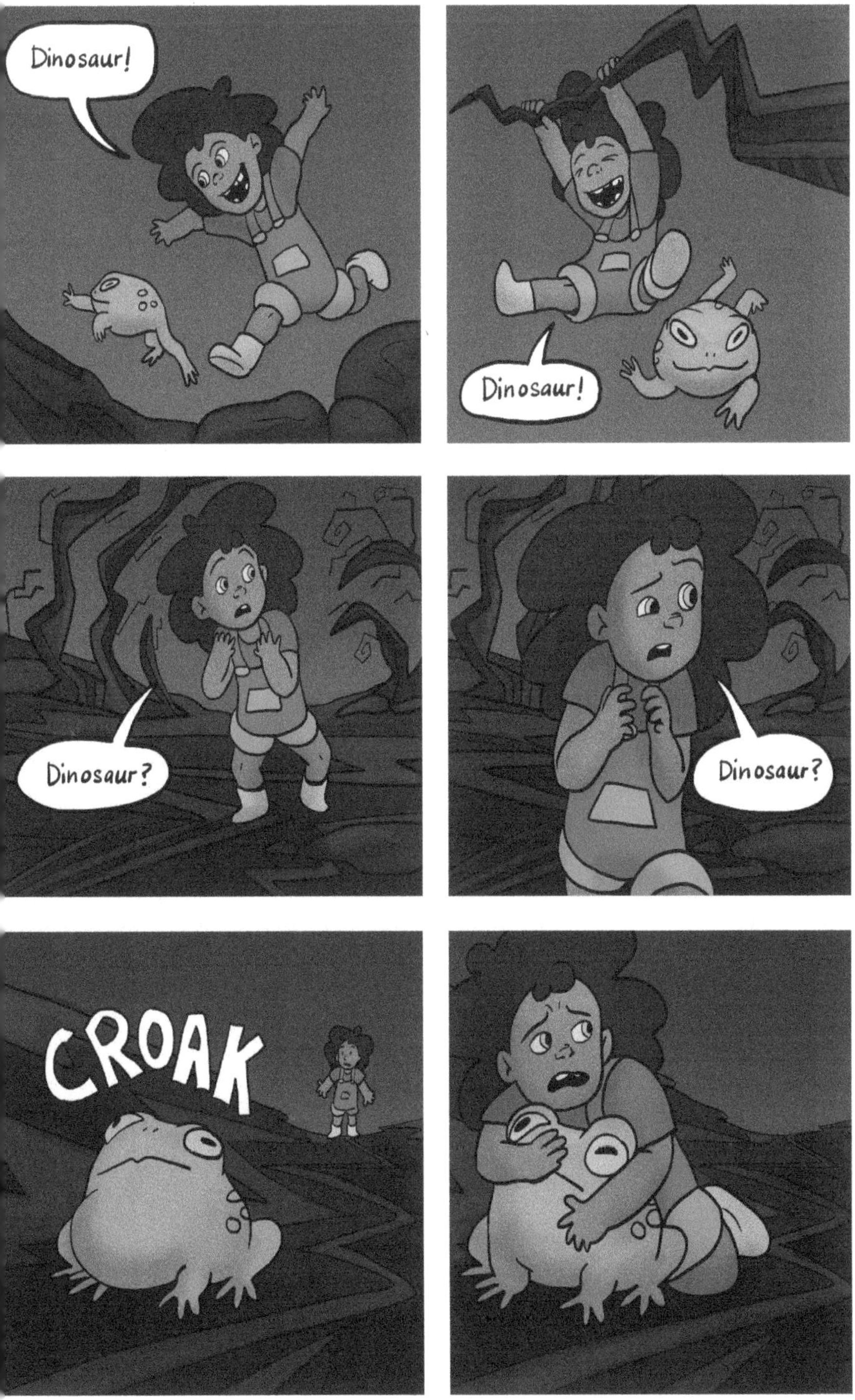
Dinosaur!
Dinosaur!
Dinosaur?
Dinosaur?
CROAK

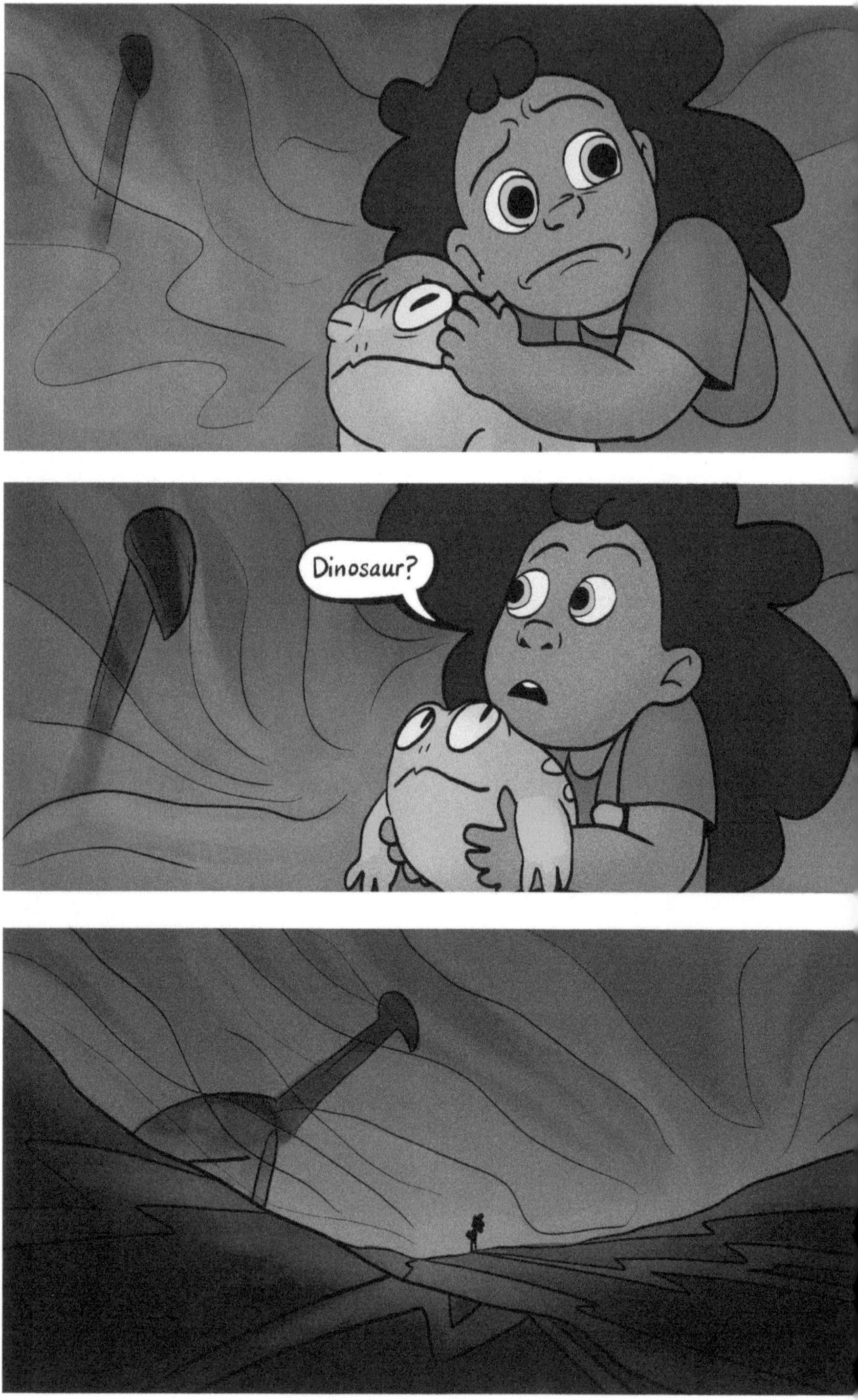
Dinosaur?

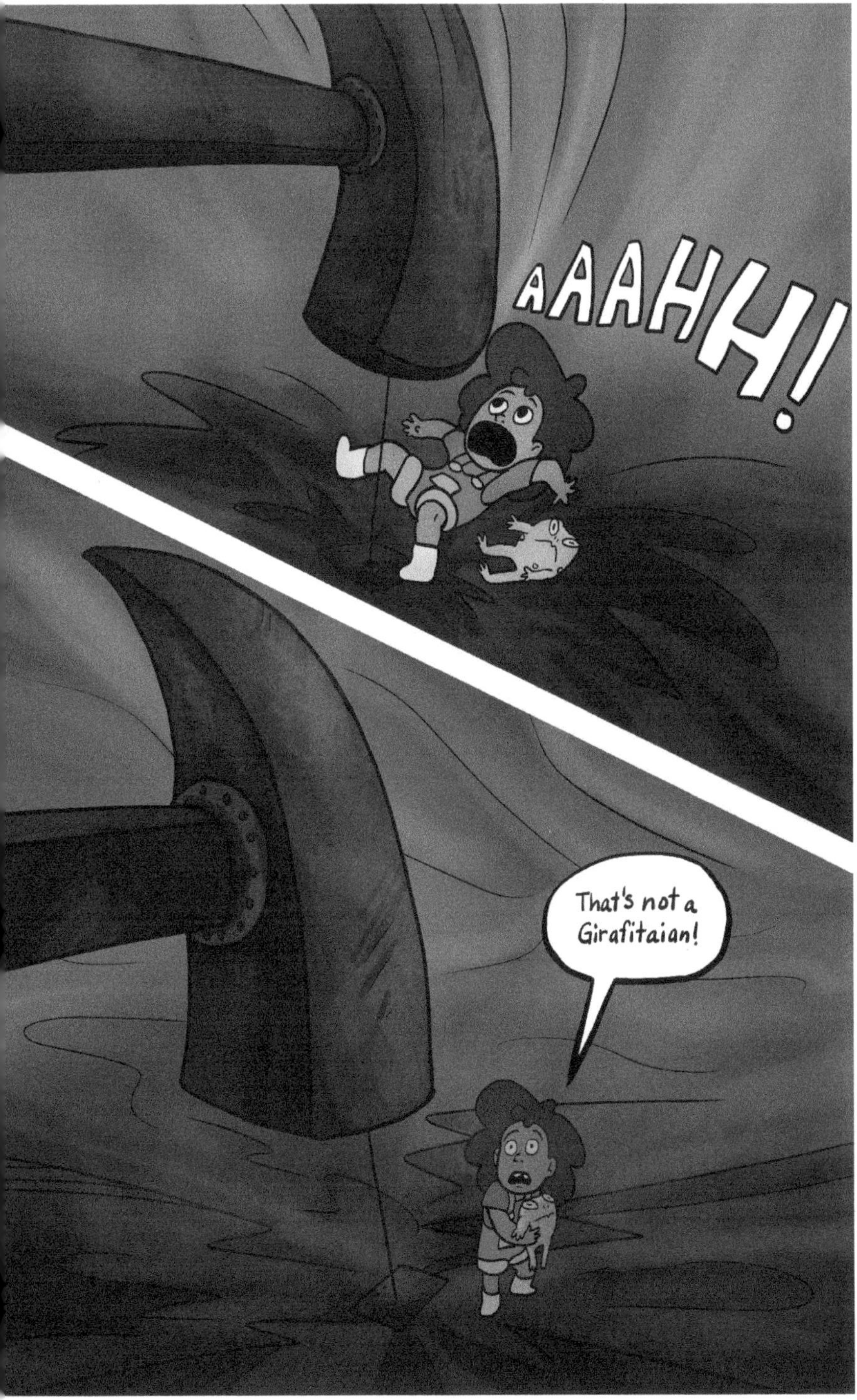
AAAHH!
That's not a Girafitaian!

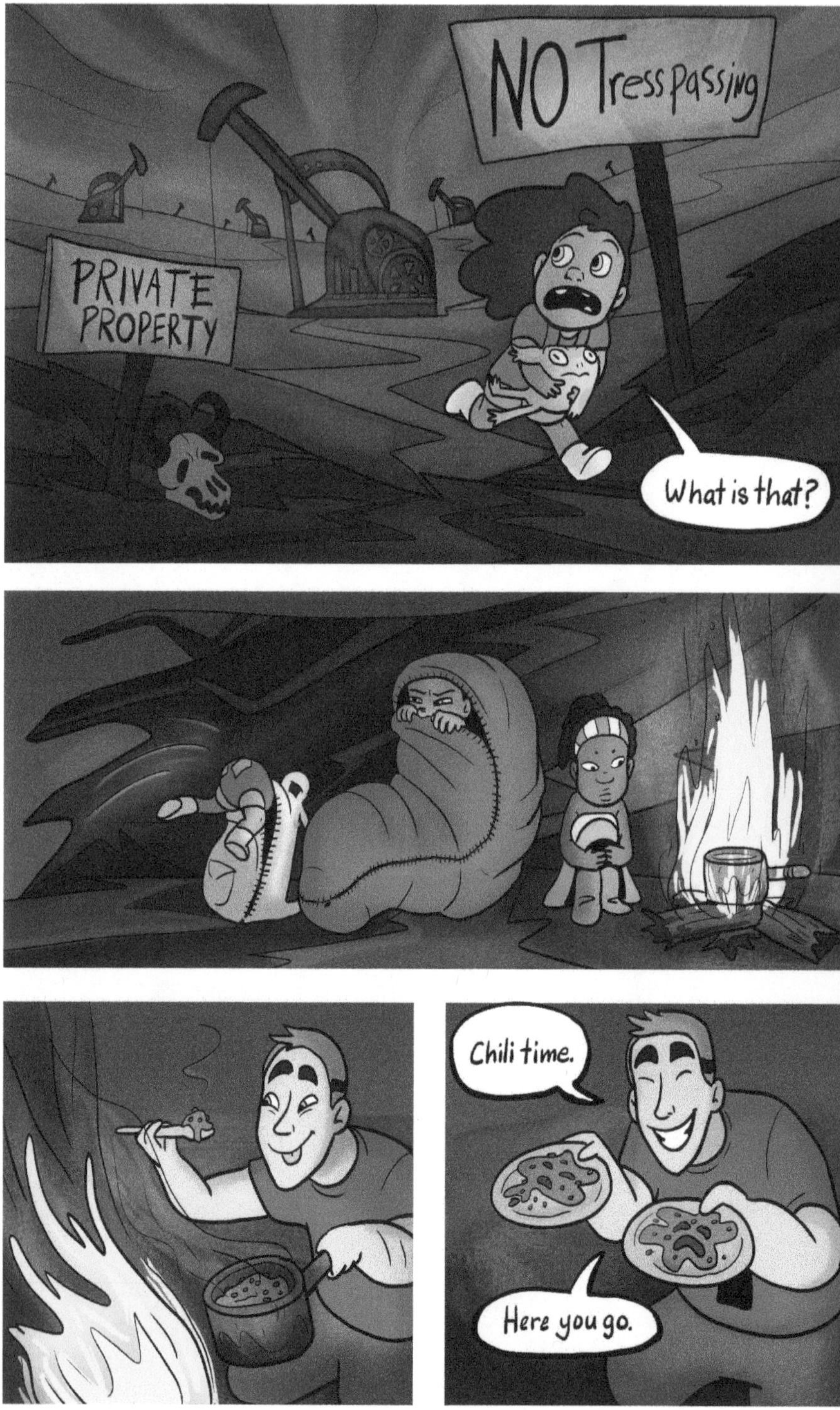
NO Tresspassing
PRIVATE PROPERTY
What is that?
Chili time.
Here you go.

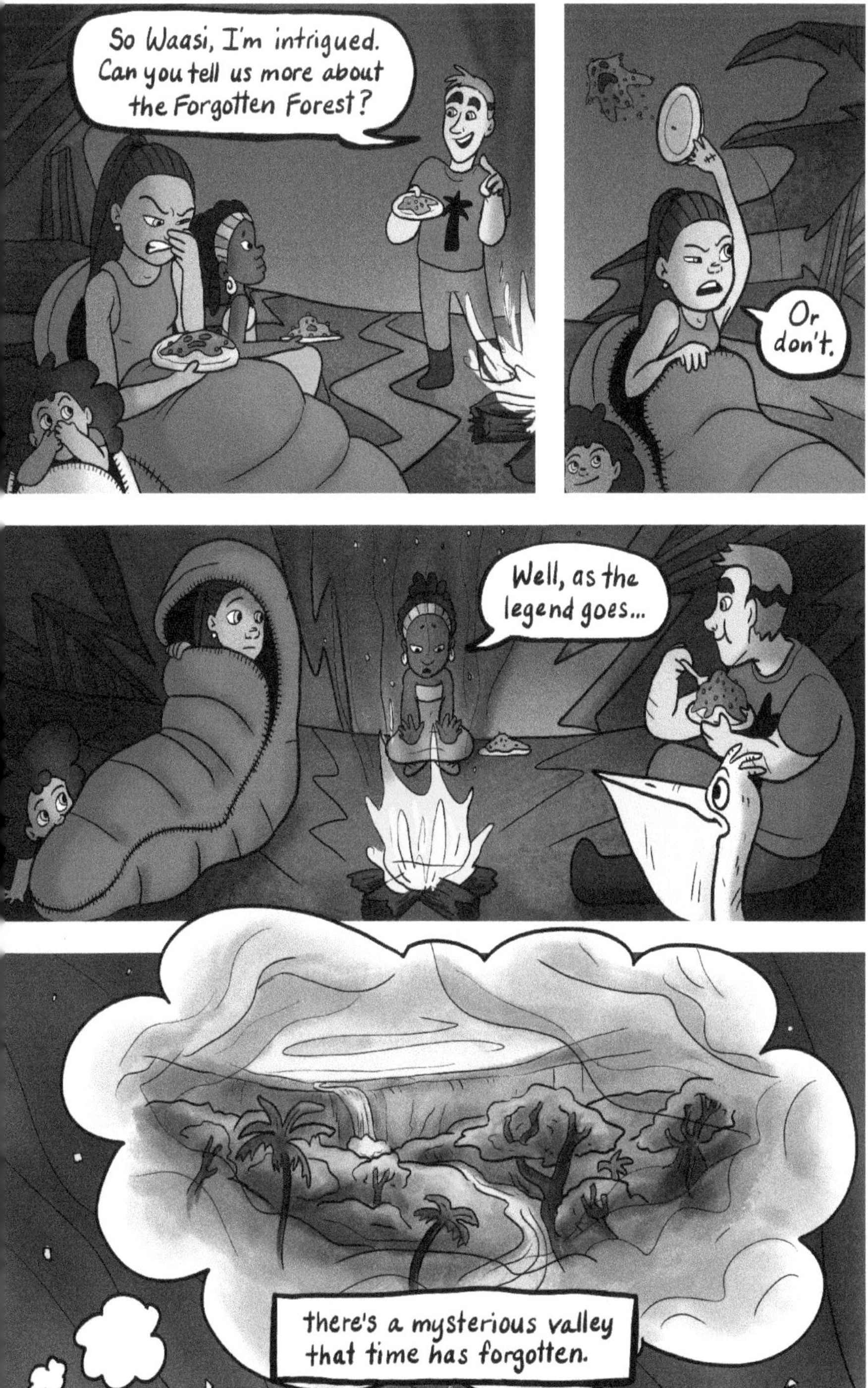
So Waasi, I'm intrigued. Can you tell us more about the Forgotten Forest?
Or don't.
Well, as the legend goes...
there's a mysterious valley that time has forgotten.

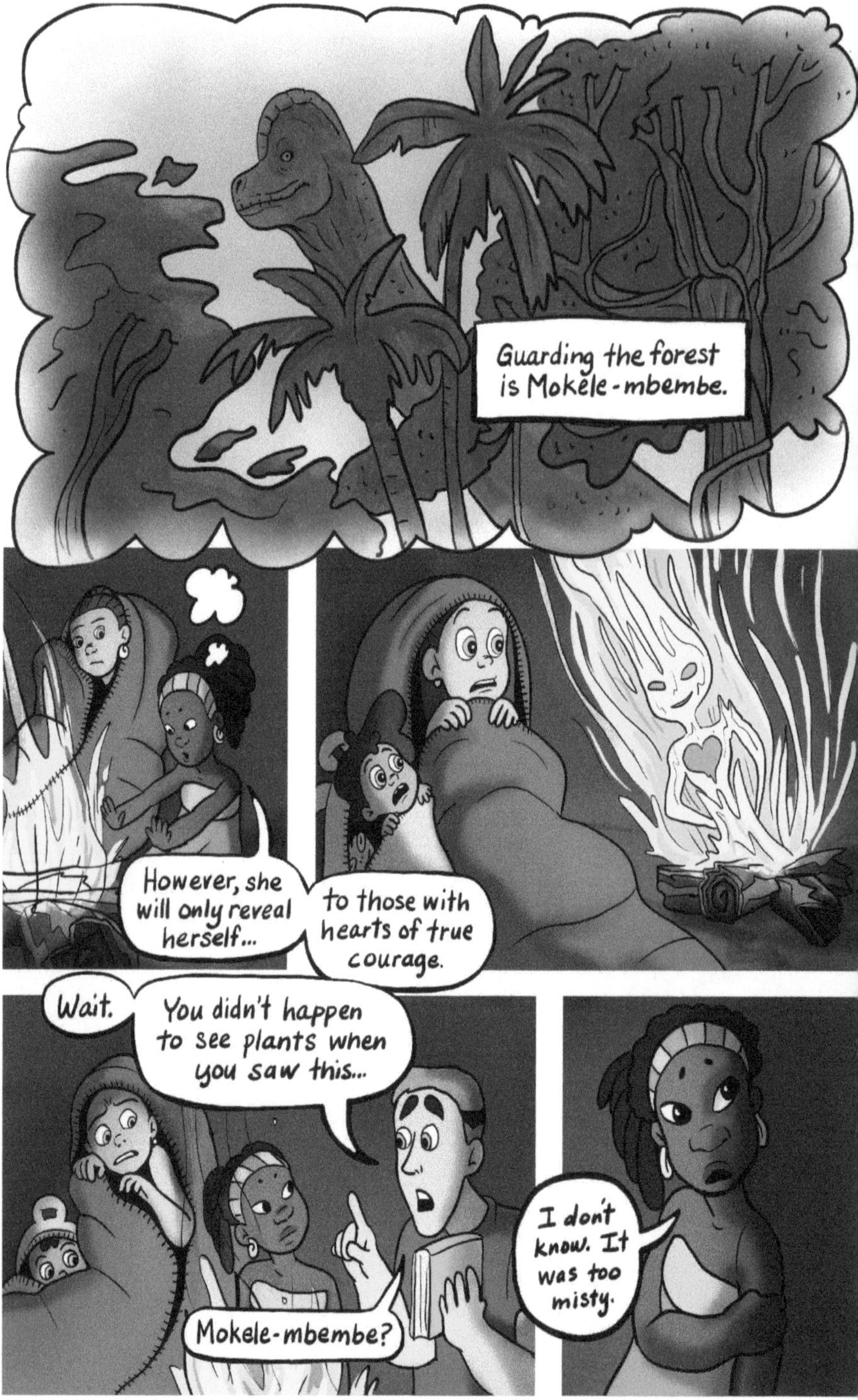
Guarding the forest is Mokele-mbembe.
However, she will only reveal herself...
to those with hearts of true courage.
Wait.
You didn't happen to see plants when you saw this...
Mokele-mbembe?
I don't know. It was too misty.

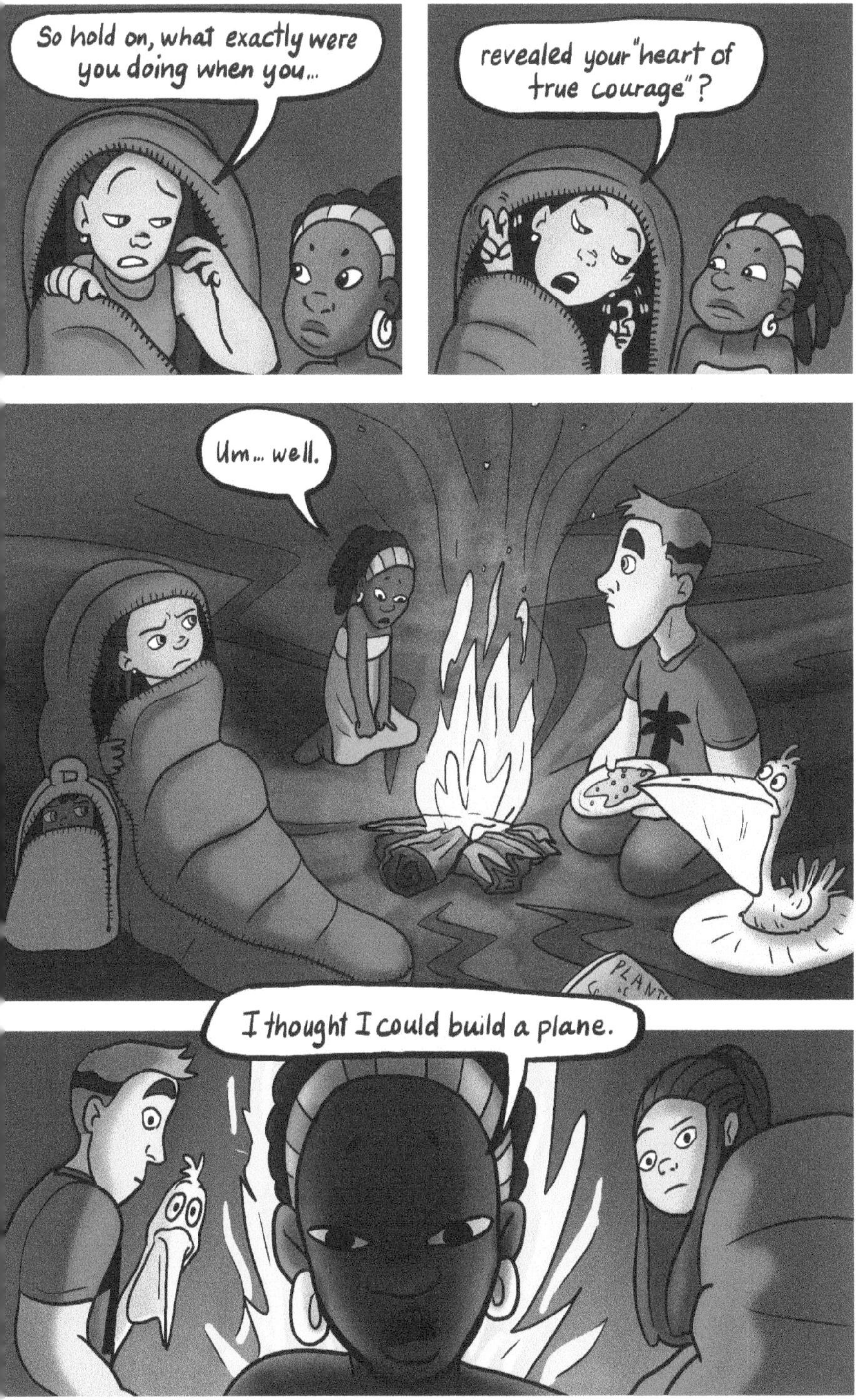
So hold on, what exactly were you doing when you...
revealed your "heart of true courage"?
Um... well.
I thought I could build a plane.

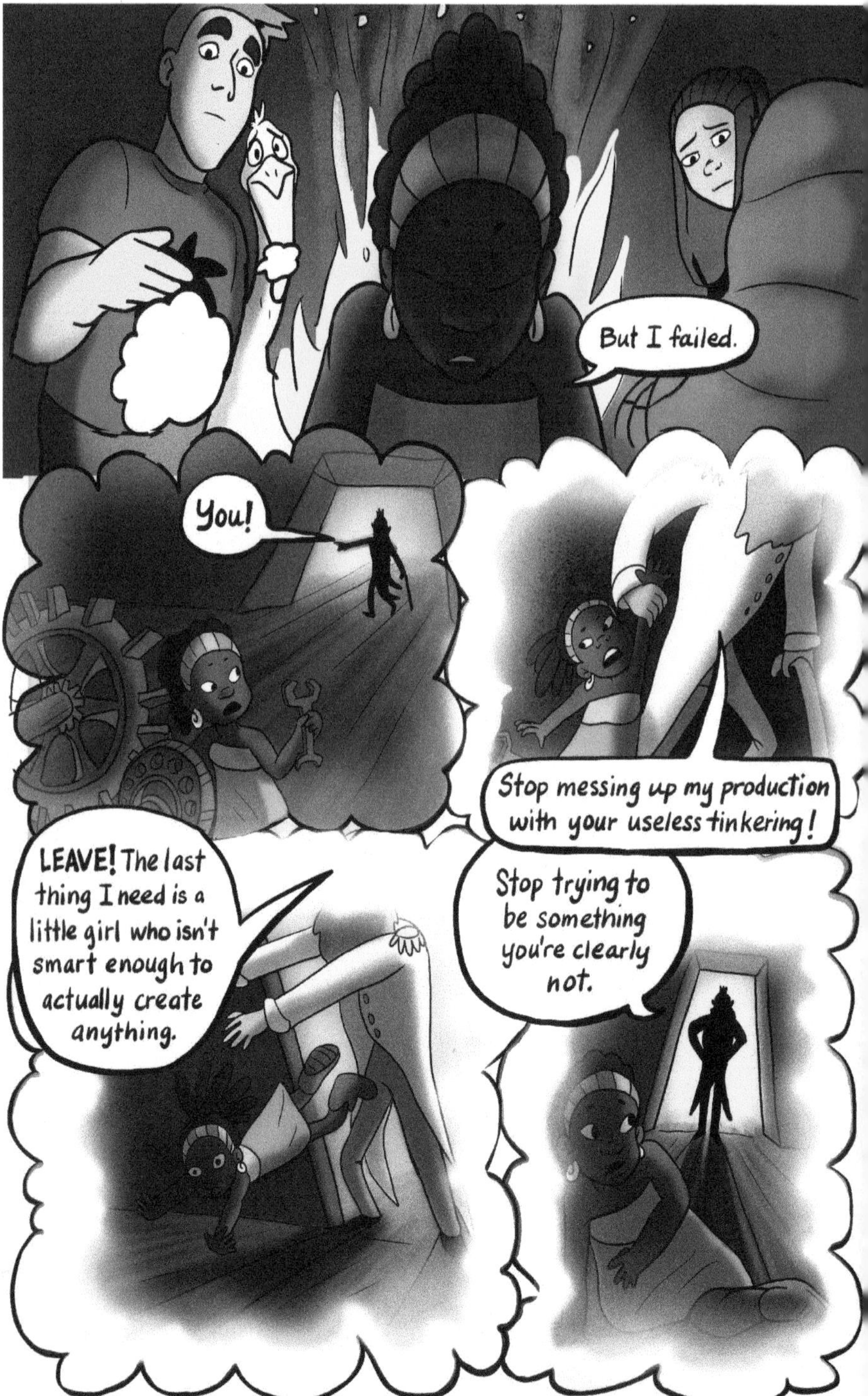
But I failed.
You!
Stop messing up my production with your useless tinkering!
LEAVE! The last thing I need is a little girl who isn't smart enough to actually create anything.
Stop trying to be something you're clearly not.

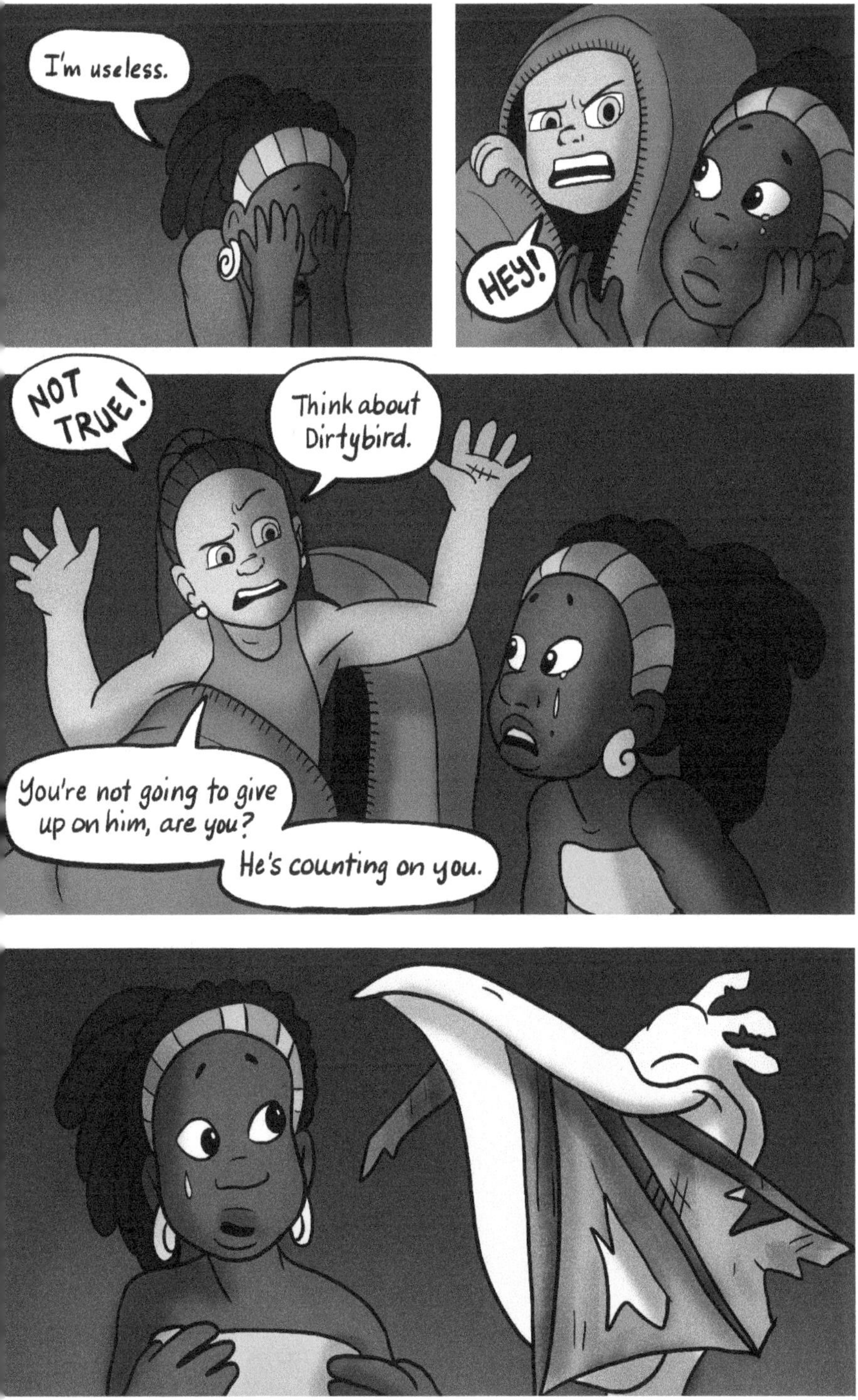
I'm useless.
HEY!
NOT TRUE!
Think about Dirtybird.
You're not going to give up on him, are you?
He's counting on you.

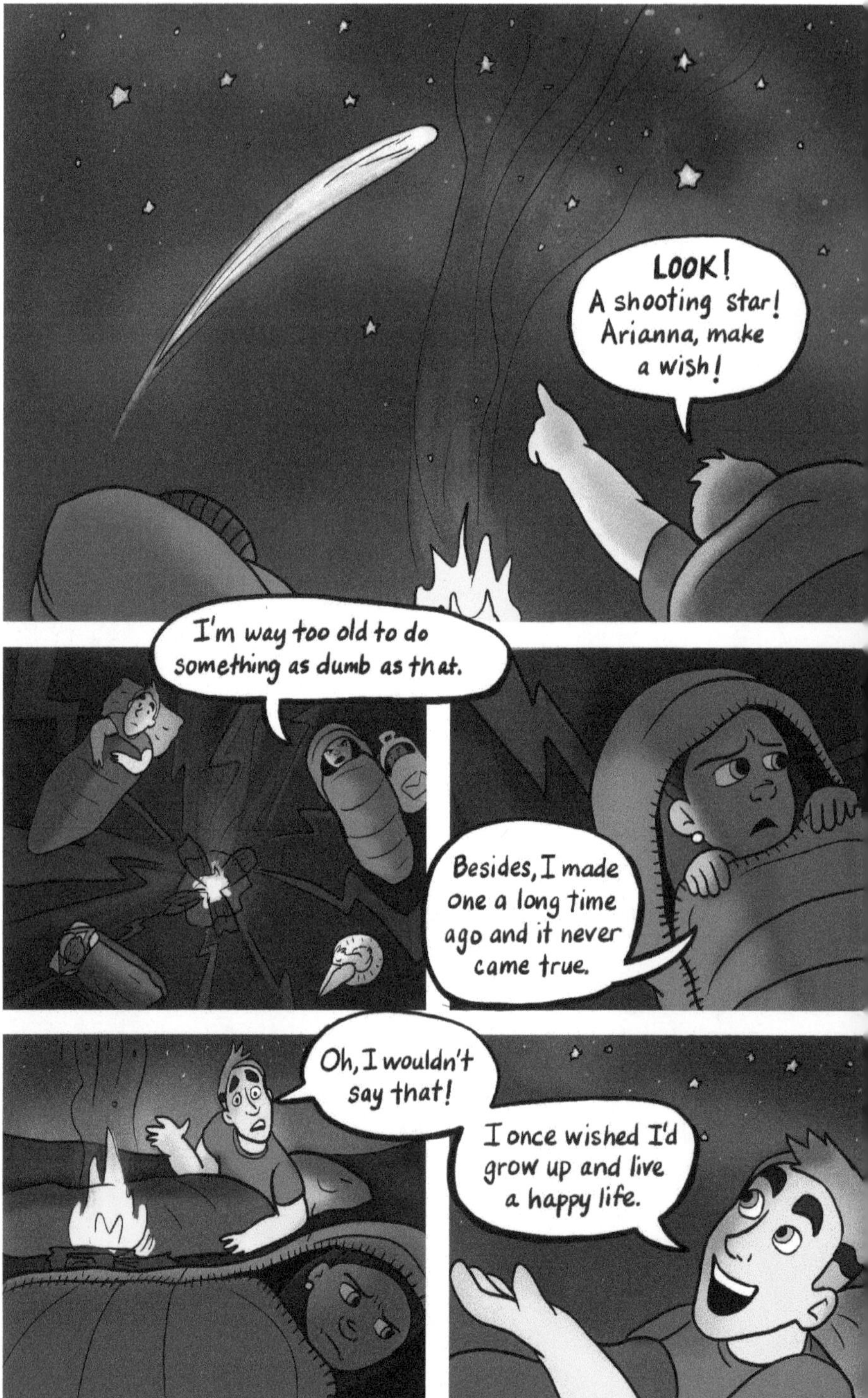
LOOK! A shooting star! Arianna, make a wish!
I'm way too old to do something as dumb as that.
Besides, I made one a long time ago and it never came true.
Oh, I wouldn't say that!
I once wished I'd grow up and live a happy life.

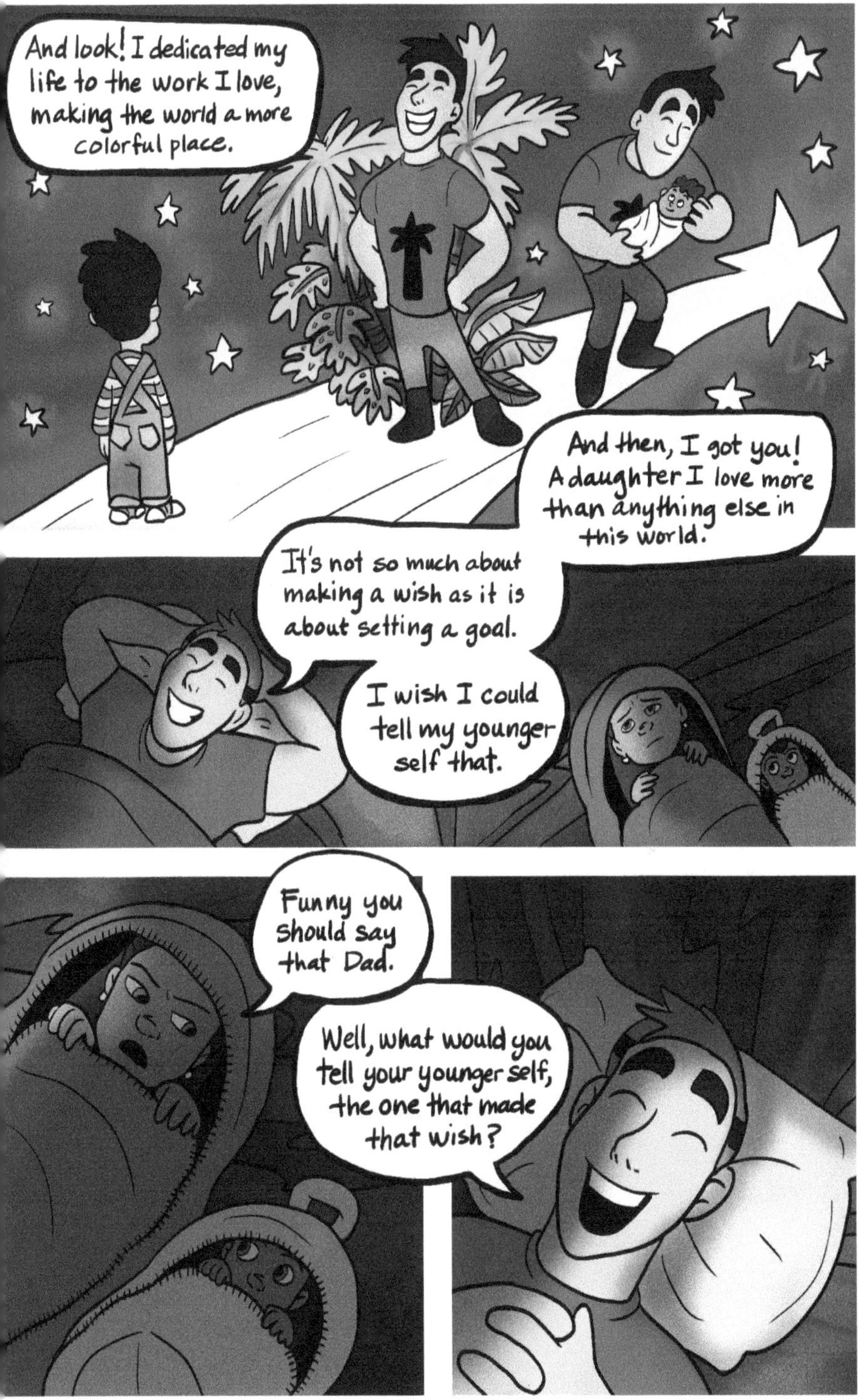
And look! I dedicated my life to the work I love, making the world a more colorful place.
And then, I got you! A daughter I love more than anything else in this world.
It's not so much about making a wish as it is about setting a goal.
I wish I could tell my younger self that.
Funny you should say that Dad.
Well, what would you tell your younger self, the one that made that wish?

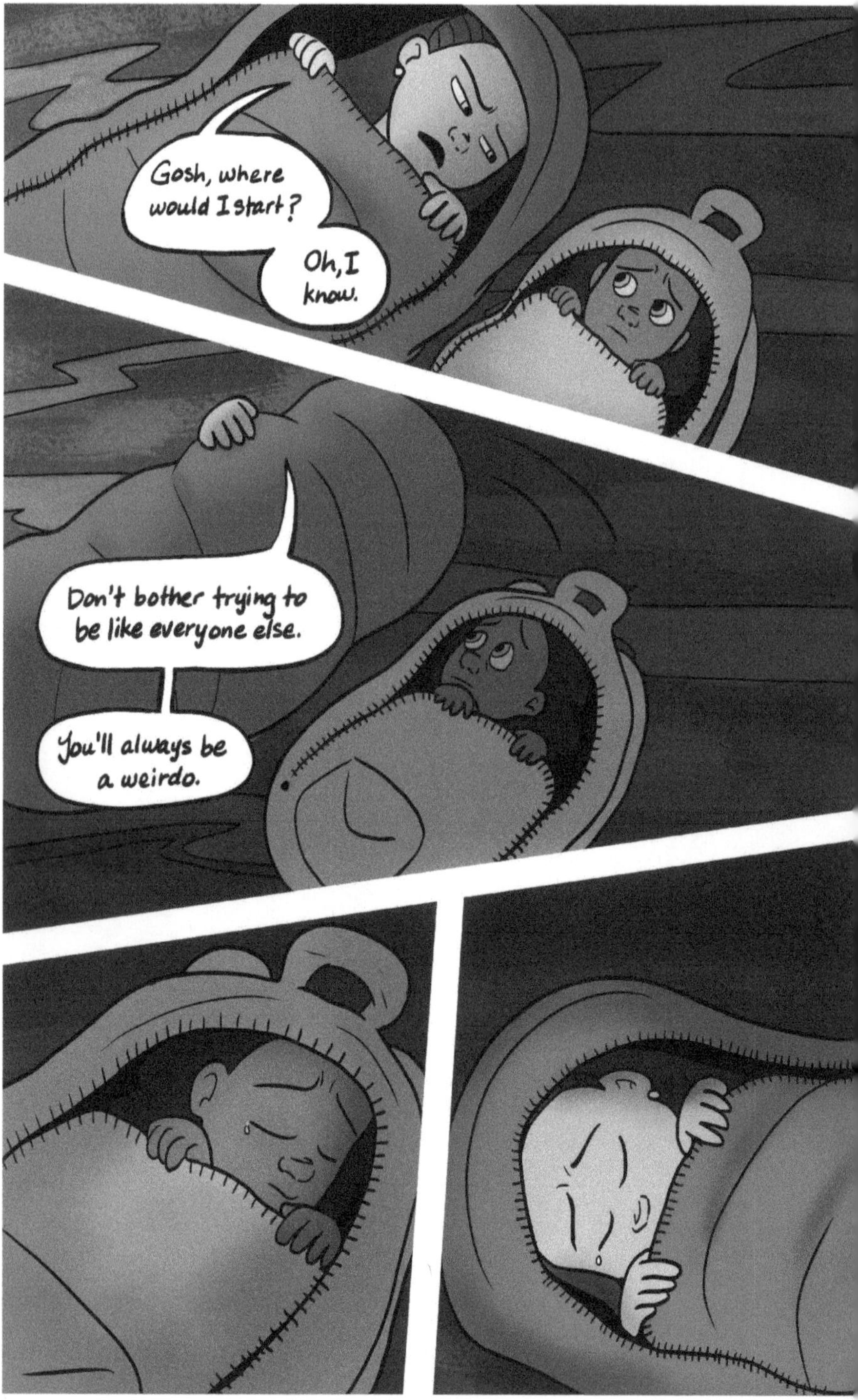
Gosh, where would I start?
Oh, I know.
Don't bother trying to be like everyone else.
You'll always be a weirdo.

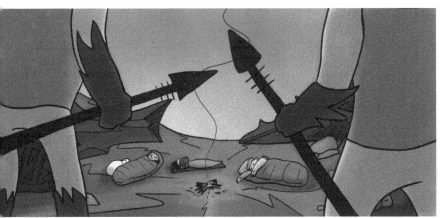

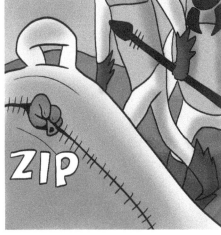

ZIP

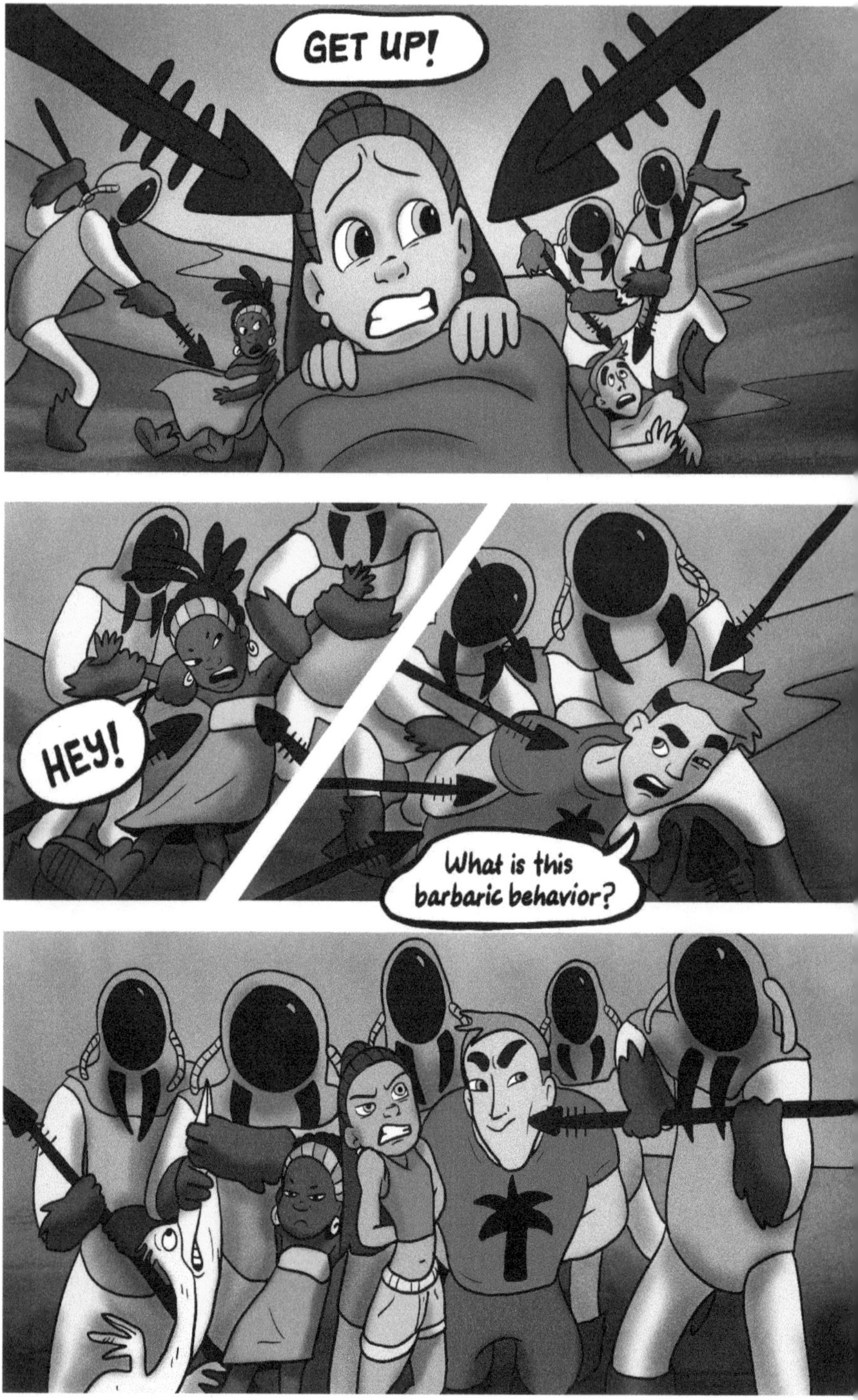
GET UP!
HEY!
What is this barbaric behavior?

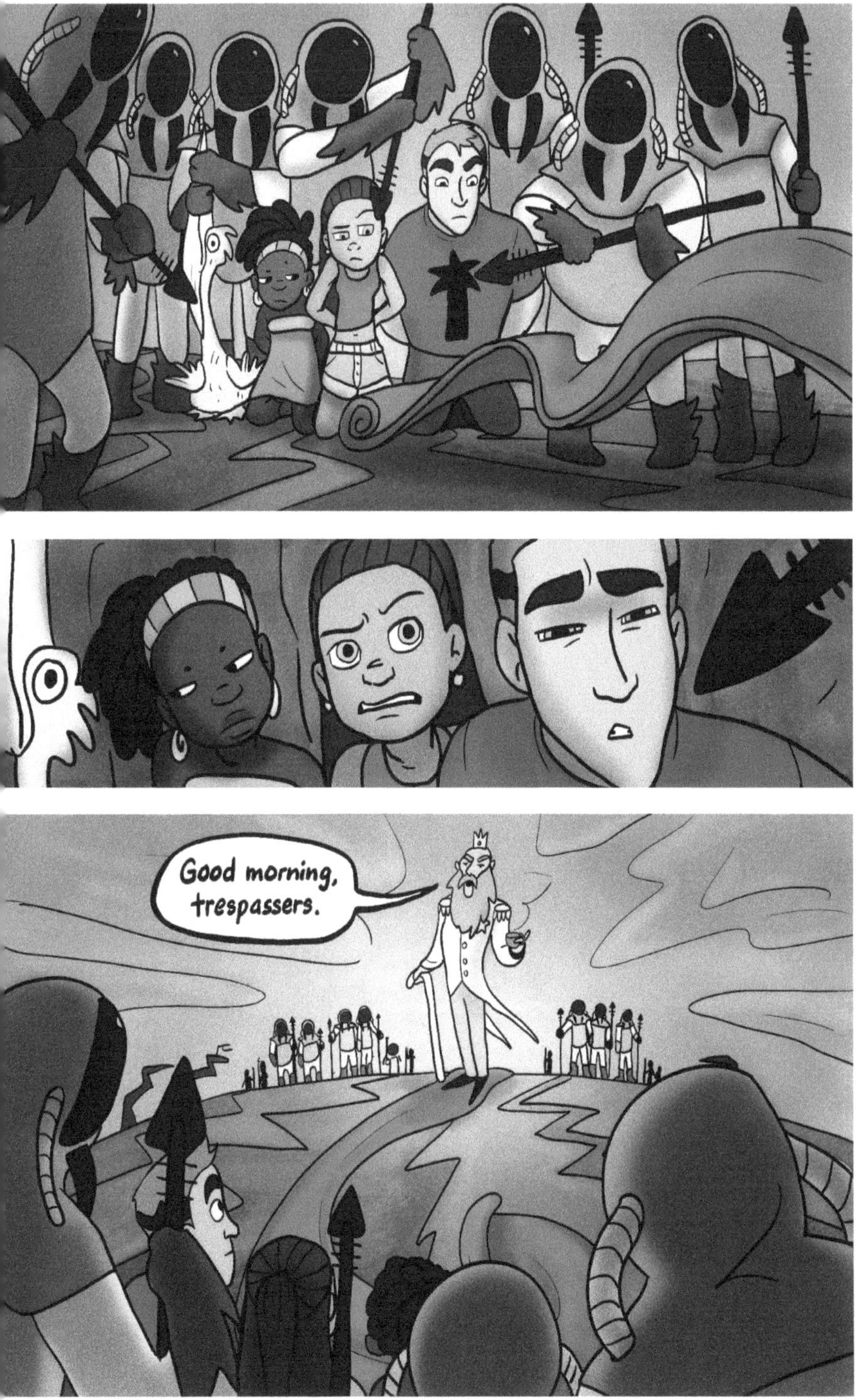
Good morning, trespassers.

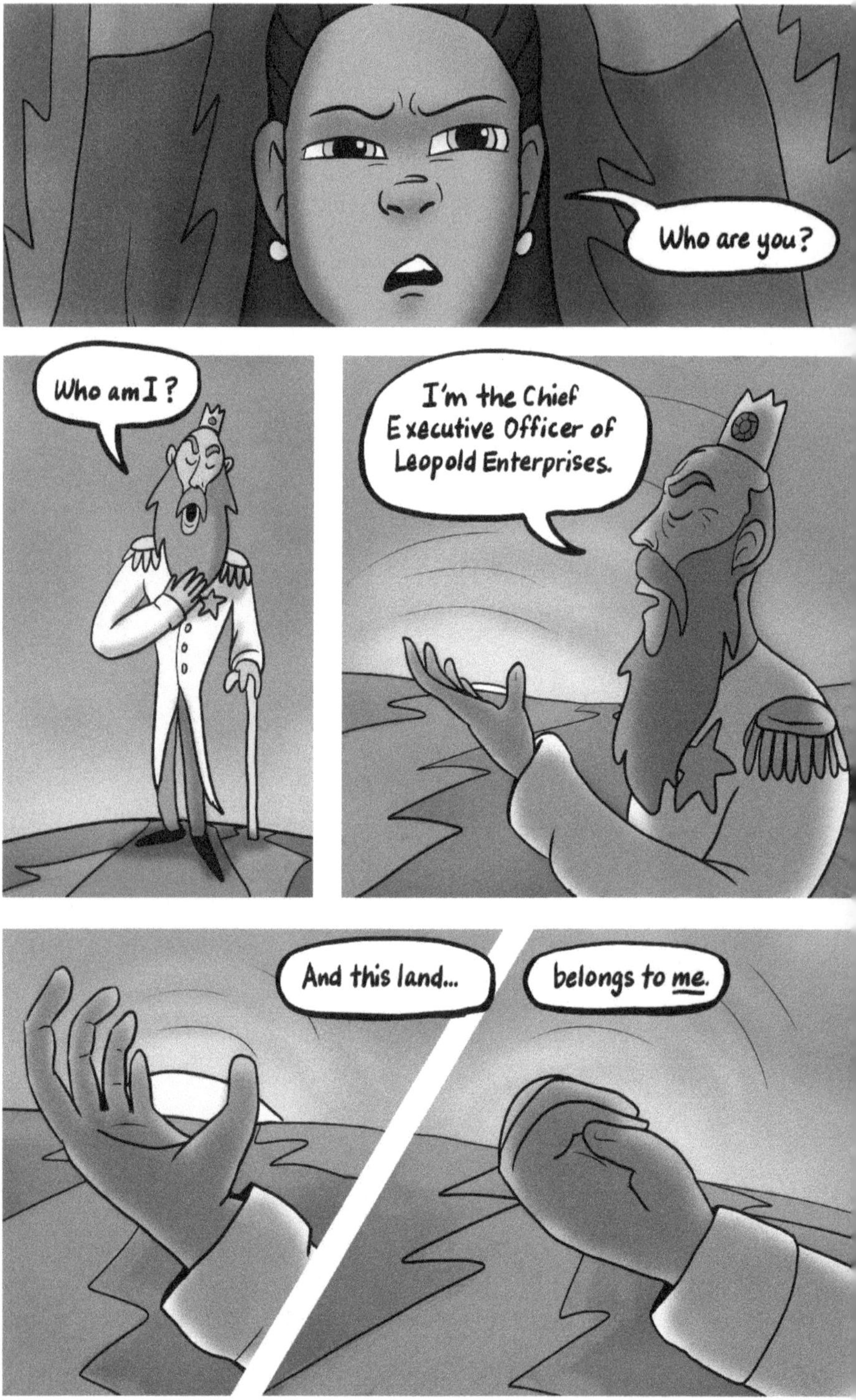
Who are you?
Who am I?
I'm the Chief Executive Officer of Leopold Enterprises.
And this land...
belongs to me.

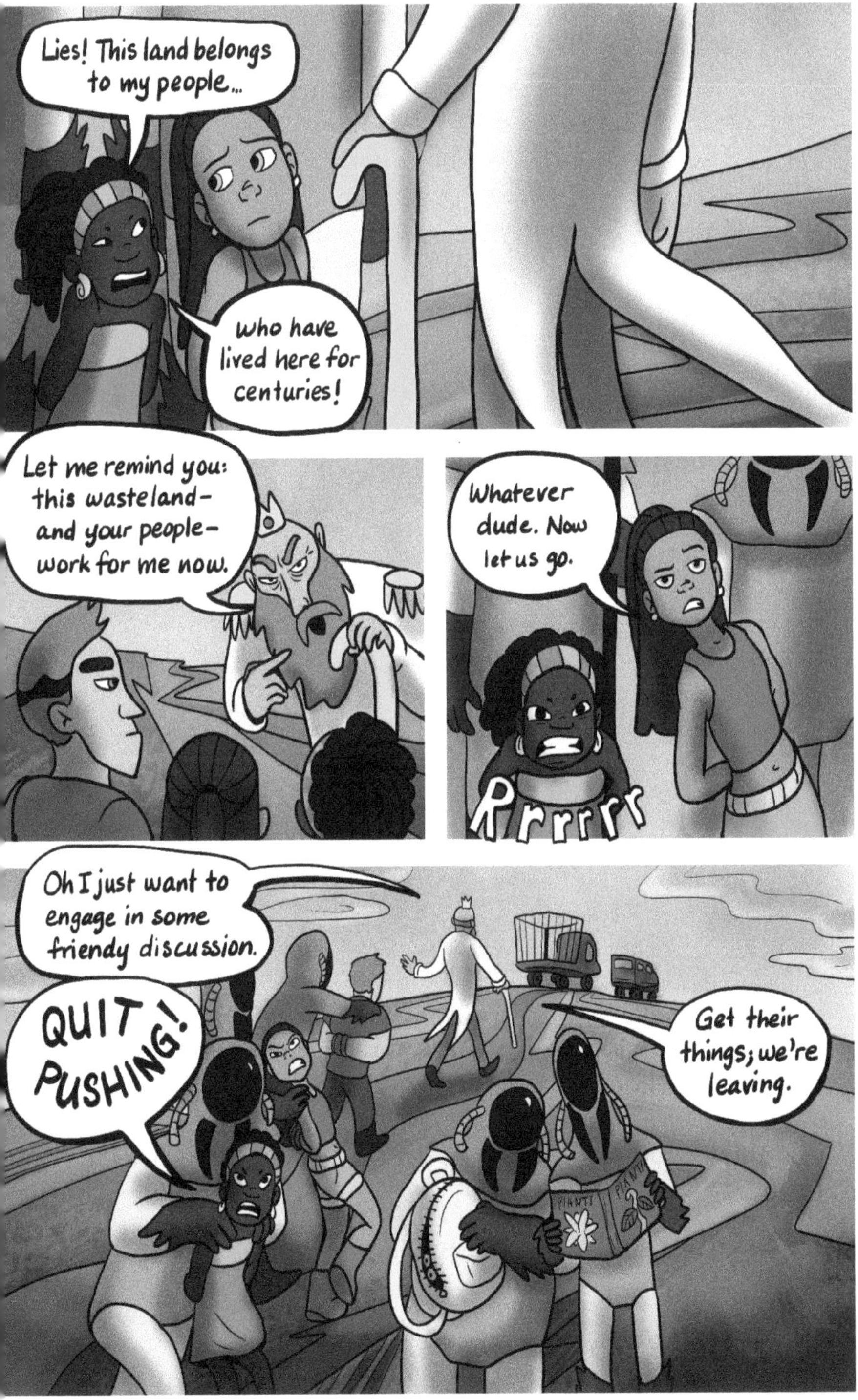
Lies! This land belongs to my people...
who have lived here for centuries!
Let me remind you: this wasteland- and your people- work for me now.
Whatever dude. Now let us go.
Rrrrrr
Oh I just want to engage in some friendy discussion.
QUIT PUSHING!
Get their things; we're leaving.

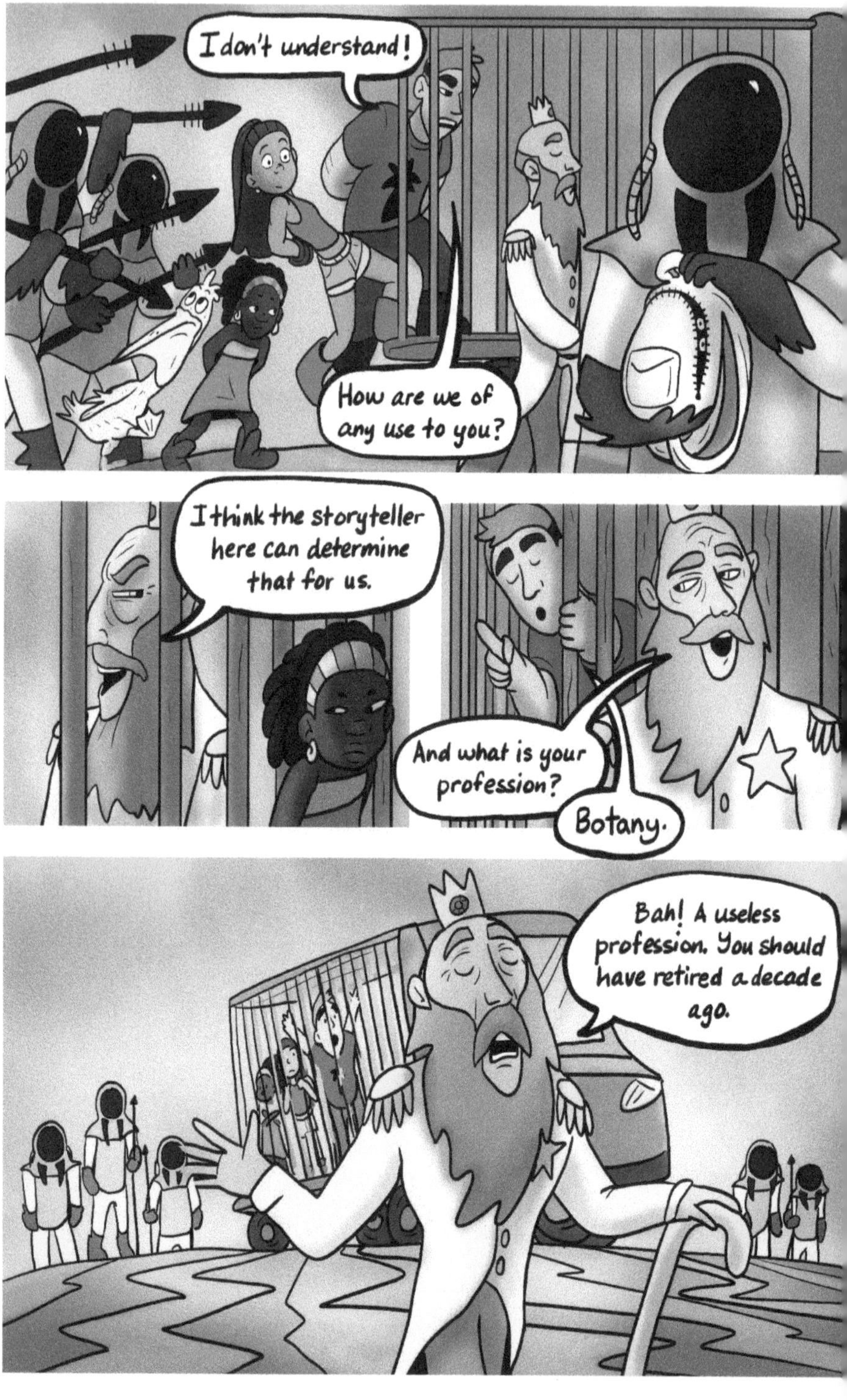
I don't understand!
How are we of any use to you?
I think the storyteller here can determine that for us.
And what is your profession?
Botany.
Bah! A useless profession. You should have retired a decade ago.

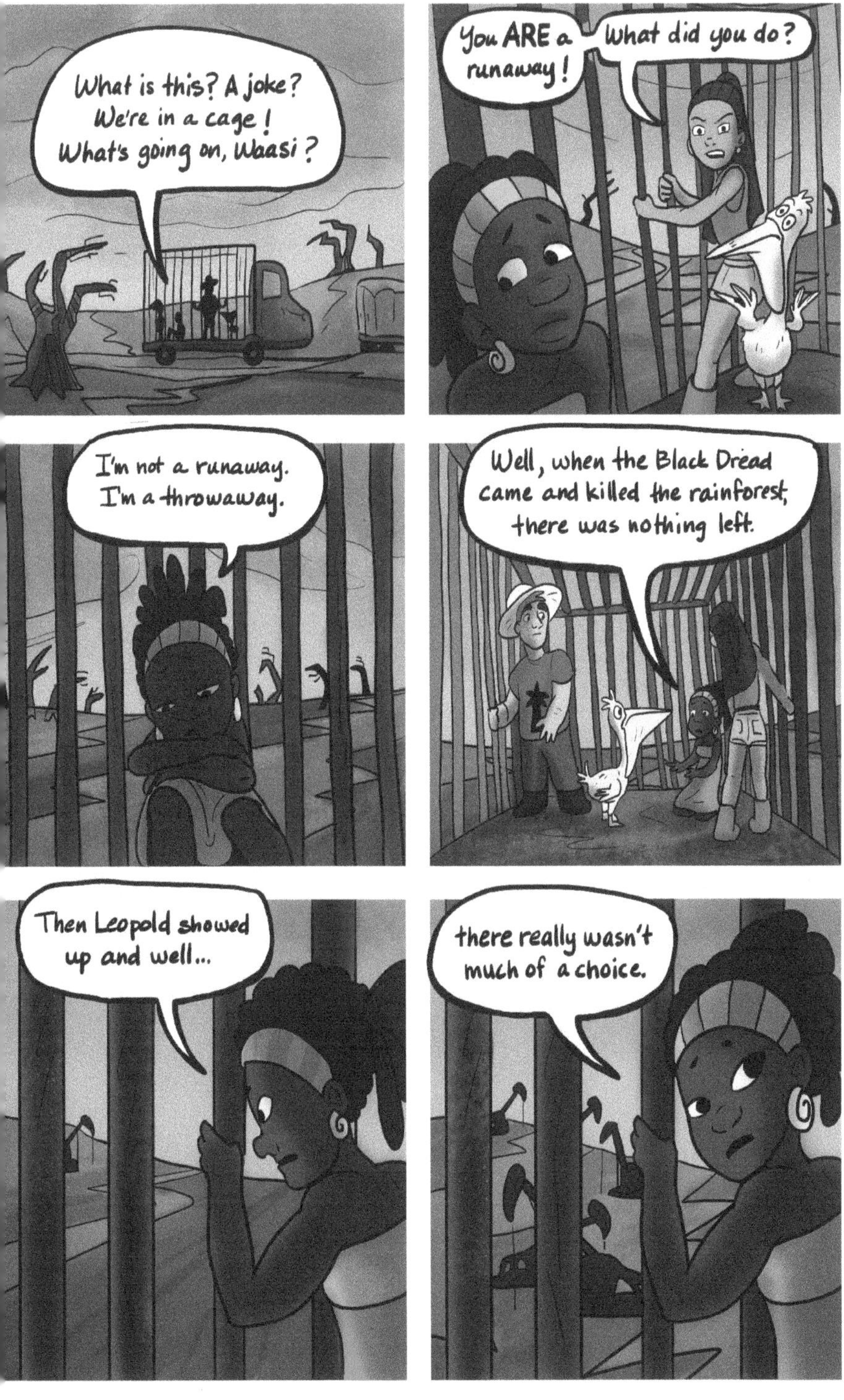
What is this? A joke? We're in a cage! What's going on, Waasi?
You ARE a runaway!
What did you do?
I'm not a runaway. I'm a throwaway.
Well, when the Black Dread came and killed the rainforest, there was nothing left.
Then Leopold showed up and well...
there really wasn't much of a choice.

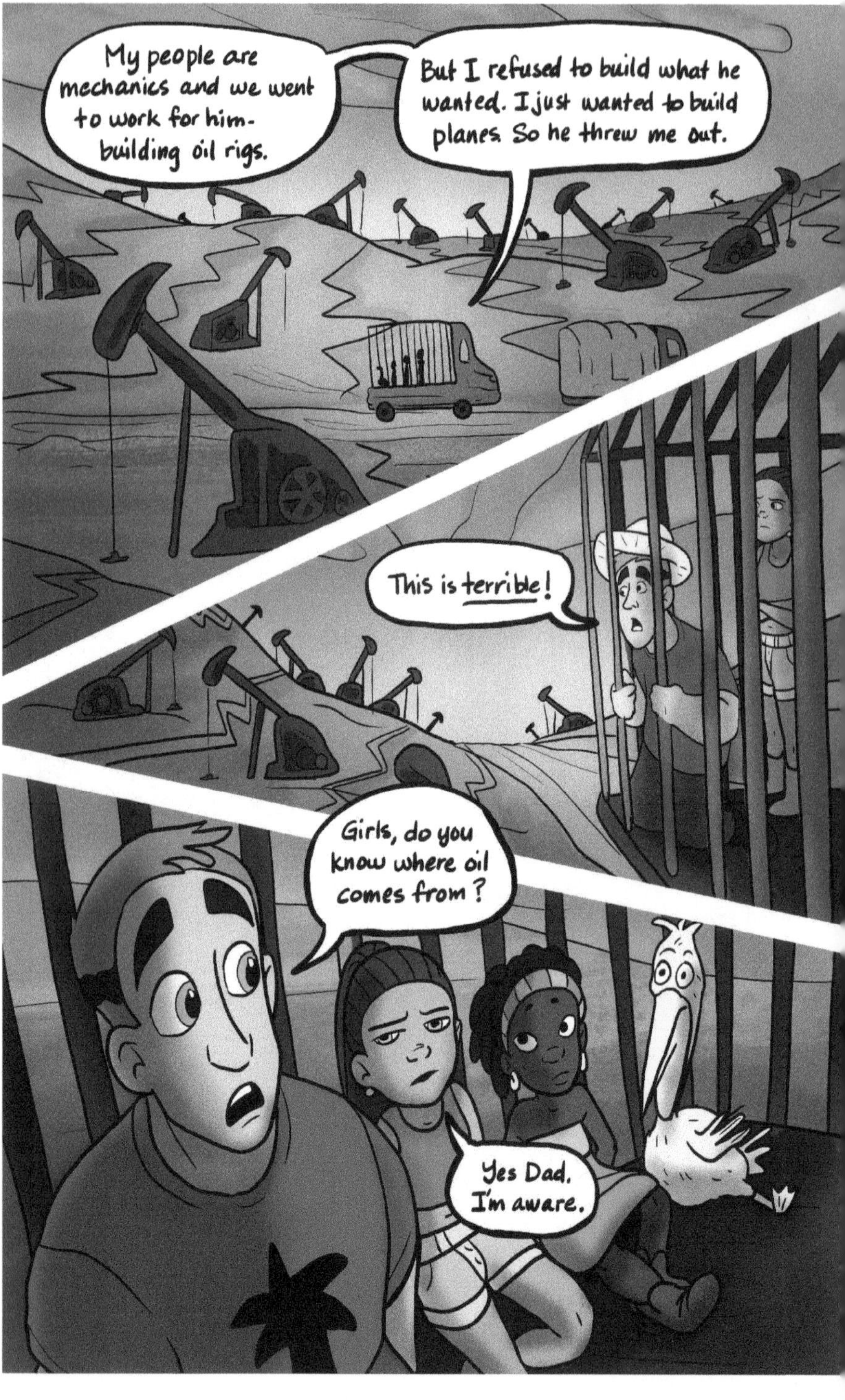
My people are mechanics and we went to work for him- building oil rigs.
But I refused to build what he wanted. I just wanted to build planes. So he threw me out.
This is terrible!
Girls, do you know where oil comes from?
Yes Dad. I'm aware.

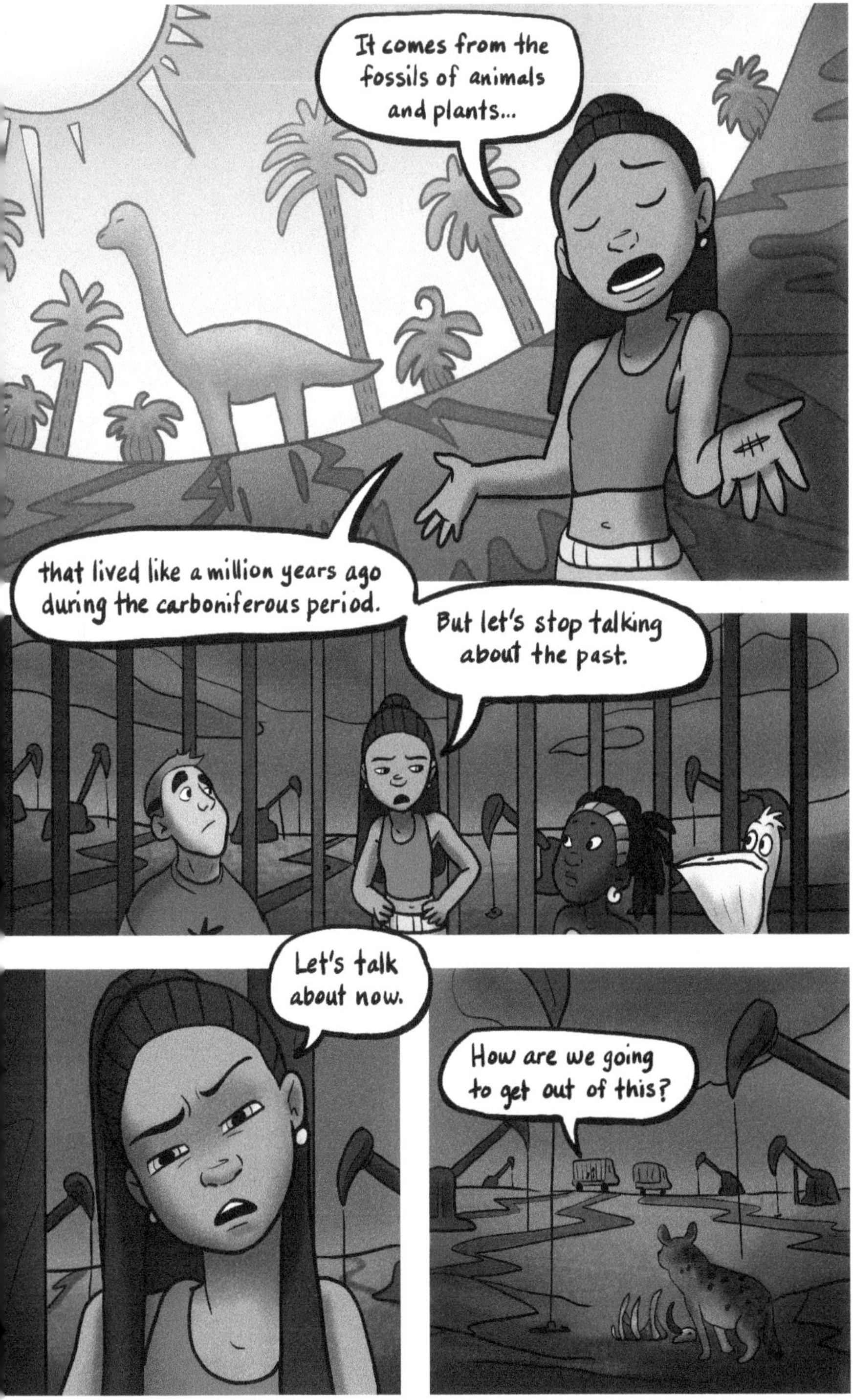
It comes from the fossils of animals and plants...
that lived like a million years ago during the carboniferous period.
But let's stop talking about the past.
Let's talk about now.
How are we going to get out of this?

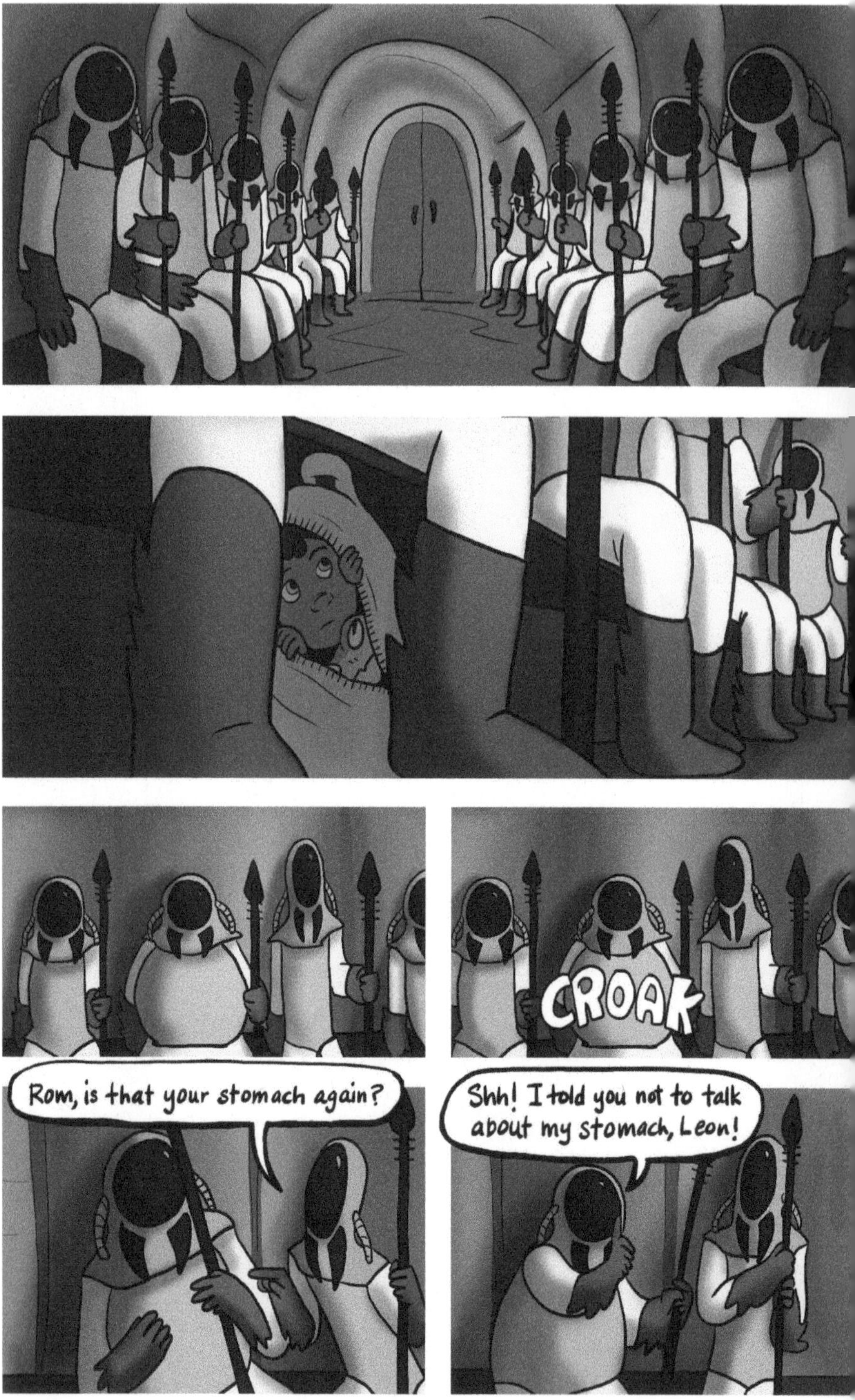
CROAK
Rom, is that your stomach again?
Shh! I told you not to talk about my stomach, Leon!

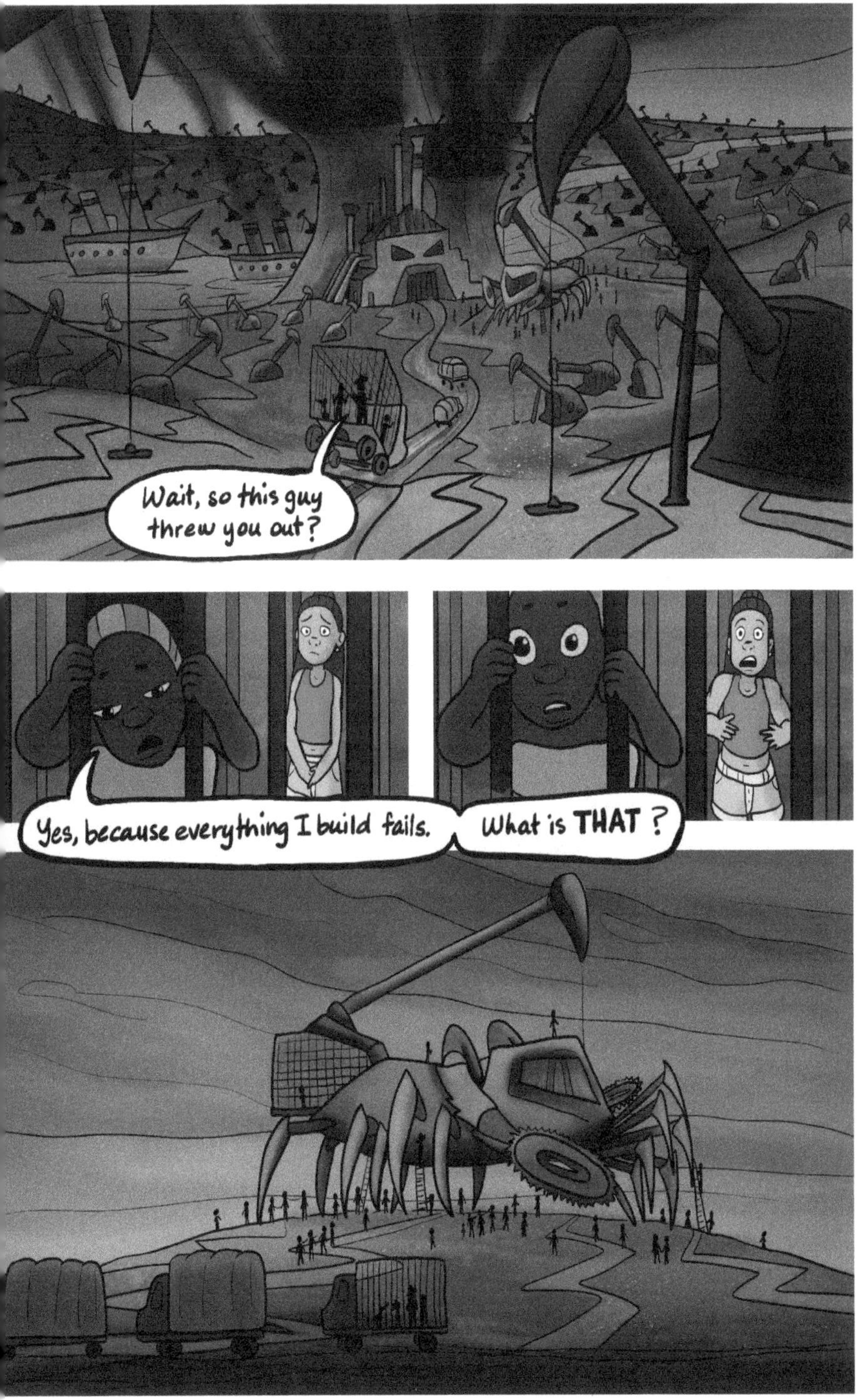
Wait, so this guy threw you out?
Yes, because everything I build fails.
What is THAT?

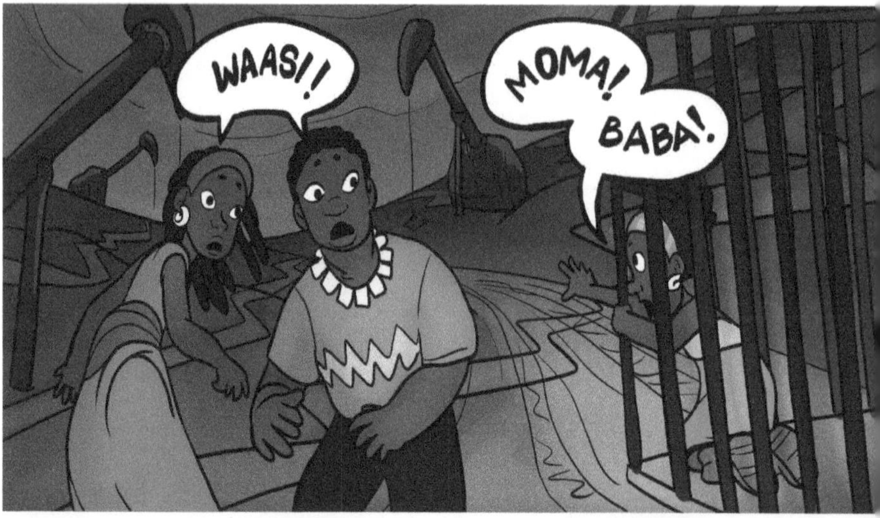
WAASI!!
MOMA! BABA!

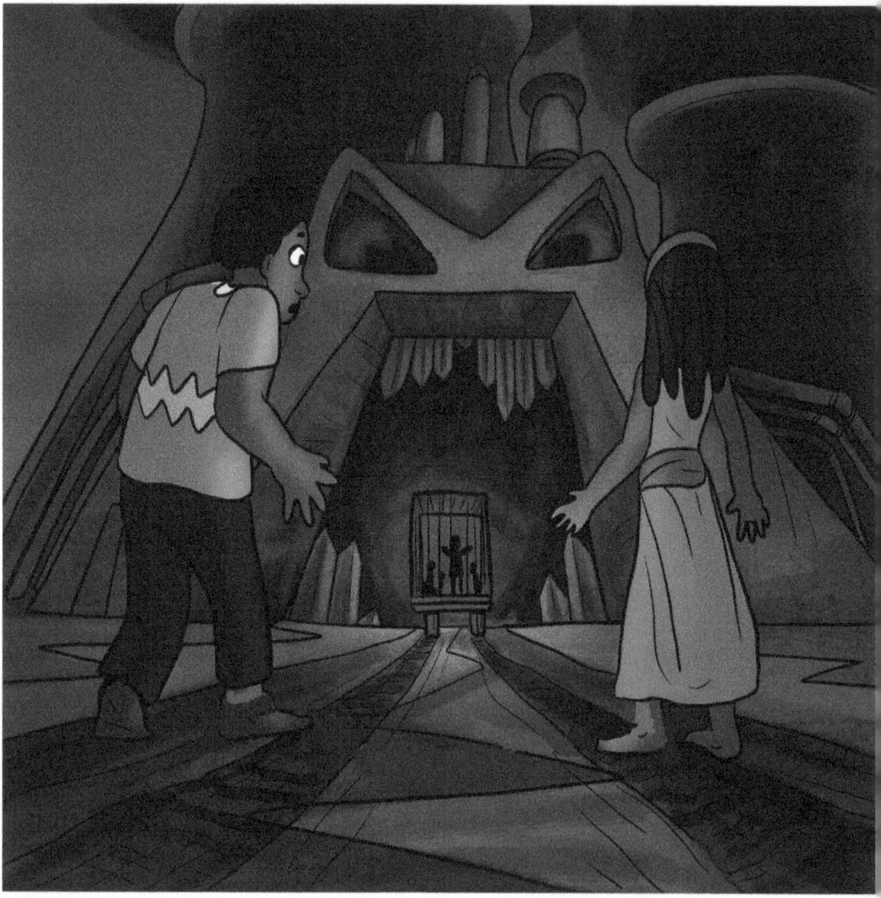

All right, old man. Cut to the chase. What do you want from us?
Yeah! What do you want?
What do I want?
I want to know the exact location of this valley.
TAP
TAP

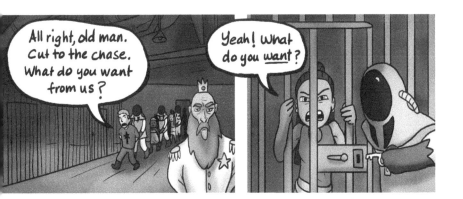

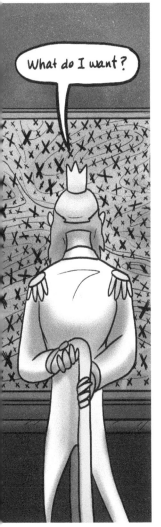

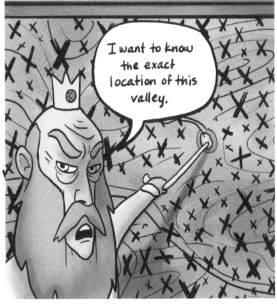

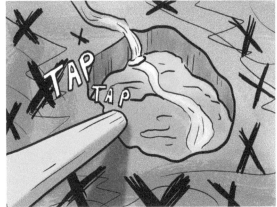

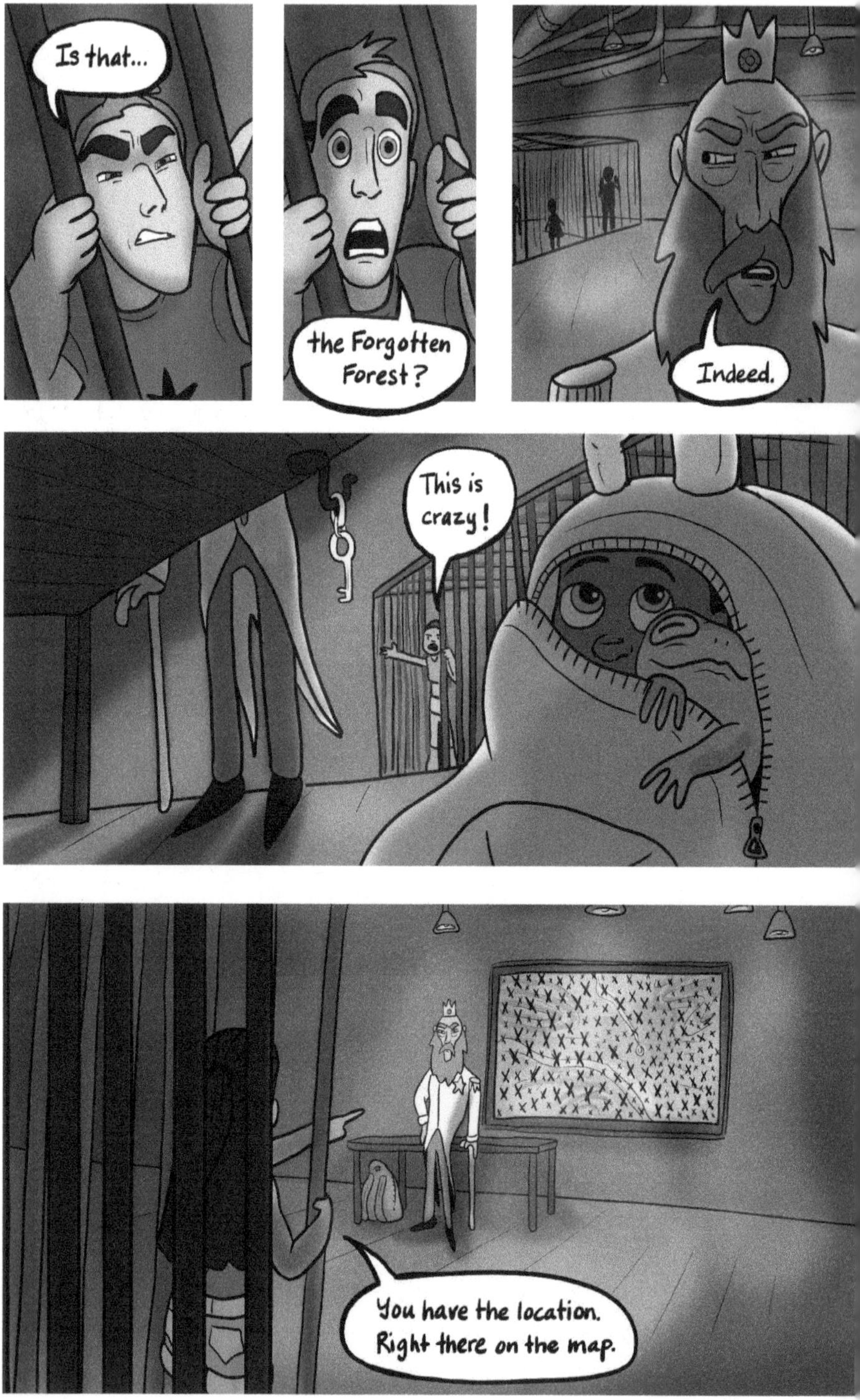
Is that...
the Forgotten Forest?
Indeed.
This is crazy!
You have the location. Right there on the map.

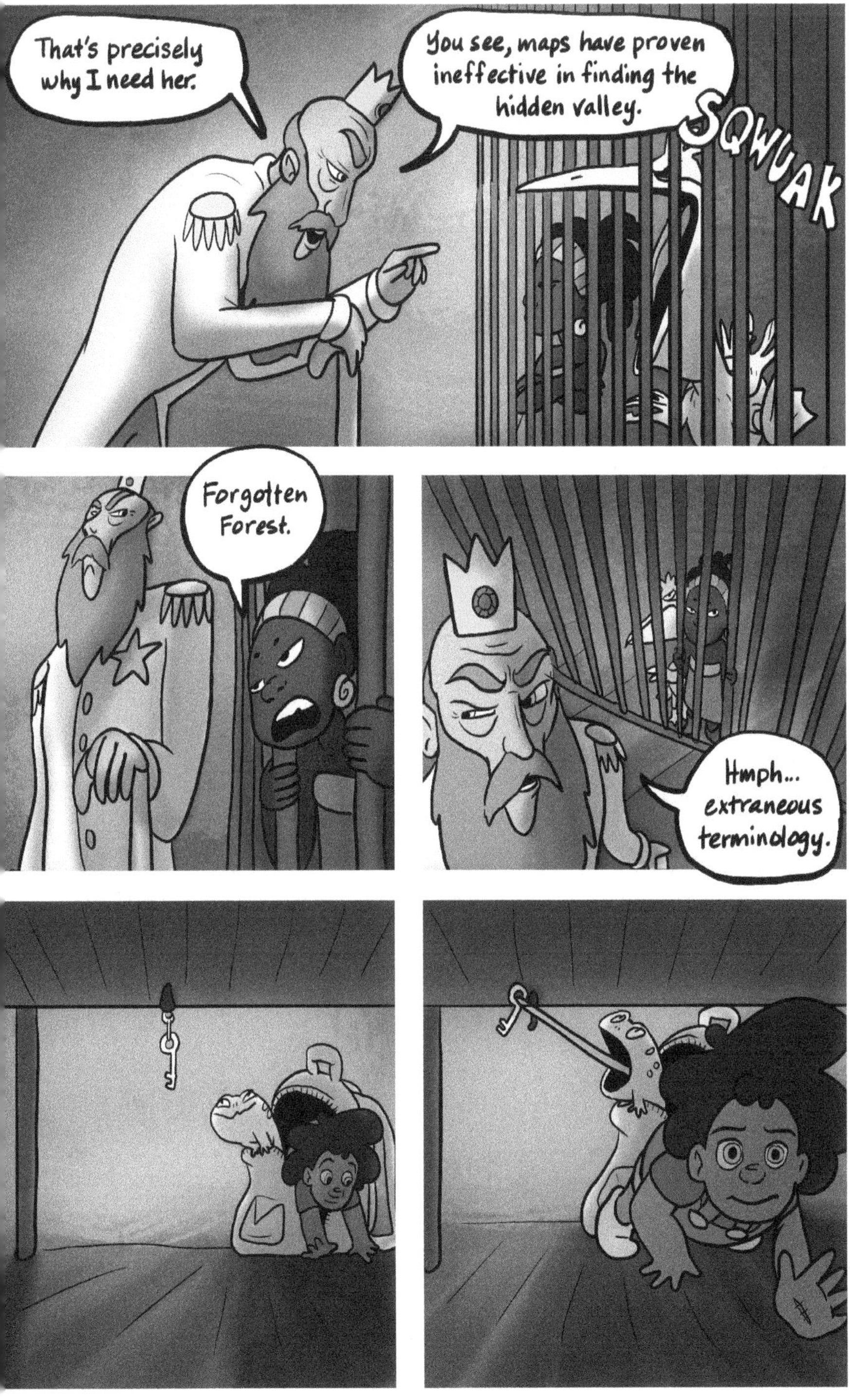
That's precisely why I need her.
You see, maps have proven ineffective in finding the hidden valley.
SQWUAK
Forgotten Forest.
Hmph... extraneous terminology.

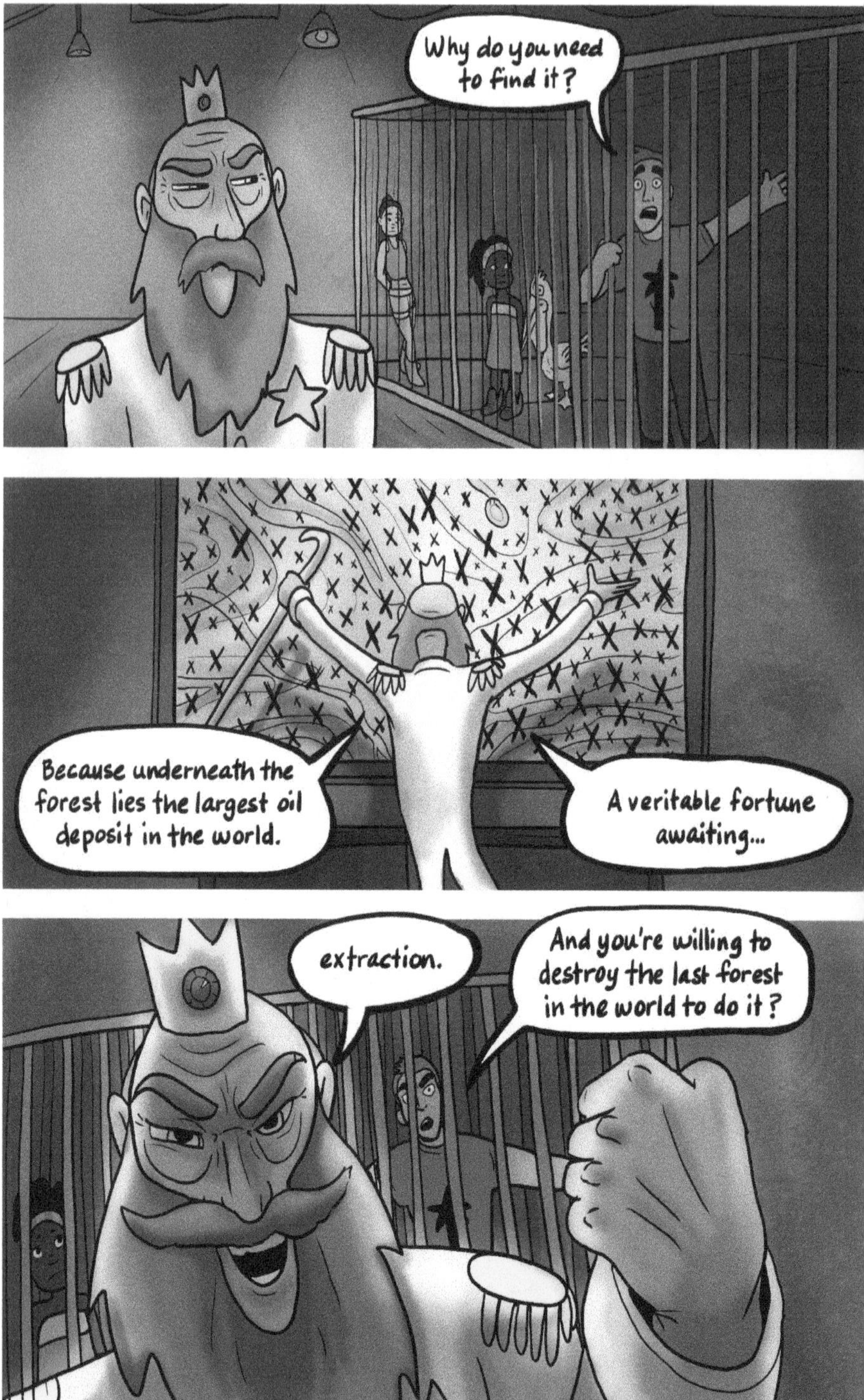
Why do you need to find it?
Because underneath the forest lies the largest oil deposit in the world.
A veritable fortune awaiting...
extraction.
And you're willing to destroy the last forest in the world to do it?

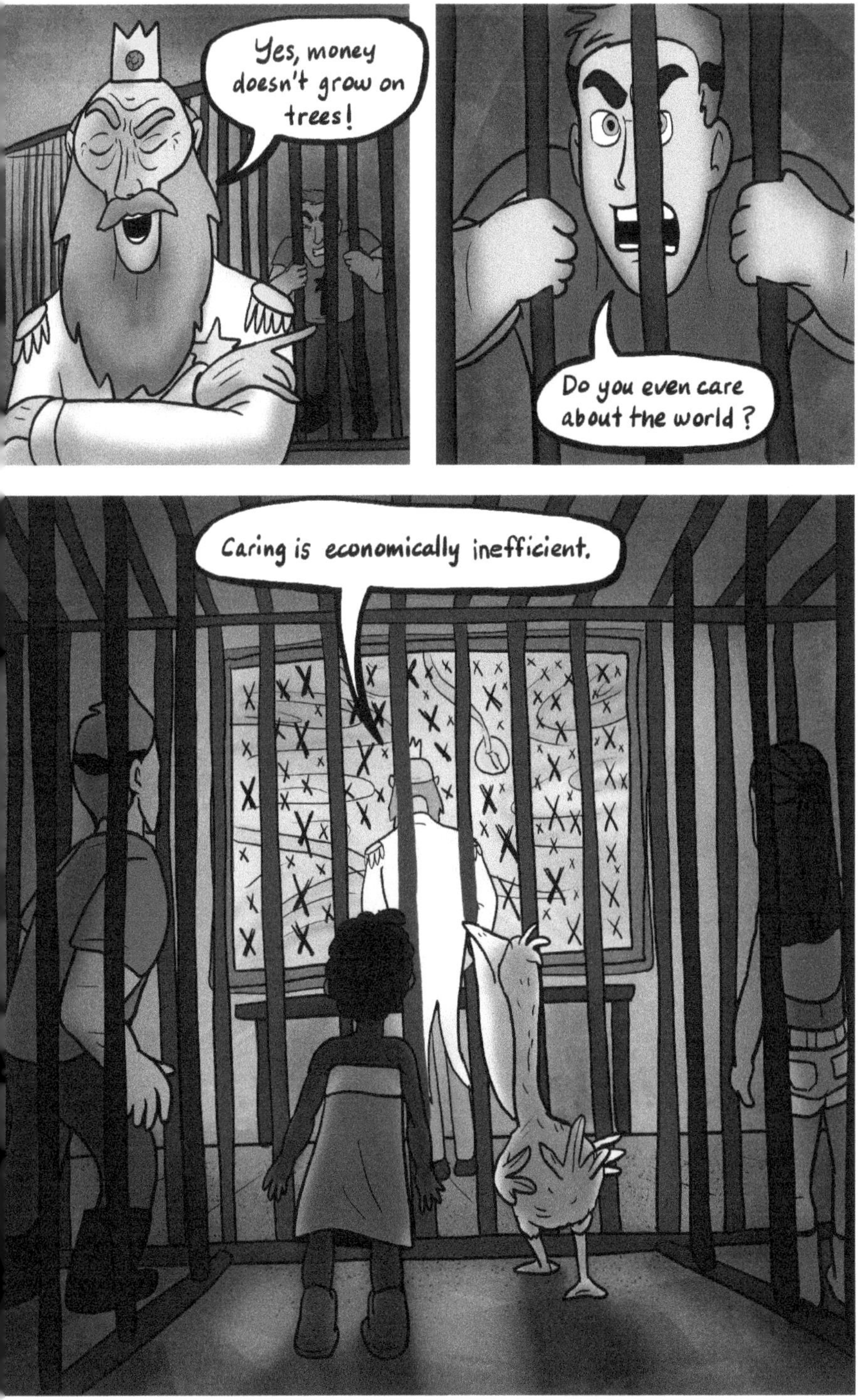
Yes, money doesn't grow on trees!
Do you even care about the world?
Caring is economically inefficient.

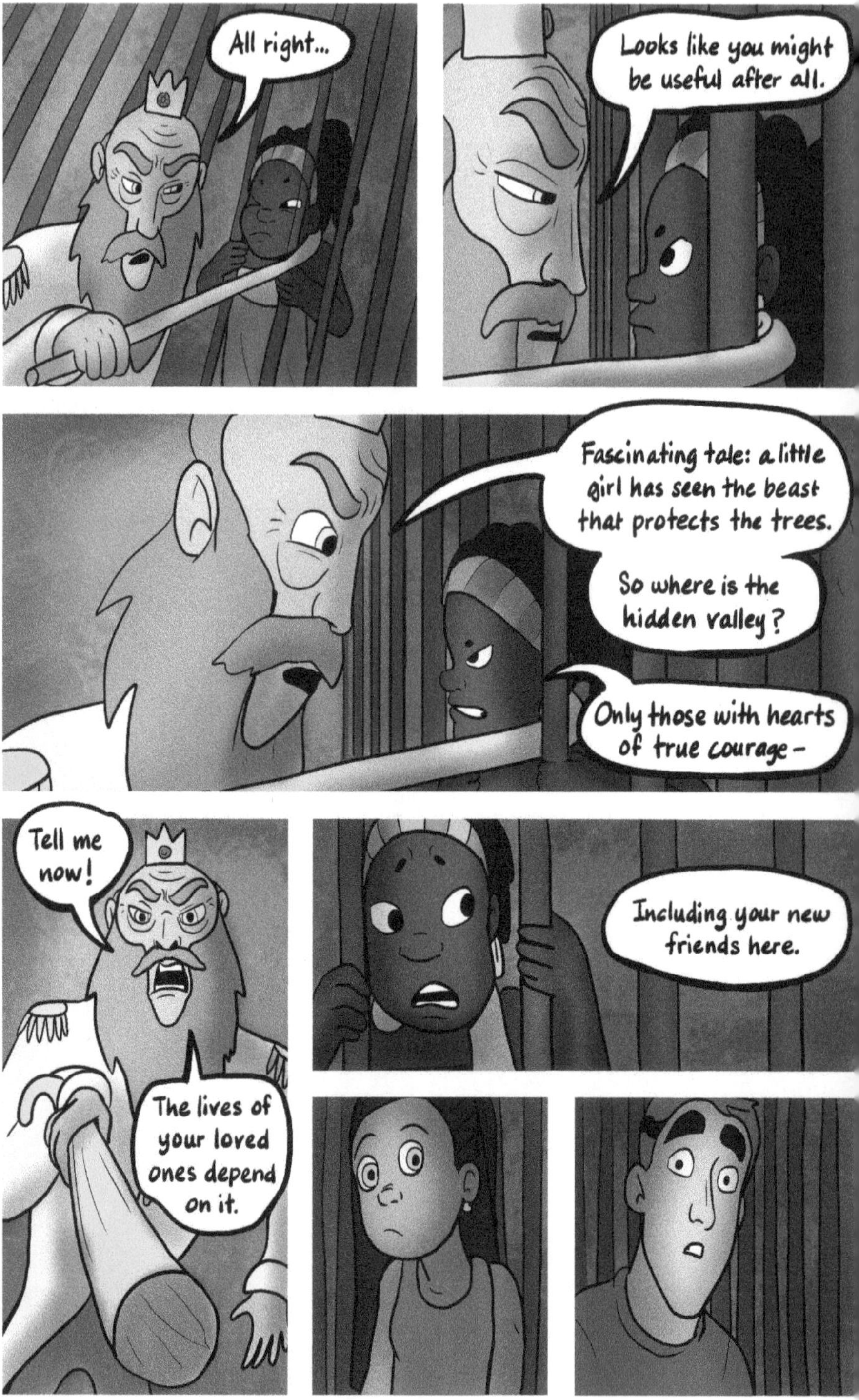
All right...
Looks like you might be useful after all.
Fascinating tale: a little girl has seen the beast that protects the trees.
So where is the hidden valley?
Only those with hearts of true courage-
Tell me now!
The lives of your loved ones depend on it.
Including your new friends here.

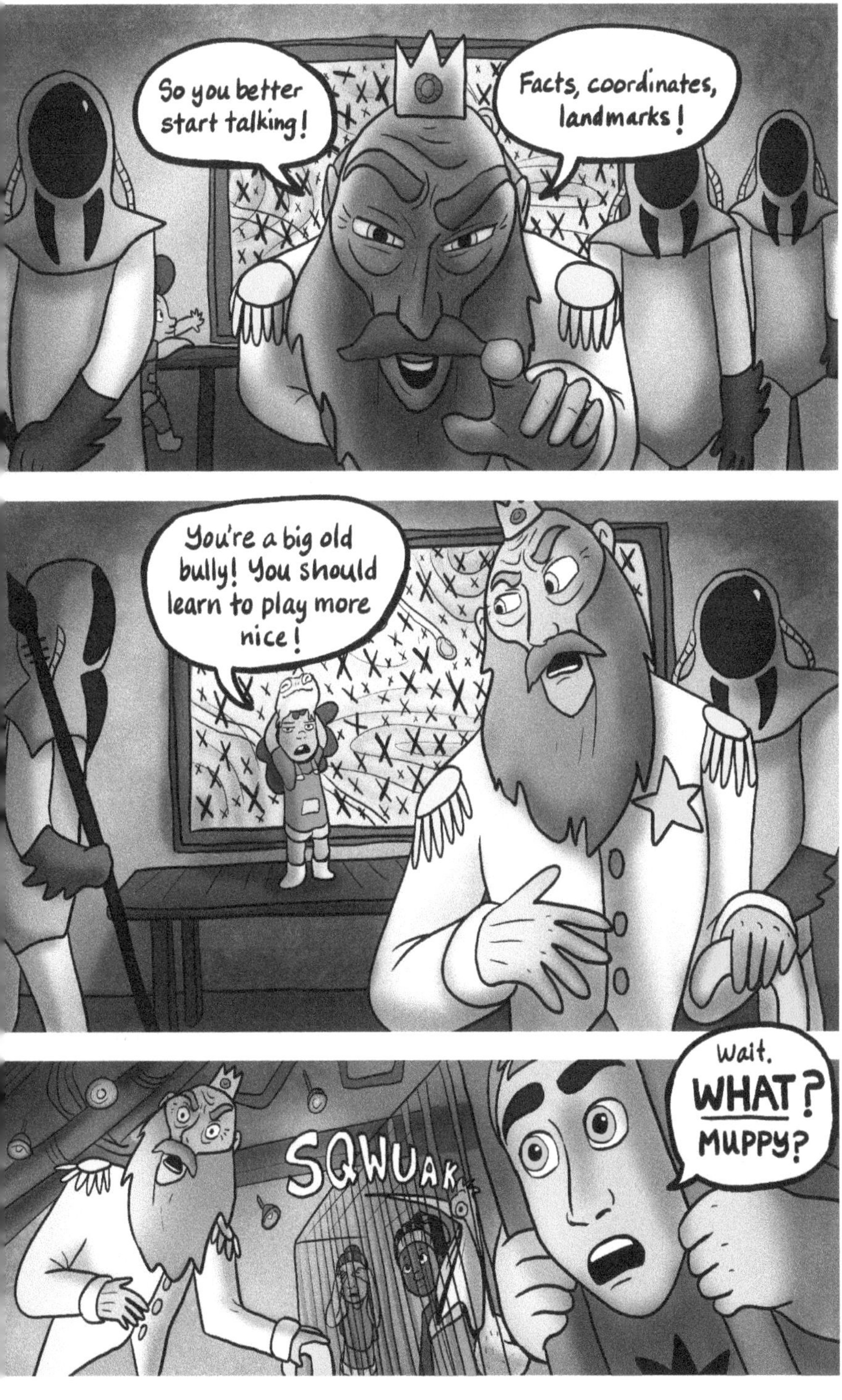
So you better start talking!
Facts, coordinates, landmarks!
You're a big old bully! You should learn to play more nice!
SQWUAK
Wait. WHAT? MUPPY?

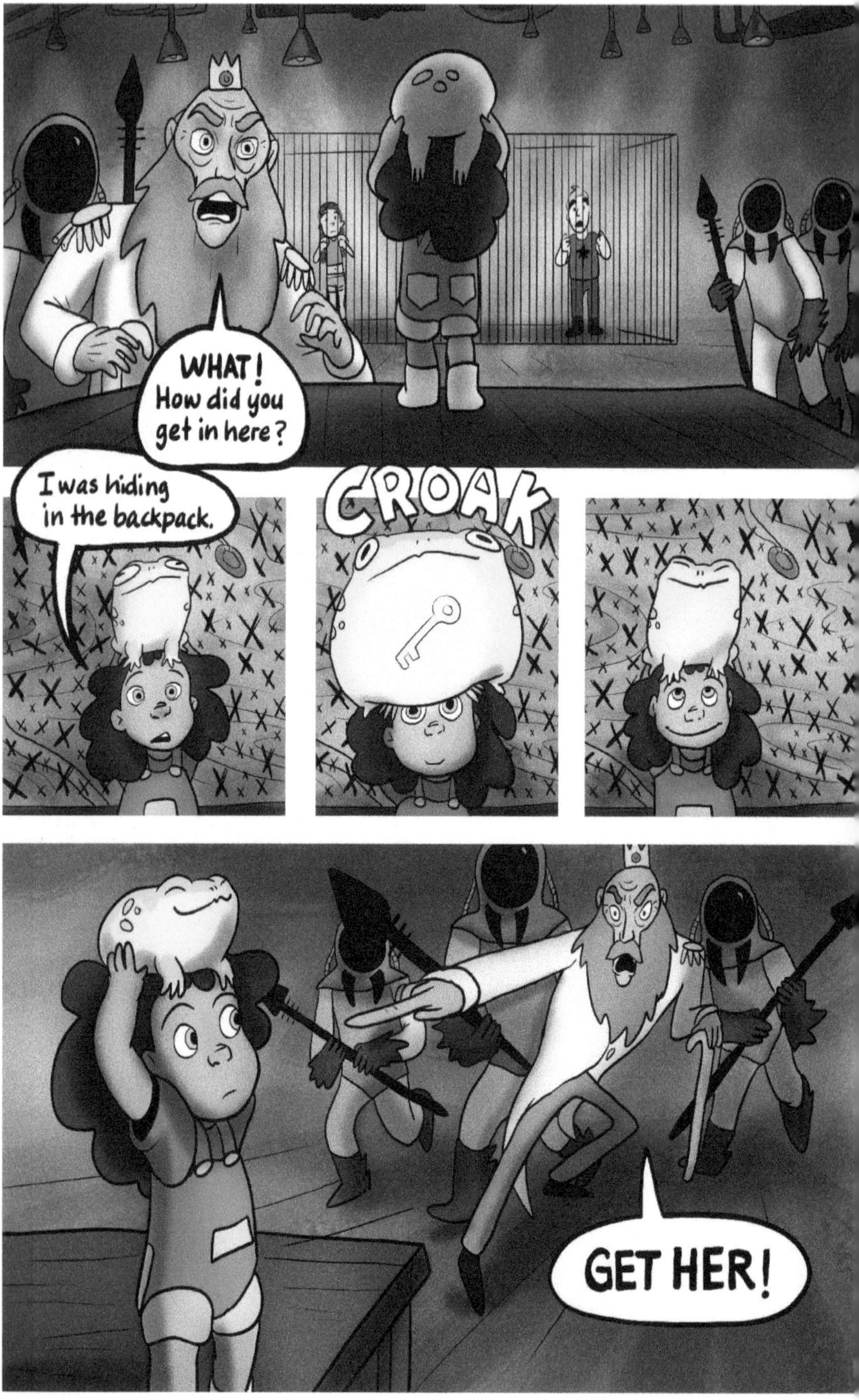
WHAT! How did you get in here?
I was hiding in the backpack.
CROAK
GET HER!

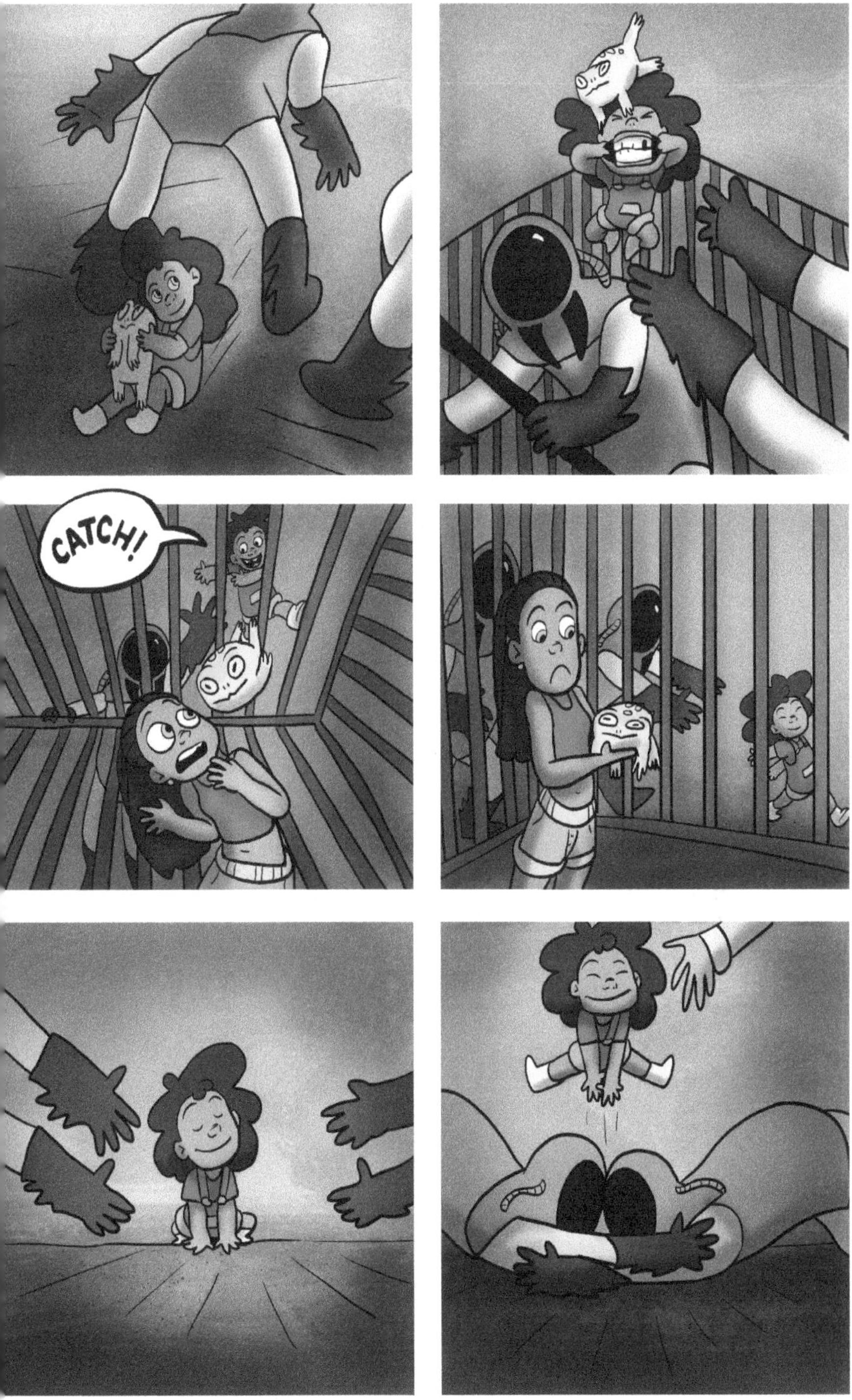
CATCH!

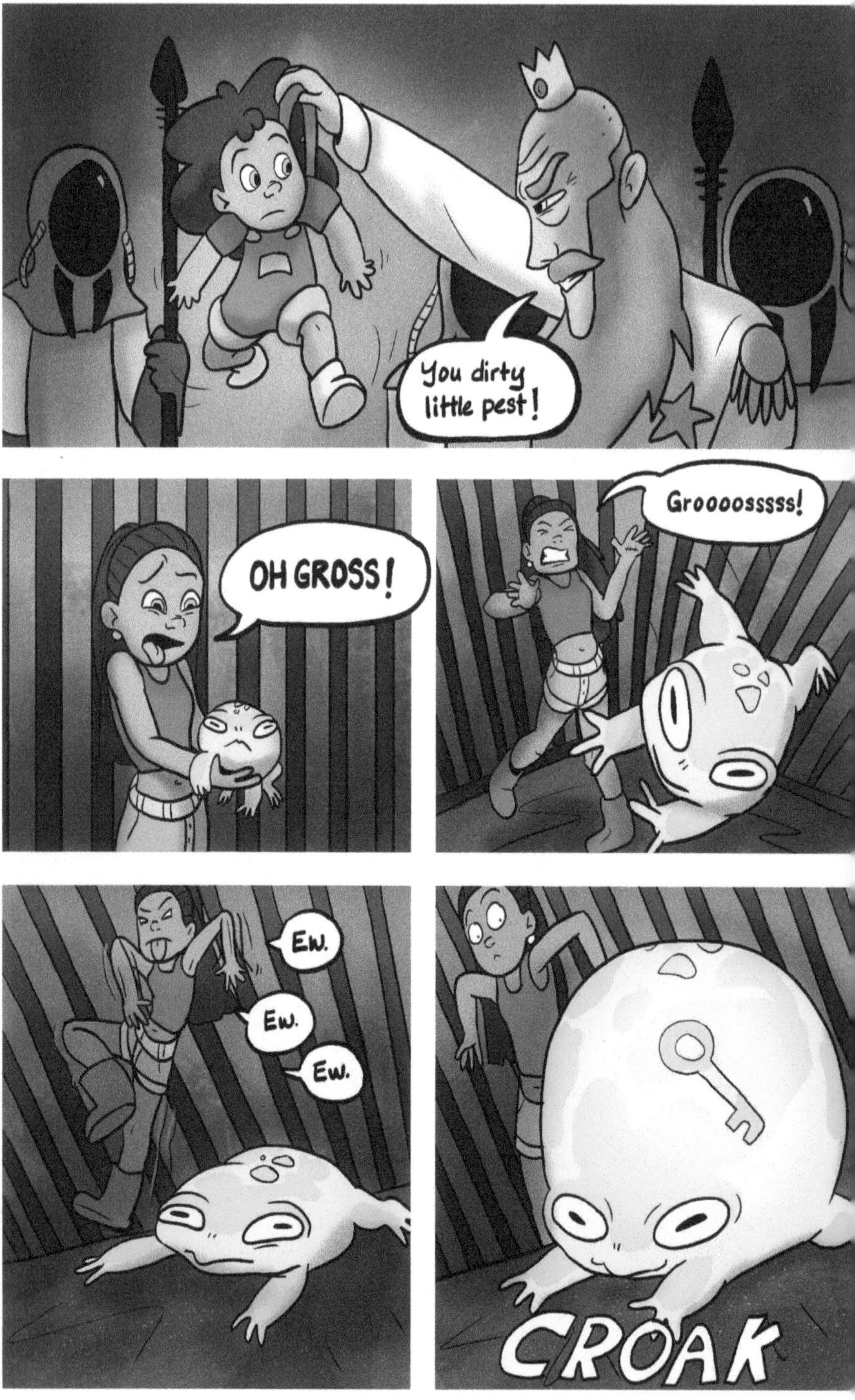
You dirty little pest!
OH GROSS!
Grooooossss!
Ew.
Ew.
Ew.
CROAK

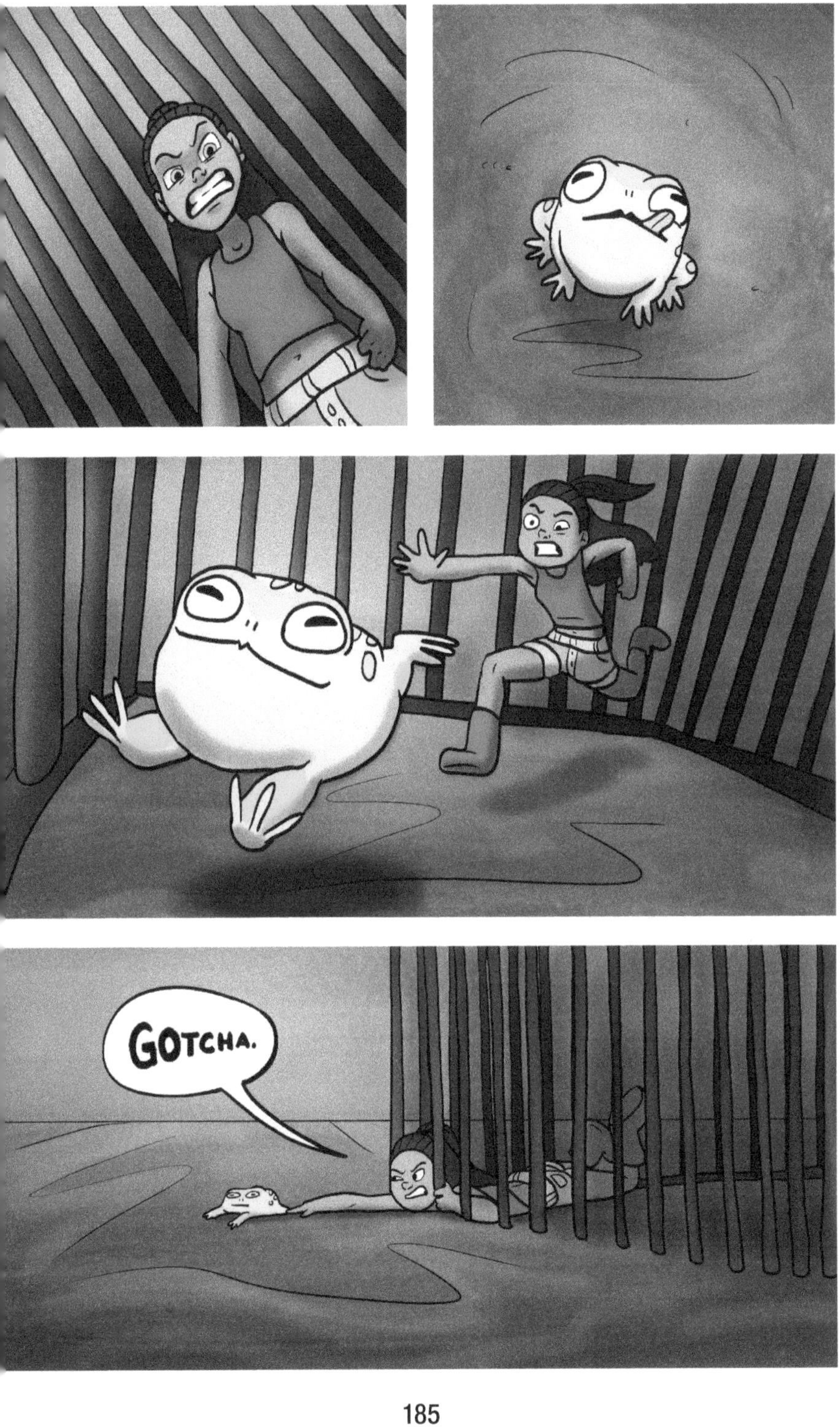
GOTCHA.

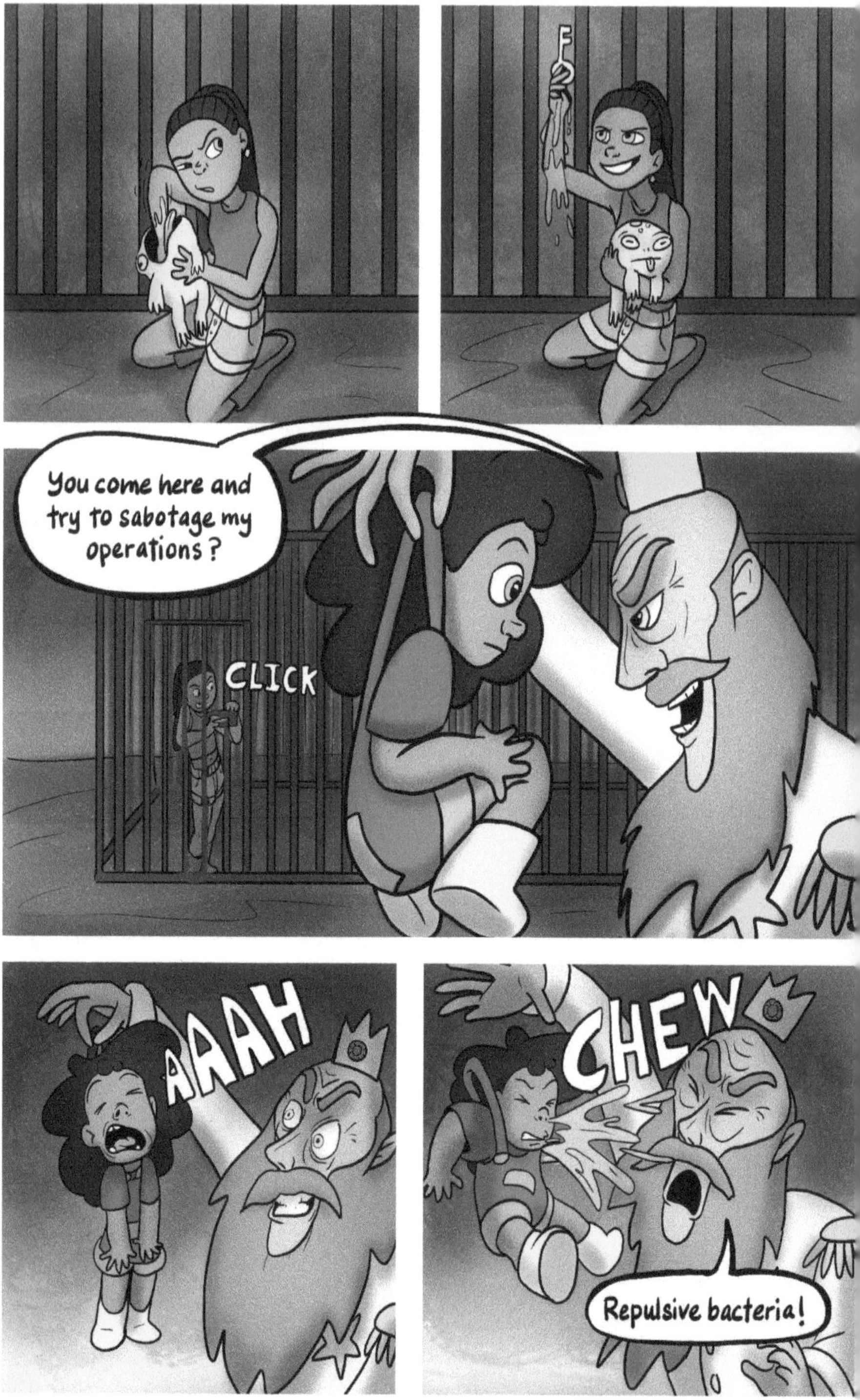
You come here and try to sabotage my operations?
CLICK
AAAH
CHEW
Repulsive bacteria!

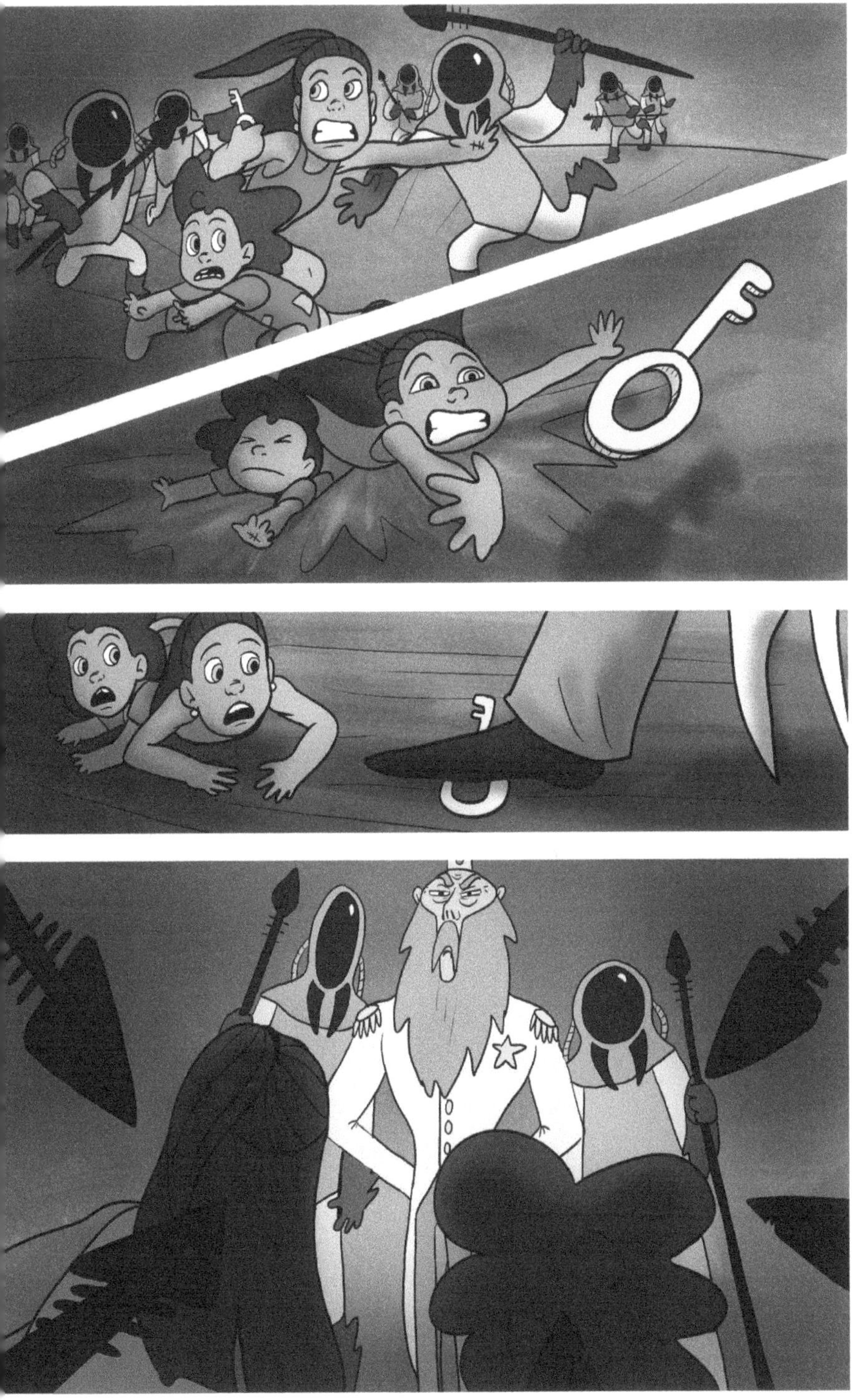

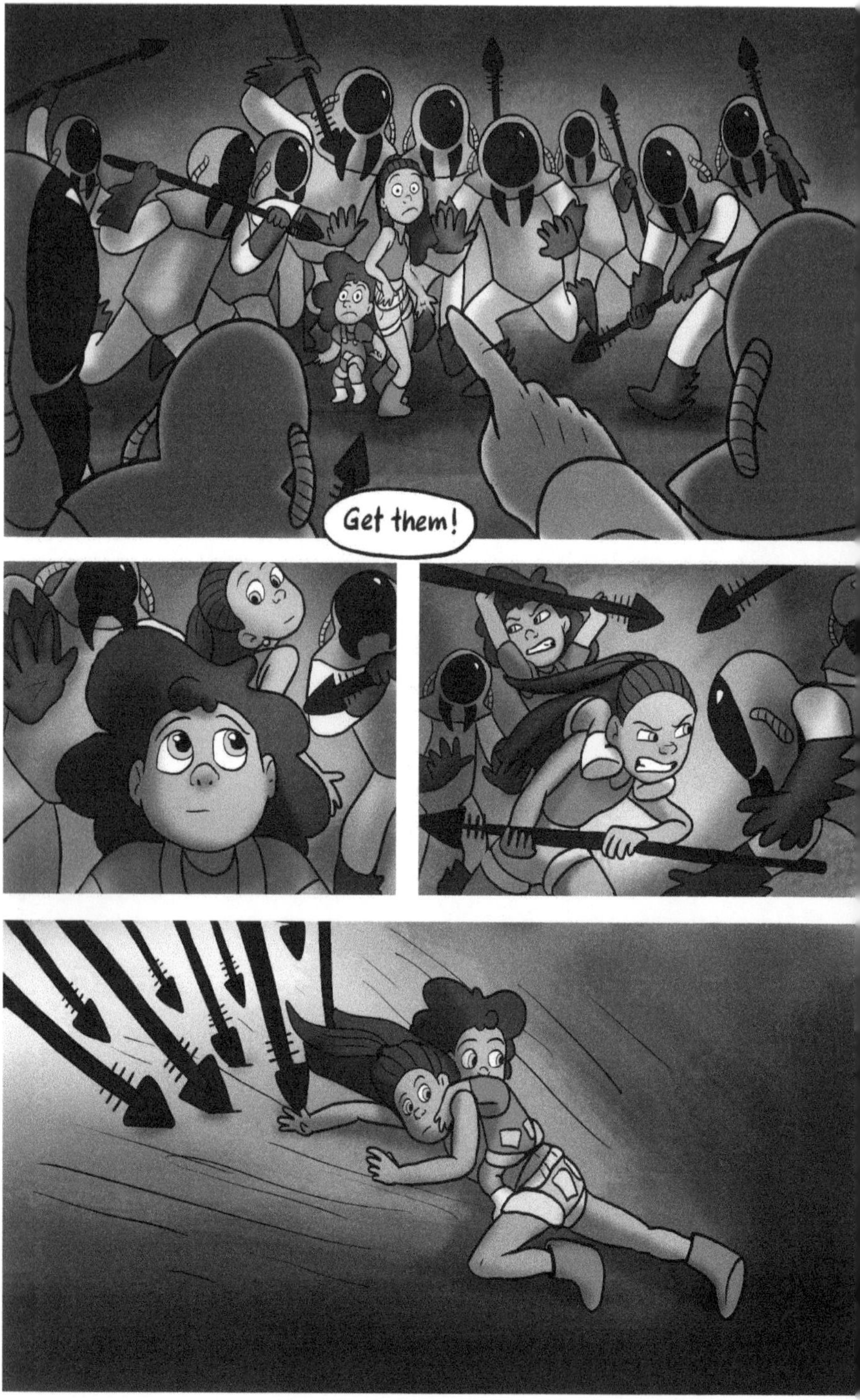
Get them!

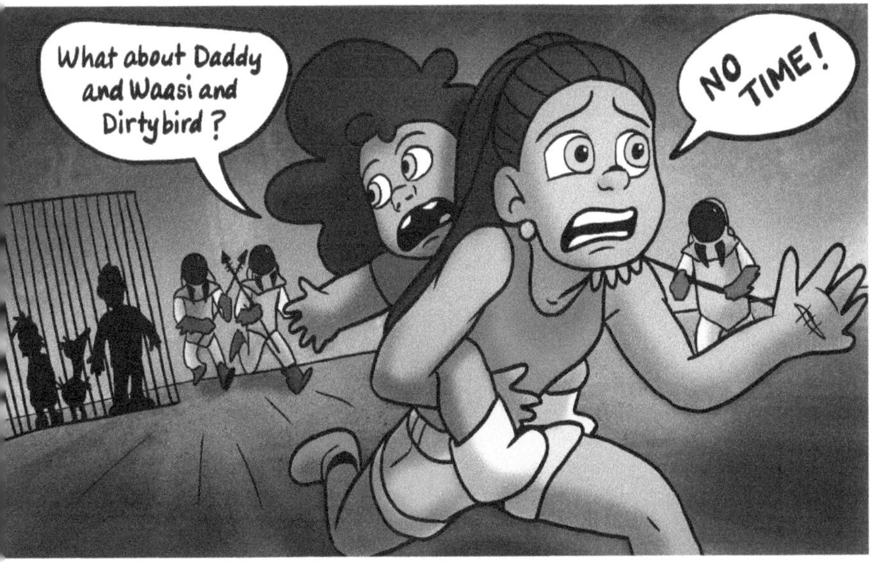
What about Daddy and Waasi and Dirtybird?
NO TIME!

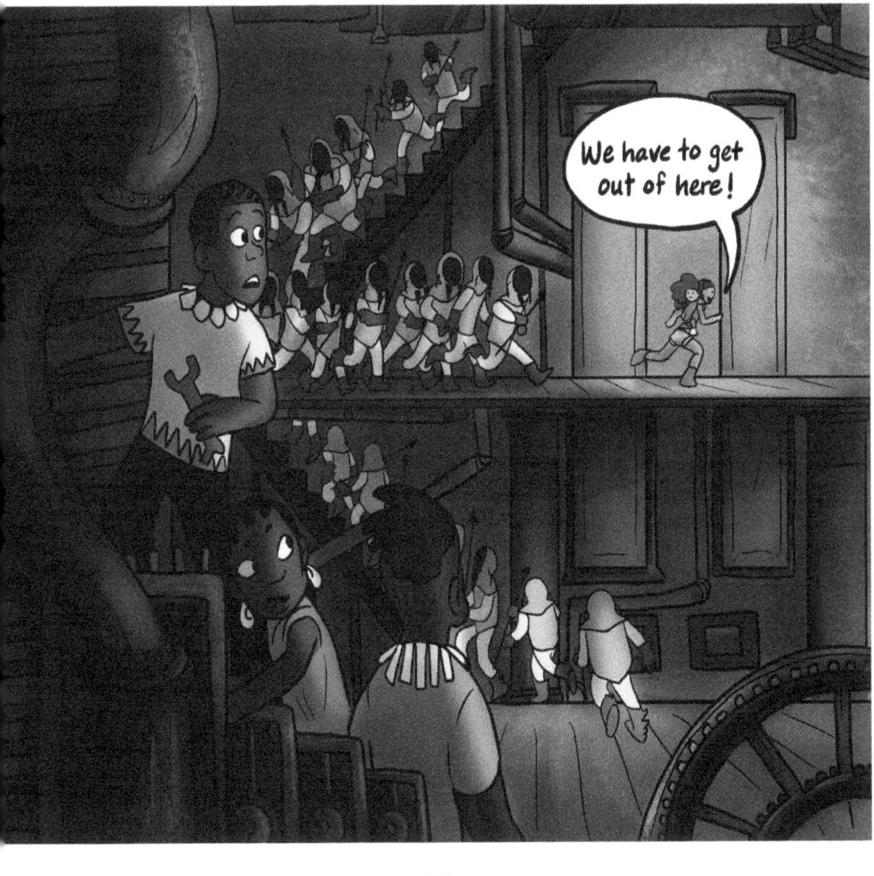
We have to get out of here!

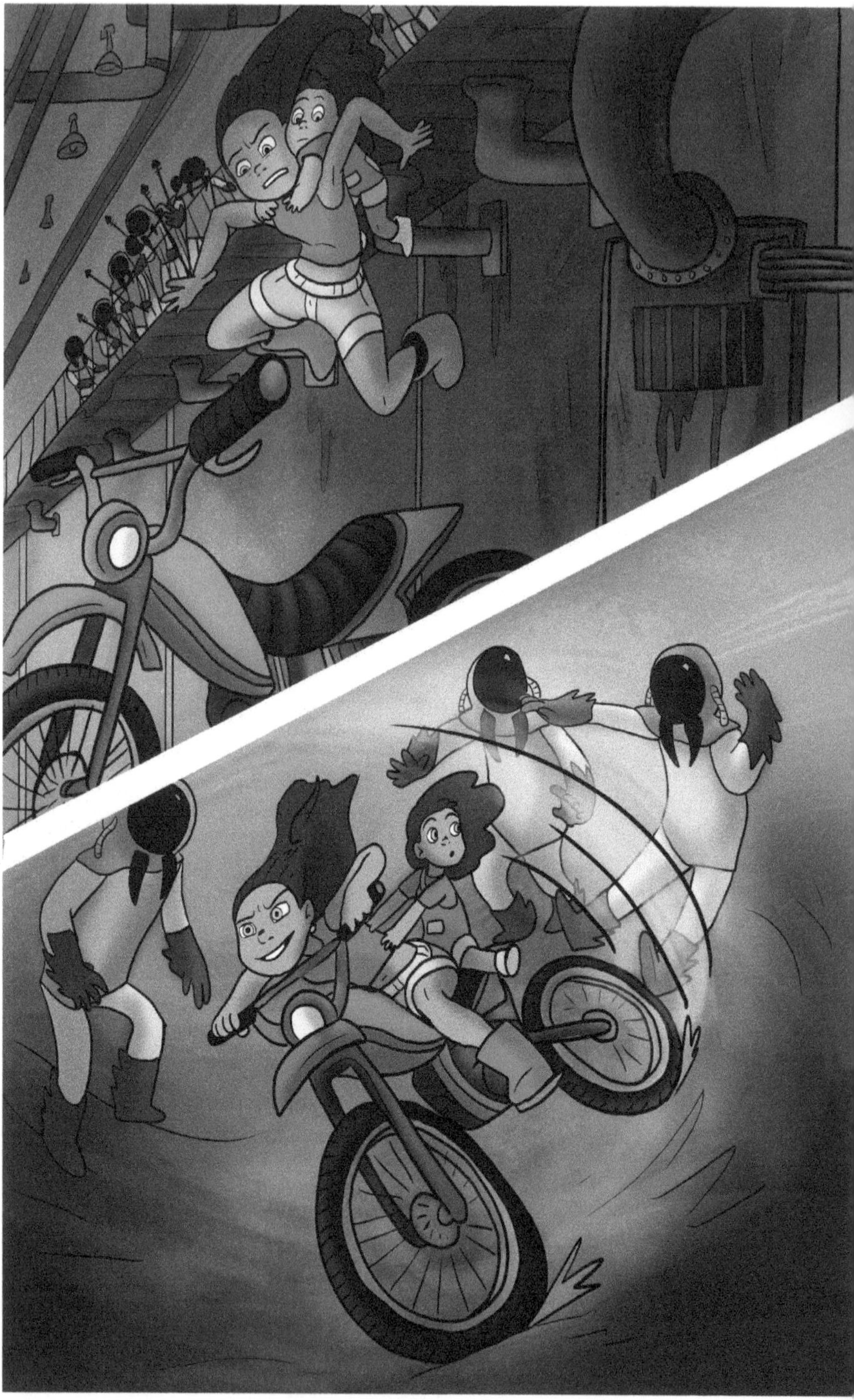

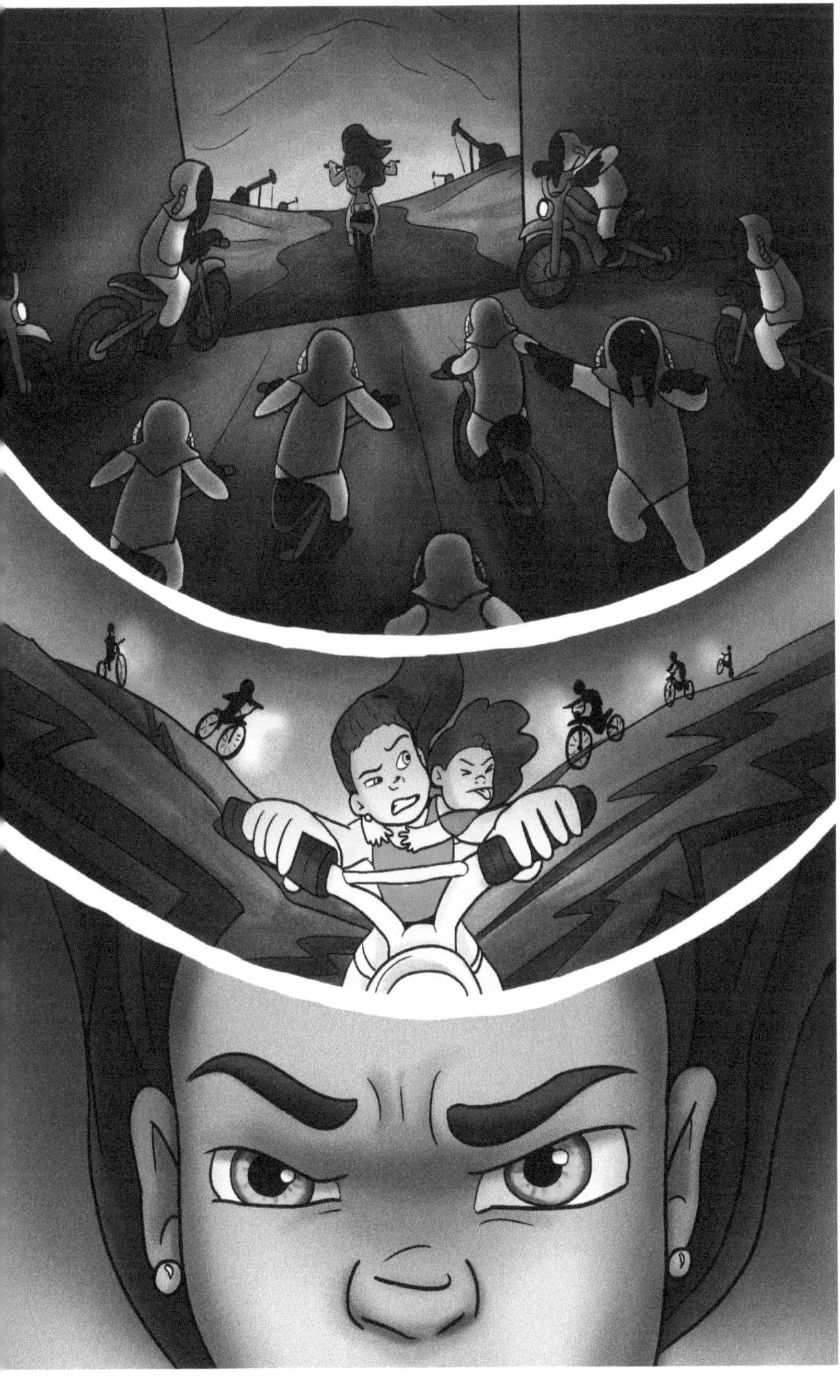

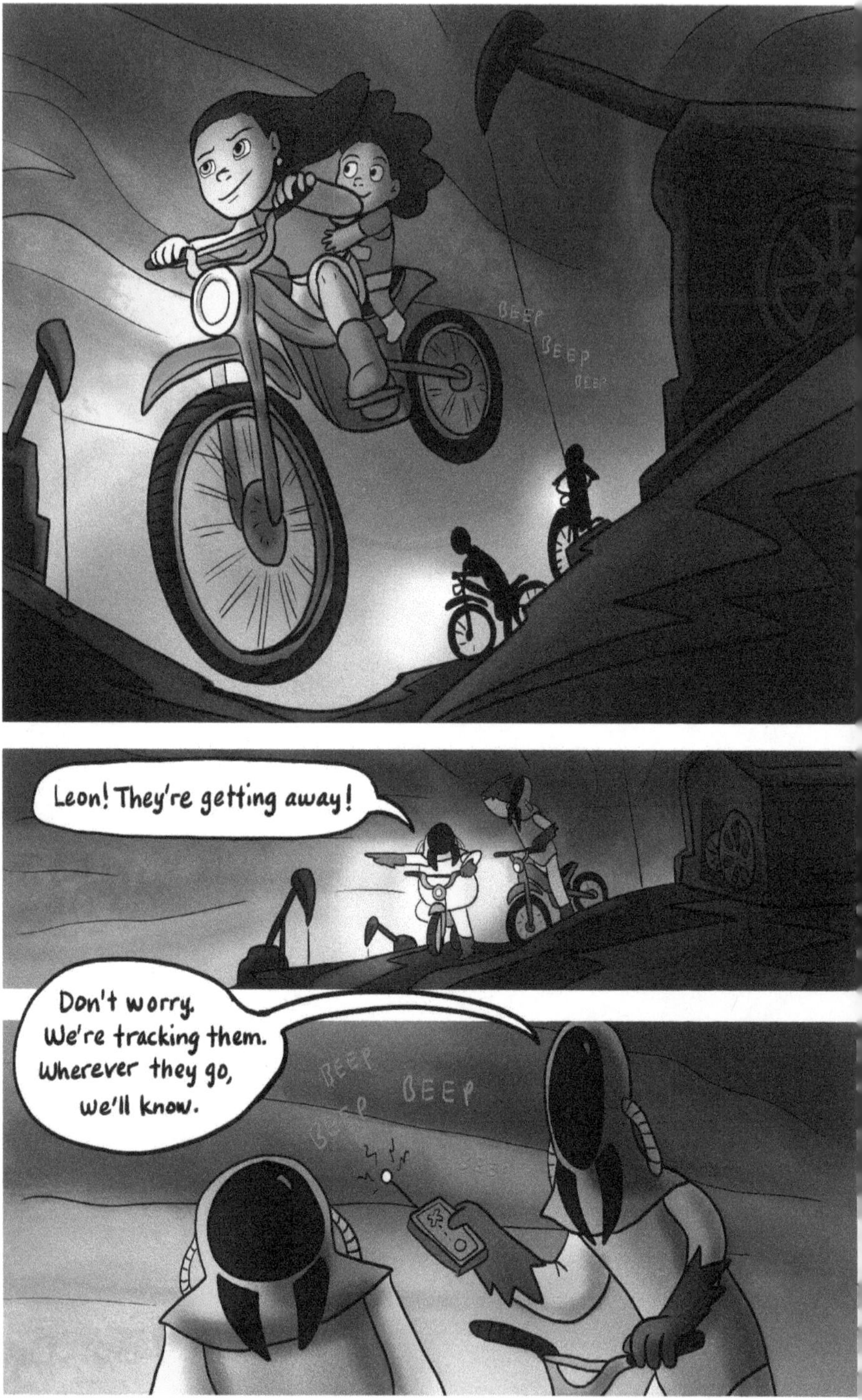
BEEP
BEEP
BEEP
Leon! They're getting away!
Don't worry.
We're tracking them.
Wherever they go,
we'll know.
BEEP
BEEP
BEEP

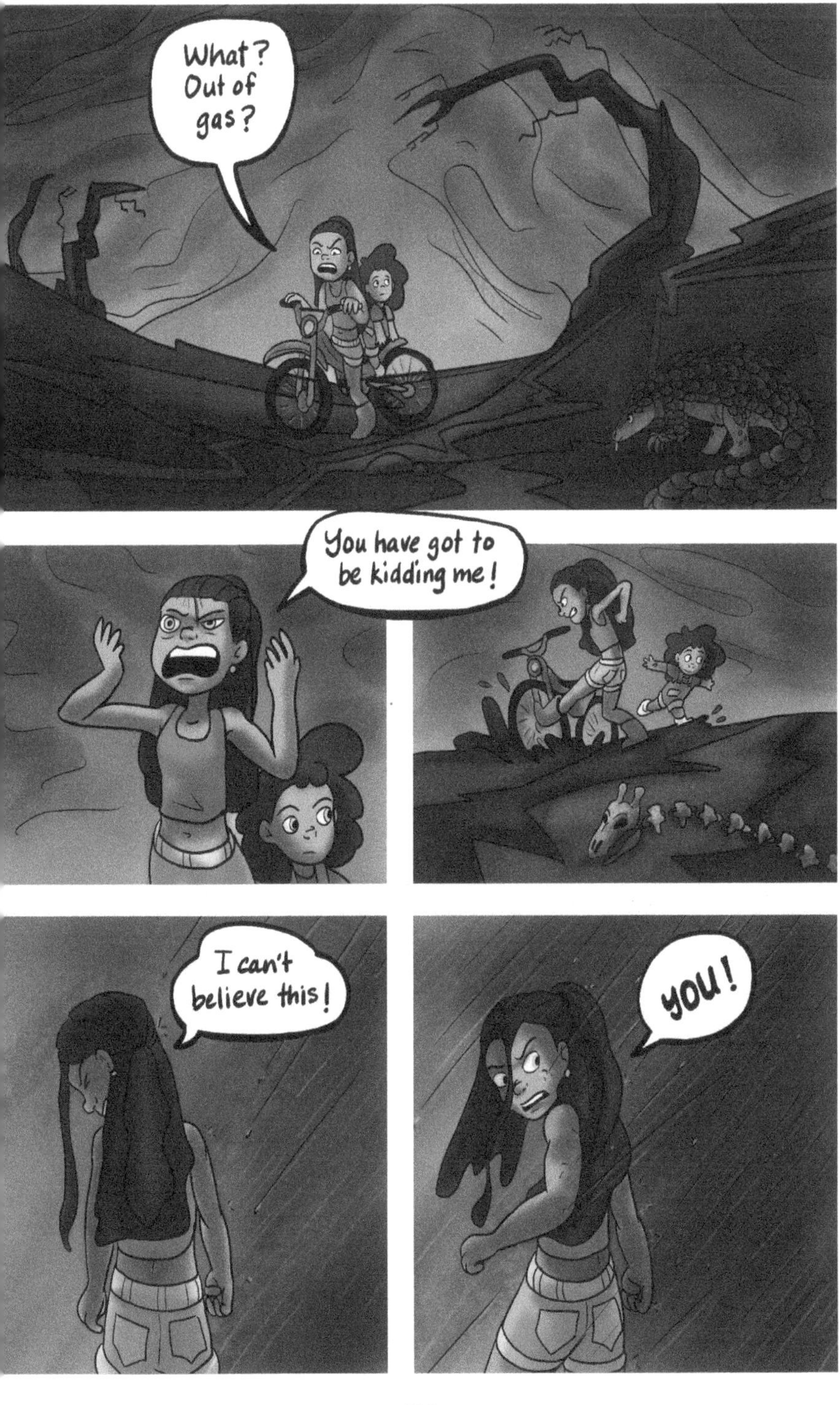
What? Out of gas?
You have got to be kidding me!
I can't believe this!
YOU!

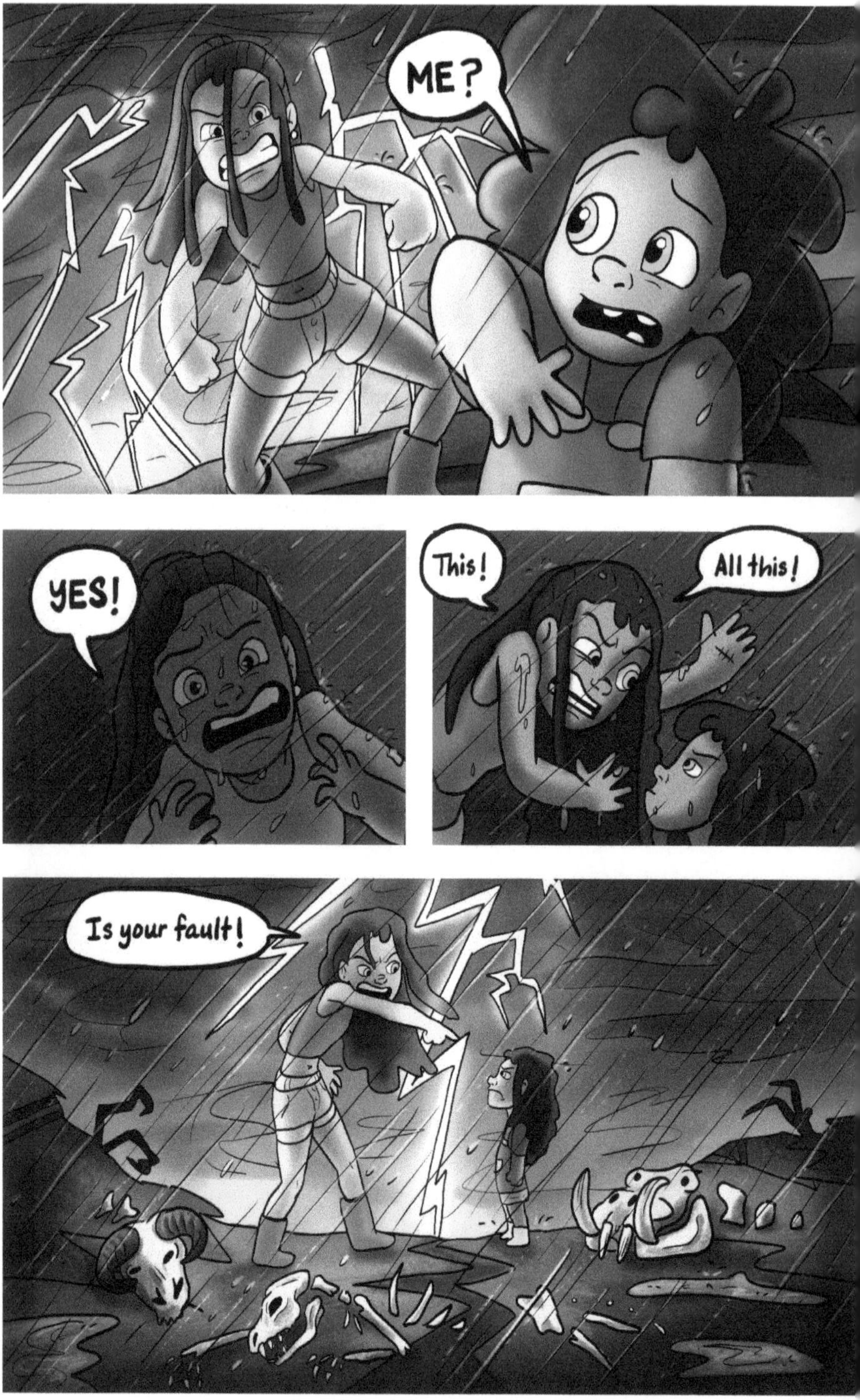
ME?
YES!
This!
All this!
Is your fault!

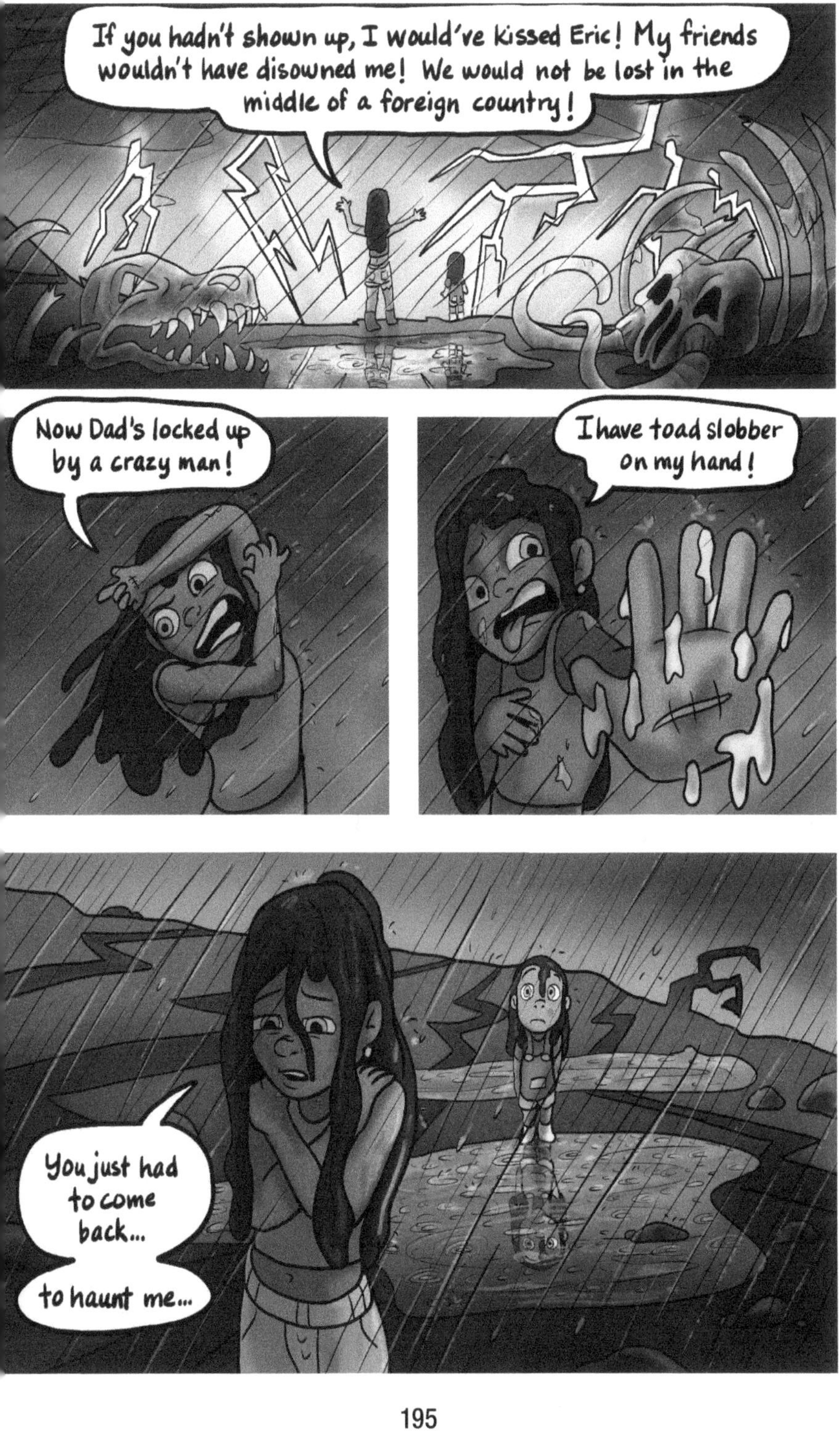
If you hadn't shown up, I would've kissed Eric! My friends wouldn't have disowned me! We would not be lost in the middle of a foreign country!
Now Dad's locked up by a crazy man!
I have toad slobber on my hand!
You just had to come back...
to haunt me...

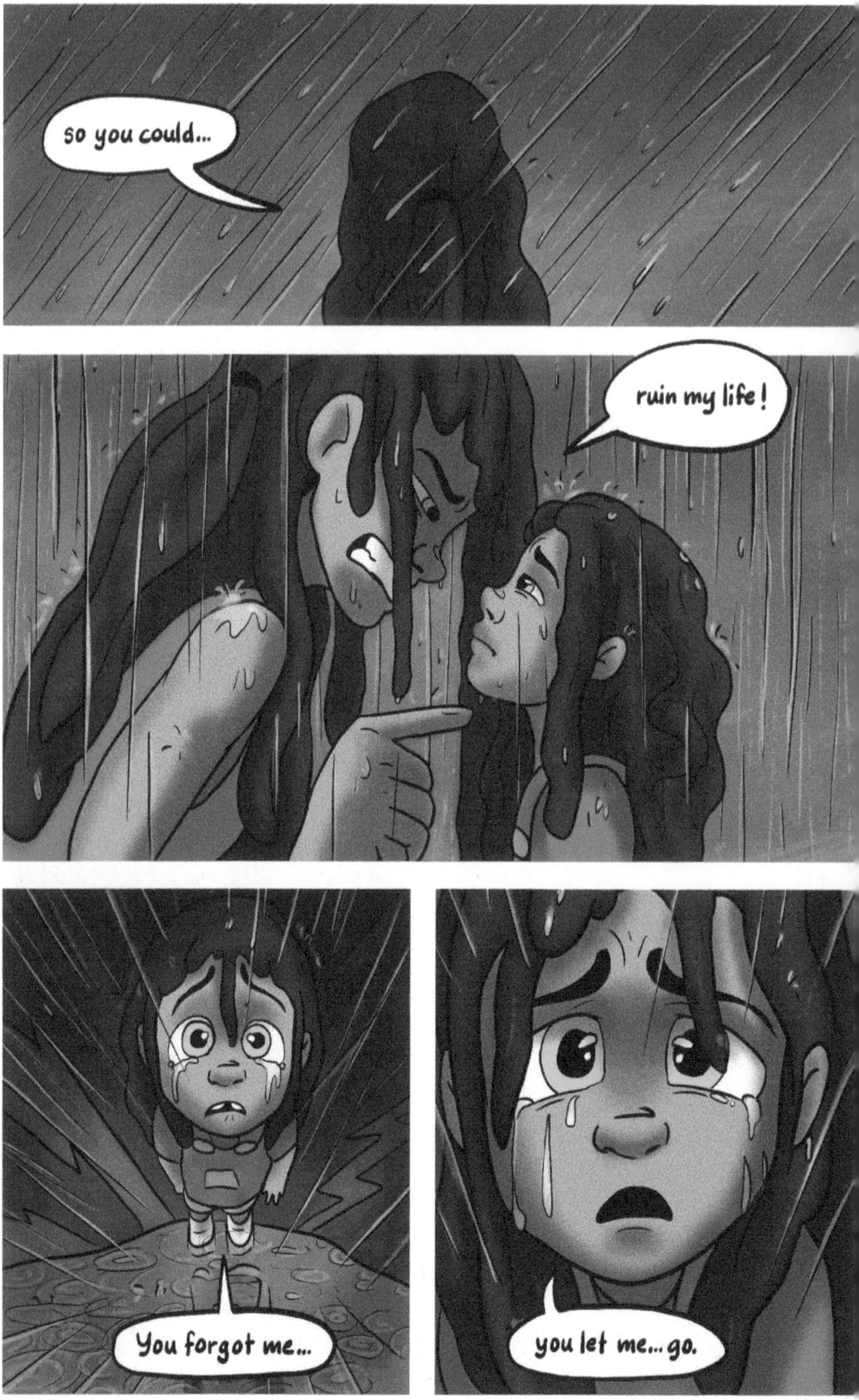
so you could...
ruin my life!
You forgot me...
you let me... go.

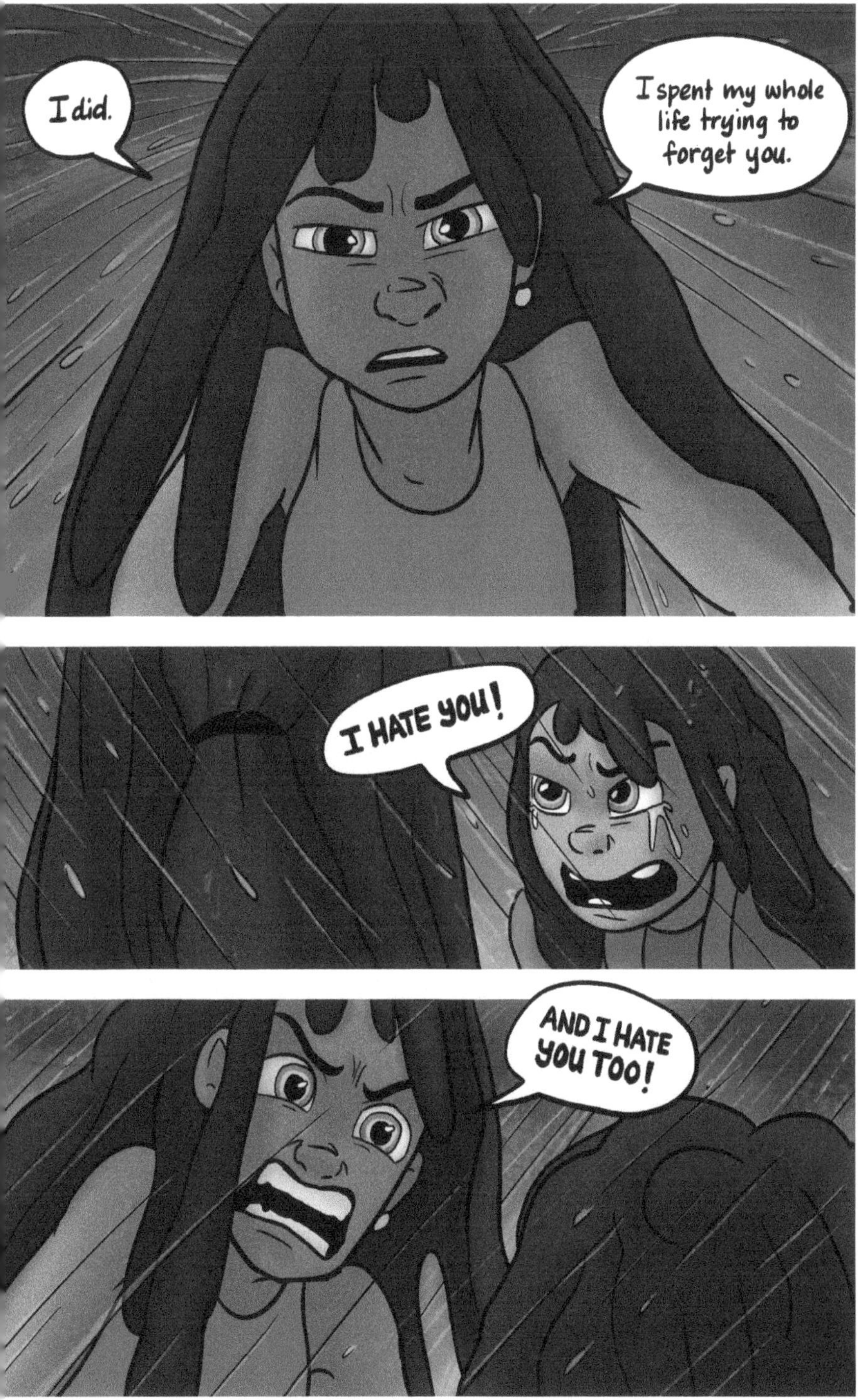
I did.
I spent my whole life trying to forget you.
I HATE YOU!
AND I HATE YOU TOO!

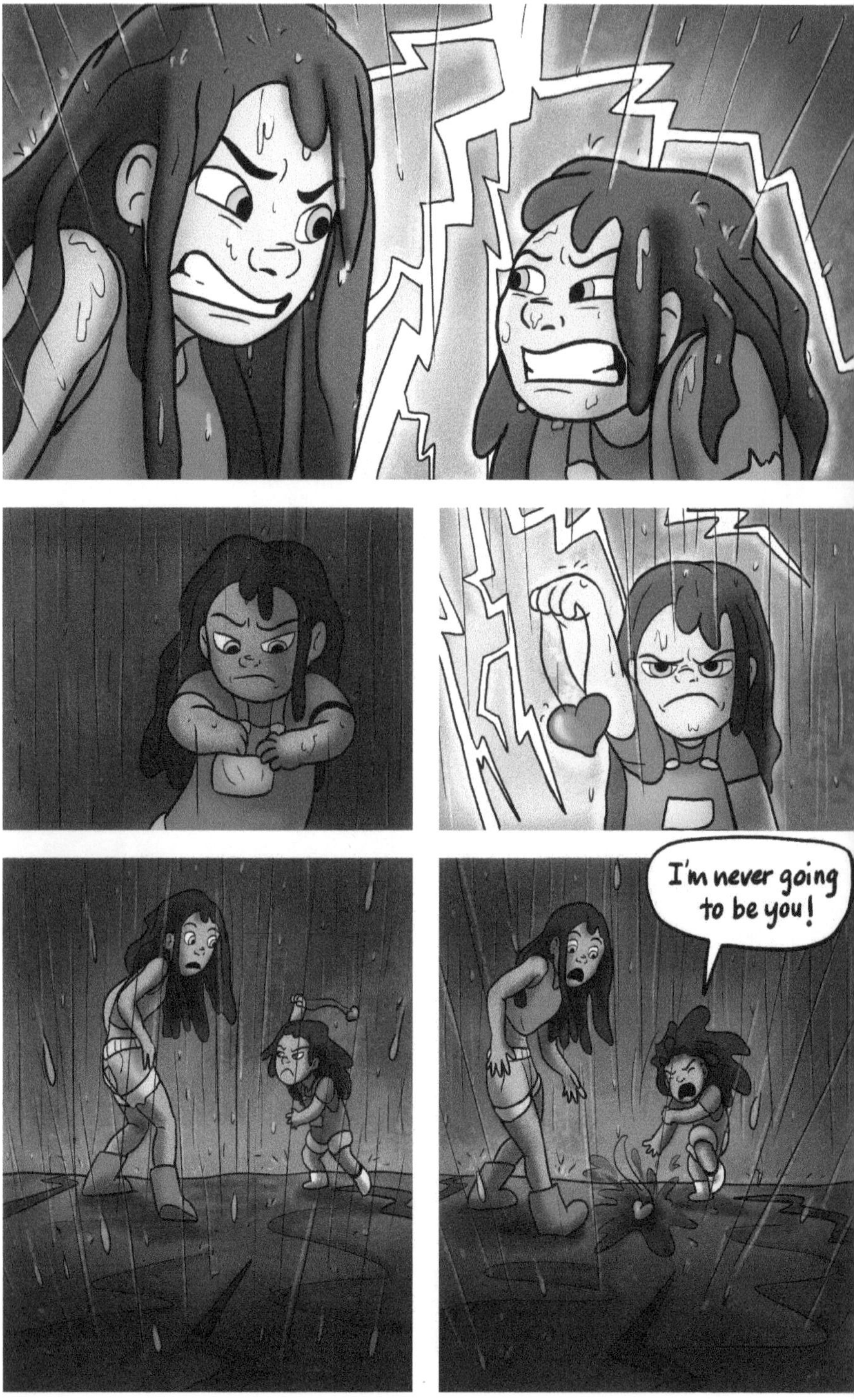
I'm never going to be you!

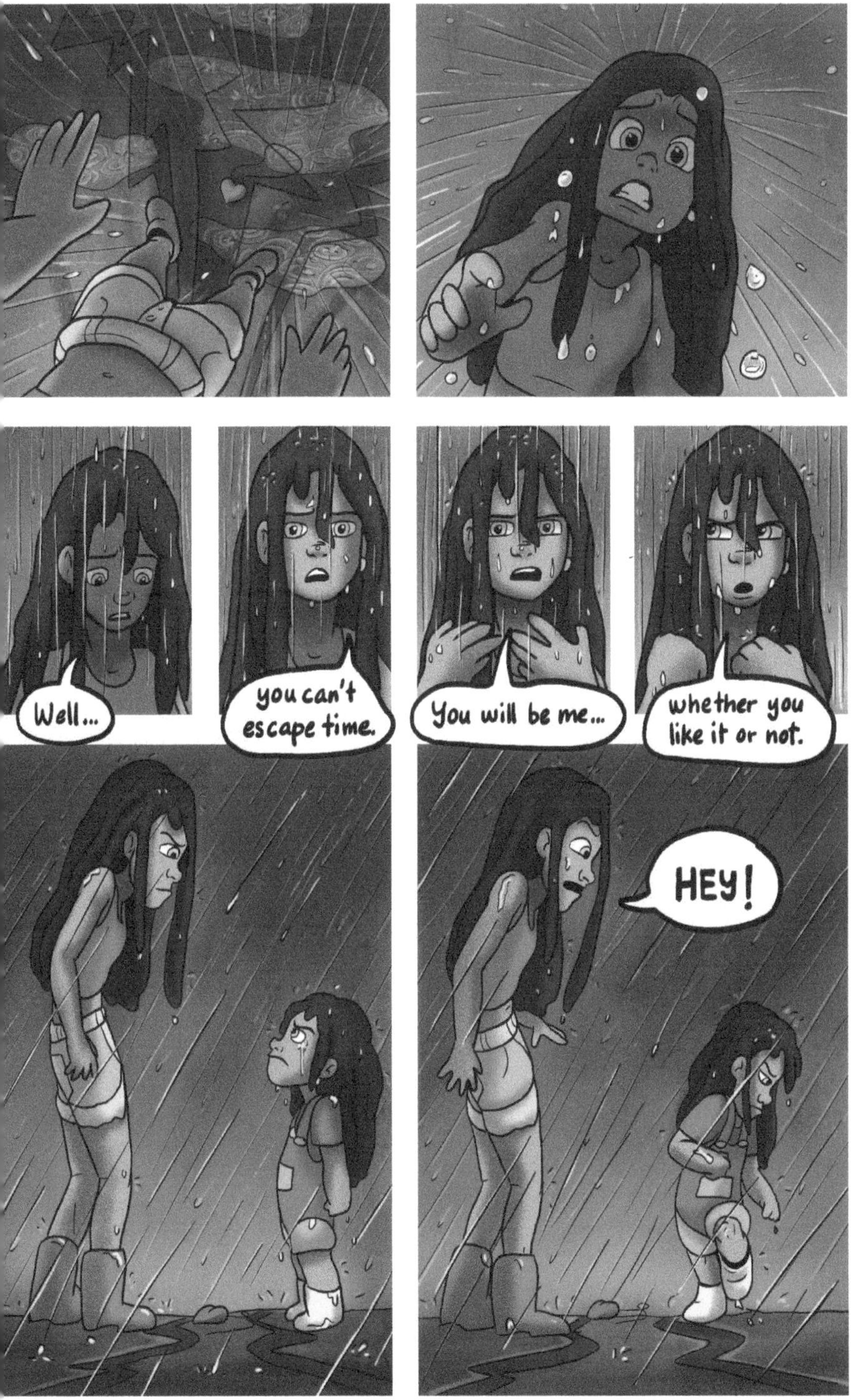

Well...
you can't escape time.
You will be me...
whether you like it or not.
HEY!

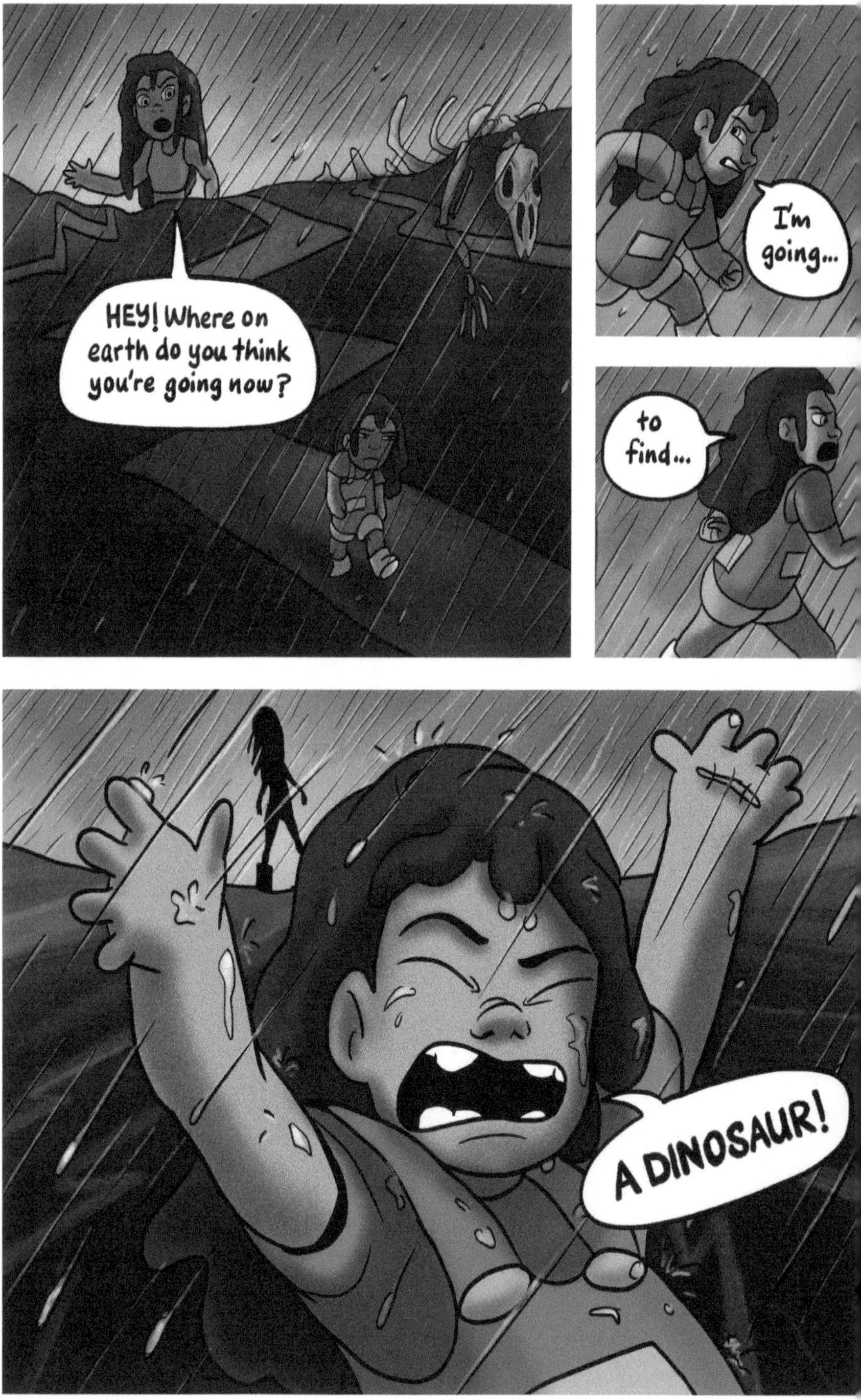
HEY! Where on earth do you think you're going now?
I'm going...
to find...
A DINOSAUR!

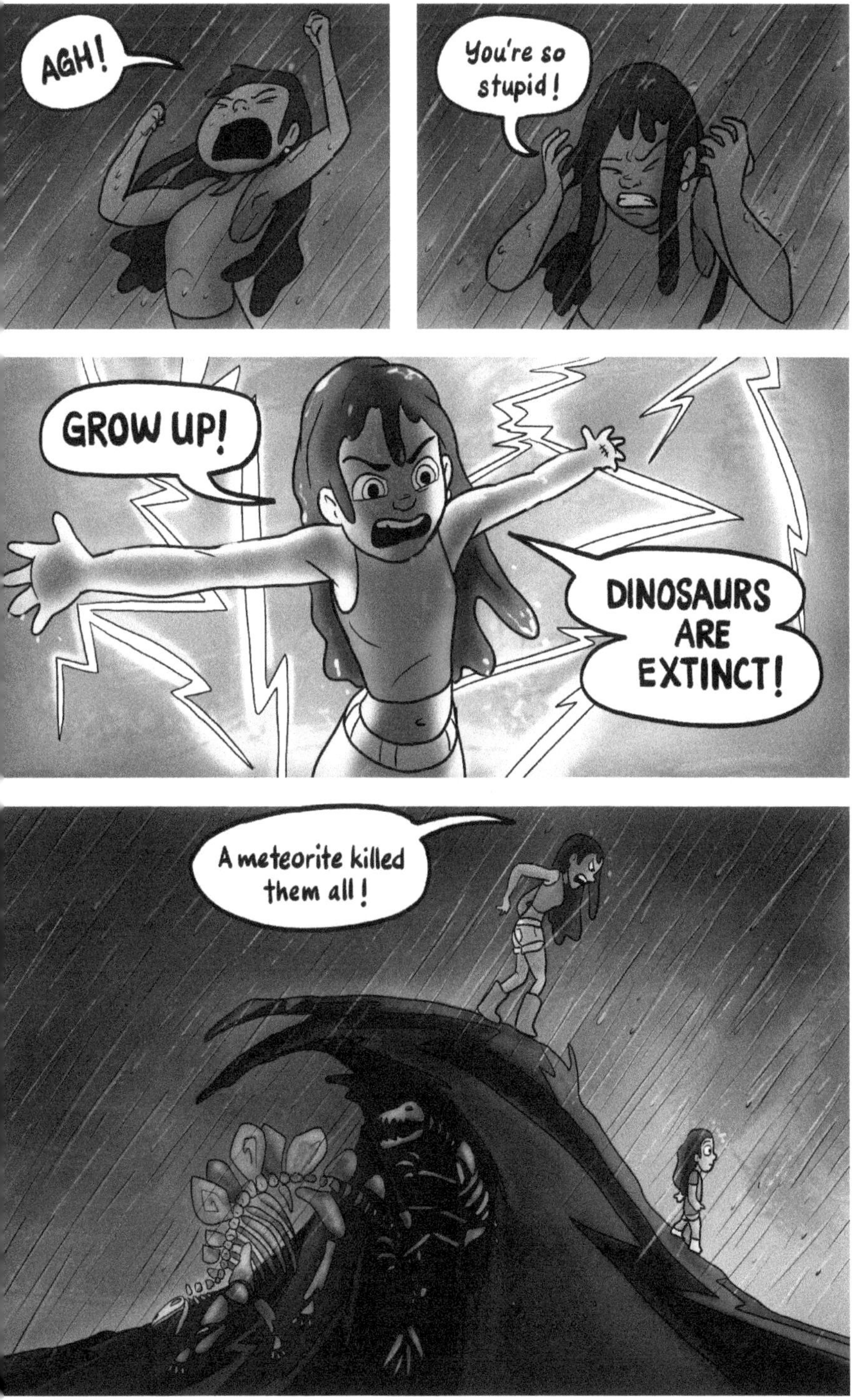
AGH!
You're so stupid!
GROW UP!
DINOSAURS ARE EXTINCT!
A meteorite killed them all!

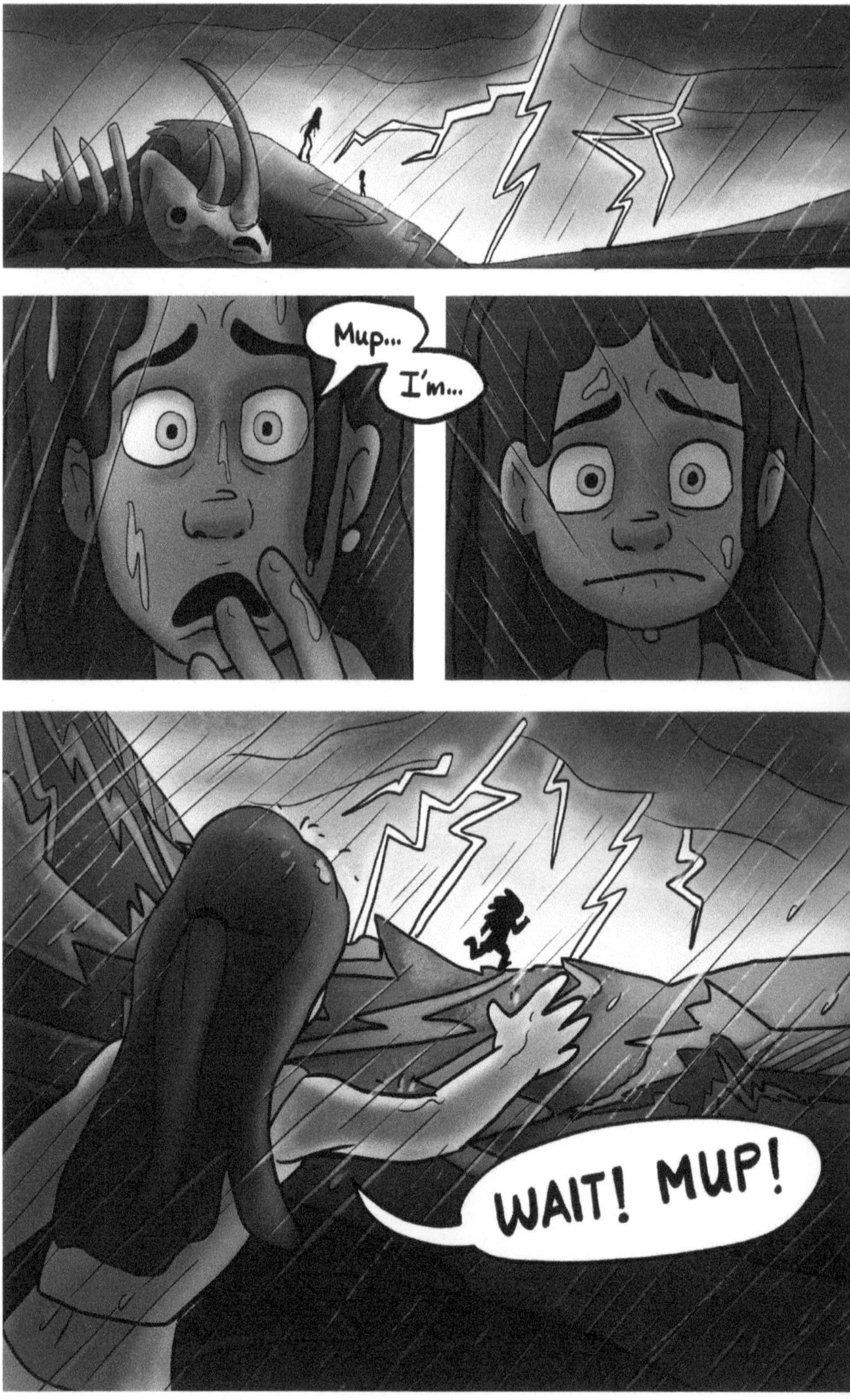
Mup...
I'm...
WAIT! MUP!

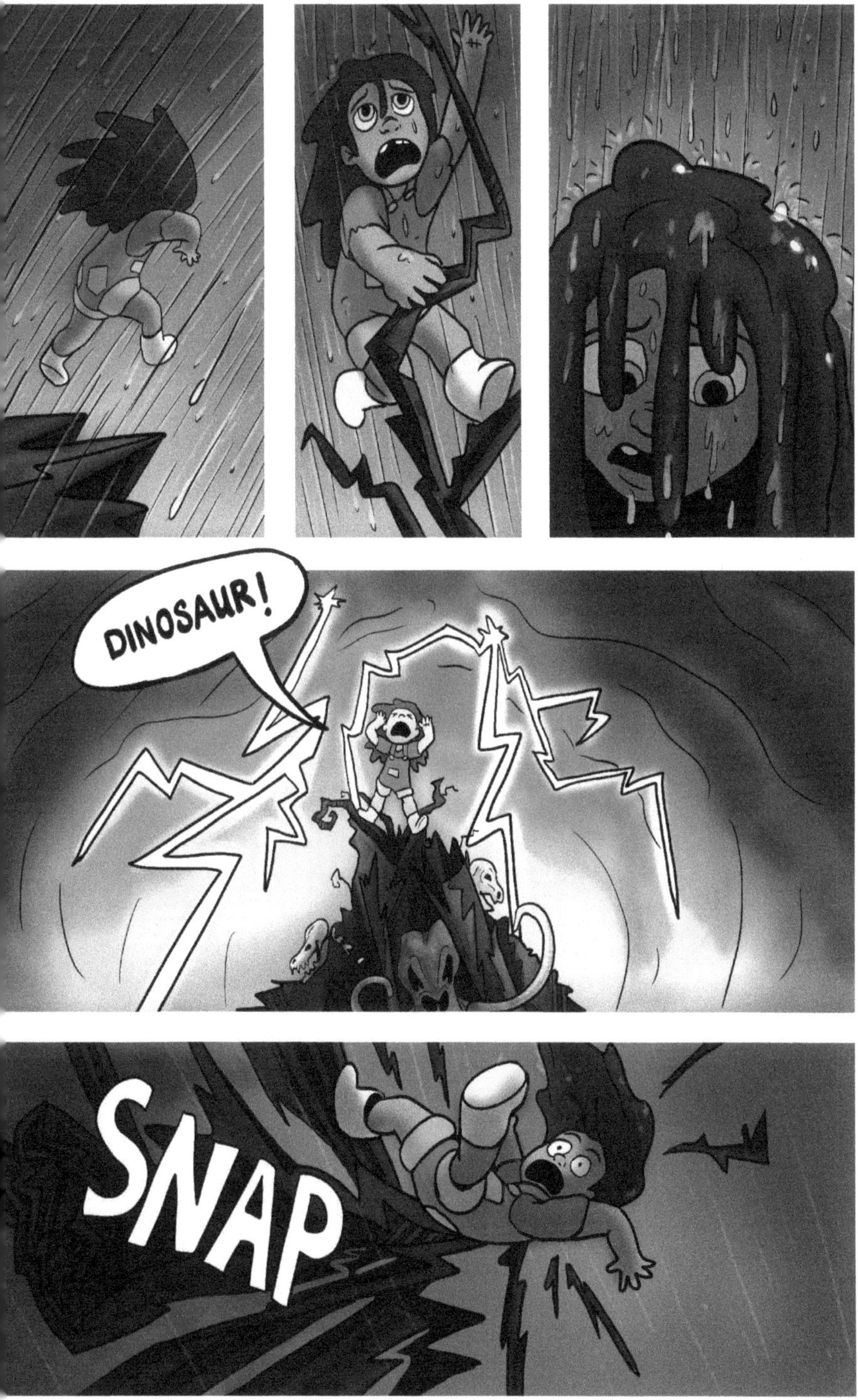
DINOSAUR!
SNAP

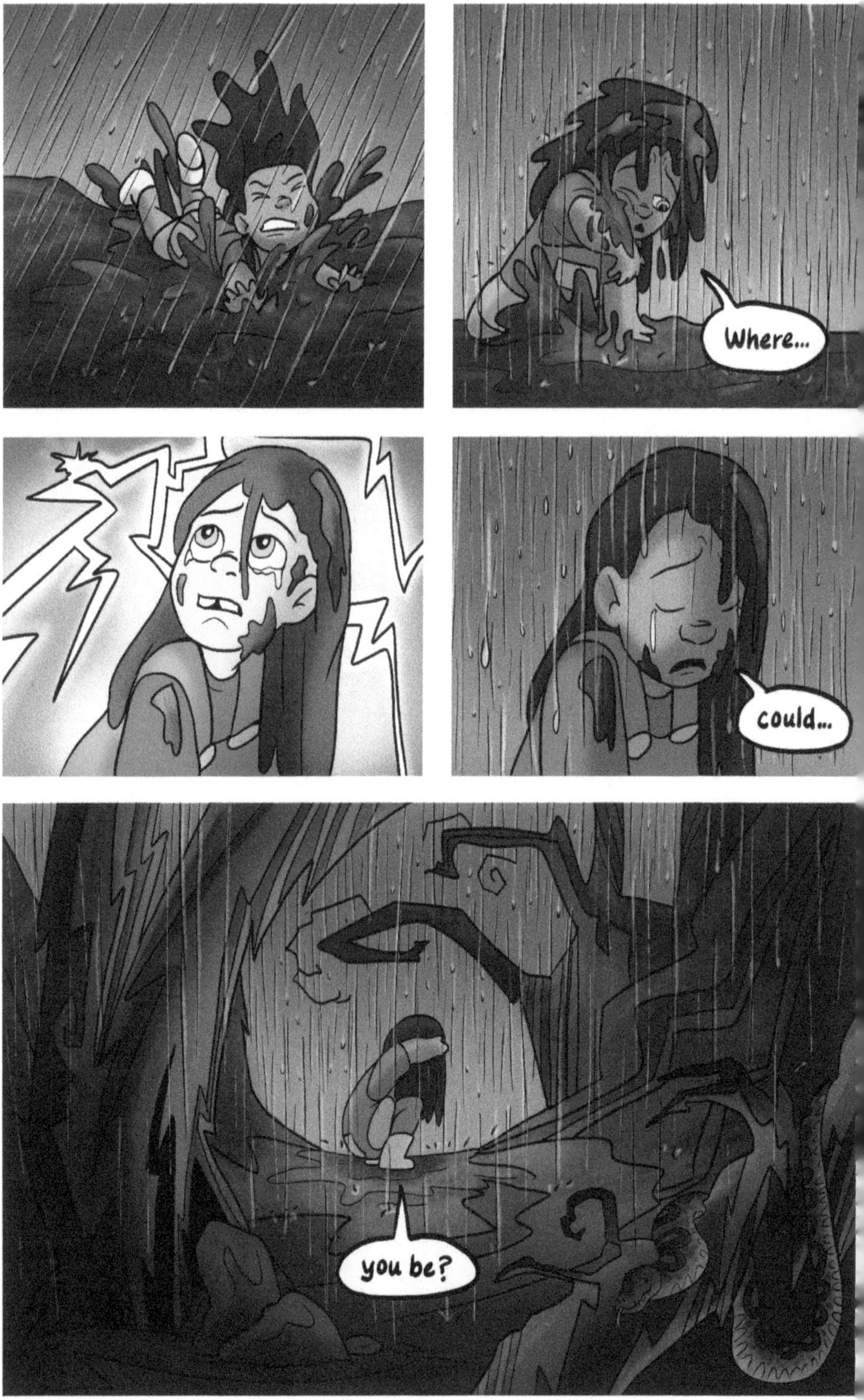
Where...
could...
you be?

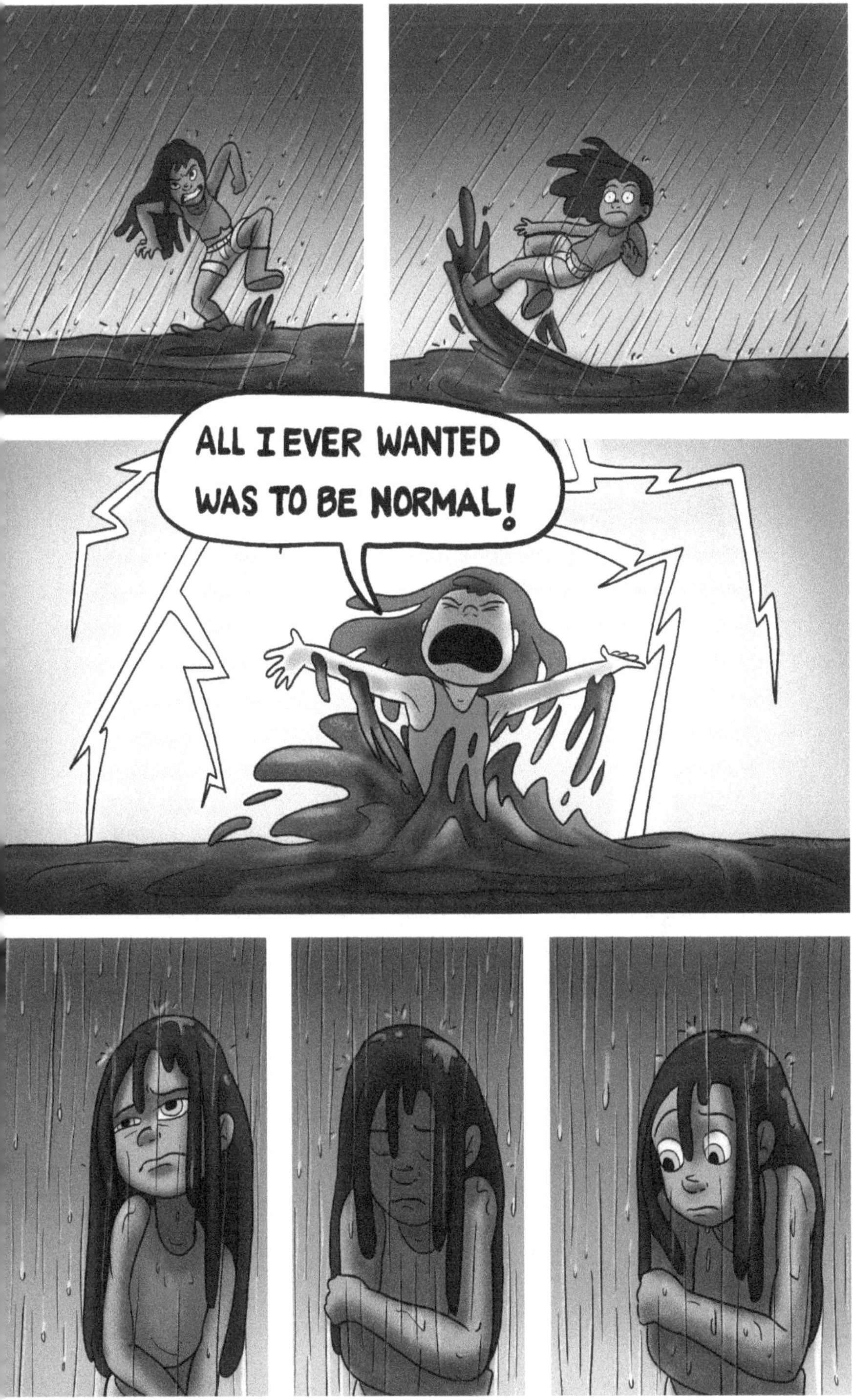
ALL I EVER WANTED
WAS TO BE NORMAL!

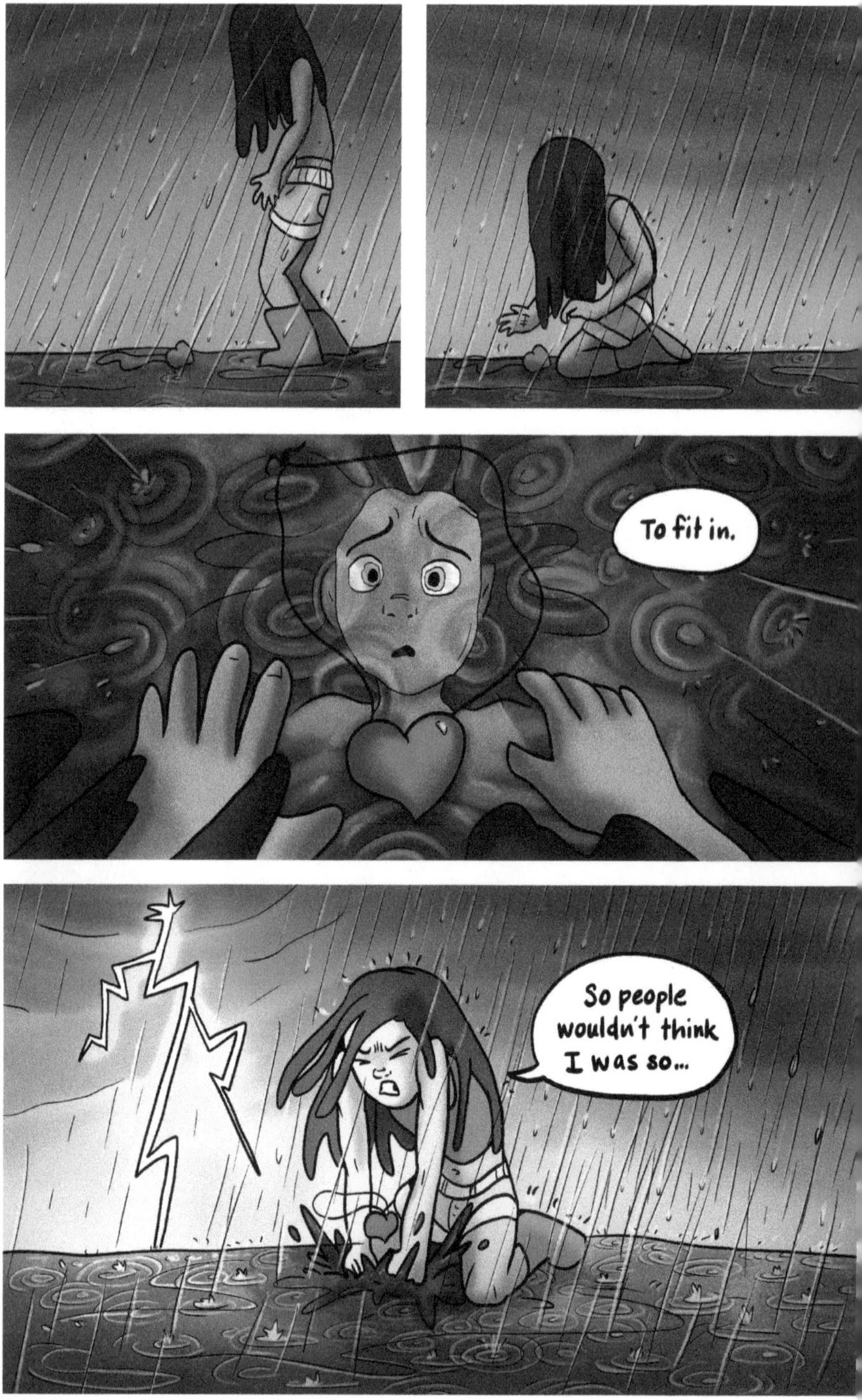
To fit in.
So people wouldn't think I was so...

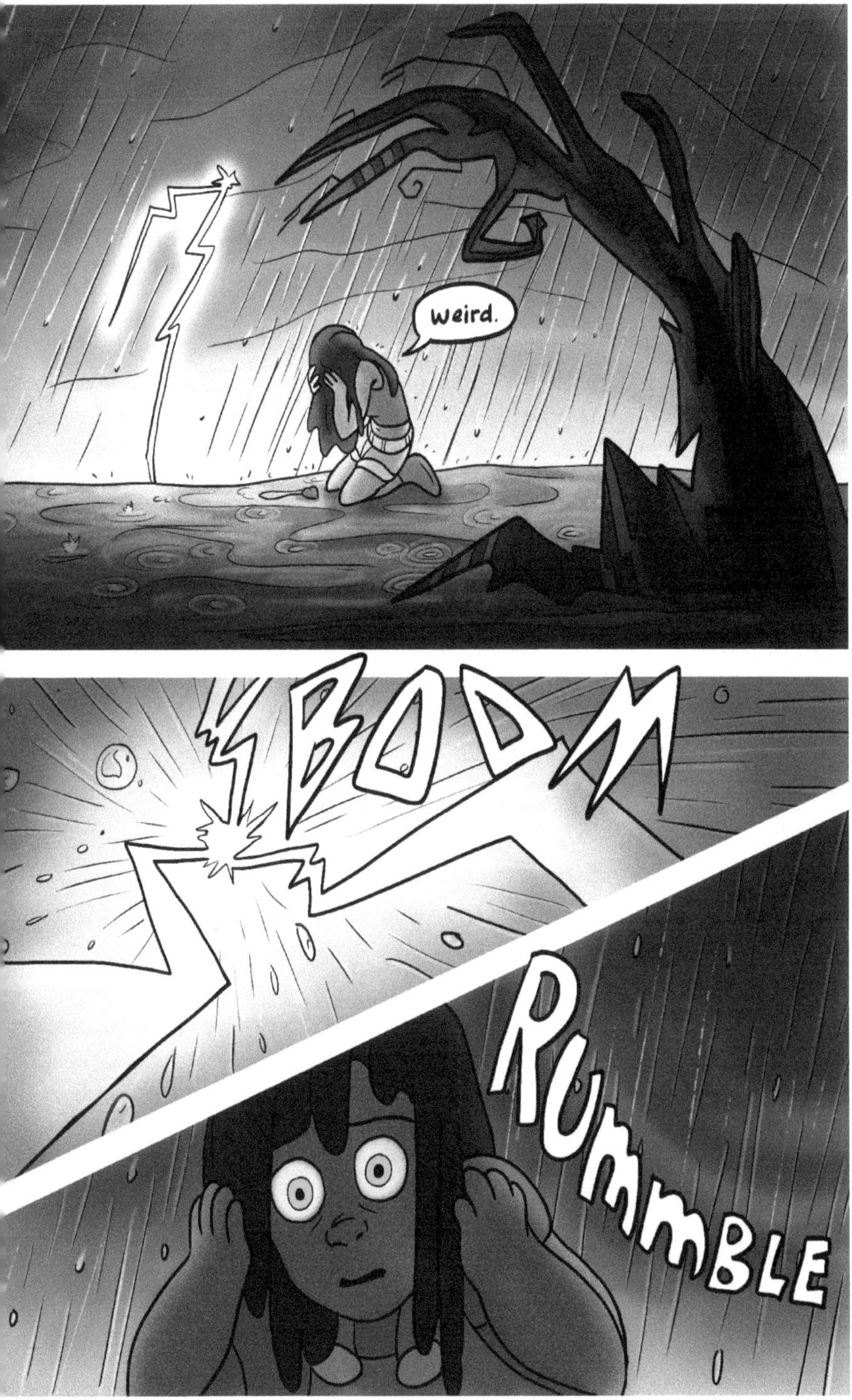
weird.
BOOM
RUMMBLE

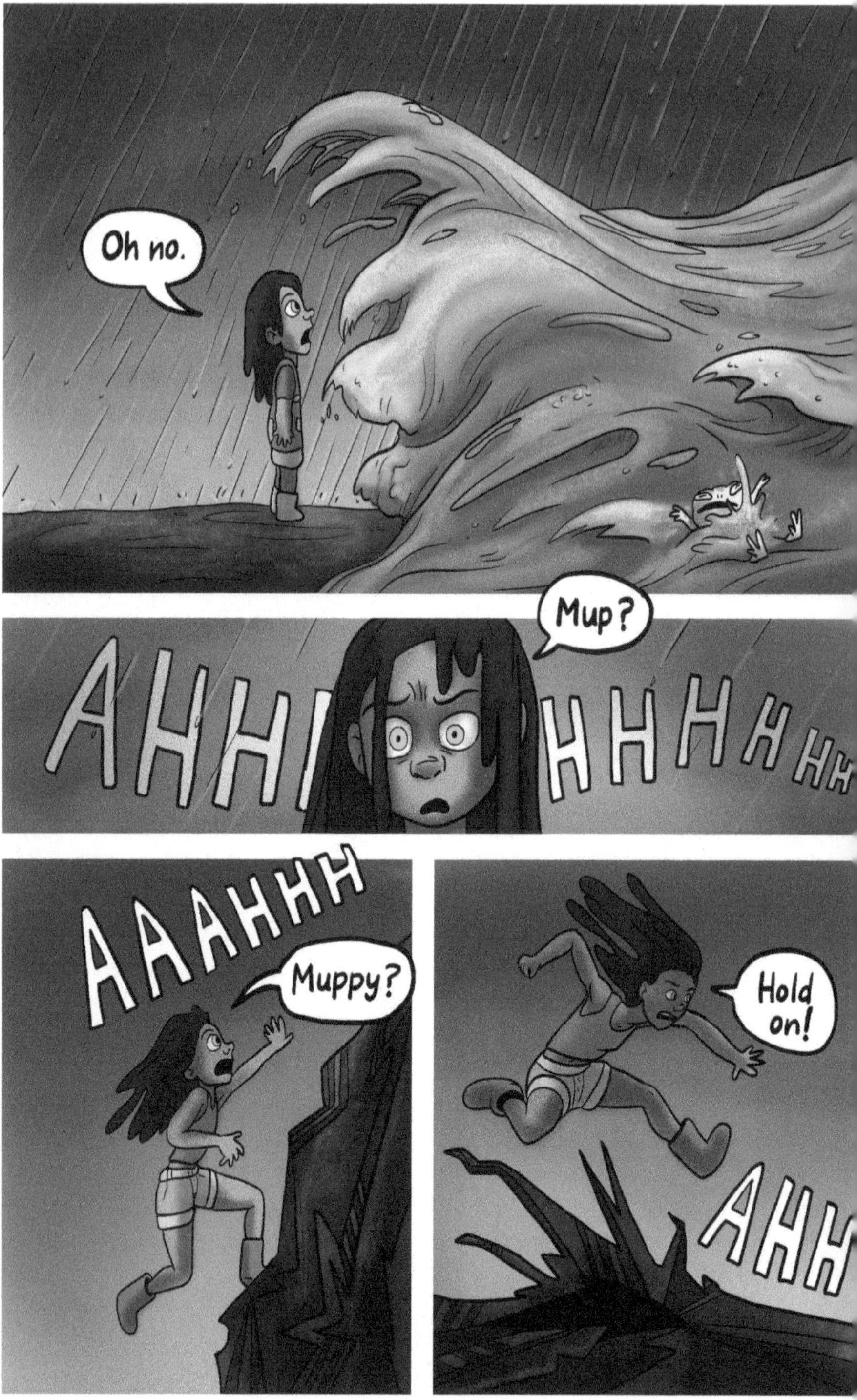
Oh no.
Mup?
AHHHHHHHHH
AAAHHH
Muppy?
Hold on!
AHH

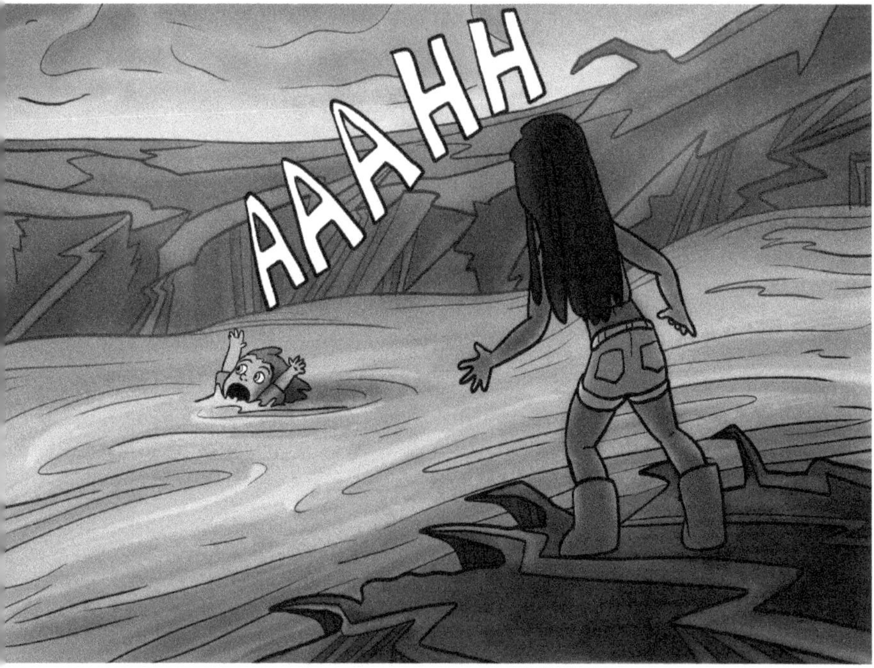
AAAHH

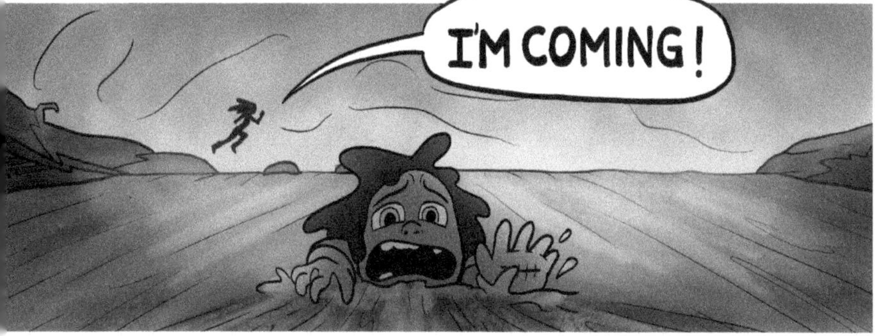
I'M COMING!

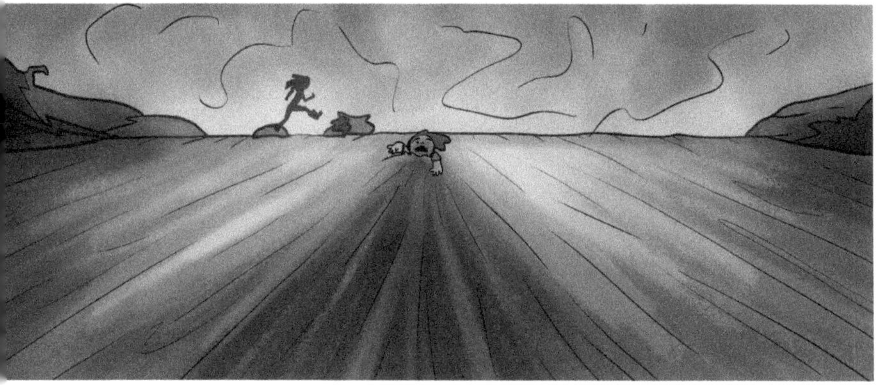

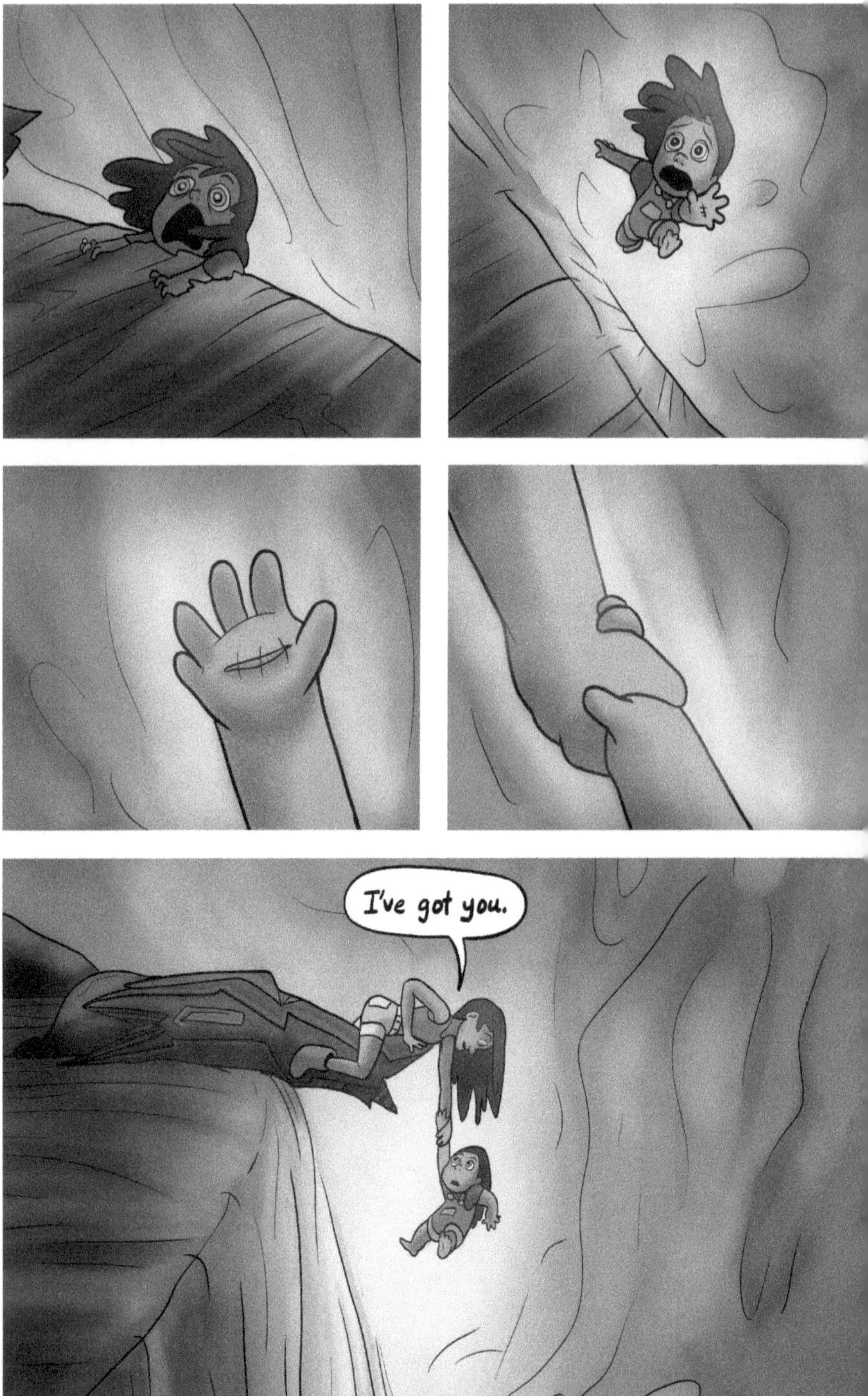
I've got you.

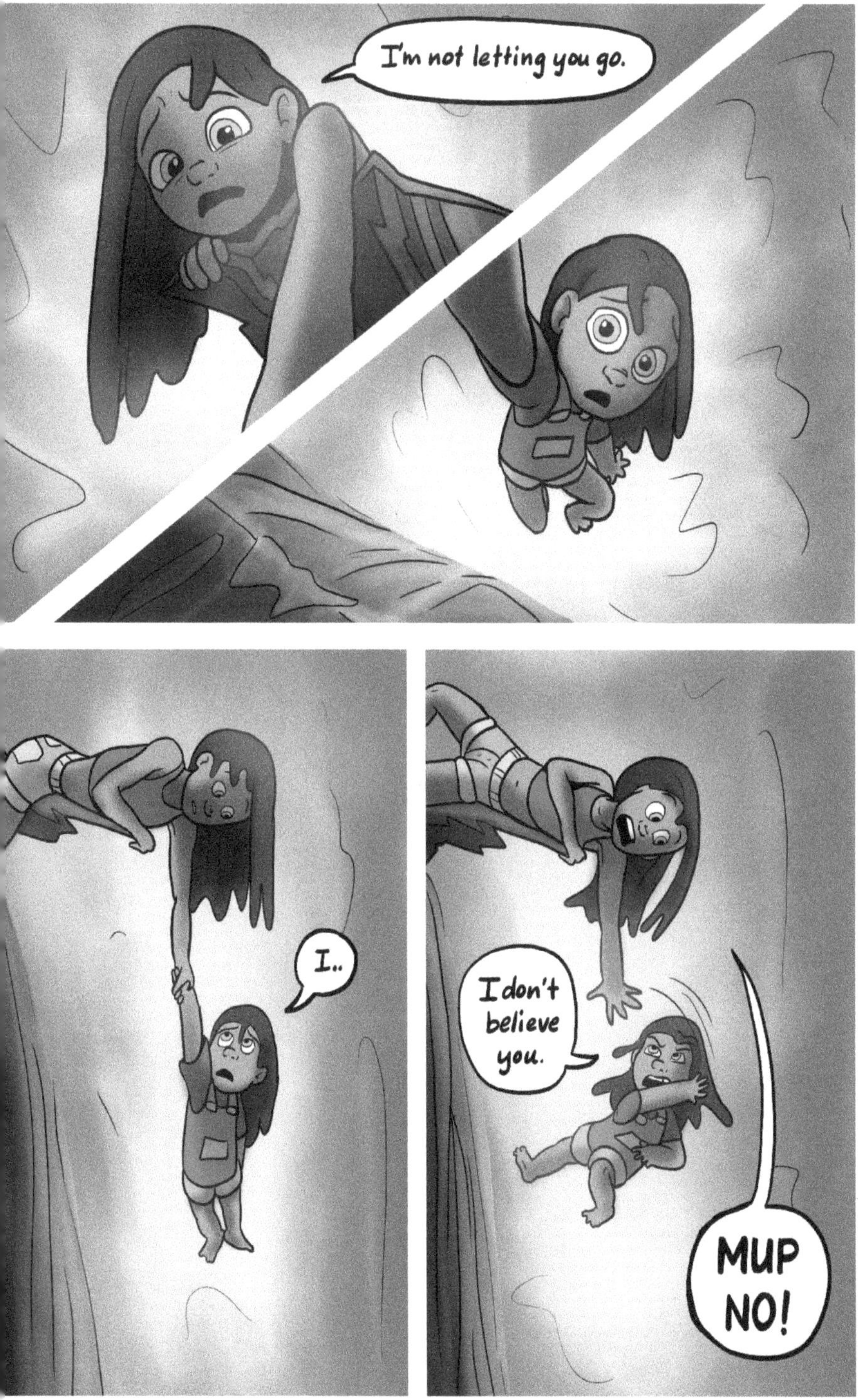
I'm not letting you go.
I..
I don't believe you.
MUP NO!

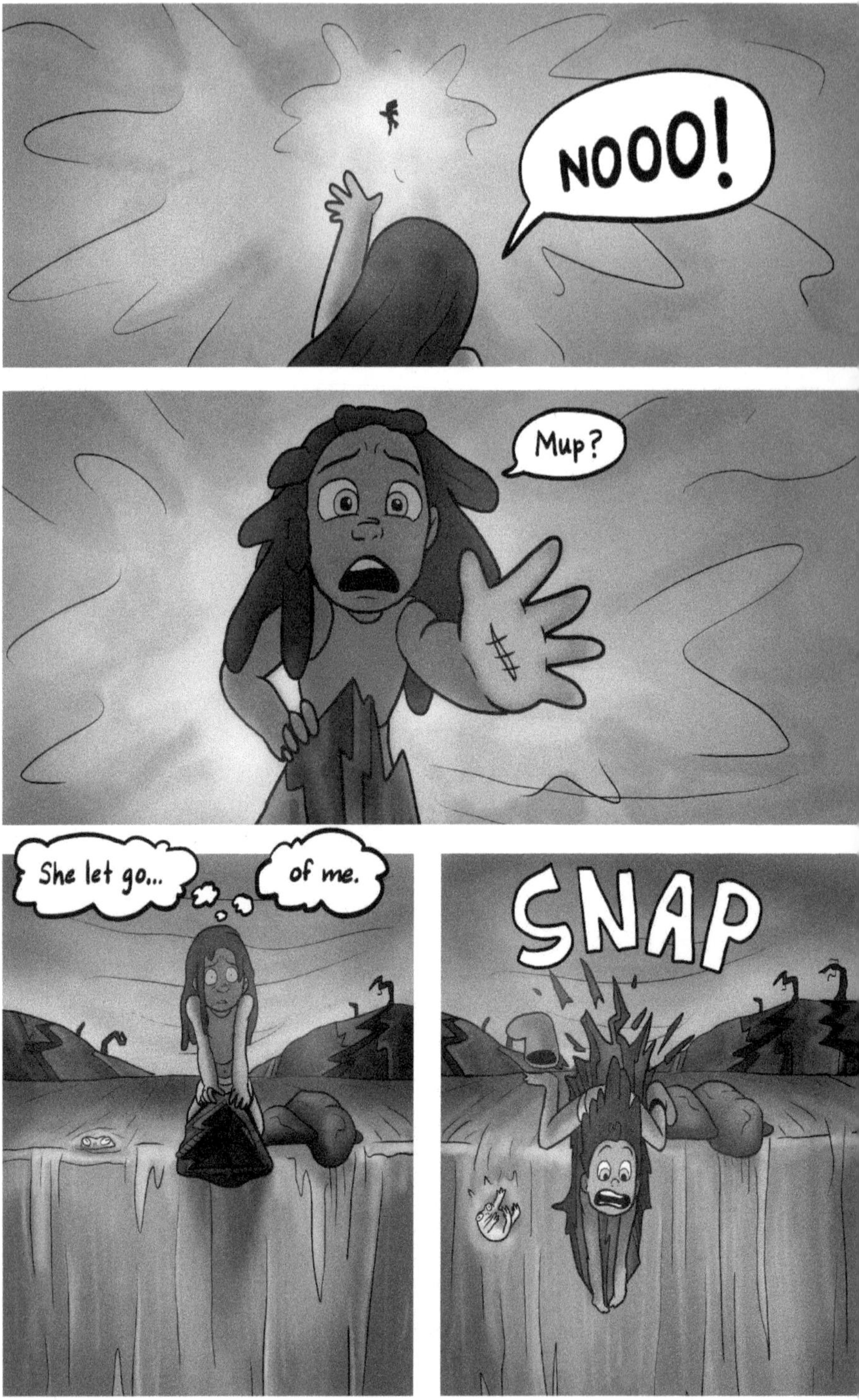
NOOO!
Mup?
She let go...
of me.
SNAP

MUP!

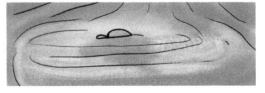

213

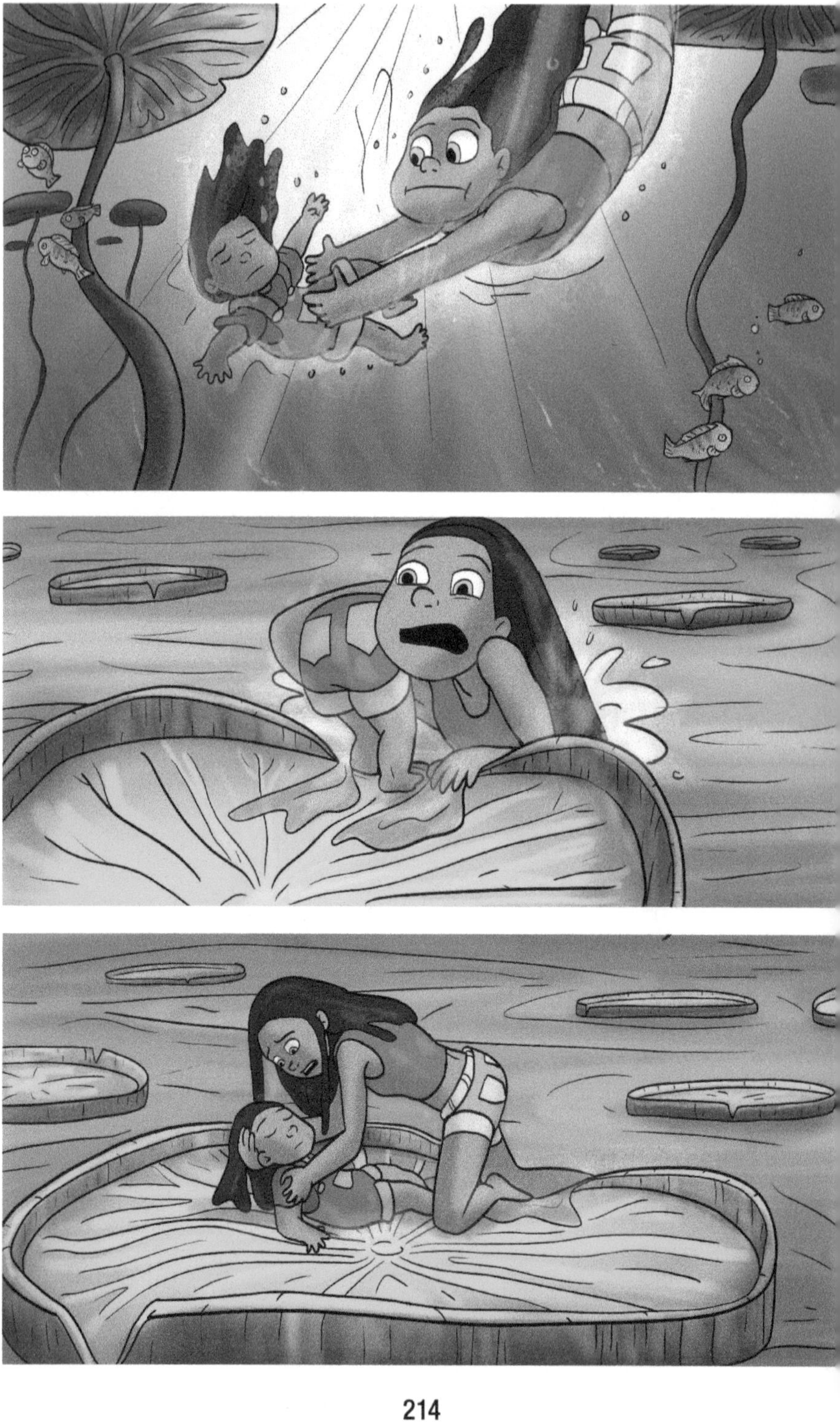

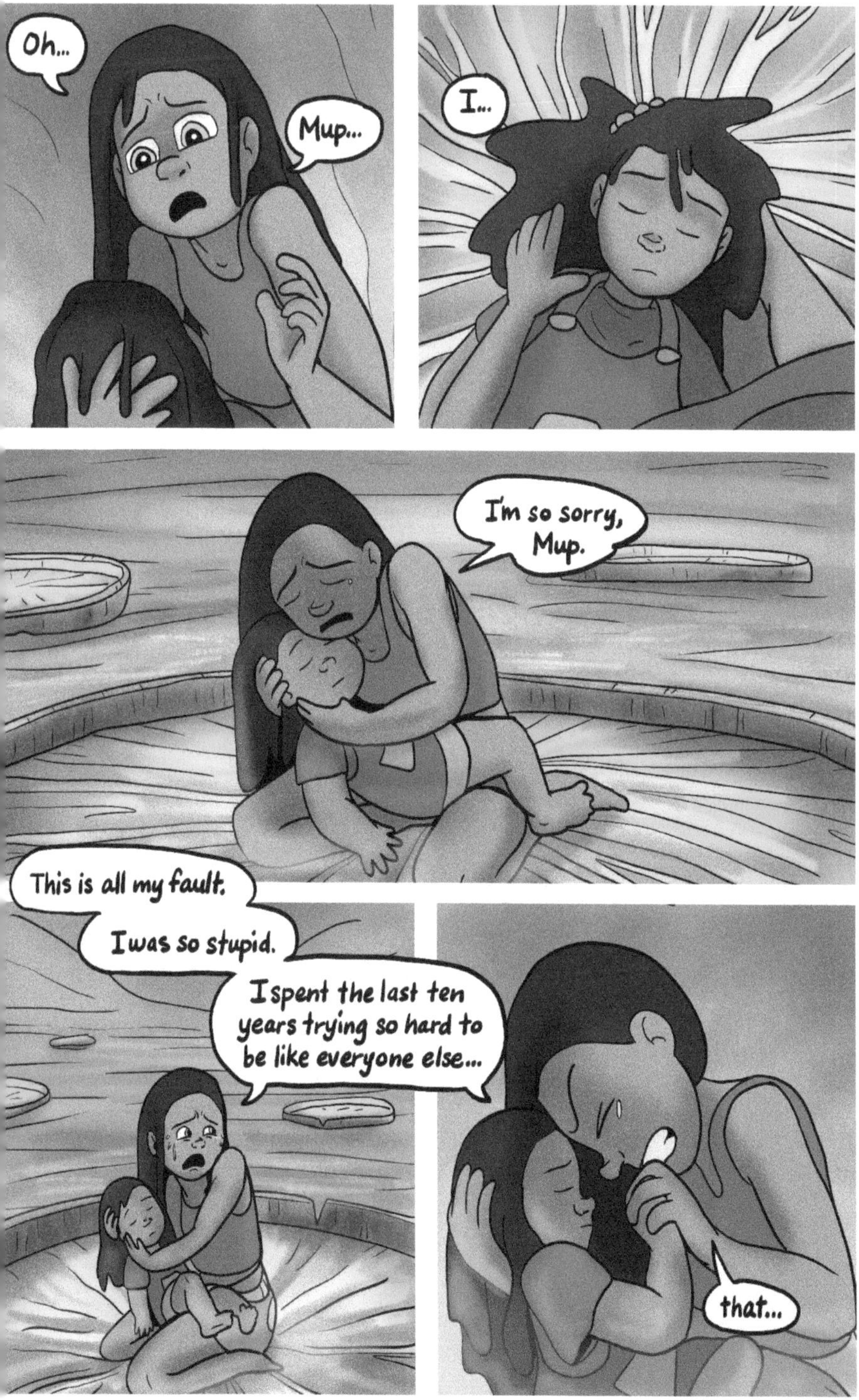
Oh...
Mup...
I...
I'm so sorry, Mup.
This is all my fault.
I was so stupid.
I spent the last ten years trying so hard to be like everyone else...
that...

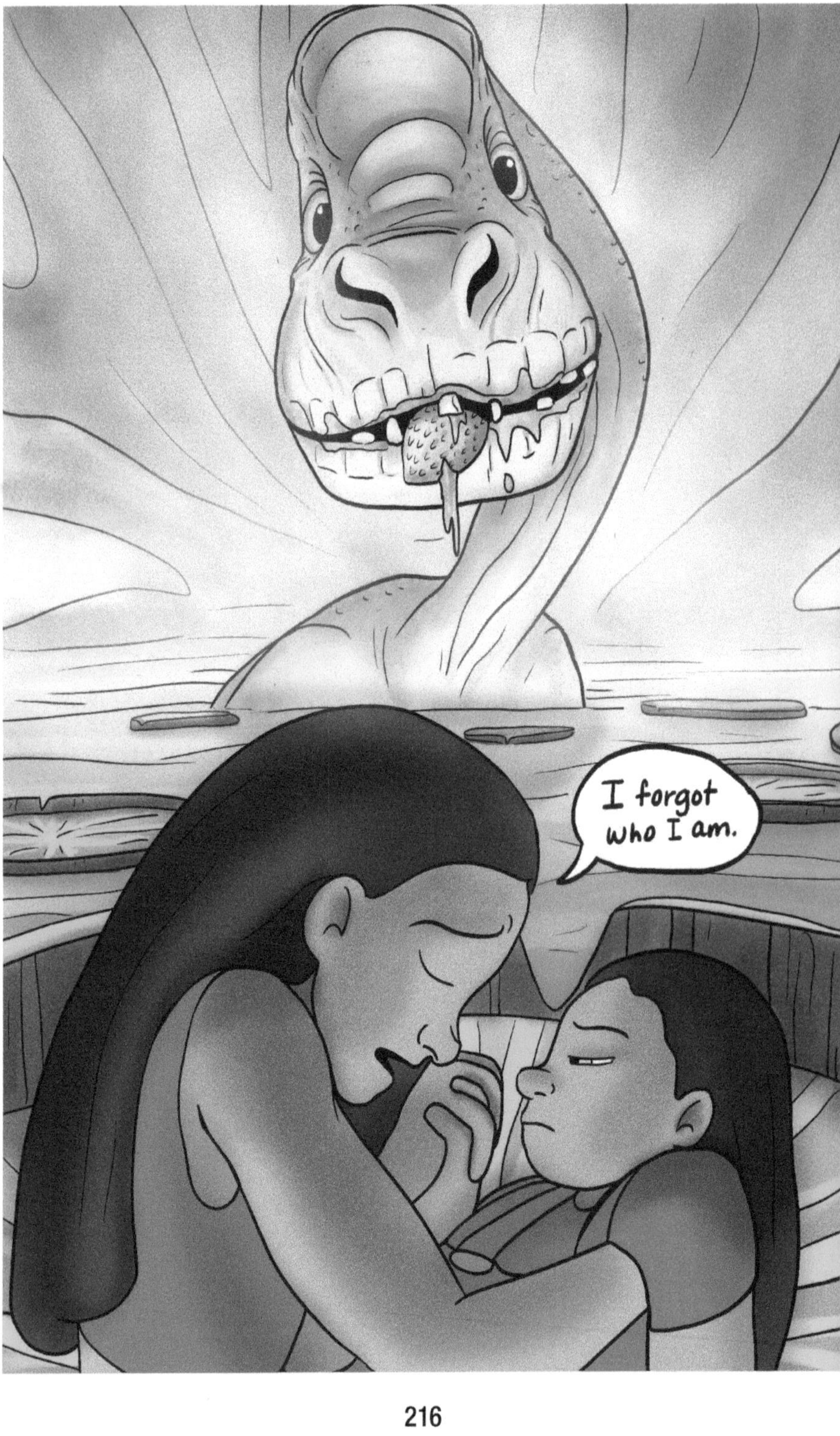
I forgot who I am.

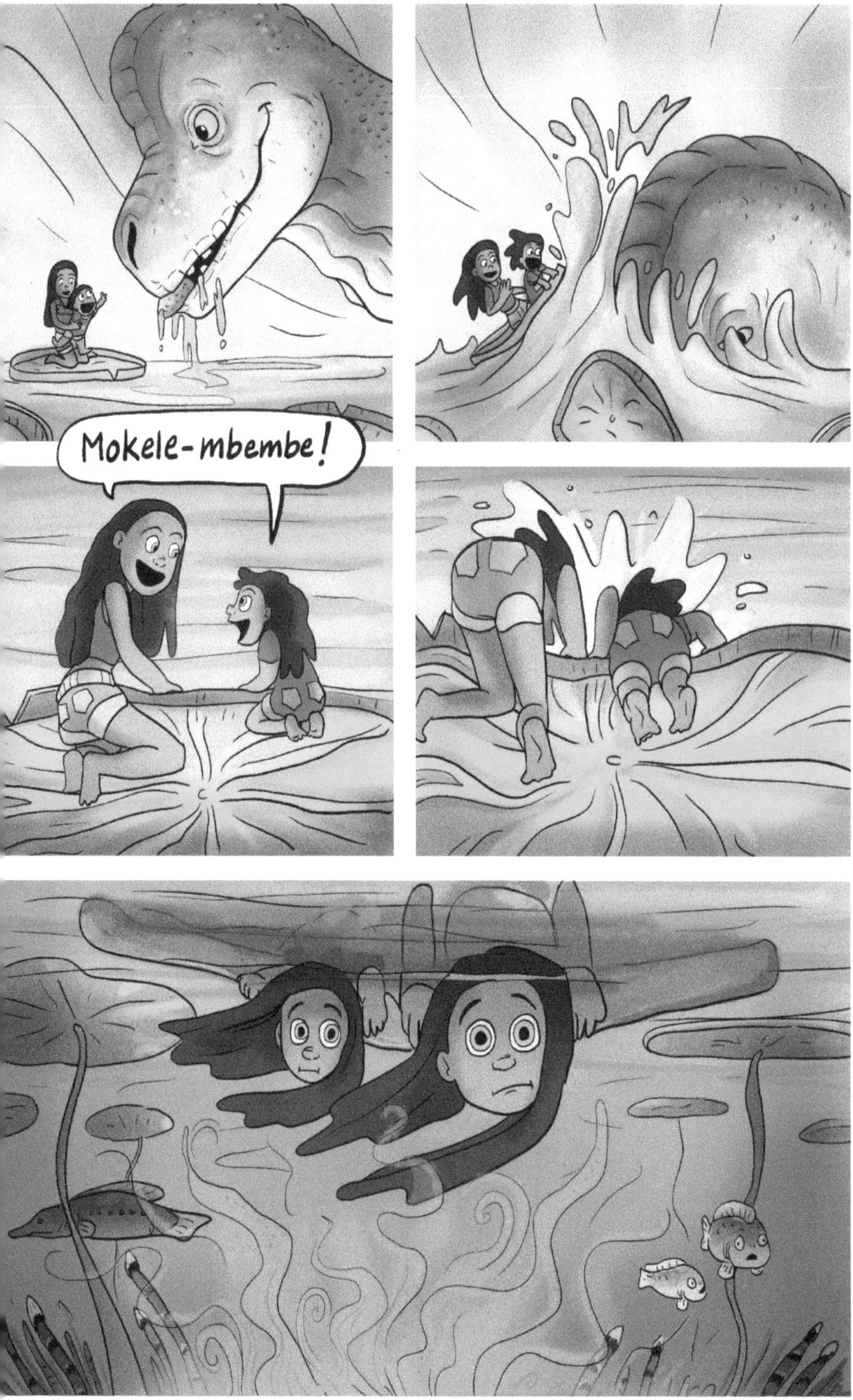
Mokele-mbembe!

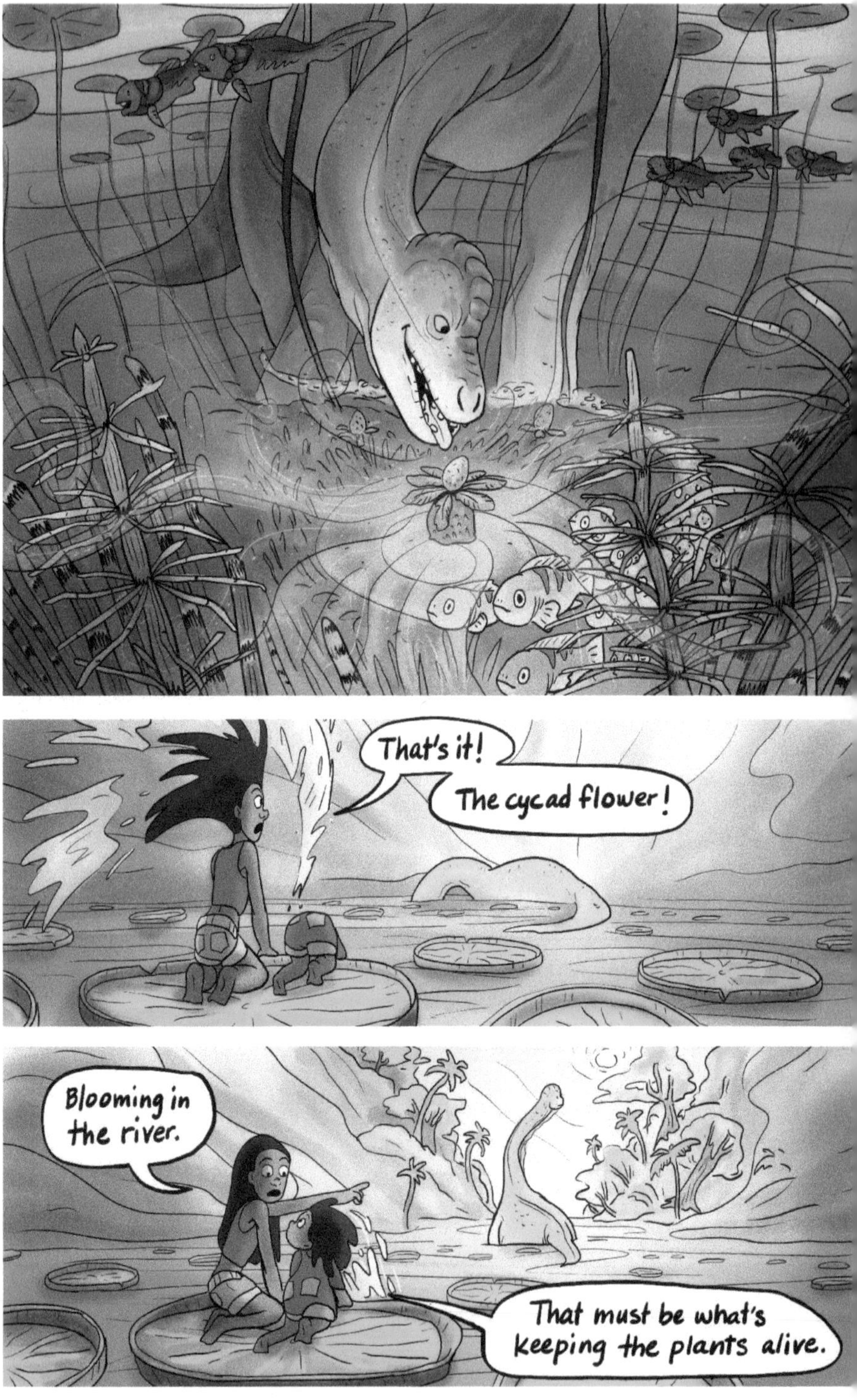
That's it!
The cycad flower!
Blooming in the river.
That must be what's keeping the plants alive.

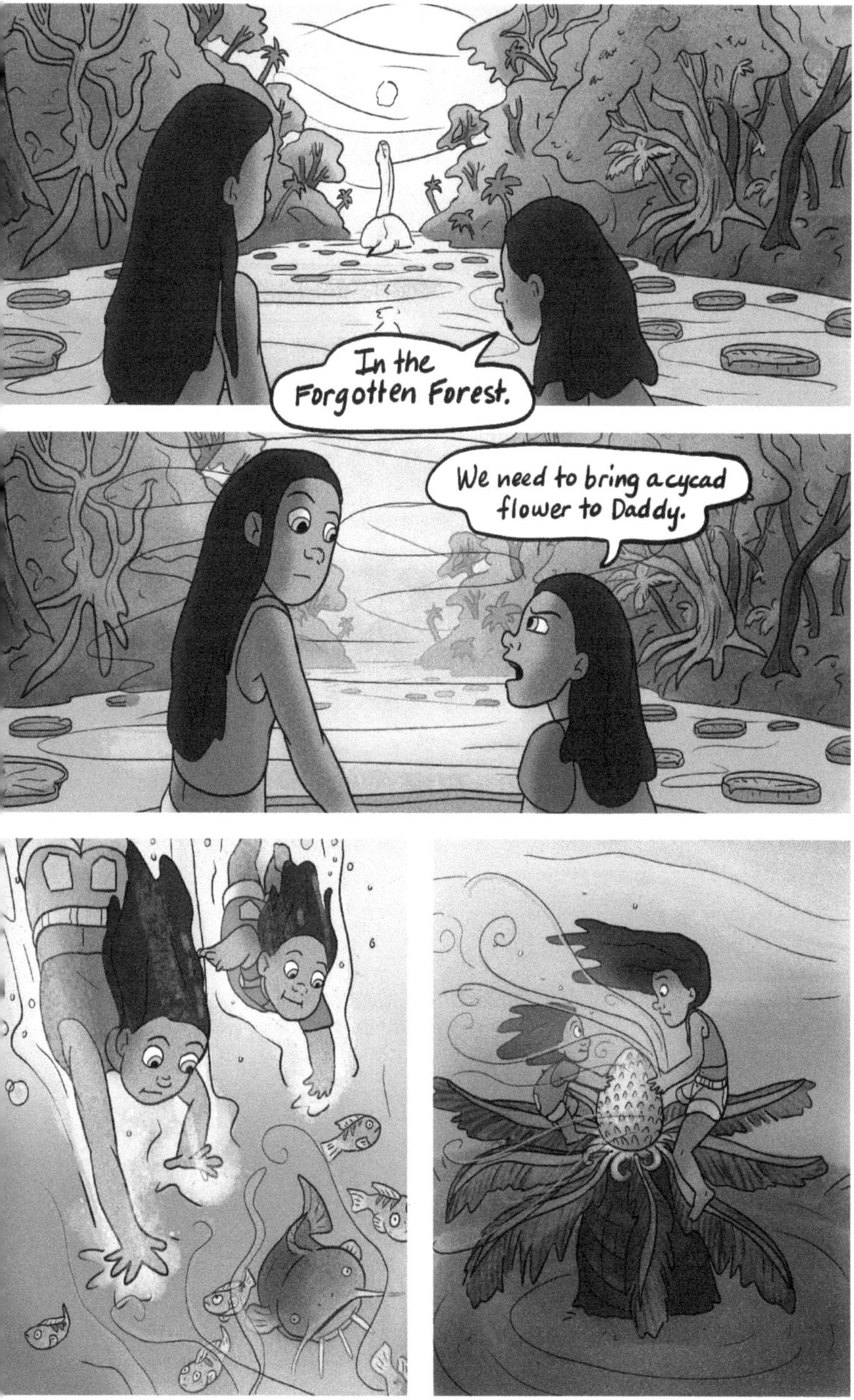
In the Forgotten Forest.
We need to bring a cycad flower to Daddy.

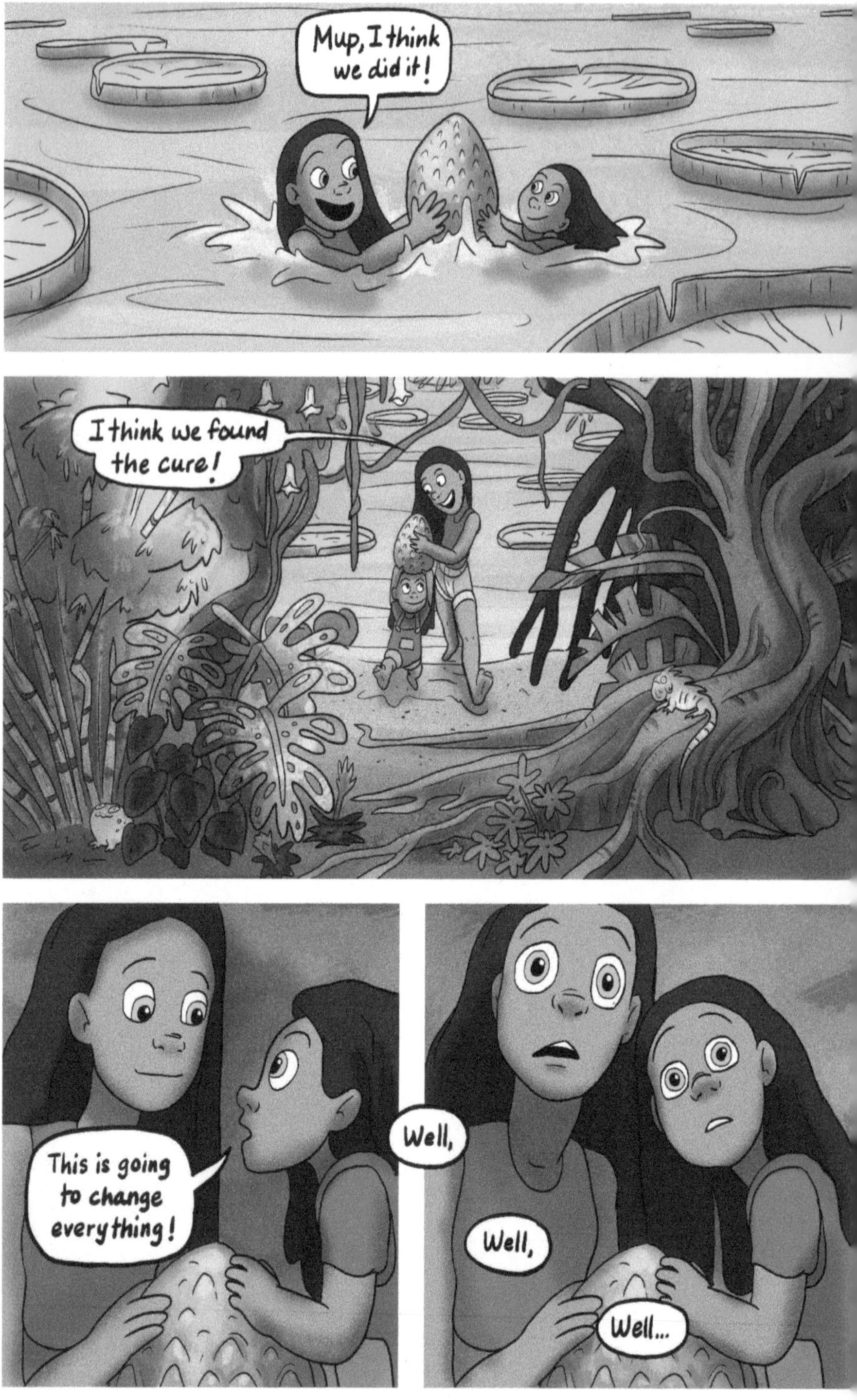

Mup, I think we did it!
I think we found the cure!
This is going to change everything!
Well,
Well,
Well...

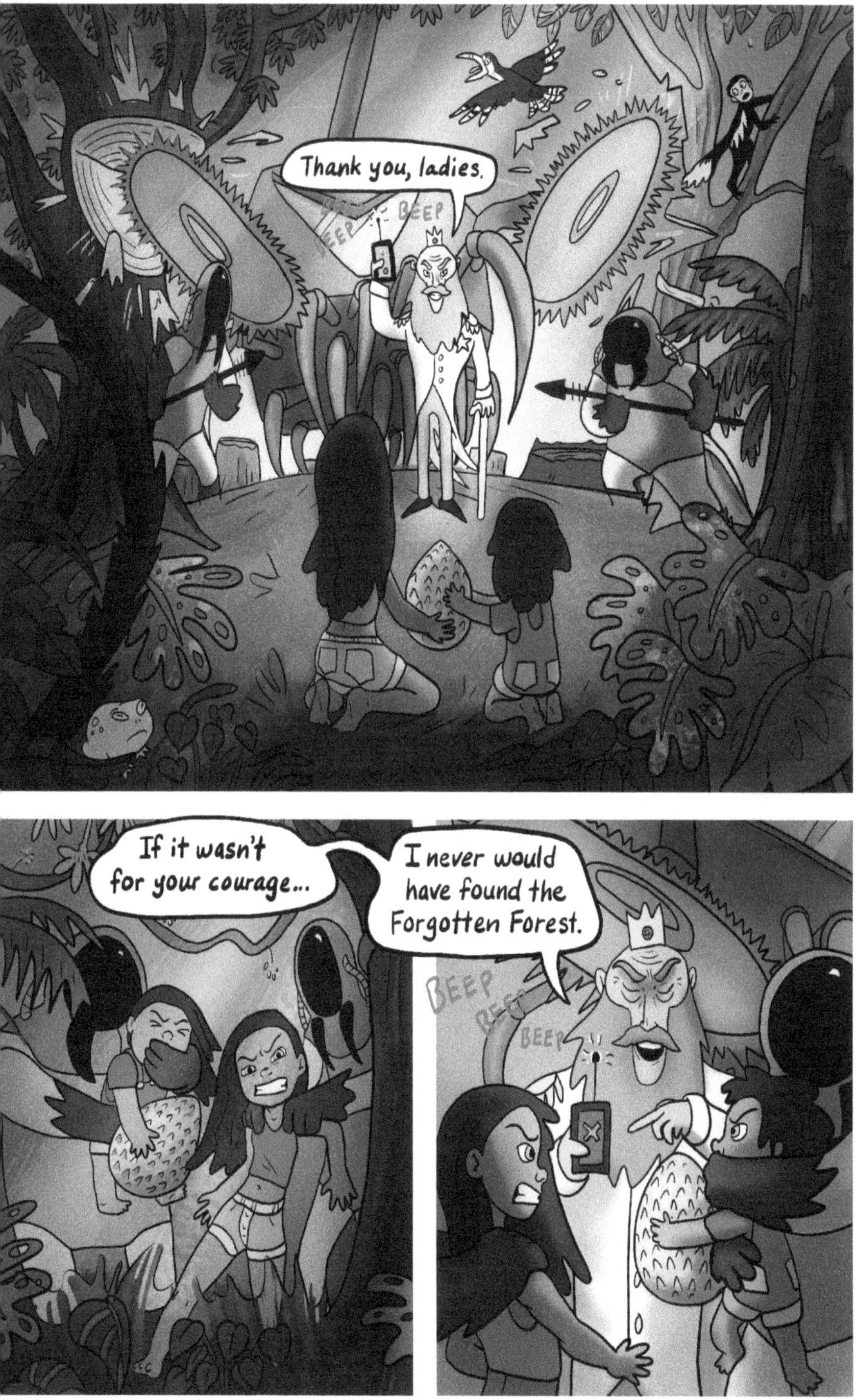

Thank you, ladies.
BEEP
BEEP
If it wasn't for your courage...
I never would have found the Forgotten Forest.
BEEP
BEEP
BEEP

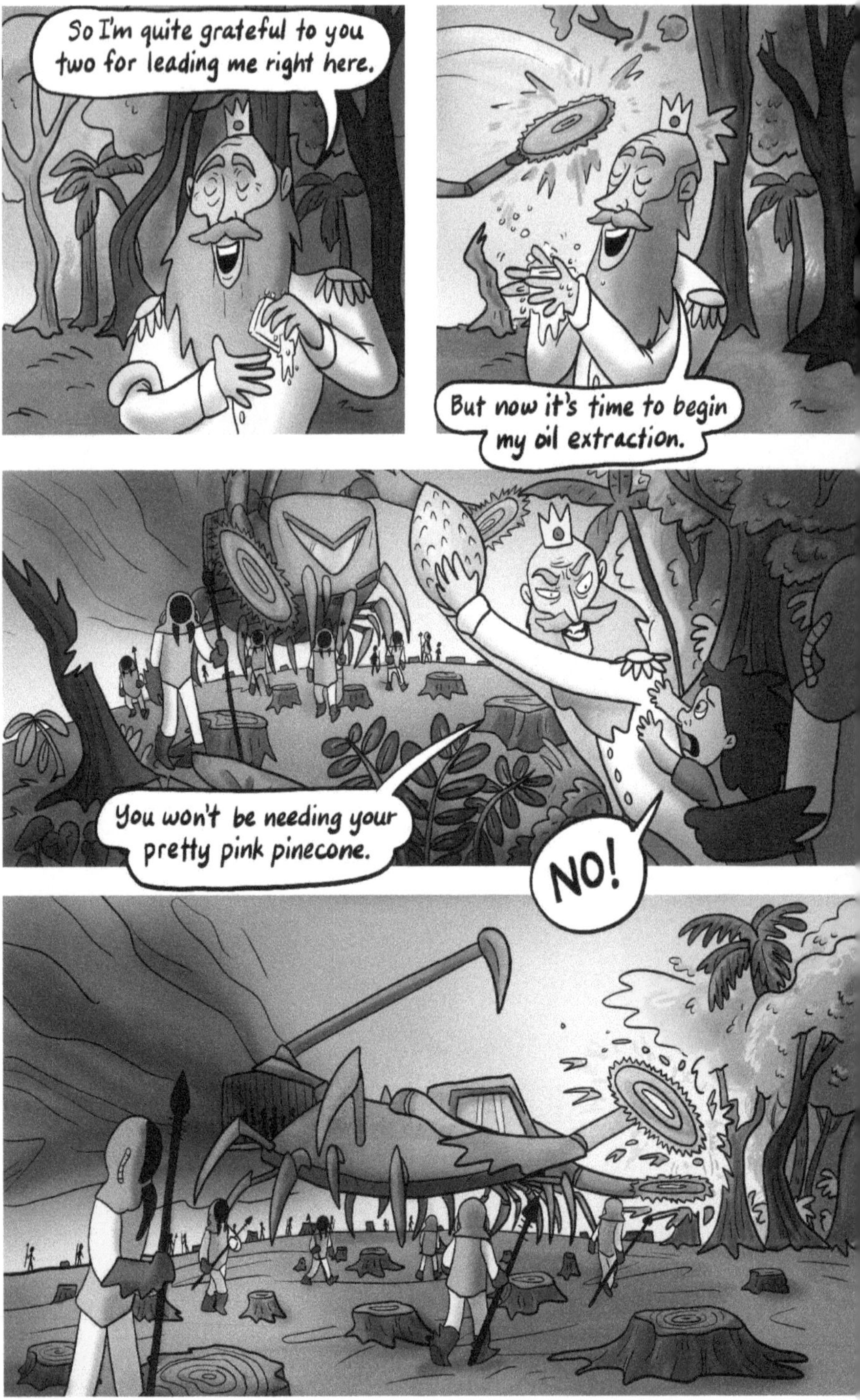

So I'm quite grateful to you two for leading me right here.
But now it's time to begin my oil extraction.
You won't be needing your pretty pink pinecone.
NO!

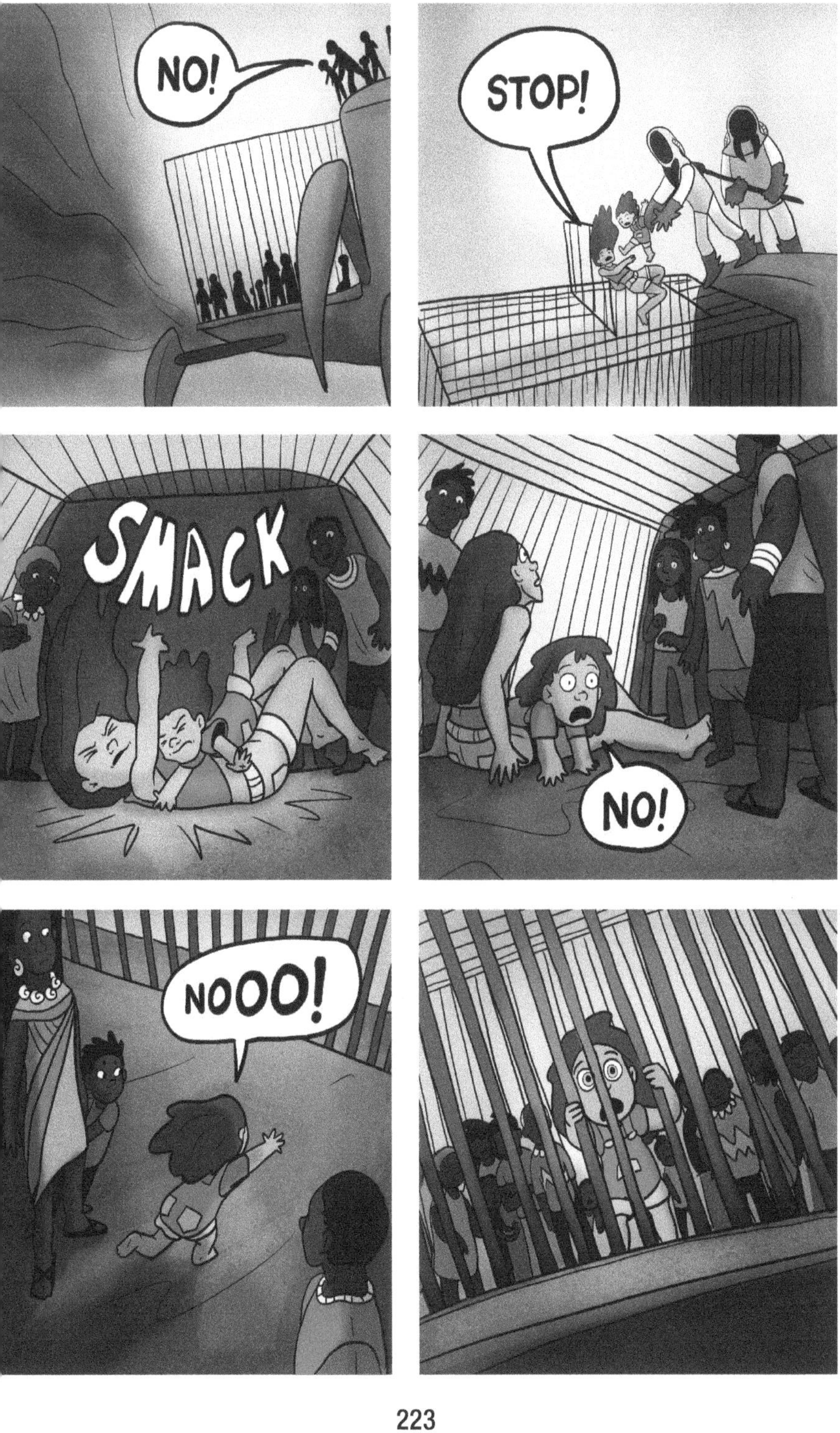
NO!
STOP!
SMACK
NO!
NOOO!

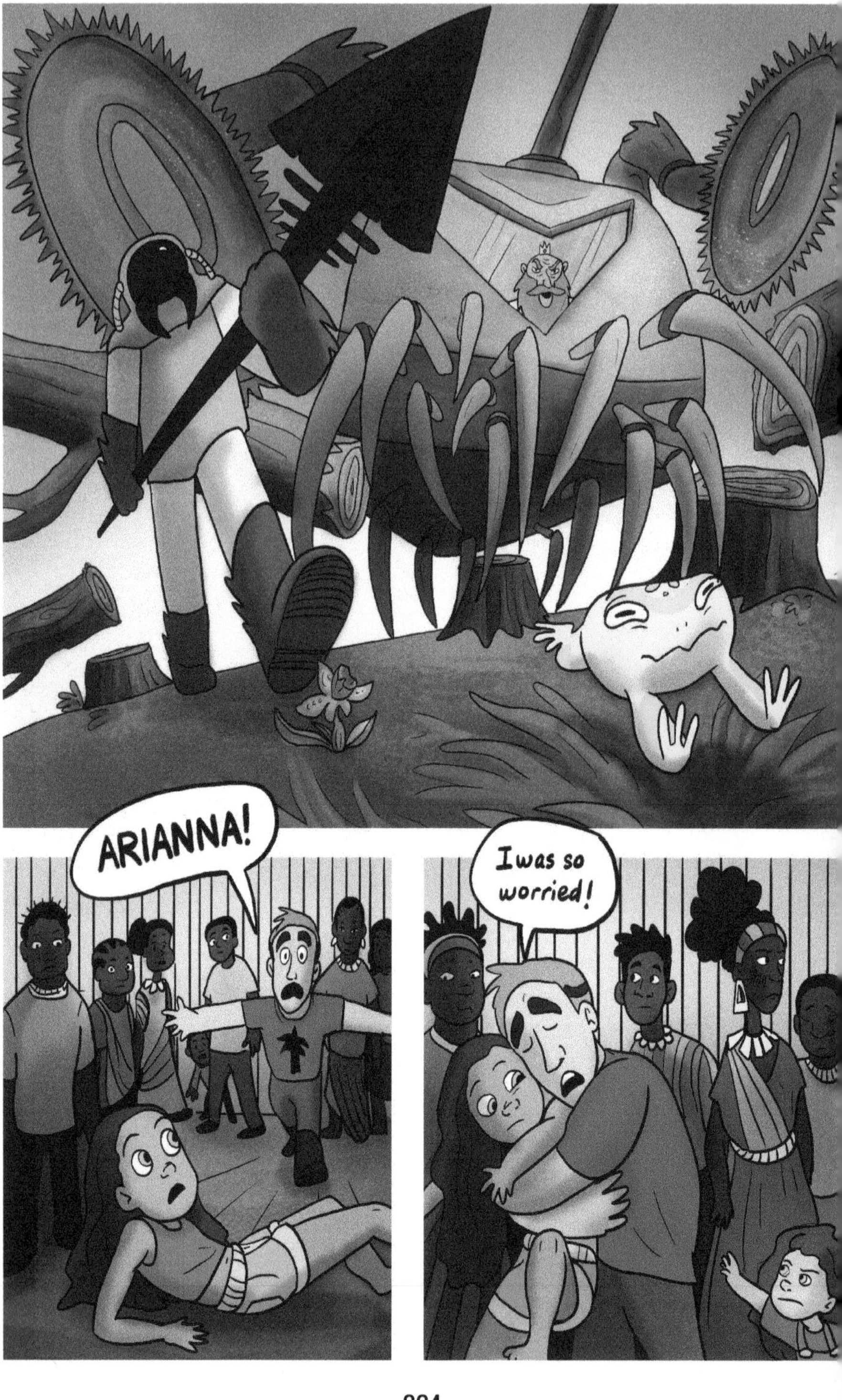
ARIANNA!
I was so worried!

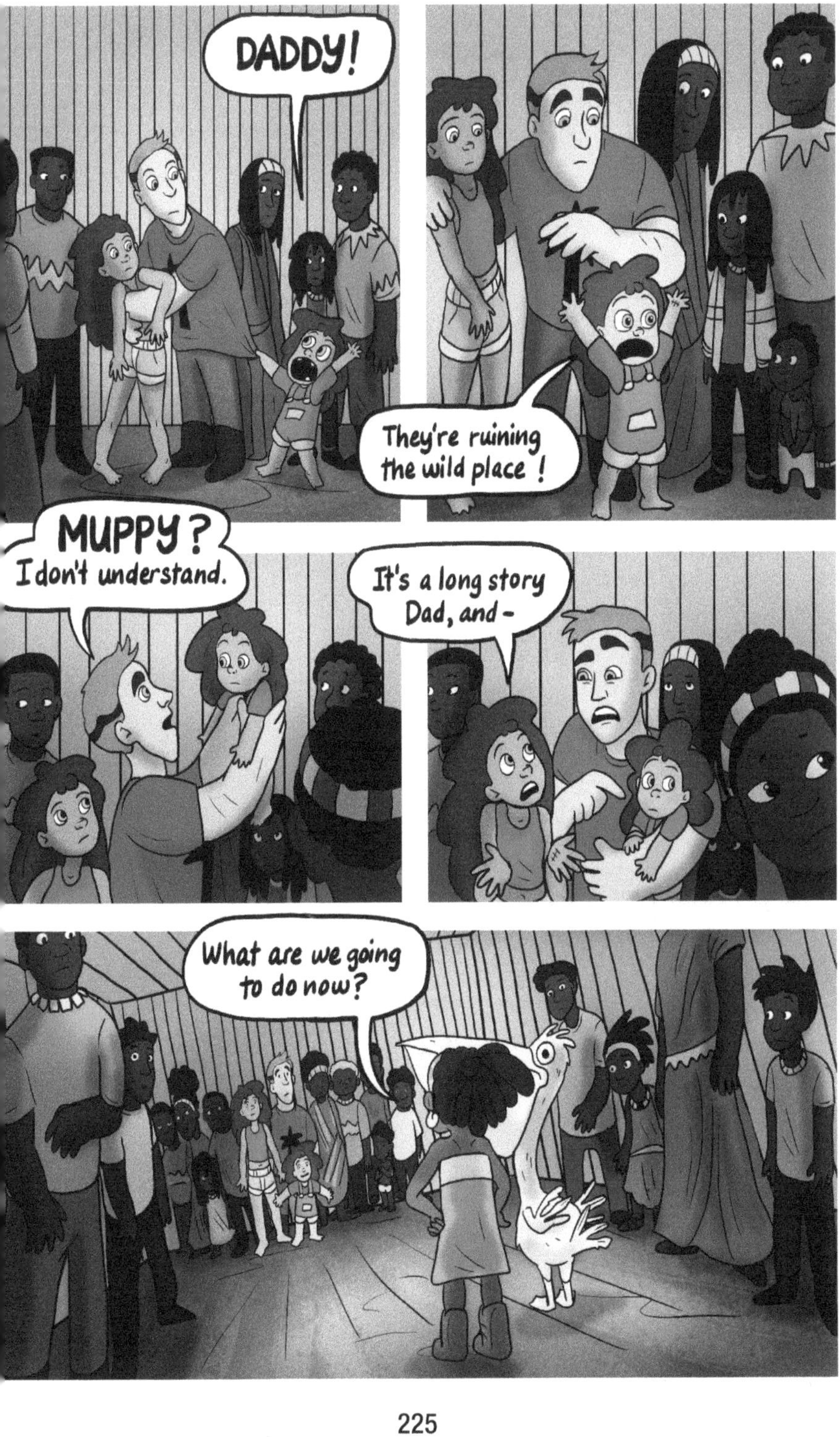
DADDY!
They're ruining the wild place !
MUPPY ? I don't understand.
It's a long story Dad, and -
What are we going to do now?

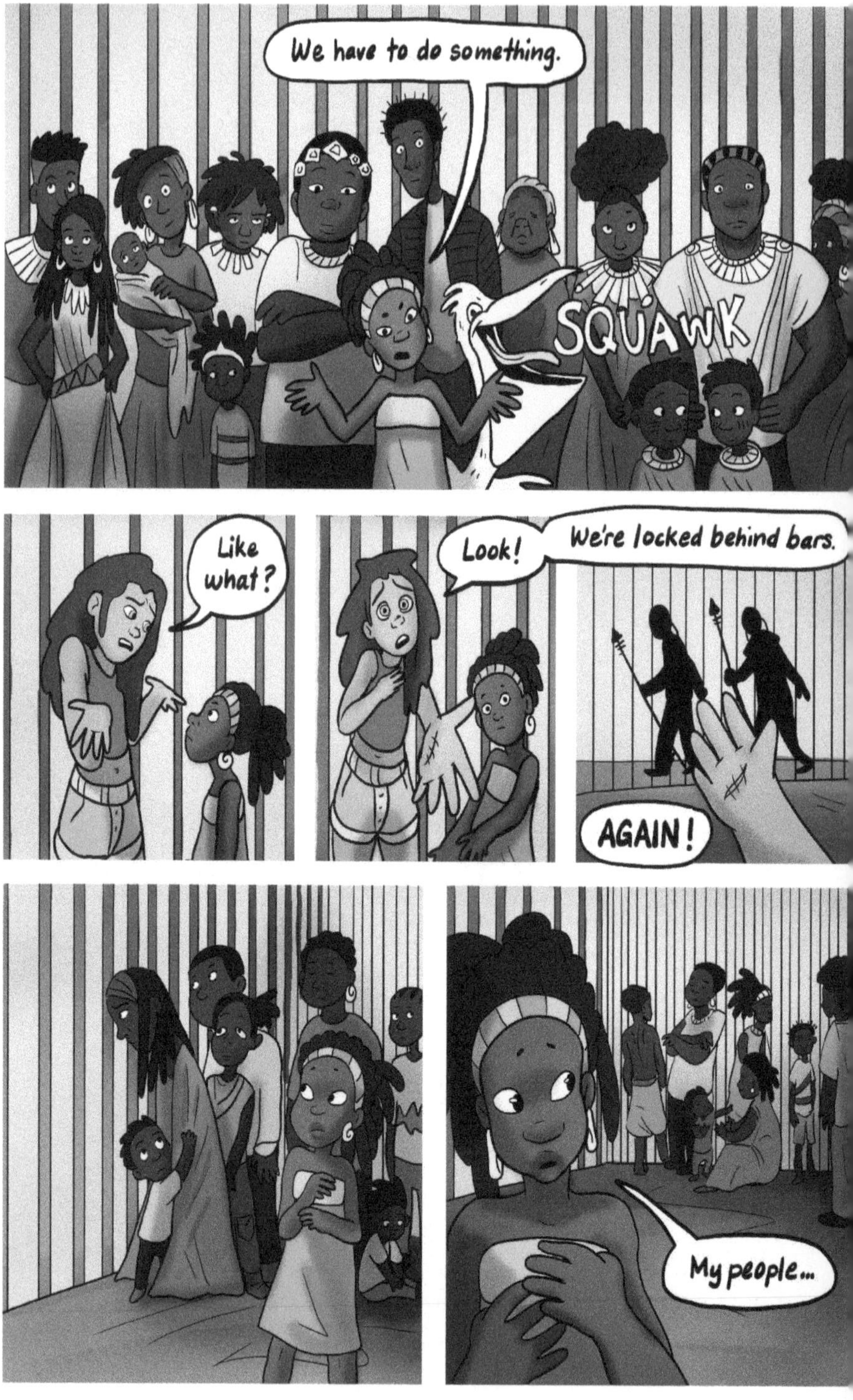
We have to do something.
SQUAWK
Like what?
Look!
We're locked behind bars.
AGAIN!
My people...

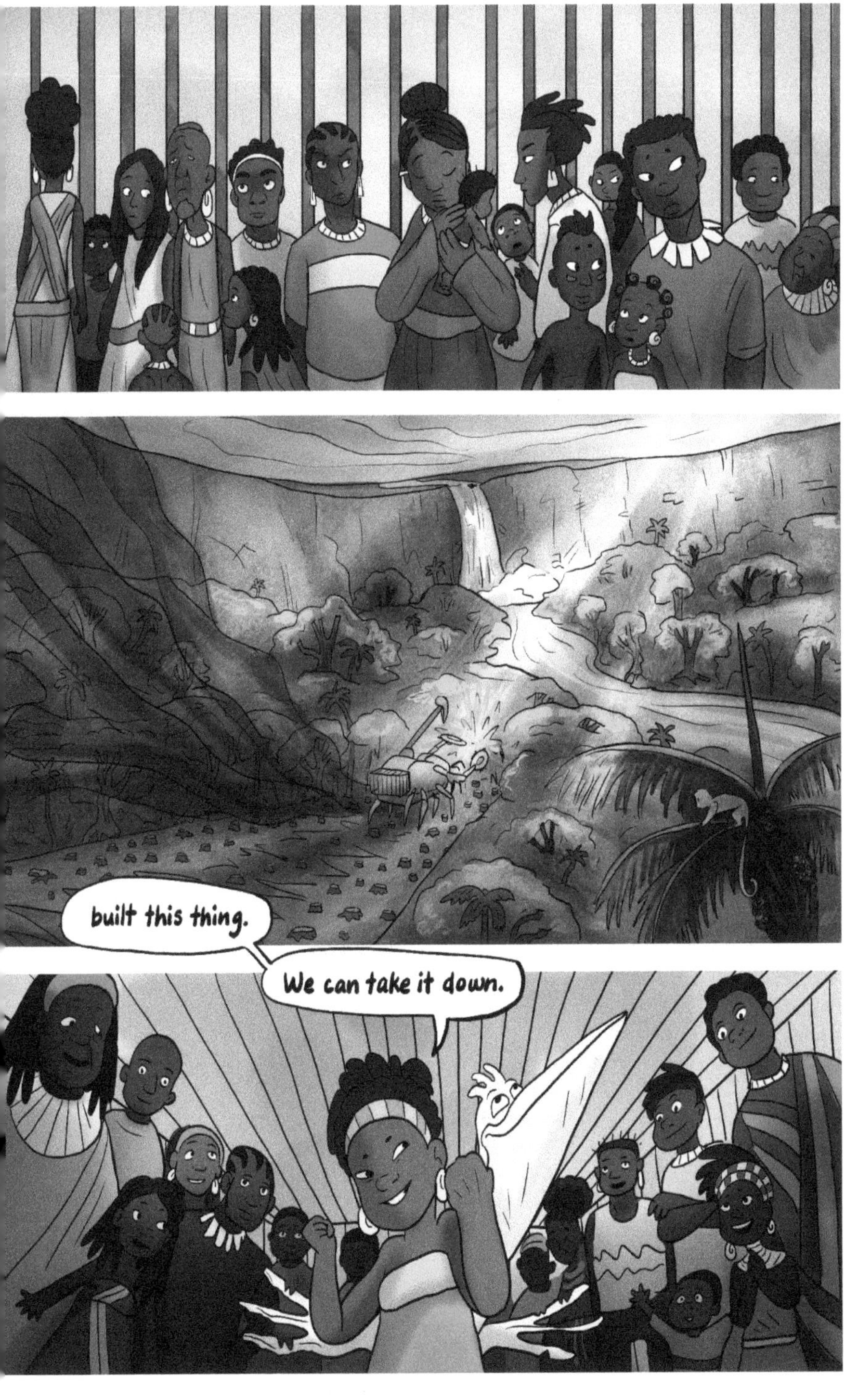
built this thing.
We can take it down.

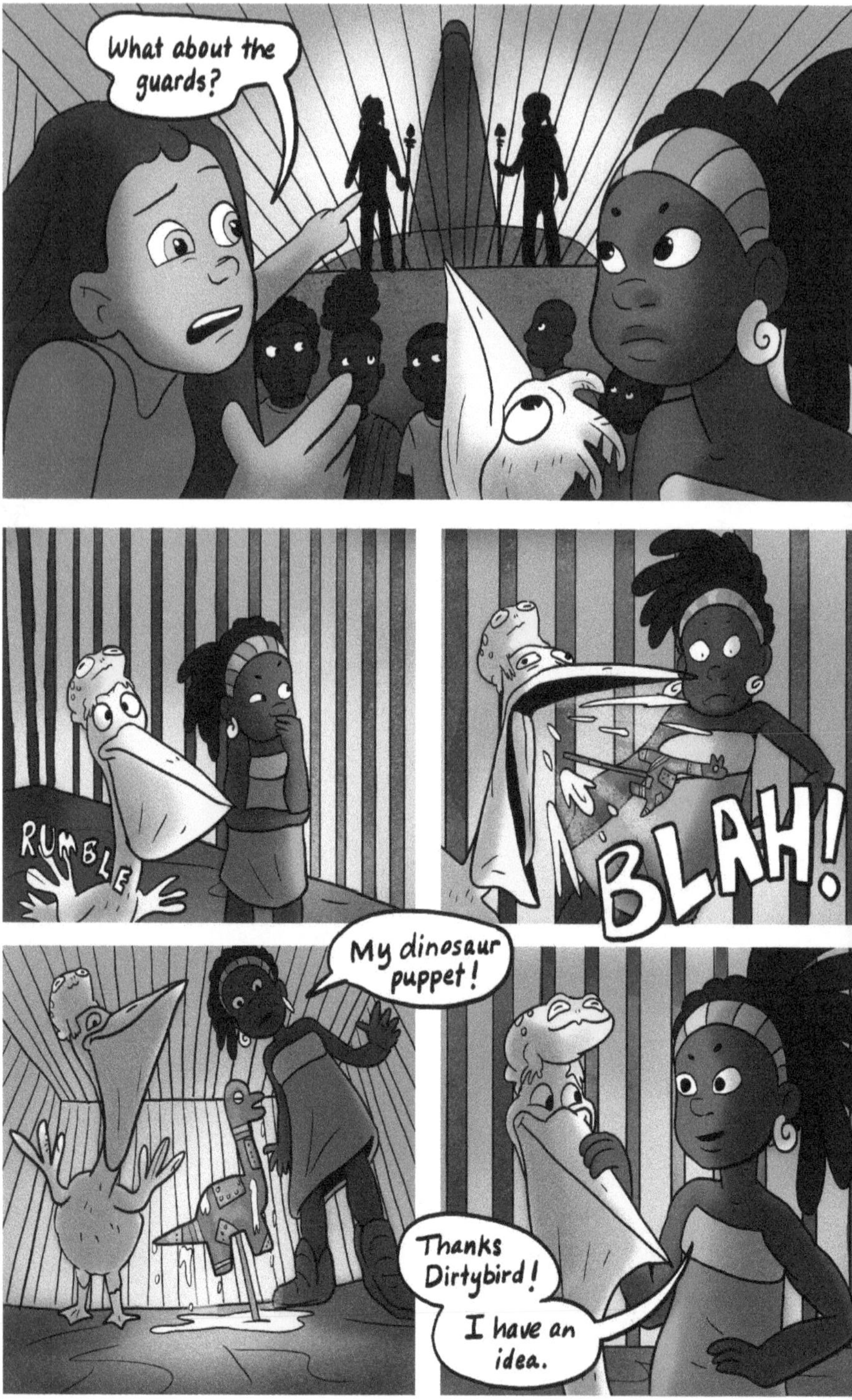
What about the guards?
RUMBLE
BLAH!
My dinosaur puppet!
Thanks Dirtybird!
I have an idea.

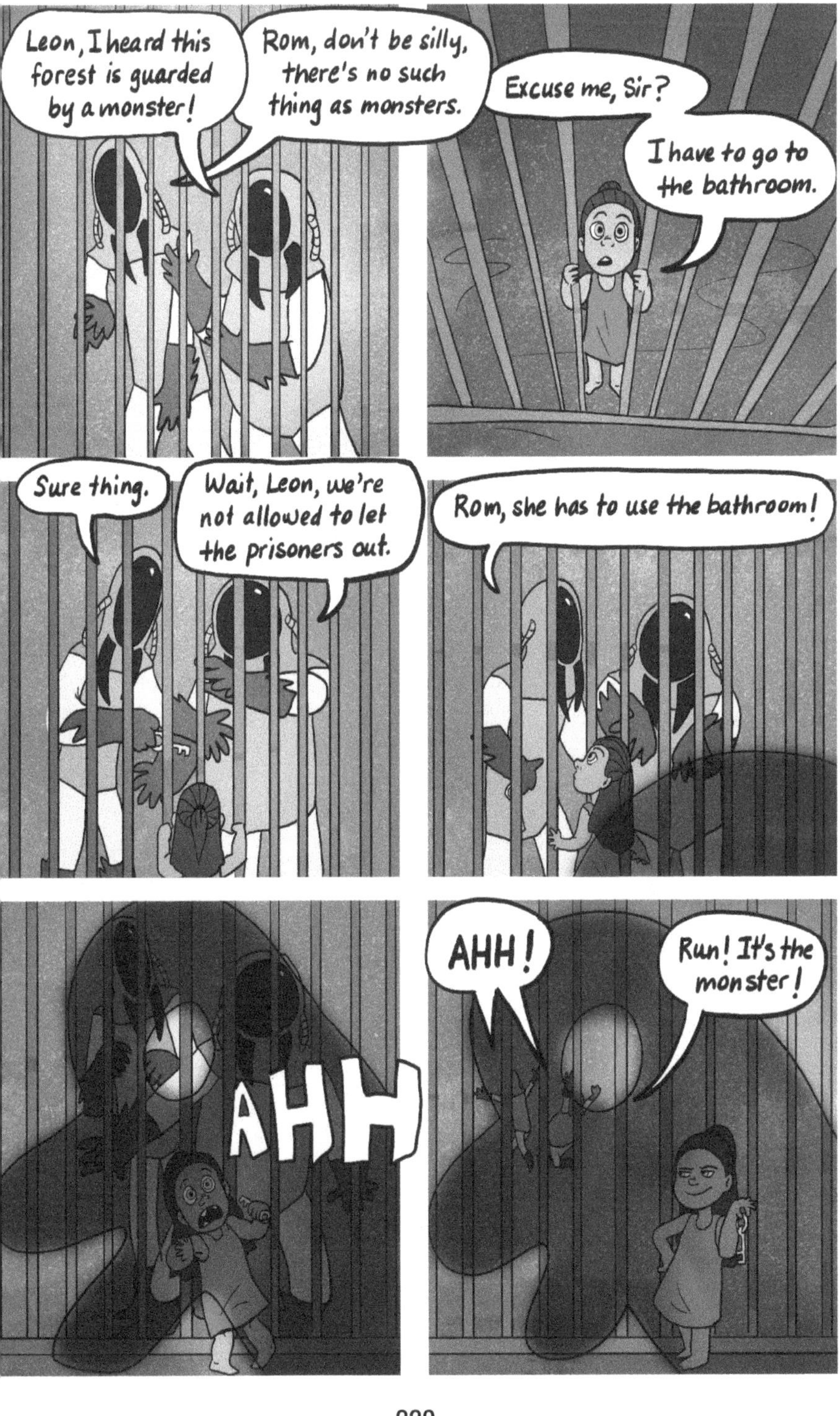
Leon, I heard this forest is guarded by a monster!
Rom, don't be silly, there's no such thing as monsters.
Excuse me, Sir?
I have to go to the bathroom.
Sure thing.
Wait, Leon, we're not allowed to let the prisoners out.
Rom, she has to use the bathroom!
AHH
AHH!
Run! It's the monster!

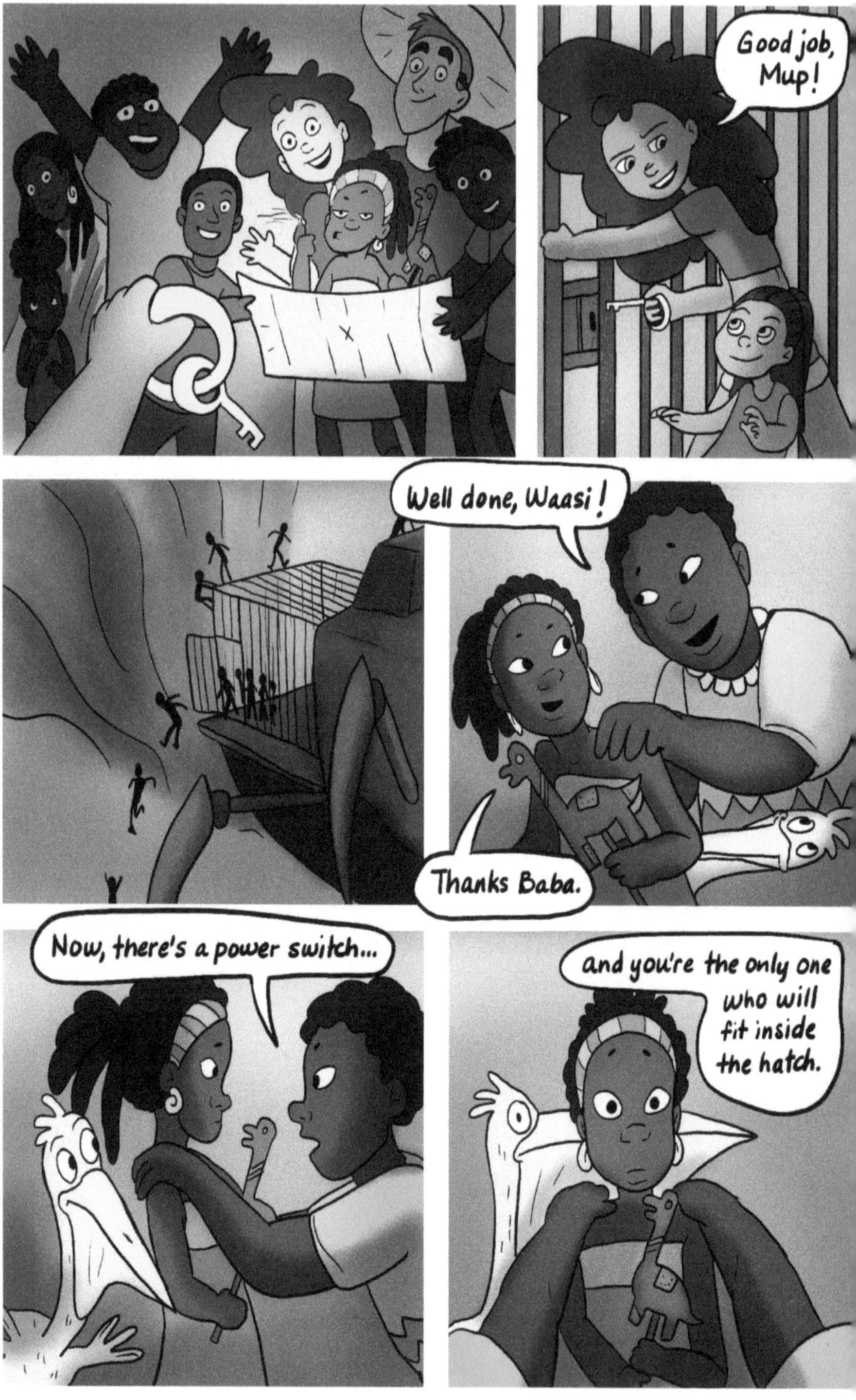
Good job, Mup!
Well done, Waasi!
Thanks Baba.
Now, there's a power switch...
and you're the only one who will fit inside the hatch.

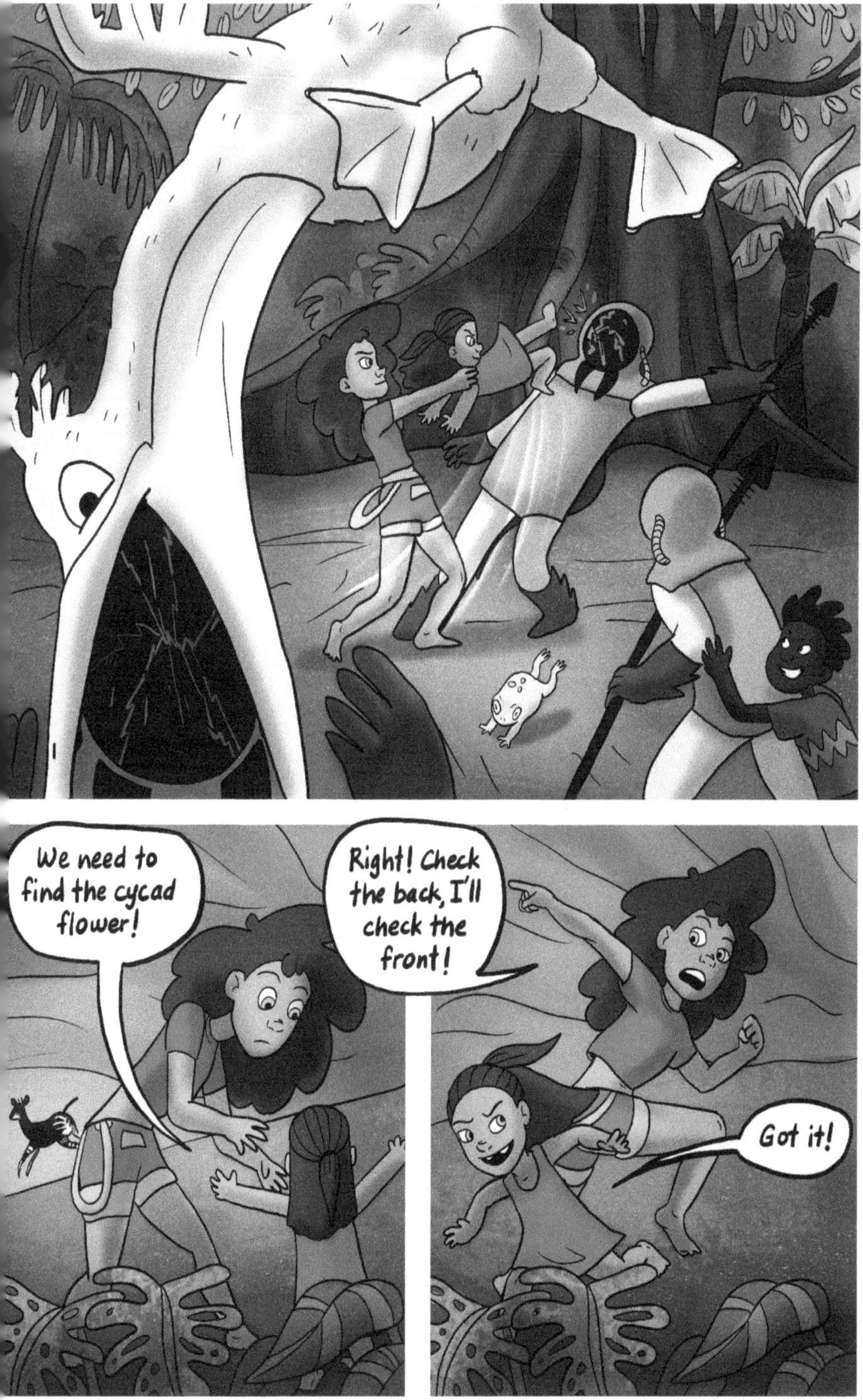
We need to find the cycad flower!
Right! Check the back, I'll check the front!
Got it!

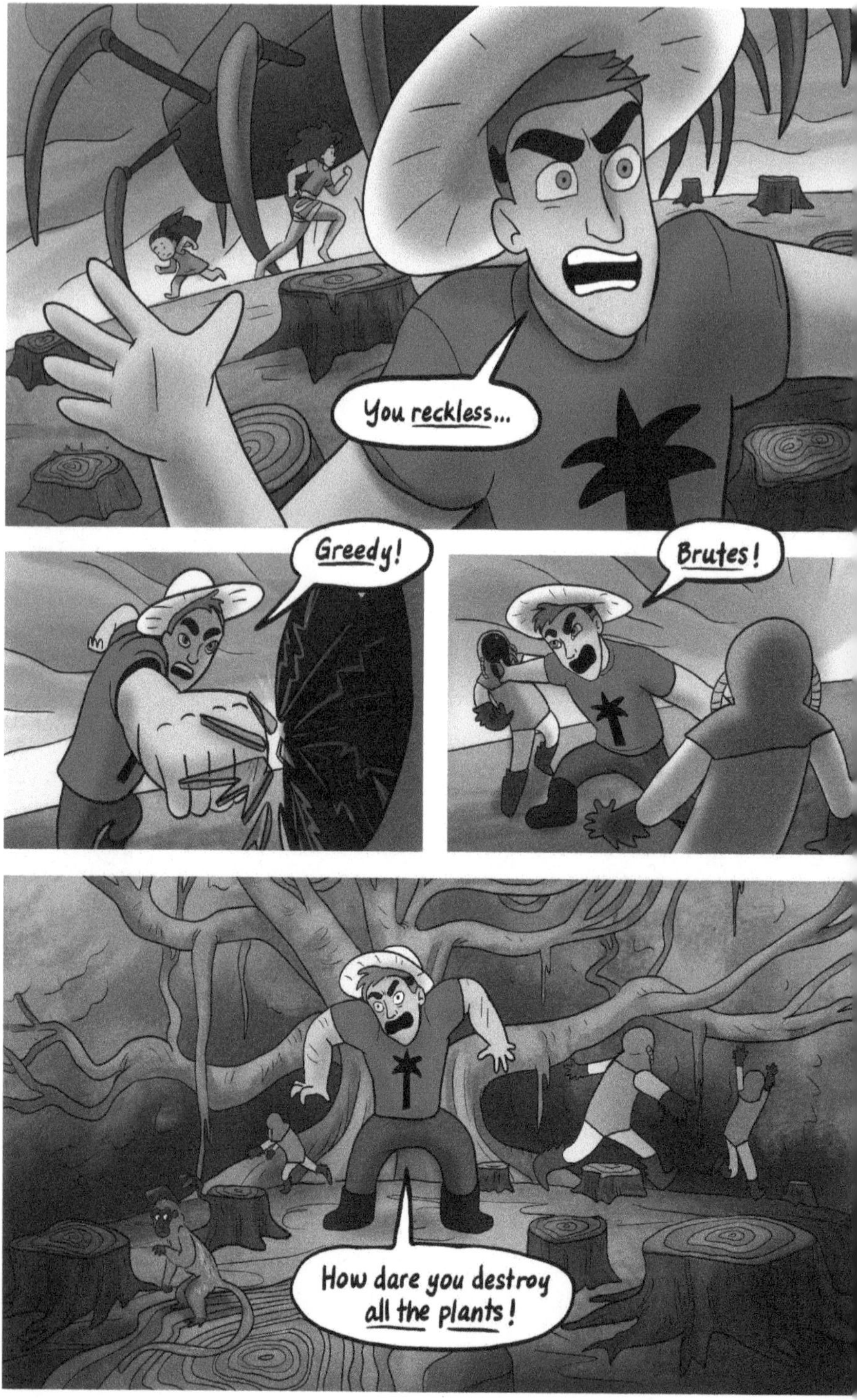
You reckless...
Greedy!
Brutes!
How dare you destroy all the plants!

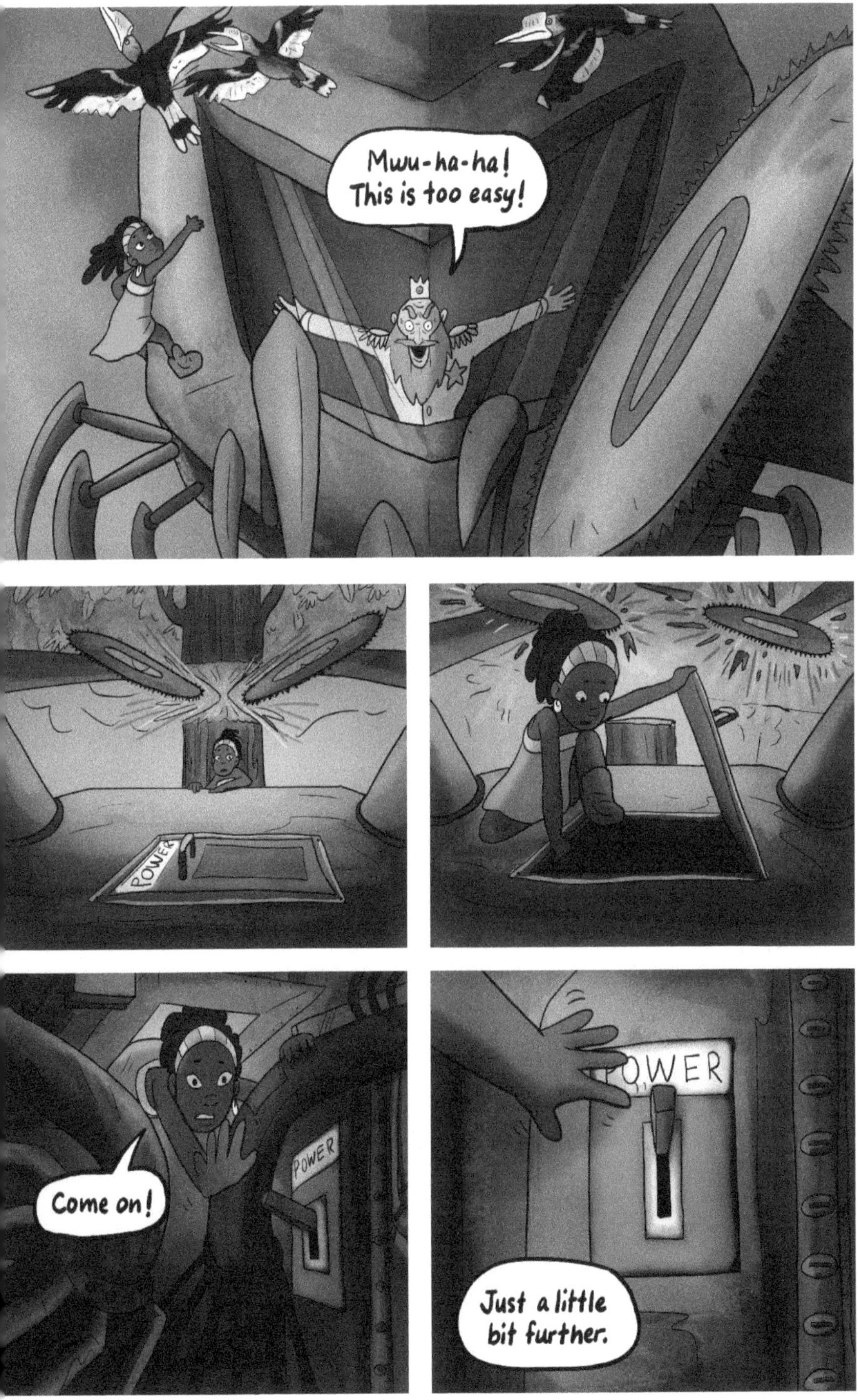
Muu-ha-ha!
This is too easy!
POWER
Come on!
POWER
POWER
Just a little bit further.

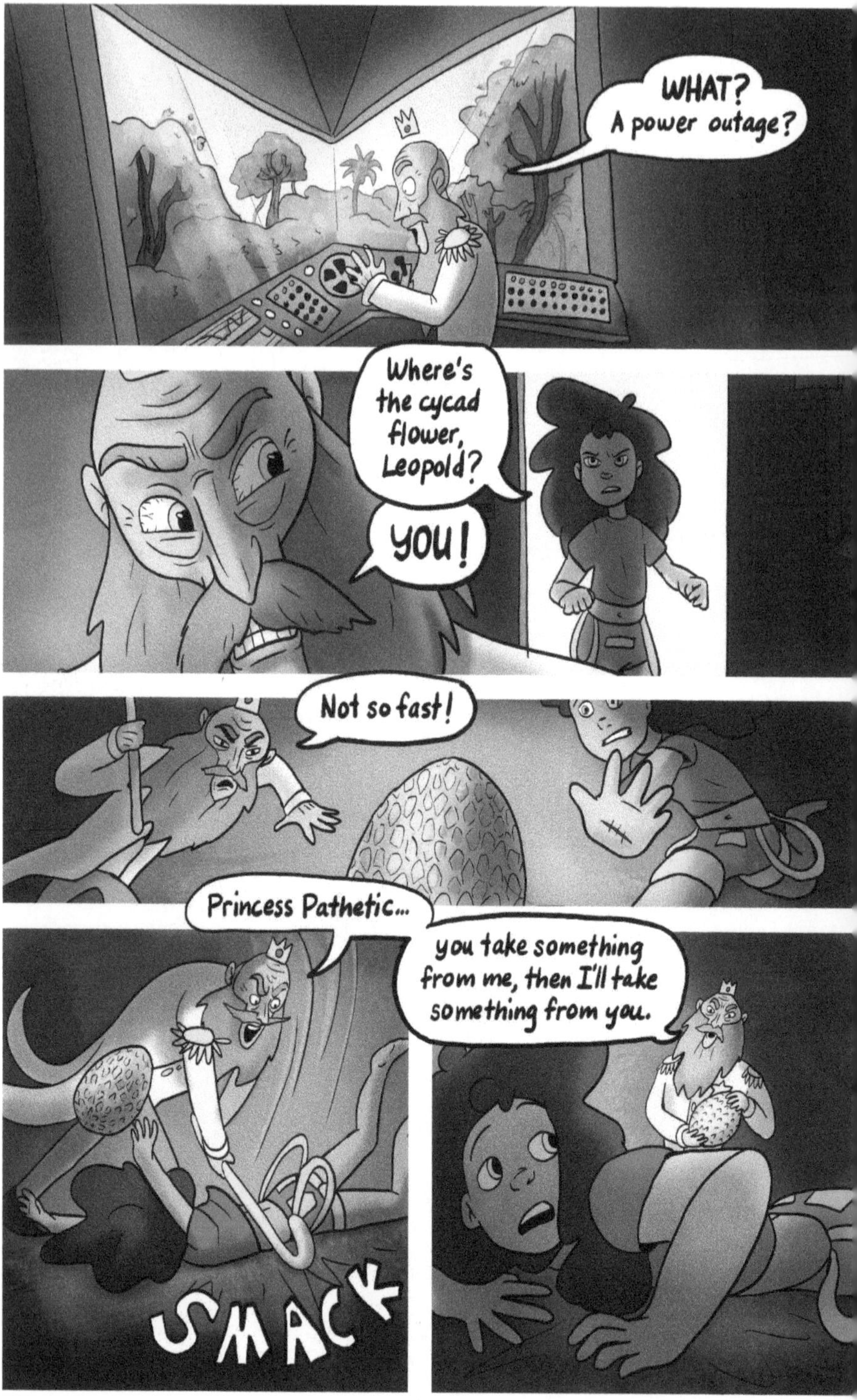
WHAT?
A power outage?
Where's the cycad flower, Leopold?
YOU!
Not so fast!
Princess Pathetic...
you take something from me, then I'll take something from you.
SMACK

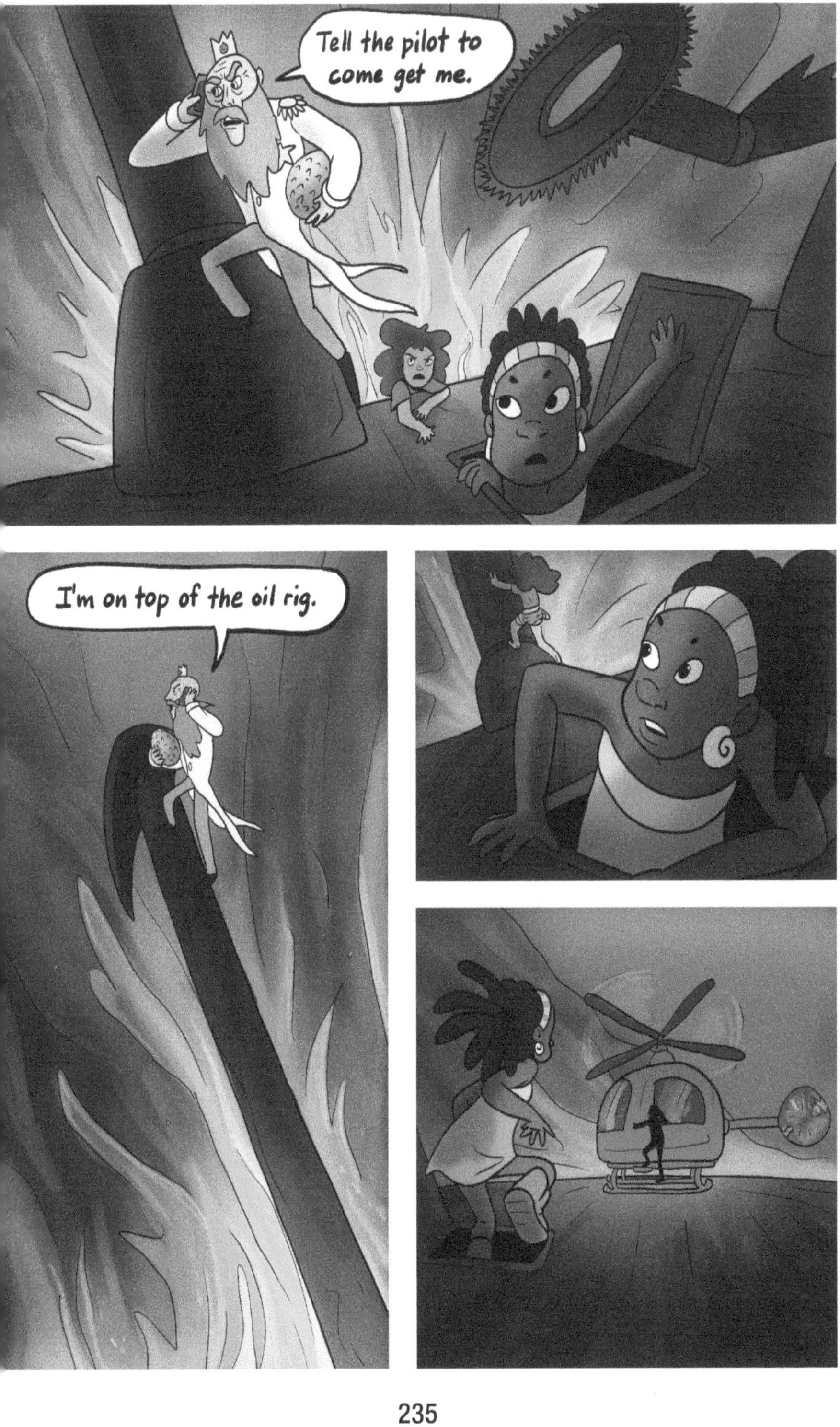
Tell the pilot to come get me.
I'm on top of the oil rig.

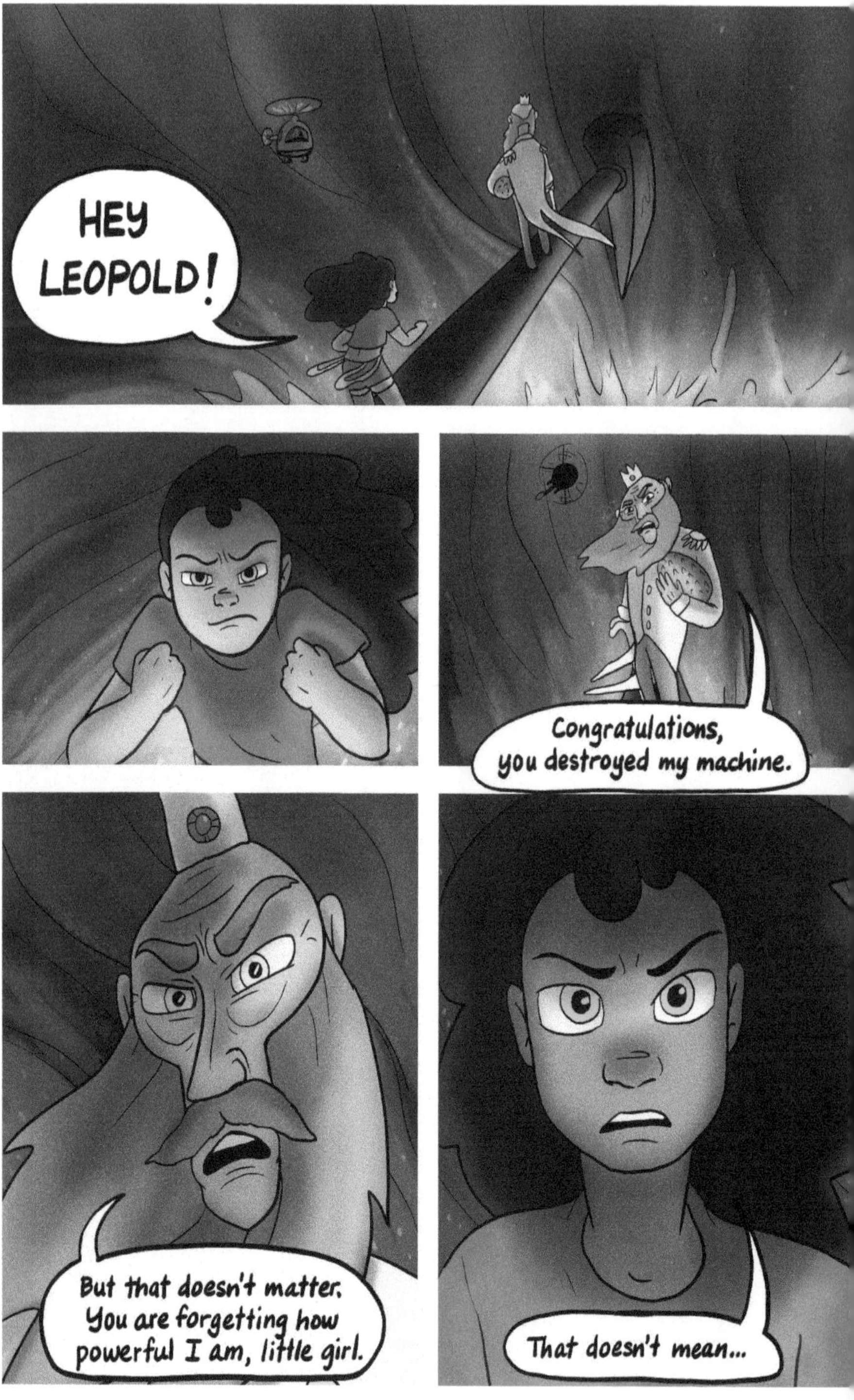
HEY LEOPOLD!
Congratulations, you destroyed my machine.
But that doesn't matter. You are forgetting how powerful I am, little girl.
That doesn't mean...

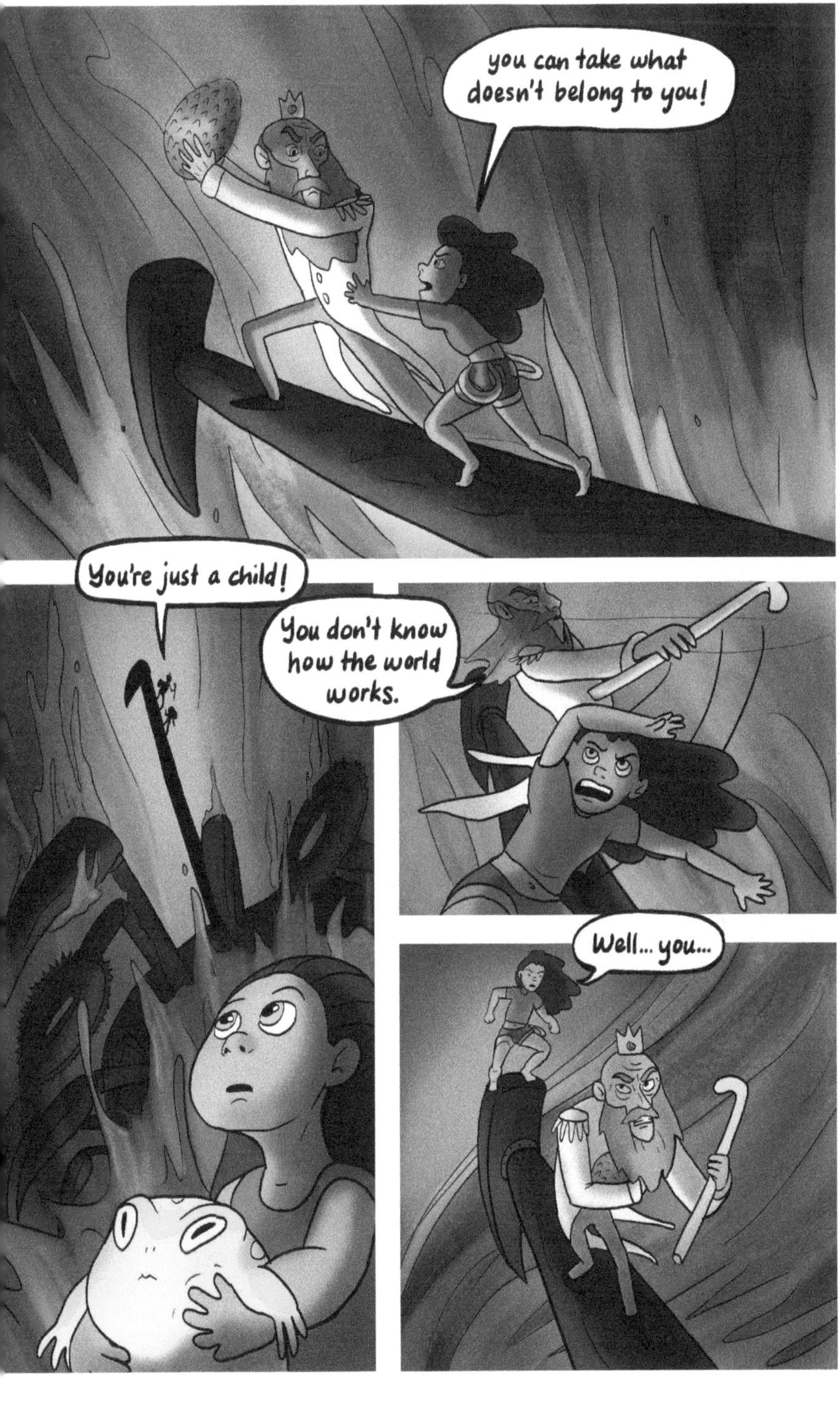
you can take what doesn't belong to you!
You're just a child!
You don't know how the world works.
Well... you...

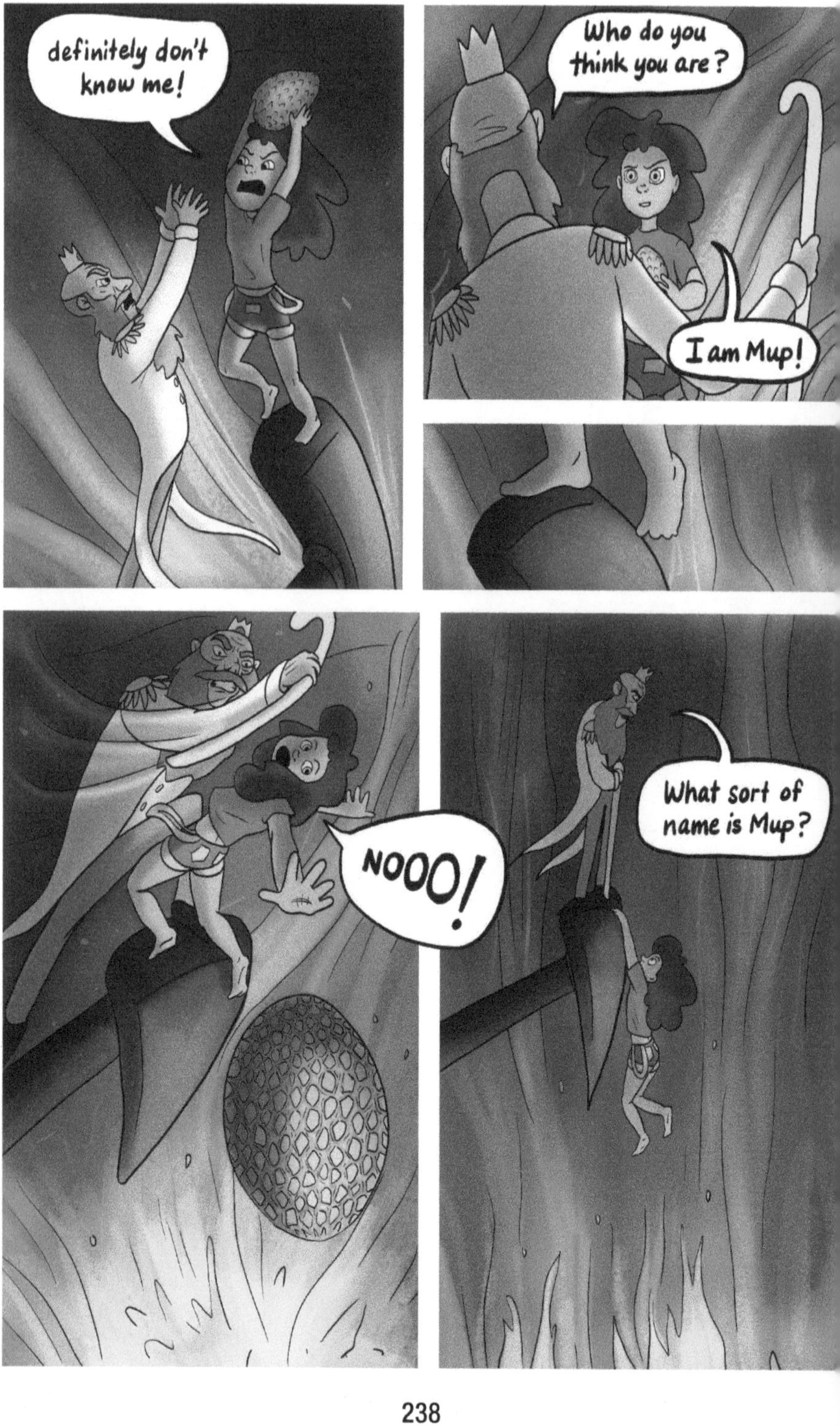
definitely don't know me!
Who do you think you are?
I am Mup!
NOOO!
What sort of name is Mup?

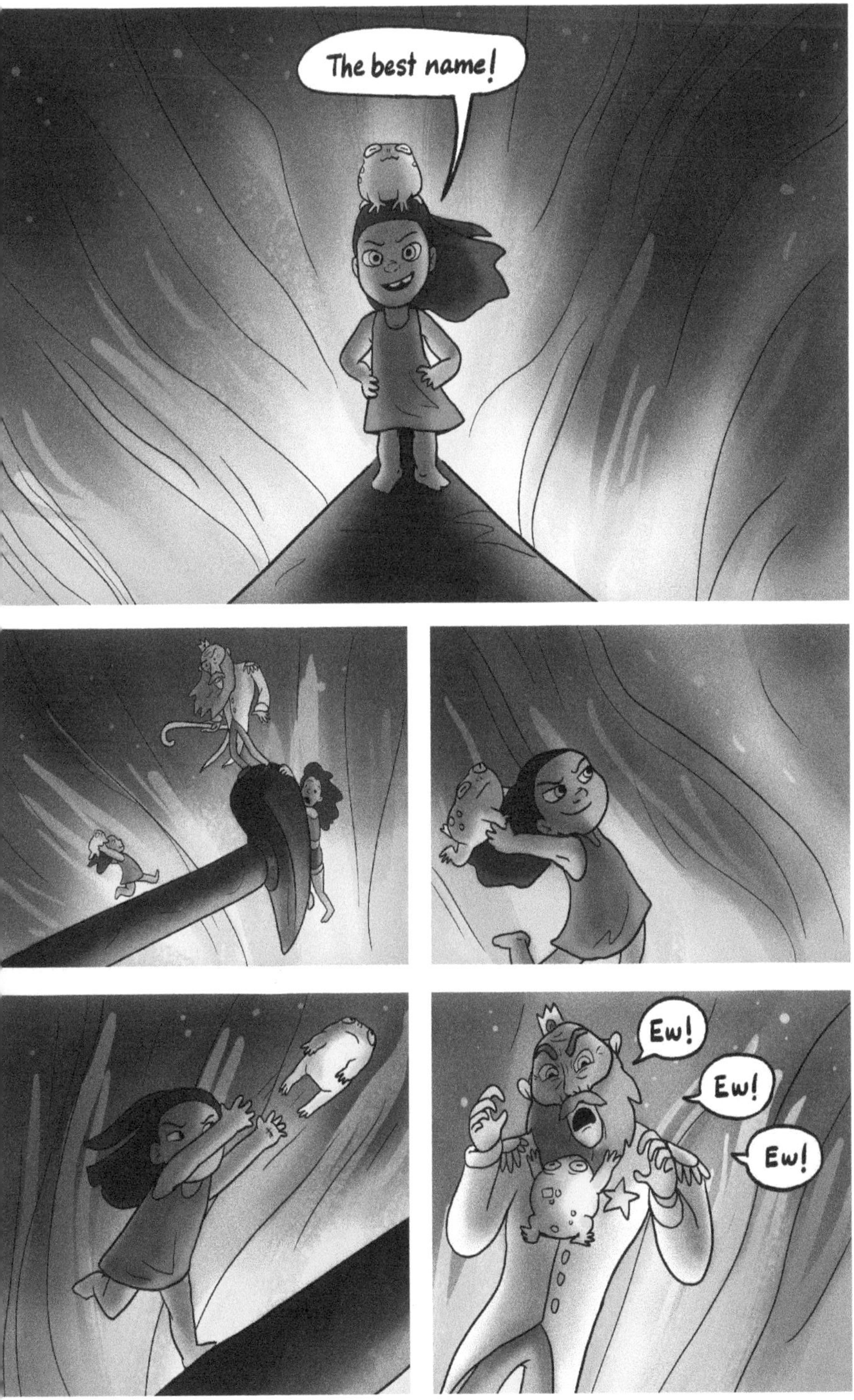
The best name!
Ew!
Ew!
Ew!

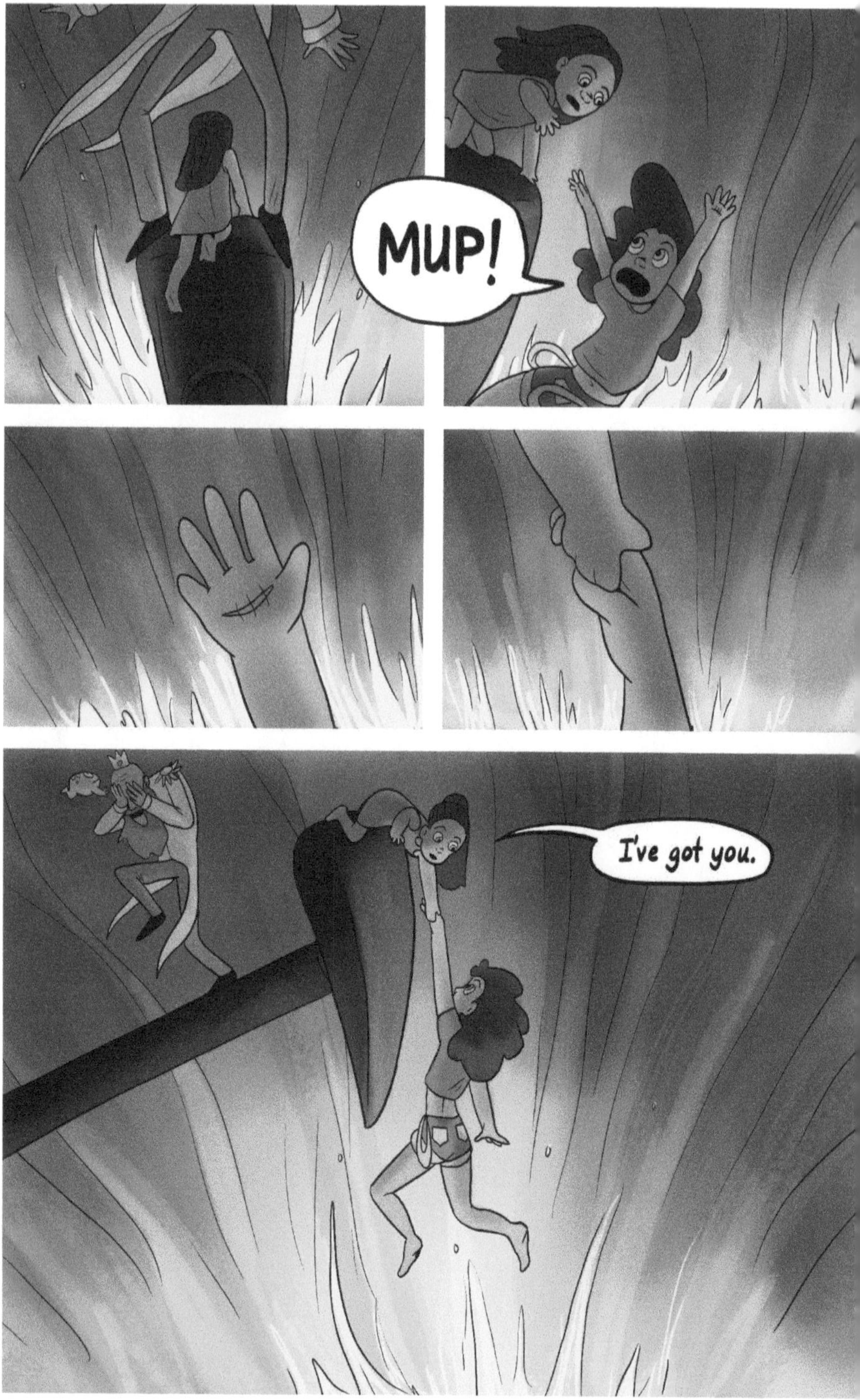
MUP!
I've got you.

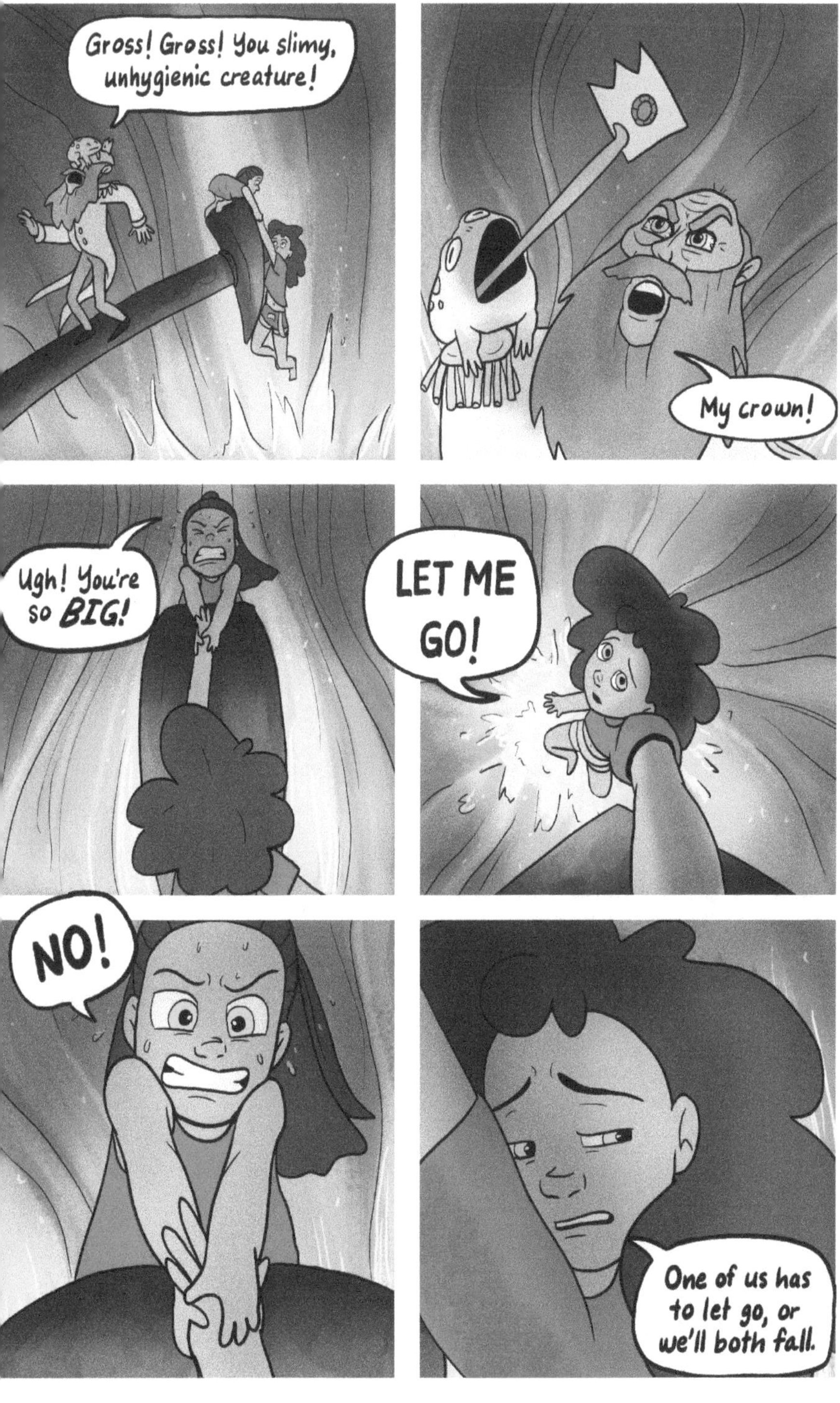
Gross! Gross! You slimy, unhygienic creature!
My crown!
Ugh! You're so BIG!
LET ME GO!
NO!
One of us has to let go, or we'll both fall.

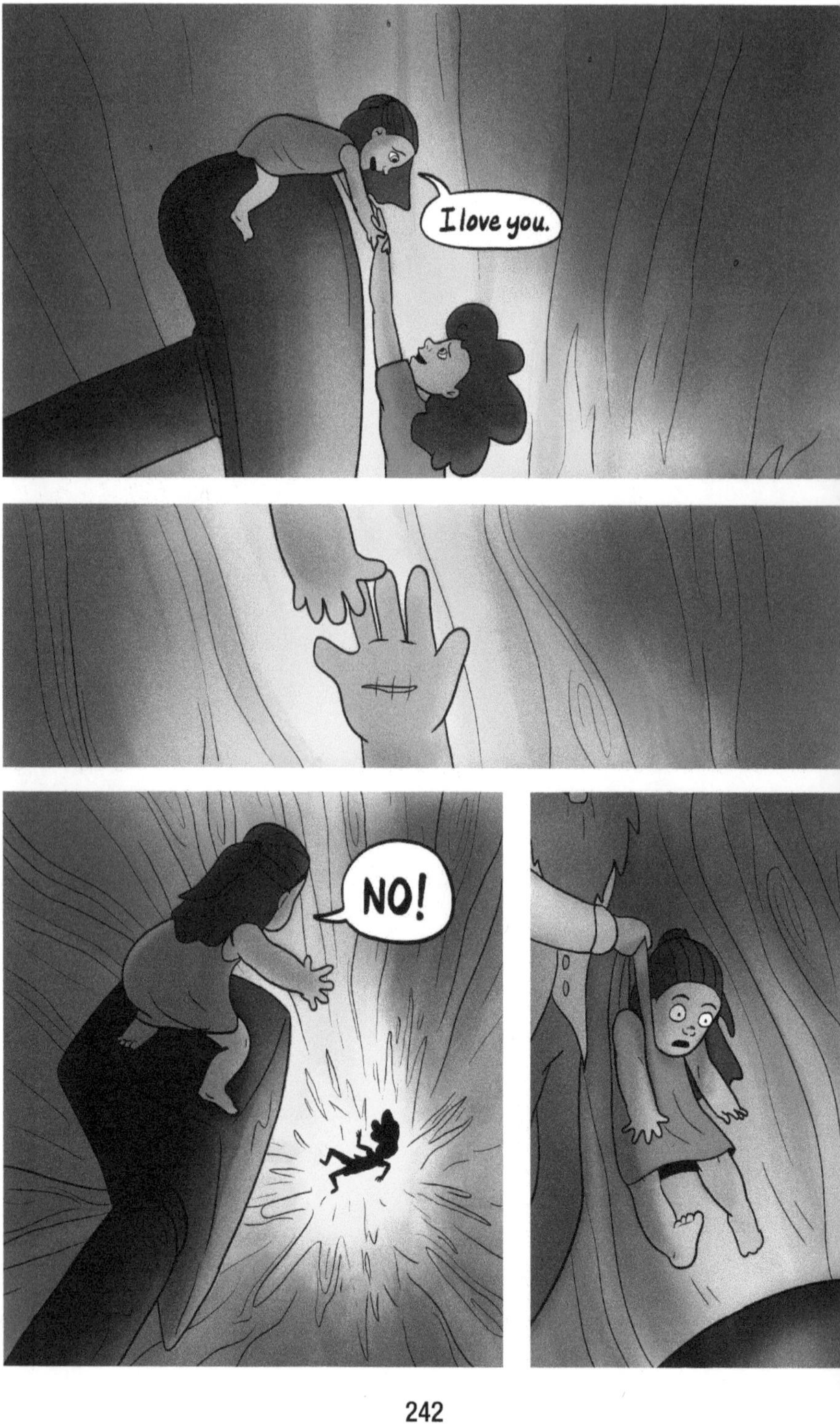
I love you.
NO!

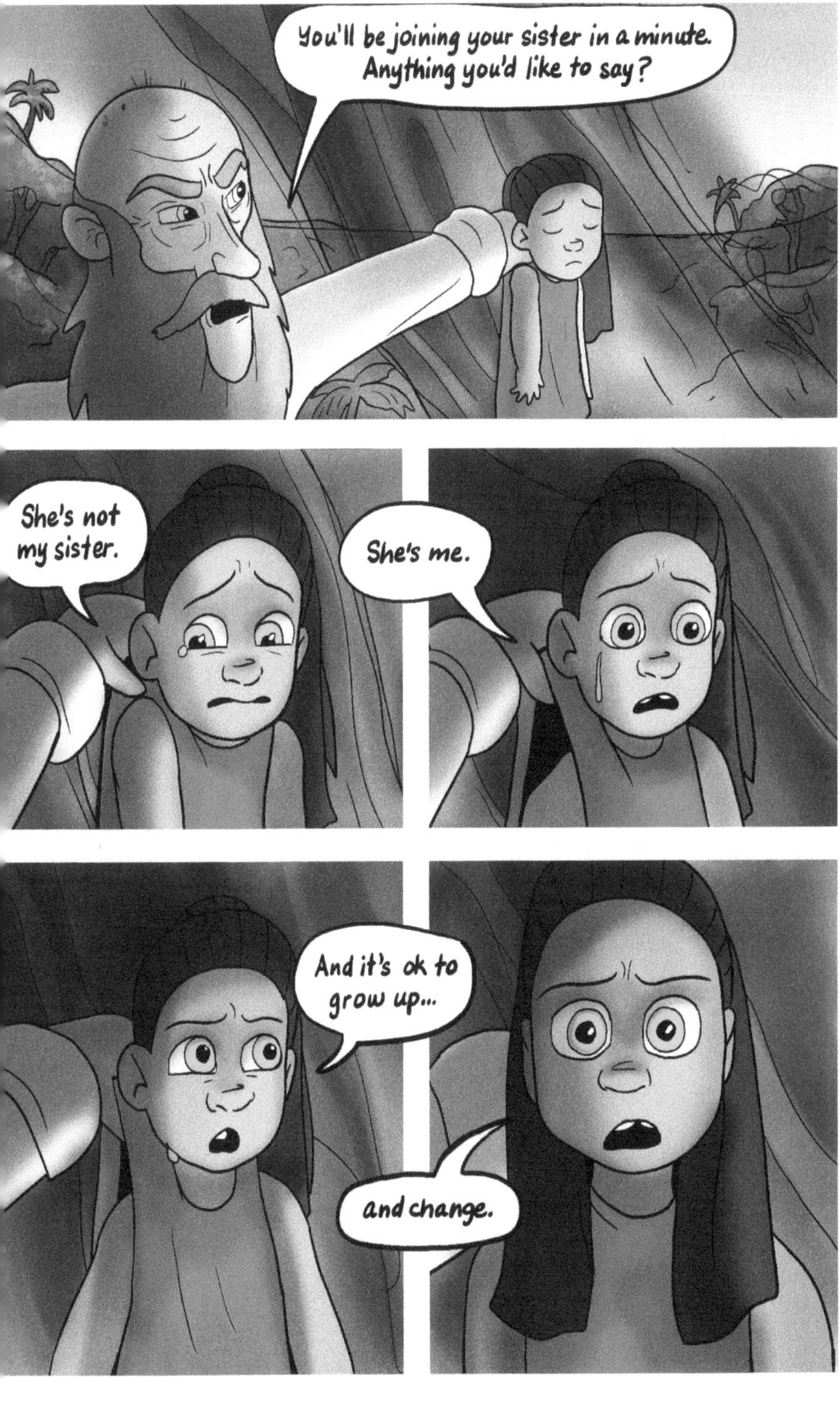
You'll be joining your sister in a minute. Anything you'd like to say?
She's not my sister.
She's me.
And it's ok to grow up...
and change.

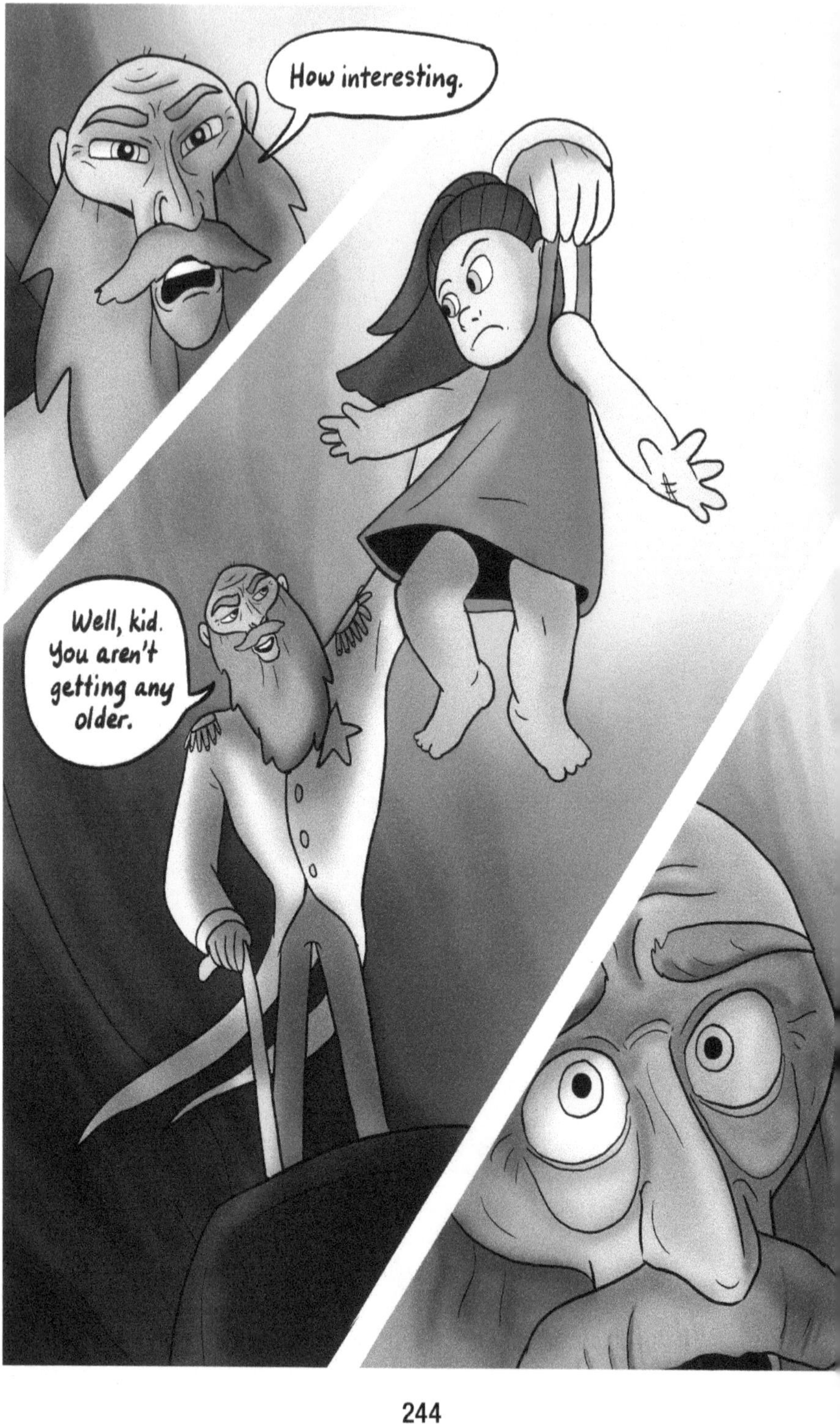
How interesting.
Well, kid. You aren't getting any older.

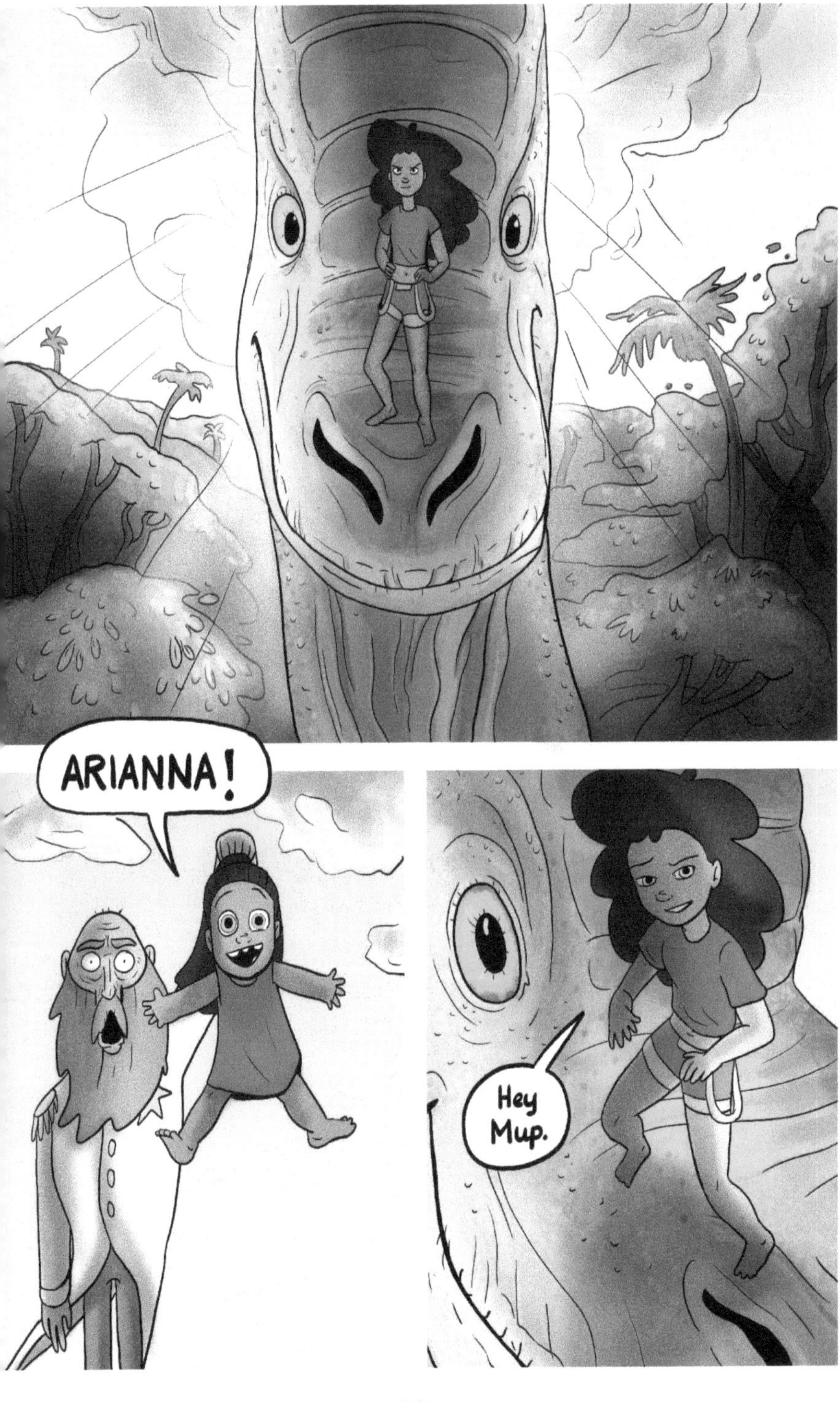
ARIANNA!
Hey Mup.

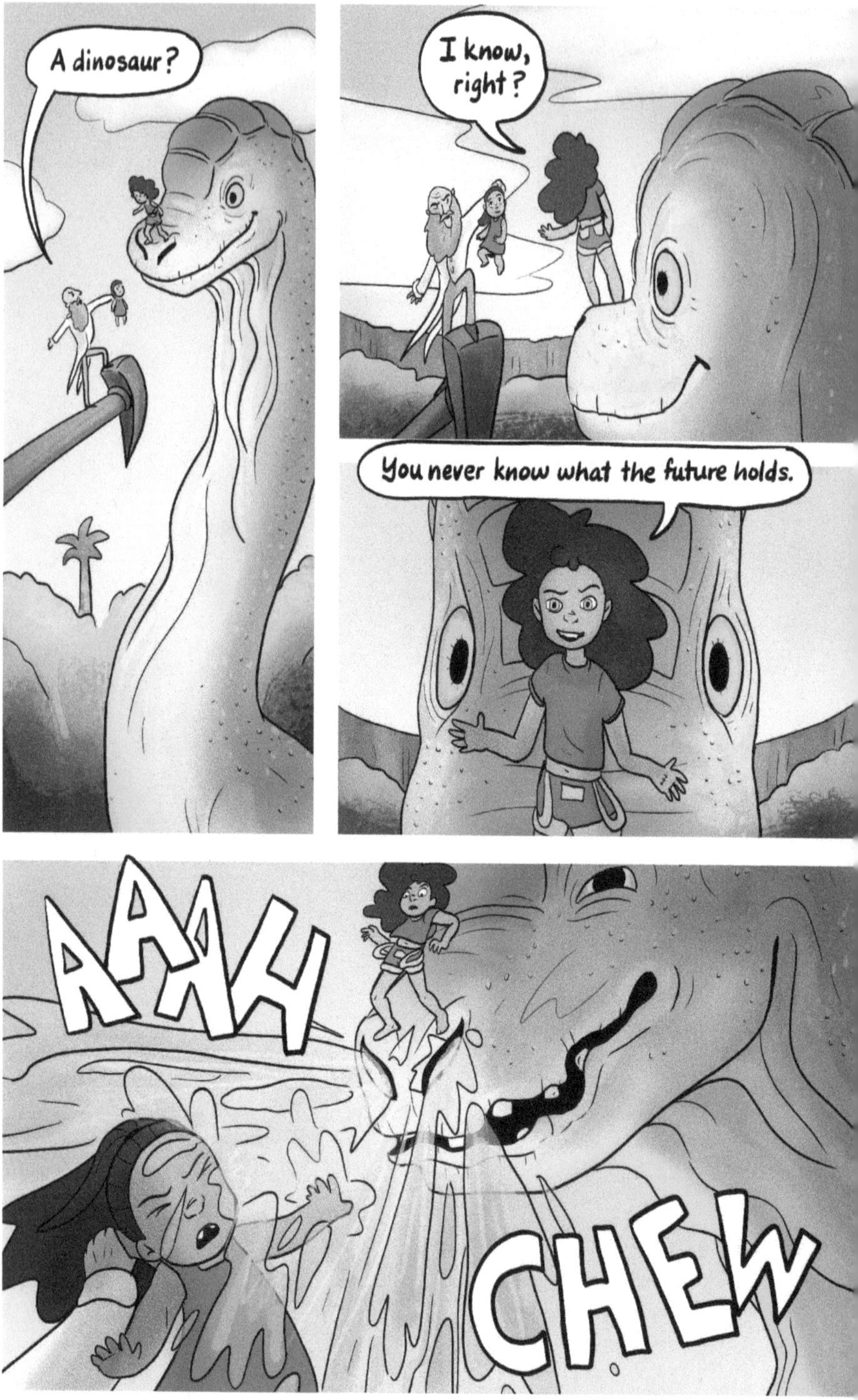
A dinosaur?
I know, right?
You never know what the future holds.
AAAH
CHEW

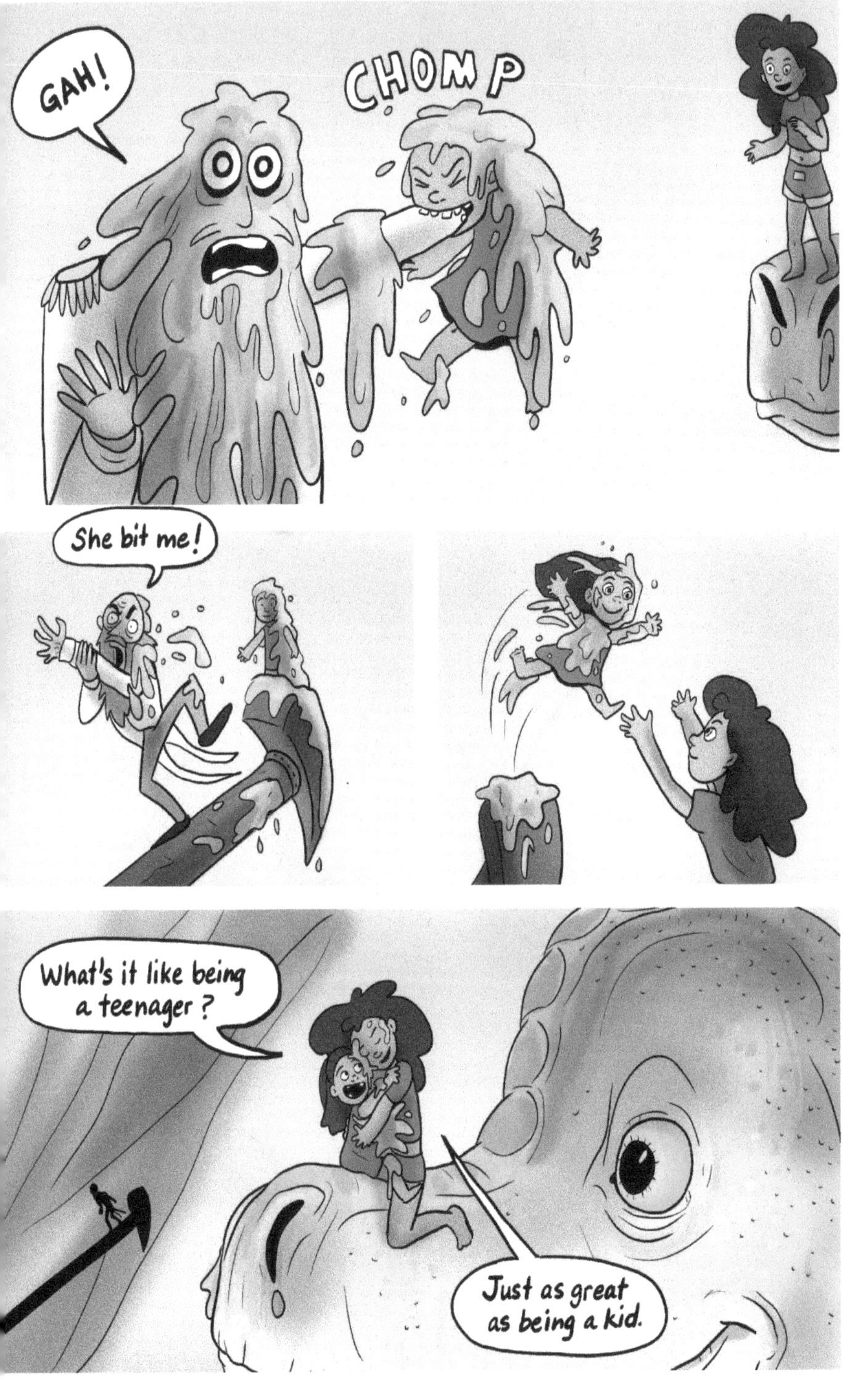
GAH!
CHOMP
She bit me!
What's it like being a teenager?
Just as great as being a kid.

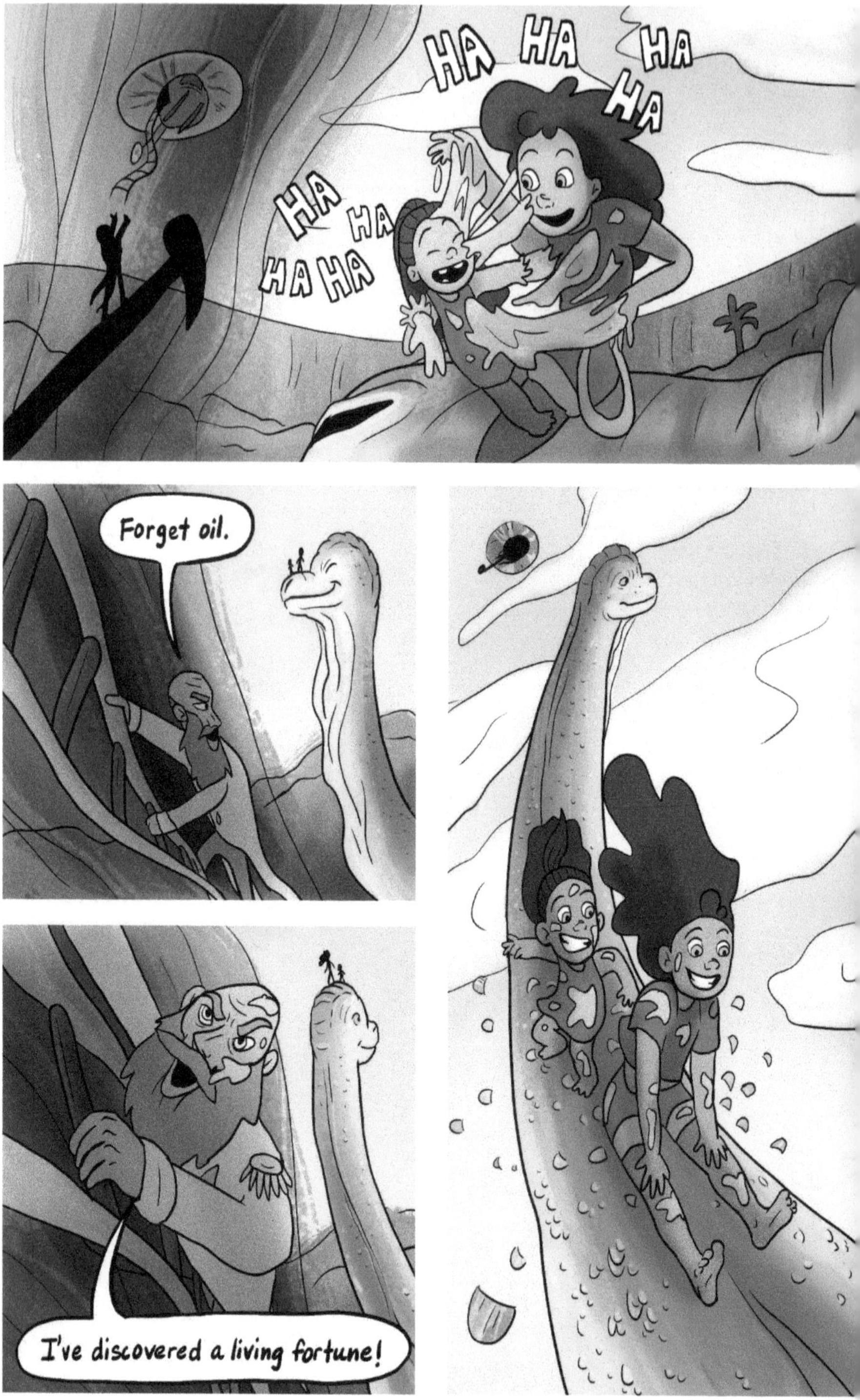
HA HA HA HA
HA HA HA HA
Forget oil.
I've discovered a living fortune!

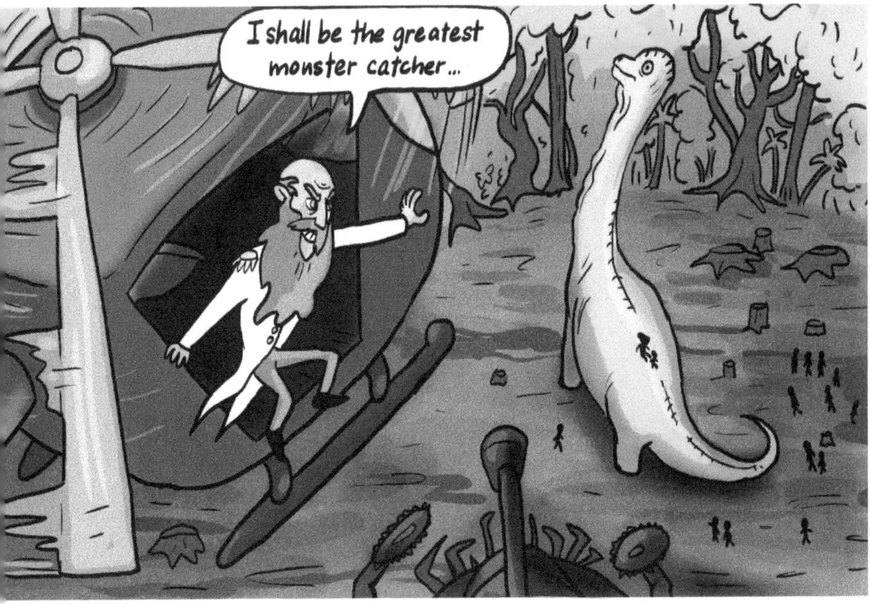
I shall be the greatest monster catcher...

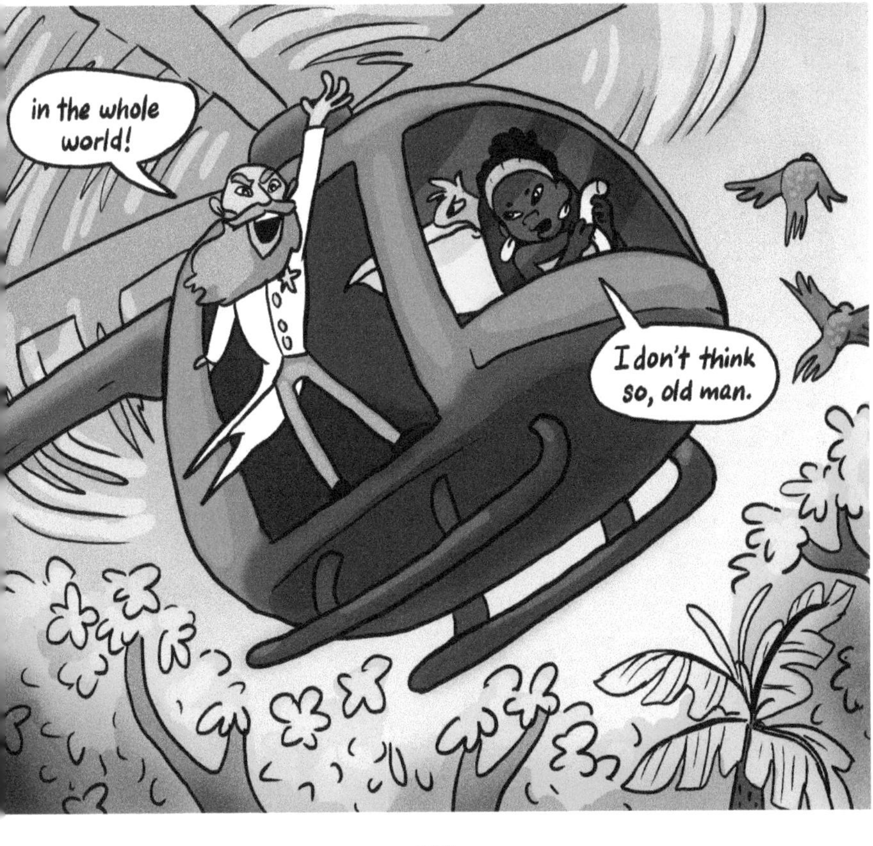
in the whole world!
I don't think so, old man.

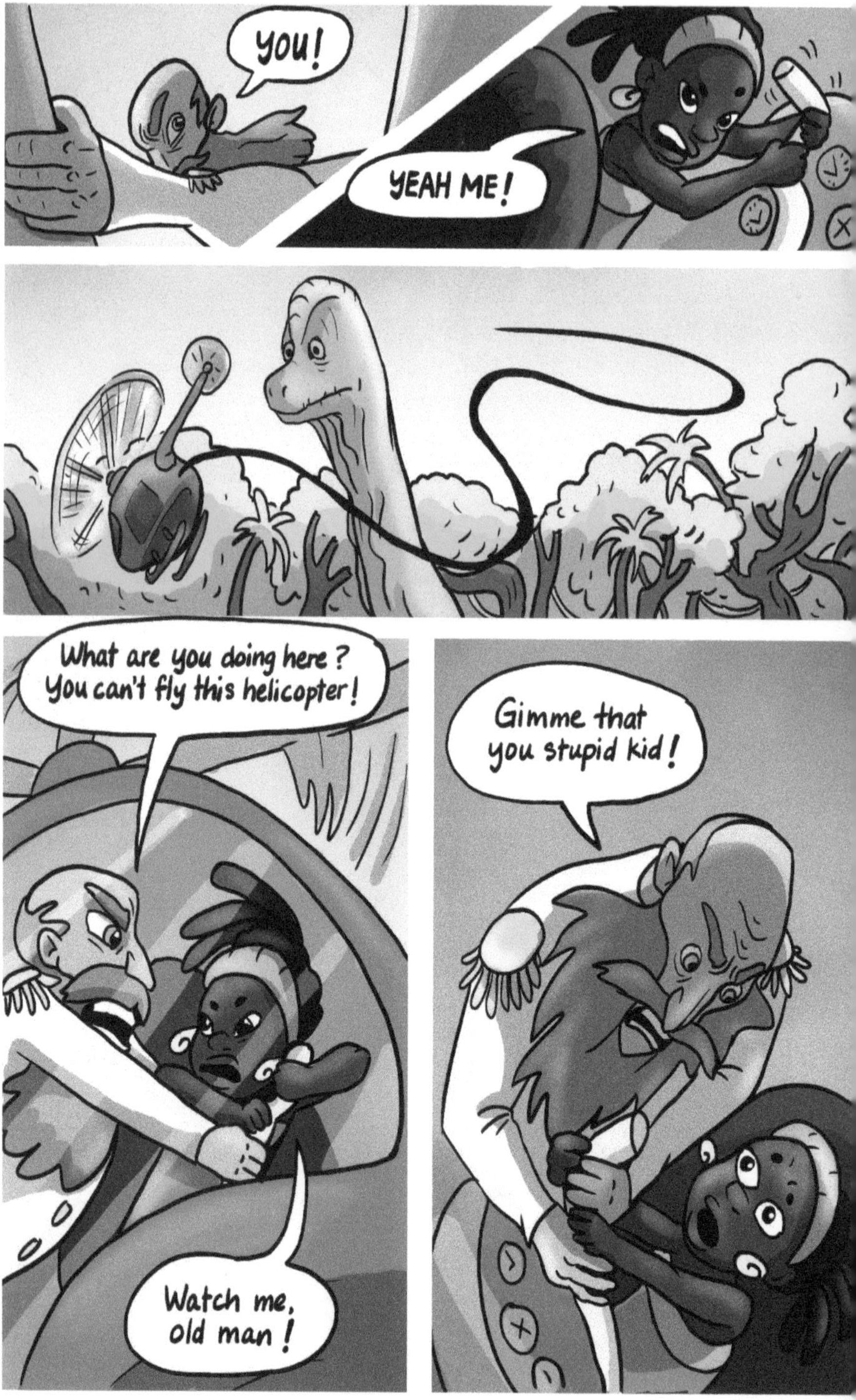
YOU!
YEAH ME!
What are you doing here? You can't fly this helicopter!
Watch me, old man!
Gimme that you stupid kid!

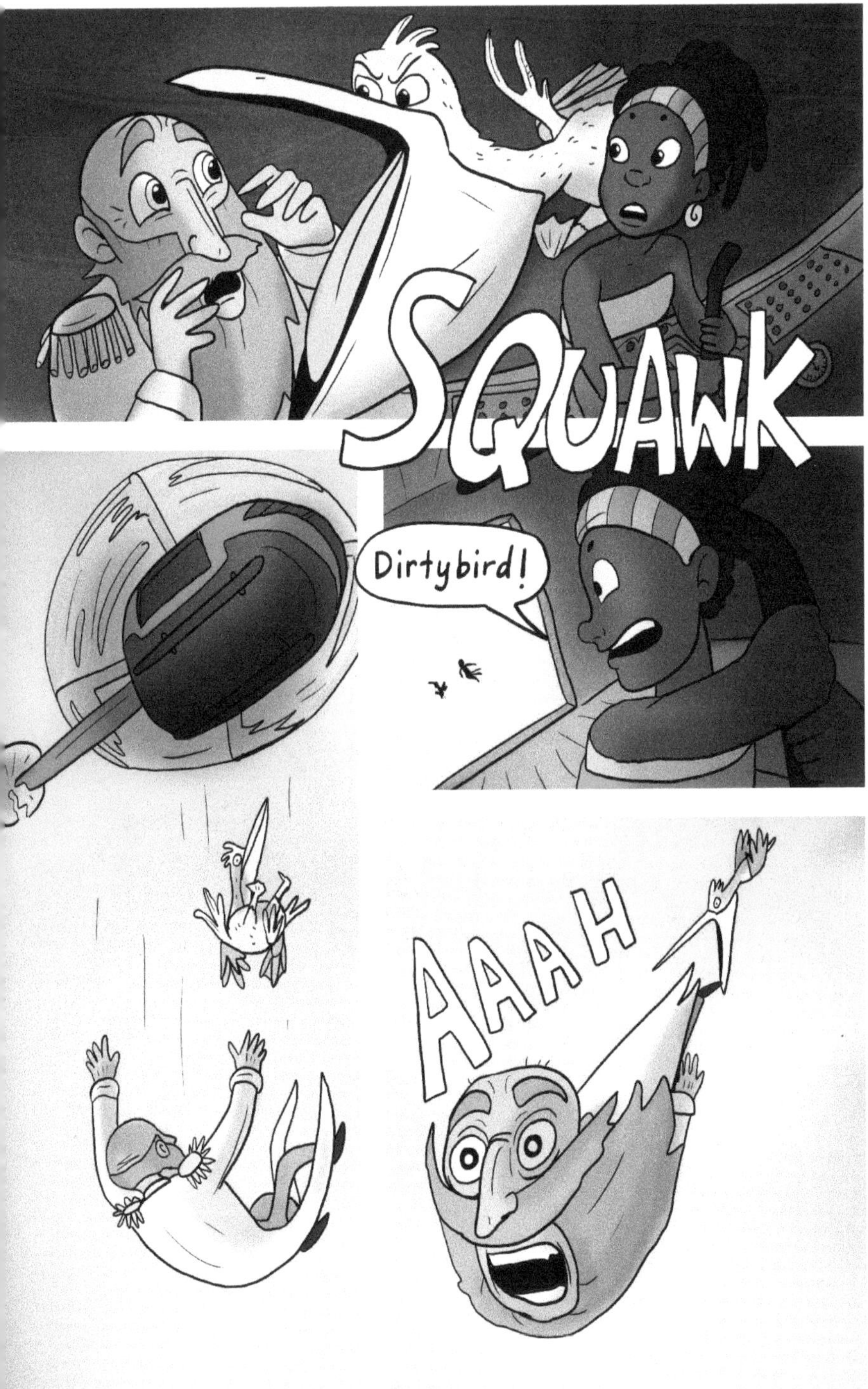
SQUAWK
Dirtybird!
AAAH

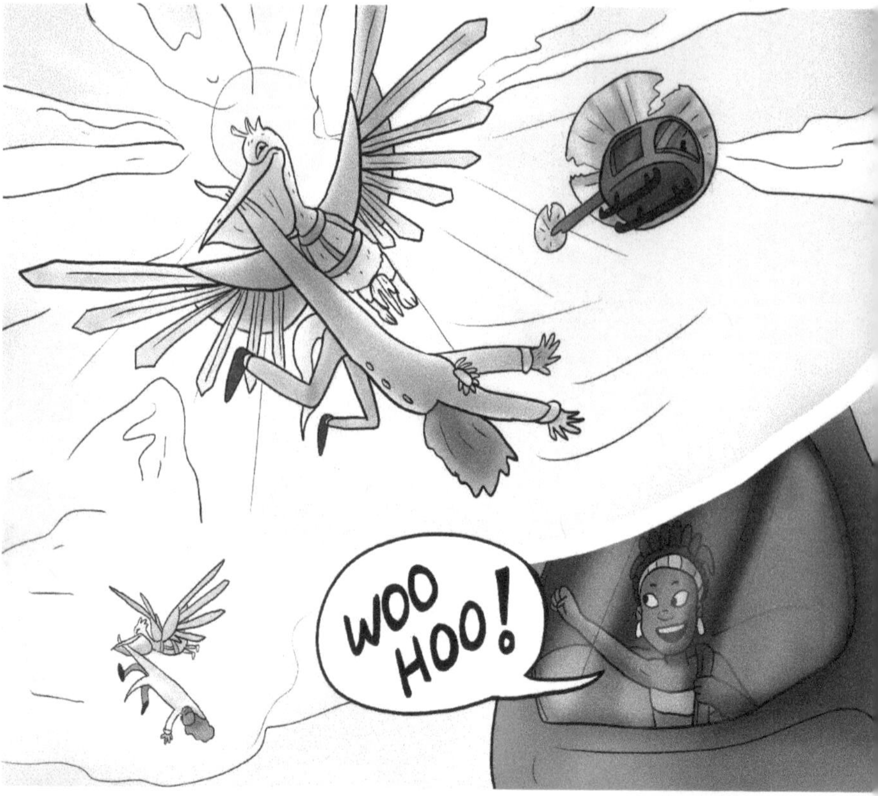
WOO HOO!

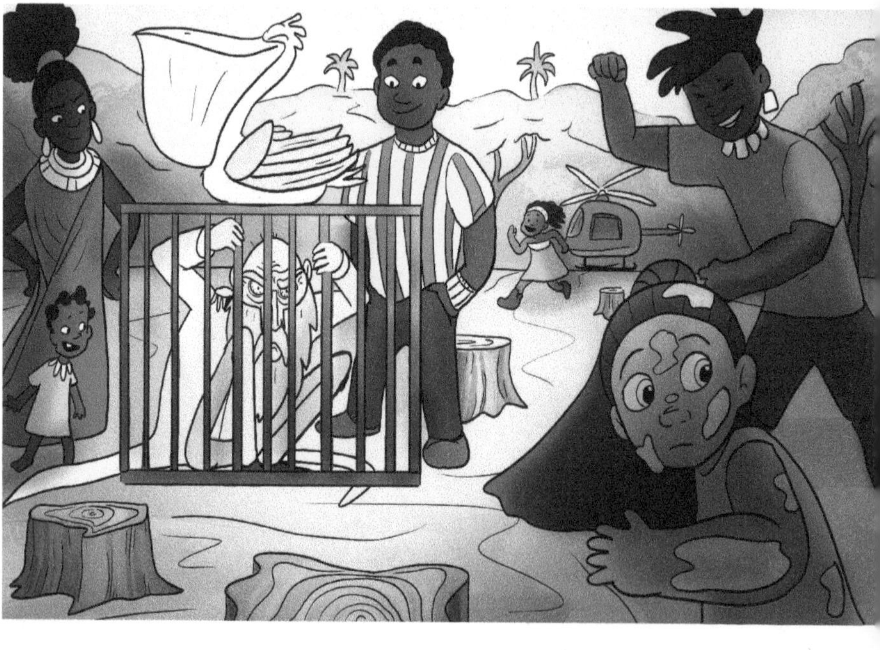

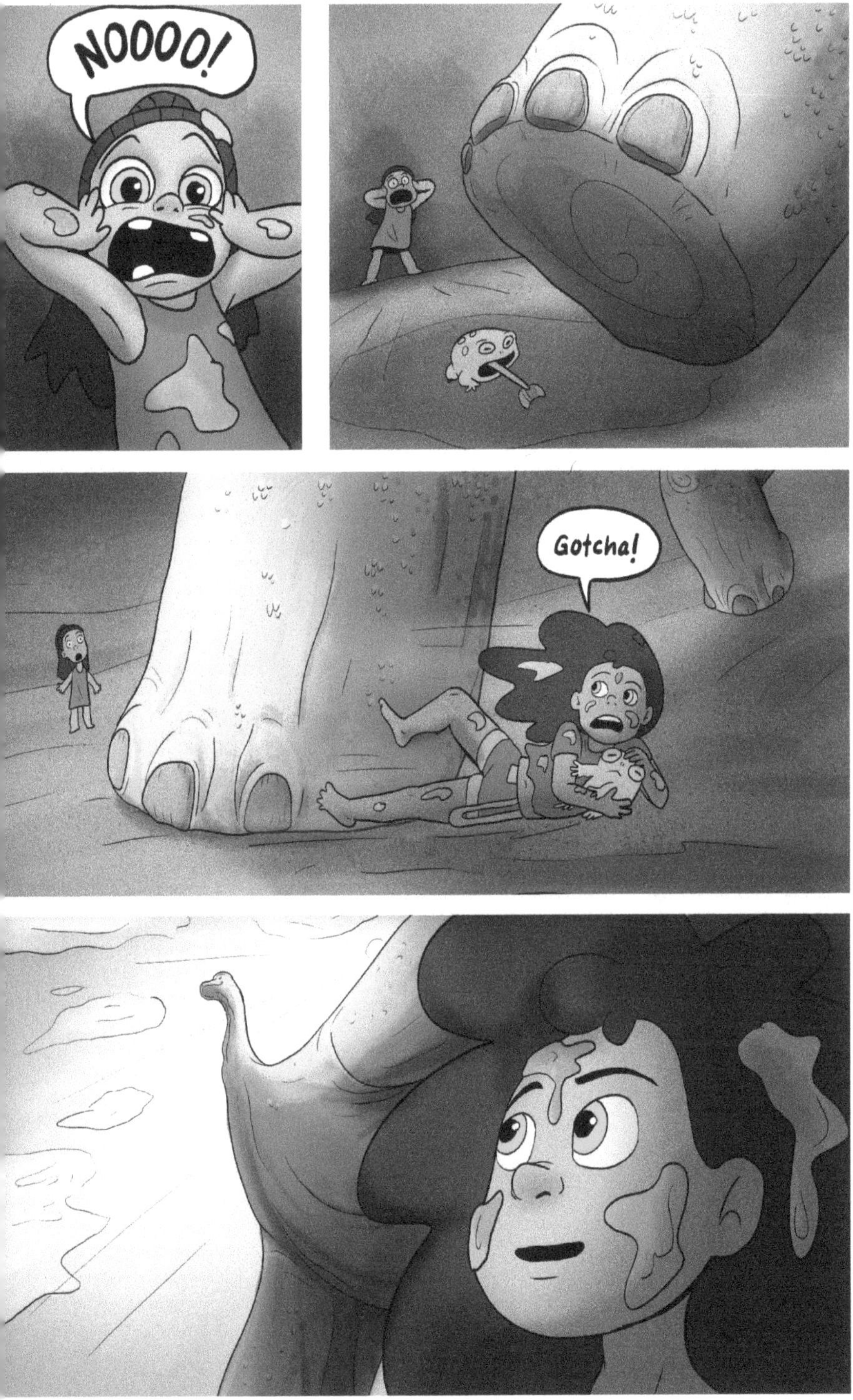
NOOOO!
Gotcha!

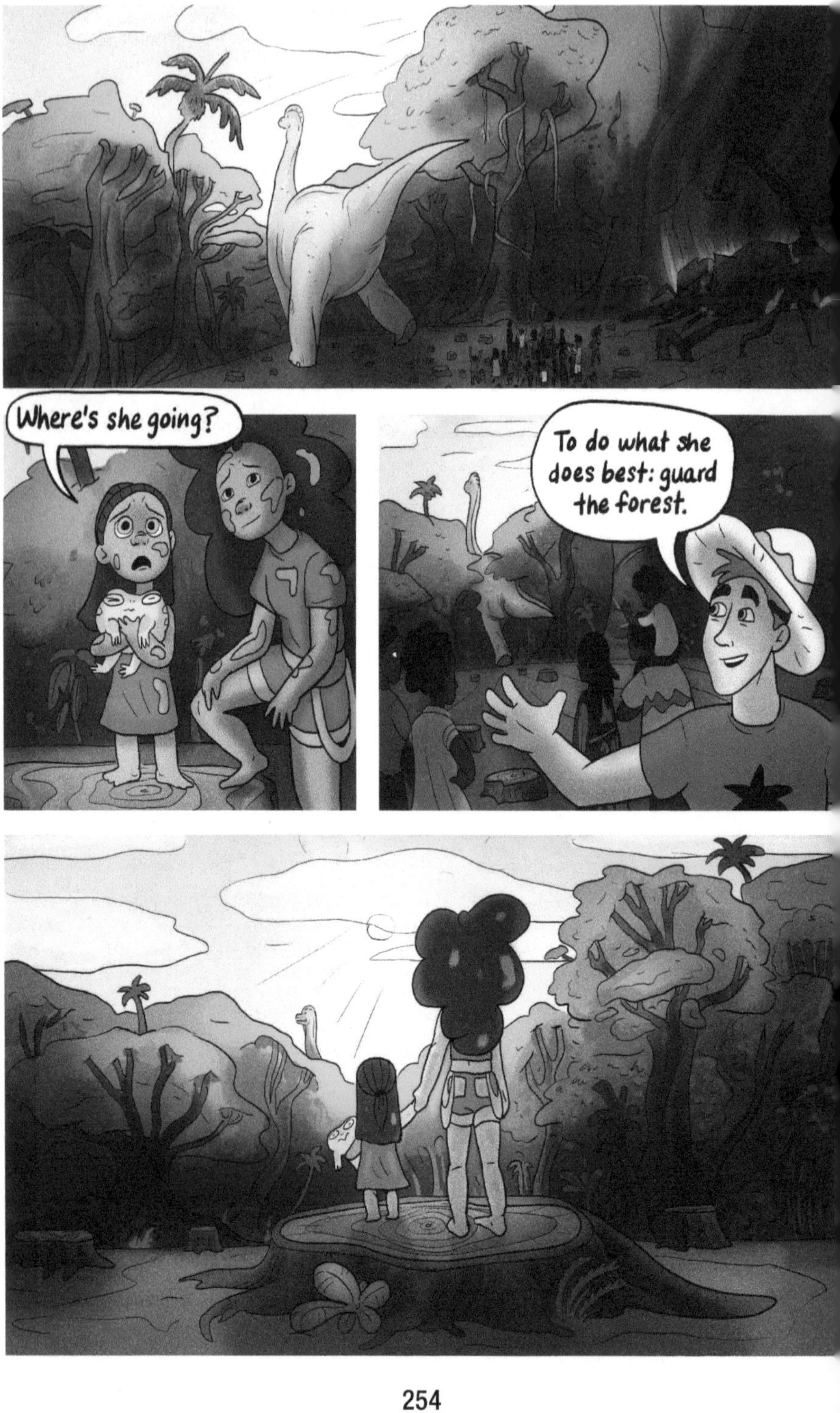
Where's she going?
To do what she does best: guard the forest.

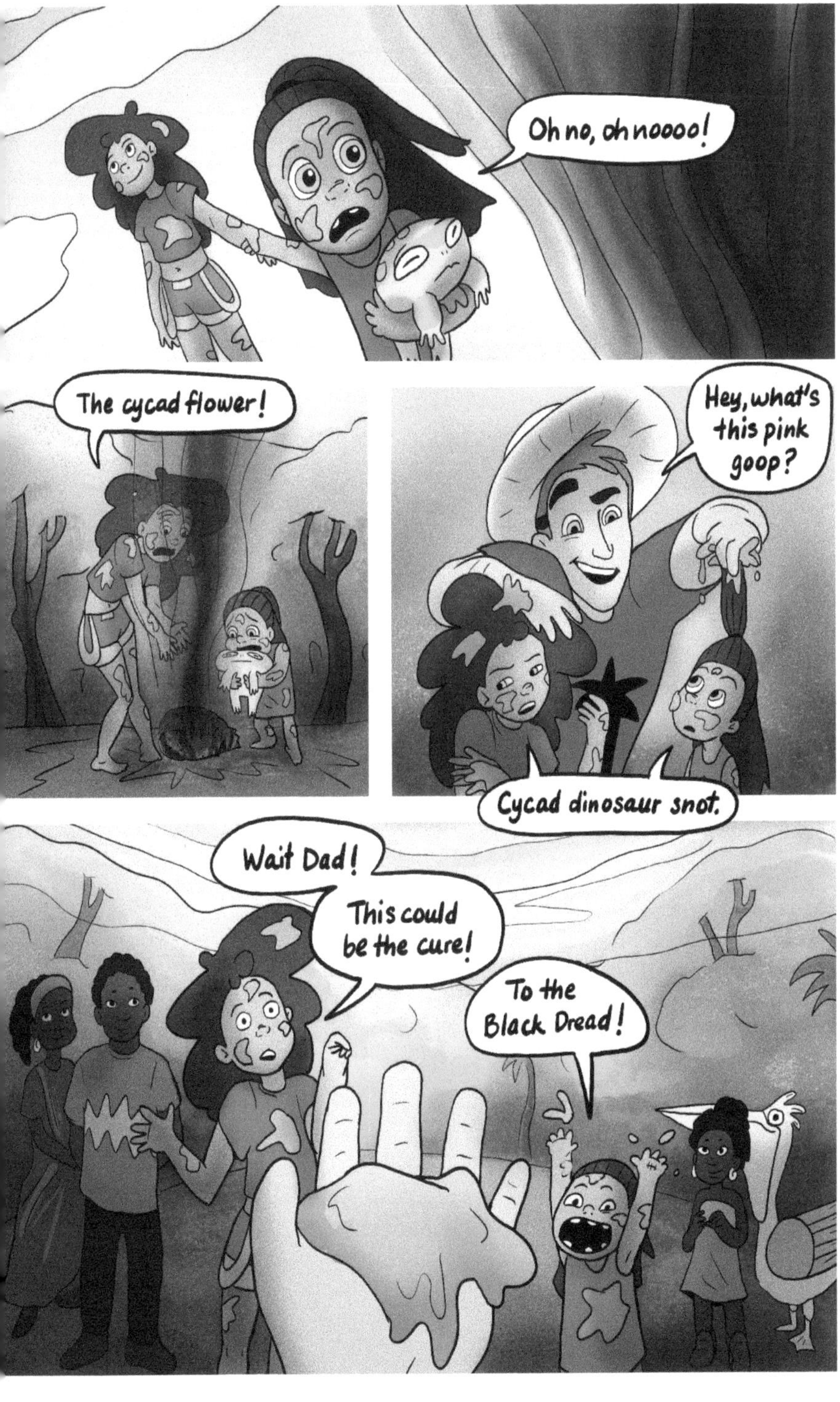
Oh no, oh noooo!
The cycad flower!
Hey, what's this pink goop?
Cycad dinosaur snot.
Wait Dad!
This could be the cure!
To the Black Dread!

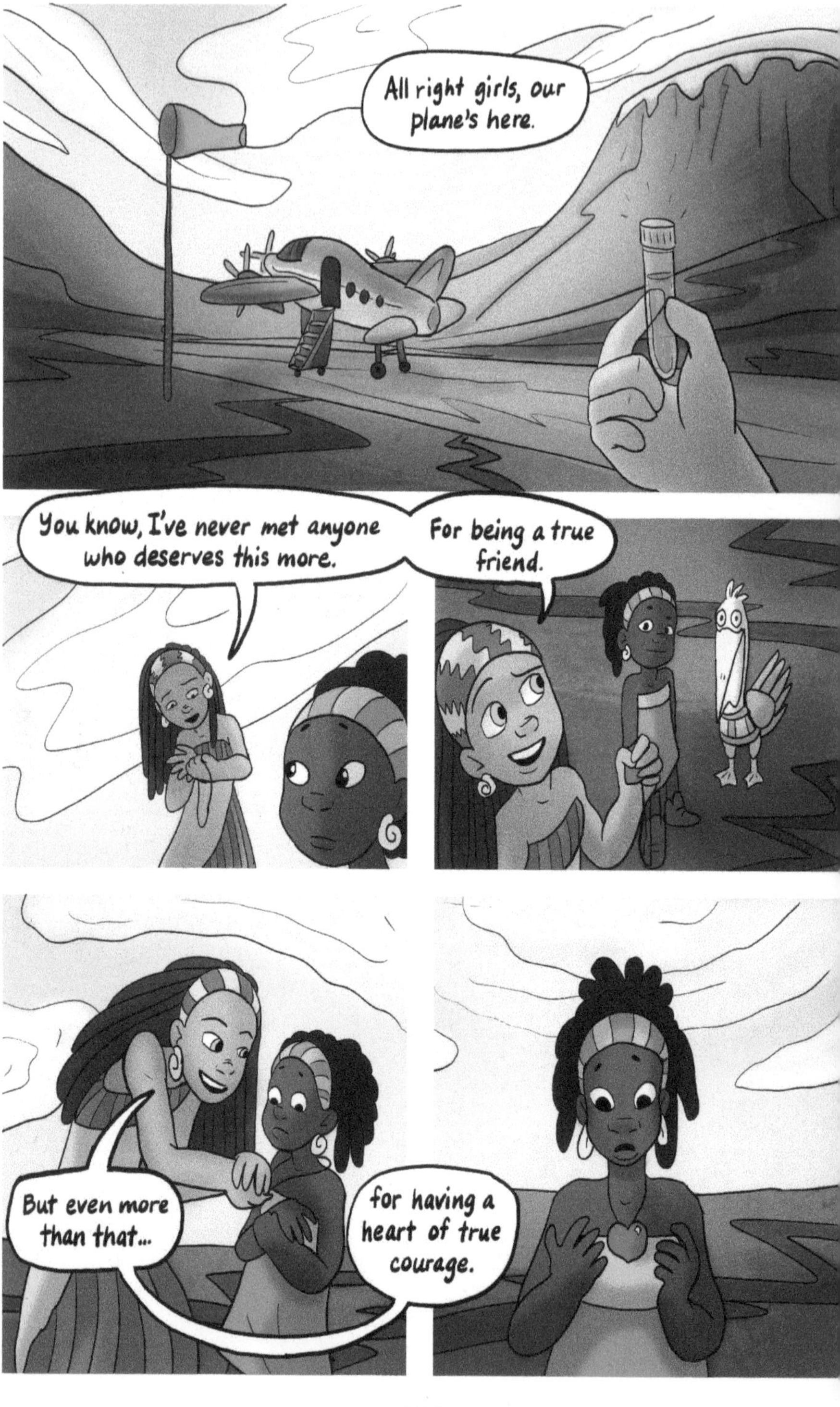
All right girls, our plane's here.
You know, I've never met anyone who deserves this more.
For being a true friend.
But even more than that...
for having a heart of true courage.

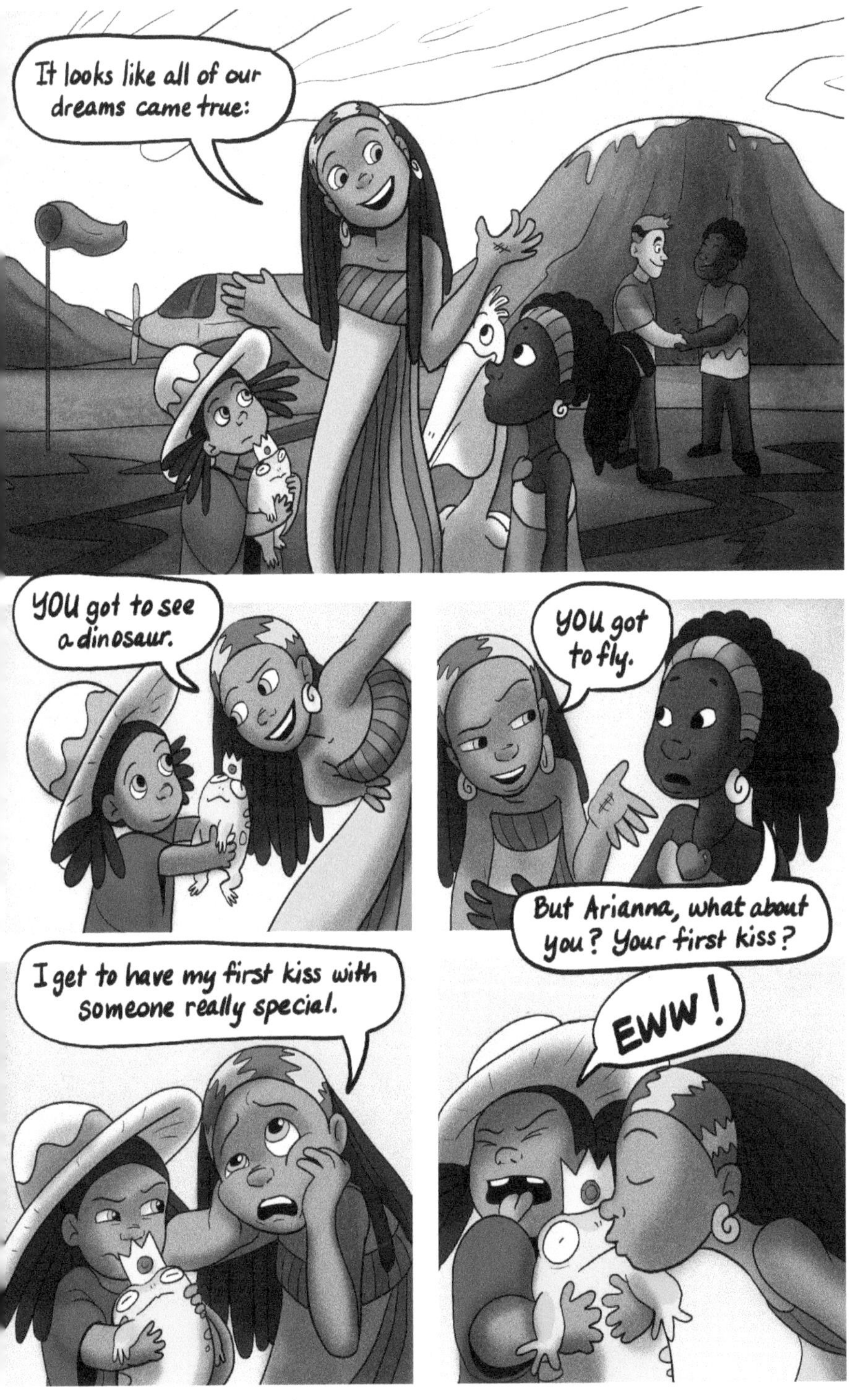
It looks like all of our dreams came true:
YOU got to see a dinosaur.
YOU got to fly.
But Arianna, what about you? Your first kiss?
I get to have my first kiss with someone really special.
EWW!

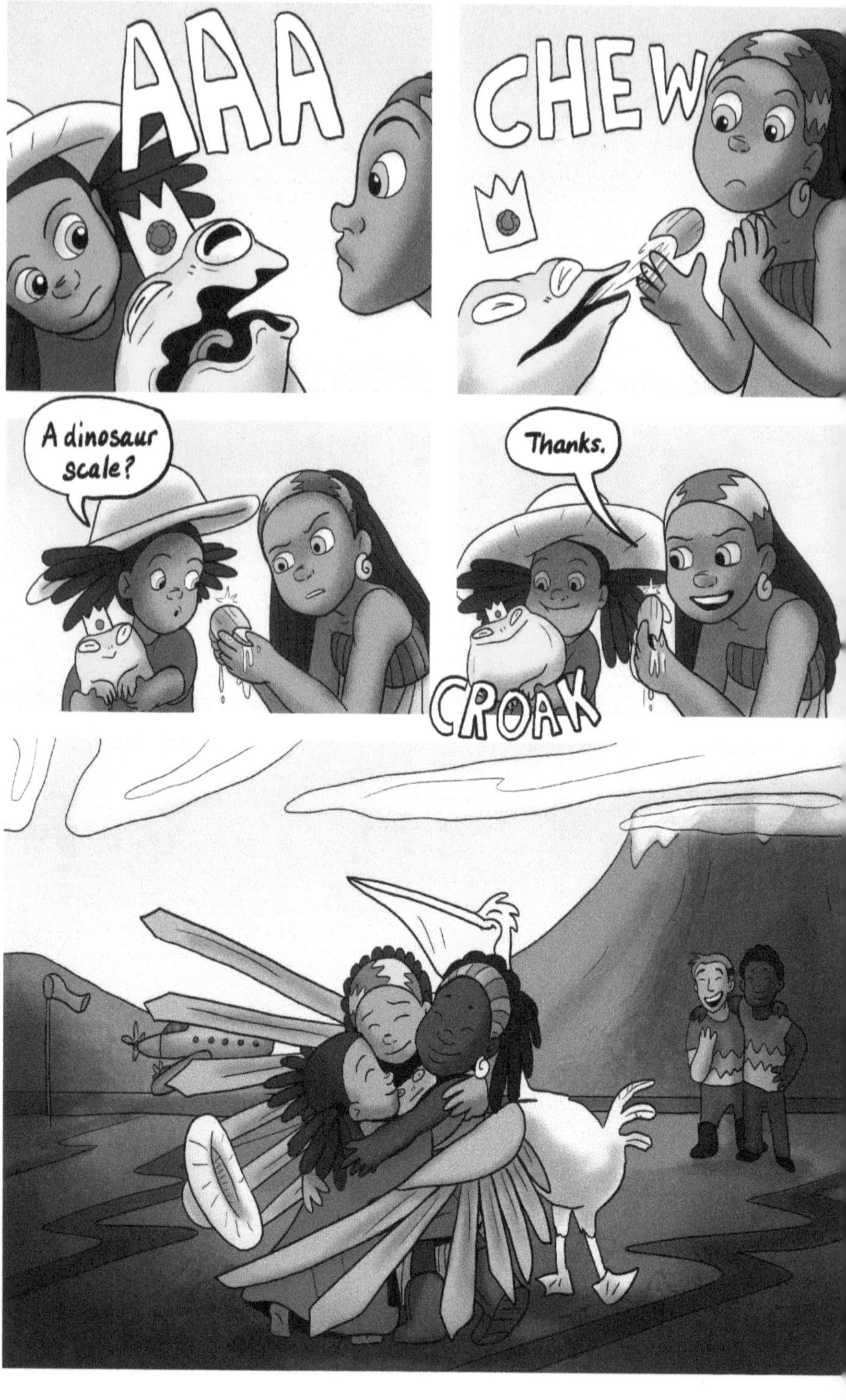
AAA
CHEW
A dinosaur scale?
Thanks.
CROAK

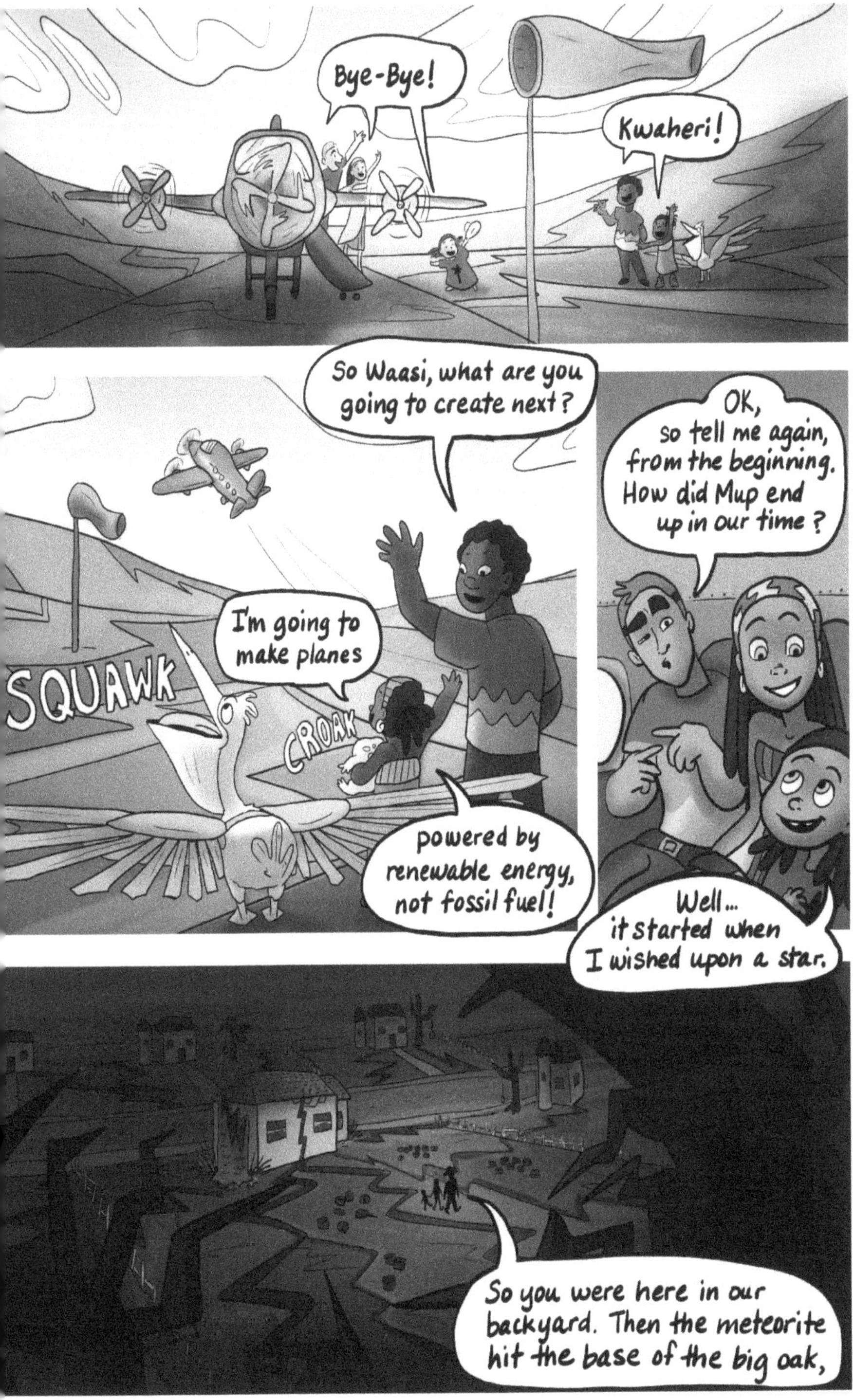
Bye-Bye!
Kwaheri!
So Waasi, what are you going to create next?
I'm going to make planes
SQUAWK
CROAK
powered by renewable energy, not fossil fuel!
OK, so tell me again, from the beginning. How did Mup end up in our time?
Well... it started when I wished upon a star.
So you were here in our backyard. Then the meteorite hit the base of the big oak,

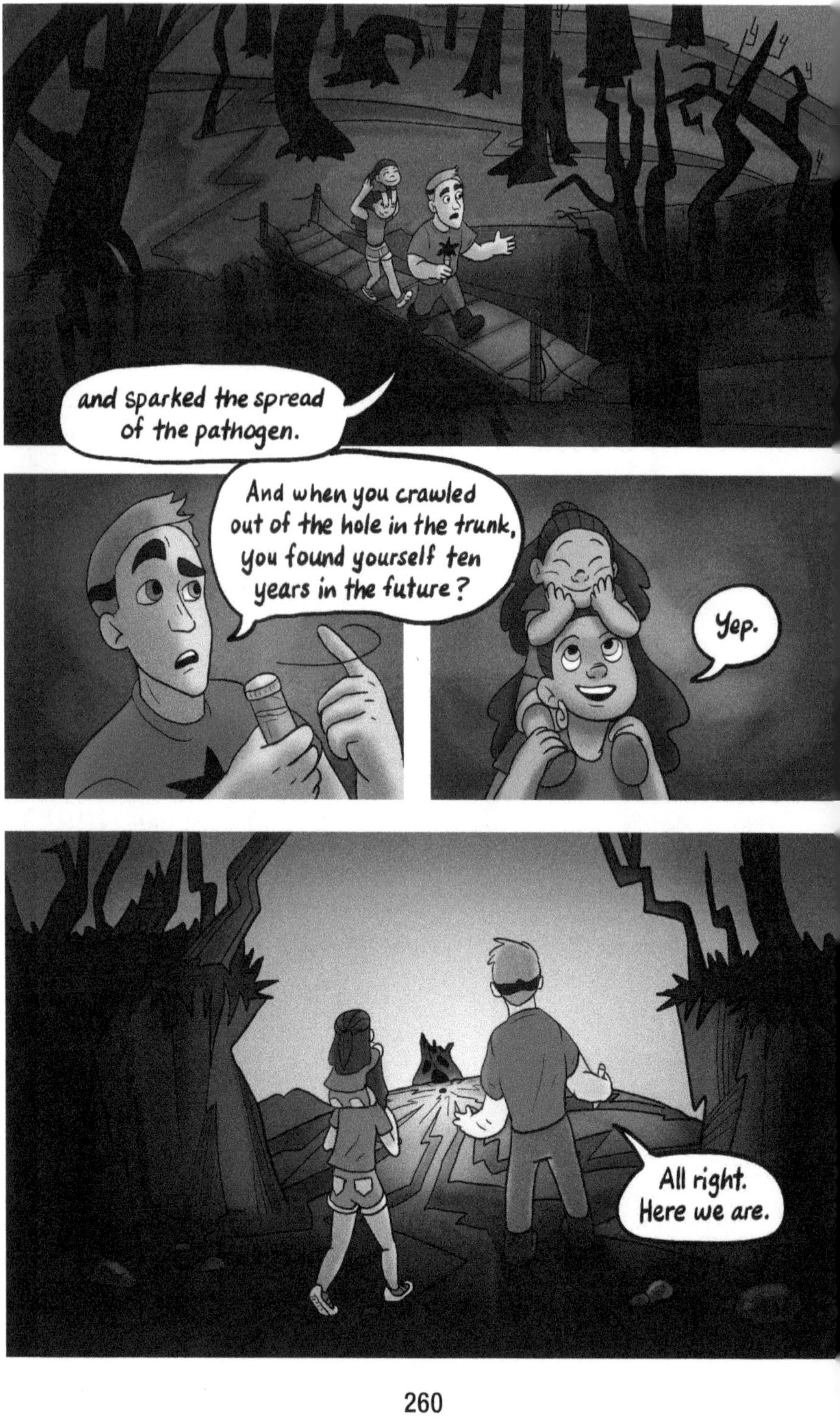
and sparked the spread of the pathogen.
And when you crawled out of the hole in the trunk, you found yourself ten years in the future?
Yep.
All right. Here we are.

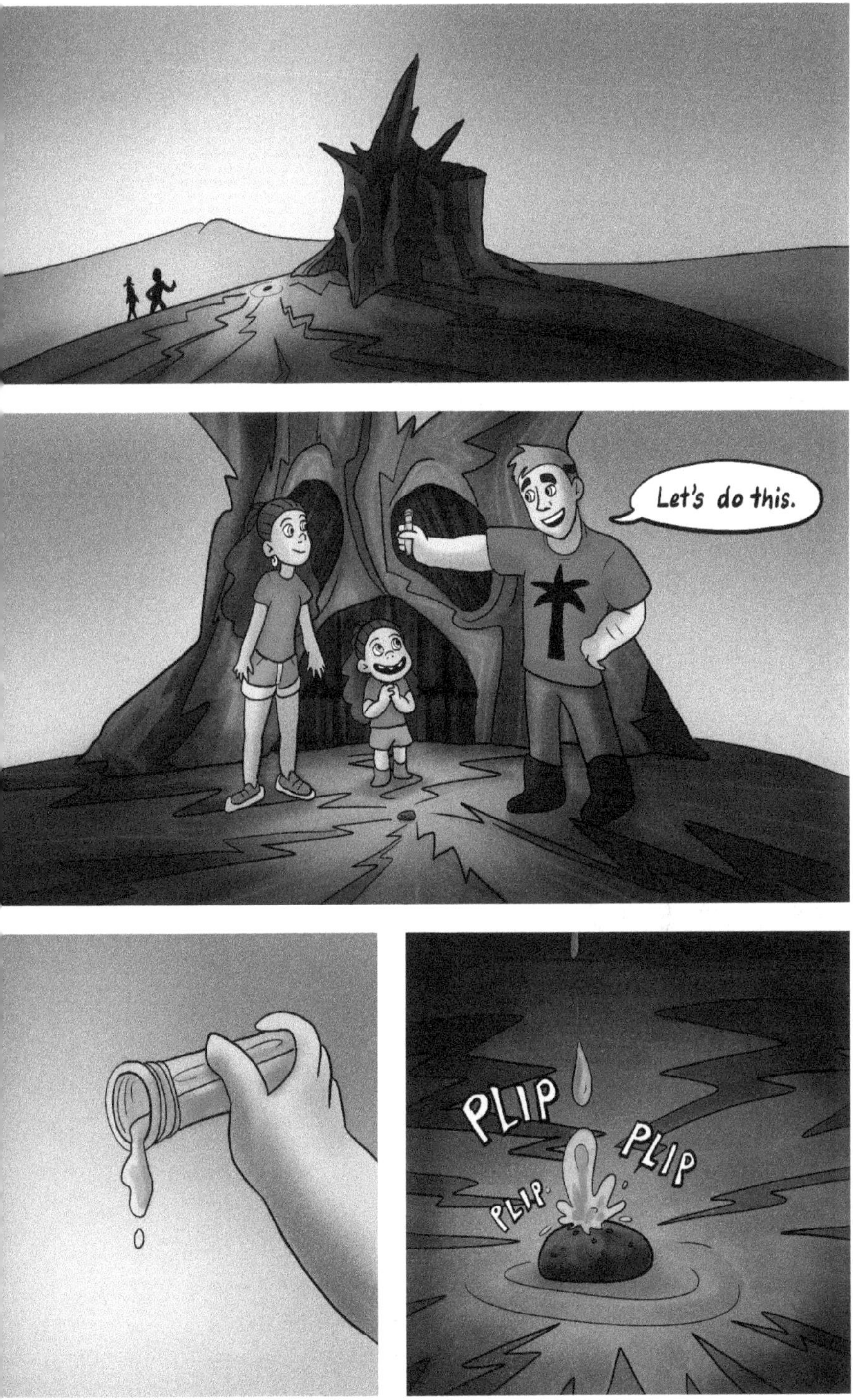
Let's do this.
PLIP
PLIP
PLIP

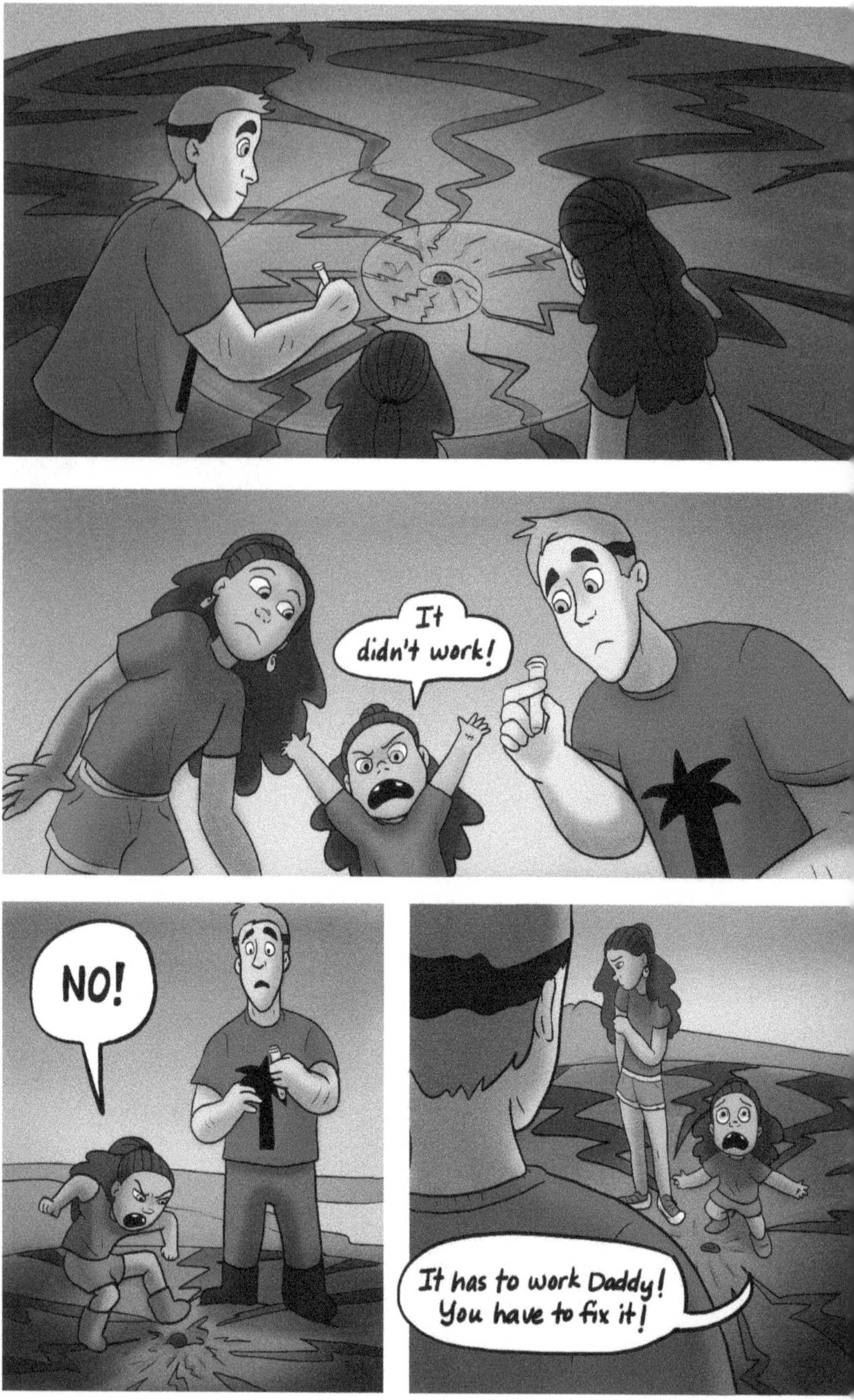
It didn't work!
NO!
It has to work Daddy! You have to fix it!

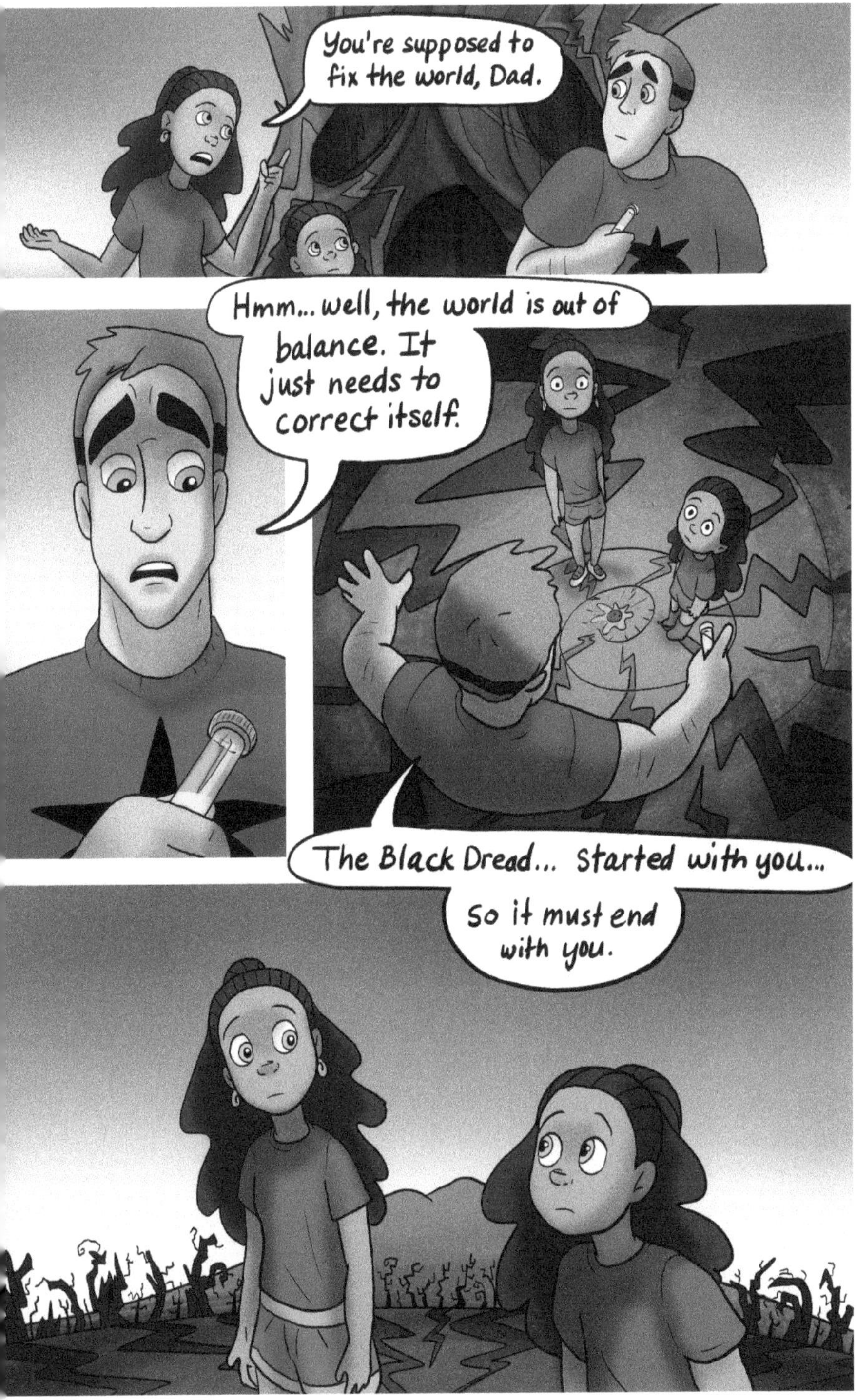
You're supposed to fix the world, Dad.
Hmm... well, the world is out of balance. It just needs to correct itself.
The Black Dread... started with you...
So it must end with you.

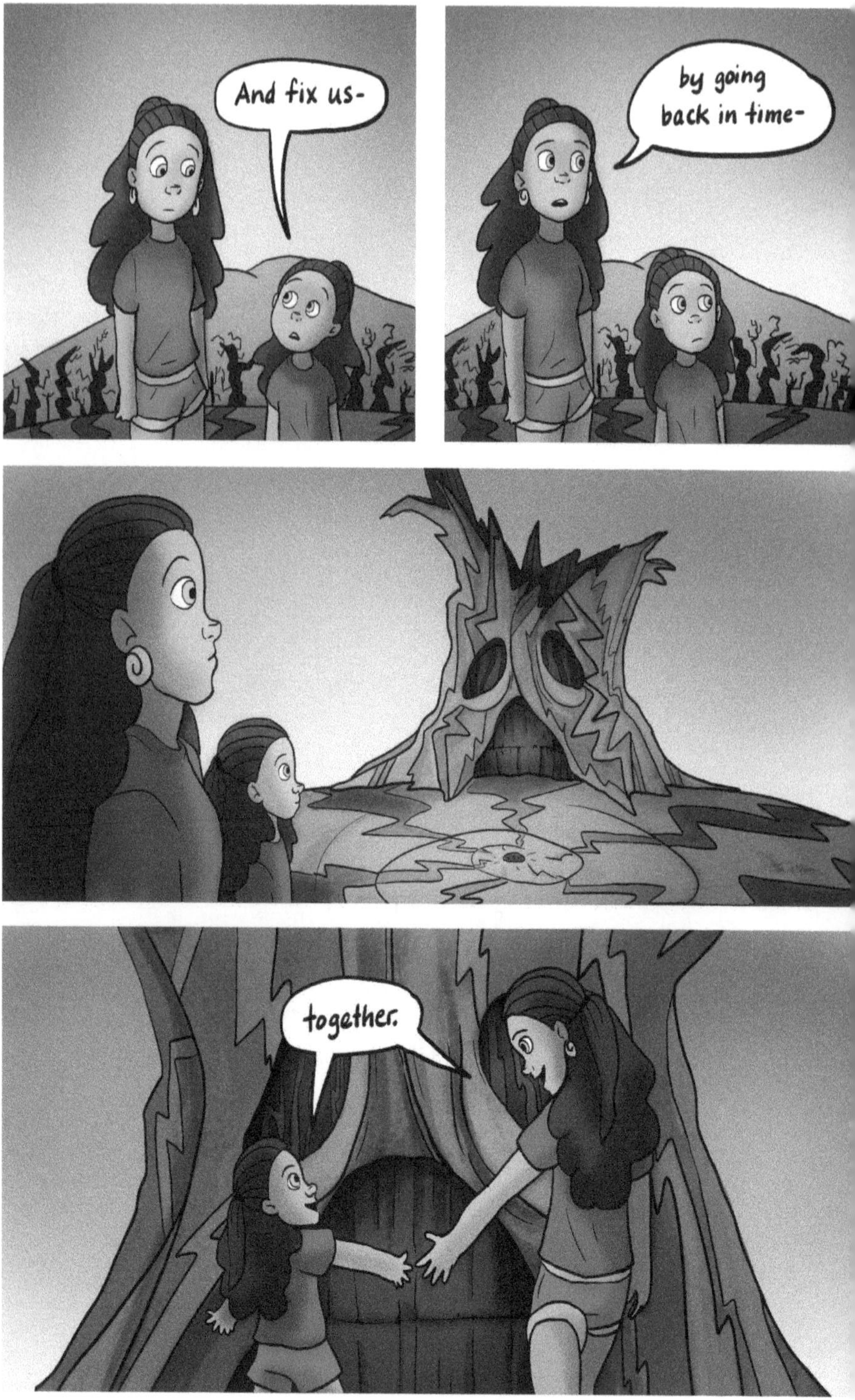
And fix us-
by going back in time-
together.

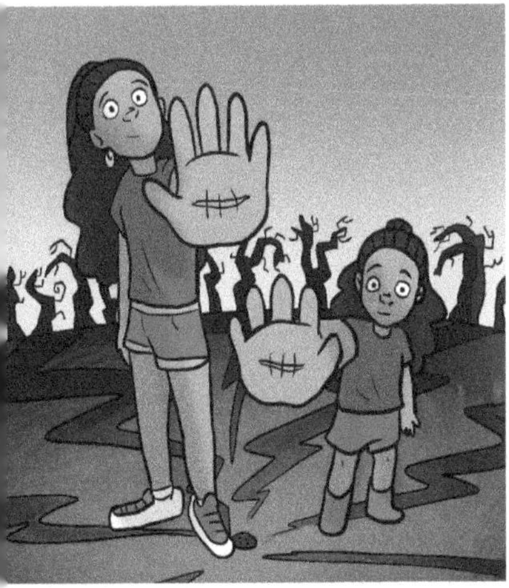

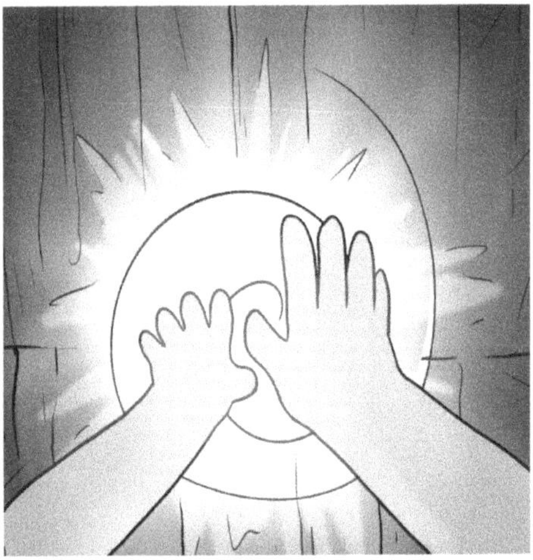

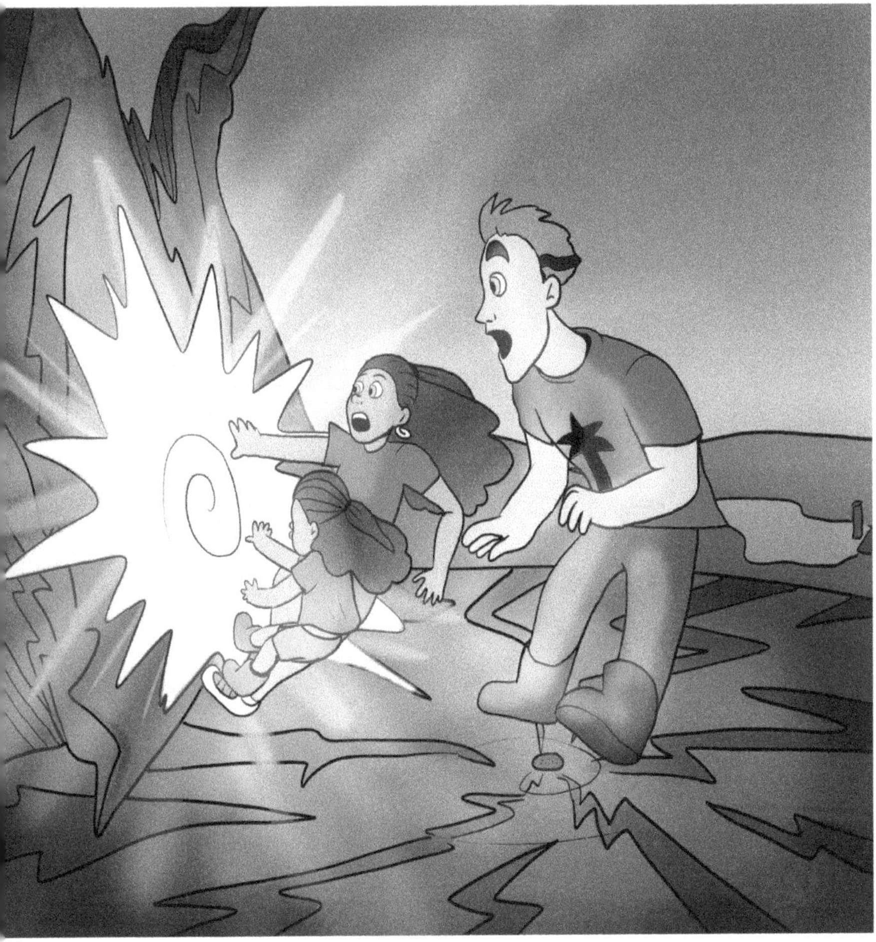

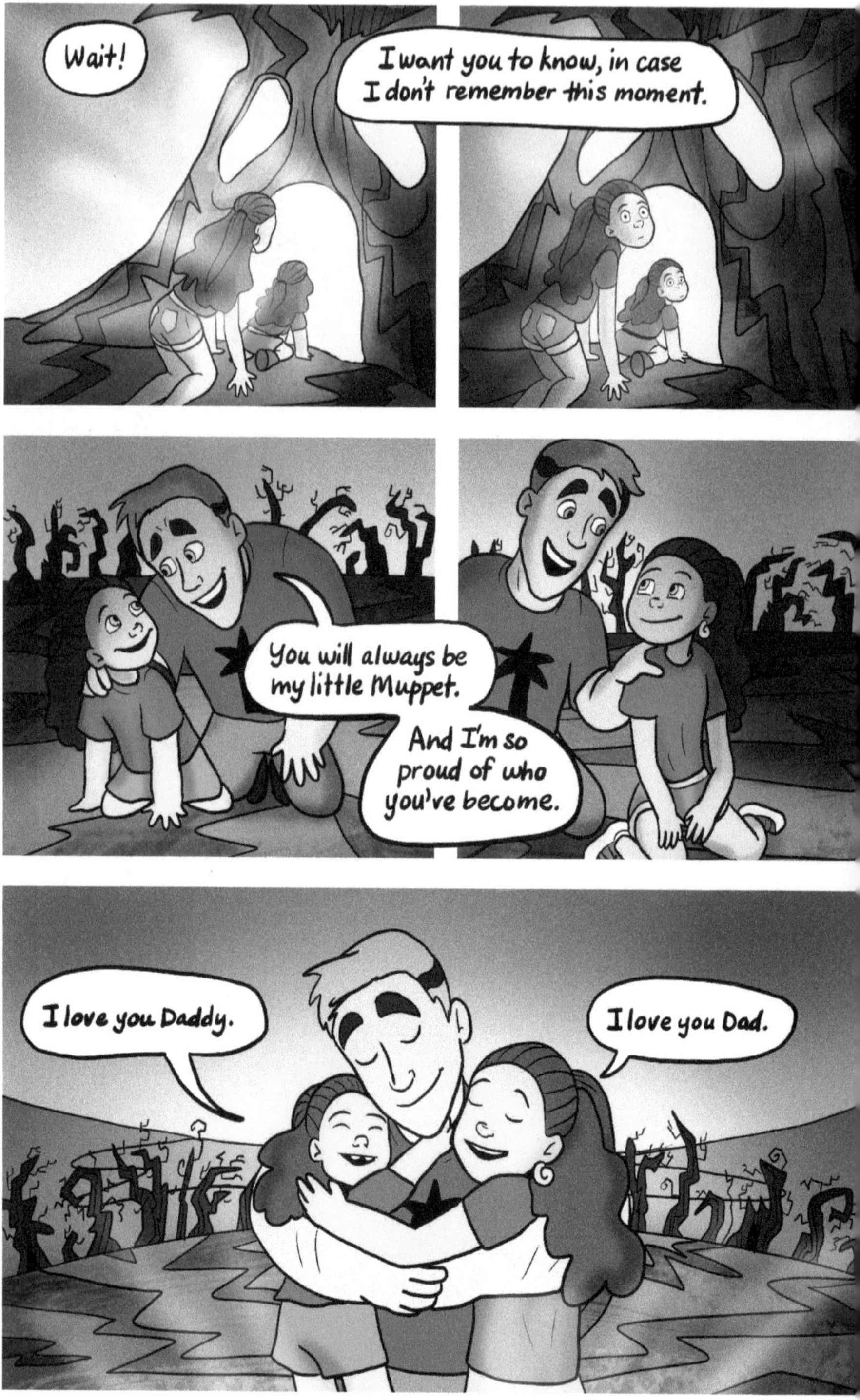
Wait!
I want you to know, in case I don't remember this moment.
You will always be my little Muppet.
And I'm so proud of who you've become.
I love you Daddy.
I love you Dad.

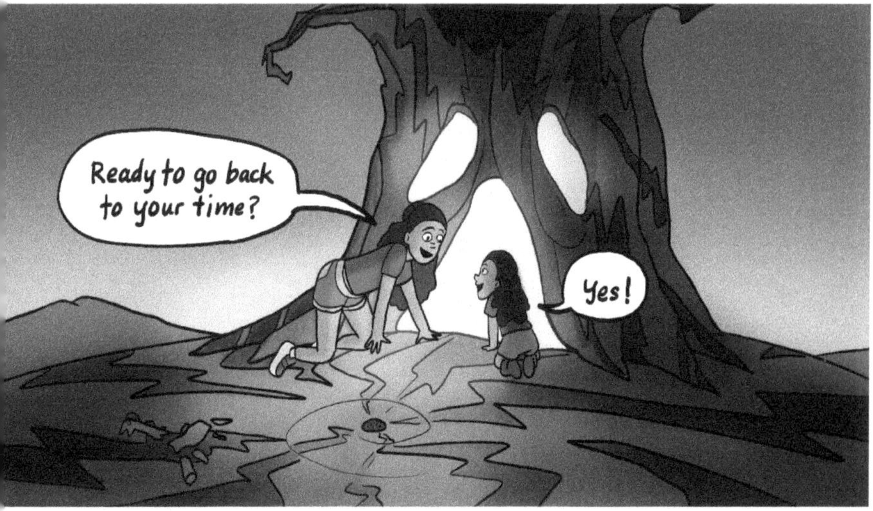
Ready to go back to your time?
Yes!

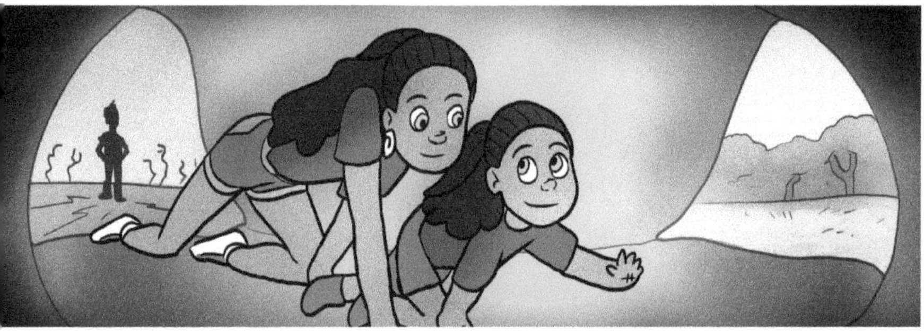

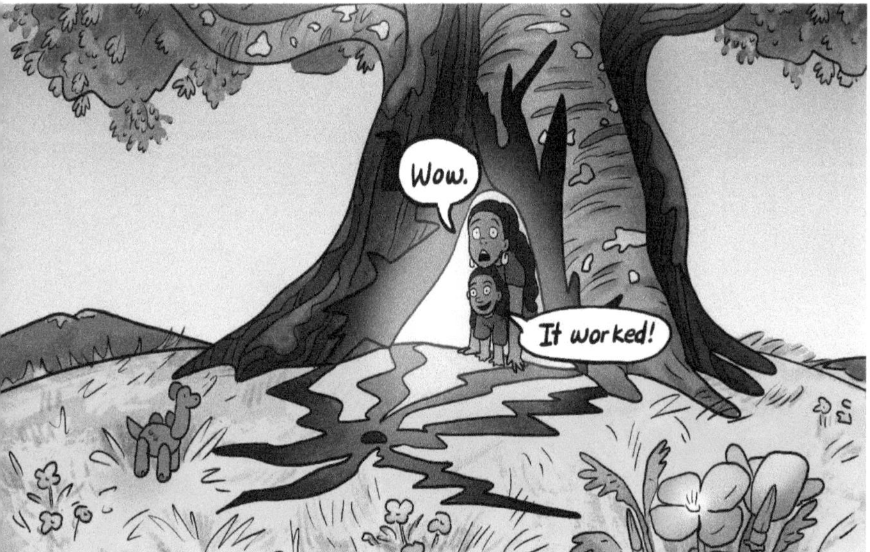
Wow.
It worked!

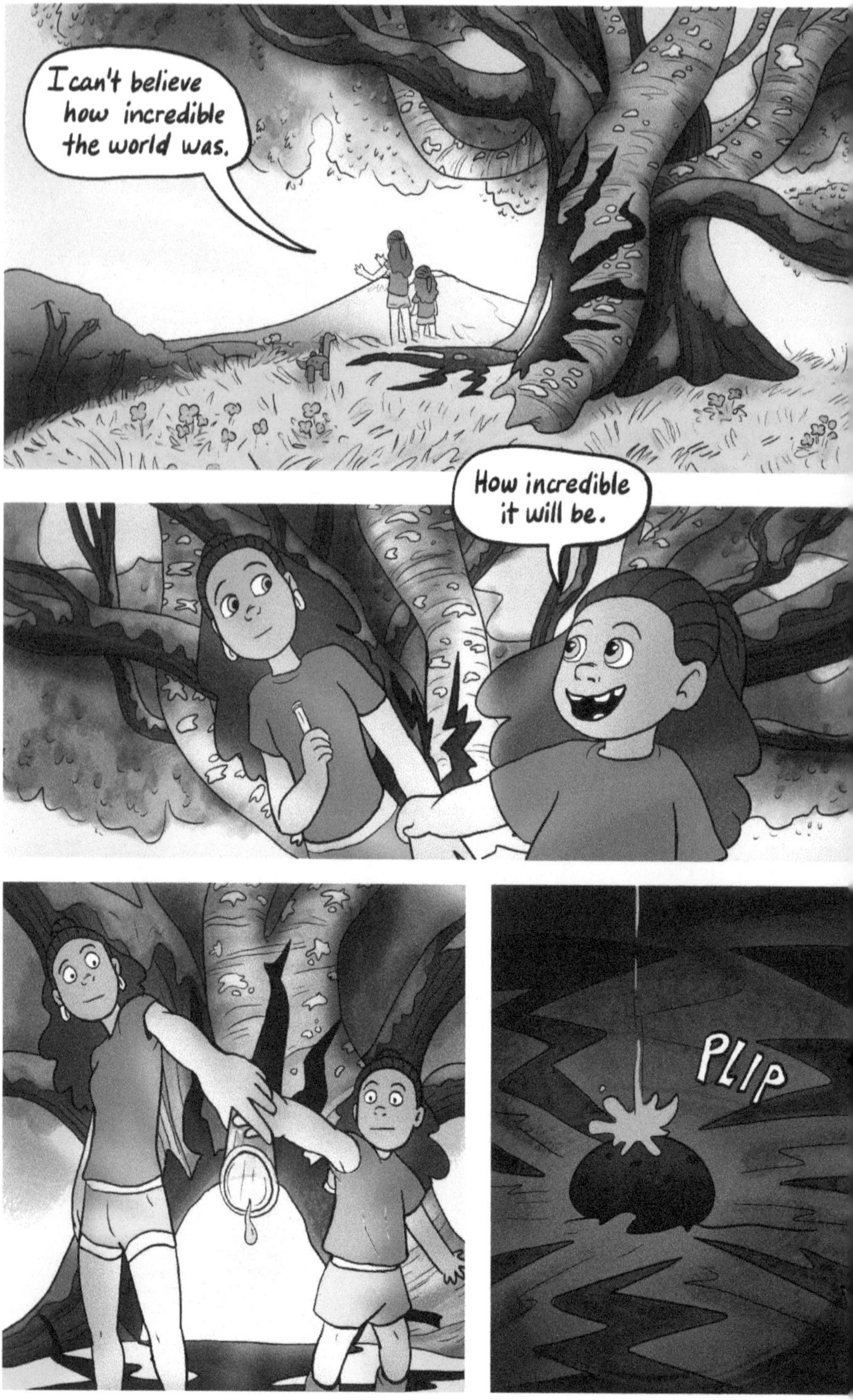

I can't believe how incredible the world was.
How incredible it will be.
PLIP

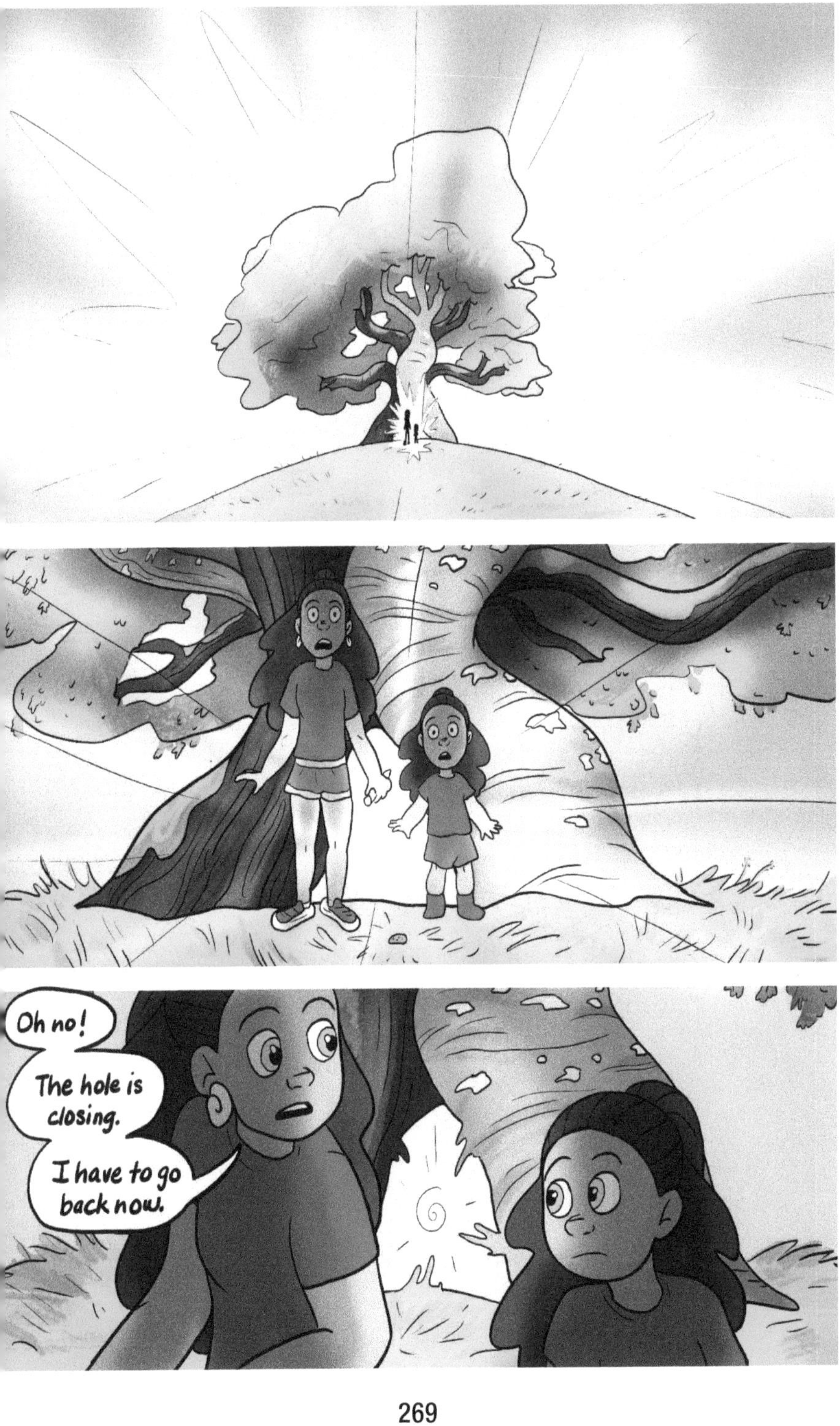
Oh no!
The hole is closing.
I have to go back now.

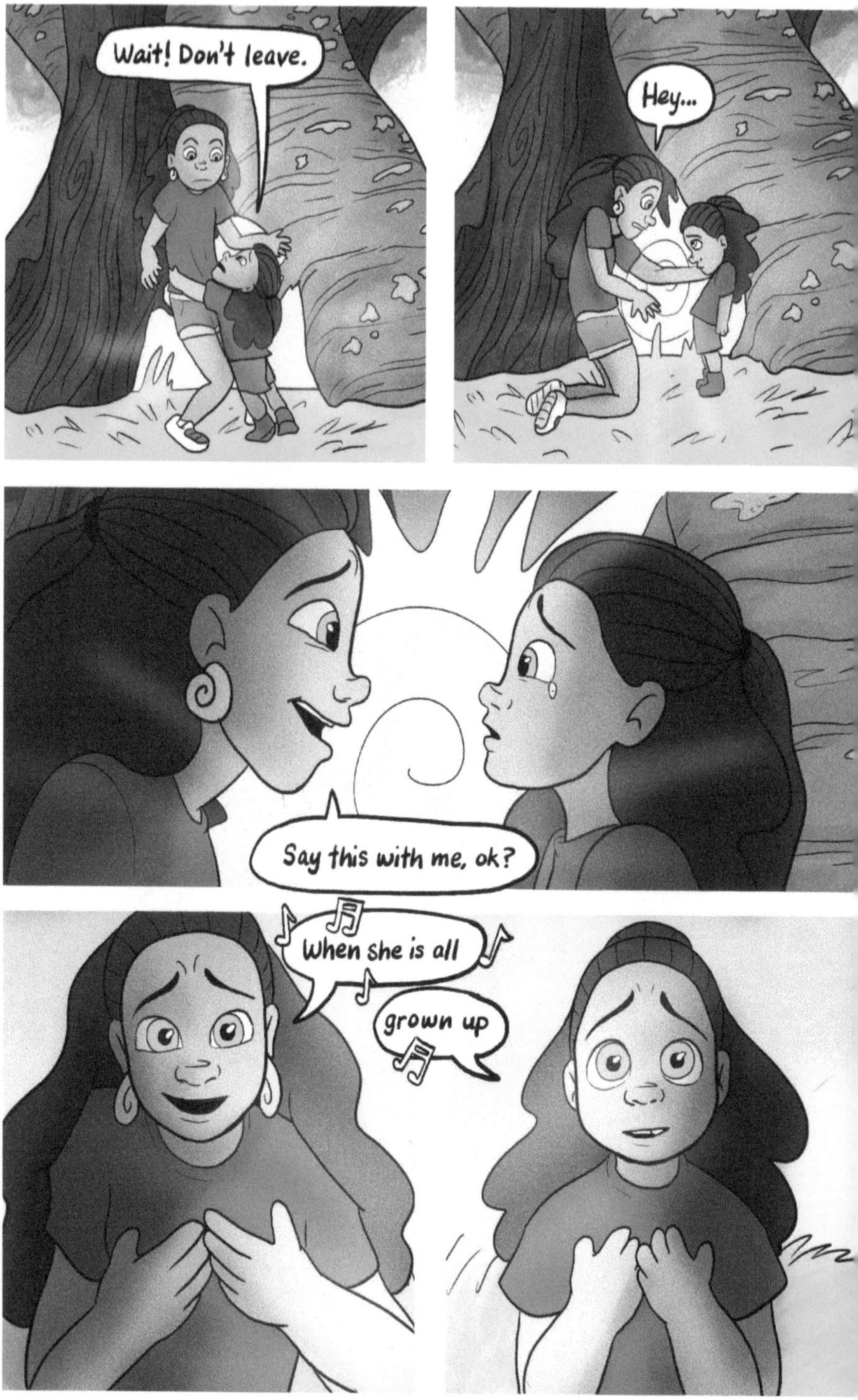
Wait! Don't leave.
Hey...
Say this with me, ok?
When she is all
grown up

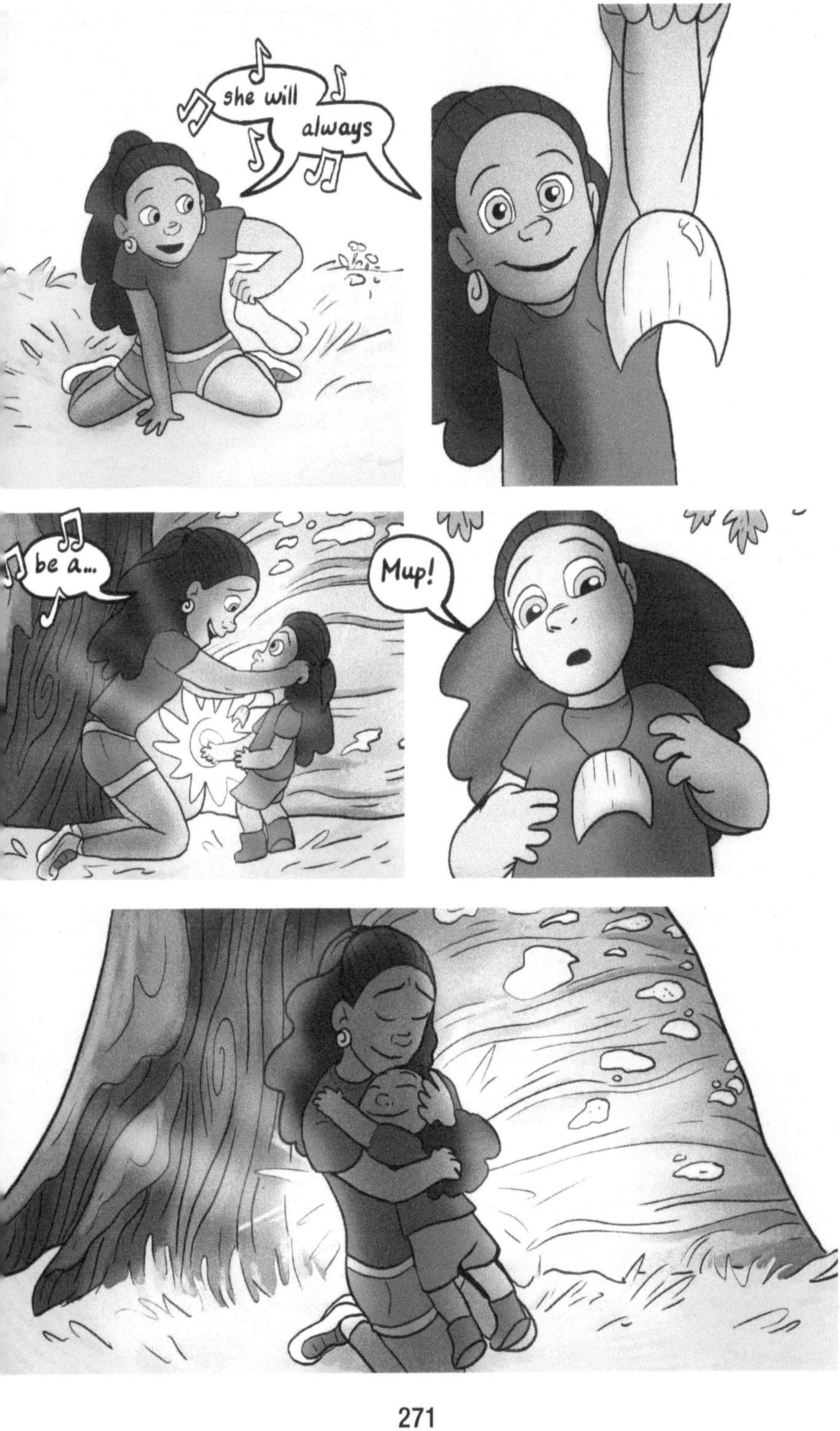
she will
always
be a...
Mup!

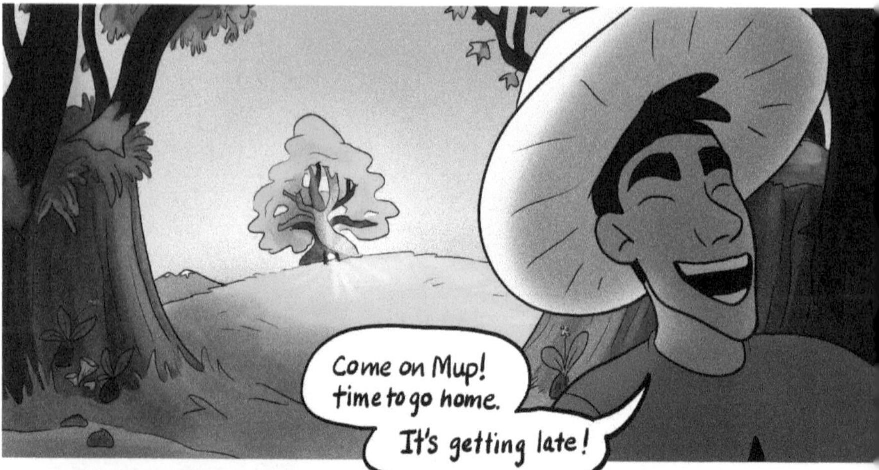
Come on Mup! time to go home.
It's getting late!

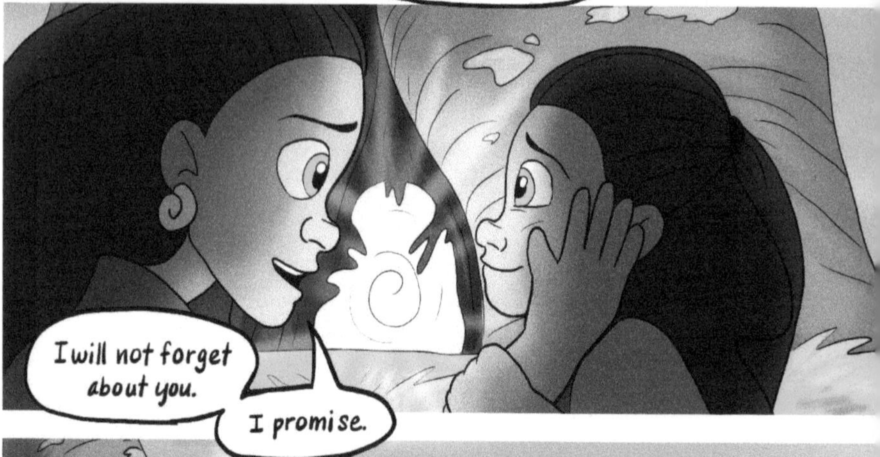
I will not forget about you.
I promise.

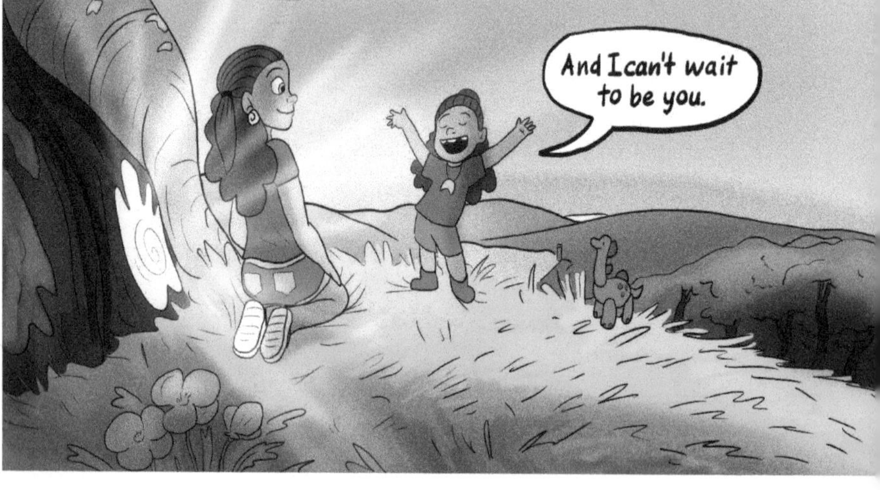
And I can't wait to be you.

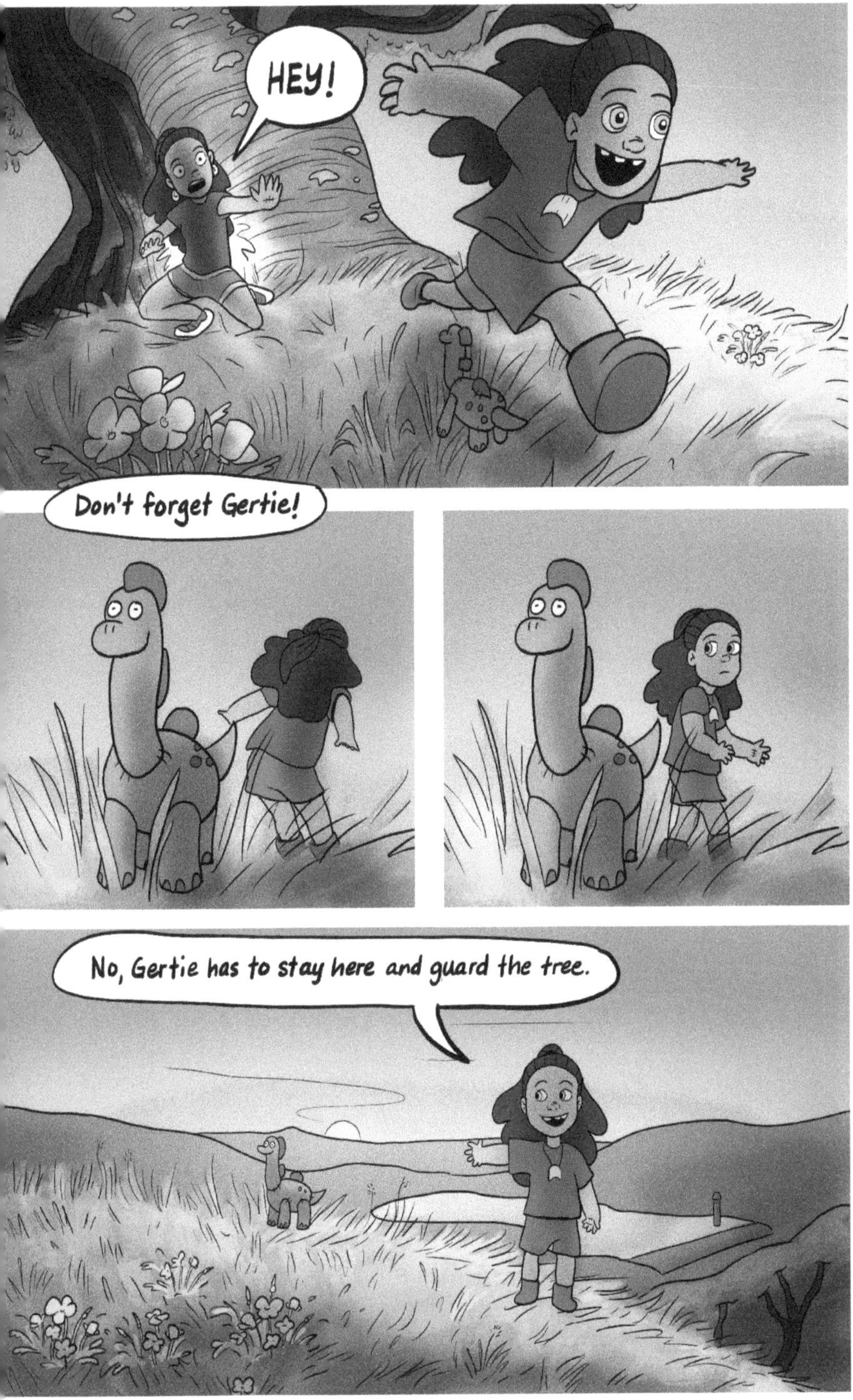
HEY!
Don't forget Gertie!
No, Gertie has to stay here and guard the tree.

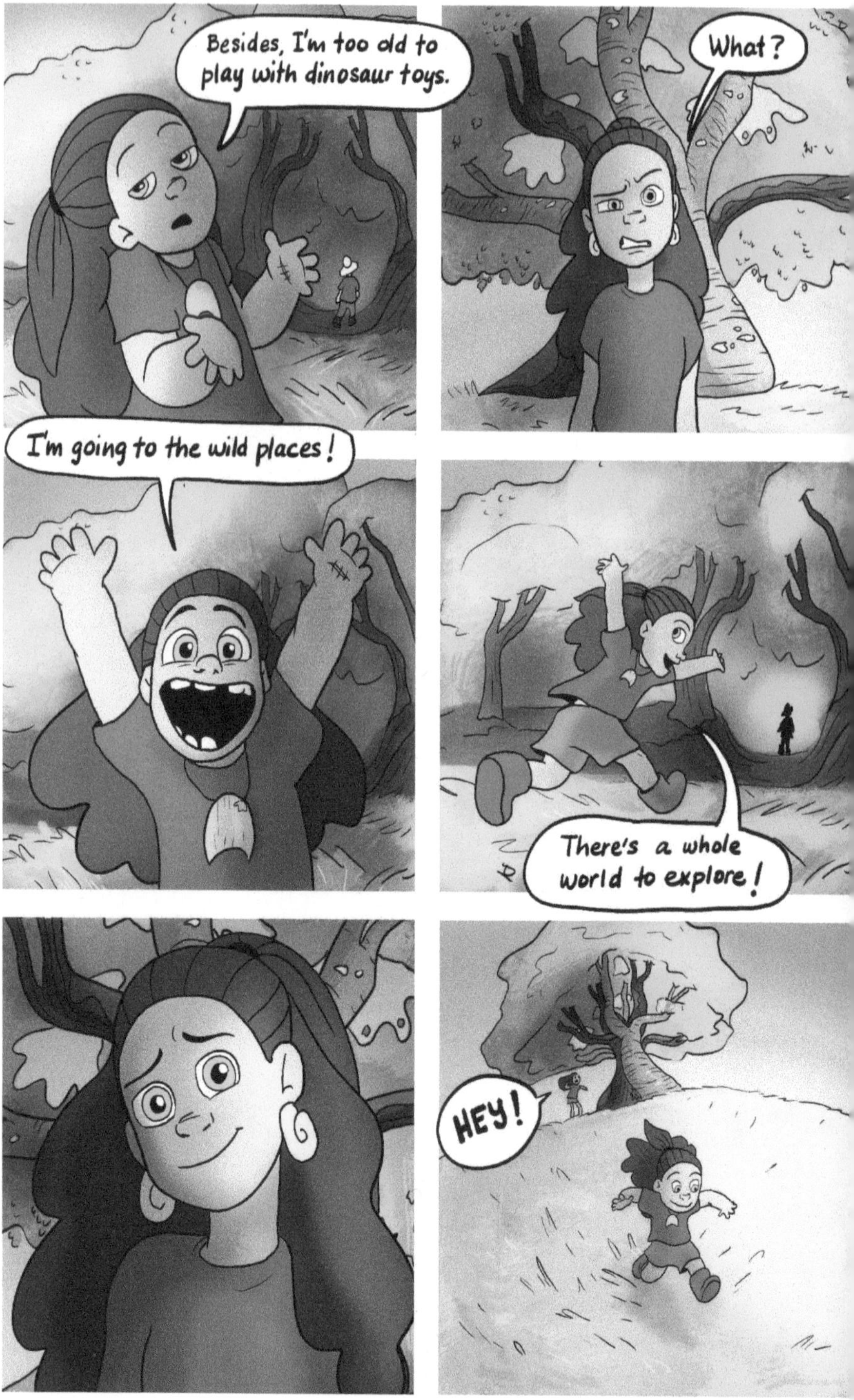

Besides, I'm too old to play with dinosaur toys.
What?
I'm going to the wild places!
There's a whole world to explore!
HEY!

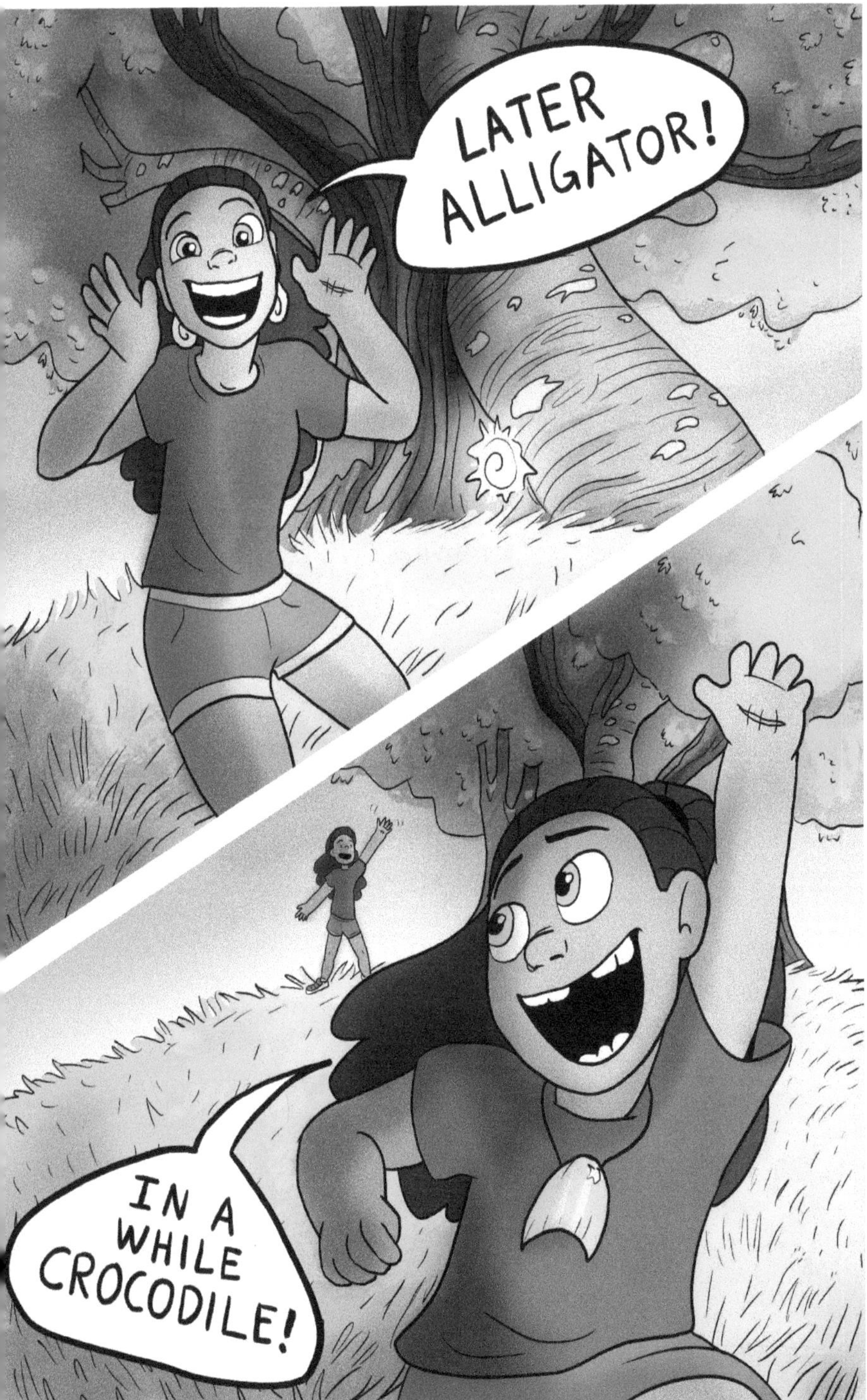
LATER ALLIGATOR!
IN A WHILE CROCODILE!

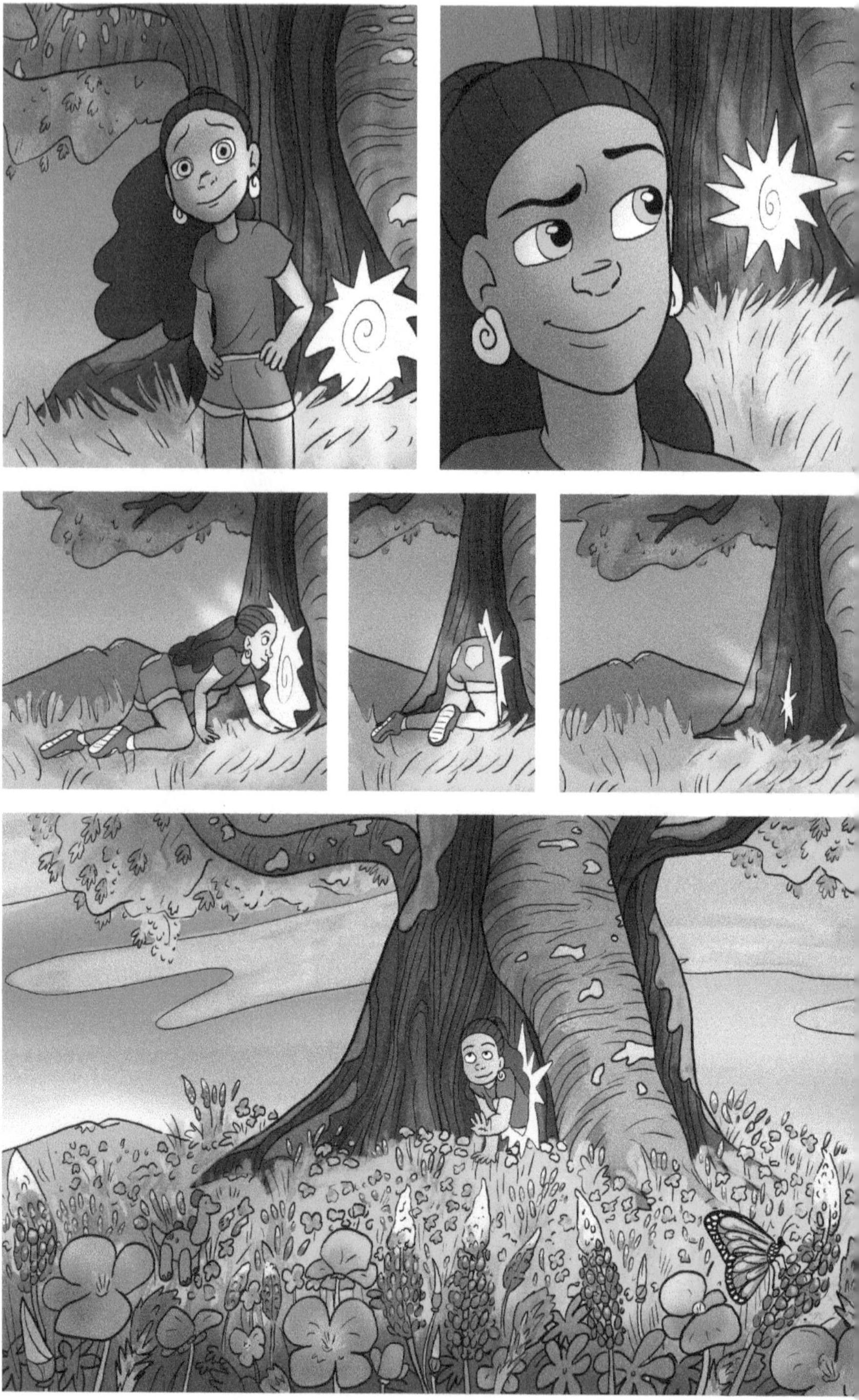

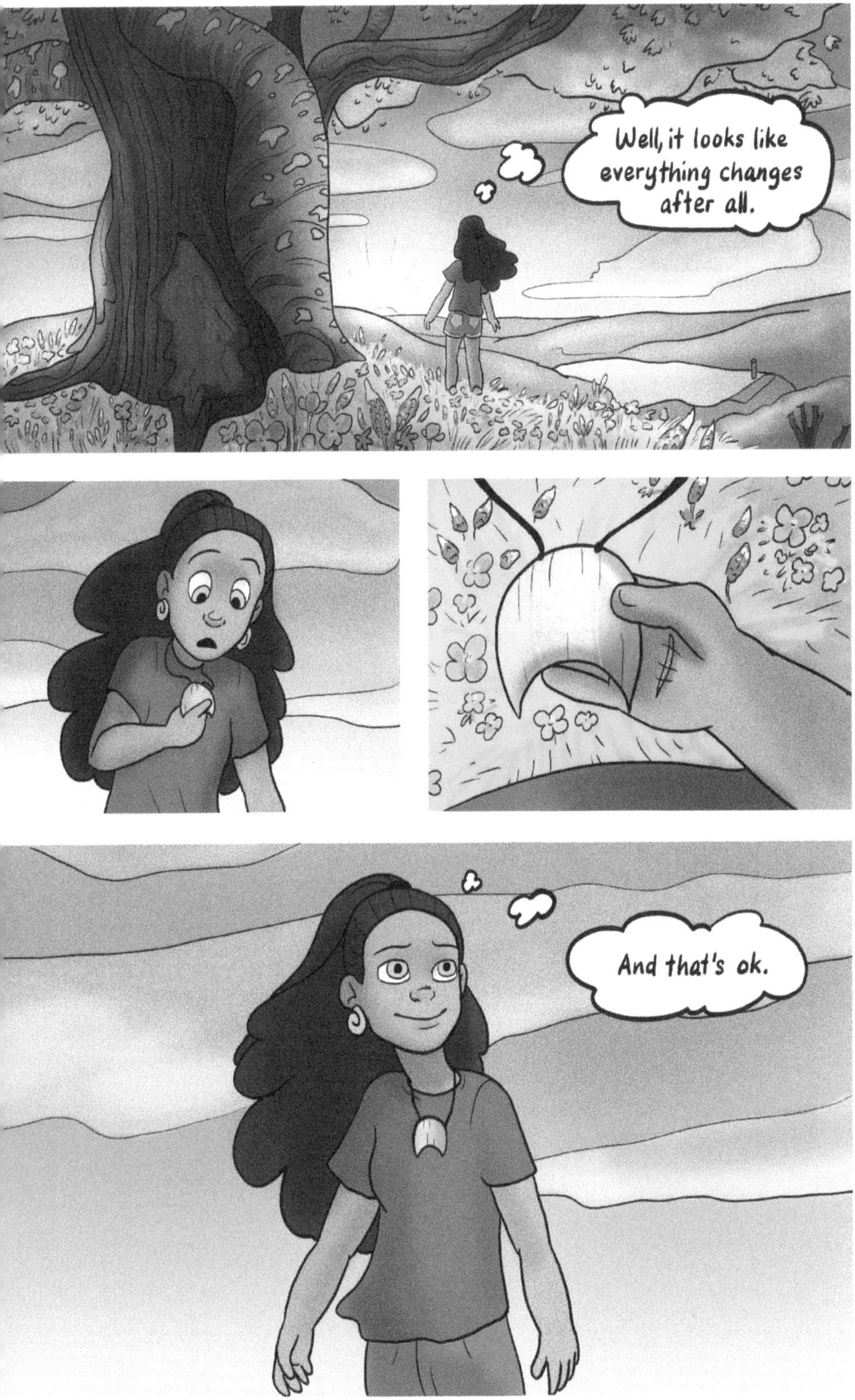
Well, it looks like everything changes after all.
And that's ok.

SPECIAL THANKS TO...

Where to begin? So many people helped bring this story to life. I'll start with Loyola Marymount University's School of Film and Television, where, through various class assignments, the idea for MUP was born.

From the Animation department: Tom Klein, Josh Morgan, Shane Acker, Ash Brannon, Adriana Jaroszewicz, Daniella Heitmuller, Sapphire Sandalo, Van Partible, Jose Garcia-Moreno, Rob Burchfield and others. Fellow Animation majors: I can't thank you guys enough for the four years spent on the third floor.

From the Screenwriting department: Frederick Ayeroff, Sally Nemeth, Kelly Younger, Margaret Oberman, Nicolaus Thatcher and others. And of course, all the screenwriting students who helped me write my initial drafts.

To all my college friends, thank you for your patience as you watched me disappear for days into the animation labs. Especially Lili Hamada: your continuous support means the world to me. Thank you Meenakshi Taneja, most excellent character colorist.

Dad: Your influence on my life is indelible and inspirational. Thank you for a lifetime of crazy botanical adventures and bestowing a load of plant knowledge upon me. For my brothers Jared and Carson: you are good sports for putting up with me and my drafts, scribbles and doodles.

And then there's Mup, my sister. Thank you for letting me turn you into a cartoon character.

And lastly Mom! I literally could not have done this without you. From the first phone call from my freshman dorm room when I pitched you the idea all the way to final publication, you were critical to the mission with your wise edits and artistic eye.

RAEA GRAGG

is a writer and illustrator, specializing in stories for children and teens. She wrote her first book at age 15 and is now developing projects for the film industry. Mup is her first graphic novel. Raea graduated from Loyola Marymount University School of Film and Television with a BA in animation in 2020 and lives in the San Francisco Bay Area. www.raeagragg.com.

CPSIA information can be obtained
at www.ICGtesting.com
Printed in the USA
LVHW050808160421
684679LV00003B/13

9 780991 626922